be
self.
efully

CHRISTMAS STORIES

Editor's Note

Charles Dickens is the Father Christmas of English literature. In some of his full-length novels, like Pickwick Papers, *and in his Christmas Stories, he keeps ablaze the Yule-tide log, brings us the pleasant aroma of long-forgotten Punch concoctions, and echoes the chirp of the cricket and the merriment round the hearth. Most of the stories in this book appeared in his two periodicals " Household Words " (1850–1859) and "All the Year Round " (1859–1871). Generally, they are slight sketches, some of which he left to be completed by collaborators like his friend Wilkie Collins. But, even so, they portray characters worthy to rank with his best—for example : the waiter in* Somebody's Luggage, *the London landlady, Mrs. Lirriper, and such termagants as Dr. Marigold's wife and the " Refreshmenters " of* Mugby Junction. *Incidentally, E. G. Dalziel's woodcut illustration to the latter story (it has been chosen as the frontispiece to this volume) is supposed to represent one of the poor public—" a merry wideawake American gent " according to the text. But the humour of the artist seems to have resulted in a happy delineation of Dickens him[self]. This edition is printed from the one car[efully] corrected by the author in 1867–1868.*

The Refreshment Room at Mugby Junction.

CHRISTMAS STORIES

FROM

"HOUSEHOLD WORDS" AND
"ALL THE YEAR ROUND"

BY

CHARLES DICKENS

ILLUSTRATED BY
E. G. DALZIEL,
TOWNLEY GREEN,
& F. A. FRASER.

LONDON:
HAZELL, WATSON & VINEY, LTD.

A CHRISTMAS TREE

[1850]

I HAVE been looking on, this evening, at a merry company of
children assembled round that pretty German toy, a Christmas
Tree. The tree was planted in the middle of a great round table, and
towered high above their heads. It was brilliantly lighted by a
multitude of little tapers; and everywhere sparkled and glittered
with bright objects. There were rosy-cheeked dolls, hiding behind the
green leaves; and there were real watches (with movable hands, at
least, and an endless capacity of being wound up) dangling from
innumerable twigs; there were French-polished tables, chairs, bedsteads, wardrobes, eight-day clocks, and various other articles of
domestic furniture (wonderfully made, in tin, at Wolverhampton),
perched among the boughs, as if in preparation for some fairy
housekeeping; there were jolly, broad-faced little men, much more
agreeable in appearance than many real men—and no wonder, for
their heads took off, and showed them to be full of sugar-plums; there
were fiddles and drums; there were tambourines, books, work-boxes,
paint-boxes, sweetmeat boxes, peep-show boxes, and all kinds of
boxes; there were trinkets for the elder girls, far brighter than any
grown-up gold and jewels; there were baskets and pincushions in all
devices; there were guns, swords, and banners; there were witches
standing in enchanted rings of pasteboard, to tell fortunes; there
were teetotums, humming-tops, needle-cases, pen-wipers, smelling-
bottles, conversation-cards, bouquet-holders, real fruit, made
artificially dazzling with gold leaf; imitation apples, pears, and wal-
nuts, crammed with surprises; in short, as a pretty child, before me,
delightedly whispered to another pretty child, her bosom friend,
"There was everything, and more." This motley collection of odd
objects, clustering on the tree like magic fruit, and flashing back the
bright looks directed towards it from every side—some of the
diamond-eyes admiring it were hardly on a level with the table, and a
few were languishing in timid wonder on the bosoms of pretty
mothers, aunts, and nurses—made a lively realisation of the fancies
of childhood; and set me thinking how all the trees that grow and all
the things that come into existence on the earth, have their wild
adornments at that well-remembered time.

Being now at home again, and alone, the only person in the house
awake, my thoughts are drawn back, by a fascination which I do not

care to resist, to my own childhood. I begin to consider, what do we all remember best upon the branches of the Christmas Tree of our own young Christmas days, by which we climbed to real life?

Straight, in the middle of the room, cramped in the freedom of its growth by no encircling walls or soon-reached ceiling, a shadowy tree arises; and, looking up into the dreamy brightness of its top—for I observe in this tree the singular property that it appears to grow downward towards the earth—I look into my youngest Christmas recollections!

All the toys at first, I find. Up yonder, among the green holly and red berries, is the Tumbler with his hands in his pockets, who wouldn't lie down, but whenever he was put upon the floor, persisted in rolling his fat body about, until he rolled himself still, and brought those lobster eyes of his to bear upon me—when I affected to laugh very much, but in my heart of hearts was extremely doubtful of him. Close beside him is that infernal snuff-box, out of which there sprang a demoniacal Counsellor in a black gown, with an obnoxious head of hair, and a red cloth mouth, wide open, who was not to be endured on any terms, but could not be put away either; for he used suddenly, in a highly magnified state, to fly out of Mammoth Snuff-boxes in dreams, when least expected. Nor is the frog with cobbler's wax on his tail, far off; for there was no knowing where he wouldn't jump; and when he flew over the candle, and came upon one's hand with that spotted back—red on a green ground—he was horrible. The cardboard lady in a blue-silk skirt, who was stood up against the candlestick to dance, and whom I see on the same branch, was milder, and was beautiful; but I can't say as much for the larger cardboard man, who used to be hung against the wall and pulled by a string; there was a sinister expression in that nose of his; and when he got his legs round his neck (which he very often did), he was ghastly, and not a creature to be alone with.

When did that dreadful Mask first look at me? Who put it on, and why was I so frightened that the sight of it is an era in my life? It is not a hideous visage in itself; it is even meant to be droll; why then were its stolid features so intolerable? Surely not because it hid the wearer's face. An apron would have done as much; and though I should have preferred even the apron away, it would not have been absolutely insupportable, like the mask. Was it the immovability of the mask? The doll's face was immovable, but I was not afraid of *her*. Perhaps that fixed and set change coming over a real face, infused into my quickened heart some remote suggestion and dread of the universal change that is to come on every face, and make it still? Nothing reconciled me to it. No drummers, from whom proceeded a melancholy chirping on the turning of a handle; no regiment of soldiers, with a mute band, taken out of a box, and fitted, one by one, upon a stiff and lazy little set of lazy-tongs; no old woman, made of wires and a brown-paper composition, cutting up a pie for two small children; could give me a permanent comfort, for a long time. Nor was it any satisfaction to be shown the Mask, and see that it was made of paper, or to have it locked up and be assured that no one wore it. The mere recollection of that fixed face, the mere knowledge of its existence anywhere, was sufficient to awake me in the night all perspiration and horror, with, "O I know it's coming! O the mask!"

I never wondered what the dear old donkey with the panniers—there he is! was made of, then! His hide was real to the touch, I recollect. And the great black horse with the round red spots all over him—the horse that I could even get upon—I never wondered what had brought him to that strange condition, or thought that such a horse was not commonly seen at Newmarket. The four horses of no colour, next to him, that went into the waggon of cheeses, and could be taken out and stabled under the piano, appear to have bits of fur-tippet for their tails, and other bits for their manes, and to stand on pegs instead of legs, but it was not so when they were brought home for a Christmas present. They were all right then; neither was their harness unceremoniously nailed into their chests, as appears to be the case now. The tinkling works of the music-cart, I *did* find out, to be made of quill toothpicks and wire; and I always thought that little tumbler in his shirt-sleeves, perpetually swarming up one side of a wooden frame, and coming down, head foremost, on the other, rather a weak-minded person—though good-natured; but the Jacob's Ladder, next him, made of little squares of red wood, that went flapping and clattering over one another, each developing a different picture, and the whole enlivened by small bells, was a mighty marvel and a great delight.

Ah! The Doll's house!—of which I was not proprietor, but where I visited. I don't admire the Houses of Parliament half so much as that stone-fronted mansion with real glass windows, and doorsteps, and a real balcony—greener than I ever see now, except at watering places; and even they afford but a poor imitation. And though it *did* open all at once, the entire house-front (which was a blow, I admit, as cancelling the fiction of a staircase), it was but to shut it up again, and I could believe. Even open, there were three distinct rooms in it: a sitting-room and bed-room, elegantly furnished, and best of all, a kitchen, with uncommonly soft fire-irons, a plentiful assortment of diminutive utensils—oh, the warming pan!—and a tin man-cook in profile, who was always going to fry two fish. What Barmecide justice have I done to the noble feasts wherein the set of wooden platters figured, each with its own peculiar delicacy, as a ham or turkey, glued tight on to it, and garnished with something green, which I recollect as moss! Could all the Temperance Societies of these later days, united, give me such a tea-drinking as I have had through the means of yonder little set of blue crockery, which really would hold liquid (it ran out of the small wooden cask, I recollect, and tasted of matches), and which made tea, nectar. And if the two legs of the ineffectual little sugar-tongs did tumble over one another, and want purpose, like Punch's hands, what does it matter? And if I did once shriek out, as a poisoned child, and strike that fashionable company with consternation, by reason of having drunk a little teaspoon, inadvertently dissolved in too hot tea, I was never the worse for it, except by a powder!

Upon the next branches of the tree, lower down, hard by the green roller and miniature gardening-tools, how thick the books begin to hang. Thin books, in themselves, at first, but many of them, and with deliciously smooth covers of bright red or green. What fat black letters to begin with! "A was an archer, and shot at a frog." Of course he was. He was an apple-pie also, and there he is. He was a good many things in his time, was A, and so were most of his friends, except X, who had so little versatility, that I never knew him to get beyond Xerxes or Xantippe—like Y, who was always confined to a Yacht or a Yew Tree; and Z condemned for ever to be a Zebra or a Zany. But, now, the very tree itself changes, and becomes a bean-stalk—the marvellous bean-stalk up which Jack climbed to the Giant's house! And now, those dreadfully interesting, double-headed giants, with their clubs over their shoulders, begin to stride along the boughs in a perfect throng, dragging knights and ladies home for dinner by the hair of their heads. And Jack—how noble, with his sword of sharpness, and his shoes of swiftness! Again those old meditations come upon me as I gaze up at him; and I debate within myself whether there was more than one Jack (which I am loth to believe possible), or only one genuine original admirable Jack, who achieved all the recorded exploits.

Good for Christmas-time is the ruddy colour of the cloak, in which —the tree making a forest of itself for her to trip through, with her basket—Little Red Riding-Hood comes to me one Christmas Eve to give me information of the cruelty and treachery of that dissembling Wolf who ate her grandmother, without making any impression on his appetite, and then ate her, after making that ferocious joke about his teeth. She was my first love. I felt that if I could have married Little Red Riding-Hood, I should have known perfect bliss. But, it was not to be; and there was nothing for it but to look out the Wolf in the Noah's Ark there, and put him late in the procession on the table, as a monster who was to be degraded. O the wonderful Noah's Ark! It was not found seaworthy when put in a washing-tub, and the animals were crammed in at the roof, and needed to have their legs well shaken down before they could be got in, even there— and then, ten to one but they began to tumble out at the door, which was but imperfectly fastened with a wire latch—but what was *that* against it! Consider the noble fly, a size or two smaller than the elephant: the lady-bird, the butterfly—all triumphs of art! Consider the goose, whose feet were so small, and whose balance was so indifferent, that he usually tumbled forward, and knocked down all the animal creation. Consider Noah and his family, like idiotic tobacco-stoppers; and how the leopard stuck to warm little fingers; and how the tails of the larger animals used gradually to resolve themselves into frayed bits of string!

Hush! Again a forest, and somebody up in a tree—not Robin Hood, not Valentine, not the Yellow Dwarf (I have passed him and all Mother Bunch's wonders, without mention), but an Eastern King with a glittering scimitar and turban. By Allah! two Eastern Kings, for I see another, looking over his shoulder! Down upon the grass, at the tree's foot, lies the full length of a coal-black Giant, stretched asleep, with his head in a lady's lap; and near them is a glass box, fastened with four locks of shining steel, in which he keeps the lady prisoner when he is awake. I see the four keys at his girdle now. The lady makes signs to the two kings in the tree, who softly descend. It is the setting-in of the bright Arabian Nights.

Oh, now all common things become uncommon and enchanted to me. All lamps are wonderful; all rings are talismans. Common flower-pots are full of treasure, with a little earth scattered on the top; trees are for Ali Baba to hide in; beef-steaks are to throw down into the Valley of Diamonds, that the precious stones may stick to them, and be carried by the eagles to their nests, whence the traders, with loud cries, will scare them. Tarts are made, according to the recipe of the Vizier's son of Bussorah, who turned pastrycook after he was set down in his drawers at the gate of Damascus; cobblers are all Mustaphas, and in the habit of sewing up people cut into four pieces, to whom they are taken blindfold.

Any iron ring let into stone is the entrance to a cave which only waits for the magician, and the little fire, and the necromancy, that will make the earth shake. All the dates imported come from the same tree as that unlucky date, with whose shell the merchant knocked out the eye of the genie's invisible son. All olives are of the stock of that fresh fruit, concerning which the Commander of the Faithful overheard the boy conduct the fictitious trial of the fraudulent olive merchant; all apples are akin to the apple purchased (with two others) from the Sultan's gardener for three sequins, and which the tall black slave stole from the child. All dogs are associated with the dog, really a transformed man, who jumped upon the baker's counter, and put his paw on the piece of bad money. All rice recalls the rice which the awful lady, who was a ghoule, could only peck by grains, because of her nightly feasts in the burial-place. My very rocking-horse,—there he is, with his nostrils turned completely inside-out, indicative of Blood!—should have a peg in his neck, by virtue thereof to fly away with me, as the wooden horse did with the Prince of Persia, in the sight of all his father's Court.

Yes, on every object that I recognise among those upper branches of my Christmas Tree, I see this fairy light! When I wake in bed, at daybreak, on the cold dark winter mornings, the white snow dimly beheld, outside, through the frost on the window-pane, I hear Dinarzade. "Sister, sister, if you are yet awake, I pray you finish the history of the Young King of the Black Islands." Scheherazade replies, "If my lord the Sultan will suffer me to live another day, sister, I will not only finish that, but tell you a more wonderful story yet." Then, the gracious Sultan goes out, giving no orders for the execution, and we all three breathe again.

At this height of my tree I begin to see, cowering among the leaves—it may be born of turkey, or of pudding, or mince pie, or of these many fancies, jumbled with Robinson Crusoe on his desert island, Philip Quarll among the monkeys, Sandford and Merton with Mr. Barlow, Mother Bunch, and the Mask—or it may be the result of indigestion, assisted by imagination and over-doctoring—a prodigious nightmare. It is so exceedingly indistinct, that I don't know why it's frightful—but I only know it is. I can only make out that it is an immense array of shapeless things, which appear to be planted on a vast exaggeration of the lazy-tongs that used to bear the toy soldiers, and to be slowly coming close to my eyes, and receding to an immeasurable distance. When it comes closest, it is worse. In connexion with it I descry remembrances of winter nights incredibly long; of being sent early to bed, as a punishment for some small offence, and waking in two hours, with a sensation of having been asleep two nights; of the leaden hopelessness of morning ever dawning; and the oppression of a weight of remorse.

And now, I see a wonderful row of little lights rise smoothly out of the ground, before a vast green curtain. Now, a bell rings—a magic bell, which still sounds in my ears unlike all other bells—and music plays, amidst a buzz of voices, and a fragrant smell of orange-peel and oil. Anon, the magic bell commands the music to cease, and the great green curtain rolls itself up majestically, and The Play begins! The devoted dog of Montargis avenges the death of his master, foully murdered in the Forest of Bondy; and a humorous Peasant with a red nose and a very little hat, whom I take from this hour forth to my bosom as a friend (I think he was a waiter or an Hostler at a village Inn, but many years have passed since he and I have met) remarks that the sassigassity of that dog is indeed surprising; and evermore this jocular conceit will live in my remembrance fresh and unfading, overtopping all possible jokes, unto the end of time. Or now I learn with bitter tears how poor Jane Shore, dressed all in white, and with her brown hair hanging down, went starving through the streets; or how George Barnwell killed the worthiest uncle that ever man had, and was afterwards so sorry for it that he ought to have been let off. Comes swift to comfort me, the Pantomime—stupendous Phenomenon!—when clowns are shot from loaded mortars into the great chandelier, bright constellation that it is; when Harlequins, covered all over with scales of pure gold, twist and sparkle, like amazing fish; when Pantaloon (whom I deem it no irreverence to compare in my own mind to my grandfather) puts red-hot pokers in his pocket, and cries "Here's somebody coming!" or taxes the Clown with petty larceny, by saying, "Now, I sawed you do it!" when Everything is capable, with the greatest ease, of being changed into Anything; and "Nothing is, but thinking makes it so." Now, too, I perceive my first experience of the dreary sensation—often to return in after-life—of being unable, next day, to get back to the dull, settled world; of wanting to live for ever in the bright atmosphere I have quitted; of doting on the little Fairy, with the wand like a celestial Barber's Pole, and pining for a Fairy immortality along with her. Ah, she comes back, in many shapes, as my eye wanders down the branches of my Christmas Tree, and goes as often, and has never yet stayed by me!

Out of this delight springs the toy-theatre,—there it is, with its familiar proscenium, and ladies in feathers, in the boxes!—and all its attendant occupation with paste and glue, and gum, and water-colours, in the getting-up of The Miller and his Men, and Elizabeth, or the Exile of Siberia. In spite of a few besetting accidents and failures (particularly an unreasonable disposition in the respectable Kelmar, and some others, to become faint in the legs, and double up, at exciting points of the drama), a teeming world of fancies so suggestive and all-embracing, that, far below it on my Christmas Tree, I see dark, dirty, real Theatres in the day-time, adorned with these associations as with the freshest garlands of the rarest flowers, and charming me yet.

But hark! The Waits are playing, and they break my childish sleep! What images do I associate with the Christmas music as I see them set forth on the Christmas Tree? Known before all the others, keeping far apart from all the others, they gather round my little bed. An angel, speaking to a group of shepherds in a field; some travellers, with eyes uplifted, following a star; a baby in a manger; a child in a spacious temple, talking with grave men; a solemn figure, with a mild and beautiful face, raising a dead girl by the hand; again, near a city gate, calling back the son of a widow, on his bier, to life; a crowd of people looking through the opened roof of a chamber where he sits, and letting down a sick person on a bed, with ropes; the same, in a tempest, walking on the water to a ship; again, on a sea-shore, teaching a great multitude; again, with a child upon his knee, and other children round; again, restoring sight to the blind, speech to the dumb, hearing to the deaf, health to the sick, strength to the lame, knowledge to the ignorant; again, dying upon a Cross, watched by armed soldiers, a thick darkness coming on, the earth beginning to shake, and only one voice heard, "Forgive them, for they know not what they do."

Still, on the lower and maturer branches of the Tree, Christmas associations cluster thick. School-books shut up; Ovid and Virgil silenced; the Rule of Three, with its cool impertinent inquiries, long disposed of; Terence and Plautus acted no more, in an arena of huddled desks and forms, all chipped, and notched, and inked; cricket-bats, stumps, and balls, left higher up, with the smell of trodden grass and the softened noise of shouts in the evening air; the tree is still fresh, still gay. If I no more come home at Christmas-time, there will be boys and girls (thank Heaven!) while the World lasts; and they do! Yonder they dance and play upon the branches of my Tree, God bless them, merrily, and my heart dances and plays too!

And I *do* come home at Christmas. We all do, or we all should. We all come home, or ought to come home, for a short holiday—the longer, the better—from the great boarding-school, where we are for ever working at our arithmetical slates, to take, and give a rest. As to going a visiting, where can we not go, if we will; where have we not been, when we would; starting our fancy from our Christmas Tree!

Away into the winter prospect. There are many such upon the tree! On, by low-lying, misty grounds, through fens and fogs, up long hills, winding dark as caverns between thick plantations, almost shutting out the sparkling stars; so, out on broad heights, until we stop at last, with sudden silence, at an avenue. The gate-bell has a deep, half-awful sound in the frosty air; the gate swings open on its hinges; and, as we drive up to a great house, the glancing lights grow larger in the windows, and the opposing rows of trees seem to fall solemnly back on either side, to give us place. At intervals, all day, a frightened hare has shot across this whitened turf; or the distant clatter of a herd of deer trampling the hard frost, has, for the minute, crushed the silence too. Their watchful eyes beneath the fern may be shining now, if we could see them, like the icy dewdrops on the leaves; but they are still, and all is still. And so, the lights growing larger, and the trees falling back before us, and closing up again, behind us, as if to forbid retreat, we come to the house.

There is probably a smell of roasted chestnuts and other good comfortable things all the time, for we are telling Winter Stories—Ghost Stories, or more shame for us—round the Christmas fire; and we have never stirred, except to draw a little nearer to it. But, no matter for that. We came to the house, and it is an old house, full of great chimneys where wood is burnt on ancient dogs upon the hearth, and grim portraits (some of them with grim legends, too) lower distrustfully from the oaken panels of the walls. We are a middle-aged nobleman, and we make a generous supper with our host and hostess and their guests—it being Christmas-time, and the old house full of company—and then we go to bed. Our room is a very old room. It is hung with tapestry. We don't like the portrait of a cavalier in green, over the fireplace. There are great black beams in the ceiling, and there is a great black bedstead, supported at the foot by two great black figures, who seem to have come off a couple of tombs in the old baronial church in the park, for our particular accommodation. But we are not a superstitious nobleman, and we don't mind. Well! we dismiss our servant, lock the door, and sit before the fire in our dressing-gown, musing about a great many things. At length we go to bed. Well! we can't sleep. We toss and tumble, and can't sleep. The embers on the hearth burn fitfully and make the room look ghostly. We can't help peeping out over the counterpane, at the two black figures and the cavalier—that wicked-looking cavalier—in green. In the flickering light they seem to advance and retire: which, though we are not by any means a superstitious nobleman, is not agreeable. Well! we get nervous—more and more nervous. We say "This is very foolish, but we can't stand this; we'll pretend to be ill, and knock up somebody." Well, we are just going to do it, when the locked door opens, and there comes in a young woman, deadly pale, and with long fair hair, who glides to the fire, and sits down in the chair we have left there, wringing her hands. Then, we notice that her clothes are wet.

Our tongue cleaves to the roof of our mouth, and we can't speak; but, we observe her accurately. Her clothes are wet; her long hair is dabbled with moist mud; she is dressed in the fashion of two hundred years ago; and she has at her girdle a bunch of rusty keys. Well! there she sits, and we can't even faint, we are in such a state about it. Presently she gets up, and tries all the locks in the room with the rusty keys, which won't fit one of them; then, she fixes her eyes on the protrait of the cavalier in green, and says, in a low, terrible voice, "The stags know it!" After that, she wrings her hands again, passes the bedside, and goes out at the door. We hurry on our dressing-gown, seize our pistols (we always travel with pistols), and are follow-ing, when we find the door locked. We turn the key, look out into the dark gallery; no one there. We wander away, and try to find our ser-vant. Can't be done. We pace the gallery till daybreak; then return to our deserted room, fall asleep, and are awakened by our servant (nothing ever haunts *him*) and the shining sun. Well! we make a wretched breakfast, and all the company say we look queer. After breakfast, we go over the house with our host, and then we take him to the portrait of the cavalier in green, and then it all comes out. He was false to a young housekeeper once attached to that family, and famous for her beauty, who drowned herself in a pond, and whose body was discovered, after a long time, because the stags refused to drink of the water. Since which, it has been whispered that she tra-verses the house at midnight (but goes especially to that room where the cavalier in green was wont to sleep), trying the old locks with the rusty keys. Well! we tell our host of what we have seen, and a shade comes over his features, and he begs it may be hushed up; and so it is. But, it's all true; and we said so, before we died (we are dead now), to many responsible people.

There is no end to the old houses, with resounding galleries, and dismal state-bedchambers, and haunted wings shut up for many years, through which we may ramble, with an agreeable creeping up our back, and encounter any number of ghosts, but (it is worthy of remark perhaps) reducible to a very few general types and classes; for, ghosts have little originality, and "walk" in a beaten track. Thus, it comes to pass, that a certain room in a certain old hall, where a certain bad lord, baronet, knight, or gentleman, shot himself, has certain planks in the floor from which the blood *will not* be taken out. You may scrape and scrape, as the present owner has done, or plane and plane, as his father did, or scrub and scrub, as his grandfather did, or burn and burn with strong acids, as his great-grandfather did, but, there the blood will still be—no redder and no paler—no more and no less—always just the same. Thus, in such another house there is a haunted door, that never will keep open; or another door that never will keep shut; or a haunted sound of a spinning-wheel, or a hammer or a footstep, or a cry, or a sigh, or a horse's tramp, or the rattling of a chain. Or else, there is a turret-clock, which, at the midnight hour, strikes thirteen when the head of the family is going to die; or a shadowy, immovable black carriage which at such a time is always seen by somebody, waiting near the great gates in the stable-yard. Or thus, it came to pass how Lady Mary went to pay a visit at a large wild house in the Scottish Highlands, and, being fatigued with her long journey, retired to bed early, and innocently said, next morning, at the breakfast-table, "How odd, to have so late a party last night, in this remote place, and not to tell of it, before I went to bed!" Then, every one asked Lady Mary what she meant? Then, Lady Mary replied, "Why, all night long, the carriages were driving round and round the terrace, underneath my window!" Then, the owner of the house turned pale, and so did his Lady, and Charles Macdoodle of Macdoodle signed to Lady Mary to say no more, and every one was silent. After breakfast, Charles Macdoodle told Lady Mary that it was a tradition in the family that those rumbling carriages on the terrace betokened death. And so it proved, for, two months afterwards, the Lady of the mansion died. And Lady Mary, who was a Maid of Honour at Court, often told this story to the old Queen Charlotte; by this token that the old King always said, "Eh, eh? What, what? Ghosts, ghosts? No such thing, no such thing!" And never left off saying so, until he went to bed.

Or, a friend of somebody's whom most of us know, when he was a young man at college, had a particular friend, with whom he made the compact that, if it were possible for the Spirit to return to this earth after its separation from the body, he of the twain who first died, should reappear to the other. In course of time, this compact was forgotten by our friend; the two young men having progressed in life, and taken diverging paths that were wide asunder. But, one night, many years afterwards, our friend being in the North of England, and staying for the night in an inn, on the Yorkshire Moors, happened to look out of bed; and there, in the moonlight, leaning on a bureau near the window, steadfastly regarding him, saw his old college friend! The appearance being solemnly addressed, replied, in a kind of whisper, but very audibly, "Do not come near me. I am dead. I am here to redeem my promise. I come from another world, but may not disclose its secrets!" Then the whole form becoming paler, melted, as it were, into the moonlight, and faded away.

Or, there was the daughter of the first occupier of the picturesque Elizabethan house, so famous in our neighbourhood. You have heard about her? No! Why, *She* went out one summer evening at twilight, when she was a beautiful girl, just seventeen years of age, to gather flowers in the garden; and presently came running, terrified, into the hall, to her father, saying, "Oh, dear father, I have met myself!" He took her in his arms, and told her it was fancy, but she said, "Oh no! met myself in the broad walk, and I was pale and gathering withered flowers, and I turned my head, and held them up!" And that night, she died; and a picture of her story was begun, though never finished, and they say it is somewhere in the house to this day, with its face to the wall.

Or, the uncle of my brother's wife was riding home on horse-back, one mellow evening at sunset, when, in a green lane close to his own house, he saw a man standing before him, in the very centre of a narrow way, "Why does that man in the cloak stand there?" he thought. "Does he want me to ride over him?" But the figure never moved. He felt a strange sensation at seeing it so still, but slackened his trot and rode forward. When he was so close to it, as almost to touch it with his stirrup, his horse shied, and the figure glided up the bank, in a curious, unearthly manner—backward, and without seeming to use its feet—and was gone. The uncle of my brother's wife, exclaiming, "Good Heaven! It's my cousin Harry, from Bombay!" put spurs to his horse, which was suddenly in a profuse sweat, and wondering at such strange behaviour, dashed round to the front of his house. There, he saw the same figure, just passing in at the long French window of the drawing-room, opening on the ground. He threw his bridle to a servant, and hastened in after it. His sister was sitting there, alone, "Alice, where's my cousin Harry?" "Your cousin, Harry, John?" "Yes. From Bombay. I met him in the lane just now, and saw him enter here, this instant." Not a creature had been seen by any one; and in that hour and minute, as it afterwards appeared, this cousin died in India.

Or, it was a certain sensible old maiden lady, who died at ninety-nine, and retained her faculties to the last, who really did see the Orphan Boy; a story which has often been incorrectly told, but, of which the real truth is this—because it is, in fact, a story belonging to our family—and she was a connexion of our family. When she was about forty years of age, and still an uncommonly fine woman (her lover died young, which was the reason why she never married, though she had many offers), she went to stay at a place in Kent, which her brother, an Indian-Merchant, had newly bought. There was a story that this place had once been held in trust, by the guardian of a young boy; who was himself the next heir, and who killed the young boy by harsh and cruel treatment. She knew nothing of that. It has been said that there was a Cage in her bedroom in which the guardian used to put the boy. There was no such thing. There was only a closet. She went to bed, made no alarm whatever in the night, and in the morning said composedly to her maid when she came in, "Who is the pretty forlorn-looking child who has been peeping out of that closet all night?" The maid replied by giving a loud scream, and instantly decamping. She was surprised; but she was a woman of remarkable strength of mind, and she dressed herself and went downstairs, and closeted herself with her brother, "Now, Walter," she said, "I have been disturbed all night by a pretty, forlorn-looking boy, who has been constantly peeping out of that closet in my room, which I can't open. This is some trick." "I am afraid not, Charlotte," said he, "for it is the legend of the house. It is the Orphan Boy. What did he do?" "He opened the door softly," said she, "and peeped out. Sometimes, he came a step or two into the room. Then, I called to him, to encourage him, and he shrunk, and shuddered, and crept in again, and shut the door." "The closet has no communication, Charlotte," said her brother, "with any other part of the house, and it's nailed up." This was undeniably true, and it took two carpenters a whole forenoon to get it open, for examination. Then, she was satisfied that she had seen the Orphan Boy. But, the wild and terrible part of the story is, that he was also seen by three of her brother's sons, in succession, who all died young. On the occasion of each child being taken ill, he came home in a heat, twelve hours before, and said, Oh, mama, he had been playing under a particular oak-tree, in a certain meadow, with a strange boy—a pretty, forlorn-looking boy, who was very timid, and made signs! From fatal experience, the parents came to know that this was the Orphan Boy, and that the course of that child whom he chose for his little playmate was surely run.

Legion is the name of the German castles, where we sit up alone to wait for the Spectre—where we are shown into a room made comparatively cheerful for our reception—where we glance round at the shadows, thrown on the blank walls by the crackling fire—where we feel very lonely when the village innkeeper and his pretty daughter have retired, after laying down a fresh store of wood upon the hearth, and setting forth on the small table such supper-cheer as a cold roast capon, bread, grapes, and a flask of old Rhine wine—where the reverberating doors close on their retreat, one after another, like so many peals of sullen thunder—and where, about the small hours of the night, we come into the knowledge of divers supernatural mysteries. Legion is the name of the haunted German students, in whose society we draw yet nearer to the fire, while the schoolboy on the corner opens his eyes wide and round, and flies off the footstool he has chosen for his seat, when the door accidentally blows open. Vast is the crop of such fruit, shining on our Christmas Tree; in blossom, almost at the very top; ripening all down the boughs!

Among the later toys and fancies hanging there—as idle often and less pure—be the images once associated with the sweet old Waits, the softened music in the night, ever unalterable! Encircled by the social thoughts of Christmas-time, still let the benignant figure of my childhood stand unchanged! In every cheerful image and suggestion that the season brings, may the bright star that rested above the poor roof, be the star of all the Christian world! a moment's pause, O vanishing tree, of which the lower boughs are dark to me as yet, and let me look once more! I know there are blank spaces on thy branches, where eyes that I have loved, have shone and smiled; from which they are departed. But, far above, I see the raiser of the dead girl, and the Widow's Son; and God is good! If Age be hiding for me in the unseen portion of thy downward growth, O may I, with a grey head, turn a child's heart to that figure yet, and a child's trustfulness and confidence!

Now, the tree is decorated with bright merriment, and song, and dance, and cheerfulness. And they are welcome. Innocent and welcome be they ever held, beneath the branches of the Christmas Tree, which cast no gloomy shadow! But, as it sinks into the ground, I hear a whisper going through the leaves. "This, in commemoration of the law of love and kindness, mercy and compassion. This, in remembrance of Me!"

WHAT CHRISTMAS IS AS WE GROW OLDER

[1851]

TIME was, with most of us, when Christmas Day encircling all our limited world like a magic ring, left nothing out for us to miss or seek; bound together all our home enjoyments, affections, and hopes! grouped everything and every one around the Christmas fire; and made the little picture shining in our bright young eyes, complete.

Time came, perhaps, all too soon, when our thoughts overleaped that narrow boundary; when there was some one (very dear, we thought then, very beautiful, and absolutely perfect) wanting to the fulness of our happiness; when we were wanting too (or we thought so, which did just as well) at the Christmas hearth by which that some one sat; and when we intertwined with every wreath and garland of our life that some one's name.

That was the time for the bright visionary Christmases which have long arisen from us to show faintly, after summer rain, in the palest edges of the rainbow! That was the time for the beatified enjoyment of the things that were to be, and never were, and yet the things that were so real in our resolute hope that it would be hard to say, now, what realities achieved since, have been stronger.

What! Did that Christmas never really come when we and the priceless pearl who was our young choice were received, after the happiest of totally impossible marriages, by the two united families previously at daggers-drawn on our account? When brothers and sisters in law who had always been rather cool to us before our relationship was effected, perfectly doted on us, and when fathers and mothers overwhelmed us with unlimited incomes? Was that Christmas dinner never really eaten, after which we arose, and generously and eloquently rendered honour to our late rival, present in the company, then and there exchanging friendship and forgiveness, and founding an attachment, not to be surpassed in Greek or Roman story, which subsisted until death? Has that same rival long ceased to care for that same priceless pearl, and married for money, and become usurious? Above all, do we really know, now, that we should probably have been miserable if we had won and worn the pearl, and that we are better without her?.

That Christmas when we had recently achieved so much fame; when we had been carried in triumph somewhere, for doing something great and good; when we had won an honoured and ennobled name, and arrived and were received at home in a shower of tears of joy; is it possible that *that* Christmas has not come yet?

And is our life, here, at the best, so constituted that, pausing as we advance at such a noticeable milestone in the track as this great birthday, we look back on the things that never were, as naturally and full as gravely as on the things that have been and are gone, or have been and still are? If it be so, and so it seems to be, must we come to the conclusion that life is little better than a dream, and little worth the loves and strivings that we crowd into it?

No! Far be such miscalled philosophy from us, dear Reader, on Christmas Day! Nearer and closer to our hearts be the Christmas spirit, which is the spirit of active usefulness, perseverance, cheerful discharge of duty, kindness and forbearance! It is in the last virtues especially, that we are, or should be, strengthened by the unaccomplished visions of our youth; for, who shall say that they are not our teachers to deal gently even with the impalpable nothings of the earth!

Therefore, as we grow older, let us be more thankful that the circle of our Christmas associations and of the lessons that they bring, expands! Let us welcome every one of them, and summon them to take their places by the Christmas hearth.

Welcome, old aspirations, glittering creatures of an ardent fancy, to your shelter underneath the holly! We know you, and have not outlived you yet. Welcome, old projects and old loves, however fleeting, to your nooks among the steadier lights that burn around us. Welcome, all that was ever real to our hearts; and for the earnestness that made you real, thanks to Heaven! Do we build no Christmas castles in the clouds now? Let our thoughts, fluttering like butterflies among these flowers of children, bear witness! Before this boy there stretches out a Future, brighter than we ever looked on in our old romantic time, but bright with honour and with truth. Around this little head on which the sunny curls lie heaped, the graces sport, as prettily, as airily, as when there was no scythe within the reach of Time to shear away the curls of our first-love. Upon another girl's face near it—placider but smiling bright—a quiet and contented little face, we see Home fairly written. Shining from the word, as rays shine from a star, we see how, when our graves are old, other hopes than ours are young, other hearts than ours are moved; how other ways are smoothed; how other happiness blooms, ripens, and decays —no, not decays, for other homes and other bands of children, not yet being nor for ages yet to be, arise, and bloom and ripen to the end of all!

Welcome, everything! Welcome, alike what has been, and what never was, and what we hope may be, to your shelter underneath the holly, to your places round the Christmas fire, where what is sits open-hearted! In yonder shadow, do we see obtruding furtively upon the blaze, an enemy's face? By Christmas Day we do forgive him! If the injury he has done us may admit of such companionship, let him come here and take his place. If otherwise, unhappily, let him go hence, assured that we will never injure nor accuse him.

On this day we shut out nothing!

"Pause," says a low voice. "Nothing? Think!"

"On Christmas Day, we will shut out from our fireside, Nothing."

"Not the shadow of a vast City where the withered leaves are lying deep?" the voice replies. "Not the shadow that darkens the whole globe? Not the shadow of the City of the Dead?"

Not even that. Of all days in the year, we will turn our faces towards that City upon Christmas Day, and from its silent hosts bring those we loved, among us. City of the Dead, in the blessed name wherein we are gathered together at this time, and in the Presence that is here among us according to the promise, we will receive, and not dismiss, the people who are dear to us!

Yes. We can look upon these children angels that alight, so solemnly, so beautifully among the living children by the fire, and can bear to think how they departed from us. Entertaining angels unawares, as the Patriarchs did, the playful children are unconscious of their guests; but we can see them—can see a radiant arm around one favourite neck, as if there were a tempting of that child away. Among the celestial figures there is one, a poor mis-shapen boy on earth, of a glorious beauty now, of whom his dying mother said it grieved her much to leave him here, alone for so many years as it was likely would elapse before he came to her—being such a little child. But he went quickly, and was laid upon her breast, and in her hand she leads him.

There was a gallant boy, who fell, far away, upon a burning sand beneath a burning sun, and said, "Tell them at home, with my last love, how much I could have wished to kiss them once, but that I died contented and had done my duty!" Or there was another, over whom they read the words, "Therefore we commit his body to the deep," and so consigned him to the lonely ocean and sailed on. Or there was another, who lay down to his rest in the dark shadows of great forests, and, on earth, awoke no more. O shall they not, from sand and sea and forest, be brought home at such a time?

There was a dear girl—almost a woman—never to be one—who made a mourning Christmas in a house of joy, and went her trackless way to the silent City. Do we recollect her, worn out, faintly whispering what could not be heard, and falling into that last sleep for weariness? O look upon her now! O look upon her beauty, her serenity, her changeless youth, her happiness! The daughter of Jairus was recalled to life, to die; but she, more blest, has heard the same voice, saying unto her, "Arise for ever!"

We had a friend who was our friend from early days, with whom we often pictured the changes that were to come upon our lives, and merrily imagined how we would speak, and walk, and think, and talk, when we came to be old. His destined habitation in the City of the Dead received him in his prime. Shall he be shut out from our Christmas remembrance? Would his love have so excluded us? Lost friend, lost child, lost parent, lost sister, brother, husband, wife, we will not so discard you! You shall hold your cherished places in our Christmas hearts, and by our Christmas fires; and in the season of immortal hope, and on the birthday of immortal mercy, we will shut out Nothing!

The winter sun goes down over town and village; on the sea it makes a rosy path, as if the Sacred tread were fresh upon the water. A few more moments, and it sinks, and night comes on, and lights begin to sparkle in the prospect. On the hillside beyond the shapelessly-diffused town, and in the quiet keeping of the trees that gird the village-steeple, remembrances are cut in stone, planted in common flowers, growing in grass entwined with lowly brambles around many a mound of earth. In town and village, there are doors and windows closed against the weather, there are flaming logs heated high, there are joyful faces, there is healthy music of voices. Be all ungentleness and harm excluded from the temples of the Household Gods, but be those remembrances admitted with tender encouragement! They are of the time and all its comforting and peaceful reassurances; and of the history that reunited even upon earth the living and the dead; and of the broad beneficence and goodness that too many men have tried to tear to narrow shreds.

THE POOR RELATION'S STORY

[1852]

HE was very reluctant to take precedence of so many respected members of the family, by beginning the round of stories they were to relate as they sat in a goodly circle by the Christmas fire; and he modestly suggested that it would be more correct if "John our esteemed host" (whose health he begged to drink) would have the kindness to begin. For as to himself, he said, he was so little used to lead the way that really——But as they all cried out here, that he must begin, and agreed with one voice that he might, could, would, and should begin, he left off rubbing his hands, and took his legs out from under his armchair, and did begin.

I have no doubt (said the poor relation) that I shall surprise the assembled members of our family, and particularly John our esteemed host to whom we are so much indebted for the great hospitality with which he has this day entertained us by the confession I am going to make. But, if you do me the honour to be surprised at anything that falls from a person so unimportant in the family as I am, I can only say that I shall be scrupulously accurate in all I relate.

I am not what I am supposed to be. I am quite another thing. Perhaps before I go further, I had better glance at what I *am* supposed to be.

It is supposed, unless I mistake—the assembled members of the family will correct me if I do, which is very likely (here the poor relation looked mildly about him for contradiction); that I am nobody's enemy but my own. That I never met with any particular success in anything. That I failed in business because I was unbusiness-like and credulous—in not being prepared for the interested designs of my partner. That I failed in love, because I was ridiculously trustful—in thinking it impossible that Christiana could deceive me. That I failed in my expectations from my uncle Chill, on account of not being as sharp as he could have wished in worldly matters. That, through life, I have been rather put upon and disappointed in a general way. That I am at present a bachelor of between fifty-nine and sixty years of age, living on a limited income in the form of a quarterly allowance, to which I see that John our esteemed host wishes me to make no further allusion.

The supposition as to my present pursuits and habits is to the following effect.

23

I live in a lodging in the Clapham Road—a very clean back room, in a very respectable house—where I am expected not to be at home in the day-time, unless poorly; and which I usually leave in the morning at nine o'clock, on pretence of going to business. I take my breakfast—my roll and butter, and my half-pint of coffee—at the old established coffee-shop near Westminster Bridge; and then I go into the City—I don't know why—and sit in Garraway's Coffee House, and on 'Change, and walk about, and look into a few offices and counting-houses where some of my relations or acquaintance are so good as to tolerate me, and where I stand by the fire if the weather happens to be cold. I get through the day in this way until five o'clock, and then I dine: at a cost, on the average, of one and threepence. Having still a little money to spend on my evening's entertainment, I look into the old-established coffee-shop as I go home, and take my cup of tea, and perhaps my bit of toast. So, as the large hand of the clock makes its way round to the morning hour again, I make my round to the Clapham Road again, and go to bed when I get to my lodging—fire being expensive, and being objected to by the family on account of its giving trouble and making a dirt.

Sometimes, one of my relations or acquaintance is so obliging as to ask me to dinner. These are holiday occasions, and then I generally walk in the Park. I am a solitary man, and seldom walk with anybody. Not that I am avoided because I am shabby; for I am not at all shabby, having always a very good suit of black on (or rather Oxford mixture, which has the appearance of black and wears much better); but I have got into a habit of speaking low, and being rather silent, and my spirits are not high, and I am sensible that I am not an attractive companion.

The only exception to this general rule is the child of my first cousin, Little Frank. I have a particular affection for that child, and he takes very kindly to me. He is a diffident boy by nature; and in a crowd he is soon run over, as I may say, and forgotten. He and I, however, get on exceedingly well. I have a fancy that the poor child will in time succeed to my peculiar position in the family. We talk but little; still, we understand each other. We walk about, hand in hand; and without much speaking he knows what I mean, and I know what he means. When he was very little indeed, I used to take him to the windows of the toy-shops, and show him the toys inside. It is surprising how soon he found out that I would have made him a great many presents if I had been in circumstances to do it.

Little Frank and I go and look at the outside of the Monument—he is very fond of the Monument—and at the Bridges, and at all the sights that are free. On two of my birthdays, we have dined on à-la-mode beef, and gone at half-price to the play and been deeply interested. I was once walking with him in Lombard Street, which we often visit on account of my having mentioned to him that there are great riches there—he is very fond of Lombard Street—when a gentleman said to me as he passed by, "Sir, your little son has dropped his glove." I assure you, if you will excuse my remarking on so trivial a circumstance, this accidental mention of the child as mine, quite touched my heart and brought the foolish tears into my eyes.

When Little Frank is sent to school in the country, I shall be very much at a loss what to do with myself, but I have the intention of walking down there once a month and seeing him on a half-holiday. I am told he will then be at play upon the Heath; and if my visits should be objected to, as unsettling the child, I can see him from a distance without his seeing me, and walk back again. His mother comes of a highly genteel family, and rather disapproves, I am aware of our being too much together. I know that I am not calculated to improve his retiring disposition; but I think he would miss me beyond the feeling of the moment if we were wholly separated.

When I die in the Clapham Road, I shall not leave much more in this world than I shall take out of it; but, I happen to have a minia-ture of a bright-faced boy, with a curling head, and an open shirt-frill waving down his bosom (my mother had it taken for me, but I can't believe that it was ever like), which will be worth nothing to sell, and which I shall beg may be given to Frank. I have written my dear boy a little letter with it, in which I have told him that I felt sorry to part from him, though bound to confess that I knew no reason why I should remain here. I have given him some short advice, the best in my power, to take warning of the consequences of being nobody's enemy but his own, and I have endeavoured to comfort him for what I fear he will consider a bereavement, by pointing out to him, that I was only a superfluous something to every one but him; and that having by some means failed to find a place in this great assembly, I am better out of it.

Such (said the poor relation, clearing his throat and beginning to speak a little louder) is the general impression about me. Now, it is a remarkable circumstance which forms the aims and purpose of my story, that this is all wrong. This is not my life, and these are not my habits. I do not even live in the Clapham Road. Comparatively speak-ing, I am very seldom there. I reside, mostly, in a—I am almost ashamed to say the word, it sounds so full of pretension—in a Castle. I do not mean that it is an old baronial habitation, but still it is a building always known to every one by the name of a Castle. In it, I preserve the particulars of my history; they run thus:

It was when I first took John Spatter (who had been my clerk) into partnership, and when I was still a young man of not more than five-and-twenty, residing in the house of my uncle Chill, from whom I had considerable expectations, that I ventured to propose to Christiana. I had loved Christiana a long time. She was very beautiful, and very winning in all respects. I rather mistrusted her widowed mother, who I feared was of a plotting and mercenary turn of mind; but, I thought as well of her as I could, for Christiana's sake. I never had loved any one but Christiana, and she had been all the world, and O far more than all the world, to me, from our childhood!

Christiana accepted me with her mother's consent, and I was rendered very happy indeed. My life at my uncle Chill's was of a spare dull kind, and my garret chamber was as dull, and bare, and cold, as an upper prison room in some stern northern fortress. But, having Christiana's love, I wanted nothing upon earth. I would not have changed my lot with any human being.

Avarice was, unhappily, my uncle Chill's master-vice. Though he was rich, he pinched, and scraped, and clutched, and lived miserably. As Christiana had no fortune, I was for some time a little fearful of confessing our engagement to him; but, at length, I wrote him a letter saying how it all truly was. I put it into his hand one night, on going to bed.

As I came downstairs next morning, shivering in the cold December air; colder in my uncle's unwarmed house than in the street, where the winter sun did sometimes shine, and which was at all events enlivened by cheerful faces and voices passing along; I carried a heavy heart towards the long, low breakfast room in which my uncle sat. It was a large room with a small fire, and there was a great bay window in it which the rain had marked in the night as if with the tears of houseless people. It stared upon a raw yard, with a cracked stone pavement, and some rusted iron railings half uprooted, whence an ugly out-building that had once been a dissecting-room (in the time of the great surgeon who had mortgaged the house to my uncle), stared at it.

We rose so early always, that at that time of the year we breakfasted by candle-light. When I went into the room, my uncle was so contracted by the cold, and so huddled together in his chair behind the one dim candle, that I did not see him until I was close to the table.

As I held out my hand to him, he caught up his stick (being infirm, he always walked about the house with a stick), and made a blow at me, and said, "You fool!"

"Uncle," I returned, "I didn't expect you to be so angry as this." Nor had I expected it, though he was a hard and angry old man.

"You didn't expect!" said he; "when did you ever expect? When did you ever calculate, or look forward, you contemptible dog?"

"These are hard words, uncle!"

"Hard words? Feathers, to pelt such an idiot as you with," said he. "Here! Betsy Snap! Look at him!"

Betsy Snap was a withered, hard-featured, yellow old woman—our only domestic—always employed, at this time of the morning, in rubbing my uncle's legs. As my uncle adjured her to look at me, he put his lean grip on the crown of her head, she kneeling beside him, and turned her face towards me. An involuntary thought connecting them both with the Dissecting Room, as it must often have been in the surgeon's time, passed across my mind in the midst of my anxiety.

"Look at the snivelling milksop!" said my uncle. "Look at the baby! This is the gentleman who, people say, is nobody's enemy but his own. This is the gentleman who can't say no. This is the gentleman who was making such large profits in his business that he must needs take a partner, t'other day. This is the gentleman who is going to marry a wife without a penny, and who falls into the hands of Jezebels who are speculating on my death!"

I knew, now, how great my uncle's rage was; for nothing short of his being almost beside himself would have induced him to utter that concluding word, which he held in such repugnance that it was never spoken or hinted at before him on any account.

"On my death," he repeated, as if he were defying me by defying his own abhorrence of the word. "On my death—death—Death! But I'll spoil the speculation. Eat your last under this roof, you feeble wretch, and may it choke you!"

You may suppose that I had not much appetite for the breakfast to which I was bidden in these terms; but, I took my accustomed seat. I saw that I was repudiated henceforth by my uncle; still I could bear that very well, possessing Christiana's heart.

He emptied his basin of bread and milk as usual, only that he took it on his knees with his chair turned away from the table where I sat. When he had done, he carefully snuffed out the candle; and the cold, slate-coloured, miserable day looked in upon us.

"Now, Mr. Michael," said he, "before we part, I should like to have a word with these ladies in your presence."

"As you will, sir," I returned; "but you deceive yourself, and wrong us, cruelly, if you suppose that there is any feeling at stake in this contract, but pure, disinterested, faithful love."

To this, he only replied, "You lie!" and not one other word.

We went, through half-thawed snow and half-frozen rain, to the house where Christiana and her mother lived. My uncle knew them very well. They were sitting at their breakfast, and were surprised to see us at that hour.

"Your servant, ma'am," said my uncle to the mother. "You divine the purpose of my visit, I dare say, ma'am. I understand there is a world of pure, disinterested, faithful love cooped up here. I am happy to bring it all it wants, to make it complete. I bring you your son-in-law, ma'am—and you, your husband, miss. The gentleman is a perfect stranger to me, but I wish him joy of his wise bargain."

He snarled at me as he went out, and I never saw him again.

It is altogether a mistake (continued the poor relation) to suppose that my dear Christiana, over-persuaded and influenced by her mother, married a rich man, the dirt from whose carriage-wheels is often, in these changed times, thrown upon me as she rides by. No, no. She married me.

The way we came to be married rather sooner than we intended was this. I took a frugal lodging and was saving and planning for her sake, when, one day, she spoke to me with great earnestness, and said:

"My dear Michael, I have given you my heart. I have said that I loved you, and I have pledged myself to be your wife. I am as much yours through all changes of good and evil as if we had been married on the day when such words passed between us. I know you well, and know that if we should be separated and our union broken off, your whole life would be shadowed, and all that might, even now, be stronger in your character for the conflict with the world would then be weakened to the shadow of what it is!"

"God help me, Christiana!" said I. "You speak the truth."

"Michael!" said she, putting her hand in mine, in all maidenly devotion, "let us keep apart no longer. It is but for me to say that I can live contented upon such means as you have, and I well know you are happy. I say so from my heart. Strive no more alone; let us strive together. My dear Michael, it is not right that I should keep secret from you what you do not suspect, but what distresses my whole life. My mother: without considering that what you have lost, you have lost for me, and on the assurance of my faith: sets her heart on riches, and urges another suit upon me, to my misery. I cannot bear this, for to bear it is to be untrue to you. I would rather share your struggles than look on. I want no better home than you can give me. I know that you will aspire and labour with a higher courage if I am wholly yours, and let it be so when you will!"

I was blest indeed, that day, and a new world opened to me. We were married in a very little while, and I took my wife to our happy home. That was the beginning of the residence I have spoken of; the Castle we have ever since inhabited together, dates from that time. All our children have been born in it. Our first child—now married—was a little girl, whom we called Christiana. Her son is so like little Frank, that I hardly know which is which.

The current impression as to my partner's dealings with me is also quite erroneous. He did not begin to treat me coldly, as a poor simpleton, when my uncle and I so fatally quarrelled; nor did he afterwards gradually possess himself of our business and edge me out. On the contrary, he behaved to me with the utmost good faith and honour.

Matters between us took this turn:—On the day of my separation from my uncle, and even before the arrival at our counting-house of my trunks (which he sent after me, *not* carriage paid), I went down to our room of business, on our little wharf, overlooking the river; and there I told John Spatter what had happened. John did not say, in reply, that rich old relatives were palpable facts, and that love and sentiment were moonshine and fiction. He addressed me thus:

"Michael," said John, "we were at school together, and I generally had the knack of getting on better than you, and making a higher reputation."

"You had, John," I returned.

"Although," said John, "I borrowed your books and lost them; borrowed your pocket-money, and never repaid it; got you to buy my damaged knives at a higher price than I had given for them new; and to own to the windows that I had broken."

"All not worth mentioning, John Spatter," said I, "but certainly true."

"When you were first established in this infant business, which promises to thrive so well," pursued John, "I came to you, in my search for almost any employment, and you made me your clerk."

"Still not worth mentioning, my dear John Spatter," said I; "still, equally true."

"And finding that I had a good head for business, and that I was really useful *to* the business, you did not like to retain me in that capacity, and thought it an act of justice soon to make me your partner."

"Still less worth mentioning, than any of those other little circumstances you have recalled, John Spatter," said I; "for I was, and am, sensible of your merits and my deficiencies."

"Now, my good friend," said John, drawing my arm through his, as he had had a habit of doing at school; while two vessels outside the windows of our counting-house—which were shaped like the stern windows of a ship—went lightly down the river with the tide, as John and I might then be sailing away in company, and in trust and confidence, on our voyage of life; "let there, under these friendly circumstances, be a right understanding between us. You are too easy, Michael. You are nobody's enemy but your own. If I were to give you that damaging character among our connexion, with a shrug, and a shake of the head, and a sigh; and if I were further to abuse the trust you place in me——"

"But you never will abuse it at all, John," I observed.

"Never!" said he; "but I am putting a case—I say, and if I were further to abuse that trust by keeping this piece of our common affair in the dark, and this other piece in the light, and again this other piece in the twilight, and so on, I should strengthen my strength, and weaken your weakness, day by day, until at last I found myself on the high road to fortune, and you left behind on some bare common, a hopeless number of miles out of the way."

"Exactly so," said I.

"To prevent this, Michael," said John Spatter, "or the remotest chance of this, there must be perfect openness between us. Nothing must be concealed, and we must have but one interest."

"My dear John Spatter," I assured him, "that is precisely what I mean."

"And when you are too easy," pursued John, his face glowing with friendship, "you must allow me to prevent that imperfection in your nature from being taken advantage of, by any one; you must not expect me to humour it——"

"My dear John Spatter," I interrupted, I *"don't* expect you to humour it. I want to correct it."

"And I, too," said John.

"Exactly so!" cried I. "We both have the same end in view; and, honourably seeking it, and fully trusting one another, and having but one interest, ours will be a prosperous and happy partnership."

"I am sure of it!" returned John Spatter. And we shook hands most affectionately.

I took John home to my Castle, and we had a very happy day. Our partnership throve well. My friend and partner supplied what I wanted, as I had foreseen that he would; and by improving both the business and myself, amply acknowledged any little rise in life to which I had helped him.

I am not (said the poor relation, looking at the fire as he slowly rubbed his hands) very rich, for I never cared to be that; but I have enough, and am above all moderate wants and anxieties. My castle is not a splendid place, but it is very comfortable, and it has a warm and cheerful air, and is quite a picture of Home.

Our eldest girl, who is very like her mother, married John Spatter's eldest son. Our two families are closely united in other ties of attachment. It is very pleasant of an evening, when we are all assembled together—which frequently happens—and when John and I talk over old times, and the one interest there has always been between us.

I really do not know, in my Castle, what loneliness is. Some of our children or grandchildren are always about it, and the young voices of my descendants are delightful—O, how delightful!—to me to hear. My dearest and most devoted wife, ever faithful, ever loving, ever helpful and sustaining and consoling, is the priceless blessing of my house; from whom all its other blessings spring. We are rather a musical family, and when Christiana sees me, at any time, a little weary or depressed, she steals to the piano and sings a gentle air she used to sing when we were first betrothed. So weak a man am I, that I cannot bear to hear it from any other source. They played it once, at the Theatre, when I was there with Little Frank; and the child said wondering, "Cousin Michael, whose hot tears are these that have fallen on my hand?"

Such is my Castle, and such are the real particulars of my life therein preserved. I often take Little Frank home there. He is very welcome to my grandchildren, and they play together. At this time of the year—the Christmas and New Year time—I am seldom out of my Castle. For, the associations of the season seem to hold me there, and the precepts of the season seem to teach me that it is well to be there.

"And the Castle is——" observed a grave, kind voice among the company.

"Yes. My Castle," said the poor relation, shaking his head as he still looked at the fire, "is in the Air. John our esteemed host suggests its situation accurately. My Castle is in the Air! I have done. Will you be so good as to pass the story!"

THE CHILD'S STORY

[1852]

ONCE upon a time, a good many years ago, there was a traveller, and he set out upon a journey. It was a magic journey, and was to seem very long when he began it, and very short when he got half way through.

He travelled along a rather dark path for some little time, without meeting anything, until at last he came to a beautiful child. So he said to the child, "What do you do here?" And the child said, "I am always at play. Come and play with me!"

So, he played with that child, the whole day long, and they were very merry. The sky was so blue, the sun was so bright, the water was so sparkling, the leaves were so green, the flowers were so lovely, and they heard such singing-birds and saw so many butterflies, that everything was beautiful. This was in fine weather. When it rained, they loved to watch the falling drops, and to smell the fresh scents. When it blew, it was delightful to listen to the wind, and fancy what it said, as it came rushing from its home—where was that, they wondered! —whistling and howling, driving the clouds before it, bending the trees, rumbling in the chimneys, shaking the house, and making the sea roar in fury. But, when it snowed, that was best of all; for they liked nothing so well as to look up at the white flakes falling fast and thick, like down from the breasts of millions of white birds; and to see how smooth and deep the drift was; and to listen to the hush upon the paths and roads.

They had plenty of the finest toys in the world, and the most astonishing picture-books: all about scimitars and slippers and turbans, and dwarfs and giants and genii and fairies, and blue-bears and bean-stalks and riches and caverns and forests and Valentines and Orsons : and all new and all true.

But, one day, of a sudden, the traveller lost the child. He called to him over and over again, but got no answer. So, he went upon his road, and went on for a little while without meeting anything, until at last he came to a handsome boy. So, he said to the boy, "What do you do here?" And the boy said, "I am always learning. Come and learn with me."

So he learned with that boy about Jupiter and Juno, and the Greeks and the Romans, and I don't know what, and learned more than I could tell—or he either, for he soon forgot a great deal of it. But, they were not always learning; they had the merriest games that ever were played. They rowed upon the river in summer, and skated on the ice in winter; they were active afoot, and active on horseback; at cricket, and all games at ball; at prisoners' base, hare and hounds, follow my leader, and more sports than I can think of; nobody could beat them. They had holidays too, and Twelfth cakes, and parties where they danced till midnight, and real Theatres where they saw palaces of real gold and silver rise out of the real earth, and saw all the wonders of the world at once. As to friends, they had such dear friends and so many of them, that I want the time to reckon them up. They were all young, like the handsome boy, and never were to be strange to one another all their lives through.

Still, one day, in the midst of all these pleasures, the traveller lost the boy as he had lost the child, and after calling to him in vain, went on upon his journey. So he went on for a little while without seeing anything, until at last he came to a young man. So, he said to the young man, "What do you do here?" And the young man said, "I am always in love. Come and love with me."

So, he went away with that young man, and presently they came to one of the prettiest girls that ever was seen—just like Fanny in the corner there—and she had eyes like Fanny, and hair like Fanny, and dimples like Fanny's, and she laughed and coloured just as Fanny does while I am talking about her. So, the young man fell in love directly—just as Somebody I won't mention, the first time he came here, did with Fanny. Well! he was teased sometimes—just as Somebody used to be by Fanny ; and they quarrelled sometimes—just as Somebody and Fanny used to quarrel; and they made it up, and sat in the dark, and wrote letters every day, and never were happy asunder, and were always looking out for one another and pretending not to, and were engaged at Christmas-time, and sat close to one another by the fire, and were going to be married very soon—all exactly like Somebody I won't mention, and Fanny!

But, the traveller lost them one day, as he had lost the rest of his friends, and, after calling to them to come back, which they never did, went on upon his journey. So, he went on for a little while without seeing anything, until at last he came to a middle-aged gentleman. So, he said to the gentleman, "What are you doing here?" And his answer was, "I am always busy. Come and be busy with me!"

So, he began to be very busy with that gentleman, and they went on through the wood together. The whole journey was through a wood, only it had been open and green at first, like a wood in spring; and now began to be thick and dark, like a wood in summer; some of the little trees that had come out earliest, were even turning brown. The gentleman was not alone, but had a lady of about the same age with him, who was his Wife; and they had children, who were with them too. So, they all went on together through the wood, cutting down the trees, and making a path through the branches and the fallen leaves, and carrying burdens, and working hard.

Sometimes, they came to a long green avenue that opened into deeper woods. Then they would hear a very little distant voice crying, " Father, father, I am another child! Stop for me!" And presently they would see a very little figure, growing larger as it came along, running to join them. When it came up, they all crowded round it, and kissed and welcomed it; and then they all went on together.

Sometimes, they came to several avenues at once, and then they all stood still, and one of the children said, "Father, I am going to sea," and another said, " Father, I am going to India," and another, " Father, I am going to seek my fortune where I can," and another, "Father, I am going to Heaven!" So, with many tears at parting, they went, solitary, down those avenues, each child upon its way; and the child who went to Heaven, rose into the golden air and vanished.

Whenever these partings happened, the traveller looked at the gentleman, and saw him glance up at the sky above the trees, where the day was beginning to decline, and the sunset to come on. He saw, too, that his hair was turning grey. But, they could never rest long, for they had their journey to perform, and it was necessary for them to be always busy.

At last, there had been so many partings that there were no children left, and only the traveller, the gentleman, and the lady, went upon their way in company. And now the wood was yellow; and now brown; and the leaves, even of the forest trees, began to fall.

So, they came to an avenue that was darker than the rest, and were pressing forward on their journey without looking down it when the lady stopped.

"My husband," said the lady. "I am called."

They listened, and they heard a voice a long way down the avenue, say, "Mother, mother!"

It was the voice of the first child who had said, "I am going to Heaven!" and the father said, "I pray not yet. The sunset is very near. I pray not yet!"

But, the voice cried, "Mother, mother!" without minding him, though his hair was now quite white, and tears were on his face.

Then, the mother, who was already drawn into the shade of the dark avenue and moving away with her arms still round his neck, kissed him, and said, "My dearest, I am summoned, and I go!" And she was gone. And the traveller and he were left alone together.

And they went on and on together, until they came to very near the end of the wood: so near, that they could see the sunset shining red before them through the trees.

Yet, once more, while he broke his way among the branches, the traveller lost his friend. He called and called, but there was no reply, and when he passed out of the wood, and saw the peaceful sun going down upon a wide purple prospect, he came to an old man sitting on a fallen tree. So, he said to the old man, "What do you do here?" And the old man said with a calm smile, "I am always remembering. Come and remember with me!"

So the traveller sat down by the side of that old man, face to face with the serene sunset; and all his friends came softly back and stood around him. The beautiful child, the handsome boy, the young man in love, the father, mother, and children: every one of them was there, and he had lost nothing. So, he loved them all, and was kind and forbearing with them all, and was always pleased to watch them all, and they all honoured and loved him. And I think the traveller must be yourself, dear Grandfather, because this is what you do to us, and what we do to you.

THE SCHOOLBOY'S STORY

[1853]

BEING rather young at present—I am getting on in years, but still I am rather young—I have no particular adventures of my own to fall back upon. It wouldn't much interest anybody here, I suppose, to know what a screw the Reverend is, or what a griffin *she* is, or how they do stick it into parents—particularly hair-cutting, and medical attendance. One of our fellows was charged in his half's account twelve and sixpence for two pills—tolerably profitable at six and threepence a-piece, I should think—and he never took them either, but put them up the sleeve of his jacket.

As to the beef, it's shameful. It's *not* beef. Regular beef isn't veins. You can chew regular beef. Besides which, there's gravy to regular beef, and you never see a drop to ours. Another of our fellows went home ill, and heard the family doctor tell his father that he couldn't account for his complaint unless it was the beer. Of course it was the beer, and well it might be!

However, beef and Old Cheeseman are two different things. So is beer. It was old Cheeseman I meant to tell about; not the manner in which our fellows get their constitutions destroyed for the sake of profit.

Why, look at the pie-crust alone. There's no flakiness in it. It's solid—like damp lead. Then our fellows get nightmares, and are bolstered for calling out and waking other fellows. Who can wonder!

Old Cheeseman one night walked in his sleep, put his hat on over his nightcap, got hold of a fishing-rod and a cricket-bat, and went down into the parlour, where they naturally thought from his appearance he was a Ghost. Why, he never would have done that if meals had been wholesome. When we all begin to walk in our sleeps, I suppose they'll be sorry for it.

Old Cheeseman wasn't second Latin Master then; he was a fellow himself. He was first brought there, very small, in a post-chaise, by a woman who was always taking snuff and shaking him—and that was the most he remembered about it. He never went home for the holidays. His accounts (he never learnt any extras) were sent to a Bank, and the Bank paid them; and he had a brown suit twice a-year, and went into boots at twelve. They were always too big for him, too.

In the Midsummer holidays some of our fellows who lived within walking distance, used to come back and climb the trees outside the playground wall, on purpose to look at Old Cheeseman reading there

by himself. He was always as mild as the tea—and *that's* pretty mild,
I should hope!—so when they whistled to him, he looked up and
nodded; and when they said, "Halloa, Old Cheeseman, what have you
had for dinner?" he said, "Boiled mutton"; and when they said,
"An't it solitary, Old Cheeseman?" he said, "It is a little dull sometimes"; and then they said, "Well, good-bye, Old Cheeseman!" and
climbed down again. Of course it was imposing on Old Cheeseman to
give him nothing but boiled mutton through a whole Vacation, but
that was just like the system. When they didn't give him boiled
mutton, they gave him rice pudding, pretending it was a treat.
And saved the butcher.

So Old Cheeseman went on. The holidays brought him into other
trouble besides the loneliness; because when the fellows began to
come back, not wanting to, he was always glad to see them; which
was aggravating when they were not at all glad to see him, and so
he got his head knocked against walls, and that was the way his
nose bled. But he was a favourite in general. Once a subscription was
raised for him; and, to keep up his spirits, he was presented before the
holidays with two white mice, a rabbit, a pigeon, and a beautiful
puppy. Old Cheeseman cried about it—especially soon afterwards,
when they all ate one another.

Of course Old Cheeseman used to be called by the names of all
sorts of cheeses—Double Glo'sterman, Family Cheshireman, Dutch-
man, North Wiltshireman, and all that. But he never minded it.
And I don't mean to say he was old in point of years—because he
wasn't—only he was called from the first, Old Cheeseman.

At last, Old Cheeseman was made second Latin Master. He was
brought in one morning at the beginning of a new half, and presented
to the school in that capacity as "Mr. Cheeseman." Then our fellows
all agreed that Old Cheeseman was a spy, and a deserter, who had
gone over to the enemy's camp, and sold himself for gold. It was no
excuse for him that he had sold himself for very little gold—two
pound ten a quarter and his washing, as was reported. It was decided
by a Parliament which sat about it, that Old Cheeseman's mercenary
motives could alone be taken into account, and that he had "coined
our blood for drachmas." The Parliament took the expression out
of the quarrel scene between Brutus and Cassius.

When it was settled in this strong way that Old Cheeseman was
a trenendous traitor, who had wormed himself into our fellows'
secrets on purpose to get himself into favour by giving up everything
he knew, all courageous fellows were invited to come forward and
enrol themselves in a Society for making a set against him. The
President of the Society was First boy, named Bob Tarter. His father
was in the West Indies, and he owned himself, that his father was
worth millions. He had great power among our fellows, and he wrote
a parody, beginning—

> "Who made believe to be so meek
> That we could hardly hear him speak,
> Yet turned out an Informing Sneak?
>   Old Cheeseman."

—and on in that way through more than a dozen verses, which he used to go and sing, every morning, close by the new master's desk. He trained one of the low boys, too, a rosy-cheeked little Brass who didn't care what he did, to go up to him with his Latin Grammar one morning, and say it so: *Nominativus pronominum*—Old Cheeseman, *raro exprimitur*—was never suspected, *nisi distinctionis*—of being an informer, *aut emphasis gratia*—until he proved one. *Ut*—for instance, *Vos damnastis*—when he sold the boys. *Quasi*—as though, *dicat*—he should say, *Præterea nemo*—I'm a Judas! All this produced a great effect on Old Cheeseman. He had never had much hair; but what he had, began to get thinner and thinner every day. He grew paler and more worn; and sometimes of an evening he was seen sitting at his desk with a precious long snuff to his candle, and his hands before his face, crying. But no member of the Society could pity him, even if he felt inclined, because the President said it was Old Cheeseman's conscience.

So Old Cheeseman went on, and didn't he lead a miserable life! Of course the Reverend turned up his nose at him, and of course *she* did—because both of them always do that at all the masters—but he suffered from the fellows most, and he suffered from them constantly. He never told about it, that the Society could find out; but he got no credit for that, because the President said it was Old Cheeseman's cowardice.

He had only one friend in the world, and that one was almost as powerless as he was, for it was only Jane. Jane was a sort of wardrobe-woman to our fellows, and took care of the boxes. She had come at first, as a kind of apprentice—some of our fellows say from a Charity, but *I* don't know—and after her time was out, had stopped at so much a year. So little a year, perhaps I ought to say, for it is far more likely. However, she had put some pounds in the Savings' Bank, and she was a very nice young woman. She was not quite pretty; but she had a very frank, honest bright face, and all our fellows were fond of her. She was uncommonly neat and cheerful, and uncommonly comfortable and kind. And if anything was the matter with a fellow's mother, he always went and showed the letter to Jane.

Jane was Old Cheeseman's friend. The more the Society went against him, the more Jane stood by him. She used to give him a good-humoured look out of her still-room window, sometimes, that seemed to set him up for the day. She used to pass out of the orchard and the kitchen garden (always kept locked, I believe you!) through the playground, when she might have gone the other way, only to give a turn of her head, as much as to say, "Keep up your spirits!" to Old Cheeseman. His slip of a room was so fresh and orderly that it was well known who looked after it while he was at his desk; and when our fellows saw a smoking hot dumpling on his plate at dinner, they knew with indignation who had sent it up.

Under these circumstances, the Society resolved, after a quantity of meeting and debating, that Jane should be requested to cut Old Cheeseman dead; and that if she refused, she must be sent to Coventry herself. So a deputation, headed by the President, was appointed to wait on Jane, and inform her of the vote the Society had been under the painful necessity of passing. She was very much respected for all her good qualities, and there was a story about her having once waylaid the Reverend in his own study, and get a fellow off from severe punishment, of her own kind comfortable heart. So the deputation didn't much like the job. However, they went up, and the President told Jane all about it. Upon which Jane turned very red, burst into tears, informed the President and the deputation, in a way not at all like her usual way, that they were a parcel of malicious young savages, and turned the whole respected body out of the room. Consequently it was entered in the Society's book (kept in astronomical cypher for fear of detection), that all communication with Jane was interdicted: and the President addressed the members on this convincing instance of Old Cheeseman's undermining.

But Jane was as true to Old Cheeseman as Old Cheeseman was false to our fellows—in their opinion, at all events—and steadily continued to be his only friend. It was a great exasperation to the Society because Jane was as much a loss to them as she was a gain to him; and being more inveterate against him than ever, they treated him worse than ever. At last, one morning, his desk stood empty, his room was peeped into, and found to be vacant, and a whisper went about among the pale faces of our fellows that Old Cheeseman, unable to bear it any longer, had got up early and drowned himself.

The mysterious looks of the other masters after breakfast, and the evident fact that Old Cheeseman was not expected, confirmed the Society in this opinion. Some began to discuss whether the President was liable to hanging or only transportation for life, and the President's face showed a great anxiety to know which. However, he said that a jury of his country should find him game; and that in his address he should put it to them to lay their hands upon their hearts and say whether they as Britons approved of informers, and how they thought they would like it themselves. Some of the Society considered that he had better run away until he found a forest where he might change clothes with a wood-cutter, and stain his face with blackberries; but the majority believed that if he stood his ground, his father—belonging as he did to the West Indies, and being worth millions—could buy him off.

All our fellows' hearts beat fast when the Reverend came in, and made a sort of a Roman, or a Field-Marshal, of himself with the ruler; as he always did before delivering an address. But their fears were nothing to their astonishment when he came out with the story that Old Cheeseman, "so long our respected friend and fellow-pilgrim in the pleasant plains of knowledge," he called him—O yes! I dare say! Much of that!—was the orphan child of a disinherited young lady, who had married against her father's wish, and whose young husband had died, and who had died of sorrow herself, and whose unfortunate baby (Old Cheeseman) had been brought up at the cost of a grandfather who would never consent to see it, baby, boy, or man: which grandfather was now dead, and serve him right—that's *my* putting in—and which grandfather's large property, there being no will, was now, and all of a sudden and for ever, Old Cheeseman's! Our so long respected friend and fellow-pilgrim in the pleasant plains of knowledge, the Reverend, wound up a lot of bothering quotations by saying, would "come among us once more" that day fortnight, when he desired to take leave of us himself, in a more particular manner. With these words, he stared severely round at our fellows, and went solemnly out.

There was precious consternation among the members of the Society, now. Lots of them wanted to resign, and lots more began to try to make out that they had never belonged to it. However, the President stuck up, and said that they must stand or fall together, and that if a breach was made it should be over his body—which was meant to encourage the Society: but it didn't. The President further said, he would consider the position in which they stood, and would give them his best opinion and advice in a few days. This was eagerly looked for, as he knew a good deal of the world on account of his father's being in the West Indies.

After days and days of hard thinking, and drawing armies all over his slate, the President called our fellows together, and made the matter clear. He said it was plain that when Old Cheeseman came on the appointed day, his first revenge would be to impeach the Society, and flogged all round. After witnessing with joy the torture of his enemies, and gloating over the cries which agony would extort from them, the probability was that he would invite the Reverend, on pretence of conversation, into a private room—say the parlour into which Parents were shown, where the two great globes were which were never used—and would there reproach him with the various frauds and oppressions he had endured at his hands. At the close of his observations he would make a signal to a Prizefighter concealed in the passage, who would then appear and pitch into the Reverend, till he was left insensible. Old Cheeseman would then make Jane a present of from five to ten pounds, and would leave the establishment in fiendish triumph.

The President explained that against the parlour part, or the Jane part, of these arrangements he had nothing to say: but, on the part of the Society, he counselled deadly resistance. With this view he recommended that all available desks should be filled with stones, and that the first word of the complaint should be the signal to every fellow to let fly at Old Cheeseman. The bold advice put the Society in better spirits, and was unanimously taken. A post about Old Cheeseman's size was put up in the playground, and all our fellows practised at it till it was dinted all over.

When the day came, and Places were called, every fellow sat down in a tremble. There had been much discussing and disputing as to how Old Cheeseman would come; but it was the general opinion that he would appear in a sort of triumphal car drawn by four horses, with two livery servants in front, and the Prizefighter in disguise up behind. So, all our fellows sat listening for the sound of wheels. But no wheels were heard, for Old Cheeseman walked after all, and came into the school without any preparation. Pretty much as he used to be, only dressed in black.

"Gentlemen," said the Reverend, presenting him, "our so long respected friend and fellow-pilgrim in the pleasant plains of knowledge, is desirous to offer a word or two. Attention, gentlemen, one and all!"

Every fellow stole his hand into his desk and looked at the President. The President was all ready, and taking aim at Old Cheeseman with his eyes.

What did Old Cheeseman then, but walk up to his old desk, look round him with a queer smile as if there was a tear in his eye, and begin in a quavering mild voice, "My dear companions and old friends!"

Every fellow's hand came out of his desk, and the President suddenly began to cry.

"My dear companions and old friends," said Old Cheeseman, "you have heard of my good fortune. I have passed so many years under this roof—my entire life so far, I may say—that I hope you have been glad to hear of it for my sake. I could never enjoy it without exchanging congratulations with you. If we have ever misunderstood one another at all, pray, my dear boys, let us forgive and forget. I have a great tenderness for you, and I am sure you return it. I want in the fulness of a grateful heart to shake hands with you every one. I have come back to do it, if you please, my dear boys."

Since the President had begun to cry, several other fellows had broken out here and there: but now, when Old Cheeseman began with him as first boy, laid his left hand affectionately on his shoulder and gave him his right; and when the President said "Indeed, I don't deserve it, sir; upon my honour I don't"; there was sobbing and crying all over the school. Every other fellow said he didn't deserve it, much in the same way; but Old Cheeseman, not minding that a bit, went cheerfully round to every boy, and wound up with every master —finishing off the Reverend last.

Then a snivelling little chap in a corner, who was always under some punishment or other, set up a shrill cry of "Success to Old Cheeseman! Hooray!" The Reverend glared upon him, and said, "*Mr.* Cheeseman, Sir." But, Old Cheeseman protesting that he liked his old name a great deal better than his new one, all our fellows took up the cry; and, for I don't know how many minutes, there was such a thundering of feet and hands, and such a roaring of Old Cheeseman, as never was heard.

After that, there was a spread in the dining-room of the most magnificent kind. Fowls, tongues, preserves, fruits, confectioneries, jellies, neguses, barley-sugar temples, trifles, crackers—eat all you can and pocket what you like—all at Old Cheeseman's expense. After that, speeches, whole holiday, double and treble sets of all manners of things for all manners of games, donkeys, pony-chaises and drive yourself, dinner for all the masters at the Seven Bells (twenty pounds a-head our fellows estimated it at), an annual holiday and feast fixed for that day every year, and another on Old Cheeseman's birthday—Reverend bound down before the fellows to allow it, so that he could never back out—all at Old Cheeseman's expense.

And didn't our fellows go down in a body and cheer outside the Seven Bells? O no!

But there's something else besides. Don't look at the next story-teller for there's more yet. Next day, it was resolved that the Society should make it up with Jane, and then be dissolved. What do you think of Jane being gone, though? "What? Gone for ever?" said our fellows, with long faces. "Yes, to be sure," was all the answer they could get. None of the people about the house would say anything more. At length, the first boy took upon himself to ask the Reverend whether our old friend Jane was really gone? The Reverend (he has got a daughter at home—turn-up nose, and red) replied severely, "Yes, Sir, Miss Pitt is gone." The idea of calling Jane, Miss Pitt! Some said she had been sent away in disgrace for taking money from Old Cheeseman; others said she had gone into Old Cheeseman's service at a rise of ten pounds a years. All that our fellows knew, was, she was gone.

It was two or three months afterwards, when, one afternoon, an open carriage stopped at the cricket field, just outside bounds, with a lady and gentleman in it, who looked at the game a long time and stood up to see it played. Nobody thought much about them, until the same little snivelling chap came in, against all rules, from the post where he was Scout, and said, "It's Jane!" Both Elevens forgot the game directly, and ran crowding round the carriage. It *was* Jane! In such a bonnet! And if you'll believe me, Jane was married to Old Cheeseman.

It soon became quite a regular thing when our fellows were hard at it in the playground, to see a carriage at the low part of the wall where it joins the high part, and a lady and gentleman standing up in it, looking over. The gentleman was always Old Cheeseman, and the lady was always Jane.

The first time I ever saw them, I saw them in that way. There had been a good many changes among our fellows then, and it had turned out that Bob Tarter's father wasn't worth Millions! He wasn't worth anything. Bob had gone for a soldier, and Old Cheeseman had purchased his discharge. But that's not the carriage. The carriage stopped, and all our fellows stopped as soon as it was seen.

"So you have never sent me to Coventry after all!" said the lady, laughing, as our fellows swarmed up the wall to shake hands with her. "Are you never going to do it?"

"Never! never! never!" on all sides.

I didn't understand what she meant then, but of course I do now. I was very much pleased with her face though, and with her good way, and I couldn't help looking at her—and at him too—with all our fellows clustering so joyfully about them.

They soon took notice of me as a new boy, so I thought I might as well swarm up the wall myself, and shake hands with them as the rest did. I was quite as glad to see them as the rest were, and was quite as familiar with them in a moment.

"Only a fortnight now," said Old Cheeseman, "to the holidays. Who stops? Anybody?"

A good many fingers pointed at me, and a good many voices cried "He does!" For it was the year when you were all away; and rather low I was about it, I can tell you.

"Oh!" said Old Cheeseman. "But it's solitary here in the holiday time. He had better come to us."

So I went to their delightful house, and was as happy as I could possibly be. They understand how to conduct themselves towards boys, *they* do. When they take a boy to the play, for instance, they *do* take him. They don't go in after it's begun, or come out before it's over. They know how to bring a boy up, too. Look at their own! Though he is very little as yet, what a capital boy he is! Why, my next favourite to Mrs. Cheeseman and Old Cheeseman, is young Cheeseman.

So, now I have told you all I know about Old Cheeseman. And it's not much after all, I am afraid. Is it?

NOBODY'S STORY

HE lived on the bank of a mighty river, broad and deep, which was always silently rolling on to a vast undiscovered ocean. It had rolled on, ever since the world began. It had changed its course sometimes, and turned into new channels, leaving its old ways dry and barren; but it had ever been upon the flow, and ever was to flow until Time should be no more. Against its strong, unfathomable stream, nothing made head. No living creature, no flower, no leaf, no particle of animate or inanimate existence, ever strayed back from the undiscovered ocean. The tide of the river set resistlessly towards it; and the tide never stopped, any more than the earth stops in its circling round the sun.

He lived in a busy place, and he worked very hard to live. He had no hope of ever being rich enough to live a month without hard work, but he was quite content, GOD knows, to labour with a cheerful will. He was one of an immense family, all of whose sons and daughters gained their daily bread by daily work, prolonged from their rising up betimes until their lying down at night. Beyond this destiny he had no prospect, and he sought none.

There was over-much drumming, trumpeting, and speech-making, in the neighbourhood where he dwelt; but he had nothing to do with that. Such clash and uproar came from the Bigwig family, at the unaccountable proceedings of which race, he marvelled much. They set up the strangest statues, in iron, marble, bronze, and brass, before his door; and darkened his house with the legs and tails of uncouth images of horses. He wondered what it all meant, smiled in a rough good-humoured way he had, and kept at his hard work.

The Bigwig family (composed of all the stateliest people thereabouts, and all the noisiest) had undertaken to save him the trouble of thinking for himself, and to manage him and his affairs. "Why truly," said he, "I have little time upon my hands; and if you will be so good as to take care of me, in return for the money I pay over" —for the Bigwig family were not above his money—"I shall be relieved and much obliged, considering that you know best." Hence the drumming, trumpeting, and speech-making, and ugly images of horses which he was expected to fall down and worship.

"I don't understand all this," said he, rubbing his furrowed brow confusedly. "But it *has* a meaning, maybe, if I could find it out."

"It means," returned the Bigwig family, suspecting something of what he said, "honour and glory in the highest, to the highest merit."

"Oh!" said he. And he was glad to hear that.

But, when he looked among the images in iron, marble, bronze, and brass, he failed to find a rather meritorious countryman of his, once the son of a Warwickshire wool-dealer, or any single countryman whomsoever of that kind. He could find none of the men whose knowledge had rescued him and his children from terrific and disfiguring disease, whose boldness had raised his forefathers from the condition of serfs, whose wise fancy had opened a new and high existence to the humblest, whose skill had filled the working man's world with accumulated wonders. Whereas, he did find others whom he knew no good of, and even others whom he knew much ill of.

"Humph!" said he. "I don't quite understand it."

So, he went home, and sat down by his fireside to get it out of his mind.

Now, his fireside was a bare one, all hemmed in by blackened streets; but it was a precious place to him. The hands of his wife were hardened with toil, and she was old before her time; but she was dear to him. His children, stunted in their growth, bore traces of unwholesome nurture; but they had beauty in his sight. Above all other things, it was an earnest desire of this man's soul that his children should be taught. "If I am sometimes misled," he said, "for want of knowledge, at least let them know better, and avoid my mistakes. If it is hard to me to reap the harvest of pleasure and instruction that is stored in books, let it be easier to them."

But, the Bigwig family broke out into violent family quarrels concerning what it was lawful to teach to this man's children. Some of the family insisted on such a thing being primary and indispensable above all other things; and others of the family insisted on such another thing being primary and indispensable above all other things; and the Bigwig family, rent into factions, wrote pamphlets, held convocations, delivered charges, orations, and all varieties of discourses; impounded one another in courts Lay and courts Ecclesiastical; threw dirt, exchanged pummellings, and fell together by the ears in unintelligible animosity. Meanwhile, this man, in his short evening snatches at his fireside, saw the demon Ignorance arise there, and take his children to itself. He saw his daughter perverted into a heavy slatternly drudge; he saw his son go moping down the ways of low sensuality, to brutality and crime; he saw the dawning light of intelligence in the eyes of his babies so changing into cunning and suspicion, that he could have rather wished them idiots.

"I don't understand this any the better," said he; "but I think it cannot be right. Nay, by the clouded Heaven above me, I protest against this as my wrong!"

Becoming peaceable again (for his passion was usually short-lived, and his nature kind), he looked about him on his Sundays and holidays, and he saw how much monotony and weariness there was, and thence how drunkenness arose with all its train of ruin. Then he appealed to the Bigwig family, and said, "We are a labouring people, and I have a glimmering suspicion in me that labouring people of whatever condition were made—by a higher intelligence than yours, as I poorly understand it—to be in need of mental refreshment and recreation. See what we fall into, when we rest without it. Come! Amuse me harmlessly, show me something, give me an escape!"

But, here the Bigwig family fell into a state of uproar absolutely deafening. When some few voices were faintly heard, proposing to show him the wonders of the world, the greatness of creation, the mighty changes of time, the workings of nature and the beauties of art—to show him these things, that is to say, at any period of his life when he could look upon them—there arose among the Bigwigs such roarings and raving, such pulpiting and petitioning, such maundering and memorialising, such name-calling and dirt-throwing, such a shrill wind of parliamentary questioning and feeble replying—where "I dare not" waited on "I would"—that the poor fellow stood aghast, staring wildly around.

"Have I provoked all this," said he, with his hands to his affrighted ears, "by what was meant to be an innocent request, plainly arising out of my familiar experience, and the common knowledge of all men who choose to open their eyes? I don't understand, and I am not understood. What is to come of such a state of things?"

He was bending over his work, often asking himself the question, when the news began to spread that a pestilence had appeared among the labourers, and was slaying them by thousands. Going forth to look about him, he soon found this to be true. The dying and the dead were mingled in the close and tainted houses among which his life was passed. New poison was distilled into the always murky, always sickening air. The robust and the weak, old age and infancy, the father and the mother, all were stricken down alike.

What means of flight had he? He remained there, where he was, and saw those who were dearest to him die. A kind preacher came to him, and would have said some prayers to soften his heart in his gloom, but he replied:

"O what avails it, missionary, to come to me, a man condemned to residence in this fœtid place, where every sense bestowed upon me for my delight becomes a torment, and where every minute of my numbered days is new mire added to the heap under which I lie oppressed! But, give me my first glimpse of Heaven, through a little of its light and air; give me pure water; help me to be clean; lighten this heavy atmosphere and heavy life, in which our spirits sink, and we welcome the indifferent and callous creatures you often see us; gently and kindly take the bodies of those who die among us, out of the small room where we grow to be so familiar with the awful change that even ITS sanctity is lost to us; and, Teacher, then I will hear— none know better than you, how willingly—of Him whose thoughts were so much with the poor, and who had compassion for all human sorrow!"

He was at work again, solitary and sad, when his Master came and stood near to him dressed in black. He, also, had suffered heavily. His young wife, his beautiful and good young wife, was dead; so, too, his only child.

"Master, 'tis hard to bear—I know it—but be comforted. I would give you comfort, if I could."

The Master thanked him from his heart, but, said he, "O you labouring men! The calamity began among you. If you had but lived more healthily and decently, I should not be the widowed and bereft mourner that I am this day."

"Master," returned the other, shaking his head, "I have begun to understand a little that most calamities will come from us, as this one did, and that none will stop at our poor doors, until we are united with that great squabbling family yonder, to do the things that are right. We cannot live healthily and decently, unless they who undertook to manage us provide the means. We cannot be instructed unless they will teach us; we cannot be rationally amused, unless they will amuse us; we cannot but have some false gods of our own, while they set up so many of theirs in all the public places. The evil consequences of imperfect instruction, the evil consequences of pernicious neglect, the evil consequences of unnatural restraint and the denial of humanising enjoyments, will all come from us, and none of them will stop with us. They will spread far and wide. They always do; they always have done—just like the pestilence. I understand so much, I think, at last."

But the Master said again, "O you labouring men! How seldom do we ever hear of you, except in connexion with some trouble!"

"Master," he replied, "I am Nobody, and little likely to be heard of (nor yet much wanted to be heard of, perhaps), except when there *is* some trouble. But it never begins with me, and it never can end with me. As sure as Death, it comes down to me, and it goes up from me."

There was so much reason in what he said, that the Bigwig family, getting wind of it, and being horribly frightened by the late desolation, resolved to unite with him to do the things that were right—at all events, so far as the said things were associated with the direct prevention, humanly speaking, of another pestilence. But, as their fear wore off, which it soon began to do, they resumed their falling out among themselves, and did nothing. Consequently the scourge appeared again—low down as before—and spread avengingly upward as before, and carried off vast numbers of the brawlers. But not a man among them ever admitted, if in the least degree he ever perceived, that he had anything to do with it.

So Nobody lived and died in the old, old way; and this, in the main, is the whole of Nobody's story.

Had he no name, you ask? Perhaps it was Legion. It matters little what his name was. Let us call him Legion.

If you were ever in the Belgian villages, near the field of Waterloo you will have seen, in some quiet little church, a monument erected by faithful companions in arms to the memory of Colonel A, Major B, Captains C, D and E, Lieutenants F and G, Ensigns H, I and J, seven non-commissioned officers, and one hundred and thirty rank and file, who fell in the discharge of their duty on the memorable day. The story of Nobody is the story of the rank and file of the earth. They bear their share of the battle; they have their part in the victory; they fall; they leave no name but in the mass. The march of the proudest of us, leads to the dusty way by which they go. O! Let us think of them this year at the Christmas fire, and not forget them when it is burnt out.

THE SEVEN POOR TRAVELLERS

IN THREE CHAPTERS

[1854]

CHAPTER I

IN THE OLD CITY OF ROCHESTER

STRICTLY speaking, there were only six Poor Travellers; but, being a Traveller myself, though an idle one, and being withal as poor as I hope to be, I brought the number up to seven. This word of explanation is due at once, for what says the inscription over the quaint old door?

> RICHARD WATTS, ESQ.
> by his Will, dated 22 Aug. 1579,
> founded this Charity
> for Six poor Travellers,
> who not being ROGUES, or PROCTORS,
> May receive gratis for one Night,
> Lodging, Entertainment,
> and Fourpence each.

It was in the ancient little city of Rochester in Kent, of all the good days in the year upon a Christmas-eve, that I stood reading this inscription over the quaint old door in question. I had been wandering about the neighbouring Cathedral, and had seen the tomb of Richard Watts, with the effigy of worthy Master Richard staring out of it like a ship's figure-head; and I had felt that I could do no less, as I gave the Verger his fee, than inquire the way to Watts's Charity. The way being very short and very plain, I had come prosperously to the inscription and the quaint old door.

"Now," said I to myself, as I looked at the knocker, "I know I am not a Proctor; I wonder whether I am a Rogue!"

Upon the whole, though Conscience reproduced two or three pretty faces which might have had smaller attraction for a moral Goliath than they had had for me, who am but a Tom Thumb in that way, I came to the conclusion that I was not a Rogue. So, beginning to regard the establishment as in some sort my property, bequeathed to me and divers co-legatees, share and share alike, by the Worshipful Master Richard Watts, I stepped backward into the road to survey my inheritance.

I found it to be a clean white house, of a staid and venerable air, with the quaint old door already three times mentioned (an arched door), choice little long low lattice-windows, and a roof of three gables. The silent High-street of Rochester is full of gables, with old beams and timbers carved into strange faces. It is oddly garnished with a queer old clock that projects over the pavement out of a grave red-brick building, as if Time carried on business there, and hung out his sign. Sooth to say, he did an active stroke of work in Rochester, in the old days of the Romans, and the Saxons and the Normans; and down to the times of King John, when the rugged castle—I will not undertake to say how many hundreds of years old then—was abandoned to the centuries of weather which have so defaced the dark apertures in its walls, that the ruin looks as if the rooks and daws had pecked its eyes out.

I was very well pleased, both with my property and its situation. While I was yet surveying it with growing content, I espied, at one of the upper lattices which stood open, a decent body, of a wholesome matronly appearance, whose eyes I caught inquiringly addressed to mine. They said so plainly, "Do you wish to see the house?" that I answered aloud, "Yes, if you please." And within a minute the old door opened, and I bent my head, and went down two steps into the entry.

"This," said the matronly presence, ushering me into a low room on the right, "is where the Travellers sit by the fire, and cook what bits of suppers they buy with their fourpences."

"O! Then they have no Entertainment?" said I. For the inscription over the outer door was still running in my head, and I was mentally repeating, in a kind of tune, "Lodging, entertainment, and fourpence each."

"They have a fire provided for 'em," returned the matron,—a mighty civil person, not, as I could make out, overpaid; "and these cooking utensils. And this what's painted on a board is the rules for their behaviour. They have their fourpences when they get their tickets from the steward over the way,—for I don't admit 'em myself, they must get their tickets first,—and sometimes one buys a rasher of bacon, and another a herring, and another a pound of potatoes, or what not. Sometimes two or three of 'em will club their fourpences together, and make a supper that way. But not much of anything is to be got for fourpence, at present, when provisions is so dear."

"True indeed," I remarked. I had been looking about the room, admiring its snug fireside at the upper end, its glimpse of the street through the low mullioned window, and its beams overhead. "It is very comfortable," said I.

"Ill-conwenient," observed the matronly presence.

I liked to hear her say so; for it showed a commendable anxiety to execute in no niggardly spirit the intentions of Master Richard Watts. But the room was really so well adapted to its purpose that I protested, quite enthusiastically, against her disparagement.

"Nay, ma'am," said I, "I am sure it is warm in winter and cool in summer. It has a look of homely welcome and soothing rest. It has a remarkably cosy fireside, the very blink of which, gleaming out into the street upon the winter night, is enough to warm all Rochester's heart. And as to the convenience of the six Poor Travellers——"

"I don't mean them," returned the presence. "I speak of its being an ill-conwenience to myself and my daughter, having no other room to sit in of a night."

This was true enough, but there was another quaint room of corresponding dimensions on the opposite side of the entry: so I stepped across to it, through the open doors of both rooms, and asked what this chamber was for.

"This," returned the presence, "is the Board Room. Where the gentlemen meet when they come here."

Let me see. I had counted from the street six upper windows besides these on the ground-story. Making a perplexed calculation in my mind, I rejoined, "Then the six Poor Travellers sleep upstairs?"

My new friend shook her head. "They sleep," she answered, "in two little outer galleries at the back, where their beds has always been, ever since the Charity was founded. It being so very ill-conwenient to me as things is at present, the gentlemen are going to take off a bit of the back yard, and make a slip of a room for 'em there, to sit in before they go to bed."

"And then the six Poor Travellers," said I, "will be entirely out of the house?"

"Entirely out of the house," assented the presence, comfortably smoothing her hands. "Which is considered much better for all parties, and much more conwenient."

I had been a little startled, in the Cathedral, by the emphasis with which the effigy of Master Richard Watts was bursting out of his tomb; but I began to think, now, that it might be expected to come across the High-street some stormy night, and make a disturbance here.

Howbeit, I kept my thoughts to myself, and accompanied the presence to the little galleries at the back. I found them on a tiny scale, like the galleries in old inn-yards; and they were very clean. While I was looking at them, the matron gave me to understand that the prescribed number of Poor Travellers were forthcoming every night from year's end to year's end; and that the beds were always occupied. My questions upon this, and her replies, brought us back to the Board Room so essential to the dignity of "the gentlemen," where she showed me the printed accounts of the Charity hanging up by the window. From them I gathered that the greater part of the property bequeathed by the Worshipful Master Richard Watts for the maintenance of this foundation was, at the period of his death, mere marshland; but that, in course of time, it had been reclaimed and built upon, and was very considerably increased in value. I found too, that about a thirtieth part of the annual revenue was now expended on the purposes commemorated in the inscription over the door; the rest being handsomely laid out in Chancery, law

expenses, collectorship, receivership, poundage, and other appendages of management, highly complimentary to the importance of
the six Poor Travellers. In short, I made the not entirely new
discovery that it may be said of an establishment like this, in dear old
England, as of the fat oyster in the American story, that it takes a
good many men to swallow it whole.

"And pray, ma'am," said I, sensible that the blankness of my
face began to brighten as the thought occurred to me, "could one see
these Travellers?"

"Well!" she returned dubiously, "no!"

"Not to-night, for instance!" said I.

"Well!" she returned more positively, "no. Nobody ever asked to
see them, and nobody ever did see them."

As I am not easily baulked in a design when I am set upon it, I
urged to the good lady that this was Christmas-eve; that Christmas
comes but once a year,—which is unhappily too true, for when it
begins to stay with us the whole year round we shall make this earth
a very different place; that I was possessed by the desire to treat the
Travellers to a supper and a temperate glass of hot Wassail; that the
voice of Fame had been heard in that land, declaring my ability to
make a hot Wassail; that if I were permitted to hold the feast, I
should be found conformable to reason, sobriety, and good hours; in
a word, that I could be merry and wise myself, and had been ever
known at a pinch to keep others so, although I was decorated with
no badge or medal, and not a brother, Orator, Apostle, Saint, or
Prophet of any denomination whatever. In the end I prevailed, to my
great joy. It was settled that at nine o'clock that night a Turkey and
a piece of Roast Beef should smoke upon the board; and that I, faint
and unworthy minister for once of Master Richard Watts, should
preside as the Christmas-supper host of the six Poor Travellers.

I went back to my inn to give the necessary directions for the Turkey and Roast Beef, and, during the remainder of the day, could
settle to nothing for thinking of the Poor Travellers. When the wind
blew hard against the windows,—it was a cold day, with dark gusts
of sleet alternating with periods of wild brightness, as if the year were
dying fitfully,—I pictured them advancing towards their resting-
place along the various cold roads, and felt delighted to think how
little they foresaw the supper that awaited them. I painted their
portraits in my mind, and indulged in little heightening touches. I
made them footsore; I made them weary; I made them carry packs
and bundles; I made them stop by finger-posts and milestones,
leaning on their bent sticks, and looking wistfully at what was written
there; I made them lose their way; and filled their five wits with
apprehensions of lying out all night, and being frozen to death. I
took up my hat, and went out, climbed to the top of the Old Castle,
and looked over the windy hills that slope down to the Medway,
almost believing that I could descry some of my Travellers in the
distance. After it fell dark, and the Cathedral bell was heard in the
invisible steeple—quite a bower of frosty time when I had last seen

it—striking five, six, seven, I became so full of my Travellers that I could eat no dinner, and felt constrained to watch them still in the coals of my fire. They were all arrived by this time, I thought, had got their tickets, and were gone in.—There my pleasure was dashed by the reflection that probably some Travellers had come too late and were shut out.

After the Cathedral bell had struck eight, I could smell a delicious savour of Turkey and Roast Beef rising to the window of my adjoining bedroom, which looked down into the inn-yard just where the lights of the kitchen reddened a massive fragment of the Castle Wall. It was high time to make the Wassail now; therefore I had up the materials (which, together with their proportions and combinations, I must decline to impart, as the only secret of my own I was ever known to keep), and made a glorious jorum. Not in a bowl; for a bowl anywhere but on a shelf is a low superstition, fraught with cooling and slopping; but in a brown earthenware pitcher, tenderly suffocated, when full, with a coarse cloth. It being now upon the stroke of nine, I set out for Watts's Charity, carrying my brown beauty in my arms. I would trust Ben, the waiter, with untold gold; but there are strings in the human heart which must never be sounded by another, and drinks that I make myself are those strings in mine.

The Travellers were all assembled, the cloth was laid, and Ben had brought a great billet of wood, and had laid it artfully on the top of the fire, so that a touch or two of the poker after supper should make a roaring blaze. Having deposited my brown beauty in a red nook on the hearth, inside the fender, where she soon began to sing like an ethereal cricket, diffusing at the same time odours as of ripe vineyards, spice forests, and orange groves,—I say, having stationed my beauty in a place of security and improvement, I introduced myself to my guests by shaking hands all round, and giving them a hearty welcome.

I found the party to be thus composed. Firstly, myself. Secondly, a very decent man indeed, with his right arm in a sling, who had a certain clean agreeable smell of wood about him, from which I judged him to have something to do with shipbuilding. Thirdly, a little sailor-boy, a mere child, with a profusion of rich dark brown hair, and deep womanly-looking eyes. Fourthly, a shabby-genteel personage in a threadbare black suit, and apparently in very bad circumstances, with a dry suspicious look; the absent buttons on his waistcoat eked out with red tape; and a bundle of extraordinarily tattered papers sticking out of an inner breast-pocket. Fifthly, a foreigner by birth, but an Englishman in speech, who carried his pipe in the band of his hat, and lost no time in telling me, in an easy, simple, engaging way, that he was a watchmaker from Geneva, and travelled all about the Continent, mostly on foot, working as a journeyman, and seeing new countries,—possibly (I thought) also smuggling a watch or so, now and then. Sixthly, a little widow, who had been very pretty and was still very young, but whose beauty had been wrecked in some great misfortune, and whose manner was remarkably timid, scared and solitary. Seventhly and lastly, a Traveller of a kind familiar to my boyhood, but now almost obsolete,—a Book Pedlar, who had a quantity of Pamphlets and Numbers with him, and who presently boasted that he could repeat more verses in an evening than he could sell in a twelvemonth.

All these I have mentioned in the order in which they sat at table. I presided, and the matronly presence faced me. We were not long in taking our places, for the supper had arrived with me, in the following procession:

Myself with the pitcher.
Ben with Beer.
Inattentive Boy with hot plates. Inattentive Boy with hot plates.
THE TURKEY.
Female carrying sauces to be heated on the spot.
THE BEEF.
Man with Tray on his head, containing Vegetables and Sundries.
Volunteer Hostler from Hotel, grinning,
And rendering no assistance.

As we passed along the High-street, comet-like, we left a long trail of fragrance behind us which caused the public to stop, sniffing in wonder. We had previously left at the corner of the inn-yard a wall-eyed young man connected with the Fly department, and well accustomed to the sound of a railway whistle which Ben always carries in his pocket, whose instructions were, so soon as he should hear the whistle blown, to dash into the kitchen, seize the hot plum-pudding and mince-pies, and speed with them to Watts's Charity, where they would be received (he was further instructed) by the sauce-female, who would be provided with brandy in a blue state of combustion.

All these arrangements were executed in the most exact and punctual manner. I never saw a finer turkey, finer beef, or greater prodigality of sauce and gravy; and my Travellers did wonderful justice to everything set before them. It made my heart rejoice to observe how their wind and frost hardened faces softened in the clatter of plates and knives and forks, and mellowed in the fire and supper heat. While their hats and caps and wrappers, hanging up, a few small bundles on the ground in a corner, and in another corner three or four old walking-sticks, worn down at the end to mere fringe, linked this snug interior with the bleak outside in a golden chain.

When supper was done, and my brown beauty had been elevated on the table, there was a general requisition to me to "take the corner"; which suggested to me comfortably enough how much my friends here made of a fire,—for when had *I* ever thought so highly of the corner, since the days when I connected it with Jack Horner? However, as I declined, Ben, whose touch on all convivial instruments is perfect, drew the table apart, and instructing my Travellers to open right and left on either side of me, and form round the fire, closed up the centre with myself and my chair, and preserved the order we had kept at table. He had already, in a tranquil manner, boxed the ears of the inattentive boys until they had been by imperceptible degrees boxed out of the room; and he now rapidly skirmished the sauce-female into the High-street, disappeared, and softly closed the door.

This was the time for bringing the poker to bear on the billet of wood. I tapped it three times, like an enchanted talisman, and a brilliant host of merry-makers burst out of it, and sported off by the chimney,—rushing up the middle in a fiery country dance, and never coming down again. Meanwhile, by their sparkling light, which threw our lamp into the shade, I filled the glasses, and gave my Travellers, CHRISTMAS!—CHRISTMAS-EVE, my friends, when the shepherds, who were Poor Travellers, too, in their way, heard the Angels sing, "On earth, peace. Good-will towards men!"

I don't know who was the first among us to think that we ought to take hands as we sat, in deference to the toast, or whether any one of us anticipated the others, but at any rate we all did it. We then drank to the memory of the good Master Richard Watts. And I wish his Ghost may never have had worse usage under that roof than it had from us.

It was the witching time for Story-telling. "Our whole life, Travellers," said I, "is a story more or less intelligible,—generally less; but we shall read it by a clearer light when it is ended. I, for one, am so divided this night between fact and fiction, that I scarce know which is which. Shall I beguile the time by telling you a story as we sit here?"

They all answered, yes. I had little to tell them, but I was bound by my own proposal. Therefore, after looking for a while at the spiral column of smoke wreathing up from my brown beauty, through which I could have almost sworn I saw the effigy of Master Richard Watts less startled than usual, I fired away.

CHAPTER II

THE STORY OF RICHARD DOUBLEDICK

IN the year one thousand seven hundred and ninety-nine, a relative of mine came limping down, on foot, to this town of Chatham. I call it this town, because if anybody present knows to a nicety where Rochester ends and Chatham begins, it is more than I do. He was a poor traveller, with not a farthing in his pocket. He sat by the fire in this very room, and he slept one night in a bed that will be occupied to-night by some one here.

My relative came down to Chatham to enlist in a cavalry regiment, if a cavalry regiment would have him; if not, to take King George's shilling from any corporal or sergeant who would put a bunch of ribbons in his hat. His object was to get shot; but he thought he might as well ride to death as be at the trouble of walking.

My relative's Christian name was Richard, but he was better known as Dick. He dropped his own surname on the road down, and took up that of Doubledick. He was passed as Richard Doubledick; age twenty-two; height five foot ten, native place, Exmouth, which he had never been near in his life. There was no cavalry in Chatham when he limped over the bridge here with half a shoe to his dusty feet, so he enlisted into a regiment of the line, and was glad to get drunk and forget all about it.

You are to know that this relative of mine had gone wrong, and run wild. His heart was in the right place, but it was sealed up. He had been betrothed to a good and beautiful girl, whom he had loved better than she—or perhaps even he—believed; but in an evil hour he had given her cause to say to him solemnly, "Richard, I will never marry another man. I will live single for your sake, but Mary Marshall's lips"—her name was Mary Marshall—"will never address another word to you on earth. Go, Richard! Heaven forgive you!" This finished him. This brought him down to Chatham. This made him Private Richard Doubledick, with a determination to be shot.

There was a more dissipated and reckless soldier in Chatham barracks, in the year one thousand seven hundred and ninety-nine, than Private Richard Doubledick. He associated with the dregs of every regiment; he was as seldom sober as he could be, and was constantly under punishment. It became clear to the whole barracks that Private Richard Doubledick would very soon be flogged.

Now the Captain of Richard Doubledick's company was a young gentleman not above five years his senior, whose eyes had an expression in them which affected Private Richard Doubledick in a very remarkable way. They were bright, handsome, dark eyes,—what are called laughing eyes generally, and, when serious, rather steady than severe,—but they were the only eyes now left in his narrowed world that Private Richard Doubledick could not stand. Unabashed by evil report and punishment, defiant of everything else and everybody else, he had but to know that those eyes looked at him for a moment, and he felt ashamed. He could not so much as salute Captain Taunton in the street like any other officer. He was reproached and confused,—troubled by the mere possibility of the captain's looking at him. In his worst moments, he would rather turn back, and go any distance out of his way, than encounter those two handsome, dark, bright eyes.

One day, when Private Richard Doubledick came out of the Black hole, where he had been passing the last eight and-forty hours, and in which retreat he spent a good deal of his time, he was ordered to betake himself to Captain Taunton's quarters. In the stale and squalid state of a man just out of the Black hole, he had less fancy than ever for being seen by the Captain; but he was not so mad yet as to disobey orders, and consequently went up to the terrace over-looking the parade-ground, where the officers' quarters were; twisting and breaking in his hands, as he went along, a bit of straw that had formed the decorative furniture of the Black hole.

"Come in!" cried the Captain, when he knocked with his knuckles at the door. Private Richard Doubledick pulled off his cap, took a stride forward, and felt very conscious that he stood in the light of the dark, bright eyes.

There was a silent pause. Private Richard Doubledick had put the straw in his mouth, and was gradually doubling it up into his windpipe and choking himself.

"Doubledick," said the Captain, "do you know where you are going to?"

"To the Devil, Sir?" faltered Doubledick.

"Yes," returned the Captain. "And very fast."

Private Richard Doubledick turned the straw of the Black hole in his mouth, and made a miserable salute of acquiescence.

"Doubledick," said the Captain, "since I entered his Majesty's service, a boy of seventeen, I have been pained to see many men of promise going that road; but I have never been so pained to see a man determined to make the shameful journey as I have been, ever since you joined the regiment, to see you."

Private Richard Doubledick began to find a film stealing over the floor at which he looked; also to find the legs of the Captain's breakfast-table turning crooked, as if he saw them through water.

"I am only a common soldier, Sir," said he. "It signifies very little what such a poor brute comes to."

"You are a man," returned the Captain, with grave indignation, "of education and superior advantages; and if you say that, meaning what you say, you have sunk lower than I had believed. How low that must be, I leave you to consider, knowing what I know of your disgrace, and seeing what I see."

"I hope to get shot soon, Sir," said Private Richard Doubledick; "and then the regiment and the world together will be rid of me."

The legs of the table were becoming very crooked. Doubledick, looking up to steady his vision, met the eyes that had so strong an influence over him. He put his hand before his own eyes, and the breast of his disgrace-jacket swelled as if it would fly asunder.

"I would rather," said the young Captain, "see this in you, Doubledick, than I would see five thousand guineas counted out upon this table for a gift to my good mother. Have you a mother?"

"I am thankful to say she is dead, Sir."

"If your praises," returned the Captain, "were sounded from mouth to mouth through the whole regiment, through the whole army, through the whole country, you would wish she had lived to say, with pride and joy, 'He is my son!'"

"Spare me, Sir," said Doubledick. "She would never have heard any good of me. She would never have had any pride and joy in owning herself my mother. Love and compassion she might have had, and would have always had, I know; but not—Spare me, Sir! I am a broken wretch, quite at your mercy!" And he turned his face to the

"God bless you, Sir!" sobbed Private Richard Doubledick.

wall, and stretched out his imploring hand.

"My friend——" began the Captain.

"God bless you, Sir," sobbed Private Richard Doubledick.

"You are at the crisis of your fate. Hold your course unchanged a little longer, and you know what must happen. I know even better than you can imagine, that, after that has happened, you are lost. No man who could shed those tears could bear those marks."

"I fully believe it, Sir," in a low, shivering voice, said Private Richard Doubledick.

"But a man in any station can do his duty," said the young Captain, "and in doing it, can earn his own respect, even if his case should be so very unfortunate and so very rare that he can earn no other man's. A common soldier, poor brute though you called him just now, has this advantage in the stormy times we live in, that he always does his duty before a host of sympathising witnesses. Do you doubt that he may so do it as to be extolled through a whole regiment, through a whole army, through a whole country? Turn while you may yet retrieve the past, and try."

"I will! I ask for only one witness, Sir," cried Richard, with a bursting heart.

"I understand you. I will be a watchful and a faithful one."

I have heard from Private Richard Doubledick's own lips, that he dropped down upon his knee, kissed that officer's hand, arose, and went out of the light of the dark, bright eyes, an altered man.

In that year, one thousand seven hundred and ninety-nine, the French were in Egypt, in Italy, in Germany, where not? Napoleon Bonaparte had likewise begun to stir against us in India, and most men could read the signs of the great troubles that were coming on. In the very next year, when we formed an alliance with Austria against him, Captain Taunton's regiment was on service in India. And there was not a finer non-commissioned officer in it,—no, nor in the whole line—than Corporal Richard Doubledick.

In eighteen hundred and one, the Indian army were on the coast of Egypt. Next year was the year of the proclamation of the short peace, and they were recalled. It had then become well known to thousands of men, that wherever Captain Taunton, with the dark, bright eyes, led, there, close to him, ever at his side, firm as a rock, true as the sun and brave as Mars, would be certain to be found, while life beat in their hearts, that famous soldier Sergeant Richard Doubledick.

Eighteen hundred and five, besides being the great year of Trafalgar, was a year of hard fighting in India. That year saw such wonders done by a Sergeant-Major, who cut his way single-handed through a solid mass of men, recovered the colours of his regiment, which had been seized from the hand of a poor boy shot through the heart, and rescued his wounded Captain, who was down, and in a very jungle of horses' hoofs and sabres,—saw such wonders done, I say, by this brave Sergeant-Major, that he was specially made the bearer of the colours he had won; and Ensign Richard Doubledick had risen from the ranks.

Sorely cut up in every battle, but always reinforced by the bravest of men,—for the fame of following the old colours, shot through and through, which Ensign Richard Doubledick had saved, inspired all breasts,—this regiment fought its way through the Peninsular war, up to the investment of Badajos in eighteen hundred and twelve. Again and again it had been cheered through the British ranks until the tears had sprung into men's eyes at the mere hearing of the mighty British voice, so exultant in their valour; and there was not a drummer-boy but knew the legend, that wherever the two friends, Major Taunton, with the dark, bright eyes, and Ensign Richard Doubledick, who was devoted to him, were seen to go, there the boldest spirits in the English army became wild to follow.

One day, at Badajos,—not in the great storming, but in repelling a hot sally of the besieged upon our men at work in the trenches, who had given way,—the two officers found themselves hurrying forward, face to face, against a party of French infantry, who made a stand. There was an officer at their head, encouraging his men,—a courageous, handsome, gallant officer of five-and-thirty, whom Doubledick saw hurriedly, almost momentarily, but saw well. He particularly noticed this officer waving his sword, and rallying his men with an eager and excited cry, when they fired in obedience to his gesture, and Major Taunton dropped.

It was over in ten minutes more, and Doubledick returned to the spot where he had laid the best friend man ever had on a coat spread upon the wet clay. Major Taunton's uniform was opened at the breast, and on his shirt were three little spots of blood.

"Dear Doubledick," said he, "I am dying."

"For the love of Heaven, no!" exclaimed the other, kneeling down beside him, and passing his arm round his neck to raise his head. "Taunton! My preserver, my guardian angel, my witness! Dearest, truest, kindest of human beings! Taunton! For God's sake!"

The bright, dark eyes—so very, very dark now, in the pale face—smiled upon him, and the hand he had kissed thirteen years ago laid itself fondly on his breast.

"Write to my mother. You will see Home again. Tell her how we became friends. It will comfort her, as it comforts me."

He spoke no more, but faintly signed for a moment towards his hair as it fluttered in the wind. The Ensign understood him. He smiled again when he saw that, and, gently turning his face over on the supporting arm as if for rest, died, with his hand upon the breast in which he had revived a soul.

No dry eye looked on Ensign Richard Doubledick that melancholy day. He buried his friend on the field, and became a lone, bereaved man. Beyond his duty he appeared to have but two remaining cares in life,—one, to preserve the little packet of hair he was to give to Taunton's mother; the other, to encounter that French officer who had rallied the men under whose fire Taunton fell. A new legend now began to circulate among our troops; and it was, that when he and the French officer came face to face once more, there would be weeping in France.

The war went on—and through it went the exact picture of the French officer on the one side, and the bodily reality upon the other—until the battle of Toulouse was fought. In the returns sent home appeared these words: "Severely wounded, but not dangerously, Lieutenant Richard Doubledick."

At Midsummer-time, in the year eighteen hundred and fourteen, Lieutenant Richard Doubledick, now a browned soldier, seven-and-thirty years of age, came home to England invalided. He brought the hair with him, near his heart. Many a French officer had he seen since that day; many a dreadful night, in searching with men and lanterns for his wounded, and he relieved French officers lying disabled; but the mental picture and the reality had never come together.

Though he was weak and suffered pain, he lost not an hour in getting down to Frome in Somersetshire, where Taunton's mother lived. In the sweet, compassionate words that naturally present themselves to the mind to-night, "he was the only son of his mother, and she was a widow."

It was a Sunday evening, and the lady sat at her quiet garden-window, reading the Bible reading to herself, in a trembling voice, that very passage in it, as I have heard him tell. He heard the words: "Young man, I say unto thee, arise!"

He had to pass the window; and the bright, dark eyes of his debased time seemed to look at him. Her heart told her who he was: she came to the door quickly, and fell upon his neck.

"He saved me from ruin, made me a human creature, won me from infamy and shame. O, God for ever bless him! As He will, He will!"

"He will!" the lady answered. "I know he is in Heaven!" Then she piteously cried, "But O, my darling boy, my darling boy!"

Never from the hour when Private Richard Doubledick enlisted at Chatham, had the Private, Corporal, Sergeant, Sergeant-Major, Ensign, or Lieutenant breathed his right name, or the name of Mary Marshall, or a word of the story of his life, into any ear except his reclaimer's. That previous scene in his existence was closed. He had firmly resolved that his expiation should be to live unknown; to disturb no more the peace that had long grown over his old offences; to let it be revealed, when he was dead, that he had striven and suffered, and had never forgotten; and then if they could forgive him and believe him—well, it would be time enough—time enough!

But that night, remembering the words he had cherished for two years, "Tell her how we became friends. It will comfort her, as it comforts me," he related everything. It gradually seemed to him as if in his maturity he had recovered a mother; it gradually seemed to her as if in her bereavement she had found a son. During his stay in England, the quiet garden into which he had slowly and painfully crept, a stranger, became the boundary of his home; when he was able to rejoin his regiment in the spring, he left the garden, thinking was this indeed the first time he had ever turned his face towards the old colours with a woman's blessing!

He followed them—so ragged, so scarred and pierced now, that they would scarcely hold together—to Quatre Bras and Ligny. He stood beside them, in an awful stillness of many men, shadowy through the mist and drizzle of a wet June forenoon, on the field of Waterloo. And down to that hour the picture in his mind of the French officer had never been compared with the reality.

The famous regiment was in action early in the battle, and received its first check in many an eventful year, when he was seen to fall. But it swept on to avenge him, and left behind it no such creature in the world of consciousness as Lieutenant Richard Doubledick.

Through pits of mire, and pools of rain; along deep ditches, once roads, that were pounded and ploughed to pieces by artillery, heavy waggons, tramp of men and horses, and the struggle of every wheeled thing that could carry wounded soldiers; jolted among the dying and the dead, so disfigured by blood and mud as to be hardly recognisable for humanity; undisturbed by the moaning of men and the shrieking of horses, which, newly taken from the peaceful pursuits of life, could not endure the sight of the stragglers lying by the wayside, never to resume their toilsome journey; dead, as to any sentient life that was in it, and yet alive,—the form that had been Lieutenant Richard Doubledick, with whose praises England rang, was conveyed to Brussels. There it was tenderly laid down in hospital; and there it lay week after week, through the long bright summer days, until the harvest, spared by war, had ripened and was gathered in.

Over and over again the sun rose and set upon the crowded city; over and over again the moonlight nights were quiet on the plains of Waterloo: and all that time was a blank to what had been Lieutenant Richard Doubledick. Rejoicing troops marched into Brussels, and marched out; brothers and fathers, sisters, mothers, and wives, came thronging thither, drew their lots of joy or agony, and departed; so many times a day the bells rang; so many times the shadows of the great buildings changed; so many lights sprang up at dusk; so many feet passed here and there upon the pavements; so many hours of sleep and cooler air of night succeeded: indifferent to all, a marble face lay on a bed, like the face of a recumbent statue on the tomb of Lieutenant Richard Doubledick.

Slowly labouring, at last, through a long heavy dream of confused time and place, presenting faint glimpses of army surgeons, whom he knew, and of faces that had been familiar to his youth,—dearest and kindest among them, Mary Marshall's, with a solicitude upon it more like reality than anything he could discern,—Lieutenant Richard Doubledick came back to life. To the beautiful life of a calm autumn evening sunset, to the peaceful life of a fresh quiet room with a large window standing open; a balcony beyond, in which were moving leaves and sweet-smelling flowers; beyond, again, the clear sky, with the sun full in his sight, pouring its golden radiance on his bed.

It was so tranquil and so lovely that he thought he had passed into another world. And he said in a faint voice, "Taunton, are you near me?"

A face bent over him. Not his, his mother's.

"I came to nurse you. We have nursed you many weeks. You were moved here long ago. Do you remember nothing?"

"Nothing."

The lady kissed his cheek, and held his hand, soothing him.

"Where is the regiment? What has happened? Let me call you mother. What has happened, mother?"

"A great victory, dear. The war is over, and the regiment was the bravest in the field."

His eyes kindled, his lips trembled, he sobbed, and the tears ran down his face. He was very weak, too weak to move his hand.

"Was it dark just now?" he asked presently.

"No."

"It was only dark to me? Something passed away like a black shadow. But as it went and the sun,—O the blessed sun, how beautiful it is!—touched my face, I thought I saw a light white cloud pass out at the door. Was there nothing that went out?"

She shook her head, and in a little while he fell asleep, she still holding his hand, and soothing him.

From that time, he recovered. Slowly, for he had been desperately wounded in the head, and had been shot in the body, but making some little advance every day. When he had gained sufficient strength to converse as he lay in bed, he soon began to remark that Mrs. Taunton always brought him back to his own history. Then he recalled his preserver's dying words, and thought, "It comforts her."

One day he awoke out of a sleep, refreshed, and asked her to read to him. But the curtain of the bed, softening the light, which she always drew back when he awoke, that she might see him from her table at the bedside where she sat at work, was held undrawn; and a woman's voice spoke, which was not hers.

"Can you bear to see a stranger?" it said softly. "Will you like to see a stranger?"

"Stranger!" he repeated. The voice awoke old memories, before the days of Private Richard Doubledick.

"A stranger now, but not a stranger once," it said in tones that thrilled him. "Richard, dear Richard, lost through so many years, my name——"

He cried out her name, "Mary," and she held him in her arms and his head lay on her bosom.

"I am not breaking a rash vow, Richard. These are not Mary Marshall's lips that speak. I have another name."

She was married.

"I have another name, Richard. Did you ever hear it?"

"Never!"

He looked into her face, so pensively beautiful, and wondered at the smile upon it through her tears.

"Think again, Richard. Are you sure you never heard my altered name?"

"Never!"

"Don't move your head to look at me, dear Richard. Let it lie here, while I tell my story. I loved a generous, noble man; loved him with my whole heart; loved him for years and years; loved him faithfully, devotedly; loved him with no hope of return; loved him, knowing nothing of his highest qualities—not even knowing that he was alive. He was a brave soldier. He was honoured and beloved by thousands of thousands, when the mother of his dear friend found me and showed me that in all his triumphs he had never forgotten me. He was wounded in a great battle. He was brought, dying, here, into Brussels. I came to watch and tend him, as I would have joyfully gone, with such a purpose, to the dreariest ends of the earth. When he knew no one else, he knew me. When he suffered most, he bore his sufferings barely murmuring, content to rest his head where yours rests now. When he lay at the point of death, he married me, that he might call me wife before he died. And the name, my dear love, that I took on that forgotten night——"

"I know it now!" he sobbed. "The shadowy remembrance strengthens. It is come back. I thank Heaven that my mind is quite restored! My Mary, kiss me; lull this weary head to rest, or I shall die of gratitude. His parting words were fulfilled. I see Home again!"

Well! They were happy. It was a long recovery, but they were happy through it all. The snow had melted on the ground, and the birds were singing in the leafless thickets of the early spring, when those three were first able to ride out together, and when people flocked about the open carriage to cheer and congratulate Captain Richard Doubledick.

But even then it became necessary for the Captain, instead of returning to England, to complete his recovery in the climate of Southern France. They found a spot upon the Rhône, within a ride of the old town of Avignon, and within view of its broken bridge, which was all they could desire; they lived there, together, six months; then returned to England. Mrs. Taunton, growing old after three years—though not so old that her bright, dark eyes were dimmed—and remembering that her strength had been benefited by the change, resolved to go back for a year to those parts. So she went with a faithful servant, who had often carried her son in arms; and she was to be rejoined and escorted home, at the year's end, by Captain Richard Doubledick.

She wrote regularly to her children (as she called them now), and they to her. She went to the neighbourhood of Aix; and there, in their own château near the farmer's house she rented, she grew into intimacy with her family belonging to that part of France. The intimacy began in her often meeting among the vineyards a pretty child, a girl, with a most compassionate heart, who was never tired of listening to the solitary English lady's stories of her poor son and the cruel wars. The family were as gentle as the child, and at length she came to know them so well that she accepted their invitation to pass the last month of her residence abroad under their roof. All this intelligence she wrote home, piecemeal as it came about, from time to time; and at last enclosed a polite note, from the head of the château, soliciting, on the occasion of his approaching mission to that neighbourhood, the honour of the company of cet homme si justement célèbre, Monsieur le Capitaine Richard Doubledick.

Captain Doubledick, now a hardy, handsome man in the full vigour of life, broader across the chest and shoulders than he had ever been before, dispatched a courteous reply, and followed it in person. Travelling through all that extent of country after three years of Peace, he blessed the better days on which the world had fallen. The corn was golden, not drenched in unnatural red; was bound in sheaves for food, not trodden underfoot by men in mortal fight. The smoke rose up from peaceful hearths, not blazing ruins. The carts were laden with the fair fruits of the earth, not with wounds and death. To him who had so often seen the terrible reverse, these things were beautiful indeed; and they brought him in a softened spirit to the old château near Aix upon a deep blue evening.

It was a large château of the genuine old ghostly kind, with round towers, and extinguishers, and a high leaden roof, and more windows than Aladdin's Palace. The lattice blinds were all thrown open after the heat of the day, and there were glimpses of rambling walls and corridors within. Then there were immense out-buildings fallen into partial decay, masses of dark trees, terrace-gardens, balustrades; tanks of water, too weak to play and too dirty to work; statues, weeds, and thickets of iron railing that seemed to have overgrown themselves like the shrubberies, and to have branched out in all manner of wild shapes. The entrance doors stood open, as doors often do in that country when the heat of the day is past; and the Captain saw no bell or knocker, and walked in.

He walked into a lofty stone hall, refreshingly cool and gloomy after the glare of a Southern day's travel. Extending along the four sides of this hall was a gallery, leading to suites of rooms; and it was lighted from the top. Still no bell was to be seen.

"Faith," said the Captain halting, ashamed of the clanking of his boots, "this is a ghostly beginning!"

He started back, and felt his face turn white. In the gallery, looking down at him, stood the French officer—the officer whose picture he had carried in his mind so long and so far. Compared with the original at last—in every lineament how like it was!

He moved, and disappeared, and Captain Richard Doubledick heard his steps coming quickly down into the hall. He entered through an archway. There was a bright, sudden look upon his face, much such a look as it had worn in that fatal moment.

Monsieur le Capitaine Richard Doubledick? Enchanted to receive him! A thousand apologies! The servants were all out in the air. There was a slight fête among them in the garden. In effect, it was the fête day of my daughter, the little cherished and protected of Madame Taunton.

He was so gracious and so frank that Monsieur le Capitaine Richard Doubledick could not withhold his hand. "It is the hand of a brave

Englishman," said the French officer, retaining it while he spoke. "I could respect a brave Englishman, even as my foe, how much more as my friend! I also am a soldier."

"He has not remembered me, as I have remembered him; he did not take such note of my face, that day, as I took of his," thought Captain Richard Doubledick. "How shall I tell him?"

The French officer conducted his guest into a garden and presented him to his wife, an engaging and beautiful woman, sitting with Mrs. Taunton in a whimsical old-fashioned pavilion. His daughter, her fair young face beaming with joy, came running to embrace him; and there was a boy-baby to tumble down among the orange trees on the broad steps, in making for his father's legs. A multitude of children visitors were dancing to sprightly music; and all the servants and peasants about the château were dancing too. It was a scene of innocent happiness that might have been invented for the climax of the scenes of peace which had soothed the Captain's journey.

He looked on, greatly troubled in his mind, until a resounding bell rang, and the French officer begged to show him his rooms. They went upstairs into the gallery from which the officer had looked down; and Monsieur le Capitaine Richard Doubledick was cordially welcomed to a grand outer chamber, and a smaller one within, all clocks and draperies, and hearths, and brazen dogs, and tiles, and cool devices, and elegance, and vastness.

"You were at Waterloo," said the French officer.

"I was," said Captain Richard Doubledick. "And at Badajos."

Left alone with the sound of his own stern voice in his ears, he sat down to consider. What shall I do, and how shall I tell him? At that time, unhappily, many deplorable duels had been fought between English and French officers, arising out of the recent war; and these duels, and how to avoid this officer's hospitality, were the uppermost thought in Captain Richard Doubledick's mind.

He was thinking, and letting the time run out in which he should have dressed for dinner, when Mrs. Taunton spoke to him outside the door, asking if he could give her the letter he had brought from Mary. "His mother, above all," the Captain thought. "How shall I tell *her?*"

"You will form a friendship with your host, I hope," said Mrs. Taunton, whom he hurriedly admitted, "that will last for life. He is so true-hearted and so generous, Richard, that you can hardly fail to esteem one another. If He had been spared," she kissed (not without tears) the locket in which she wore his hair, "he would have appreciated him with his own magnanimity, and would have been truly happy that the evil days were past which made such a man his enemy."

She left the room; and the Captain walked, first to one window, whence he could see the dancing in the garden, then to another window, whence he could see the smiling prospect and the peaceful vineyards.

"Spirit of my departed friend," said he, "is it through thee these better thoughts are rising in my mind? Is it thou who hast shown me, all the way I have been drawn to meet this man, the blessings pervading sensation of getting up to be hanged which I have usually found inseparable from untimely rising under such circumstances.

How well I remember the forlorn aspect of Fleet-street when I came out of the Temple! The street-lamps flickering in the gusty north-east wind, as if the very gas were contorted with cold; the white-topped houses; the bleak, star-lighted sky; the market people and other early stragglers, trotting to circulate their almost frozen blood; the hospitable light and warmth of the few coffee-shops and public-houses that were open for such customers; the hard, dry, frosty rime with which the air was charged (the wind had already beaten it into every crevice), and which lashed my face like a steel whip.

It wanted nine days to the end of the month, and end of the year. The Post-office packet for the United States was to depart from Liverpool, weather permitting, on the first of the ensuing month, and I had the intervening time on my hands. I had taken this into consideration, and had resolved to make a visit to a certain spot (which I need not name) on the farther borders of Yorkshire. It was endeared to me by my having first seen Angela at a farmhouse in that place, and my melancholy was gratified by the idea of taking a wintry leave of it before my expatriation. I ought to explain, that, to avoid being sought out before my resolution should have been rendered irrevocable by being carried into full effect, I had written to Angela overnight, in my usual manner, lamenting that urgent business, of which she should know all particulars by-and-by—took me unexpectedly away from her for a week or ten days.

There was no Northern Railway at that time, and in its place there were stage-coaches; which I occasionally find myself, in common with some other people, affecting to lament now, but which everybody dreaded as a very serious penance then. I had secured the box-seat on the fastest of these, and my business in Fleet-street was to get into a cab with my portmanteau, so to make the best of my way to the Peacock at Islington, where I was to join this coach. But when one of our Temple watchmen, who carried my portmanteau into Fleet-street for me, told me about the huge blocks of ice that had for some days past been floating in the river, having closed up in the night, and made a walk from the Temple Gardens over to the Surrey shore, I began to ask myself the question, whether the box-seat would not be likely to put a sudden and a frosty end to my unhappiness. I was heart-broken, it is true, and yet I was not quite so far gone as to wish to be frozen to death.

When I got up to the Peacock,—where I found everybody drinking hot purl, in self-preservation,—I asked if there were an inside seat to spare. I then discovered that, inside or out, I was the only passenger. This gave me a still livelier idea of the great inclemency of the weather, since that coach always loaded particularly well. However, I took a little purl (which I found uncommonly good), and got into the coach. When I was seated, they built me up with straw to the waist, and, conscious of making a rather ridiculous appearance,

I began my journey.

It was still dark when we left the Peacock. For a little while, pale, uncertain ghosts of houses and trees appeared and vanished, and then it was hard, black, frozen day. People were lighting their fires; smoke was mounting straight up high into the rarefied air; and we were rattling for Highgate Archway over the hardest ground I have ever heard the ring of iron shoes on. As we got into the country, everything seemed to have grown old and gray. The roads, the trees, thatched roofs of cottages and homesteads, the ricks in farmers' yards. Out-door work was abandoned, horse-troughs at roadside inns were frozen hard, no stragglers lounged about, doors were close shut, little turnpike houses had blazing fires inside, and children (even turnpike people have children, and seem to like them) rubbed the frost from the little panes of glass with their chubby arms, that their bright eyes might catch a glimpse of the solitary coach going by. I don't know when the snow began to set in; but I know that we were changing horses somewhere when I heard the guard remark, "That the old lady up in the sky was picking her geese pretty hard to-day." Then, indeed, I found the white down falling fast and thick.

The lonely day wore on, and I dozed it out, as a lonely traveller does. I was warm and valiant after eating and drinking,—particularly after dinner; cold and depressed at all other times. I was always bewildered as to time and place, and always more or less out of my senses. The coach and horses seemed to execute in chorus Auld Lang Syne, without a moment's intermission. They kept the time and tune with the greatest regularity, and rose into the swell at the beginning of the Refrain, with a precision that worried me to death. While we changed horses, the guard and coachman went stumping up and down the road, printing off their shoes in the snow, and poured so much liquid consolation into themselves without being any the worse for it, that I began to confound them, as it darkened again, with two great white casks standing on end. Our horses tumbled down in solitary places, and we got them up,—which was the pleasantest variety *I* had, for it warmed me. And it snowed and snowed, and still it snowed, and never left off snowing. All night long we went on in this manner. Thus we came round the clock, upon the Great North Road, to the performance of Auld Lang Syne all day again. And it snowed and snowed, and still it snowed, and never left off snowing.

I forget now where we were at noon on the second day, and where we ought to have been; but I know that we were scores of miles behindhand, and that our case was growing worse every hour. The drift was becoming prodigiously deep; landmarks were getting snowed out; the road and the fields were all one; instead of having fences and hedge-rows to guide us, we went crunching on over an unbroken surface of ghastly white that might sink beneath us at any moment and drip us down a whole hillside. Still the coachman and guard— who kept together on the box, always in council, and looking well about them—made out the track with astonishing sagacity.

When we came in sight of a town, it looked, to my fancy, like a large drawing on a slate, with abundance of slate-pencil expended on the churches and houses where the snow lay thickest. When we came within a town, and found the church clocks all stopped, the dial-faces choked with snow, and the inn-signs blotted out, it seemed as if the whole place were overgrown with white moss. As to the coach, it was a mere snowball; similarly, the men and boys who ran along beside us to the town's end, turning our clogged wheels and encouraging our horses, were men and boys of snow; and the bleak wild solitude to which they at last dismissed us was a snowy Sahara. One would have thought this enough: notwithstanding which, I pledge my word that it snowed and snowed, and still it snowed, and never left off snowing.

We performed Auld Lang Syne the whole day; seeing nothing, out of towns and villages, but the track of stoats, hares, and foxes, and sometimes of birds. At nine o'clock at night, on a Yorkshire moor, a cheerful burst from our horn, and a welcome sound of talking, with a glimmering and moving about of lanterns, roused me from my drowsy state. I found that we were going to change.

They helped me out, and I said to a waiter, whose bare head became as white as King Lear's in a single minute, "What Inn is this?"

"The Holly-Tree, Sir," said he.

"Upon my word, I believe," said I, apologetically, to the guard and coachman, "that I must stop here."

Now the landlord, and the landlady, and the ostler, and the post-boy, and all the stable authorities, had already asked the coachman, to the wide-eyed interest of all the rest of the establishment, if he meant to go on. The coachman had already replied, "Yes, he'd take her through it,"—meaning by Her the coach,—"if so be as George would stand by him." George was the guard, and he had already sworn that he *would* stand by him. So the helpers were already getting the horses out.

My declaring myself beaten, after this parley, was not an announcement without preparation. Indeed, but for the way to the announcement being smoothed by the parley, I more than doubt whether, as an innately bashful man, I should have had confidence to make it. As it was, it received the approval even of the guard and coachman. Therefore, with many confirmations of my inclining, and many remarks from one bystander to another, that the gentleman could go for'ard by the mail to-morrow, whereas to-night he would only be froze and, where was the good of a gentleman being froze,—ah, let alone buried alive (which latter clause was added by a humorous helper as a joke at my expense, and was extremely well received), I saw my portmanteau got off stiff, like a frozen body; did the handsome thing by the guard and coachman; wished them good-night, and a prosperous journey; and, a little ashamed of myself, after all, for leaving them to fight it out alone, followed the landlord, landlady, and waiter of the Holly-tree upstairs.

I thought I had never seen such a large room as that into which they showed me. It had five windows, with dark red curtains that would have absorbed the light of a general illumination; and there were complications of drapery at the top of the curtains, that went wandering about the wall in a most extraordinary manner. I asked for a smaller room, and they told me there was no smaller room. They could screen me in, however, the landlord said. They brought a great old japanned screen, with natives (Japanese, I suppose) engaged in a variety of idiotic pursuits all over it; and left me roasting whole before an immense fire.

My bedroom was some quarter of a mile off, up a great staircase at the end of a long gallery; and nobody knows what a misery this is to a bashful man who would rather not meet people on the stairs. It was the grimmest room I have ever had the nightmare in; and all the furniture, from the four posts of the bed to the two old silver candle-sticks, was tall, high-shouldered, and spindle-waisted. Below, in my sitting-room, if I looked round my screen, the wind rushed at me like a mad bull; if I stuck to my armchair, the fire scorched me to the colour of a new brick. The chimneypiece was very high, and there was a bad glass—what I may call a wavy glass—above it, which, when I stood up, just showed me my anterior phrenological developments, —and these never look well, in any subject, cut short off at the eye-brow. If I stood with my back to the fire, a gloomy vault of darkness above and beyond the screen insisted on being looked at; and, in its dim remoteness, the drapery of the ten curtains of the five windows went twisting and creeping about, like a nest of gigantic worms.

I suppose that what I observe in myself must be observed by some other men of similar character in *themselves;* therefore I am emboldened to mention, that, when I travel, I never arrive at a place but I immediately want to go away from it. Before I had finished my supper of broiled fowl and mulled port, I had impressed upon the waiter in detail my arrangements for departure in the morning. Breakfast and bill at eight. Fly at nine. Two horses, or, if needful, even four.

Tired though I was, the night appeared about a week long. In cases of nightmare, I thought of Angela, and felt more depressed than ever by the reflection that I was on the shortest road to Gretna Green. What had *I* to do with Gretna Green? I was not going *that* way to the devil, but by the American route, I remarked in my bitterness.

In the morning I found that it was snowing still, that it had snowed alll night, and that I was snowed up. Nothing could get out of that spot on the moor, or could come at it, until the road had been cut out by labourers from the market-town. When they might cut their way to the Holly-Tree nobody could tell me.

It was now Christmas-eve. I should have had a dismal Christmas-time of it anywhere, and consequently that did not so much matter; still, being snowed up was like dying of frost, a thing I had not bargained for. I felt very lonely. Yet I could no more have proposed to the landlord and landlady to admit me to their society (though I should have liked it very much) than I could have asked them to little Inn in Switzerland, while I was staying there. It was a very homely place, in a village of one narrow zigzag street, among mountains, and you went in at the main door through the cow-house, and among the mules and the dogs and the fowls, before ascending a great bare staircase to the rooms; which were all of unpainted wood, without plastering or papering,—like rough packing-cases. Outside there was nothing but the straggling street, a little toy church with a copper-coloured steeple, a pine forest, a torrent, mists, and mountainsides. A young man belonging to this Inn had disappeared eight weeks before (it was winter-time), and was supposed to have had some undiscovered love affair, and to have gone for a soldier. He had got up in the night, and dropped into the village street from the loft in which he slept with another man; and he had done it so quietly, that his companion and fellow-labourer had heard no movement when he was awakened in the morning, and they said, "Louis, where is Henri?" They looked for him high and low, in vain, and gave him up. Now, outside this Inn, there stood, as there stood outside every dwelling in the village, a stack of firewood; but the stack belonging to the Inn was higher than any of the rest, because the Inn was the richest house, and burnt the most fuel. It began to be noticed, while they were looking high and low, that a Bantam cock, part of the live stock of the Inn, put himself wonderfully out of his way to get to the top of this wood-stack; and that he would stay there for hours and hours, crowing, until he appeared in danger of splitting himself. Five weeks went on,—six weeks,—and still this terrible Bantam, neglecting his domestic affairs, was always on the top of the wood-stack, crowing the very eyes out of his head. By this time it was perceived that Louis had become inspired with a violent animosity towards the terrible Bantam, and one morning he was seen by a woman, who sat nursing her goître at a little window in a gleam of sun, to catch up a rough billet of wood, with a great oath, hurl it at the terrible Bantam crowing on the wood-stack, and bring him down dead. Hereupon the woman, with a sudden light in her mind, stole round to the back of the wood-stack, and, being a good climber, as all those women are, climbed up, and soon was seen upon the summit, screaming, looking down the hollow within, and crying, "Seize Louis, the murderer! Ring the church bell! Here is the body!" I saw the murderer that day, and I saw him as I sat by my fire at the Holly-Tree Inn, and I see him now, lying shackled with cords on the stable litter, among the mild eyes and the smoking breath of the cows, waiting to be taken away by the police, and stared at by the fearful village. A heavy animal,—the dullest animal in the stables,—with a stupid head, and a lumpish face devoid of any trace of sensibility, who had been, within the knowledge of the murdered youth, an embezzler of certain small moneys belonging to his master, and who had taken this hopeful mode of putting a possible accuser out of his way. All of which he confessed next day, like a sulky wretch who couldn't be troubled any more, now that they had got hold of him, and meant to make an end of him. I saw him once again, on the day of my departure from the Inn. In that Canton the headsman still does his office with a sword; and I came upon this murderer, sitting bound to a chair, with his eyes bandaged, on a scaffold in a little market-place. In that instant, a great sword (loaded with quicksilver in the thick part of the blade) swept round him like a gust of wind or fire, and there was no such creature in the world. My wonder was, not that he was so suddenly dispatched, but that any head was left unreaped, within a radius of fifty yards of that tremendous sickle.

That was a good Inn, too, with the kind, cheerful landlady and the honest landlord, where I lived in the shadow of Mont Blanc, and where one of the apartments has a zoological papering on the walls, not so accurately joined but that the elephant occasionally rejoices in a tiger's hind legs and tail, while the lion puts on a trunk and tusks, and the bear, moulting as it were, appears as to portions of himself like a leopard. I made several American friends at that Inn, who all called Mont Blanc Mount Blank,—except one good-humoured gentleman, of a very sociable nature, who became on such intimate terms with it that he spoke of it familiarly as " Blank " ; observing, at breakfast, " Blank looks pretty tall this morning " ; or considerably doubting in the courtyard in the evening, whether there warn't some go-ahead naters in our country, Sir, that would make out the top of Blank in a couple of hours from first start—now!

Once I passed a fortnight at an Inn in the North of England, where I was haunted by the ghost of a tremendous pie. It was a Yorkshire pie, like a fort,—an abandoned fort with nothing in it; but the waiter had a fixed idea that it was a point of ceremony at every meal to put the pie on the table. After some days I tried to hint, in several delicate ways, that I considered the pie done with; as, for example, by emptying fag-ends of glasses of wine into it; putting cheese-plates and spoons into it, as into a basket; putting wine-bottles into it, as into a cooler; but always in vain, the pie being invariably cleaned out again and brought up as before. At last, beginning to be doubtful whether I was not the victim of a spectral illusion, and whether my health and spirits might not sink under the horrors of an imaginary pie, I cut a triangle out of it, fully as large as the musical instrument of that name in a powerful orchestra. Human prevision could not have foreseen the result—but the waiter mended the pie. With some effectual species of cement, he adroitly fitted the triangle in again, and I paid my reckoning and fled.

The Holly-Tree was getting rather dismal. I made an overland expedition beyond the screen, and penetrated as far as the fourth window. Here I was driven back by stress of weather. Arrived at my winter-quarters once more, I made up the fire, and took another Inn.

It was in the remotest part of Cornwall. A great annual Miner's Feast was being holden at the Inn, when I and my travelling companions presented ourselves at night among the wild crowd that were dancing before it by torchlight. We had had a break-down in the dark, on a stony morass some miles away ; and I had the honour of leading one of the unharnessed post-horses. If any lady or gentleman, on perusal of the present lines, will take any very tall post-horse with his traces hanging about his legs, and will conduct him by the bearing-rein into the heart of a country dance of a hundred and fifty couples, that lady or gentleman will then, and only then, form an adequate idea of the extent to which that post-horse will tread on his conductor's toes. Over and above which, the post-horse, finding three hundred people whirling about him, will probably rear, and also lash out with his hind legs, in a manner incompatible with dignity or self-respect on his conductor's part. With such little drawbacks on my usually impressive aspect, I appeared at this Cornish Inn, to the unutterable wonder of the Cornish Miners. It was full, and twenty times full, and nobody could be received but the post-horse, —though to get rid of that noble animal was something. While my fellow-travellers and I were discussing how to pass the night and so much of the next day as must intervene before the jovial blacksmith and the jovial wheelwright would be in a condition to go out on the morass and mend the coach, an honest man stepped forth from the crowd and proposed his unlet floor of two rooms, with supper of eggs and bacon, ale and punch. We joyfully accompanied him home to the strangest of clean houses, where we were well entertained to the satisfaction of all parties. But the novel feature of the entertainment was, that our host was a chairmaker, and that the chairs assigned to us were mere frames, altogether without bottoms of any sort; so that we passed the evening on perches. Nor was this the absurdest consequence; for when we unbent at supper, and any one of us gave way to laughter, he forgot the peculiarity of his position, and instantly disappeared. I myself, doubled up into an attitude from which self-extrication was impossible, was taken out of my frame, like a clown in a comic pantomime who has tumbled into a tub, five times by the taper's light during the eggs and bacon.

The Holly-Tree was fast reviving within me a sense of loneliness. I began to feel conscious that my subject would never carry on until I was dug out. I might be a week here,—weeks!

There was a story with a singular idea in it, connected with an Inn I once passed a night at in a picturesque old town on the Welsh border. In a large double-bedded room of this Inn there had been a suicide committed by poison, in one bed, while a tired traveller slept unconscious in the other. After that time, the suicide bed was never used, but the other constantly was; the disused bedstead remaining in the room empty, though as to all other respects in its old state. The story ran, that whosoever slept in this room, though never so entire a stranger, from never so far off, was invariably observed to come down in the morning with an impression that he smelt Laudanum, and that his mind always turned upon the subject to suicide; to which, whatever kind of man he might be, he was certain to make some reference if he conversed with any one. This went on for years, until it at length induced the landlord to take the disused bedstead down, and bodily burn it,—bed, hangings, and all. The strange influence (this was the story) now changed to a fainter one, but never changed afterwards. The occupant of that room, with occasional but very rare exceptions, would come down in the morning, trying to recall a forgotten dream he had had in the night. The landlord, on his mentioning his perplexity, would suggest various commonplace subjects, not one of which, as he very well knew, was the true subject. But the moment the landlord suggested " Poison," the traveller started, and cried, "Yes!" He never failed to accept that suggestion, and he never recalled any more of the dream.

This reminiscence brought the Welsh Inns in general before me; with the women in their round hats, and the harpers with their white beards (venerable, but humbugs, I am afraid), playing outside the door while I took my dinner. The transition was natural to the Highland Inns, with the oatmeal bannocks, the honey, the venison steaks, the trout from the loch, the whisky, and perhaps (having the materials so temptingly at hand) the Athol brose. Once was I coming south from the Scottish Highlands in hot haste, hoping to change quickly at the station at the bottom of a certain wild historical glen, when these eyes did with mortification see the landlord come out with a telescope and sweep the whole prospect for the horses; which horses were away picking up their own living, and did not heave in sight under four hours. Having thought of the loch-trout, I was taken by quick association to the Anglers' Inns of England (I have assisted at innumerable feats of angling by lying in the bottom of the boat, whole summer days, doing nothing with the greatest perseverance; which I have generally found to be as effectual towards the taking of fish as the finest tackle and the utmost science), and to the pleasant white, clean, flower-pot-decorated bedrooms of those inns, overlooking the river, and the ferry, and the green ait, and the church-spire, and the country bridge; and to the peerless Emma with the bright eyes and the pretty smile, who waited, bless her! with a natural grace that would have converted Blue-Beard. Casting my eyes upon my Holly-Tree fire, I next discerned among the glowing coals the pictures of a score or more of those wonderful English posting-inns which we are all so sorry to have lost, which were so large and so comfortable, and which were such monuments of British submission to rapacity and extortion. He who would see these houses pining away, let him walk from Basingstoke, or even Windsor, to London, by way of Hounslow, and moralise on their perishing remains; the stables crumbling to dust; unsettled labourers and wanderers bivouacking in the outhouses; grass growing in the yards; the rooms, where erst so many hundred beds of down were made up, let off to Irish lodgers at eighteenpence a week; a little ill-looking beer-shop shrinking in the tap of former days, burning coach-house gates for firewood, having one of its two windows bunged up, as if it had received punishment in a fight with the Railroad; a low, bandy-legged, brick-making bulldog standing in the doorway. What could I next see in my fire so naturally as the new railway-house of these times near the dismal country station; with nothing particular on draught but cold air and damp, nothing worth mentioning in the larder but new mortar, and no business doing beyond a conceited affectation of luggage in the hall? Then I came to the Inns of Paris, with the pretty apartment of four pieces up one hundred and seventy-five waxed stairs, the privilege of ringing the bell all day long without influencing anybody's mind or body but your own, and the not-too-much-for-dinner, considering the price. Next to the provincial Inns of France, with the great church-tower rising above the courtyard, the horse-bells jingling merrily up and down the street beyond, and the clocks of all descriptions in all the rooms, which are never right, unless taken at the precise minute when, by getting exactly twelve hours too fast or too slow, they unintentionally become so. Away I went, next, to the lesser roadside Inns of Italy; where all the dirty clothes in the house (not in wear) are always lying in your anteroom; where the mosquitoes make a raisin pudding of your face in summer, and the cold bites it blue in winter; where you get what you can, and forget what you can't; where I should again like to be boiling my tea in a pocket-handkerchief dumpling, for want of a teapot. So to the old palace Inns and old monastery Inns, in towns and cities of the same bright country; with their massive quadrangular staircases, whence you may look from among clustering pillars high into the blue vault of heaven; with their stately banqueting-rooms, and vast refectories; with their labyrinths of ghostly bedchambers, and their glimpses into gorgeous streets that have no appearance of reality or possibility. So to the close little Inns of the Malaria districts, with their pale attendants, and their peculiar smell of never letting in the air. So to the immense fantastic Inns of Venice, with the cry of the gondolier below, as he skims the corner; the grip of the watery odours on one particular little bit of the bridge of your nose (which is never released while you stay there); and the great bell of St. Mark's Cathedral tolling midnight. Next I put up for a minute at the restless Inns upon the Rhine, where your going to bed, no matter at what hour, appears to be the tocsin for everybody else's getting up; and where, in the table-d'hôte room at the end of the long table (with several Towers of Babel on it at the other end, all made of white plates), one knot of stoutish men, entirely dressed in jewels and dirt, and having nothing else upon them, *will* remain all night, clinking glasses, and singing about the river that flows, and the grape that grows, and Rhine wine that beguiles, and Rhine woman that smiles and hi drink drink my friend and ho drink drink my brother, and all the rest of it. I departed thence, as a matter of course, to other German Inns, where all the eatables are soddened down to the same flavour, and where the mind is disturbed by the apparition of hot puddings, and boiled cherries, sweet and slab, at awfully unexpected periods of the repast. After a draught of sparkling beer from a foaming glass jug, and a glance of recognition through the windows of the student beer-houses at Heidelberg and elsewhere, I put out to sea for the Inns of America, with their four hundred beds apiece, and their eight or nine hundred ladies and gentlemen at dinner every day. Again I stood in the bar-rooms thereof, taking my evening cobbler, julep, sling, or cocktail. Again I listened to my friend the General,—whom I had known for five minutes, in the course of which period he had made me intimate for life with two Majors, who again had made me intimate for life with three Colonels, who again had made me brother to twenty-two civilians,—again, I say, I listened to my friend the General, leisurely expounding the resources of the establishment, as to gentlemen's morning-room, Sir; ladies' morning-room, Sir; gentlemen's evening-room, Sir; ladies' evening-room, Sir; ladies' and gentlemen's evening reuniting-room, Sir; music-room, Sir; reading-room, Sir; over four hundred sleeping-rooms, Sir; and the entire planned and finished within twelve calendar months from the first clearing off of the old encumbrances on the plot, at a cost of five hundred thousand dollars, Sir. Again I found, as to my individual way of thinking, that the greater, the more gorgeous, and the more dollarous the establishment was, the less desirable it was. Nevertheless, again I drank my cobbler, julep, sling, or cocktail, in all good-will, to my friend the General, and my friends the Majors, Colonels, and civilians all; full well knowing that, whatever little motes my beamy eyes may have described in theirs, they belong to a kind, generous, large-hearted, and great people.

I had been going on lately at a quick pace to keep my solitude out of my mind; but here I broke down for good, and gave up the subject. What was I to do? What was to become of me? Into what extremity was I submissively to sink? Supposing that, like Baron Trenck, I looked out for a mouse or spider, and found one, and beguiled my imprisonment by training it? Even that might be dangerous with a view to the future. I might be so far gone when the road did come to be cut through the snow, that, on my way forth, I might burst into tears, and beseech, like the prisoner who was released in his old age from the Bastille, to be taken back again to the five windows, the ten curtains, and the sinuous drapery.

A desperate idea came into my head. Under any other circumstances I should have rejected it; but, in the strait at which I was, I held it fast. Could I so far overcome the inherent bashfulness which withheld me from the landlord's table and the company I might find there, as to call up the Boots, and ask him to take a chair,—and something in a liquid form,—and talk to me? I could. I would. I did.

SECOND BRANCH

THE BOOTS

WHERE had he been in his time? he repeated, when I asked him the question. Lord, he had been everywhere! And what had he been? Bless you, he had been everything you could mention a'most!

Seen a good deal? Why, of course he had. I should say so, he could assure me, if I only knew about a twentieth part of what had come in *his* way. Why, it would be easier for him, he expected, to tell what he hadn't seen than what he had. Ah! A deal, it would.

What was the curiousest thing he had seen? Well! He didn't know. He couldn't momently name what was the curiousest thing he had seen,—unless it was a Unicorn,—and he see *him* once at a Fair. But supposing a young gentleman not eight year old was to run away with a fine young woman of seven, might I think *that* a queer start? Certainly. Then that was a start as he himself had had his blessed eyes on, and he had cleaned the shoes they run away in—and they was so little that he couldn't get his hand into 'em.

Master Harry Walmers' father, you see, he lived at the Elmses, down away by Shooter's Hill there, six or seven miles from Lunnon. He was a gentleman of spirit, and good-looking, and held his head up when he walked, and had what you may call Fire about him. He wrote poetry, and he rode, and he ran, and he cricketed, and he danced, and he acted, and he done it all equally beautiful. He was uncommon proud of Master Harry as was his only child; but he didn't spoil him neither. He was a gentleman that had a will of his own and a eye of his own, and that would be minded. Consequently, though he made quite a companion of the fine bright boy, and was delighted to see him so fond of reading his fairy books, and was never tired of hearing him say my name is Norval, or hearing him sing his songs about Young May Moons is beaming love, and When he as adores thee has left but the name, and that; still he kept the command over the child, and the child *was* a child, and it's to be wished more of 'em was!

How did Boots happen to know all this? Why, through being under-gardener. Of course he couldn't be under-gardener, and be always about, in the summer-time, near the windows on the lawn, a mowing, and sweeping, and weeding, and pruning, and this and that, without getting acquainted with the ways of the family. Even supposing Master Harry hadn't come to him one morning early, and said, "Cobbs, how should you spell Norah, if you was asked?" and then began cutting it in print all over the fence.

He couldn't say he had taken particular notice of children before that; but really it was pretty to see them two mites a going about the place together, deep in love. And the courage of the boy! Bless your soul, he'd have throwed off his little hat, and tucked up his little sleeves, and gone in at a Lion, he would, if they had happened to meet one, and she had been frightened of him. One day he stops, along with her, where Boots was hoeing weeds in the gravel, and says, speaking up, "Cobbs," he says, "I like *you*." "Do you, Sir? I'm proud to hear it." "Yes, I do, Cobbs. Why do I like you, do you think, Cobbs?" "Don't know, Master Harry, I am sure." "Because Norah likes you, Cobbs." "Indeed, Sir? That's very gratifying." "Gratifying, Cobbs? It's better than millions of the brightest diamonds to be liked by Norah." "Certainly, Sir," "You're going away, ain't you, Cobbs?" "Yes, Sir." "Would you like another situation, Cobbs?" "Well, Sir, I shouldn't object, if it was a good 'un." "Then, Cobbs," says he, "you shall be our Head Gardener when we are married." And he tucks her, in her little sky-blue mantle, under his arm, and walks away.

Boots could assure me that it was better than a picter, and equal to a play, to see them babies, with their long, bright, curling hair, their sparkling eyes, and their beautiful light tread, a rambling about the garden, deep in love. Boots was of opinion that the birds believed they was birds, and kept up with 'em, singing to please 'em. Sometimes they would creep under the Tulip-tree, and would sit there with their arms round one another's necks, and their soft cheeks touching, a reading about the Prince and the Dragon, and the good and bad enchanters, and the king's fair daughter. Sometimes he would hear them planning about having a house in a forest, keeping bees and a cow, and living entirely on milk and honey. Once he came upon them by the pond, and heard Master Harry say, "Adorable Norah, kiss me, and say you love me to distraction, or I'll jump in head-foremost." And Boots made no question he would have done it if she hadn't complied. On the whole, Boots said it had a tendency to make him feel as if he was in love himself—only he didn't exactly know who with.

"Cobbs," said Master Harry, one evening, when Cobbs was watering the flowers, "I am going on a visit, this present Midsummer, to my grandmamma's at York."

"Are you indeed, Sir? I hope you'll have a pleasant time. I am going into Yorkshire, myself, when I leave here."

"Are you going to your grandmamma's, Cobbs?"

"No, Sir. I haven't got such a thing."

"Not as a grandmamma, Cobbs?"

"No, Sir."

The boy looked on at the watering of the flowers for a little while, and then said, "I shall be very glad indeed to go, Cobbs,—Norah's going."

"You'll be all right then, Sir," says Cobbs, "with your beautiful sweetheart by your side."

"Cobbs," returned the boy, flushing, "I never let anybody joke about it, when I can prevent them."

"It wasn't a joke, Sir," says Cobbs, with humility,—"wasn't so meant."

"I am glad of that, Cobbs, because I like you, you know, and you're going to live with us.—Cobbs!"

"Sir."

"What do you think my grandmamma gives me when I go down there?"

"I couldn't so much as make a guess, Sir."

"A Bank of England five-pound note, Cobbs."

"Whew!" says Cobbs, "that's a spanking sum of money, Master Harry."

"A person could do a good deal with such a sum of money as that, —couldn't a person, Cobbs?"

"I believe you, Sir!"

"Cobbs," said the boy, "I'll tell you a secret. At Norah's house, they have been joking her about me, and pretending to laugh at our being engaged,—pretending to make game of it, Cobbs!"

"Such, Sir," says Cobbs, "is the depravity of human natur.'"

The boy, looking exactly like his father, stood for a few minutes with his glowing face towards the sunset, and then departed with, "Good-night, Cobbs. I'm going in."

If I was to ask Boots how it happened that he was a going to leave that place just at that present time, well, he couldn't rightly answer me. He did suppose he might have stayed there till now if he had been anyways inclined. But, you see, he was younger then, and he wanted change. That's what he wanted,—change. Mr. Walmers, he said to him when he gave him notice of his intentions to leave, "Cobbs," he says, "have you anythink to complain of? I make the inquiry because if I find that any of my people really has anythink to complain of, I wish to make it right if I can." "No, Sir," says Cobbs; "thanking you, Sir, I find myself as well sitiwated here as I could hope to anywheres. The truth is, Sir, that I'm a-going to seek my fortun'." "O, indeed, Cobbs!" he says; "I hope you may find it." And Boots could assure me—which he did, touching his hair with his bootjack, as a salute in the way of his present calling—that he hadn't found it yet.

Well, Sir! Boots left the Elmses when his time was up, and Master Harry, he went down to the old lady's at York, which old lady would have given that child the teeth out of her head (if she had had any), she was so wrapped up in him. What does that Infant do,—for Infant you may call him and be within the mark,—but cut away from that old lady's with his Norah, on a expedition to go to Gretna Green and be married!

Sir, Boots was at this identical Holly-Tree Inn (having left it several times since to better himself, but always come back through one thing or another), when, one summer afternoon, the coach drives up, and out of the coach gets them two children. The Guard says to our Governor, "I don't quite make out these little passengers, but the young gentleman's words was, that they was to be brought here." The young gentleman gets out; hands his lady out; gives the Guard something for himself; says to our Governor, "We're to stop here to-night, please. Sitting-room and two bedrooms will be required. Chops and cherry-pudding for two!" and tucks her, in her little sky-blue mantle, under his arm, and walks into the house much bolder than Brass.

Boots leaves me to judge what the amazement of that establishment was, when these two tiny creatures all alone by themselves was marched into the Angel,—much more so, when he, who had seen them without their seeing him, give the Governor his views of the expedition they was upon. "Cobbs," says the Governor, "if this is so, I must set off myself to York, and quiet their friends' minds. In which case you must keep your eye upon 'em, and humour 'em, till I come back. But before I take these measures, Cobbs, I should wish you to find from themselves whether your opinion is correct. "Sir, to you," says Cobbs, "that shall be done directly."

So Boots goes upstairs to the Angel, and there he finds Master Harry on a e-normous sofa,—immense at any time, but looking like the Great Bed of Ware, compared with him,—a drying the eyes of Miss Norah with his pocket-hankercher. Their little legs was entirely off the ground, of course, and it really is not possible for Boots to express to me how small them children looked.

"It's Cobbs! It's Cobbs!" cried Master Harry, and comes running to him, and catching hold of his hand. Miss Norah comes running to him on t'other side and catching hold of his t'other hand, and they both jump for joy.

"I see you a getting out, Sir," says Cobbs, "I thought it was you. I thought I couldn't be mistaken in your height and figure. What's the object of your journey, Sir?—Matrimonial?"

"We are going to be married, Cobbs, at Gretna Green," returned the boy. "We have run away on purpose. Norah has been in rather low spirits, Cobbs; but she'll be happy, now we have found you to be our friend."

"Thank you, Sir, and thank *you*, Miss," says Cobbs, "for your good opinion. *Did* you bring any luggage with you, Sir?"

If I will believe Boots when he gives me his word and honour upon it, the lady had got a parasol, a smelling-bottle, a round and a half of cold buttered toast, eight peppermint drops, and a hair-brush,—seemingly a doll's. The gentleman had got about half-a-dozen yards of string, a knife, three or four sheets of writing-paper folded up surprising small, a orange, and a Chaney mug with his name upon it.

"What may be the exact natur of your plans, Sir?" says Cobbs.

"To go on," replied the boy,—which the courage of that boy was somethingwonderful!—"in the morning, and be married to-morrow."

"Just so, Sir," says Cobbs. "Would it meet your views, Sir, if I was to accompany you?"

When Cobbs said this, they both jumped for joy again, and cried out, "Oh, yes, yes, Cobbs! Yes!"

"Well, Sir," says Cobbs. "If you will excuse my having the freedom to give an opinion, what I should recommend would be this. I'm acquainted with a pony, Sir, which, put in a pheayton that I could borrow, would take you and Mrs. Harry Walmers, Junior, (myself driving, if you approved,) to the end of your journey in a very short space of time. I am not altogether sure, Sir, that this pony will be at liberty to-morrow, but even if you had to wait over to-morrow for him, it might be worth your while. As to the small account here, Sir, in case you was to find yourself running at all short, that don't signify; because I'm a part proprietor of this inn, and it could stand over."

Boots assures me that when they clapped their hands, and jumped for joy again, and called him "Good Cobbs!" and "Dear Cobbs!" and bent across him to kiss one another in the delight of their confiding hearts, he felt himself the meanest rascal for deceiving 'em that ever was born.

"Is there anything you want just at present, Sir?" says Cobbs, mortally ashamed of himself.

"We should like some cakes after dinner," answered Master Harry, folding his arms, putting out one leg, and looking straight at him, "and two apples,—and jam. With dinner we should like to have toast-and-water. But Norah has always been accustomed to half a glass of currant wine at dessert. And so have I."

"It shall be ordered at the bar, Sir," says Cobbs; and away he went.

Boots has the feeling as fresh upon him at this minute of speaking as he had then, that he would far rather have had it out in half-a-dozen rounds with the Governor than have combined with him; and that he wished with all his heart there was any impossible place where those two babies could make an impossible marriage, and live impossibly happy ever afterwards. However, as it couldn't be, he went into the Governor's plans, and the Governor set off for York in half an hour.

The way in which the women of that house—without exception—every one of 'em—married *and* single—took to that boy when they heard the story, Boots considers surprising. It was as much as he could do to keep 'em from dashing into the room and kissing him. They climbed up all sorts of places, at the risk of their lives, to look at him through a pane of glass. They was seven deep at the keyhole. They was out of their minds about him and his bold spirit.

In the evening, Boots went into the room to see how the runaway couple was getting on. The gentleman was on the window-seat, supporting the lady in his arms. She had tears upon her face, and was lying, very tired and half asleep, with her head upon his shoulder.

"Mrs. Harry Walmers, Junior, fatigued, Sir?" says Cobbs.

"Yes, she is tired, Cobbs; but she is not used to be away from home, and she has been in low spirits again. Cobbs, do you think you could bring a biffin, please?"

"I ask your pardon, Sir," says Cobbs, "What was it you——?"

"I think a Norfolk biffin would rouse her, Cobbs. She is very fond of them."

Boots withdrew in search of the required restorative, and, when he brought it in, the gentleman handed it to the lady, and fed her with a spoon, and took a little himself; the lady being heavy with sleep, and rather cross. "What should you think, Sir," says Cobbs, "of a chamber candlestick?" The gentleman approved; the chamber-maid went first, up the great staircase; the lady, in her sky-blue mantle, followed, gallantly escorted by the gentleman; the gentleman embraced her at her door, and retired to his own apartment, where Boots softly locked him up.

Boots couldn't but feel with increased acuteness what a base deceiver he was, when they consulted him at breakfast (they had ordered sweet milk-and-water, and toast and currant jelly overnight) about the pony. It really was as much as he could do, he don't mind confessing to me, to look them two young things in the face, and think what a wicked old father of lies he had grown to be. Howsom-

ever, he went on a lying like a Trojan about the pony. He told 'em
that it did so unfort'nately happen that the pony was half clipped,
you see, and that he couldn't be taken out in that state, for fear it
should strike to his inside. But that he'd be finished clipping in the
course of the day, and that to-morrow morning at eight o'clock the
pheayton would be ready. Boots's view of the whole case, looking
back on it in my room, is, that Mrs. Harry Walmers, Junior, was
beginning to give in. She hadn't had her hair curled when she went
to bed, and she didn't seem quite up to brushing it herself, and its
getting in her eyes put her out. But nothing put out Master Harry.
He sat behind his breakfast-cup, a tearing away at the jelly, as if he
had been his own father.

After breakfast, Boots is inclined to consider that they drawed
soldiers,—at least, he knows that many such was found in the fireplace, all on horseback. In the course of the morning, Master Harry
rang the bell,—it was surprising how that there boy did carry on,—
and said, in a sprightly way, "Cobbs, is there any good walks in this
neighbourhood?"

"Yes, Sir," says Cobbs. "There's Love-lane."

"Get out with you, Cobbs!" —that was that there boy's expression
—"you're joking."

"Begging your pardon, Sir," says Cobbs, "there really is Love-lane.
And a pleasant walk it is, and proud shall I be to show it to yourself
and Mrs. Harry Walmers, Junior."

"Norah, dear," said Master Harry, "this is curious. We really
ought to see Love-lane. Put on your bonnet, my sweetest darling,
and we will go there with Cobbs."

Boots leaves me to judge what a Beast he felt himself to be, when
that young pair told him, as they all three jogged along together,
that they had made up their minds to give him two thousand guineas
a year as head-gardener, on account of his being so true a friend to
'em. Boots could have wished at the moment that the earth would
have opened and swallowed him up, he felt so mean, with their beaming eyes a looking at him, and believing him. Well, Sir, he turned the
conversation as well as he could, and he took 'em down Love-lane
to the water-meadows, and there Master Harry would have drowned
himself in half a moment more, a getting out a water-lily for her,—
but nothing daunted that boy. Well, Sir, they was tired out. All being
so new and strange to 'em, they was tired as tired could be. And they
laid down on a bank of daisies, like the children in the wood, least-
ways meadows, and fell asleep.

Boots don't know—perhaps I do,—but never mind, it don't signify
either way—why it made a man fit to make a fool of himself to see
them two pretty babies a lying there in the clear still sunny day, not
dreaming half so hard when they was asleep as they done when they
was awake. But, Lord! when you come to think of yourself, you know,
and what a game you have been up to ever since you was in your own
cradle, and what a poor sort of a chap you are, and how it's always
either Yesterday with you, or else To-morrow, and never To-day,

that's where it is!

Well, Sir, they woke up at last, and then one thing was getting pretty clear to Boots, namely, that Mrs. Harry Walmerses, Junior's, temper was on the move. When Master Harry took her round the waist, she said he "teased her so"; and when he says, "Norah, my young May Moon, your Harry tease you?" she tells him, "Yes; and I want to go home!"

A biled fowl, and baked bread-and-butter pudding, brought Mrs. Walmers up a little; but Boots could have wished, he must privately own to me, to have seen her more sensible of the woice of love, and less abandoning of herself to currants. However, Master Harry, he kept up, and his noble heart was as fond as ever. Mrs. Walmers turned very sleepy about dusk, and began to cry. Therefore, Mrs. Walmers went off to bed as per yesterday; and Master Harry ditto repeated.

About eleven or twelve at night comes back the Governor in a chaise, along with Mr. Walmers and a elderly lady. Mr. Walmers looks amused and very serious, both at once, and says to our missis, "We are much indebted to you, ma'am, for your kind care of our little children, which we can never sufficiently acknowledge. Pray, ma'am, where is my boy?" Our missis says, "Cobbs has the dear child in charge, Sir. Cobbs, show Forty!" Then he says to Cobbs, "Ah, Cobbs, I am glad to see *you!* I understood you was here!" And Cobbs says, "Yes, Sir. Your most obedient, Sir."

I may be surprised to hear Boots say it, perhaps; but Boots assures me that his heart beat like a hammer, going upstairs. "I beg your pardon, Sir," says he, while unlocking the door; "I hope you are not angry with Master Harry. For Master Harry is a fine boy, Sir, and will do you credit and honour." And Boots signifies to me, that, if the fine boy's father had contradicted him in the daring state of mind in which he then was, he thinks he should have "fetched him a crack," and taken the consequences.

But Mr. Walmers only says, "No, Cobbs. No, my good fellow. Thank you!" And, the door being opened, goes in.

Boots goes in too, holding the light, and he sees Mr. Walmers go up to the bedside, bend gently down, and kiss the little sleeping face. Then he stands looking at it for a minute, looking wonderfully like it (they do say he ran away with Mrs. Walmers); and then he gently shakes the little shoulder.

"Harry, my dear boy! Harry!"

Master Harry starts up and looks at him. Looks at Cobbs too. Such is the honour of that mite, that he looks at Cobbs, to see whether he has brought him into trouble.

"I am not angry, my child. I only want you to dress yourself and come home."

"Yes, pa."

Master Harry dresses himself quickly. His breast begins to swell when he has nearly finished, and it swells more and more as he stands, at last, a looking at his father: his father standing a looking at him, the quiet image of him.

"Please may I"—the spirit of that little creatur, and the way he kept his rising tears down!—"please, dear pa—may I—kiss Norah before I go?"

"You may, my child."

So he takes Master Harry in his hand, and Boots leads the way with the candle, and they come to that other bedroom, where the elderly lady is seated by the bed, and poor little Mrs. Harry Walmers, Junior, is fast asleep. There the father lifts the child up to the pillow, and he lays his little face down for an instant by the little warm face of poor unconscious little Mrs. Harry Walmers, Junior, and gently draws it to him,—a sight so touching to the chambermaids who are peeping through the door, that one of them calls out, "It's a shame to part 'em!" But this chambermaid was always, as Boots informs me, a soft-hearted one. Not that there was any harm in that girl. Far from it.

Finally, Boots says, that's all about it. Mr. Walmers drove away in the chaise, having hold of Master Harry's hand. The elderly lady and Mrs. Harry Walmers, Junior, that was never to be (she married a Captain long afterwards, and died in India), went off next day. In conclusion, Boots put it to me whether I hold with him in two opinions: firstly, that there are not many couples on their way to be married who are half as innocent of guile as those two children; secondly, that it would be a jolly good thing for a great many couples on their way to be married, if they could only be stopped in time, and brought back separately.

THIRD BRANCH

THE BILL

I HAD been snowed up a whole week. The time had hung so lightly on my hands, that I should have been in great doubt of the fact but for a piece of documentary evidence that lay upon my table.

The road had been dug out of the snow on the previous day, and the document in question was my bill. It testified emphatically to my having eaten and drunk, and warmed myself, and slept among the sheltering branches of the Holly-Tree, seven days and nights.

I had yesterday allowed the road twenty-four hours to improve itself, finding that I required that additional margin of time for the completion of my task. I had ordered my bill to be upon the table and a chaise to be at the door, "at eight o'clock to-morrow evening." It was eight o'clock to-morrow evening when I buckled up my travelling writing-desk in its leather case, paid my bill, and got on my warm coats and wrappers. Of course, no time now remained for my travelling on to add a frozen tear to the icicles which were doubtless hanging plentifully about the farmhouse where I had first seen Angela. What I had to do was to get across to Liverpool by the shortest open road, there to meet my heavy baggage and embark

It was quite enough to do, and I had not an hour too much time to do it in.

I had taken leave of all my Holly-Tree friends—almost, for the time being, of my bashfulness too—and was standing for half a minute at the Inn door watching the ostler as he took another turn at the cord which tied my portmanteau on the chaise, when I saw lamps coming down towards the Holly-Tree. The road was so padded with snow that no wheels were audible; but all of us who were standing at the Inn door saw lamps coming on, and at a lively rate too, between the walls of snow that had been heaped up on either side of the track. The chambermaid instantly divined how the case stood, and called to the ostler, "Tom, this is a Gretna job!" The ostler, knowing that her sex instinctively scented a marriage, or anything in that direction, rushed up the yard bawling, "Next four out!" and in a moment the whole establishment was thrown into commotion.

I had a melancholy interest in seeing the happy man who loved and was beloved; and therefore, instead of driving off at once, I remained at the Inn door when the fugitives drove up. A bright-eyed fellow, muffled in a mantle, jumped out so briskly that he almost overthrew me. He turned to apologise, and, by Heaven, it was Edwin!

"Charley!" said he, recoiling. "Gracious powers, what do you do here?"

"Edwin," said I, recoiling, "gracious powers, what do *you* do here?" I struck my forehead as I said it, and an insupportable blaze of light seemed to shoot before my eyes.

He hurried me into the little parlour (always kept with a low fire in it and no poker), where posting company waited while their horses were putting to, and, shutting the door, said:

"Charley, forgive me!"

"Edwin!" I returned. "Was this well? When I loved her so dearly! When I had garnered up my heart so long!" I could say no more.

He was shocked when he saw how moved I was, and made the cruel observation that he had not thought I should have taken it so much to heart.

I looked at him. I reproached him no more. But I looked at him.

"My dear, dear Charley," said he, "don't think ill of me, I beseech you! I know you have a right to my utmost confidence, and, believe me, you have ever had it until now. I abhor secrecy. Its meanness is intolerable to me. But I and my dear girl have observed it for your sake."

He and his dear girl! It steeled me.

"You have observed it for my sake, Sir?" said I, wondering how his frank face could face it out so.

"Yes!—and Angela's," said he.

I found the room reeling round in an uncertain way, like a labouring humming-top. "Explain yourself," said I, holding on by one hand to an armchair.

"Dear old darling Charley!" returned Edwin, in his cordial manner, "consider! When you were going on so happily with Angela, why should I compromise you with the old gentleman by making you a party to our engagement, and (after he had declined my proposals to our secret intention? Surely it was better that you should be able honourably to say, 'He never took counsel with me, never told me, never breathed a word of it.' If Angela suspected it, and showed me all the favour and support she could—God bless her for a precious creature and a priceless wife!—I couldn't help that. Neither I nor Emmeline ever told her, any more than we told you. And for the same good reason, Charley; trust me, for the same good reason, and no other upon earth!"

Emmeline was Angela's cousin. Lived with her. Had been brought up with her. Was her father's ward. Had property.

"Emmeline is in the chaise, my dear Edwin!" said I, embracing him with the greatest affection.

"My good fellow!" said he, "do you suppose I should be going to Gretna Green without her?"

I ran out with Edwin, I opened the chaise door, I took Emmeline in my arms, I folded her to my heart. She was wrapped in soft white fur, like the snowy landscape: but was warm, and young, and lovely. I put their leaders to with my own hands, I gave the boys a five-pound note apiece, I cheered them as they drove away, I drove the other way myself as hard as I could pelt.

I never went to Liverpool, I never went to America, I went straight back to London, and I married Angela. I have never until this time, even to her, disclosed the secret of my character, and the mistrust and the mistaken journey into which it led me. When she, and they, and our eight children and their seven—I mean Edwin's and Emme-line's, whose eldest girl is old enough now to wear white for herself, and to look very like her mother in it—come to read these pages, as of course they will, I shall hardly fail to be found out at last. Never mind! I can bear it. I began at the Holly-Tree, by idle accident, to associate the Christmas-time of year with human interest, and with some inquiry into, and some care for, the lives of those by whom I find myself surrounded. I hope that I am none the worse for it, and that no one near me or afar off is the worse for it. And I say, May the green Holly-Tree flourish, striking its roots deep into our English ground, and having its germinating qualities carried by the birds of Heaven all over the world!

THE WRECK OF THE GOLDEN MARY

[1856]

THE WRECK

I WAS apprenticed to the Sea when I was twelve years old, and I have encountered a great deal of rough weather, both literal and metaphorical. It has always been my opinion since I first possessed such a thing as an opinion, that the man who knows only one subject is next tiresome to the man who knows no subject. Therefore, in the course of my life I have taught myself whatever I could, and although I am not an educated man, I am able, I am thankful to say, to have an intelligent interest in most things.

A person might suppose, from reading the above, that I am in the habit of holding forth about number one. That is not the case. Just as if I was to come into a room among strangers, and must either be introduced or introduce myself, so I have taken the liberty of passing these few remarks, simply and plainly, that it may be known who and what I am. I will add no more of the sort than that my name is William George Ravender, that I was born at Penrith half a year after my own father was drowned, and that I am on the second day of this present blessed Christmas week of one thousand eight hundred and fifty-six, fifty-six years of age.

When the rumour first went flying up and down that there was gold in California—which, as most people know, was before it was discovered in the British colony of Australia—I was in the West Indies, trading among the Islands. Being in command and likewise part-owner of a smart schooner, I had my work cut out for me, and I was doing it. Consequently, gold in California was no business of mine.

But, by the time when I came home to England again, the thing was as clear as your hand held up before you at noonday. There was Californian gold in the museums and in the goldsmith's shops, and the very first time I went upon 'Change, I met a friend of mine (a seafaring man like myself), with a Californian nugget hanging to his watch-chain. I handled it. It was as like a peeled walnut with bits unevenly broken off here and there, and then electrotyped all over, as ever I saw anything in my life.

I am a single man (she was too good for this world and for me, and she died six weeks before our marriage-day), so when I am ashore, I live in my house at Poplar. My house at Poplar is taken care of and kept ship-shape by an old lady who was my mother's maid before I was born. She is as handsome and as upright as any old lady in the world. She is as fond of me as if she had ever had an only son, and I was he. Well do I know wherever I sail that she never lays down her head at night without having said, "Merciful Lord! bless and preserve William George Ravender, and send him safe home, through Christ our Saviour!" I have thought of it in many a dangerous moment, when it has done me no harm, I am sure.

In my house at Poplar, along with this old lady, I lived quiet for best part of a year: having had a long spell of it among the Islands, and having (which was very uncommon in me) taken the fever rather badly. At last, being strong and hearty, and having read every book I could lay hold of, right out, I was walking down Leadenhall Street in the City of London, thinking of turning-to again, when I met what I call Smithick and Watersby of Liverpool. I chanced to lift up my eyes from looking in a ship's chronometer in a window, and I saw him bearing down upon me, head on.

It is, personally, neither Smithick nor Watersby, that I here mention, nor was I ever acquainted with any man of either of those names, nor do I think that there has been any one of either of those names in that Liverpool House for years back. But, it is in reality the House itself that I refer to; and a wiser merchant or a truer gentleman never stepped.

"My dear Captain Ravender," says he. "Of all the men on earth, I wanted to see you most. I was on my way to you."

"Well!" says I. "That looks as if you *were* to see me, don't it?" With that I put my arm in his, and we walked on towards the Royal Exchange, and when we got there, walked up and down at the back of it where the Clock-Tower is. We walked an hour and more, for he had much to say to me. He had a scheme for chartering a new ship of their own to take out cargo to the diggers and emigrants in California, and to buy and bring back gold. Into the particulars of that scheme I will not enter, and I have no right to enter. All I say of it is, that it was a very original one, a very fine one, a very sound one, and a very lucrative one beyond doubt.

He imparted it to me as freely as if I had been a part of himself. After doing so, he made me the handsomest sharing offer that ever was made to me, boy or man—or I believe to any other captain in the Merchant Navy—and he took this round turn to finish with:

"Ravender, you are well aware that the lawlessness of that coast and country at present, is as special as the circumstances in which it is placed. Crews of vessels outward-bound, desert as soon as they make the land; crews of vessels homeward-bound, ship at enormous wages, with the express intention of murdering the captain and seizing the gold freight; no man can trust another, and the devil seems let loose. Now," says he, "you know my opinion of you, and you know I am only expressing it, and with no singularity, when I tell you that you are almost the only man on whose integrity, discretion, and energy——'' etc., etc. For, I don't want to repeat what he said, though I was and am sensible of it.

Notwithstanding my being, as I have mentioned, quite ready for a voyage, still I had some doubts of this voyage. Of course I knew, without being told, that there were peculiar difficulties and dangers in it, a long way over and above those which attend all voyages. It must not be supposed that I was afraid to face them; but, in my opinion a man has no manly motive or sustainment in his own breast for facing dangers, unless he has well considered what they are, and is able quietly to say to himself, "None of these perils can now take me by surprise; I shall know what to do for the best in any of them; all the rest lies in the higher and greater hands to which I humbly commit myself." On this principle I have so attentively considered (regarding it as my duty) all the hazards I have ever been able to think of, in the ordinary way of storm, shipwreck, and fire at sea, that I hope I should be prepared to do, in any of those cases, whatever could be done, to save the lives intrusted to my charge.

As I was thoughtful, my good friend proposed that he should leave me to walk there as long as I liked, and that I should dine with him by-and-by at his club in Pall Mall. I accepted the invitation and I walked up and down there, quarter-deck fashion, a matter of a couple of hours; now and then looking up at the weathercock as I might have looked up aloft; and now and then taking a look into Cornhill, as I might have taken a look over the side.

All dinner-time, and all after dinner-time, we talked it over again. I gave him my views of his plan, and he very much approved of the same. I told him I had nearly decided, but not quite. "Well, well," says he, "come down to Liverpool to-morrow with me, and see the Golden Mary." I liked the name (her name was Mary, and she was golden, if golden stands for good), so I began to feel that it was almost done when I said I would go to Liverpool. On the next morning but one we were on board the Golden Mary. I might have known, from his asking me to come down and see her, what she was. I declare her to have been the completest and most exquisite Beauty that ever I set my eyes upon.

We had inspected every timber in her, and had come back to the gangway to go ashore from the dock-basin, when I put out my hand to my friend. "Touch upon it," says I, "and touch heartily. I take command of this ship, and I am hers and yours, if I can get John Steadiman for my chief mate."

John Steadiman had sailed with me four voyages. The first voyage John was third mate out to China, and came home second. The other three voyages he was my first officer. At this time of chartering the Golden Mary, he was aged thirty-two. A brisk, bright, blue-eyed fellow, a very neat figure and rather under the middle size, never out of the way and never in it, a face that pleased everybody and that all children took to, a habit of going about singing as cheerily as a blackbird, and a perfect sailor.

We were in one of those Liverpool hackney-coaches in less than a minute, and we cruised about in her upwards of three hours, looking for John. John had come home from Van Diemen's Land barely a month before, and I had heard of him as taking a frisk in Liverpool. We asked after him, among many other places, at the two boarding-houses he was fondest of, and we found he had had a week's spell at each of them; but, he had gone here and gone there, and had set off "to lay out on the main-to'-gallant-yard of the highest Welsh mountain" (so he had told the people of the house), and where he might be then, or when he might come back, nobody could tell us. But it was surprising, to be sure, to see how every face brightened the moment there was mention made of the name of Mr. Steadiman.

We were taken aback at meeting with no better luck, and we had wore ship and put her head for my friends, when as we were jogging through the streets, I clap my eyes on John himself coming out of a toyshop! He was carrying a little boy, and conducting two uncommon pretty women to their coach, and he told me afterwards that he had never in his life seen one of the three before, but that he was so taken with them on looking in at the toyshop while they were buying the child a cranky Noah's ark, very much down by the head, that he had gone in and asked the ladies' permission to treat him to a tolerably correct Cutter there was in the window, in order that such a handsome boy might not grow up with a lubberly idea of naval architecture.

We stood off and on until the ladies' coachman began to give way, and then we hailed John. On his coming aboard of us, I told him, very gravely, what I had said to my friend. It struck him, as he said himself, amidships. He was quite shaken by it. "Captain Ravender," were John Steadiman's word, "such an opinion from you is true commendation, and I'll sail round the world with you for twenty years if you hoist the signal, and stand by you for ever!" And now indeed I felt that it was done, and that the Golden Mary was afloat.

Grass never grew yet under the feet of Smithick and Watersby. The riggers were out of that ship in a fortnight's time, and we had begun taking in cargo. John was always aboard, seeing everything stowed with his own eyes; and whenever I went aboard myself early or late, whether he was below in the hold or on deck at the hatchway, or overhauling his cabin, nailing up pictures in it of the Blush Roses of England, the Blue Bells of Scotland, and the female Shamrock of Ireland: of a certainty I heard John singing like a blackbird.

We had room for twenty passengers. Our sailing advertisement was no sooner out, than we might have taken these twenty times over. In entering our men, I and John (both together) picked them, and we entered none but good hands—as good as were to be found in that port. And so, in a good ship of the best build, well owned, well arranged, well officered, well manned, well found in all respects, we parted with our pilot at a quarter past four o'clock in the afternoon of the seventh of March, one thousand eight hundred and fifty-one, and stood with a fair wind out to sea.

It may be easily believed that up to that time I had had no leisure to be intimate with my passengers. The most of them were then in their berths sea-sick; however, in going among them, telling them what was good for them, persuading them not to be there, but to come up on deck and feel the breeze, and in rousing them with a joke, or a comfortable word, I made acquaintance with them, perhaps, in a more friendly and confidential way from the first, than I might have done at the cabin table.

Of my passengers, I need only particularise, just at present, a bright-eyed blooming young wife who was going out to join her husband in California, taking with her their only child, a little girl of three years old, whom he had never seen; a sedate young woman in black, some five years older (about thirty as I should say), who was going out to join a brother; and an old gentleman, a good deal like a hawk if his eyes had been better and not so red, who was always talking, morning, noon, and night, about the gold discovery. But, whether he was making the voyage, thinking his old arms could dig for gold, or whether his speculation was to buy it, or to barter for it, or to cheat for it, or to snatch it anyhow from other people, was his secret. He kept his secret.

These three and the child were the soonest well. The child was a most engaging child, to be sure, and very fond of me: though I am bound to admit that John Steadiman and I were borne on her pretty little books in reverse order, and that he was captain there, and I was mate. It was beautiful to watch her with John, and it was beautiful to watch John with her. Few would have thought it possible, to see John playing at bo-peep round the mast, that he was the man who had caught up an iron bar and struck a Malay and a Maltese dead, as they were gliding with their knives down the cabin stair aboard the barque Old England, when the captain lay ill in his cot, off Saugar Point. But he was; and give him his back against a bulwark, he would have done the same by half-a-dozen of them. The name of the young mother was Mrs. Atherfield, the name of the young lady in black was Miss Coleshaw, and the name of the old gentleman was Mr. Rarx.

As the child had a quantity of shining fair hair, clustering in curls all about her face, and as her name was Lucy, Steadiman gave her the name of the Golden Lucy. So, we had the Golden Lucy and the Golden Mary; and John kept up the idea to that extent as he and the child went playing about the decks, that I believe she used to think the ship was alive somehow—a sister or companion, going to the same place as herself. She liked to be by the wheel, and in fine weather, I have often stood by the man whose trick it was at the wheel, only to hear her, sitting near my feet, talking to the ship. Never had a child such a doll before, I suppose; but she made a doll of the Golden Mary, and used to dress her up by tying ribbons and little bits of finery to the belaying-pins; and nobody ever moved them, unless it was to save them from being blown away.

Of course I took charge of the two young women, and I called them "my dear," and they never minded, knowing that whatever I said was said in a fatherly and protecting spirit. I gave them their places on each side of me at dinner, Mrs. Atherfield on my right and Miss Coleshaw on my left; and I directed the unmarried lady to serve out the breakfast, and the married lady to serve out the tea. Likewise I said to my black steward in their presence, "Tom Snow, these two ladies are equally the mistresses of this house, and do you obey their orders equally"; at which Tom laughed, and they all laughed.

Old Mr. Rarx was not a pleasant man to look at, nor yet to talk to, or to be with, for no one could help seeing that he was a sordid and selfish character, and that he had warped further and further out of the straight with time. Not but what he was on his best behaviour with us, as everybody was; for we had no bickering among us, for'-ard or aft. I only mean to say, he was not the man one would have chosen for a messmate. If choice there had been, one might even have gone a few points out of one's course, to say, "No! Not him!" But, there was one curious inconsistency in Mr. Rarx. That was, that he took an astonishing interest in the child. He looked, and I may add, he was, one of the last of men to care at all for a child, or to care much for any human creature. Still, he went so far as to be habitually uneasy, if the child was long on deck, out of his sight. He was always afraid of her falling overboard, or falling down a hatchway, or of a block or what not coming down upon her from the rigging in the working of the ship, or of her getting some hurt or other. He used to look at her and touch her, as if she was something precious to him. He was always solicitous about her not injuring her health, and constantly entreated her mother to be careful of it. This was so much the more curious, because the child did not like him, but used to shrink away from him, and would not even put out her hand to him without coaxing from others. I believe that every soul on board frequently noticed this, and not one of us understood it. However, it was such a plain fact, that John Steadiman said more than once when old Mr. Rarx was not within earshot, that if the Golden Mary felt a tenderness for the dear old gentleman she carried in her lap, she must be bitterly jealous of the Golden Lucy.

Before I go any further with this narrative, I will state that our ship was a barque of three hundred tons, carrying a crew of eighteen men, a second mate in addition to John, a carpenter, an armourer or smith, and two apprentices (one a Scotch boy, poor little fellow). We had three boats; the Long-boat, capable of carring twenty-five men; the Cutter, capable of carrying fifteen; and the Surf-boat, capable of carrying ten. I put down the capacity of these boats according to the numbers they were really meant to hold.

We had tastes of bad weather and head-winds, of course; but, on the whole we had as fine a run as any reasonable man could expect, for sixty days. I then began to enter two remarks in the ship's Log and in my Journal; first, that there was an unusual and amazing quantity of ice; second, that the nights were most wonderfully dark, in spite of the ice.

For five days and a half, it seemed quite useless and hopeless to alter the ship's course so as to stand out of the way of this ice. I made what southing I could; but, all that time, we were beset by it. Mrs. Atherfield after standing by me on deck once, looking for some time in an awed manner at the great bergs that surrounded us, said in a whisper, "O, Captain Ravender, it looks as if the whole solid earth had changed into ice, and broken up!" I said to her, laughing, "I don't wonder that it does, to your inexperienced eyes, my dear." But I had never seen a twentieth part of the quantity, and, in reality, I was pretty much of her opinion.

However, at two P.M. on the afternoon of the sixth day, that is to say, when we were sixty-six days out, John Steadiman who had gone aloft, sang out from the top, that the sea was clear ahead. Before four P.M. a strong breeze springing up right astern, we were in open water at sunset. The breeze then freshening into half a gale of wind, and the Golden Mary being a very fast sailer, we went before the wind merrily, all night.

I had thought it impossible that it could be darker than it had been, until the sun, moon, and stars should fall out of the Heavens, and Time should be destroyed; but, it had been next to light, in comparison with what it was now. The darkness was so profound, that looking into it was painful and oppressive—like looking, without a ray of light, into a dense black bandage put as close before the eyes as it could be, without touching them. I doubled the look-out, and John and I stood in the bow side-by-side, never leaving it all night. Yet I should no more have known that he was near me when he was silent, without putting out my arm and touching him, than I should if he had turned in and been fast asleep below. We were not so much looking out, all of us, as listening to the utmost, both with our eyes and ears.

Next day, I found that the mercury in the barometer, which had risen steadily since we cleared the ice, remained steady. I had had very good observations, with now and then the interruption of a day or so, since our departure. I got the sun at noon, and found that we were in Lat. 58° S., Long. 60° W., off New South Shetland; in the neighbourhood of Cape Horn. We were sixty-seven days out, that day. The ship's reckoning was accurately worked and made up. The ship did her duty admirably, all on board were well, and all hands were as smart, efficient, and contented as it was possible to be.

When the night came on again as dark as before, it was the eighth night I had been on deck. Nor had I taken more than a very little sleep in the daytime, my station being always near the helm, and often at it, while we were among the ice. Few but those who have tried it can imagine the difficulty and pain of only keeping the eyes open—physically open—under such circumstances, in such darkness. They get struck by the darkness, and blinded by the darkness. They make patterns in it, and they flash in it, as if they had gone out of your head to look at you. On the turn of midnight, John Steadiman, who was alert and fresh (for I had always made him turn in by day), said to me, "Captain Ravender, I entreat of you to go below. I am sure you can hardly stand, and your voice is getting weak, Sir. Go below, and take a little rest. I'll call you if a block chafes." I said to John in answer, "Well, well, John! Let us wait till the turn of one o'clock, before we talk about that." I had just had one of the ship's lanterns held up, that I might see how the night went by my watch, and it was then twenty minutes after twelve.

At five minutes before one, John sang out to the boy to bring the lantern again, and when I told him once more what the time was, entreated and prayed of me to go below. "Captain Ravender," says he, "all's well; we can't afford to have you laid up for a single hour; and I respectfully and earnestly beg of you to go below." The end of it was, that I agreed to do so, on the understanding that if I failed to come up of my own accord within three hours, I was to be punctually called. Having settled that, I left John in charge. But I called him to me once afterwards, to ask him a question. I had been to look at the barometer, and had seen the mercury still perfectly steady, and had come up the companion again to take a last look about me— if I can use such a word in reference to such darkness—when I thought that the waves, as the Golden Mary parted them and shook them off, had a hollow sound in them; something that I fancied was a rather unusual reverberation. I was standing by the quarter-deck rail on the starboard side, when I called John aft to me, and bade him listen. He did so with the greatest attention. Turning to me he then said, "Rely upon it, Captain Ravender, you have been without rest too long, and the novelty is only in the state of your sense of hearing." I thought so too by that time, and I think so now, though I can never know for absolute certain in this world, whether it was or not.

When I left John Steadiman in charge, the ship was still going at a great rate through the water. The wind still blew right astern. Though she was making great way, she was under shortened sail, and had no more than she could easily carry. All was snug, and nothing complained. There was a pretty sea running, but not a very high sea neither, not at all a confused one.

I turned in, as we seamen say, all standing. The meaning of that is, I did not pull my clothes off—no, not even so much as my coat: though I did my shoes, for my feet were badly swelled with the deck. There was a little swing-lamp alight in my cabin. I thought, as I looked at it before shutting my eyes, that I was so tired of darkness, that I could have gone to sleep best in the midst of a million of flaming gas-lights. That was the last thought I had before I went off, except the prevailing thought that I should not be able to get to sleep at all.

I dreamed that I was back at Penrith again, and was trying to get round the church, which had altered its shape very much since I last saw it, and was cloven all down the middle of the steeple in a most singular manner. Why I wanted to get round the church I don't know; but I was so anxious to do it as if my life depended upon it.

Indeed, I believe it did in the dream. For all that, I could not get round the church. I was still trying, when I came against it with a violent shock, and was flung out of my cot against the ship's side. Shrieks and a terrific outcry struck me far harder than the bruising timbers, and amidst sounds of grinding and crashing, and a heavy rushing and breaking of water—sounds I understood too well—I made my way on deck. It was not an easy thing to do, for the ship heeled over frightfully, and was beating in a furious manner.

I could not see the men as I went forward, but I could hear that they were hauling in sail, in disorder. I had my trumpet in my hand, and, after directing and encouraging them in this till it was done, I hailed first John Steadiman, and then my second mate, Mr. William Rames. Both answered clearly and steadily. Now, I had practised them and all my crew, as I have ever made it a custom to practise all who sail with me, to take certain stations and wait my orders, in case of any unexpected crisis. When my voice was heard hailing, and their voices were heard answering, I was aware, through all the noises of the ship and sea, and all the crying of the passengers below, that there was a pause. "Are you ready, Rames?"—"Ay, ay, Sir!"— "Then light up, for God's sake!" In a moment he and another were burning blue-lights, and the ship and all on board seemed to be enclosed in a mist of light, under a great black dome.

The light shone up so high that I could see the huge Iceberg upon which we had struck, cloven at the top and down the middle, exactly like Penrith Church in my dream. At the same moment I could see the watch last relieved, crowding up and down on deck; I could see Mrs. Atherfield and Miss Coleshaw thrown about on the top of the companion as they struggled to bring the child up from below; I could see that the masts were going with the shock and the beating of the ship; I could see the frightful breach stove in on the starboard side, half the length of the vessel, and the sheathing and timbers spirting up; I could see that the Cutter was disabled, in a wreck of broken fragments; and I could see every eye turned upon me. It is my belief that if there had been ten thousand eyes there, I should have seen them all, with their different looks. And all this in a moment. But you must consider what a moment.

I saw the men, as they looked at me, fall towards their appointed stations, like good men and true. If she had not righted, they could have done very little there or anywhere but die—not that it is little for a man to die at his post—I mean they could have done nothing to save the passengers and themselves. Happily, however, the violence of the shock with which we had so determinedly borne down direct on that fatal Iceberg, as if it had been our destination instead of our destruction, had so smashed and pounded the ship that she got off in this same instant and righted. I did not want the carpenter to tell me she was filling and going down; I could see and hear that. I gave Rames the word to lower the Long-boat, and the Surf-boat, and I myself told off the men for each duty. Not one hung back, or came before the other. I now whispered to John Steadiman, "John, I stand at the gangway here, to see every soul on board safe over the side. You shall have the next post of honour, and shall be the last but one to leave the ship. Bring up the passengers, and range them behind me; and put what provision and water you can get at, in the boats. Cast your eye for'ard, John, and you'll see you have not a moment to lose."

My noble fellows got the boats over the side as orderly as I ever saw boats lowered with any sea running, and, when they were launched, two or three of the nearest men in them as they held on, rising and falling with the swell, called out, looking up at me, "Captain Ravender, if anything goes wrong with us, and you are saved, remember we stood by you!"—"We'll all stand by one another ashore, yet, please God, my lads!" says I. "Hold on bravely, and be tender with the women."

The women were an example to us. They trembled very much, but they were quiet and perfectly collected. "Kiss me, Captain Ravender," says Mrs. Atherfield, "and God in heaven bless you, you good man!" "My dear," says I, "those words are better for me than a lifeboat." I held her child in my arms till she was in the boat, and then kissed the child and handed her safe down. I now said to the people in her, "You have got your freight, my lads, all but me, and I am not coming yet awhile. Pull away from the ship, and keep off!"

That was the Long-boat. Old Mr. Rarx was one of her complement, and he was the only passenger who had greatly misbehaved since the ship struck. Others had been a little wild, which was not to be wondered at, and not very blamable; but, he had made a lamentation and uproar which it was dangerous for the people to hear, as there is always contagion in weakness and selfishness. His incessant cry had been that he must not be separated from the child, that he couldn't see the child, and that he and the child must go together. He had even tried to wrest the child out of my arms, that he might keep her in his. "Mr. Rarx," said I to him when it came to that, "I have a loaded pistol in my pocket; and if you don't stand out of the gangway, and keep perfectly quiet, I shall shoot you through the heart, if you have got one." Says he, "You won't do murder, Captain Ravender!" "No, Sir," says I, "I won't murder forty-four people to humour you, but I'll shoot you to save them." After that he was quiet, and stood shivering a little way off, until I named him to go over the side.

The Long-boat being cast off, the Surf-boat was soon filled. There only remained aboard the Golden Mary, John Mullion, the man who had kept on burning the blue-lights (and who had lighted every new one at every old one before it went out, as quietly as if he had been at an illumination); John Steadiman; and myself. I hurried those two into the Surf-boat, called to them to keep off, and waited with a grateful and relieved heart for the Long-boat to come and take me in, if she could. I looked at my watch, and it showed me, by the blue-light, ten minutes past two. They lost no time. As soon as she was near enough, I swung myself into her, and called to the men, "With a will, lads! She's reeling!" We were not an inch too far out of the inner vortex of her going down, when, by the blue-light which John Mullion still burnt in the bow of the Surf-boat, we saw her lurch, and plunge to the bottom head-foremost. The child cried, weeping wildly, "O the dear Golden Mary! O look at her! Save her! Save the poor Golden Mary!" And then the light burnt out, and the black dome seemed to come down upon us.

I suppose if we had all stood a-top of a mountain, and seen the whole remainder of the world sink away from under us, we could hardly have felt more shocked and solitary than we did when we knew we were alone on the wide ocean and that the beautiful ship in which most of us had been securely asleep within half an hour was gone for ever. There was an awful silence in our boat, and such a kind of palsy on the rowers and the man at the rudder, that I felt they were scarcely keeping her before the sea. I spoke out then, and said, "Let every one here thank the Lord for our preservation!" All the voices answered (even the child's), "We thank the Lord!" I then said the Lord's Prayer, and all hands said it after me with a solemn murmuring. Then I gave the word "Cheerily, O men, Cheerily!" and I felt that they were handling the boat again as a boat ought to be handled.

The Surf-boat now burnt another blue-light to show us where they were, and we made for her, and laid ourselves as nearly alongside of her as we dared. I had always kept my boats with a coil or two or good stout stuff in each of them, so both boats had a rope at hand. We made a shift, with much labour and trouble, to get near enough to one another to divide the blue-lights (they were no use after that night, for the sea-water soon got at them), and to get a tow-rope out between us. All night long we kept together, sometimes obliged to cast off the rope, and sometimes getting it out again, and all of us wearying for the morning—which appeared so long in coming that old Mr. Rarx screamed out, in spite of his fears of me, "The world is drawing to an end, and the sun will never rise any more!"

When the day broke, I found that we were all huddled together in a miserable manner. We were deep in the water; being, as I found on mustering, thirty-one in number, or at least six too many. In the Surf-boat they were fourteen in number, being at least four too many. The first thing I did, was to get myself passed to the rudder—which I took from that time—and to get Mrs. Atherfield, her child, and Miss Coleshaw, passed on to sit next me. As to old Mr. Rarx, I put him in the bow, as far from us as I could. And I put some of the best men near us in order that if I should drop there might be a skilful hand ready to take the helm.

The sea moderating as the sun came up, though the sky was cloudy and wild, we spoke the other boat, to know what stores they had, and to overhaul what we had. I had a compass in my pocket, a small telescope, a double-barrelled pistol, a knife, and a fire-box and matches. Most of my men had knives, and some had a little tobacco: some, a pipe as well. We had a mug among us, and an iron spoon. As to provisions, there were in my boat two bags of biscuit, one piece of raw beef, one piece of raw pork, a bag of coffee, roasted but not ground (thrown in, I imagine, by mistake, for something else), two small casks of water, and about half-a-gallon of rum in a keg. The Surf-boat, having rather more rum than we, and fewer to drink it, gave us, as I estimated, another quart into our keg. In return, we gave then three double handfuls of coffee, tied up in a piece of a handkerchief; they reported that they had aboard besides, a bag of biscuit, a piece of beef, a small cask of water, a small box of lemons, and a Dutch cheese. It took a long time to make these exchanges, and they were not made without risk to both parties; the sea running quite high enough to make our approaching near to one another very hazardous. In the bundle with the coffee, I conveyed to John Steadiman (who had a ship's compass with him), a paper written in pencil, and torn from my pocket-book, containing the course I meant to steer, in the hope of making land, or being picked up by some vessel— I say in the hope, though I had little hope of either deliverance. I then sang out to him, so as all might hear, that if we two boats could live or die together, we would; but, that if we should be parted by the weather, and join company no more, they should have our prayers and blessings, and we asked for theirs. We then gave them three cheers, which they returned, and I saw the men's heads droop in both boats as they fell to their oars again.

These arrangements had occupied the general attention advantageously for all, though (as I expressed in the last sentence) they ended in a sorrowful feeling. I now said a few words to my fellow-voyagers on the subject of the small stock of food on which our lives depended if they were preserved from the great deep, and on the rigid necessity of our eking it out in the most frugal manner. One and all replied that whatever allowance I thought best to lay down should be strictly kept to. We made a pair of scales out of a thin strap of iron-plating and some twine, and I got together for weights such of the heaviest buttons among us as I calculated made up some fraction over two ounces. This was the allowance of solid food served out once a-day to each, from that time to the end; with the addition of a coffee-berry, or sometimes half a one, when the weather was very fair, for breakfast. We had nothing else whatever, but half a pint of water each per day, and sometimes, when we were coldest and weakest, a teaspoonful of rum each, served out as a dram. I know how learnedly it can be shown that rum is poison, but I also know that in this case, as in all similar cases I have ever read of—which are numerous—no words can express the comfort and support derived from it. Nor have I the least doubt that it saved the lives of far more than half our number. Having mentioned half a pint of water as our daily allowance, I ought to observe that sometimes we had less, and sometimes we had more; for much rain fell, and we caught it in a canvas stretched for the purpose.

Thus, at that tempestuous time of the year, and in that tempestuous part of the world, we shipwrecked people rose and fell with the waves. It is not my intention to relate (if I can avoid it) such circumstances appertaining to our doleful condition as have been better told in many other narratives of the kind that I can be expected to tell them. I will only note, in so many passing words, that day after day and night after night we received the sea upon our backs to prevent it from swamping the boat; that one party was always kept baling, and that every hat and cap among us soon got worn out, though patched up fifty times, as the only vessels we had for that service; that another party lay down in the bottom of the boat, while a third rowed; and that we were soon all in boils and blisters and rags.

The other boat was a source of such anxious interest to all of us that I used to wonder whether, if we were saved, the time could ever come when the survivors in this boat of ours could be at all indifferent to the fortunes of the survivors in that. We got out a tow-rope whenever the weather permitted, but that did not often happen, and how we two parties kept within the same horizon, as we did, He, who mercifully permitted it to be so for our consolation, only knows. I never shall forget the looks with which, when the morning light came, we used to gaze about us over the stormy waters, for the other boat. We once parted company for seventy-two hours, and we believed them to have gone down, as they did us. The joy on both sides when we came within view of one another again, had something in a manner Divine in it; each was so forgetful of individual suffering, in tears of delight and sympathy for the people in the other boat.

I have been wanting to get round to the individual or personal part of my subject, as I call it, and the foregoing incident puts me in the right way. The patience and good disposition aboard of us was wonderful. I was not surprised by it in the women; for all men born of women know what great qualities they will show when men will fail; but, I own I was a little surprised by it in some of the men. Among one-and-thirty people assembled at the best of times, there will usually, I should say, be two or three uncertain tempers. I knew that I had more than one rough temper with me among my own people, for I had chosen those for the Long-boat that I might have them under my eye. But, they softened under their misery, and were as considerate of the ladies, and as compassionate of the child, as the best among us, or among men—they could not have been more so. I heard scarcely any complaining. The party lying down would moan a good deal in their sleep, and I would often notice a man—not always the same man, it is to be understood, but nearly all of them at one time or other—sitting moaning at his oar, or in his place, as he looked mistily over the sea. When it happened to be long before I could catch his eye, he would go on moaning all the time in the dismallest manner; but, when our looks met, he would brighten and leave off. I almost always got the impression that he did not know what sound he had been making, but that he thought he had been humming a tune.

Our sufferings from cold and wet were far greater than our sufferings from hunger. We managed to keep the child warm; but, I doubt if any one else among us ever was warm for five minutes together; and the shivering, and the chattering of teeth, were sad to hear. The child cried a little at first for her lost playfellow, the Golden Mary; but hardly ever whimpered afterwards; and when the state of the weather made it possible, she used now and then to be held up in the arms of some of us, to look over the sea for John Steadiman's boat. I see the golden hair and the innocent face now, between me and the driving clouds, like an angel going to fly away.

It had happened on the second day, towards night, that Mrs. Atherfield, in getting Little Lucy to sleep, sang her a song. She had a soft, melodious voice, and, when she had finished it, our people up and begged for another. She sang them another, and after it had fallen dark ended with the Evening Hymn. From that time, whenever anything could be heard above the sea and wind, and while she had any voice left, nothing would serve the people but that she should sing at sunset. She always did, and always ended with the Evening Hymn. We mostly took up the last line, and shed tears when it was done, but not miserably. We had a prayer night and morning, also, when the weather allowed of it.

Twelve nights and eleven days we had been driving in the boat, when old Mr. Rarx began to be delirious, and to cry out to me to throw the gold overboard or it would sink us, and we should all be lost. For days past the child had been declining, and that was the great cause of his wildness. He had been over and over again shrieking out to me to give her all the remaining meat, to give her all the remaining rum, to save her at any cost, or we should all be ruined. At this time, she lay in her mother's arms at my feet. One of her little hands was almost always creeping about her mother's neck or chin. I had watched the wasting of the little hand, and I knew it was nearly over.

The old man's cries were so discordant with the mother's love and submission, that I called out to him in an angry voice, unless he held his peace on the instant, I would order him to be knocked on the head and thrown overboard. He was mute then, until the child died, very peacefully, an hour afterwards, which was known to all in the boat by the mother's breaking out into lamentations for the first time since the wreck—for, she had great fortitude and constancy, though she was a little gentle woman. Old Mr. Rarx then became quite ungovernable, tearing what rags he had on him, raging in imprecations, and calling to me that if I had thrown the gold overboard (always the gold with him!) I might have saved the child. "And now," says he, in a terrible voice, "we shall founder, and all go to the Devil, for our sins will sink us, when we have no innocent child to bear us up!" We so discovered with amazement, that this old wretch had only cared for the life of the pretty little creature dear to all of us, because of the influence he superstitiously hoped she might have in preserving him! Altogether it was too much for the smith or armourer, who was sitting next the old man, to bear. He took him by the throat and rolled him under the thwarts, where he lay still enough for hours afterwards.

All that thirteenth night, Miss Coleshaw, lying across my knees as

I kept the helm, comforted and supported the poor mother. Her child, covered with a pea-jacket of mine, lay in her lap. It troubled me all night to think that there was no Prayer-Book among us, and that I could remember but very few of the exact words of the burial service. When I stood up at broad day, all knew what was going to be done, and I noticed that my poor fellows made the motion of uncovering their heads, though their heads had been stark bare to the sky and sea for many a weary hour. There was a long heavy swell on, but otherwise it was a fair morning, and there were broad fields of sunlight on the waves in the east. I said no more than this. "I am the Resurrection and the Life, saith the Lord. He raised the daughter of Jairus the ruler, and said she was not dead but slept. He raised the widow's son. He arose Himself, and was seen of many. He loved little children, saying, Suffer them to come unto Me, and rebuke them not, for of such is the kingdom of heaven. In His name, my friends, and committed to His merciful goodness!" With those words I laid my rough face softly on the placid little forehead and buried the Golden Lucy in the grave of the Golden Mary.

Having had it on my mind to relate the end of this dear little child, I have omitted something from its exact place, which I will supply here. It will come quite as well here as anywhere else.

Foreseeing that if the boat lived through the stormy weather, the time must come, and soon come, when we should have absolutely no morsel to eat, I had one momentous point often in my thoughts. Although I had, years before that, fully satisfied myself that the instances in which human beings in the last distress have fed upon each other, are exceedingly few, and have very seldom indeed (if ever) occurred when the people in distress, however dreadful their extremity, have been accustomed to moderate forbearance and restraint; I say, though I had long before quite satisfied my mind on this topic, I felt doubtful whether there might not have been in former cases some harm and danger from keeping it out of sight and pretending not to think of it. I felt doubtful whether some minds, growing weak with fasting and exposure and having such a terrific idea to dwell upon in secret, might not magnify it until it got to have an awful attraction about it. This was not a new thought of mine, for it had grown out of my reading. However, it came over me stronger than it had ever done before—as it had reason for doing —in the boat, and on the fourth day I decided that I would bring out into the light that unformed fear which must have been more or less darkly in every brain among us. Therefore, as a means of beguiling the time and inspiring hope, I gave them the best summary in my power of Bligh's voyage of more than three thousand miles, in an open boat, after the Mutiny of the Bounty, and of the wonderful preservation of that boat's crew. They listened throughout with great interest, and I concluded by telling them, that, in my opinion, the happiest circumstance in the whole narrative was, that Bligh, who was no delicate man either, had solemnly placed it on record therein that he was sure and certain that under no conceivable circumstances whatever would that emaciated party, who had gone through all the pains of famine, have preyed on one another. I cannot describe the visible relief which this spread through the boat, and how the tears stood in every eye. From that time I was as well convinced as Bligh himself that there was no danger, and that this phantom, at any rate, did not haunt us.

Now, it was a part of Bligh's experience that when the people in his boat were most cast down, nothing did them so much good as hearing a story told by one of their number. When I mentioned that, I saw that it struck the general attention as much as it did my own, for I had not thought of it until I came to it in my summary. This was on the day after Mrs. Atherfield first sang to us. I proposed that, whenever the weather would permit, we should have a story two hours after dinner (I always issued the allowance I have mentioned at one o'clock, and called it by that name), as well as our song at sunset. The proposal was received with a cheerful satisfaction that warmed my heart within me; and I do not say too much when I say that those two periods in the four-and-twenty hours were expected with positive pleasure, and were really enjoyed by all hands. Spectres as we soon were in our bodily wasting, our imaginations did not perish like the gross flesh upon our bones. Music and Adventure, two of the great gifts of Providence to mankind, could charm us long after that was lost.

The wind was almost always against us after the second day; and for many days together we could not nearly hold our own. We had all varieties of bad weather. We had rain, hail, snow, wind, mist, thunder, and lightning. Still the boats lived through the heavy seas, and still we perishing people rose and fell with the great waves.

Sixteen nights and fifteen days, twenty nights and nineteen days, twenty-four nights and twenty-three days. So the time went on. Disheartening as I knew that our progress, or want of progress, must be, I never deceived them as to my calculations of it. In the first place, I felt that we were all too near eternity for deceit; in the second place, I knew that if I failed, or died, the man who followed me must have a knowledge of the true state of things to begin upon. When I told them at noon, what I reckoned we had made or lost, they generally received what I said in a tranquil and resigned manner, and always gratefully towards me. It was not unusual at any time of the day for some one to burst out weeping loudly without any new cause; and, when the burst was over, to calm down a little better than before. I had seen exactly the same thing in a house of mourning.

During the whole of this time, old Mr. Rarx had had his fits of calling out to me to throw the gold (always the gold!) overboard, and of heaping violent reproaches upon me for not having saved the child; but now, the food being all gone, and I having nothing left to serve out but a bit of coffee-berry now and then, he began to be too weak to do this, and consequently fell silent. Mrs. Atherfield and Miss Coleshaw generally lay, each with an arm across one of my knees, and her head upon it. They never complained at all. Up to the time of her child's death, Mrs. Atherfield had bound up her own beautiful hair every day; and I took particular notice that this was always before she sang her song at night, when every one looked at her. But she never did it after the loss of her darling; and it would have been now all tangled with dirt and wet, but that Miss Coleshaw was careful of it long after she was herself, and would sometimes smooth it down with her weak thin hands.

We were past mustering a story now; but one day, at about this period, I reverted to the superstition of old Mr. Rarx, concerning the Golden Lucy, and told them that nothing vanished from the eye of God, though much might pass away from the eyes of men. "We were all of us," says I, "children once; and our baby feet have strolled in green woods ashore; and our baby hands have gathered flowers in gardens, where the birds were singing. The children that we were, are not lost to the great knowledge of our Creator. Those innocent creatures will appear with us before Him, and plead for us. What we were in the best time of our generous youth will arise and go with us too. The purest part of our lives will not desert us at the pass to which all of us here present are gliding. What we were then, will be as much in existence before Him, as what we are now." They were no less comforted by this consideration, than I was myself; and Miss Coleshaw, drawing my ear nearer to her lips, said, "Captain Ravender, I was on my way to marry a disgraced and broken man, whom I dearly loved when he was honourable and good. Your words seem to have come out of my own poor heart." She pressed my hand upon it, smiling.

Twenty-seven nights and twenty-six days. We were in no want of rain-water, but we had nothing else. And yet, even now, I never turned my eyes upon a waking face but it tried to brighten before mine. O, what a thing it is, in a time of danger and in the presence of death, the shining of a face upon a face! I have heard it broached that orders should be given in great new ships by electric telegraph. I admire machinery as much as any man and am as thankful to it as any man can be for what it does for us. But it will never be a substitute for the face of a man, with his soul in it, encouraging another man to be brave and true. Never try it for that. It will break down like a straw.

I now began to remark certain changes in myself which I did not like. They caused me much disquiet. I often saw the Golden Lucy in the air above the boat. I often saw her I have spoken of before, sitting beside me. I saw the Golden Mary go down, as she really had gone down, twenty times in a day. And yet the sea was mostly, to my thinking, not sea neither, but moving country and extraordinary mountainous regions, the like of which have never been beheld. I felt it time to leave my last words regarding John Steadiman, in case any lips should last out to repeat them to any living ears. I said that John had told me (as he had on deck) that he had sung out "Breakers ahead!" the instant they were audible, and had tried to wear ship, but she struck before it could be done. (His cry, I dare say, had made my dream.) I said that the circumstances were altogether without warning, and out of any course that could have been guarded against; that the same loss would have happened if I had been in charge; and that John was not to blame, but from first to last had done his duty nobly, like the man he was. I tried to write it down in my pocket-book, but could make no words, though I knew what the words were that I wanted to make. When it had come to that, her hands—though she was dead so long—laid me down gently in the bottom of the boat, and she and the Golden Lucy swung me to sleep.

All that follows, was written by John Steadiman, Chief Mate:

On the twenty-sixth day after the foundering of the Golden Mary at sea, I, John Steadiman, was sitting in my place in the stern-sheets of the Surf-boat, with just sense enough left in me to steer—that is to say, with my eyes strained, wide-awake, over the bows of the boat, and my brains fast alseep and dreaming—when I was roused upon a sudden by our second mate, Mr. William Rames.

"Let me take a spell in your place," says he. "And look you out for the Long-boat astern. The last time she rose on the crest of a wave, I thought I made out a signal flying aboard her."

We shifted our places, clumsily and slowly enough, for we were both of us weak and dazed with wet, cold, and hunger. I waited some time, watching the heavy rollers astern, before the Long-boat rose a-top of one of them at the same time with us. At last, she was heaved up for a moment well in view, and there, sure enough, was the signal flying aboard of her—a strip of rag of some sort, rigged to an oar, and hoisted in her bows.

"What does it mean?" says Rames to me in a quavering, trembling sort of voice. "Do they signal a sail in sight?"

"Hush, for God's sake!" says I, clapping my hand over his mouth. "Don't let the people hear you. They'll all go mad together if we mislead them about that signal. Wait a bit, till I have another look at it."

I held on by him, for he had set me all of a tremble with his notion of a sail in sight, and watched for the Long-boat again. Up she rose on the top of another roller. I made out the signal clearly, that second time, and saw that it was rigged half-mast high.

"Rames," says I, "it's a signal of distress. Pass the word forward to keep her before the sea, and no more. We must get the Long-boat within hailing distance of us, as soon as possible."

I dropped down into my old place at the tiller without another word—for the thought went through me like a knife that something had happened to Captain Ravender. I should consider myself unworthy to write another line of this statement, if I had not made up my mind to speak the truth, the whole truth, and nothing but the truth—and I must, therefore, confess plainly that now, for the first time, my heart sank within me. This weakness on my part was produced in some degree, as I take it, by the exhausting effects of previous anxiety and grief.

Our provisions—if I may give that name to what we had left— were reduced to the rind of one lemon and about a couple of handsfull of coffee-berries. Besides these great distresses, caused by the death, the danger, and the suffering among my crew and passengers, I had had a little distress of my own to shake me still more, in the death of the child whom I had got to be very fond of on the voyage out—so fond that I was secretly a little jealous of her being taken in the Long-boat instead of mine when the ship foundered. It used to be a great comfort to me, and I think to those with me also, after we had seen the last of the Golden Mary, to see the Golden Lucy, held up by the men in the Long-boat, when the weather allowed it, as the best and brightest sight they had to show. She looked, at the distance we saw her from, almost like a little white bird in the air. To miss her for the first time, when the weather lulled a little again, and we all looked out for our white bird and looked in vain, was a sore disappointment. To see the men's heads bowed down and the captain's hand pointing into the sea when we hailed the Long-boat, a few days after, gave me as heavy a shock and as sharp a pang of heartache to bear as ever I remember suffering in all my life. I only mention these things to show that if I did give way a little at first, under the dread that our captain was lost to us, it was not without having been a good deal shaken beforehand by more trials of one sort or another than often fall to one man's share.

I had got over the choking in my throat, with the help of a drop of water, and had steadied my mind again so as to be prepared against the worst, when I heard the hail (Lord help the poor fellows, how weak it sounded!)—

"Surf-boat ahoy!"

I looked up, and there were our companions in misfortune tossing abreast of us; not so near that we could make out the features of any of them, but near enough, with some exertion for people in our condition, to make their voices heard in the intervals when the wind was weakest.

I answered the hail, and waited a bit, and heard nothing, and then sung out the Captain's name. The voice that replied did not sound like his; the words that reached us were:

"Chief-mate wanted on board!"

Every man of my crew knew what that meant as well as I did. As second officer in command, there could be but one reason for wanting me on board the Long-boat. A groan went all round us, and my men looked darkly in each other's faces, and whispered under their breaths:

"The captain is dead!"

I commanded them to be silent, and not to make too sure of bad news, at such a pass as things had now come to with us. Then, hailing the Long-boat, I signified that I was ready to go on board when the weather would let me—stopped a bit to draw a good long breath—and then called out as loud as I could the dreadful question:

"Is the captain dead?"

The black figures of three or four men in the after-part of the Long-boat all stooped down together as my voice reached them. They were lost to view for about a minute; then appeared again—one man among them was held up on his feet by the rest, and he hailed back the blessed words (a very faint hope went a very long way with people in our desperate situation): "Not yet!"

The relief felt by me, and by all with me, when we knew that our captain, though unfitted for duty, was not lost to us, it is not in words —at least, not in such words as a man like me can command—to express. I did my best to cheer the men, by telling them what a good sign it was that we were not as badly off yet as we had feared; and then communicated what instructions I had to give, to William Rames, who was to be left in command in my place when I took charge of the Long-boat. After that, there was nothing to be done, but to wait for the chance of the wind dropping at sunset, and the sea going down afterwards, so as to enable our weak crews to lay the two boats alongside of each other, without undue risk—or, to put it plainer, without saddling ourselves with the necessity for any extraordinary exertion of strength or skill. Both the one and the other had now been starved out of us for days and days together.

At sunset the wind suddenly dropped, but the sea, which had been running high for so long a time past, took hours after that before it showed any signs of getting to rest. The moon was shining, the sky was wonderfully clear, and it could not have been, according to my calculations, far off midnight, when the long, slow, regular swell of the calming ocean fairly set in, and I took the responsibility of lessening the distance between the Long-boat and ourselves.

It was, I dare say, a delusion of mine; but I thought I had never seen the moon shine so white and ghastly anywhere, either at sea or on land, as she shone that night while we were approaching our companions in misery. When there was not much more than a boat's length between us, and the white light streamed cold and clear over all our faces, both crews rested on their oars with one great shudder, and stared over the gunwale of either boat, panic-stricken, at the first sight of each other.

"Any lives lost among you?" I asked, in the midst of that frightful silence.

The men in the Long-boat huddled together like sheep at the sound of my voice.

"None yet, but the child, thanks be to God!" answered one among them.

And at the sound of his voice, all my men shrank together like the men in the Long-boat. I was afraid to let the horror produced by our first meeting at closer quarters after the dreadful changes that wet, cold, and famine had produced, last one moment longer than could be helped; so without giving time for any more questions and answers, I commanded the men to lay the two boats close alongside of each other. When I rose up and committed the tiller to the hands of Rames, all my poor fellows raised their white faces imploringly to mine. "Don't leave us, Sir," they said, "don't leave us." "I leave you," says I, "under the command and guidance of Mr. William Rames, as good a sailor as I am, and as trusty and kind a man as ever stepped. Do your duty by him, as you have done it by me; and remember to the last, that while there is life there is hope. God bless and help you all!'' With those words I collected what strength I had left, and caught at two arms that were held out to me, and so got from the stern-sheets of one boat into the stern-sheets of the other.

''Mind where you step, Sir,'' whispered one of the men who had helped me into the Long-boat. I looked down as he spoke. Three figures were huddled up below me, with the moonshine falling on them in ragged streaks through the gaps between the men standing or sitting above them. The first face I made out was the face of Miss Coleshaw; her eyes were wide open and fixed on me. She seemed still to keep her senses, and, by the alternate parting and closing of her lips, to be trying to speak, but I could not hear that she uttered a single word. On her shoulder rested the head of Mrs. Atherfield. The mother of our poor little Golden Lucy must, I think, have been dreaming of the child she had lost; for there was a faint smile just ruffling the white stillness of her face, when I first saw it turned upward, with peaceful closed eyes towards the heavens. From her, I looked down a little, and there, with his head on her lap, and with one of her hands resting tenderly on his cheeks—there lay the Captain, to whose help and guidance, up to this miserable time, we had never looked in vain,—there, worn out at last in our service, and for our sakes, lay the best and bravest man of all our company. I stole my hand in gently through his clothes and laid it on his heart, and felt a little feeble warmth over it, though my cold dulled touch could not detect even the faintest beating. The two men in the stern-sheets with me, noticing what I was doing—knowing I loved him like a brother—and seeing, I suppose, more distress in my face than I myself was conscious of its showing, lost command over themselves altogether, and burst into a piteous moaning, sobbing lamentation over him. One of the two drew aside a jacket from his feet, and showed me that they were bare, except where a wet, ragged strip of stocking still clung to one of them. When the ship struck the Iceberg, he had run on deck leaving his shoes in his cabin. All through the voyage in the boat his feet had been unprotected; and not a soul had discovered it until he dropped! As long as he could keep his eyes open, the very look of them had cheered the men, and comforted and upheld the women. Not one living creature in the boat, with any sense about him, but had felt the good influence of that brave man in one way or another. Not one but had heard him, over and over again, give the credit to others which was due only to himself; praising this man for patience, and thanking that man for help, when the patience and the help had really and truly, as to the best part of both, come only from him. All this, and much more, I heard pouring confusedly from the men's lips while they crouched down, sobbing and crying over their commander, and wrapping the jacket as warmly and tenderly as they could over his cold feet. It went to my heart to check them; but I knew that if this lamenting spirit spread any further, all chance of keeping alight any last sparks of hope and resolution among the boat's company would be lost for ever. Accordingly I sent them to their places, spoke a few encouraging words to the men forward, promising to serve out, when the morning came, as much as I dared, of any eatable thing left in the lockers; called to Rames, in my old boat, to keep as near us as he safely could; drew the garment and coverings of the two poor suffering women more closely about them; and, with a secret prayer to be directed for the best in bearing the awful responsibility now laid on my shoulders, took my Captain's vacant place at the helm of the Long-boat.

This, as well as I can tell it, is the full and true account of how I came to be placed in charge of the lost passengers and crew of the Golden Mary, on the morning of the twenty-seventh day after the ship struck the Iceberg, and foundered at sea.

THE PERILS OF
CERTAIN ENGLISH PRISONERS

IN TWO CHAPTERS

[1857]

CHAPTER I

THE ISLAND OF SILVER-STORE

IT was in the year of our Lord one thousand seven hundred and forty-four, that I, Gill Davis to command, His Mark, having then the honour to be a private in the Royal Marines, stood a-leaning over the bulwarks of the armed sloop Christopher Columbus, in the South American waters off the Mosquito shore.

My lady remarks to me, before I go any further, that there is no such Christian-name as Gill, and that her confident opinion is, that the name given to me in the baptism wherein I was made, etc., was Gilbert. She is certain to be right, but I never heard of it. I was a foundling child, picked up somewhere or another, and I always understood my Christian name to be Gill. It is true that I was called Gills when employed at Snorridge Bottom betwixt Chatham and Maidstone to frighten birds; but that had nothing to do with the baptism wherein I was made, etc., and wherein a number of things were promised for me by somebody, who let me alone ever afterwards as to performing any of them, and who, I consider, must have been the Beadle. Such name of Gills was entirely owing to my cheeks, or gills, which at that time of my life were of a raspy description.

My lady stops me again, before I go any further, by laughing exactly in her old way and waving the feather of her pen at me. That action on her part, calls to my mind as I look at her hand with the rings on it——Well! I won't! To be sure it will come in, in its own place. But it's always strange to me, noticing the quiet hand, and noticing it (as I have done, you know, so many times) a-fondling children and grandchildren asleep, to think that when blood and honour were up—there! I won't! not at present!—Scratch it out.

She won't scratch it out, and quite honourable; because we have made an understanding that everything is to be taken down, and that nothing that is once taken down shall be scratched out. I have the great misfortune not to be able to read and write, and I am speaking my true and faithful account of those Adventures, and my lady is writing it, word for word.

I say, there I was, a-leaning over the bulwarks of the sloop Christopher Columbus in the South American waters off the Mosquito shore: a subject of his Gracious Majesty King George of England, and a private in the Royal Marines.

In those climates, you don't want to do much. I was doing nothing. I was thinking of the shepherd (my father, I wonder?) on the hillsides by Snorridge Bottom, with a long staff, and with a rough white coat in all weathers all the year round, who used to let me lie in a corner of his hut by night, and who used to let me go about with him and his sheep by day when I could get nothing else to do, and who used to give me so little of his victuals and so much of his staff, that I ran away from him—which was what he wanted all along, I expect —to be knocked about the world in preference to Snorridge Bottom. I had been knocked about the world for nine-and-twenty years in all, when I stood looking along those bright blue South American Waters. Looking after the shepherd, I may say. Watching him in a half-waking dream, with my eyes half shut, as he, and his flock of sheep, and his two dogs, seemed to move away from the ship's side, far away over the blue water, and go right down into the sky.

"It's rising out of the water steady," a voice said close to me. I had been thinking on so, that it like woke me with a start, though it was no stranger voice than the voice of Harry Charker, my own comrade.

"What's rising out of the water, steady?" I asked my comrade.

"What?" says he. "The Island."

"O! The Island!" says I, turning my eyes towards it. "True. I forgot the Island."

"Forgot the port you're going to?   That's odd, ain't it?"

"It is odd," says I.

"And odd," he said, slowly considering with himself, "ain't even. Is it, Gill?"

He had always a remark just like that to make, and seldom another. As soon as he had brought a thing round to what it was not, he was satisfied. He was one of the best of men, and, in a certain sort of a way, one with the least to say for himself, I qualify it, because, besides being able to read and write like a Quarter-master, he had always one most excellent idea in his mind. That was, Duty. Upon my soul, I don't believe, though I admire learning beyond everything, that he could have got a better idea out of all the books in the world, if he had learnt them every word, and been the cleverest of scholars.

My comrade and I had been quartered in Jamaica, and from there we had been drafted off to the British settlement of Belize, lying away West and North of the Mosquito coast. At Belize there had been great alarm of one cruel gang of pirates (there were always more pirates than enough in those Caribbean Seas), and as they got the better of our English cruisers by running into out-of-the-way creeks and shallows, and taking the land when they were hotly pressed, the governor of Belize had received orders from home to keep a sharp look-out for them along shore. Now, there was an armed sloop came once a-year from Port Royal, Jamaica, to the Island, laden with all manner of necessaries, to eat, and to drink, and to wear, and to use in various ways; and it was aboard of that sloop which had touched at Belize, that I was a-standing, leaning over the bulwarks.

The Island was occupied by a very small English colony. It had been given the name of Silver-Store. The reason of its being so called, was, that the English colony owned and worked a silver mine over on the mainland, in Honduras, and used this Island as a safe and convenient place to store their silver in, until it was annually fetched away by the sloop. It was brought down from the mine to the coast on the backs of mules, attended by friendly Indians and guarded by white men; from thence it was conveyed over to Silver-Store, when the weather was fair, in the canoes of that country; from Silver-Store, it was carried to Jamaica by the armed sloop once a-year, as I have already mentioned; from Jamaica, it went, of course, all over the world.

How I came to be aboard the armed sloop, is easily told. Four-and-twenty marines under command of a lieutenant—that officer's name was Linderwood—had been told off at Belize, to proceed to Silver-Store, in aid of boats and seamen stationed there for the chase of the Pirates. The Island was considered a good post of observation against the pirates, both by land and sea; neither the pirate ship nor yet her boats had been seen by any of us, but they had been so much heard of, that the reinforcement was sent. Of that party, I was one. It included a corporal and a sergeant. Charker was corporal, and the sergeant's name was Drooce. He was the most tyrannical non-commissioned officer in His Majesty's service.

The night came on, soon after I had had the foregoing words with Charker. All the wonderful bright colours went out of the sea and sky in a few minutes, and all the stars in the Heavens seemed to shine out together, and to look down at themselves in the sea, over one another's shoulders, millions deep. Next morning, we cast anchor off the Island. There was a snug harbour within a little reef; there was a sandy beach; there were cocoa-nut trees with high straight stems, quite bare, and foliage at the top like plumes of magnificent green feathers; there were all the objects that are usually seen in those parts, and I am not going to describe them, having something else to tell about.

Great rejoicings, to be sure, were made on our arrival. All the flags in the place were hoisted, all the guns in the place were fired, and all the people in the place came down to look at us. One of those Sambo fellows—they call those natives Sambos, when they are half-negro and half-Indian—had come off outside the reef, to pilot us in, and remained on board after we had let go our anchor. He was called Christian George King, and was fonder of all hands than anybody else was. Now, I confess, for myself, that on that first day, if I had been captain of the Christopher Columbus, instead of private in the Royal Marines, I should have kicked Christian George King—who was no more a Christian than he was a King or a George—over the side, without exactly knowing why, except that it was the right thing to do.

But, I must likewise confess, that I was not in a particularly pleasant humour, when I stood under arms that morning, aboard the Christopher Columbus in the harbour of the Island of Silver-Store. I had had a hard life, and the life of the English on the Island seemed too easy and too gay to please me. "Here you are," I thought to myself, "good scholars and good livers; able to read what you like, able to write what you like, able to eat and drink what you like, and spend what you like, and do what you like; and much *you* care for a poor, ignorant Private in the Royal Marines! Yet it's hard, too, I think, that you should have all the halfpence, and I all the kicks; you all the smooth, and I all the rough; you all the oil, and I all the vinegar." It was as envious a thing to think as might be, let alone its being nonsensical; but, I thought it. I took it so much amiss, that, when a very beautiful young English lady came aboard, I grunted to myself, "Ah! *you* have got a lover, I'll be bound!" As if there was any new offence to me in that, if she had!

She was sister to the captain of our sloop, who had been in a poor way for some time, and who was so ill then that he was obliged to be carried ashore. She was the child of a military officer, and had come out there with her sister, who was married to one of the owners of the silver mine, and who had three children with her. It was easy to see that she was the light and spirit of the Island. After I had got a good look at her, I grunted to myself again, in an even worse state of mind than before, "I'll be damned, if I don't hate him, whoever he is!"

My officer, Lieutenant Linderwood, was as ill as the captain of the sloop, and was carried ashore, too. They were both young men of about my age, who had been delicate in the West India climate. I even took *that* in bad part. I thought I was much fitter for the work than they were, and that if all of us had our deserts, I should be both of them rolled into one. (It may be imagined what sort of an officer of marines I should have made, without the power of reading a written order. And as to any knowledge how to command the sloop —Lord! I should have sunk her in a quarter of an hour!)

However, such were my reflections; and when we men were ashore and dismissed, I strolled about the place along with Charker, making my observations in a similar spirit.

It was a pretty place: in all its arrangements partly South American and partly English, and very agreeable to look at on that account, being like a bit of home that had got chipped off and had floated away to that spot, accommodating itself to circumstances as it drifted along. The huts of the Sambos, to the number of five-and-twenty, perhaps, were down by the beach to the left of the anchorage. On the right was a sort of barrack, with a South-American Flag and the Union Jack, flying from the same staff, where the little English colony could all come together, if they saw occasion. It was a walled square of building, with a sort of pleasure-ground inside, and inside that again a sunken block like a powder magazine, with a little square trench round it, and steps down to the door. Charker and I were looking in at the gate, which was not guarded; and I had said to Charker, in reference to the bit like a powder magazine, "That's where they keep the silver you see"; and Charker had said to me, after thinking it over, "And silver ain't gold. Is it, Gill?" when the beautiful young English lady I had been so bilious about, looked out of a door, or a window—at all events looked out, from under a bright awning. She no sooner saw us two in uniform, than she came out so quickly that she was still putting on her broad Mexican hat of plaited straw when we saluted.

"Would you like to come in," she said, "and see the place? It is rather a curious place."

We thanked the young lady, and said we didn't wish to be troublesome; but, she said it could be no trouble to an English soldier's daughter, to show English soldiers how their countrymen and countrywomen fared, so far away from England; and consequently we saluted again, and went in. Then, as we stood in the shade, she showed us (being as affable as beautiful), how the different families lived in their separate houses, and how there was a general house for stores, and a general reading-room, and a general room for music and dancing, and a room for Church; and how there were other houses on the rising ground called the Signal Hill, where they lived in the hotter weather.

"Your officer has been carried up there," she said, "and my brother, too, for the better air. At present, our few residents are dispersed over both spots: deducting, that is to say, such of our number as are always going to, or coming from, or staying at, the Mine."

("He is among one of those parties," I thought, "and I wish somebody would knock his head off.")

"Some of our married ladies live here," she said, "during at least half the year, as lonely as widows, with their children."

"Many children here, ma'am?"

"Seventeen. There are thirteen married ladies, and there are eight like me."

There were not eight like her—there was not one like her—in the world. She meant single.

"Which, with about thirty Englishmen of various degrees," said the young lady, "form the little colony now on the Island. I don't count the sailors, for they don't belong to us. Nor the soldiers," she gave us a gracious smile when she spoke of the soldiers, "for the same reason."

"Nor the Sambos, ma'am," said I.

"No."

"Under your favour, and with your leave, ma'am," said I, "are they trustworthy?"

"Perfectly! We are all very kind to them, and they are very grateful to us."

"Indeed, ma'am? Now—Christian George King——?"

"Very much attached to us all. Would die for us."

She was, as in my uneducated way I have observed very beautiful women almost always to be, so composed, that her composure gave great weight to what she said, and I believed it.

Then, she pointed out to us the building like a powder magazine, and explained to us in what manner the silver was brought from the mine, and was brought over from the mainland, and was stored there. The Christopher Columbus would have a rich lading, she said, for there had been a great yield that year, a much richer yield than usual, and there was a chest of jewels besides the silver.

When we had looked about us, and were getting sheepish, through fearing we were troublesome, she turned us over to a young woman, English born but West-India bred, who served her as her maid. This young woman was the widow of a non-commissioned officer in a regiment of the line. She had got married and widowed at St. Vincent, with only a few months between the two events. She was a little saucy woman, with a bright pair of eyes, rather a neat little foot and figure, and rather a neat little turned-up nose. The sort of young woman, I considered at the time, who appeared to invite you to give her a kiss, and who would have slapped your face if you accepted the invitation.

I couldn't make out her name at first; for, when she gave it in answer to my inquiry, it sounded like Belltott, which didn't sound right. But, when we became better acquainted—which was while Charker and I were drinking sugar-cane sangaree, which she made in a most excellent manner—I found that her Christian name was Isabella, which they shortened into Bell, and that the name of the deceased non-commissioned officer was Tott. Being the kind of neat little woman it was natural to make a toy of—I never saw a woman so like a toy in my life—she had got the plaything name of Belltott. In short, she had no other name on the Island. Even Mr. Commissioner Pordage (and *he* was a grave one!) formally addressed her as Mrs. Belltott. But, I shall come to Mr. Commissioner Pordage presently.

The name of the captain of the sloop was Captain Maryon, and therefore it was no news to hear from Mrs. Belltott, that his sister, the beautiful unmarried young English lady, was Miss Maryon. The novelty was, that her Christian name was Marion too. Marion Maryon. Many a time I have run off those two names in my thoughts, like a bit of verse. Oh many, and many, and many a time!

We saw out all the drink that was produced, like good men and true, and then took our leaves, and went down to the beach. The weather was beautiful; the wind steady, low, and gentle; the Island, a picture; the sea, a picture; the sky, a picture. In that country there are two rainy seasons in the year. One sets in at about our English Midsummer; the other, about a fortnight after our English Michaelmas. It was the beginning of August at that time; the first of these rainy seasons was well over; and everything was in its most beautiful growth, and had its loveliest look upon it.

"They enjoy themselves here," I says to Charker, turning surly again. "This is better than private-soldiering."

We had come down to the beach, to be friendly with the boat's-crew who had camped and hutted there; and we were approaching towards their quarters over the sand, when Christian George King comes up from the landing-place at a wolf's-trot, crying, "Yup, So-Jeer!"—which was that Sambo Pilot's barbarous way of saying, Hallo, Soldier! I have stated myself to be a man of no learning, and, if I entertain prejudices, I hope allowance may be made. I will now confess to one. It may be a right one or it may be a wrong one; but, I never did like Natives, except in the form of oysters.

So, when Christian George King, who was individually unpleasant to me besides, comes a trotting along the sand, clucking, "Yup, So-Jeer!" I had a thundering good mind to let fly at him with my right. I certainly should have done it, but that it would have exposed me to reprimand.

"Yup, So-Jeer!" says he. "Bad job."

"What do you mean?" says I.

"Yup, So-Jeer!" says he, "Ship Leakee."

"Ship leaky?" says I.

"Iss," says he, with a nod that looked as if it was jerked out of him by a most violent hiccup—which is the way with those savages.

I cast my eyes at Charker, and we both heard the pumps going aboard the sloop, and saw the signal run up, "Come on board; hands wanted from the shore." In no time some of the sloop's liberty-men were already running down to the water's edge, and the party of seamen, under orders against the Pirates, were putting off to the Columbus in two boats.

"O Christian George King sar berry sorry!" says that Sambo vagabond, then. "Christian George King cry, English fashion!" His English fashion of crying was to screw his black knuckles into his eyes, howl like a dog, and roll himself on his back on the sand. It was trying not to kick him, but I gave Charker the word, "Double-quick, Harry!" and we got down to the water's edge, and got on board the sloop.

By some means or other, she had sprung such a leak, that no pumping would keep her free; and what between the two fears that she would go down in the harbour, and that, even if she did not, all the supplies she had brought for the little colony would be destroyed by the sea-water as it rose in her, there was great confusion. In the midst of it, Captain Maryon was heard hailing from the beach. He had been carried down in his hammock, and looked very bad; but he insisted on being stood there on his feet; and I saw him, myself, come off in the boat, sitting upright in the stern-sheets, as if nothing was wrong with him.

A quick sort of council was held, and Captain Maryon soon re-

solved that we must all fall to work to get the cargo out, and that
when that was done, the guns and heavy matters must be got out,
and that the sloop must be hauled ashore, and careened, and the
leak stopped. We were all mustered (the Pirate-Chase party volun-
teering), and told off into parties, with so many hours of spell and
so many hours of relief, and we all went at it with a will. Christian
George King was entered one of the party in which I worked, at his
own request, and he went at it with as good a will as any of the rest.
He went at it with so much heartiness, to say the truth, that he rose
in my good opinion almost as fast as the water rose in the ship.
Which was fast enough, and faster.

Mr. Commissioner Pordage kept in a red-and-black japanned box,
like a family lump-sugar box, some document or other, which some
Sambo chief or other had got drunk and spilt some ink over (as well
as I could understand the matter), and by that means had given up
lawful possession of the Island. Through having hold of this box,
Mr. Pordage got his title of Commissioner. He was styled Consul too,
and spoke of himself as "Government."

He was a stiff-jointed, high-nosed old gentleman, without an
ounce of fat on him, of a very angry temper and a very yellow complexion. Mrs. Commissioner Pordage, making allowance for difference of sex, was much the same. Mr. Kitten, a small, youngish, bald,
botanical and mineralogical gentleman, also connected with the
mine—but everybody there was that, more or less—was sometimes
called by Mr. Commissioner Pordage, his Vice-commissioner, and
sometimes his Deputy-consul. Or sometimes he spoke of Mr. Kitten,
merely as being "under Government."

The beach was beginning to be a lively scene with the preparations
for careening the sloop, and, with cargo, and spars, and rigging, and
water-casks, dotted about it, and with temporary quarters for the
men rising up there out of such sails and odds and ends as could be
best set on one side to make them, when Mr. Commissioner Pordage
comes down in a high fluster, and asks for Captain Maryon. The
Captain, ill as he was, was slung in his hammock betwixt two
trees, that he might direct; and he raised his head, and answered for
himself.

"Captain Maryon," cries Mr. Commissioner Pordage, "this is not
official. This is not regular."

"Sir," says the Captain, "it hath been arranged with the clerk and
supercargo, that you should be communicated with, and requested
to render any little assistance that may lie in your power. I am quite
certain that hath been duly done."

"Captain Maryon," replies Mr. Commissioner Pordage, "there hath
been no written correspondence. No documents have passed, no
memoranda have been made, no minutes have been made, no entries
and counter-entries appear in the official muniments. This is indecent. I call upon you, Sir, to desist, until all is regular, or Government will take this up."

"Sir," says Captain Maryon, chafing a little, as he looked out of his hammock; "between the chances of Government taking this up, and my ship taking herself down, I much prefer to trust myself to the former."

"You do, Sir?" cries Mr. Commissioner Pordage.

"I do, Sir," says Captain Maryon, lying down again.

"Then, Mr. Kitten," says the Commissioner, "send up instantly for my Diplomatic coat."

He was dressed in a linen suit at that moment; but, Mr. Kitten started off himself and brought down the Diplomatic coat, which was a blue cloth one, gold-laced, and with a crown on the button.

"Now, Mr. Kitten," says Pordage, "I instruct you, as Vice-commissioner, and Deputy-consul of this place, to demand of Captain Maryon, of the sloop Christopher Columbus, whether he drives me to the act of putting this coat on?"

"Mr. Pordage," says Captain Maryon, looking out of his hammock again, "as I can hear what you say, I can answer it without troubling the gentleman. I should be sorry that you should be at the pains of putting on too hot a coat on my account; but, otherwise, you may put it on hind-side before, or inside-out, or with your legs in the sleeves, or your head in the skirts, for any objection that I have to offer to your thoroughly pleasing yourself."

"Very good, Captain Maryon," says Pordage, in a tremendous passion. "Very good, Sir. Be the consequences on your own head! Mr. Kitten, as it has come to this, help me on with it."

When he had given that order, he walked off in the coat, and all our names were taken, and I was afterwards told that Mr. Kitten wrote from his dictation more than a bushel of large paper on the subject, which cost more before it was done with, than ever could be calculated, and which only got done with after all, by being lost.

Our work went on merrily, nevertheless, and the Christopher Columbus, hauled up, lay helpless on her side like a great fish out of water. While she was in that state, there was a feast, or a ball, or an entertainment, or more properly all three together, given us in honour of the ship, and the ship's company, and the other visitors. At that assembly, I believe, I saw all the inhabitants then upon the Island, without any exception. I took no particular notice of more than a few, but I found it very agreeable in that little corner of the world to see the children, who were of all ages, and mostly very pretty—as they mostly are. There was one handsome elderly lady, with very dark eyes and grey hair, that I inquired about. I was told that her name was Mrs. Venning; and her married daughter, a fair slight thing, was pointed out to me by the name of Fanny Fisher. Quite a child she looked, with a little copy of herself holding to her dress; and her husband, just come back from the mine, exceeding proud of her. They were a good-looking set of people on the whole, but I didn't like them. I was out of sorts; in conversation with Charker, I found fault with all of them. I said of Mrs. Venning, she was proud ; of Mrs. Fisher, she was a delicate little baby-fool. What did I think of this one? Why, he was a fine gentleman. What did I say to that one? Why, she was a fine lady. What could you expect them to be (I asked Charker), nursed in that climate, with the tropical night shining for them, musical instruments playing to them, great trees bending over them, soft lamps lighting them, fire-flies sparkling in among them, bright flowers and birds brought into existence to please their eyes, delicious drinks to be had for the pouring out, delicious fruits to be got for the picking, and every one dancing and murmuring happily in the scented air, with the sea breaking low on the reef for a pleasant chorus.

"Fine gentlemen and fine ladies, Harry?" I says to Charker. "Yes, I think so! Dolls! Dolls! Not the sort of stuff for wear, that comes of poor private-soldiering in the Royal Marines!"

However, I could not gainsay that they were very hospitable people, and that they treated us uncommonly well. Every man of us was at the entertainment, and Mrs. Belltott had more partners than she could dance with: though she danced all night, too. As to Jack (whether of the Christopher Columbus, or of the Pirate pursuit party, it made no difference), he danced with his brother Jack, danced with himself, danced with the moon, the stars, the trees, the prospect, anything. I didn't greatly take to the chief-officer of that party, with his bright eyes, brown face, and easy figure. I didn't much like his way when he first happened to come where we were, with Miss Maryon on his arm. "O, Captain Carton," she says, "here are two friends of mine!" He says, "Indeed? These two Marines?"—meaning Charker and self. "Yes," says she, "I showed these two friends of mine when they first came, all the wonders of Silver-Store." He gave us a laughing look, and says he, "You are in luck, men. I would be disrated and go before the mast to-morrow, to be shown the way upward again by such a guide. You are in luck, men." When we had saluted, and he and the lady had waltzed away, I said, "You are a pretty fellow, too, to talk of luck. You may go to the Devil!"

Mr. Commissioner Pordage and Mrs. Commissioner, showed among the company on that occasion like the King and Queen of a much Greater Britain than Great Britain. Only two other circumstances in that jovial night made much separate impression on me. One was this. A man in our draft of marines, named Tom Packer, a wild unsteady young fellow, but the son of a respectable shipwright in Portsmouth Yard, and a good scholar who had been well brought up, comes to me after a spell of dancing, and takes me aside by the elbow, and says, swearing angrily:

"Gill Davis, I hope I may not be the death of Sergeant Drooce one day!"

Now, I knew Drooce had always borne particularly hard on this man, and I knew this man to be of a very hot temper: so, I said:

"Tut, nonsense! don't talk so to me! If there's a man in the corps who scorns the name of an assassin, that man and Tom Packer are one."

Tom wipes his head, being in a mortal sweat, and says he:

"I hope so, but I can't answer for myself when he lords it over me, as he has just now done, before a woman. I tell you what, Gill! Mark my words! It will go hard with Sergeant Drooce, if ever we are in an engagement together, and he has to look to me to save him. Let him say a prayer then, if he knows one, for it's all over with him, and he is on his deathbed. Mark my words!"

I did mark his words, and very soon afterwards, too, as will shortly be taken down.

The other circumstance that I noticed at that ball, was, the gaiety and attachment of Christian George King. The innocent spirits that Sambo Pilot was in, and the impossibility he found himself under of showing all the little colony, but especially the ladies and children, how fond he was of them, how devoted to them, and how faithful to them for life and death, for present, future, and everlasting, made a great impression on me. If ever a man, Sambo or no Sambo, was trustful and trusted, to what may be called quite an infantine and sweetly beautiful extent, surely, I thought that morning when I did at last lie down to rest, it was that Sambo Pilot, Christian George King.

This may account for my dreaming of him. He stuck in my sleep, cornerwise, and I couldn't get him out. He was always flitting about me, dancing round me, and peeping in over my hammock, though I woke and dozed off again fifty times. At last, when I opened my eyes, there he really was, looking in at the open side of the little dark hut; which was made of leaves, and had Charker's hammock slung in it as well as mine.

"So-Jeer!" says he, in a sort of a low croak. "Yup!"

"Hallo!" says I, starting up. "What? You *are* there, are you?"

"Iss," says he. "Christian George King got news."

"What news has he got?"

"Pirates out!"

I was on my feet in a second. So was Charker. We were both aware that Captain Carton, in command of the boats, constantly watched the mainland for a secret signal, though, of course, it was not known to such as us what the signal was.

Christian George King had vanished before we touched the ground. But, the word was already passing from hut to hut to turn out quietly, and we knew that the nimble barbarian had got hold of the truth, or something near it.

In a space among the trees behind the encampment of us visitors, naval and military, was a snugly-screened spot, where we kept the stores that were in use, and did our cookery. The word was passed to assemble here. It was very quickly given, and was given (so far as we were concerned) by Sergeant Drooce, who was as good in a soldier point of view, as he was bad in a tyrannical one. We were ordered to drop into this space, quietly, behind the trees, one by one. As we assembled here, the seamen assembled too. Within ten minutes, as I should estimate, we were all here, except the usual guard upon the beach. The beach (we could see it through the wood) looked as it always had done in the hottest time of the day. The guard were in the shadow of the sloop's hull, and nothing was moving but the sea, and that moved very faintly. Work had always been knocked off at that hour, until the sun grew less fierce, and the sea-breeze rose; so that its being holiday with us, made no difference, just them, in the look of the place. But I may mention that it was a holiday, and the first we had had since our hard work began. Last night's ball had been given, on the leak's being repaired, and the careening done. The worst of the work was over, and to-morrow we were to begin to get the sloop afloat again.

We marines were now drawn up here under arms. The chase-party were drawn up separate. The men of the Columbus were drawn up separate. The officers stepped out into the midst of the three parties, and spoke so as all might hear. Captain Carton was the officer in command, and he had a spy-glass in his hand. His coxswain stood by him with another spy-glass, and with a slate on which he seemed to have been taking down signals.

"Now, men!" says Captain Carton; "I have to let you know, for your satisfaction: Firstly, that there are ten pirate-boats, strongly manned and armed, lying hidden up a creek yonder on the coast, under the overhanging branches of the dense trees. Secondly, that they will certainly come out this night when the moon rises, on a pillaging and murdering expedition, of which some part of the main-land is the object. Thirdly—don't cheer, men!—that we will give chase, and, if we can get at them, rid the world of them, please God!"

Nobody spoke, that I heard, and nobody moved, that I saw. Yet there was a kind of ring, as if every man answered and approved with the best blood that was inside of him.

"Sir," says Captain Maryon, "I beg to volunteer on this service, with my boats. My people volunteer, to the ship's boys."

"In His Majesty's name and service," the other answers, touching his hat, "I accept your aid with pleasure. Lieutenant Linderwood, how will you divide your men?"

I was ashamed—I give it out to be written down as large and plain as possible—I was heart and soul ashamed of my thoughts of those two sick officers, Captain Maryon and Lieutenant Linderwood, when I saw them, then and there. The spirit in those two gentlemen beat down their illness (and very ill I knew them to be) like Saint George beating down the Dragon. Pain and weakness, want of ease and want of rest, had no more place in their minds than fear itself. Meaning now to express for my lady to write down, exactly what I felt then and there, I felt this: "You two brave fellows that I had been so grudgeful of, I know that if you were dying you would put it off to get up and do your best, and then you would be so modest that in lying down again to die, you would hardly say, 'I did it!'"

It did me good. It really did me good.

But, to go back to where I broke off. Says Captain Carton to Lieutenant Linderwood, "Sir, how will you divide your men? There is not room for all; and a few men should, in any case, be left here."

There was some debate about it. At last, it was resolved to leave
eight Marines and four seamen on the island, besides the sloop's
two boys. And because it was considered that the friendly Sambos
would only want to be commanded in case of any danger (though
none at all was apprehended there), the officers were in favour of
leaving the two non-commissioned officers, Drooce and Charker. It
was a heavy disappointment to them, just as my being one of the
left was a heavy disappointment to me—then, but not soon afterwards. We men drew lots for it, and I drew "Island." So did Tom
Packer. So, of course, did four more of our rank and file.

When this was settled, verbal instructions were given to all hands
to keep the intended expedition secret, in order that the women and
children might not be alarmed, or the expedition put in a difficulty
by more volunteers. The assembly was to be on that same spot at
sunset. Every man was to keep up an appearance, meanwhile, of
occupying himself in his usual way. That is to say, every man
excepting four old trusty seamen, who were appointed, with an
officer, to see to the arms and ammunition, and to muffle the rullocks
of the boats, and to make everything as trim and swift and silent
as it could be made.

The Sambo Pilot had been present all the while, in case of his
being wanted, and had said to the officer in command, five hundred
times over if he had said it once, that Christian George King would
stay with the So-Jeers, and take care of the booffer ladies and the
booffer childs—booffer being that native's expression for beautiful.
He was now asked a few questions concerning the putting off of the
boats, and in particular whether there was any way of embarking
at the back of the Island: which Captain Carton would have half
liked to do, and then have dropped round in its shadow and slanted
across to the main. But, "No," says Christian George King. "No, no,
no! Told you so, ten times. No, no, no! All reef, all rock, all swim,
all drown!" Striking out as he said it, like a swimmer gone mad,
and turning over on his back on dry land, and spluttering himself
to death, in a manner that made him quite an exhibition.

The sun went down, after appearing to be a long time about it,
and the assembly was called. Every man answered to his name, of
course, and was at his post. It was not yet black dark, and the roll
was only just gone through, when up comes Mr. Commissioner
Pordage with his Diplomatic coat on.

" Captain Carton," says he, "Sir, what is this?"

"This, Mr. Commissioner" (he was very short with him), "is an
expedition against the Pirates. It is a secret expedition, so please
to keep it a secret."

"Sir," says Commissioner Pordage, "I trust there is going to be
no unnecessary cruelty committed?"

"Sir," returns the officer, "I trust not."

"That is not enough, Sir," cries Commissioner Pordage, getting
wroth. "Captain Carton, I give you notice. Government requires
you to treat the enemy with great delicacy, consideration, clemency,

and forbearance."

"Sir," says Captain Carton, "I am an English officer, commanding English Men, and I hope I am not likely to disappoint the Government's just expectations. But, I presume you know that these villains under their black flag have despoiled our countrymen of their property, burnt their homes, barbarously murdered them and their little children, and worse than murdered their wives and daughters?"

"Perhaps I do, Captain Carton," answers Pordage, waving his hand, with dignity; "perhaps I do not. It is not customary, Sir, for Government to commit itself."

"It matters very little, Mr. Pordage, whether or no. Believing that I hold my commission by the allowance of God, and not that I have received it direct from the Devil, I shall certainly use it, with all avoidance of unnecessary suffering and with all merciful swiftness of execution, to exterminate these people from the face of the earth. Let me recommend you to go home, Sir, and to keep out of the night-air."

Never another syllable did that officer say to the Commissioner, but turned away to his men. The Commissioner buttoned his Diplomatic coat to the chin, said, "Mr. Kitten, attend me!" gasped, half choked himself, and took himself off. It now fell very dark, indeed. I have seldom, if ever, seen it darker, nor yet so dark. The moon was not due until one in the morning, and it was but a little after nine when our men lay down where they were mustered. It was pretended that they were to take a nap, but everybody knew that no nap was to be got under the circumstances. Though all were very quiet, there was a restlessness among the people; much what I have seen among the people on a race-course, when the bell has rung for the saddling for a great race with large stakes on it.

At ten, they put off; only one boat putting off at a time; another followed in five minutes; both then lying on their oars until another followed. Ahead of all, paddling his own outlandish little canoe without a sound, went the Sambo pilot, to take them safely outside the reef. No light was shown but once, and that was in the commanding officer's own hand. I lighted the dark lantern for him, and he took it from me when he embarked. They had blue-lights and such like with them, but kept themselves as dark as Murder.

The expedition got away with wonderful quietness, and Christian George King soon came back dancing with joy.

"Yup, So-Jeer," says he to myself in a very objectionable kind of convulsions, "Christian George King sar berry glad. Pirates all be blown a-pieces. Yup! Yup!"

My reply to that cannibal was, "However glad you may be, hold your noise, and don't dance jigs and slap your knees about it, for I can't abear to see you do it."

I was on duty then; we twelve who were left being divided into four watches of three each, three hours' spell. I was relieved at twelve. A little before that time, I had challenged, and Miss Maryon and Mrs. Belltott had come in.

"Good Davis," says Miss Maryon, "what is the matter? Where is my brother?"

I told her what was the matter, and where her brother was.

"O Heaven help him!" says she, clasping her hands and looking up—she was close in front of me, and she looked most lovely to be sure; " he is not sufficiently recovered, not strong enough for such strife!"

"If you had seen him, miss," I told her, "as I saw him when he volunteered, you would have known that his spirit is strong enough for any strife. It will bear his body, miss, to wherever duty calls him. It will always bear him to an honourable life, or a brave death."

"Heaven bless you!" says she, touching my arm. "I know it. Heaven bless you!"

Mrs. Belltott surprised me by trembling and saying nothing. They were still standing looking towards the sea and listening, after the relief had come round. It continuing very dark, I asked to be allowed to take them back. Miss Maryon thanked me, and she put her arm in mine, and I did take them back. I have now got to make a confession that will appear singular. After I had left them, I laid myself down on my face on the beach, and cried for the first time since I had frightened birds as a boy at Snorridge Bottom, to think what a poor, ignorant, low-placed, private soldier I was.

It was only for half a minute or so. A man can't at all times be quite master of himself, and it was only for half a minute or so. Then I up and went to my hut, and turned into my hammock, and fell asleep with wet eyelashes, and a sore, sore heart. Just as I had often done when I was a child, and had been worse used than usual.

I slept (as a child under those circumstances might) very sound, and yet very sore at heart all through my sleep. I was awoke by the words, "He is a determined man." I had sprung out of my hammock, and had seized my firelock, and was standing on the ground, saying the words myself. "He is a determined man." But, the curiosity of my state was, that I seemed to be repeating them after somebody, and to have been wonderfully startled by hearing them.

As soon as I came to myself, I went out of the hut, and away to where the guard was. Charker challenged:

"Who goes there?"

"A friend."

"Not Gill?" says he, as he shouldered his piece.

"Gill," says I.

"Why, what the deuce do you do out of your hammock?" says he.

"Too hot for sleep," says I; "is all right?"

"Right!" says Charker, "yes, yes; all's right enough here; what should be wrong here? It's the boats that we want to know of. Except for fire-flies winkling about, and the lonesome splashes of great creatures as they drop into the water, there's nothing going on here to ease a man's mind from the boats."

The moon was above the sea, and had risen, I should say, some half-an-hour. As Charker spoke, with his face towards the sea, I,

looking landward, suddenly laid my right hand on his breast, an
said, "Don't move. Don't turn. Don't raise your voice! You neve
saw a Maltese face here?"

"No. What do you mean!" he asks, staring at me.

"Nor yet an English face, with one eye and a patch across th
nose?"

"No. What ails you? What do you mean?"

I had seen both, looking at us round the stem of a cocoa-nut tree
where the moon struck them. I had seen that Sambo Pilot, with on
hand laid on the stem of the tree, drawing them back into the heav
shadow. I had seen their naked cutlasses twinkle and shine, like bit
of the moonshine in the water that had got blown ashore among th
trees by the light wind. I had seen it all, in a moment. And I saw in
moment (as any man would), that the signalled move of the pirate
on the mainland was a plot and a feint; that the leak had been mad
to disable the sloop; that the boats had been tempted away, to leav
the Island unprotected; that the pirates had landed by some secrete
way at the back; and that Christian George King was a double-dye
traitor, and a most infernal villain.

I considered, still all in one and the same moment, that Charke
was a brave man, but not quick with his head; and that Sergean
Drooce, with a much better head, was close by. All I said to Charke
was, "I am afraid we are betrayed. Turn your back full to the moon
light on the sea, and cover the stem of the cocoa-nut tree which wil
then be right before you, at the height of a man's heart. Are yo
right?"

"I am right," says Charker, turning instantly, and falling into th
position with a nerve of iron; "and right ain't left. Is it, Gill?"

A few seconds brought me to Sergeant Drooce's hut. He was fas
asleep, and being a heavy sleeper, I had to lay my hand upon him t
rouse him. The instant I touched him he came rolling out of hi
hammock, and upon me like a tiger. And a tiger he was, except tha
he knew what he was up to, in his utmost heat, as well as any man.

I had to struggle with him pretty hard to bring him to his senses
panting all the while (for he gave me a breather), "Sergeant, I an
Gill Davis! Treachery! Pirates on the Island!"

The last words brought him round, and he took his hands off
"I have seen two of them within this minute," said I. And so I tol
him what I had told Harry Charker.

His soldierly, though tyrannical, head was clear in an instant. H
didn't waste one word, even of surprise. "Order the guard," says he
"to draw off quietly into the Fort." (They called the enclosure I hav
before mentioned, the Fort, though it was not much of that.) "The
get you to the Fort as quick as you can, rouse up every soul there, an
fasten the gate. I will bring in all those who are up at the Signal Hil
If we are surrounded before we can join you, you must make a sall
and cut us out if you can. The word among our men is, 'Women an
children!'"

He burst away, like fire going before the wind over dry reeds. H used up the seven men who were off duty, and had them bursting way with him, before they knew they were not asleep. I reported orders to Charker, and ran to the Fort, as I have never run at any other time in all my life: no, not even in a dream.

The gate was not fast, and had no good fastening: only a double wooden bar, a poor chain, and a bad lock. Those, I secured as well as they could be secured in a few seconds by one pair of hands, and so an to that part of the building where Miss Maryon lived. I called to her loudly by her name until she answered. I then called loudly all he names I knew—Mrs. Macey (Miss Maryon's married sister), Mr. Macey, Mrs. Venning, Mr. and Mrs. Fisher, even Mr. and Mrs. Pordage. Then I called out, "All you gentlemen here, get up and defend the place! We are caught in a trap. Pirates have landed. We re attacked!"

At the terrible word "Pirates!"—for, those villains had done such deeds in those seas as never can be told in writing, and can scarcely e so much as thought of—cries and screams rose up from every part f the place. Quickly lights moved about from window to window, and the cries moved about with them, and men, women, and children came flying down into the square. I remarked to myself, even then, what a number of things I seemed to see at once. I noticed Mrs. Macey coming towards me, carrying all her three children together. I noticed Mr. Pordage in the greatest terror, in vain trying to get on his Diplomatic coat; and Mr. Kitten respectfully tying his pocket-handkerchief over Mrs. Pordage's nightcap. I noticed Mrs. Belltott run out screaming, and shrink upon the ground near me, and cover her face in her hands, and lie all of a bundle, shivering. But, what I noticed with the greatest pleasure was, the determined eyes with which those men of the Mine that I had thought fine gentlemen, came round me with what arms they had: to the full as cool and resolute as I could be, for my life—ay, and for my soul, to, into the bargain!

The chief person being Mr. Macey, I told him how the three men of the guard would be at the gate directly, if they were not already here, and how Sergeant Drooce and the other seven were gone to bring in the outlying part of the people of Silver-Store. I next urged him, for the love of all who were dear to him, to trust no Sambo, and, above all, if he could get any good chance at Christian George King, not to lose it, but to put him out of the world.

"I will follow your advice to the letter, Davis," says he; "what next?"

My answer was, "I think, Sir, I would recommend you next, to order down such heavy furniture and lumber as can be moved, and make a barricade within the gate."

"That's good again," says he: "will you see it done?"

"I'll willingly help to do it," says I, "unless or until my superior, Sergeant Drooce, gives me other orders."

He shook me by the hand, and having told off some of his companions to help me, bestirred himself to look to the arms and ammunition. A proper quick, brave, steady, ready gentleman!

One of their three little children was deaf and dumb. Miss Maryon had been from the first with all the children, soothing them, and dressing them (poor little things, they had been brought out of their beds), and making them believe that it was a game of play, so that some of them were now even laughing. I had been working hard with the others at the barricade, and had got up a pretty good breastwork within the gate. Drooce and the seven had come back, bringing in the people from the Signal Hill, and had worked along with us: but, I had not so much as spoken a word to Drooce, nor had Drooce so much as spoken a word to me, for we were both too busy. The breastwork was now finished, and I found Miss Maryon at my side, with a child in her arms. Her dark hair was fastened round her head with a band. She had a quantity of it, and it looked even richer and more precious, put up hastily out of her way, than I had seen it look when it was carefully arranged. She was very pale, but extraordinarily quiet and still.

"Dear good Davis," said she, "I have been waiting to speak one word to you."

I turned to her directly. If I had received a musket-ball in the heart, and she had stood there, I almost believe I should have turned to her before I dropped.

"This pretty little creature," said she, kissing the child in her arms, who was playing with her hair and trying to pull it down, "cannot hear what we say—can hear nothing. I trust you so much, and have such great confidence in you, that I want you to make me a promise."

"What is it, Miss?"

"That if we are defeated, and you are absolutely sure of my being taken, you will kill me."

"I shall not be alive to do it, Miss. I shall have died in your defence before it comes to that. They must step across my body to lay a hand on you."

"But if you are alive, you brave soldier." How she looked at me! "And if you cannot save me from the Pirates, living, you will save me, dead. Tell me so."

Well! I told her I would do that at the last, if all else failed. She took my hand—my rough, coarse hand—and put it to her lips. She put it to the child's lips, and the child kissed it. I believe I had the strength of half-a-dozen men in me, from that moment, until the fight was over.

All this time, Mr. Commissioner Pordage had been wanting to make a Proclamation to the Pirates to lay down their arms and go away; and everybody had been hustling him about and tumbling over him, while he was calling for pen and ink to write it with. Mrs. Pordage, too, had some curious ideas about the British respectability of her nightcap (which had as many frills to it, growing in layers one inside another, as if it was a white vegetable of the artichoke sort), and she wouldn't take the nightcap off, and would be angry when it got crushed by the other ladies who were handing things about, and, n short, she gave as much trouble as her husband did. But, as we were now forming for the defence of the place, they were both poked out of the way with no ceremony. The children and ladies were got into the little trench which surrounded the silver-house (we were afraid of leaving them in any of the light buildings, lest they should be set on fire), and we made the best disposition we could. There was a pretty good store, in point of amount, of tolerable swords and cutlasses. Those were issued. There were, also, perhaps a score or so of spare muskets, Those were brought out. To my astonishment, little Mrs. Fisher that I had taken for a doll and a baby, was not only very active in that service, but volunteered to load the spare arms.

"For, I understand it well," says she, cheerfully, without a shake in her voice.

"I am a soldier's daughter and a sailor's sister, and I understand it too," says Miss Maryon, just in the same way.

Steady and busy behind where I stood, those two beautiful and delicate young women fell to handling the guns, hammering the flints, looking to the locks, and quietly directing others to pass up powder and bullets from hand to hand, as unflinching as the best of tried soldiers.

Sergeant Drooce had brought in word that the Pirates were very strong in numbers—over a hundred was his estimate—and that they were not, even then, all landed; for, he had seen them in a very good position on the further side of the Signal Hill, evidently waiting for the rest of their men to come up. In the present pause, the first we had had since the alarm, he was telling this over again to Mr. Macey, when Mr. Macey suddenly called out: "The signal! Nobody had thought of the signal!"

We knew of no signal, so we could not have thought of it.

"What signal may you mean, Sir?" says Sergeant Drooce, looking sharp at him.

"There is a pile of wood, upon the Signal Hill. If it could be lighted—which never has been done yet—it would be a signal of distress to the mainland."

Charker cries, directly: "Sergeant Drooce, dispatch me on that duty. Give me the two men who were on guard with me to-night, and I'll light the fire, if it can be done."

"And if it can't, Corporal——" Mr. Macey strikes in.

"Look at these ladies and children, Sir!" says Charker. "I'd sooner *light myself*, than not try any chance to save them."

We gave him a Hurrah!—it burst from us, come of it what might—and he got his two men, and was let out at the gate, and crept away. I had no sooner come back to my place from being one of the party to handle the gate, than Miss Maryon said in a low voice behind me:

"Davis, will you look at the powder? This is not right."

I turned my head. Christian George King again, and treachery again! Sea-water had been conveyed into the magazine, and every grain of powder was spoiled!

"Stay a moment," said Sergeant Drooce, when I had told him,

without causing a movement in a muscle of his face: "look to your pouch, my lad. You Tom Packer, look to your pouch, confound you! Look to your pouches, all you Marines."

The same artful savage had got at them, somehow or another, and the cartridges were all unserviceable. "Hum!" says the Sergeant. "Look to your loading, men. You are right so far?"

Yes; we were right so far.

"Well, my lads, and gentlemen all," says the Sergeant, "this will be a hand-to-hand affair, and so much the better."

He treated himself to a pinch of snuff, and stood up, square-shouldered and broad-chested, in the light of the moon—which was now very bright—as cool as if he was waiting for a play to begin. He stood quiet, and we all stood quiet, for a matter of something like half an hour. I took notice from such whispered talk as there was, how little we that the silver did not belong to, thought about it, and how much the people that it did belong to, thought about it. At the end of the half hour, it was reported from the gate that Charker and the two were falling aback on us, pursued by about a dozen.

"Sally! Gate-party, under Gill Davis," says the Sergeant, "and bring 'em in! Like men, now!"

We were not long about it, and we brought them in. "Don't take me," says Charker, holding me round the neck, and stumbling down at my feet when the gate was fast, "don't take me near the ladies or to the children, Gill. They had better not see Death, till it can't be helped. They'll see it soon enough."

"Harry!" I answered, holding up his head. "Comrade!"

He was cut to pieces. The signal had been secured by the first pirate party that landed; his hair was all singed off, and his face was blackened with the running pitch from a torch.

He made no complaint of pain, of or anything. "Good-bye, old chap," was all he said, with a smile. "I've got my death. And Death ain't life. Is it, Gill?"

Having helped to lay his poor body on one side, I went back to my post. Sergeant Drooce looked at me, with his eyebrows a little lifted. I nodded. "Close up here, men, and gentlemen all!" said the Sergeant. "A place too many, in the line."

The pirates were so close upon us at this time, that the foremost of them were already before the gate, with a great noise, and shouting loudly. When we believed from the sound that they were all there, we gave three English cheers. The poor little children joined, and we were so fully convinced of our being at play, that they enjoyed the noise, and were heard clapping their hands in the silence that followed.

Our disposition was this, beginning with the rear. Mrs. Venning, holding her daughter's child in her arms, sat on the steps of the little square trench surrounding the silver-house, encouraging and directing those women and children as she might have done in the happiest and easiest time of her life. Then, there was an armed line, under Mr. Macey, across the width of the enclosure, facing that way and having their backs towards the gate, in order that they might watch the walls and prevent our being taken by surprise. Then there was a space of eight or ten feet deep, in which the spare arms were, and in which Miss Maryon and Mrs.Fisher, their hands and dresses blackened with the spoilt gunpowder, worked on their knees tying such things as knives, old bayonets, and spear-heads, to the muzzles of the useless muskets. Then, there was a second armed line, under Sergeant Drooce, also across the width of the enclosure, but facing to the gate. Then came the breastwork we had made, with a zig-zag way through it for me and my little party to hold good in retreating, as long as we could, when we were driven from the gate. We all knew that it was impossible to hold the place long, and that our only hope was in the timely discovery of the plot by the boats, and in their coming back.

I and my men were now thrown forward to the gate. From a spy-hole, I could see the whole crowd of Pirates. There were Malays among them, Dutch, Maltese, Greeks, Sambos, Negroes, and Convict Englishmen from the West India Islands; among the last, him with the one eye and the patch across the nose. There were some Portuguese, too, and a few Spaniards. The captain was a Portuguese; a little man with very large earrings under a very broad hat, and a great bright shawl twisted about his shoulders. They were all strongly armed, but like a boarding party, with pikes, swords, cutlasses, and axes. I noticed a good many pistols, but not a gun of any kind among them. This gave me to understand that they had considered that a continued roll of musketry might perhaps have been heard on the mainland; also, that for the reason that fire would be seen from the mainland they would not set the Fort in flames and roast us alive; which was one of their favourite ways of carrying on. I looked about for Christian George King, and if I had seen him I am much mistaken if he would not have received my one round of ball-cartridge in his head. But, no Christian George King was visible.

A sort of wild Portuguese demon, who seemed either fierce-mad or fierce-drunk—but, they all seemed one or the other—came forward with the black flag, and gave it a wave or two. After that, the Portuguese captain called out in shrill English, "I say you! English fools! Open the gate! Surrender!"

As we kept close and quiet, he said something to his men which I didn't understand, and when he had said it, the one-eyed English rascal with the patch (who had stepped out when he began), said it again in English. It was only this. "Boys of the back flag, this is to be quickly done. Take all the prisoners you can. If they don't yield, kill the children to make them. Forward!" Then, they all came on at the gate, and, in another half minute were smashing and splitting it in.

We struck at them through the gaps and shivers, and we dropped many of them, too; but, their very weight would have carried such a gate, if they had been unarmed. I soon found Sergeant Drooce at my side, forming us six remaining marines in line—Tom Packer next to me—and ordering us to fall back three paces, and, as they broke in, to give them our one little volley at short distance. "Then," says he, "receive them behind your breastwork on the bayonet, and at least let every man of you pin one of the cursed cock-chafers through the body."

We checked them by our fire, slight as it was, and we checked them at the breastwork. However, they broke over it like swarms of devils—they were, really and truly, more devils than men—and then it was hand to hand indeed,.

We clubbed our muskets and laid about us; even then, those two ladies—always behind me—were steady and ready with the arms. I had a lot of Maltese and Malays upon me, and, but for a broadsword that Miss Maryon's own hand put in mine should have got my end from them. But, was that all? No. I saw a heap of banded dark hair and a white dress come thrice between me and them, under my own raised right arm, which each time might have destroyed the wearer of the white dress; and each time one of the lot went down, struck dead.

Drooce was armed with a broadsword, too, and did such things with it, that there was a cry in half-a-dozen languages of "Kill that sergeant!" as I knew, by the cry being raised in English, and taken up in other tongues. I had received a severe cut across the left arm a few moments before, and should have known nothing of it, except supposing that somebody had struck me a smart blow, if I had not felt weak, and seen myself covered with spouting blood, and, at the same instant of time, seen Miss Maryon tearing her dress and binding it with Mrs. Fisher's help round the wound. They called to Tom Packer, who was scouring by, to stop and guard me for one minute, while I was bound, or I should bleed to death in trying to defend myself. Tom stopped directly, with a good sabre in his hand.

In that same moment—all things seem to happen in that same moment, at such a time—half a dozen had rushed howling at Sergeant Drooce. The Sergeant, stepping back against the wall, stopped one howl for ever with such a terrible blow, and waited for the rest to come on, with such a wonderfully unmoved face, that they stopped and looked at him.

"See him now!" cried Tom Packer. "Now, when I could cut him out! Gill! Did I tell you to mark my words?"

I implored Tom Packer in the Lord's name, as well as I could in my faintness, to go to the Sergeant's aid.

"I hate and detest him," says Tom, moodily wavering. "Still, he is a brave man." Then he calls out, "Sergeant Drooce, Sergeant Drooce! Tell me you have driven me too hard, and are sorry for it."

The Sergeant, without turning his eyes from his assailants, which would have been instant death to him, answers:

"No. I won't."

"Sergeant Drooce!" cries Tom in a kind of an agony. "I have passed my word that I would never save you from Death, if I could, but would leave you to die. Tell me you have driven me too hard and are sorry for it, and that shall go for nothing."

One of the group laid the Sergeant's bald head open. The Sergeant laid him dead.

"I tell you," says the Sergeant, breathing a little short, and waiting for the next attack, "no. I won't. If you are not man enough to strike for a fellow soldier because he wants help, and because of nothing else, I'll go into the other world and look for a better man."

Tom swept upon them, and cut him out. Tom and he fought their way through another knot of them, and sent them flying, and came over to where I was beginning again to feel, with inexpressible joy, that I had got a sword in my hand.

They had hardly come to us, when I heard, above all the other noises, a tremendous cry of women's voices. I also saw Miss Maryon, with quite a new face, suddenly clap her two hands over Mrs. Fisher's eyes. I looked towards the silver-house, and saw Mrs. Venning— standing upright on the top of the steps of the trench, with her gray hair and her dark eyes—hide her daughter's child behind her, among the folds of her dress, strike a pirate with her other hand, and fall, shot by his pistol.

The cry arose again, and there was a terrible and confusing rush of the women into the midst of the struggle. In another moment, something came tumbling down upon me that I thought was the wall. It was a heap of Sambos who had come over the wall; and of four men who clung to my legs like serpents, one who clung to my right leg was Christian George King.

"Yup, So-Jeer," says he, "Christian George King sar berry glad So-Jeer a prisoner. Christian George King been waiting for So-Jeer sech long time. Yup, yup!"

What could I do, with five-and-twenty of them on me, but be tied hand and foot? So, I was tied hand and foot. It was all over now— boats not come back—all lost! When I was fast bound and was put up against the wall, the one-eyed English convict came up with the Portuguese Captain, to have a look at me.

"See!" says he. "Here's the determined man! If you had slept sounder, last night, you'd have slept your soundest last night, my determined man."

The Portuguese Captain laughed in a cool way, and with the flat of his cutlass, hit me crosswise, as if I was the bough of a tree that he played with: first on the face, and across the chest and wounded arm. I looked him steadily in the face without tumbling while he looked at me, I am happy to say; but, when they went away, I fell, and lay there.

The sun was up, when I was roused and told to come down to the beach and be embarked. I was full of aches and pains, and could not at first remember; but, I remembered quite soon enough. The killed were lying about all over the place, and the Pirates were burying their dead, and taking away their wounded on hastily-made litters, to the back of the Island. As for us prisoners, some of their boats had come round to the usual harbour, to carry us off. We looked a wretched few, I thought, when I got down there; still, it was another sign that we had fought well, and made the enemy suffer.

The Portuguese Captain had all the women already embarked in the boat he himself commanded, which was just putting off when I got down. Miss Maryon sat on one side of him, and gave me a moment's look, as full of quiet courage, and pity, and confidence, as if it had been an hour long. On the other side of him was poor little Mrs. Fisher, weeping for her child and her mother. I was shoved into the same boat with Drooce and Packer, and the remainder of our party of marines: of whom we had lost two privates, besides Charker, my poor, brave comrade. We all made a melancholy passage, under the hot sun over to the mainland. There, we landed in a solitary place, and were mustered on the sea sand. Mr. and Mrs. Macy and their children were amongst us, Mr. and Mrs. Pordage, Mr. Kitten, Mr. Fisher, and Mrs. Belltott. We mustered only fourteen men, fifteen women, and seven children. Those were all that remained of the English who had lain down to sleep last night, unsuspecting and happy, on the Island of Silver-Store.

[The second chapter, which was not written by Mr. Dickens, describes the Prisoners (twenty-two women and children) taken into the interior by the Pirate Captain, who makes them the material guarantee for the precious metal and jewels left on the Island; declaring that, if the latter be wrested by English ships from the pirates in charge, he will murder the captives. From their "Prison in the Woods," however (this being the title of the second chapter), they escape by means of rafts down the river; and the sequel is told in a third and concluding chapter by Mr. Dickens.]

CHAPTER III

THE RAFTS ON THE RIVER

WE contrived to keep afloat all that night, and, the stream running strong with us, to glide a long way down the river. But, we found the night to be a dangerous time for such navigation, on account of the eddies and rapids, and it was therefore settled next day that in future we would bring-to at sunset, and encamp on the shore. As we knew no boats that the Pirates possessed, up at the Prison in the Woods, we settled always to encamp on the opposite side of the stream, so as to have the breadth of the river between our sleep and them. Our opinion was, that if they were acquainted with any near way by land to the mouth of this river, they would come up it in force, and retake us or kill us, according as they could; but if that was not the case, and if the river ran by none of their secret stations, we might escape.

When I say we settled this or that, I do not mean that we planned anything with any confidence as to what might happen an hour hence. So much had happened in one night, and such great changes had been violently and suddenly made in the fortunes of many among us, that we had got better used to uncertainty, in a little while, than I dare say most people do in the course of their lives.

The difficulties we soon got into, through the off-settings and point-currents of the stream, made the likelihood of our being drowned, alone—to say nothing of our being retaken—as broad and plain as the sun at noonday to all of us. But, we all worked hard at managing the rafts, under the direction of the seamen (of our own skill, I think we never could have prevented them from oversetting), and we also worked hard at making good the defects in their first hasty construction—which the water soon found out. While we humbly resigned ourselves to going down, if it was the will of Our Father that was in Heaven, we humbly made up our minds, that we could all do the best that was in us.

And so we held on, gliding with the stream. It drove us to this bank, and it drove us to that bank, and it turned us, and whirled us; but yet it carried us on. Sometimes much too slowly; sometimes much too fast, but yet it carried us on.

My little deaf and dumb boy slumbered a good deal now, and that was the case with all the children. They caused very little trouble to any one. They seemed, in my eyes, to get more like one another, not only in the quiet manner, but in face, too. The motion of the raft was usually so much the same, the scene was usually so much the same, the sound of the soft wash and the ripple of the water was usually so much the same, that they were made drowsy, as they might have been by the constant playing of one tune. Even on the grown people, who worked hard and felt anxiety, the same things produced something of the same effect. Every day was so like the other, that I soon lost count of the days, myself, and had to ask Miss Maryon, for instance, whether this was the third or fourth? Miss Maryon had a pocket-book and pencil, and she kept the log; that is to say, she entered up a clear little journal of the time, and of the distances our seamen thought we had made, each night.

So, as I say, we kept afloat and glided on. All day long, and every day, the water, and the woods, and sky; all day long, and every day, the constant watching of both sides of the river, and far ahead at every bold turn and sweep it made, for any signs of Pirate-boats, or Pirate-dwellings. So, as I say, we kept afloat and glided on. The days melting themselves together to that degree, that I could hardly believe my ears when I asked "How many, now, Miss?" and she answered "Seven."

To be sure, poor Mr. Pordage had, by about now, got his Diplomatic coat into such a state as never was seen. What with the mud of the river, what with the water of the river, what with the sun, and the dews, and the tearing boughs, and the thickets, it hung about him in discoloured shreds like a mop. The sun had touched him a bit. He had taken to always polishing one particular button, which just held on to his left wrist, and to always calling for stationery. I suppose that man called for pens, ink, and paper, tape, and sealing-wax, upwards of one thousand times in four-and-twenty hours. He had an idea that we should never get out of that river unless we were written out of it in a formal Memorandum; and the more we laboured at navigating the rafts, the more he ordered us not to touch them at our peril, and the more he sat and roared for stationery.

Mrs. Pordage, similarly, persisted in wearing her nightcap. I doubt if any one but ourselves who had seen the progress of that article of dress, could by this time have told what it was meant for. It had got so limp and ragged that she couldn't see out of her eyes for it. It was so dirty, that whether it was vegetable matter out of a swamp, or weeds out of the river, or an old porter's-knot from England, I don't think any new spectator could have said. Yet, this unfortunate old woman had a notion that it was not only vastly genteel, but that it was the correct thing as to propriety. And she really did carry herself over the other ladies who had no nightcaps, and who were forced to tie up their hair how they could, in a superior manner that was perfectly amazing.

I don't know what she looked like, sitting in that blessed nightcap, on a log of wood, outside the hut or cabin upon our raft. She would have rather resembled a fortune-teller in one of the picture-books that used to be in shop-windows in my boyhood, except for her stateliness. But, Lord bless my heart, the dignity with which she sat and moped, with her head in that bundle of tatters, was like nothing else in the world! She was not on speaking terms with more than three of the ladies. Some of them had, what she called, "taken precedence" of her—in getting into, or out of, that miserable little shelter! and others had not called to pay their respects, or something of that kind. So, there she sat, in her own state and ceremony, while her husband sat on the same log of wood, ordering us one and all to let the raft go to the bottom, and to bring him stationery.

What with this noise on the part of Mr. Commissioner Pordage, and what with the cries of Sergeant Drooce on the raft astern (which were sometimes more than Tom Packer could silence), we often made our slow way down the river, anything but quietly. Yet, that it was of great importance that no ears should be able to hear us from the woods, on the banks, could not be doubted. We were looked for, to a certainty, and we might be retaken at any moment. It was an anxious time; it was, indeed, indeed, an anxious time.

On the seventh night of our voyage on the rafts, we made fast, as usual, on the opposite side of the river to that from which we had started, in as dark a place as we could pick out. Our little encampment was soon made, and supper was eaten, and the children fell asleep. The watch was set, and everything made orderly for the night. Such a starlight night, with such blue in the sky, and such black in the places of heavy shade on the banks of the great stream!

Those two ladies, Miss Maryon and Mrs. Fisher, had always kept near me since the night of the attack. Mr. Fisher, who was untiring in the work of the raft, had said to me:

"My dear little childless wife has grown so attached to you, Davis, and you are such a gentle fellow, as well as such a determined one;" our party had adopted that last expression from the one-eyed English pirate, and I repeat what Mr. Fisher said, only because he said it; "that it takes a load off my mind to leave her in your charge."

I said to him: "Your lady is in far better charge than mine, Sir, having Miss Maryon to take care of her; but, you may rely upon it, that I will guard them both faithful and true."

Says he: "I do rely upon it, Davis, and I heartily wish all the silver on our old Island was yours."

That seventh starlight night, as I have said, we made our camp, and got our supper, and set our watch, and the children fell asleep. It was solemn and beautiful in those wild and solitary parts, to see them, every night before they lay down, kneeling under the bright sky, saying their little prayers at women's laps. At that time we men all uncovered, and mostly kept at a distance. When the innocent creatures rose up, we murmured "Amen!" all together. For, though we had not heard what they said, we knew it must be good for us.

At that time, too, as was only natural, those poor mothers in our company, whose children had been killed, shed many tears. I thought the sight seemed to console them while it made them cry; but, whether I was right or wrong in that, they wept very much. On this seventh night, Mrs. Fisher had cried for her lost darling until she cried herself asleep. She was lying on a little couch of leaves and such-like (I made the best little couch I could for them every night), and Miss Maryon had covered her, and sat by her, holding her hand. The stars looked down upon them. As for me, I guarded them.

"Davis!" says Miss Maryon. (I am not going to say what a voice she had. I couldn't if I tried.)

"I am here, Miss."

"The river sounds as if it were swollen to-night."

"We all think, Miss, that we are coming near the sea."

"Do you believe we shall escape?"

"I do now, Miss, really believe it." I had always said I did; but, I had in my own mind been doubtful.

"How glad you will be, my good Davis, to see England again!"

I have another confession to make that will appear singular. When she said these words, something rose in my throat; and the stars I looked away at, seemed to break into sparkles that fell down my face and burnt it.

"England is not much to me, Miss, except as a name."

"O, so true an Englishman should not say that!—Are you not well to-night, Davis?" Very kindly, and with a quick change.

"Quite well, Miss."

"Are you sure? Your voice sounds altered in my hearing."

"No, Miss, I am stronger than ever. But, England is nothing to me."

Miss Maryon sat silent for so long a while, that I believed she had done speaking to me for one time. However, she had not; for by-and-by she said in a distinct clear tone:

"No, good friend; you must not say that England is nothing to you. It is to be much to you yet,—everything to you. You have to take back to England the good name you have earned here, and the gratitude and attachment and respect you have won here: and you have to make some good English girl very happy and proud, by marrying her; and I shall one day see her, I hope, and make her happier and prouder still, by telling her what noble services her husband's were in South America, and what a noble friend he was to me there."

Though she spoke these kind words in a cheering manner, she spoke them compassionately. I said nothing. It will appear to be another strange confession, that I paced to and fro, within call, all that night, a most unhappy man, reproaching myself all the night long. "You are as ignorant as any man alive; you are as obscure as any man alive; you are as poor as any man alive; you are no better than the mud under your foot." That was the way in which I went on against myself until the morning.

With the day, came the day's labour. What I should have done without the labour, I don't know. We were afloat again at the usual hour, and were again making our way down the river. It was broader, and clearer of obstructions than it had been, and it seemed to flow faster. This was one of Drooce's quiet days; Mr. Pordage, besides being sulky, had almost lost his voice; and we made good way, and with little noise.

There was always a seaman forward on the raft, keeping a bright look-out. Suddenly, in the full heat of the day, when the children were slumbering, and the very trees and reeds appeared to be slumbering, this man—it was Short—holds up his hand, and cries with great caution: "Avast! Voices ahead!"

We held on against the stream as soon as we could bring her up, and the other raft followed suit. At first, Mr. Macey, Mr. Fisher, and myself, could hear nothing; though both the seamen aboard of us agreed that they could hear voices and oars. After a little pause, however, we united in thinking that we *could* hear the sound of voices, and the dip of oars. But, you can hear a long way in those countries, and there was a bend of the river before us, and nothing was to be seen except such waters and such banks as we were now in the eighth day (and might, for the matter of our feeling, have been in the eightieth), of having seen with anxious eyes.

It was soon decided to put a man ashore, who should creep through the wood, see what was coming, and warn the rafts. The rafts in the meantime to keep the middle of the stream. The man to be put ashore, and not to swim ashore, as the first thing could be more quickly done than the second. The raft conveying him, to get back into midstream, and to hold on along with the other, as well as it could, until signalled by the man. In case of danger, the man to shift for himself until it should be safe to take him on board again. I volunteered to be the man.

We knew that the voices and oars must come up slowly against the stream; and our seamen knew, by the set of the stream, under which bank they would come. I was put ashore accordingly. The raft got off well, and I broke into the wood.

Steaming hot it was, and a tearing place to get through. So much the better for me, since it was nothing to contend against and do. I cut off the bend of the river, at a great saving of space, came to the water's edge again, and hid myself, and waited. I could now hear the dip of the oars very distinctly; the voices had ceased.

The sound came on in a regular tune, and as I lay hidden, I fancied the tune so played to be, "Chris'en—George—King! Chris'en—George —King! Chris'en—George—King!" over and over again, always the same, with the pauses always at the same places. I had likewise time to make up my mind that if these were the Pirates, I could and would (barring my being shot) swim off to my raft, in spite of my wound, the moment I had given the alarm, and hold my old post by Miss Maryon.

"Chris'en—George—King! Chris'en—George—King! Chris'en— George—King!" coming on, now, very near.

I took a look at the branches about me, to see where a shower of bullets would be most likely to do me least hurt; and I took a look back at the track I had made in forcing my way in; and now I was wholly prepared and fully ready for them.

"Chris'en—George—King! Chris'en—George—King! Chris'en— George—King!" Here they were!

Who were they? The barbarous Pirates, scum of all nations, headed by such men as the hideous little Portuguese monkey, and the one-eyed English convict with the gash across his face, that ought to have gashed his wicked head off? The worst men in the world picked out from the worst, to do the cruellest and most atrocious deeds that ever stained it? The howling, murdering, black-flag waving, mad, and drunken crowds of devils that had overcome us by numbers and by treachery? No. These were English men in English boats—good blue-jackets and red-coats—marines that I knew myself, and sailors that knew our seamen! At the helm of the first boat, Captain Carton, eager and steady. At the helm of the second boat, Captain Maryon, brave and bold. At the helm of the third boat, an old seaman, with deter-mination carved into his watchful face, like the figure-head of a ship. Every man doubly and trebly armed from head to foot. Every man lying-to at his work, with a will that had all his heart and soul in it. Every man looking out for any trace of friend or enemy, and burning to be the first to do good or avenge evil. Every man with his face on fire when he saw me, his countryman who had been taken prisoner, and hailed me with a cheer, as Captain Carton's boat ran in and took men on board.

I reported, "All escaped, sir! All well, all safe, all here!"

God bless me—and God bless them—what a cheer! It turned me weak; as I was passed on from hand to hand to the stern of the boat: every hand patting me or grasping me in some way or other, in the moment of my going by.

"Hold up, my brave fellow," says Captain Carton, clapping me on the shoulder like a friend, and giving me a flask. "Put your lips to that, and they'll be red again. Now, boys, give way!"

The banks flew by us as if the mightiest stream that ever ran was with us; and so it was, I am sure, meaning the stream to those men's ardour and spirit. The banks flew by us, and we came in sight of the rafts—the banks flew by us, and we came alongside of the rafts—

the banks stopped; and there was a tumult of laughing and crying, and kissing and shaking of hands, and catching up of children and setting of them down again, and a wild hurry of thankfulness and joy that melted every one and softened all hearts.

I had taken notice, in Captain Carton's boat, that there was a curious and quite new sort of fitting on board. It was a kind of a little bower made of flowers, and it was set up behind the captain, and betwixt him and the rudder. Not only was this arbour, so to call it, neatly made of flowers, but it was ornamented in a singular way. Some of the men had taken the ribbons and buckles off their hats, and hung them among the flowers; others had made festoons and streamers of their handkerchiefs, and hung them there; others had intermixed such trifles as bits of glass and shining fragments of lockets and tobacco-boxes with the flowers; so that altogether it was a very bright and lively object in the sunshine. But why there, or what for, I did not understand.

Now, as soon as the first bewilderment was over, Captain Carton gave the order to land for the present. But this boat of his, with two hands left in her, immediately put off again when the men were out of her, and kept off, some yards from the shore. As she floated there, with the two hands gently backing water to keep her from going down the stream, this pretty little arbour attracted many eyes. None of the boat's crew, however, had anything to say about it, except that it was the captain's fancy.

The captain—with the women and children clustering round him, and the men of all ranks grouped outside them, and all listening—stood telling how the Expedition, deceived by its bad intelligence, had chased the light Pirate boats all that fatal night, and had still followed in their wake next day, and had never suspected until many hours too late that the great Pirate body had drawn off in the darkness when the chase began, and shot over to the Island. He stood telling how the Expedition, supposing the whole array of armed boats to be ahead of it, got tempted into shallows and went aground; but not without having its revenge upon the two decoy-boats, both of which it had come up with, overhand, and sent to the bottom with all on board. He stood telling how the Expedition, fearing then that the case stood as it did, got afloat again, by great exertion, after the loss of four more tides, and returned to the Island, where they found the sloop scuttled and the treasure gone. He stood telling how my officer, Lieutenant Linderwood, was left upon the Island, with as strong a force as could be got together hurriedly from the mainland, and how the three boats we saw before us were manned and armed and had come away, exploring the coast and inlets, in search of any tidings of us. He stood telling all this, with his face to the river; and, as he stood telling it, the little arbour of flowers floated in the sunshine before all the faces there.

Leaning on Captain Carton's shoulder, between him and Miss Maryon, was Mrs. Fisher, her head drooping on her arm. She asked him, without raising it, when he had told so much, whether he had found her mother?

"Be comforted! She lies," said the Captain gently, "under the cocoa-nut trees on the beach."

"And my child, Captain Carton, did you find my child, too? Does my darling rest with my mother?"

"No. Your pretty child sleeps," said the Captain, "under a shade of flowers."

His voice shook; but there was something in it that struck all the hearers. At that moment there sprung from the arbour in his boat a little creature, clapping her hands and stretching out her arms, and crying, "Dear papa! Dear mamma! I am not killed. I am saved. I am coming to kiss you. Take me to them, take me to them, good kind sailors!"

Nobody who saw that scene has ever forgotten it, I am sure, or ever will forget it. The child had kept quite still, where her brave grandmamma had put her (first whispering in her ear, "Whatever happens to me, do not stir, my dear!"), and had remained quiet until the fort was deserted; she had then crept out of the trench, and gone into her mother's house; and there, alone on the solitary Island, in her mother's room, and asleep on her mother's bed, the Captain had found her. Nothing could induce her to be parted from him after he took her up in his arms, and he had brought her away with him, and the men had made the bower for her. To see those men now, was a sight. The joy of the women was beautiful; the joy of those women who had lost their own children, was quite sacred and divine; but the ecstasies of Captain Carton's boat's crew, when their pet was restored to her parents, were wonderful for the tenderness they showed in the midst of roughness. As the Captain stood with the child in his arms, and the child's own little arms now clinging round his neck, now round her father's, now round her mother's, now round some one who pressed up to kiss her, the boat's crew shook hands with one another, waved their hats over their heads, laughed, sang, cried, danced—and all among themselves, without wanting to interfere with anybody—in a manner never to be represented. At last, I saw the coxswain and another, two very hard-faced men, with grizzled heads, who had been the heartiest of the hearty all along, close with one another, get each of them the other's head under his arm, and pommel away at it with his fist as hard as he could, in his excess of joy.

When we had well rested and refreshed ourselves—and very glad we were to have some of the heartening things to eat and drink that had come up in the boats—we recommenced our voyage down the river: rafts, and boats, and all. I said to myself, it was a very different kind of voyage now, from what it had been; and I fell into my proper place and station among my fellow-soldiers.

But, when we halted for the night, I found that Miss Maryon had spoken to Captain Carton concerning me. For, the Captain came straight up to me, and says he, "My brave fellow, you have been Miss Maryon's body-guard all along, and you shall remain so. Nobody shall supersede you in the distinction and pleasure of protecting that young lady." I thanked his honour in the fittest words I could find, and that night I was placed on my old post of watching the place where she slept. More than once in the night, I saw Captain Carton come out into the air, and stroll about there, to see that all was well. I have now this other singular confession to make, that I saw him with a heavy heart. Yes; I saw him with a heavy, heavy heart.

In the daytime, I had the like post in Captain Carton's boat. I had a special station of my own, behind Miss Maryon, and no hands but hers ever touched my wound. (It has been healed these many long years; but, no other hands have ever touched it.) Mr. Pordage was kept tolerably quiet now, with pen and ink, and began to pick up his senses a little. Seated in the second boat, he made documents with Mr. Kitten, pretty well all day; and he generally handed in a Protest about something whenever we stopped. The Captain, however, made so very light of these papers, that it grew into a saying among the men, when one of them wanted a match for his pipe, "Hand us over a Protest, Jack!" As to Mrs. Pordage, she still wore the nightcap, and she now had cut all the ladies on account of her not having been formally and separately rescued by Captain Carton before anybody else. The end of Mr. Pordage, to bring to an end all I know about him, was, that he got great compliments at home for his conduct on these trying occasions, and that he died of yellow jaundice, a Governor and a K.C.B.

Sergeant Drooce had fallen from a high fever into a low one. Tom Packer—the only man who could have pulled the Sergeant through it—kept hospital aboard the old raft, and Mrs. Belltott, as brisk as ever again (but the spirit of that little woman, when things tried it, was not equal to appearances), was head-nurse under his directions. Before we got down to the Mosquito coast, the joke had been made by one of our men, that we should see her gazetted Mrs. Tom Packer, *vice* Belltott exchanged.

When we reached the coast, we got native boats as substitutes for the rafts; and we rowed along under the land; and in that beautiful climate, and upon that beautiful water, the blooming days were like enchantment. Ah! They were running away, faster than any sea or river, and there was no tide to bring them back. We were coming very near the settlement where the people of Silver-Store were to be left, and from which we Marines were under orders to return to Belize.

Captain Carton had, in the boat by him, a curious long-barrelled Spanish gun, and he had said to Miss Maryon one day that it was the best of guns, and had turned his head to me, and said:

"Gill Davis, load her fresh with a couple of slugs, against a chance of showing how good she is."

So, I had discharged the gun over the sea, and had loaded her, according to orders, and there it had lain at the Captain's feet, convenient to the Captain's hand.

The last day but one of our journey was an uncommonly hot day. We started very early; but, there was no cool air on the sea as the day got on, and by noon the heat was really hard to bear, considering that there were women and children to bear it. Now, we happened to open, just at that time, a very pleasant little cove or bay, where there was a deep shade from a great growth of trees. Now, the Captain, therefore, made this signal to the other boats to follow him in and lie by a while.

The men who were off duty went ashore, and lay down, but were ordered, for caution's sake, not to stray, and to keep within view. The others rested on their oars, and dozed. Awnings had been made of one thing and another, in all the boats, and the passengers found it cooler to be under them in the shade, when there was room enough, than to be in the thick woods. So, the passengers were all afloat, and mostly sleeping. I kept my post behind Miss Maryon, and she was on Captain Carton's right in the boat, and Mrs. Fisher sat on her right again. The Captain had Mrs. Fisher's daughter on his knee. He and the two ladies were talking about the Pirates, and were talking softly ; partly, because people do talk softly under such indolent circumstances, and partly because the little girl had gone off asleep.

I think I have before given it out for my Lady to write down, that Captain Carton had a fine bright eye of his own. All at once, he darted me a side look, as much as to say, "Steady—don't take on—I see something!"—and gave the child into her mother's arms. That eye of his was so easy to understand, that I obeyed it by not so much as looking either to the right or to the left out of a corner of my own, or changing my attitude the least trifle. The Captain went on talking in the same mild and easy way; but began—with his arms resting across his knees, and his head a little hanging forward, as if the heat were rather too much for him—began to play with the Spanish gun.

"They had laid their plans, you see," says the Captain, taking up the Spanish gun across his knees, and looking, lazily, at the inlaying on the stock, "with a great deal of art; and the corrupt or blundering local authorities were so easily deceived;" he ran his left hand idly along the barrel, but I saw, with my breath held, that he covered the action of cocking the gun with his right—"so easily deceived, that they summoned us out to come into the trap. But my intention as to future operations——" In a flash the Spanish gun was at his bright eye, and he fired.

All started up; innumerable echoes repeated the sound of the discharge; a cloud of bright-coloured birds flew out of the wood screaming; a handful of leaves were scattered in the place where the shot had struck; a crackling of branches was heard; and some lithe but heavy creature sprang into the air, and fell forward, head down, over the muddy bank.

"What is it?" cries Captain Maryon from his boat. All silent then, but the echoes rolling away.

"It is a Traitor and a Spy," said Captain Carton, handing me the gun to load again. "And I think the other name of the animal is Christian George King!"

Shot through the heart. Some of the people ran round to the spot, and drew him out, with the slime and wet trickling down his face;

but his face itself would never stir any more to the end of time.

"Leave him hanging to that tree," cried Captain Carton; his boat's crew giving way, and he leaping ashore. "But first into this wood, every man in his place. And boats! Out of gunshot!"

It was a quick change, well meant and well made, though it ended in disappointment. No Pirates were there; no one but the Spy was found. It was supposed that the Pirates, unable to retake us, and expecting a great attack upon them to be the consequences of our escape, had made from the ruins in the Forest, taken to their ship along with the Treasure, and left the Spy to pick up what intelligence he could. In the evening we went away, and he was left hanging to the tree, all alone, with the red sun making a kind of a dead sunset on his black face.

Next day, we gained the settlement on the Mosquito coast for which we were bound. Having stayed there to refresh seven days, and having been much commended, and highly spoken of and finely entertained, we Marines stood under orders to march from the Town-gate (it was neither much of a town nor much of a gate), at five in the morning.

My officer had joined us before then. When we turned out at the gate, all the people were there; in the front of them all those who had been our fellow-prisoners, and all the seamen.

"Davis," says Lieutenant Linderwood. "Stand out, my friend!"

I stood out from the ranks, and Miss Maryon and Captain Carton came up to me.

"Dear Davis," says Miss Maryon, while the tears fell fast down her face, "your grateful friends, in most unwillingly taking leave of you, ask the favour that, while you bear away with you their affectionate remembrance, which nothing can ever impair, you will also take this purse of money—far more valuable to you, we all know, for the deep attachment and thankfulness with which it is offered, than for its own contents, though we hope those may prove useful to you, too, in after life."

I got out, in answer, that I thankfully accepted the attachment and affection, but not the money. Captain Carton looked at me very attentively, and stepped back, and moved away. I made him my bow as he stepped back, to thank him for being so delicate.

"No, Miss," said I, "I think it would break my heart to accept of money. But, if you could condescend to give to a man so ignorant and common as myself, any little thing you have worn—such as a bit of ribbon——"

She took a ring from her finger, and put it in my hand. And she rested her hand in mine, while she said these words:

" The brave gentlemen of old—but not one of them was braver, or had a nobler nature than you—took such gifts from ladies, and did all their good actions for the givers' sakes. If you will do yours for mine, I shall think with pride that I continue to have some share in the life of a gallant and generous man."

For the second time in my life she kissed my hand. I made so bold, for the first time, as to kiss hers; and I tied the ring at my breast, and I fell back to my place.

Then, the horse-litter went out at the gate with Sergeant Drooce in it; and the horse-litter went out at the gate with Mrs. Belltott in it; and Lieutenant Linderwood gave the word of command, "Quick march!" and, cheered and cried for, we went out of the gate too, marching along the level plain towards the serene blue sky, as if we were marching straight to Heaven.

When I have added here that the Pirate scheme was blown to shivers, by the Pirate-ship which had the Treasure on board being so vigorously attacked by one of His Majesty's cruisers, among the West-India Keys, and being so swiftly boarded and carried, that nobody suspected anything about the scheme until three-fourths of the Pirates were killed, and the other fourth were in irons, and the Treasure was recovered; I come to the last singular confession I have got to make.

It is this. I well knew what an immense and hopeless distance there was between me and Miss Maryon; I well knew that I was no fitter company for her than I was for the angels; I well knew that she was as high above my reach as the sky over my head; and yet I loved her. What put it in my low heart to be so daring, or whether such a thing ever happened before or since, as that a man so uninstructed and obscure as myself got his unhappy thoughts lifted up to such a height, while knowing very well how presumptuous and impossible to be realised they were, I am unable to say; still, the suffering to me was just as great as if I had been a gentleman. I suffered agony—agony. I suffered hard, and I suffered long. I thought of her last words to me, however, and I never disgraced them. If it had not been for those dear words, I think I should have lost myself in despair and recklessness.

The ring will be found lying on my heart, of course, and will be laid with me wherever I am laid. I am getting on in years now, though I am able and hearty. I was recommended for promotion, and everything was done to reward me that could be done; but my total want of all learning stood in my way, and I found myself so completely out of the road to it, that I could not conquer any learning, though I tried. I was long in the service, and I respected it, and was respected in it, and the service is dear to me at this present hour.

At this present hour, when I give this out to my Lady to be written down, all my old pain has softened away, and I am as happy as a man can be, at this present fine old country-house of Admiral Sir George Carton, Baronet. It was my Lady Carton who herself sought me out, over a great many miles of the wide world, and found me in Hospital wounded, and brought me here. It is my Lady Carton who writes down my words. My Lady was Miss Maryon. And now, that I conclude what I had to tell, I see my Lady's honoured gray hair droop over her face, as she leans a little lower at her desk; and I fervently thank her for being so tender as I see she is, towards the past pain and trouble of her poor, old, faithful, humble soldier.

GOING INTO SOCIETY

[1858]

AT one period of its reverses, the House fell into the occupation of a Showman. He was found registered as its occupier, on the parish books of the time when he rented the House, and there was therefore no need of any clue to his name. But, he himself was less easy to be found; for, he had led a wandering life, and settled people had lost sight of him, and people who plumed themselves on being respectable were shy of admitting that they had ever known anything of him. At last, among the marsh lands near the river's level, that lie about Deptford and the neighbouring market-gardens, a Grizzled Personage in velveteen, with a face so cut up by varieties of weather that he looked as if he had been tattooed, was found smoking a pipe at the door of a wooden house on wheels. The wooden house was laid up in ordinary for the winter, near the mouth of a muddy creek; and everything near it, the foggy river, the misty marshes, and the steaming market-gardens, smoked in company with the grizzled man. In the midst of this smoking party, the funnel-chimney of the wooden house on wheels was not remiss, but took its pipe with the rest in a companionable manner.

On being asked if it were he who had once rented the House to Let, Grizzled Velveteen looked surprised, and said yes. Then his name was Magsman? That was it, Toby Magsman—which lawfully christened Robert; but called in the line, from a infant, Toby. There was nothing agin Toby Magsman, he believed? If there was suspicion of such— mention it!

There was no suspicion of such, he might rest assured. But, some inquiries were making about that House, and would he object to say why he left it?

Not at all; why should he? He left it, along of a Dwarf.

Along of a Dwarf?

Mr. Magsman repeated, deliberately and emphatically, Along of a Dwarf.

Might it be compatible with Mr. Magsman's inclination and convenience to enter, as a favour, into a few particulars?

Mr. Magsman entered into the following particulars.

It was a long time ago, to begin with;—afore lotteries and a deal more was done away with. Mr. Magsman was looking about for a good pitch, and he see that house, and he says to himself, "I'll have you, if you're to be had. If money'll get you, I'll have you."

The neighbours cut up rough, and made complaints; but Mr. Magsman don't know what they *would* have had. It was a lovely thing. First of all, there was the canvas, representing the picter of the Giant, in Spanish trunks and a ruff, who was himself half the heighth of the house, and was run up with a line and pulley to a pole on the roof, so that his Ed was coeval with the parapet. Then, there was the canvas, representin the picter of the Albina lady, showing her white air to the Army and Navy in correct uniform. Then, there was the canvas, representin the picter of the Wild Indian a scalpin a member of some foreign nation. Then, there was the canvas, representin the picter of a child of a British Planter, seized by two Boa Constrictors—not that *we* never had no child, nor no Constrictors neither. Similarly, there was the canvas, representin the picter of the Wild Ass of the Prairies—not that *we* never had no wild asses, nor wouldn't have had 'em at a gift. Last, there was the canvas, representin the picter of the Dwarf, and like him too (considerin), with George the Fourth in such a state of astonishment at him as His Majesty couldn't with his utmost politeness and stoutness express. The front of the House was so covered with canvases, that there wasn't a spark of daylight ever visible on that side. "MAGSMAN'S AMUSEMENTS," fifteen foot long by two foot high, ran over the front door and parlour winders. The passage was a Arbour of green baize and gardenstuff. A barrel-organ performed there unceasing. And as to respectability,—if threepence ain't respectable, what is?

But, the Dwarf is the principal article at present, and he was worth the money. He was wrote up as MAJOR TPSCHOFFKI, OF THE IMPERIAL BULGRADERIAN BRIGADE. Nobody couldn't pronounce the name, and it never was intended anybody should. The public always turned it, as a regular rule, into Chopski. In the line he was called Chops; partly on that account, and partly because his real name, if he ever had any real name (which was very dubious), was Stakes.

He was a uncommon small man, he really was. Certainly not so small as he was made out to be, but were *is* your Dwarf as is? He was a most uncommon small man, with a most uncommon large Ed; and what he had inside that Ed, nobody never knowed but himself: even supposin himself to have ever took stock of it, which it would have been a stiff job for even him to do.

The kindest little man as never growed! Spirited, but not proud. When he travelled with the Spotted Baby—though he knowed himself to be a nat'ral Dwarf, and knowed the Baby's spots to be put upon him artificial, he nursed that baby like a mother. You never heerd him give a ill-name to a Giant. He *did* allow himself to break out into strong language respectin the Fat Lady from Norfolk; but that was an affair of the 'art; and when a man's 'art has been trifled with by a lady, and the preference giv to a Indian, he ain't master of his actions.

He was always in love, of course; every human nat'ral phenomenon is. And he was always in love with a large woman; *I* never knowed the Dwarf as could be got to love a small one. Which helps to keep 'em the Curiosities they are.

One sing'ler idea he had in that Ed of his, which must have meant something, or it wouldn't have been there. It was always his opinion that he was entitled to property. He never would put his name to anything. He had been taught to write, by the young man without arms, who got his living with his toes (quite a writing-master *he* was, and taught scores in the line), but Chops would have starved to death afore he'd have gained a bit of bread by putting his hand to a paper. This is the more curious to bear in mind, because HE had no property, nor hope of property except his house and a sarser. When I say his house, I mean the box, painted and got up outside like a reg'lar six-roomer, that he used to creep into, with a diamond ring (or quite as good to look at) on his forefinger, and ring a little bell out of what the Public believed to be the Drawing-room window. And when I say a sarser, I mean a Chaney sarser in which he made a collection for himself at the end of every Entertainment. His cue for that, he took from me; "Ladies and gentlemen, the little man will now walk three times round the Cairawan, and retire behind the curtain." When he said anything important, in private life, he mostly wound it up with this form of words, and they was generally the last thing he said to me at night afore he went to bed.

He had what I consider a fine mind—a poetic mind. His ideas respectin his property never come upon him so strong as when he sat upon a barrel-organ and had the handle turned. Arter the wibration had run through him a little time, he would screech out, "Toby, I feel my property coming—grind away! I'm counting my guineas by thousands, Toby—grind away! Toby, I shall be a man of fortun! I feel the Mint a jingling in me, Toby, and I'm swelling out into the Bank of England!" Such is the influence of music on a poetic mind. Not that he was partial to any other music but a barrel-organ; on the contrary, hated it.

He had a kind of everlasting grudge agin the Public; which is a thing you may notice in many phenomenons that get their living out of it. What riled him most in the nater of his occupation was, that it kep him out of Society. He was continiwally saying, "Toby, my ambition is, to go into Society. The curse of my position towards the Public is, that it keeps me hout of Society. This don't signify to a low beast of a Indian; he an't formed for Society. This don't signify to a Spotted Baby; *he* an't formed for Society.—I am."

Nobody never could make out what Chops done with his money. He had a good salary, down on the drum every Saturday as the day came round, besides having the run of his teeth—and he was a Woodpecker to eat—but all Dwarfs are. The sarser was a little income bringing him in so many halfpence that he'd carry 'em for a week together, tied up in a pocket-handkercher. And yet he never had money. And it couldn't be the Fat Lady from Norfolk, as was once supposed; because it stands to reason that when you have a animosity towards a Indian, which makes you grind your teeth at him to his face, and which can hardly hold you from Goosing him audible when he's going through his War-Dance—it stands to reason you wouldn't under them circumstances deprive yourself to support that Indian in the lap of luxury.

Most unexpected, the mystery came out one day at Egham Races. The Public was shy of bein pulled in, and Chops was ringin his little bell out of his drawing-room winder, and was snarling to me over his shoulder as he kneeled down with his legs out at the back-door—for he couldn't be shoved into his house without kneeling down, and the premises wouldn't accommodate his legs—was snarlin, "Here's a precious Public for you; why the Devil don't they tumble up?" when a man in the crowd holds up a carrier-pigeon, and cries out, "If there's any person here as has got a ticket, the Lottery's just drawed, and the number as has come up for the great prize is three, seven, forty-two! Three, seven, forty-two!" I was givin the man to the Furies myself, for calling off the Public's attention—for the Public will turn away, at any time, to look at anything in preference to the thing showed 'em; and if you doubt it, get 'em together for any indiwidual purpose on the face of the earth, and send only two people in late, and see if the whole company an't far more interested in takin particular notice of them two than of you—I say, I wasn't best pleased with the man for callin out, and wasn't blessin him in my own mind, when I see Chops's little bell fly out of winder at a old lady, and he gets up and kicks his box over, exposin the whole secret, and he catches hold of the calves of my legs and he says to me, "Carry me into the wan, Toby, and throw a pail of water over me or I'm a dead man, for I've come into my property!"

Twelve thousand odd hundred pound, was Chops's winnins. He had bought a half-ticket for the twenty-five thousand prize, and it had come up. The first use he made of his property, was to offer to fight the Wild Indian for five hundred pound a side, him with a poisoned darnin-needle and the Indian with a club; but the Indian being in want of backers to that amount, it went no further.

Arter he had been mad for a week—in a state of mind, in short, in which, if I had let him sit on the organ for only two minutes, I believe he would have bust—but we kep the organ from him—Mr. Chops come round, and behaved liberal and beautiful to all. He then sent for a young man he knowed, as had a wery genteel appearance and was a Bonnet at a gaming-booth (most respectable brought up, father having been imminent in the livery stable line but unfort'nate in a commercial crisis, through paintin a old gray, ginger-bay, and sellin him with a Pedigree), and Mr. Chops said to this Bonnet, who said his name was Normandy, which it wasn't:

"Normandy, I'm a goin into Society. Will you go with me?"

Says Normandy: "Do I understand you, Mr. Chops, to hintimate that the 'ole of the expenses of that move will be borne by yourself?"

"Correct," says Mr. Chops. "And you shall have a princely allowance too."

The Bonnet lifted Mr. Chops upon a chair, to shake hands with him, and replied in poetry, with his eyes seemingly full of tears:

> "My boat is on the shore,
> And my bark is on the sea,
> And I do not ask for more,
> But I'll Go:—along with thee."

They went into Society, in a chay and four grays with silk jackets. They took lodgings in Pall Mall, London, and they blazed away.

In consequence of a note that was brought to Bartlemy Fair in the autumn of next year by a servant, most wonderful got up in milk-white cords and tops, I cleaned myself and went to Pall Mall, one evening appointed. The gentlemen was at their wine arter dinner, and Mr. Chops's eyes was more fixed in that Ed of his than I thought good for him. There was three of 'em (in company, I mean) and I knowed the third well. When last met, he had on a white Roman shirt, and a bishop's mitre covered with leopard-skin, and played the clarionet all wrong, in a band at a Wild Beast Show.

This gent took on not to know me, and Mr. Chops said: "Gentlemen, this is a old friend of former days:" and Normandy looked at me through a eye-glass, and said, "Magsman, glad to see you!"—which I'll take my oath he wasn't. Mr. Chops, to git him convenient to the table, had his chair on a throne (much of the form of George the Fourth's in the canvas), but he hardly appeared to me to be King there in any other pint of view, for his two gentlemen ordered about like Emperors. They was all dressed like May-Day—gorgeous!—and as to Wine, they swam in all sorts.

I made the round of the bottles, first separate (to say I had done it), and then mixed 'em all together (to say I had done it), and then tried two of 'em as half-and-half, and then t'other two. Altogether, I passed a pleasin evenin, but with a tendency to feel muddled, until I considered it good manners to get up and say, "Mr. Chops, the best of friends must part, I thank you for the wariety of foreign drains you have stood so 'ansome, I looks towards you in red wine, and I takes my leave," Mr. Chops replied, "If you'll just hitch me out of this over your right arm, Magsman, and carry me downstairs, I'll see you out." I said I couldn't think of such a thing, but he would have it, so I lifted him off his throne. He smelt strong of Maideary, and I couldn't help thinking as I carried him down that it was like carrying a large bottle full of wine, with a rayther ugly stopper, a good deal out of proportion.

When I set him on the door-mat in the hall, he kep me close to him by holding on to my coat-collar, and he whispers:

"I ain't 'appy, Magsman."

"What's on your mind, Mr. Chops?"

"They don't use me well. They ain't grateful to me. They puts me on the mantel-piece when I won't have in more Champagne-wine, and they locks me in the sideboard when I won't give up my property."

"Get rid of 'em, Mr. Chops."

"I can't. We're in Society together and what would Society say?"

"Come out of Society!" says I.

"I can't. You don't know what you're talking about. When you have once gone into Society, you mustn't come out of it."

"Then if you'll excuse the freedom, Mr. Chops," were my remark, shaking my head grave, "I think it's a pity you ever went in."

Mr. Chops shook that deep Ed of his, to a surprisin extent, and slapped it half-a-dozen times with his hand, and with more Wice than I thought were in him. Then, he says, "You're a good fellow, but you don't understand. Good night, go along. Magsman, the little man will now walk three times round the Cairawan, and retire behind the curtain." The last I see of him on that occasion was his tryin, on the extremest werge of insensibility, to climb up the stairs, one by one, with his hands and knees. They'd have been much too steep for him, if he had been sober; but he wouldn't be helped.

It warn't long after that, that I read in the newspaper of Mr. Chops's being presented at court. It was printed, "It will be recollected"—and I've noticed in my life, that it is sure to be printed that it *will* be recollected, whenever it won't—"that Mr. Chops is the individual of small stature, whose brilliant success in the last State Lottery attracted so much attention." Well, I says to myself, Such is Life! He has been and done it in earnest at last! He has astonished George the Fourth!

(On account of which, I had that canvas new-painted, him with a bag of money in his hand, a presentin it to George the Fourth, and a lady in Ostrich Feathers fallin in love with him in a bag-wig, sword, and buckles correct.)

I took the House as is the subject of present inquiries—though not the honour of bein acquainted—and I run Magsman's Amusements in it thirteen months—sometimes one thing, sometimes another, sometimes nothin particular, but always all the canvases outside. One night, when we had played the last company out, which was a shy company, through its raining Heavens hard, I was takin a pipe in the one pair back along with the young man with the toes, which I had taken on for a month (though he never drawed—except on paper), and I heard a kickin at the street door. "Halloa!" I says to the young man, "what's up?" He rubs his eyebrows with his toes, and he says, "I can't imagine, Mr. Magsman"—which he never could imagine nothin, and was monotonous company.

The noise not leavin off, I laid down my pipe, and I took up a candle, and I went down and opened the door. I looked out into the street; but nothin could I see, and nothin was I aware of, until I turned round quick, because some creetur run between my legs into the passage. There was Mr. Chops!

"Magsman," he says, "take me, on the old terms, and you've got me; if it's done, say done!"

I was all of a maze, but I said, "Done, Sir."

"Done to your done, and double done!" says he. "Have you got a bit of supper in the house?"

Bearin in mind them sparklin warieties of foreign drains as we'd guzzled away at in Pall Mall, I was ashamed to offer him cold sassages and gin-and-water; but he took 'em both and took 'em free; havin a chair for his table, and sittin down at it on a stool, like hold times. I, all of a maze all the while.

It was arter he had made a clean sweep of the sassages (beef, and to the best of my calculations two pound and a quarter), that the wisdom as was in that little man began to come out of him like perspiration.

"Magsman," he says, "look upon me! You see afore you, One as has both gone into Society and come out."

"O! You *are* out of it, Mr. Chops? How did you get out, Sir?"

"SOLD OUT!" says he. You never saw the like of the wisdom as his Ed expressed, when he made use of them two words.

"My friend Magsman, I'll impart to you a discovery I've made. It's wallable; it's cost twelve thousand five hundred pound; it may do you good in life.—The secret of this matter is, that it ain't so much that a person goes into Society, as that Society goes into a person."

Not exactly keepin up with his meanin, I shook my head, put on a deep look, and said, "You're right there, Mr. Chops."

"Magsman," he says, twitchin me by the leg, "Society has gone into me, to the tune of every penny of my property."

I felt that I went pale, and though nat'rally a bold speaker, I couldn't hardly say, "Where's Normandy?"

"Bolted. With the plate," said Mr. Chops.

"And t'other one?" meaning him as formerly wore the bishop's mitre.

"Bolted. With the jewels," said Mr. Chops.

I sat down and looked at him, and he stood up and looked at me.

"Magsman," he says, and he seemed to myself to get wiser as he got hoarser; "Society, taken in the lump, is all dwarfs. At the court of St. James's, they was all a doing my old business—all a going three times round the Cairawan, in the hold court-suits and properties. Elsewheres, they was most of 'em ringin their little bells out of make-believes. Everywheres, the sarser was a goin round. Magsman, the sarser is the uniwersal Institution!"

I perceived, you understand, that he was soured by his misfortuns, and I felt for Mr. Chops.

"As to Fat Ladies," says he, giving his head a tremendious one agin the wall, "there's lots of *them* in Society, and worse than the original. *Hers* was a outrage upon Taste—simply a outrage upon Taste—awaken in contempt—carryin its own punishment in the form of a Indian!" Here he giv himself another tremendious one. "But *theirs*, Magsman, *theirs* is mercenary outrages. Lay in Cashmeer shawls, buy bracelets, strew 'em and a lot of 'andsome fans and things about your rooms, let it be known that you give away like water to all as come to admire, and the Fat Ladies that don't exhibit for so much down upon the drum, will come from all the pints of the compass to flock about you, whatever you are. They'll drill holes in

Mayor Tpschoffki, the Dwarf, Returns to Magsman's Show.

our 'art, Magsman, like a Cullender. And when you've no more left
o give, they'll laugh at you to your face, and leave you to have your
bones picked dry by Wulturs, like the dead Wild Ass of the Prairies
hat you deserve to be!" Here he giv himself the most tremendious
one of all, and dropped.

I thought he was gone. His Ed was so heavy, and he knocked it so
hard, and he fell so stoney, and the sassagerial disturbance in him
must have been so immense, that I thought he was gone. But, he
soon come round with care, and he sat up on the floor, and he said to
me, with wisdom comin out of his eyes, if ever it come:

"Magsman! The most material difference between the two states
of existence through which your unappy friend has passed;" he
reached out his poor little hand, and his tears dropped down on the
moustachio which it was a credit to him to have done his best to grow,
out it is not in mortals to command success,—"the difference is this.
When I was out of Society, I was paid light for being seen. When I
went into Society, I paid heavy for being seen. I prefer the former,
even if I wasn't forced upon it. Give me out through the trumpet, in
the hold way, to-morrow."

Arter that, he slid into the line again as easy as if he had been iled
all over. But the organ was kep from him, and no allusions was ever
made, when a company was in, to his property. He got wiser every
day; his views of Society and the Public was luminous, bewilderin,
awful; and his Ed got bigger and bigger as his Wisdom expanded it.

He took well, and pulled 'em in most excellent for nine weeks. At
the expiration of that period, when his Ed was a sight, he expressed
one evenin, the last Company havin been turned out, and the door
shut, a wish to have a little music.

"Mr. Chops," I said (I never dropped the "Mr." with him; the
world might do it, but not me); "Mr. Chops, are you sure as you are
in a state of mind and body to sit upon the organ?"

His answer was this: "Toby, when next met with on the tramp, I
orgive her and the Indian. And I am."

It was with fear and trembling that I began to turn the handle; but
he sat like a lamb. It will be my belief to my dying day, that I see his
Ed expand as he sat; you may therefore judge how great his thoughts
was. He sat out all the changes, and then he come off.

"Toby," he says, with a quiet smile, "the little man will now walk
three times round the Cairawan, and retire behind the curtain."

When we called him in the morning, we found him gone into a
much better Society than mine or Pall Mall's. I giv Mr. Chops as
comfortable a funeral as lay in my power, followed myself as Chief,
and had the George the Fourth canvas carried first, in the form of a
banner. But, the House was so dismal arterwards, that I giv it up, and
took to the Wan again.

"I don't triumph," said Jarber, folding up the second manuscript,
and looking hard at Trottle. "I don't triumph over this worthy
creature. I merely ask him if he is satisfied now?"

"How can he be anything else?" I said, answering for Trottle, wh sat obstinately silent. "This time, Jarber, you have not only read a delightfully amusing story, but you have also answered the questic about the House. Of course it stands empty now. Who would thin of taking it after it had been turned into a caravan?" I looked Trottle, as I said those last words, and Jarber waved his hand indu gently in the same direction.

"Let this excellent person speak," said Jarber. "You were abov to say, my good man——?"

"I only wished to ask, Sir," said Trottle doggedly, "if you coul kindly oblige me with a date or two in connexion with that last story

"A date!" repeated Jarber. "What does the man want with dates?

"I should be glad to know, with great respect," persisted Trottl "if the person named Magsman was the last tenant who lived in tl House. It's my opinion—if I may be excused for giving it—that I most decidedly was not."

With those words, Trottle made a low bow, and quietly left tl room.

There is no denying that Jarber, when we were left together, looke sadly discomposed. He had evidently forgotten to inquire about date and, in spite of his magnificent talk about his series of discoveries, was quite as plain that the two stories he had just read, had reall and truly exhausted his present stock. I thought myself bound, i common gratitude, to help him out of his embarrassment by a timel suggestion. So I proposed that he should come to tea again, on tl next Monday evening, the thirteenth, and should make such inquiri in the meantime, as might enable him to dispose triumphantly Trottle's objection.

He gallantly kissed my hand, made a neat little speech of acknov ledgement, and took his leave. For the rest of the week I would n encourage Trottle by allowing him to refer to the House at all. I su pected he was making his own inquiries about dates, but I put i questions to him.

On Monday evening, the thirteenth, that dear unfortunate Jarb came, punctual to the appointed time. He looked so terribly harasse that he was really quite a spectacle of feebleness and fatigue. I sav at a glance, that the question of dates had gone against him, that M Magsman had not been the last tenant of the House, and that tl reason of its emptiness was still to seek.

"What I have gone through," said Jarber, "words are not eloque enough to tell. O Sophonisba, I have begun another series of di coveries! Accept the last two as stories laid on your shrine; and wa to blame me for leaving your curiosity unappeased, until you hav heard Number Three."

Number Three looked like a very short manuscript, and I said much. Jarber explained to me that we were to have some poetry th time. In the course of his investigations he had stepped into the Ci culating Library, to seek for information on the one important sul ject. All the Library-people knew about the House was, that a fema

elative of the last tenant, as they believed, had, just after that
enant left, sent a little manuscript poem to them, which she des-
ribed as referring to events that had actually passed in the House;
.nd which she wanted the proprietor of the Library to publish. She
1ad written no address on her letter; and the proprietor had kept the
nanuscript ready to be given back to her (the publishing of poems
1ot being in his line) when she might call for it. She had never called
or it; and the poem had been lent to Jarber, at his express request,
:o read to me.

Before he began, I rang the bell for Trottle; being determined to
1ave him present at the new reading, as a wholesome check on his
obstinacy. To my surprise Peggy answered the bell, and told me that
Trottle had stepped out without saying where. I instantly felt the
strongest possible conviction that he was at his old tricks: and that
his stepping out in the evening, without leave, meant—Philandering.

Controlling myself on my visitor's account, I dismissed Peggy,
stifled my indignation, and prepared, as politely as might be, to
listen to Jarber.

THE HAUNTED HOUSE

IN TWO CHAPTERS *

[1859]

THE MORTALS IN THE HOUSE

UNDER none of the accredited ghostly circumstances, and environed by none of the conventional ghostly surroundings, did I first make acquaintance with the house which is the subject of this Christmas piece. I saw it in the daylight, with the sun upon it. There was no wind, no rain, no lightning, no thunder, no awful or unwonted circumstance, of any kind, to heighten its effect. More than that : I had come to it direct from a railway station: it was more than a mile distant from the railway station; and, as I stood outside the house, looking back upon the way I had come, I could see the goods train running smoothly along the embankment in the valley. I will not say that everything was utterly commonplace, because I doubt if anything can be that, except to utterly commonplace people—and there my vanity steps in; but, I will take it on myself to say that anybody might see the house as I saw it, any fine autumn morning.

The manner of my lighting on it was this.

I was travelling towards London out of the North, intending to stop by the way, to look at the house. My health required a temporary residence in the country; and a friend of mine who knew that, and who had happened to drive past the house, had written to me to suggest it as a likely place. I had got into the train at midnight, and had fallen asleep, and had woke up and had sat looking out of the window at the brilliant Northern Lights in the sky, and had fallen asleep again, and had woke up again to find the night gone, with the usual discontented conviction on me that I hadn't been to sleep at all;—upon which question, in the first imbecility of that condition, I am ashamed to believe that I would have done wager by battle with the man who sat opposite me. That opposite man had had, through the night—as that opposite man always has—several legs too many, and all of them too long. In addition to this unreasonable conduct (which was only to be expected of him), he had had a pencil and a pocket-book, and had been perpetually listening and taking notes. It had

* The original has eight chapters, which will be found in *All the Year Round*, vol. ii., old series; but those not printed here, excepting a page at the close, were not written by Mr. Dickens.

appeared to me that these aggravating notes related to the jolts and bumps of the carriage, and I should have resigned myself to his taking them, under a general supposition that he was in the civil-engineering way of life, if he had not sat staring straight over my head whenever he listened. He was a goggle-eyed gentleman of a perplexed aspect, and his demeanour became unbearable.

It was a cold, dead morning (the sun not being up yet), and when I had out-watched the paling light of the fires of the iron country, and the curtain of heavy smoke that hung at once between me and the stars and between me and the day, I turned to my fellow-traveller and said:

"I *beg* your pardon, Sir, but do you observe anything particular in me?" For, really, he appeared to be taking down, either my travelling-cap or my hair, with a minuteness that was a liberty.

The goggle-eyed gentleman withdrew his eyes from behind me, as if the back of the carriage were a hundred miles off, and said, with a lofty look of compassion for my insignificance:

"In you, Sir?—B."

"B, Sir?" said I, growing warm.

"I have nothing to do with you, Sir," returned the gentleman; "pray let me listen—O."

He enunciated this vowel after a pause, and noted it down.

At first I was alarmed, for an Express lunatic and no communication with the guard, is a serious position. The thought came to my relief that the gentleman might be what is popularly called a Rapper : one of a sect for (some of) whom I have the highest respect, but whom I don't believe in. I was going to ask him the question, when he took the bread out of my mouth.

"You will excuse me," said the gentleman contemptuously, "if I am too much in advance of common humanity to trouble myself at all about it. I have passed the night—as indeed I pass the whole of my time now—in spiritual intercourse."

"O!" said I, something snappishly.

"The conferences of the night began," continued the gentleman, turning several leaves of his note-book, "with this message: 'Evil communications corrupt good manners.'"

"Sound," said I; "but, absolutely new?"

"New from spirits," returned the gentleman.

I could only repeat my rather snappish "O!" and ask if I might be favoured with the last communication.

"'A bird in the hand,'" said the gentleman, reading his last entry with great solemnity, "'is worth two in the Bosh.'"

"Truly I am of the same opinion," said I; "but shouldn't it be Bush?"

"It came to me, Bosh," returned the gentleman.

The gentleman then informed me that the spirit of Socrates had delivered this special revelation in the course of the night. "My friend, I hope you are pretty well. There are two in this railway carriage. How do you do? There are seventeen thousand four hundred

and seventy-nine spirits here, but you cannot see them. Pythagoras i
here. He is not at liberty to mention it, but hopes you like travelling.
Galileo likewise had dropped in, with this scientific intelligence, "
am glad to see you, *amico. Come sta?* Water will freeze when it is col
enough. *Addio*!" In the course of the night, also, the following pheno
mena had occurred. Bishop Butler had insisted on spelling his name
"Bubler," for which offence against orthography and good manner
he had been dismissed as out of temper. John Milton (suspected o
wilful mystification) had repudiated the authorship of Paradise Los
and had introduced, as joint authors of that poem, two Unknow
gentlemen, respectively named Grungers and Scadgingtone. An
Prince Arthur, nephew of King John of England, had described him
self as tolerably comfortable in the seventh circle, where he was learn
ing to paint on velvet, under the direction of Mrs. Trimmer and Mar
Queen of Scots.

If this should meet the eye of the gentleman who favoured m
with these disclosures, I trust he will excuse my confessing that th
sight of the rising sun, and the contemplation of the magnificen
Order of the vast Universe, made me impatient of them. In a word
I was so impatient of them, that I was mightily glad to get out at th
next station, and to exchange these clouds and vapours for the fre
air of Heaven.

By that time it was a beautiful morning. As I walked away amon
such leaves as had already fallen from the golden, brown, and russe
trees; and as I looked around me on the wonders of Creation, an
thought of the steady, unchanging, and harmonious laws by whic
they are sustained; the gentleman's spiritual intercourse seemed t
me as poor a piece of journey-work as ever this world saw. In whic
heathen state of mind, I came within view of the house, and stoppe
to examine it attentively.

It was a solitary house, standing in a sadly neglected garden:
pretty even square of some two acres. It was a house of about th
time of George the Second; as stiff, as cold, as formal, and in as ba
taste, as could possibly be desired by the most loyal admirer of th
whole quartet of Georges. It was uninhabited, but had, within a yea
or two, been cheaply repaired to render it habitable; I say cheaply
because the work had been done in a surface manner, and wa
already decaying as to the paint and plaster, though the colours wer
fresh. A lop-sided board drooped over the garden wall, announcin
that it was "to let on very reasonable terms, well furnished." It wa
much too closely and heavily shadowed by trees, and, in particular
there were six tall poplars before the front windows, which were ex
cessively melancholy, and the site of which had been extremely il
chosen.

It was easy to see that it was an avoided house—a house that wa
shunned by the village, to which my eye was guided by a churc
spire some half a mile off—a house that nobody would take. And th
natural inference was, that it had the reputation of being a haunte
house.

No period within the four-and-twenty hours of day and night is so solemn to me, as the early morning. In the summer time, I often rise very early, and repair to my room to do a day's work before breakfast, and I am always on those occasions deeply impressed by the stillness and solitude around me. Besides that there is something awful in the being surrounded by familiar faces asleep—in the knowledge that those who are dearest to us and to whom we are dearest, are profoundly unconscious of us, in an impassive state, anticipative of that mysterious condition to which we are all tending—the stopped life, the broken threads of yesterday, the deserted seat, the closed book, the unfinished but abandoned occupation, all are images of Death. The tranquillity of the hour is the tranquillity of Death. The colour and the chill have the same association. Even a certain air that familiar household objects take upon them when they first emerge from the shadows of the night into the morning, of being newer, and as they used to be long ago, has its counterpart in the subsidence of the worn face of maturity or age, in death, into the old youthful look. Moreover, I once saw the apparition of my father, at this hour. He was alive and well, and nothing ever came of it, but I saw him in the daylight, sitting with his back towards me, on a seat that stood beside my bed. His head was resting on his hand, and whether he was slumbering or grieving, I could not discern. Amazed to see him there, I sat up, moved my position, leaned out of bed, and watched him. As he did not move, I spoke to him more than once. As he did not move then, I became alarmed and laid my hand upon his shoulder, as I thought—and there was no such thing.

For all these reasons, and for others less easily and briefly statable, I find the early morning to be my most ghostly time. Any house would be more or less haunted, to me, in the early morning; and a haunted house could scarcely address me to greater advantage than then.

I walked on into the village, with the desertion of this house upon my mind, and I found the landlord of the little inn, sanding his door-step. I bespoke breakfast, and broached the subject of the house.

"Is it haunted?" I asked.

The landlord looked at me, shook his head, and answered, "I say nothing."

"Then it *is* haunted?"

"Well!" cried the landlord, in an outburst of frankness that had the appearance of desperation—"I wouldn't sleep in it."

"Why not?"

"If I wanted to have all the bells in a house ring, with nobody to ring 'em; and all the doors in a house bang, with nobody to bang 'em; and all sorts of feet treading about, with no feet there; why, then," said the landlord, "I'd sleep in that house."

"Is anything seen there?"

The landlord looked at me again, and then, with his former appearance of desperation, called down his stable-yard for "Ikey!"

The call produced a high-shouldered young fellow, with a round red face, a short crop of sandy hair, a very broad humorous mouth, a turned-up nose, and a great sleeved waistcoat of purple bars, with mother-of-pearl buttons, that seemed to be growing upon him, and to be in a fair way—if it were not pruned—of covering his head and overrunning his boots.

"This gentleman wants to know," said the landlord, "if anything's seen at the Poplars."

" 'Ooded woman with a howl," said Ikey, in a state of great freshness.

"Do you mean a cry?"

"I mean a bird, Sir."

"A hooded woman with an owl. Dear me! Did you ever see her?"

"I seen the howl."

"Never the woman?"

"Not so plain as the howl, but they always keeps together."

"Has anybody ever seen the woman as plainly as the owl?"

"Lord bless you, Sir! Lots."

"Who?"

"Lord bless you, Sir! Lots."

"The general-dealer opposite, for instance, who is opening his shop?"

"Perkins? Bless you, Perkins wouldn't go a-nigh the place. No!" observed the young man, with considerable feeling; "he an't over wise, an't Perkins, but he an't such a fool as *that*."

(Here, the landlord murmured his confidence in Perkins's knowing better.)

"Who is—or who was—the hooded woman with the owl? Do you know?"

"Well!" said Ikey, holding up his cap with one hand while he scratched his head with the other, "they say, in general, that she was murdered, and the howl he 'ooted the while."

This very concise summary of the facts was all I could learn, except that a young man, as hearty and likely a young man as ever I see, had been took with fits and held down in 'em, after seeing the hooded woman. Also, that a personage, dimly described as "a hold chap, a sort of one-eyed tramp, answering to the name of Joby, unless you challenged him as Greenwood, and then he said, 'Why not? and even if so, mind your own business,' " had encountered the hooded woman, a matter of five or six times. But, I was not materially assisted by these witnesses: inasmuch as the first was in California, and the last was, as Ikey said (and he was confirmed by the landlord), Anywheres.

Now, although I regard with a hushed and solemn fear, the mysteries, between which and this state of existence is interposed the barrier of the great trial and change that fall on all the things that live; and although I have not the audacity to pretend that I know anything of them; I can no more reconcile the mere banging of doors, ringing of bells, creaking of boards, and such-like insignificances, with the majestic beauty and pervading analogy of all the Divine rules that I am permitted to understand, than I had been able, a little while before, to yoke the spiritual intercourse of my fellow-traveller to the chariot of the rising sun. Moreover, I had lived in two haunted houses—both abroad. In one of these, an old Italian palace, which bore the reputation of being very badly haunted indeed, and which had recently been twice abandoned on that account, I lived eight months, most tranquilly and pleasantly: notwithstanding that the house had a score of mysterious bedrooms, which were never used, and possessed, in one large room in which I sat reading, times out of number at all hours, and next to which I slept, a haunted chamber of the first pretensions. I gently hinted these considerations to the landlord. And as to this particular house having a bad name—I reasoned with him, Why, how many things had bad names undeservedly, and how easy it was to give bad names, and did he not think that if he and I were persistently to whisper in the village that any weird-looking old drunken tinker of the neighbourhood had sold himself to the Devil, he would come in time to be suspected of that commercial venture! All this wise talk was perfectly ineffective with the landlord, I am bound to confess, and was as dead a failure as ever I made in my life.

To cut this part of the story short, I was piqued about the haunted house, and was already half resolved to take it. So, after breakfast, I got the keys from Perkins's brother-in-law (a whip and harness maker, who keeps the Post Office, and is under submission to a most rigorous wife of the Doubly Seceding Little Emmanuel persuasion), and went up to the house, attended by my landlord and by Ikey.

Within, I found it, as I had expected, transcendently dismal. The slowly changing shadows waved on it from the heavy trees, were doleful in the last degree; the house was ill-placed, ill-built, ill-planned, and ill-fitted. It was damp, it was not free from dry rot, there was a flavour of rats in it, and it was the gloomy victim of that indescribable decay which settles on all the work of man's hands whenever it is not turned to man's account. The kitchens and offices were too large, and too remote from each other. Above stairs and below, waste tracts of passage intervened between patches of fertility represented by rooms; and there was a mouldy old well with a green growth upon it, hiding like a murderous trap, near the bottom of the back-stairs, under the double row of bells. One of these bells was labelled, on a black ground in faded white letters, MASTER B. This, they told me, was the bell that rang the most.

"Who was Master B.?" I asked. "Is it known what he did while the owl hooted?"

"Rang the bell," said Ikey.

I was rather struck by the prompt dexterity with which this young man pitched his fur cap at the bell, and rang it himself. It was a loud, unpleasant bell, and made a very disagreeable sound. The other bells were inscribed according to the names of the rooms to which their wires were conducted: as "Picture Room," "Double Room," "Clock Room," and the like. Following Master B.'s bell to its source, I found that young gentleman to have had but indifferent third-class accommodation in a triangular cabin under the cock-loft, with a corner fireplace which Master B. must have been exceedingly small if he were ever able to warm himself at, and a corner chimneypiece like a pyramidal staircase to the ceiling for Tom Thumb. The papering of one side of the room had dropped down bodily, with fragments of plaster adhering to it, and almost blocked up the door. It appeared that Master B., in his spiritual condition, always made a point of pulling the paper down. Neither the landlord nor Ikey could suggest why he made such a fool of himself.

Except that the house had an immensely large rambling loft at top, I made no other discoveries. It was moderately well furnished, but sparely. Some of the furniture—say, a third—was as old as the house; the rest was of various periods within the last half-century. I was referred to a corn-chandler in the market-place of the county town to treat for the house. I went that day, and I took it for six months.

It was just the middle of October when I moved in with my maiden sister (I venture to call her eight-and-thirty, she is so very handsome, sensible, and engaging). We took with us, a deaf stableman, my bloodhound Turk, two women servants, and a young person called an Odd Girl. I have reason to record of the attendant last enumerated, who was one of the Saint Lawrence's Union Female Orphans, that she was a fatal mistake and a disastrous engagement.

The year was dying early, the leaves were falling fast, it was a raw cold day when we took possession, and the gloom of the house was most depressing. The cook (an amiable woman, but of a weak turn of intellect) burst into tears on beholding the kitchen, and requested that her silver watch might be delivered over to her sister (2 Tuppintock's Gardens, Liggs's Walk, Clapham Rise), in the event of anything happening to her from the damp. Streaker, the housemaid, feigned cheerfulness, but was the greater martyr. The Odd Girl, who had never been in the country, alone was pleased, and made arrangements for sowing an acorn in the garden outside the scullery window, and rearing an oak.

We went, before dark, through all the natural—as opposed to supernatural—miseries incidental to our state. Dispiriting reports ascended (like the smoke) from the basement in volumes, and descended from the upper rooms. There was no rolling-pin, there was no salamander (which failed to surprise me, for I don't know what it is), there was nothing in the house, what there was, was broken, the last people must have lived like pigs, what could the meaning of the landlord be? Through these distresses, the Odd Girl was cheerful and exemplary. But within four hours after dark we had got into a supernatural groove, and the Odd Girl had seen "Eyes," and was in hysterics.

My sister and I had agreed to keep the haunting strictly to ourselves, and my impression was, and still is, that I had not left Ikey, when he helped to unload the cart, alone with the women or any one of them, for one minute. Nevertheless, as I say, the Odd Girl had

seen "Eyes" (no other explanation could ever be drawn from her),
before nine, and by ten o'clock had had as much vinegar applied to
her as would pickle a handsome salmon.

I leave a discerning public to judge of my feelings, when, under
these untoward circumstances, at about half-past ten o'clock Master
B.'s bell began to ring in a most infuriated manner, and Turk howled
until the house resounded with his lamentations!

I hope I may never again be in a state of mind so unchristian as the
mental frame in which I lived for some weeks, respecting the memory
of Master B. Whether his bell was rung by rats, or mice, or bats, or
wind, or what other accidental vibration, or sometimes by one cause,
sometimes another, and sometimes by collusion, I don't know; but,
certain it is, that it did ring two nights out of three, until I conceived
the happy idea of twisting Master B.'s neck—in other words, breaking
his bell short off—and silencing that young gentleman, as to my
experience and belief, for ever.

But, by that time, the Odd Girl had developed such improving
powers of catalepsy, that she had become a shining example of that
very inconvenient disorder. She would stiffen, like a Guy Fawkes
endowed with unreason, on the most irrelevant occasions. I would
address the servants in a lucid manner, pointing out to them that I
had painted Master B.'s room and balked the paper, and taken
Master B.'s bell away and balked the ringing, and if they could
suppose that that confounded boy had lived and died, to clothe
himself with no better behaviour than would most unquestionably
have brought him and the sharpest particles of a birch-broom into
close acquaintance in the present imperfect state of existence, could
they also suppose a mere poor human being, such as I was, capable
by those contemptible means of counteracting and limiting the
powers of the disembodied spirits of the dead, or of any spirits?—
I say I would become emphatic and cogent, not to say rather com-
placent, in such an address, when it would all go for nothing by
reason of the Odd Girl's suddenly stiffening from the toes upward,
and glaring among us like a parochial petrifaction.

Streaker, the housemaid, too, had an attribute of a most dis-
comfiting nature. I am unable to say whether she was of an unusually
lymphatic temperament, or what else was the matter with her, but
this young woman became a mere Distillery for the production of the
largest and most transparent tears I ever met with. Combined with
these characteristics, was a peculiar tenacity of hold in those
specimens, so that they didn't fall, but hung upon her face and nose.
In this condition, and mildly and deplorably shaking her head, her
silence would throw me more heavily than the Admirable Crichton
could have done in a verbal disputation for a purse of money. Cook,
likewise, always covered me with confusion as with a garment, by
neatly winding up the session with the protest that the Ouse was
wearing her out, and by meekly repeating her last wishes regarding
her silver watch.

As to our nightly life, the contagion of suspicion and fear was among us, and there is no such contagion under the sky. Hooded woman? According to the accounts, we were in a perfect Convent of hooded women. Noises? With that contagion downstairs, I myself have sat in the dismal parlour, listening, until I have heard so many and such strange noises, that they would have chilled my blood if I had not warmed it by dashing out to make discoveries. Try this in bed, in the dead of the night; try this at your own comfortable fireside, in the life of the night. You can fill any house with noises, if you will, until you have a noise for every nerve in your nervous system.

I repeat; the contagion of suspicion and fear was among us, and there is no such contagion under the sky. The women (their noses in a chronic state of excoriation from smelling-salts) were always primed and loaded for a swoon, and ready to go off with hair-triggers. The two elder detached the Odd Girl on all expeditions that were considered doubly hazardous, and she always established the reputation of such adventures by coming back cataleptic. If Cook or Streaker went overhead after dark, we knew we should presently hear a bump on the ceiling; and this took place so constantly, that it was as if a fighting man were engaged to go about the house, administering a touch of his art which I believe is called the Auctioneer, to every domestic he met with.

It was in vain to do anything. It was in vain to be frightened, for the moment in one's own person, by a real owl, and then to show the owl. It was in vain to discover, by striking an accidental discord on the piano, that Turk always howled at particular notes and combinations. It was in vain to be a Rhadamanthus with the bells, and if an unfortunate bell rang without leave, to have it down inexorably and silence it. It was in vain to fire up chimneys, let torches down the well, charge furiously into suspected rooms and recesses. We changed servants, and it was no better. The new set ran away, and a third set came, and it was no better. At last, our comfortable house-keeping got to be so disorganised and wretched, that I one night dejectedly said to my sister: "Patty, I begin to despair of our getting people to go on with us here, and I think we must give this up."

My sister, who is a woman of immense spirit, replied, "No, John, don't give it up. Don't be beaten, John. There is another way."

"And what is that?" said I.

"John," returned my sister, "if we are not to be driven out of this house, and that for no reason whatever, that is apparent to you or me, we must help ourselves and take the house wholly and solely into our own hands."

"But the servants," said I.

"Have no servants," said my sister, boldly.

Like most people in my grade of life, I had never thought of the possibility of going on without those faithful obstructions. The notion was so new to me when suggested, that I looked very doubtful.

"We know they come here to be frightened and infect one another, and we know they are frightened and do infect one another," said my sister.

"With the exception of Bottles," I observed, in a meditative tone.

(The deaf stable-man. I kept him in my service, and still keep him, as a phenomenon of moroseness not to be matched in England.)

"To be sure, John," assented my sister; "except Bottles. And what does that go to prove? Bottles talks to nobody, and hears nobody unless he is absolutely roared at, and what alarm has Bottles ever given, or taken? None."

This was perfectly true; the individual in question having retired, every night at ten o'clock, to his bed over the coach-house, with no other company than a pitchfork and a pail of water. That the pail of water would have been over me, and the pitchfork through me, if I had put myself without announcement in Bottles's way after that minute, I had deposited in my own mind as a fact worth remembering. Neither had Bottles ever taken the least notice of any of our many uproars. An imperturbable and speechless man, he had sat at his supper, with Streaker present in a swoon, and the Odd Girl marble, and had only put another potato in his cheek, or profited by the general misery to help himself to beefsteak pie.

" And so," continued my sister, "I exempt Bottles. And considering, John, that the house is too large, and perhaps too lonely, to be kept well in hand by Bottles, you, and me, I propose that we cast about among our friends for a certain selected number of the most reliable and willing—form a Society here for three months—wait upon ourselves and one another—live cheerfully and socially—and see what happens."

I was so charmed with my sister, that I embraced her on the spot, and went into her plan with the greatest ardour.

We were then in the third week of November, but, we took our measures so vigorously, and were so well seconded by the friends in whom we confided, that there was still a week of the month unexpired, when our party all came down together merrily, and mustered in the haunted house.

I will mention, in this place, two small changes that I made while my sister and I were yet alone. It occurring to me as not improbable that Turk howled in the house at night, partly because he wanted to get out of it, I stationed him in his kennel outside, but unchained; and I seriously warned the village that any man who came in his way must not expect to leave him without a rip in his own throat. I then casually asked Ikey if he were a judge of a gun? On his saying, "Yes, Sir, I knows a good gun when I sees her," I begged the favour of his stepping up to the house and looking at mine.

"*She's* a true one, Sir," said Ikey, after inspecting a double-barrelled rifle that I bought in New York a few years ago. "No mistake about *her*, Sir."

"Ikey," said I, "don't mention it; I have seen something in this house."

"No, Sir?" he whispered, greedily opening his eyes. " 'Ooded lady, Sir?"

"Don't be frightened," said I. "It was a figure rather like you."

"Lord, Sir?"

"Ikey!" said I, shaking hands with him warmly: I may say affectionately: "if there is any truth in these ghost-stories, the greatest service I can do you, is, to fire at that figure. And I promise you, by Heaven and earth, I will do it with this gun if I see it again!"

The young man thanked me, and took his leave with some little precipitation, after declining a glass of liquor. I imparted my secret to him, because I had never quite forgotten his throwing his cap at the bell; because I had, on another occasion, noticed something very like a fur cap, lying not far from the bell, one night when it had burst out ringing; and because I had remarked that we were at our ghostliest whenever he came up in the evening to comfort the servants. Let me do Ikey no injustice. He was afraid of the house, and believed in its being haunted; and yet he would play false on the haunting side, so surely as he got an opportunity. The Odd Girl's case was exactly similar. She went about the house in a state of real terror, and yet lied monstrously and wilfully, and invented many of the alarms she spread, and made many of the sounds we heard. I had had my eye on the two, and I know it. It is not necessary for me, here, to account for this preposterous state of mind; I content myself with remarking that it is familiarly known to every intelligent man who has had fair medical, legal, or other watchful experience; that it is as well established and as common a state of mind as any with which observers are acquainted; and that it is one of the first elements, above all others, rationally to be suspected in, and strictly looked for, and separated from, any question of this kind.

To return to our party. The first thing we did when we were all assembled, was, to draw lots for bedrooms. That done, and every bedroom, and, indeed, the whole house, having been minutely examined by the whole body, we allotted the various household duties, as if we had been on a gipsy party, or a yachting party, or a hunting party, or were shipwrecked. I then recounted the floating rumours concerning the hooded lady, the owl, and Master B.; with others, still more filmy, which had floated about during our occupation, relative to some ridiculous old ghost of the female gender who went up and down, carrying the ghost of a round table; and also to an impalpable Jackass, whom nobody was ever able to catch. Some of these ideas I really believe our people below had communicated to one another in some diseased way, without conveying them in words. We then gravely called one another to witness, that we were not there to be deceived, or to deceive—which we considered pretty much the same thing—and that, with a serious sense of responsibility, we would be strictly true to one another, and would strictly follow out the truth. The understanding was established, that any one who heard unusual noises in the night, and who wished to trace them, should knock at my door; lastly, that on Twelfth Night, the last night of holy Christmas, all our individual experiences since that then present hour of our coming together in the haunted house, should be brought to light for the good of all; and that we would hold our peace on the subject till then, unless on some remarkable provocation to break silence.

We were, in number and in character, as follows:

First—to get my sister and myself out of the way—there were we two. In the drawing of lots, my sister drew her own room, and I drew Master B.'s. Next, there was our first cousin, John Herschel, so called after the great astronomer: than whom I suppose a better man at a telescope does not breathe. With him, was his wife: a charming creature to whom he had been married in the previous spring. I thought it (under the circumstances) rather imprudent to bring her, because there is no knowing what even a false alarm may do at such a time; but I suppose he knew his own business best, and I must say that if she had been *my* wife, I never could have left her endearing and bright face behind. They drew the Clock Room. Alfred Starling, an uncommonly agreeable young fellow of eight-and-twenty for whom I have the greatest liking, was in the Double Room; mine, usually, and designated by that name from having a dressing-room within it, with two large and cumbersome windows, which no wedges *I* was ever able to make, would keep from shaking, in any weather, wind or no wind. Alfred is a young fellow who pretends to be "fast" (another word for loose, as I understand the term), but who is much too good and sensible for that nonsense, and who would have distinguished himself before now, if his father had not unfortunately left him a small independence of two hundred a year, on the strength of which his only occupation in life has been to spend six. I am in hopes, however, that his Banker may break, or that he may enter into some speculation guaranteed to pay twenty per cent.; for, I am convinced that if he could only be ruined, his fortune is made. Belinda Bates, bosom friend of my sister, and a most intellectual, amiable, and delightful girl, got the Picture Room. She has a fine genius for poetry, combined with real business earnestness, and "goes in"—to use an expression of Alfred's—for Woman's mission, Woman's rights, Woman's wrongs, and everything that is woman's with a capital W, or is not and ought to be, or is and ought not to be. "Most praiseworthy, my dear, and Heaven prosper you!" I whispered to her on the first night of my taking leave of her at the Picture-Room door, "but don't overdo it. And in respect of the great necessity there is, my darling, for more employments being within the reach of Woman than our civilisation has as yet assigned to her, don't fly at the unfortunate men, even those men who are at first sight in your way, as if they were the natural oppressors of your sex; for, trust me, Belinda, they do sometimes spend their wages among wives and daughters, sisters, mothers, aunts, and grandmothers; and the play is, really, not *all* Wolf and Red Riding-Hood, but has other parts in it." However, I digress.

Belinda, as I have mentioned, occupied the Picture Room. We had but three other chambers: the Corner Room, the Cupboard Room, and the Garden Room. My old friend, Jack Governor, "slung his hammock," as he called it, in the Corner Room. I have always regarded Jack as the finest-looking sailor that ever sailed. He is gray now, but as handsome as he was a quarter of a century ago—nay, handsomer. A portly, cheery, well-built figure of a broad-shouldered man, with a frank smile, a brilliant dark eye, and a rich dark eyebrow. I remember those under darker hair, and they look all the better for their silver setting. He has been wherever his Union namesake flies, has Jack, and I have met old shipmates of his, away in the Mediterranean and on the other side of the Altantic, who have beamed and brightened at the casual mention of his name, and have cried, "You know Jack Governor? Then you know a prince of men!" That he is! And so unmistakably a naval officer, that if you were to meet him coming out of an Esquimaux snow-hut in a seal's skin, you would be vaguely persuaded he was in full naval uniform.

Jack once had that bright clear eye of his on my sister; but, it fell out that he married another lady and took her to South America, where she died. This was a dozen years ago or more. He brought down with him to our haunted house a little cask of salt beef; for, he is always convinced that all salt beef not of his own pickling, is mere carrion, and invariably, when he goes to London, packs a piece in his portmanteau. He had also volunteered to bring with him one "Nat Beaver," an old comrade of his, captain of a merchantman. Mr. Beaver, with a thick-set wooden face and figure, and apparently as hard as a block all over, proved to be an intelligent man, with a world of watery experiences in him, and great practical knowledge. At times, there was a curious nervousness about him, apparently the lingering result of some old illness; but, it seldom lasted many minutes. He got the Cupboard Room, and lay there next to Mr. Undery, my friend and solicitor: who came down, in an amateur capacity, "to go through with it," as he said, and who plays whist better than the whole Law List, from the red cover at the beginning to the red cover at the end.

I never was happier in my life, and I believe it was the universal feeling among us. Jack Governor, always a man of wonderful resources, was Chief Cook, and made some of the best dishes I ever ate, including unapproachable curries. My sister was pastrycook and confectioner. Starling and I were Cook's Mate, turn and turn about, and on special occasions the chief cook "pressed" Mr. Beaver. We had a great deal of out-door sport and exercise, but nothing was neglected within, and there was no ill-humour or misunderstanding among us, and our evenings were so delightful that we had at least one good reason for being reluctant to go to bed.

We had a few night alarms in the beginning. On the first night, I was knocked up by Jack with a most wonderful ship's lantern in his hand, like the gills of some monster of the deep, who informed me that he "was going aloft to the main truck," to have the weathercock down. It was a stormy night, and I remonstrated; but Jack called my atten-

"Jack ... stood upon nothing particular, coolly knocking the weathercock off."

tion to its making a sound like a cry of despair, and said somebody would be "hailing a ghost" presently, if it wasn't done. So, up to the top of the house, where I could hardly stand for the wind, we went, accompanied by Mr. Beaver; and there Jack, lantern and all, with Mr. Beaver after him, swarmed up to the top of a cupola, some two dozen feet above the chimneys, and stood upon nothing particular, coolly knocking the weathercock off, until they both got into such good spirits with the wind and the height, that I thought they would never come down. Another night, they turned out again, and had a chimney-cowl off. Another night, they cut a sobbing and gulping water-pipe away. Another night, they found out something else. On several occasions, they both, in the coolest manner, simultaneously dropped out of their respective bedroom windows, hand over hand by their counterpanes, to "overhaul" something mysterious in the garden.

The engagement among us was faithfully kept, and nobody revealed anything. All we knew was, if any one's room were haunted, no one looked the worse for it.

THE GHOST IN MASTER B.'S ROOM

WHEN I established myself in the triangular garret which had gained so distinguished a reputation, my thoughts naturally turned to Master B. My speculations about him were uneasy and manifold. Whether his Christian name was Benjamin, Bissextile (from his having been born in Leap Year), Bartholomew, or Bill. Whether the initial letter belonged to his family name, and that was Baxter. Black, Brown, Barker, Buggins, Baker, or Bird. Whether he was a foundling, and had been baptized B. Whether he was a lion-hearted boy, and B. was short for Briton, or for Bull. Whether he could possibly have been kith and kin to an illustrious lady who brightened my own childhood, and had come of the blood of the brilliant Mother Bunch?

With these profitless meditations I tormented myself much. I also carried the mysterious letter into the appearance and pursuits of the deceased; wondering whether he dressed in Blue, wore Boots (he couldn't have been Bald), was a boy of Brains, liked Books, was good at Bowling, had any skill as a Boxer, even in his Buoyant Boyhood Bathed from a Bathing Machine at Bognor. Bangor, Bournemouth, Brighton, or Broadstairs, like a Bounding Billiard Ball?

So, from the first, I was haunted by the letter B.

It was not long before I remarked that I never by any hazard had a dream of Master B., or of anything belonging to him. But, the instant I awoke from sleep, at whatever hour of the night, my thoughts took him up, and roamed away, trying to attach his initial letter to something that would fit it and keep it quiet.

For six nights, I had been worried thus in Master B.'s room, when I began to perceive that things were going wrong.

The first appearance that presented itself was early in the morning when it was just daylight and no more. I was standing shaving at my glass, when I suddenly discovered, to my consternation and amazement, that I was shaving—not myself—I am fifty—but a boy. Apparently Master B.

I trembled and looked over my shoulder; nothing there. I looked again in the glass, and distinctly saw the features and expression of a boy, who was shaving, not to get rid of a beard, but to get one. Extremely troubled in my mind, I took a few turns in the room, and went back to the looking-glass, resolved to steady my hand and complete the operation in which I had been disturbed. Opening my eyes, which I had shut while recovering my firmness, I now met in the glass, looking straight at me, the eyes of a young man of four or five and twenty. Terrified by this new ghost, I closed my eyes, and made a strong effort to recover myself. Opening them again, I saw, shaving his cheek in the glass, my father, who has long been dead. Nay, I even saw my grandfather too, whom I never did see in my life.

Although naturally much affected by these remarkable visitations, I determined to keep my secret, until the time agreed upon for the present general disclosure. Agitated by a multitude of curious thoughts, I retired to my room, that night, prepared to encounter some new experience of a spectral character. Nor was my preparation needless, for, waking from an uneasy sleep at exactly two o'clock in the morning, what were my feelings to find that I was sharing my bed with the skeleton of Master B.!

I sprang up, and the skeleton sprang up also. I then heard a plaintive voice saying, "Where am I? What is become of me?" and, looking hard in that direction, perceived the ghost of Master B.

The young spectre was dressed in an obsolete fashion : or rather, was not so much dressed as put into a case of inferior pepper-and-salt cloth, made horrible by means of shining buttons. I observed that these buttons went, in a double row, over each shoulder of the young ghost, and appeared to descend his back. He wore a frill round his neck. His right hand (which I distinctly noticed to be inky) was laid upon his stomach; connecting this action with some feeble pimples on his countenance, and his general air of nausea, I concluded this ghost to be the ghost of a boy who had habitually taken a great deal too much medicine.

"Where am I?" said the little spectre, in a pathetic voice. "And why was I born in the Calomel days, and why did I have all that Calomel given me?"

I replied, with sincere earnestness, that upon my soul I couldn't tell him.

"Where is my little sister," said the ghost, "and where my angelic little wife, and where is the boy I went to school with?"

I entreated the phantom to be comforted, and above all things to take heart respecting the loss of the boy he went to school with. I represented to him that probably that boy never did, within human experience, come out well, when discovered. I urged that I myself had, in later life, turned up several boys whom I went to school with, and none of them had at all answered. I expressed my humble belief that

that boy never did answer. I represented that he was a mythic character, a delusion, and a snare. I recounted how, the last time I found him, I found him at a dinner party behind a wall of white cravat, with an inconclusive opinion on every possible subject, and a power of silent boredom absolutely Titanic. I related how, on the strength of our having been together at "Old Doylance's," he had asked himself to breakfast with me (a social offence of the largest magnitude); how, fanning my weak embers of belief in Doylance's boys, I had let him in; and how, he had proved to be a fearful wanderer about the earth, pursuing the race of Adam with inexplicable notions concerning the currency, and with a proposition that the Bank of England should, on pain of being abolished, instantly strike off and circulate, God knows how many thousand millions of ten-and-sixpenny notes.

The ghost heard me in silence, and with a fixed stare. "Barber!" it apostrophised me when I had finished.

"Barber?" I repeated—for I am not of that profession.

"Condemned," said the ghost, "to shave a constant change of customers—now, me—now, a young man—now, thyself as thou art —now, thy father—now, thy grandfather; condemned, too, to lie down with a skeleton every night, and to rise with it every morning ——"

(I shuddered on hearing this dismal announcement.)

"Barber! Pursue me!"

I had felt, even before the words were uttered, that I was under a spell to pursue the phantom. I immediately did so, and was in Master B.'s room no longer.

Most people know what long and fatiguing night journeys had been forced upon the witches who used to confess, and who, no doubt, told the exact truth—particularly as they were always assisted with leading questions, and the Torture was always ready. I asseverate that, during my occupation of Master B.'s room, I was taken by the ghost that haunted it, on expeditions fully as long and wild as any of those. Assuredly, I was presented to no shabby old man with a goat's horns and tail (something between Pan and an old clothesman), holding conventional receptions, as stupid as those of real life and less decent, but, I came upon other things which appeared to me to have more meaning.

Confident that I speak the truth and shall be believed, I declare without hesitation that I followed the ghost, in the first instance on a broom-stick, and afterwards on a rocking-horse. The very smell of the animal's paint—especially when I brought it out, by making him warm—I am ready to swear to. I followed the ghost, afterwards, in a hackney coach; an institution with the peculiar smell of which, the present generation is unacquainted, but to which I am again ready to swear as a combination of stable, dog with the mange, and very old bellows. (In this, I appeal to previous generations to confirm or refute me.) I pursued the phantom, on a headless donkey: at least, upon a donkey who was so interested in the state of his stomach that his head was always down there, investigating it; on ponies, expressly born to kick up behind; on roundabouts and swings, from fairs; in the first cab—another forgotten institution where the fare regularly got into bed, and was tucked up with the driver.

Not to trouble you with a detailed account of all my travels in pursuit of the ghost of Master B., which were longer and more wonderful than those of Sinbad the Sailor, I will confine myself to one experience from which you may judge of many.

I was marvellously changed. I was myself, yet not myself. I was conscious of something within me, which has been the same all through my life, and which I have always recognised under all its phases and varieties as never altering, and yet I was not the I who had gone to bed in Master B.'s room. I had the smoothest of faces and the shortest of legs, and I had taken another creature like myself, also with the smoothest of faces and the shortest of legs, behind a door, and was confiding to him a proposition of the most astounding nature.

This proposition was, that we should have a Seraglio.

The other creature assented warmly. He had no notion of respectability, neither had I. It was the custom of the East, it was the way of the good Caliph Haroun Alraschid (let me have the corrupted name again for once, it is so scented with sweet memories!), the usage was highly laudable, and most worthy of imitation. "O, yes! Let us," said the other creature with a jump, "have a Seraglio."

It was not because we entertained the faintest doubts of the meritorious character of the Oriental establishment we proposed to import, that we perceived it must be kept a secret from Miss Griffin. It was because we knew Miss Griffin to be bereft of human sympathies, and incapable of appreciating the greatness of the great Haroun. Mystery impenetrably shrouded from Miss Griffin then, let us entrust it to Miss Bule.

We were ten in Miss Griffin's establishment by Hampstead Ponds; eight ladies and two gentlemen. Miss Bule, whom I judge to have attained the ripe age of eight or nine, took the lead in society. I opened the subject to her in the course of the day, and proposed that she should become the Favourite.

Miss Bule, after struggling with the diffidence so natural to, and charming in, her adorable sex, expressed herself as flattered by the idea, but wished to know how it was proposed to provide for Miss Pipson? Miss Bule—who was understood to have vowed towards that young lady, a friendship, halves, and no secrets, until death, on the Church Service and Lessons complete in two volumes with case and lock—Miss Bule said she could not, as the friend of Pipson, disguise from herself, or me, that Pipson was not one of the common.

Now, Miss Pipson, having curly light hair and blue eyes (which was my idea of anything mortal and feminine that was called Fair), I promptly replied that I regarded Miss Pipson in the light of a Fair Circassian.

"And what then?" Miss Bule pensively asked.

I replied that she must be inveigled by a Merchant, brought to me veiled, and purchased as a slave.

[The other creature had already fallen into the second male place in the State, and was set apart for Grand Vizier. He afterwards resisted this disposal of events, but had his hair pulled until he yielded.]

"Shall I not be jealous?" Miss Bule inquired, casting down her eyes.

"Zobeide, no," I replied; "you will ever be the favourite Sultana; the first place in my heart, and on my throne, will be ever yours."

Miss Bule, upon that assurance, consented to propound the idea to her seven beautiful companions. It occurring to me, in the course of the same day, that we knew we could trust a grinning and good-natured soul called Tabby, who was the serving drudge of the house, and had no more figure than one of the beds, and upon whose face there was always more or less black-lead, I slipped into Miss Bule's hand after supper, a little note to that effect: dwelling on the black-lead as being in a manner deposited by the finger of Providence, pointing Tabby out for Mesrour, the celebrated chief of the Blacks of the Hareem.

There were difficulties in the formation of the desired institution, as there are in all combinations. The other creature showed himself of a low character, and, when defeated in aspiring to the throne, pretended to have conscientious scruples about prostrating himself before the Caliph; wouldn't call him Commander of the Faithful; spoke of him slightingly and inconsistently as a mere "chap"; said he, the other creature, "wouldn't play"—Play!—and was otherwise coarse and offensive. This meanness of disposition was, however, put down by the general indignation of an united Seraglio, and I became blessed in the smiles of eight of the fairest of the daughters of men.

The smiles could only be bestowed when Miss Griffin was looking another way, and only then in a very wary manner, for there was a legend among the followers of the Prophet that she saw with a little round ornament in the middle of the pattern on the back of her shawl. But every day after dinner, for an hour, we were all together, and then the Favourite and the rest of the Royal Hareem competed who should most beguile the leisure of the Serene Haroun reposing from the cares of State—which were generally, as in most affairs of State, of an arithmetical character, the Commander of the Faithful being a fearful boggler at a sum.

On these occasions, the devoted Mesrour, chief of the Blacks of the Hareem, was always in attendance (Miss Griffin usually ringing for that officer, at the same time, with great vehemence), but never acquitted himself in a manner worthy of his historical reputation. In the first place, his bringing a broom into the Divan of the Caliph, even when Haroun wore on his shoulders the red robe of anger (Miss Pipson's pelisse), though it might be got over for the moment, was never to be quite satisfactorily accounted for. In the second place, his breaking out into grinning exclamations of "Lork you pretties!" was neither Eastern nor respectful. In the third place, when specially instructed to say "Bismillah! he always said "Hallelujah!" This officer, unlike his class, was too good-humoured altogether, kept his mouth open far too wide, expressed approbation to an incongruous extent, and even once—it was on the occasion of the purchase of the Fair Circassian for five hundred thousand purses of gold, and cheap, too—embraced the Slave, the Favourite, and the Caliph, all round. (Parenthetically let me say God bless Mesrour, and may there have been sons and daughters on that tender bosom, softening many a hard day since!)

Miss Griffin was a model of propriety, and I am at a loss to imagine what the feelings of the virtuous woman would have been, if she had known, when she paraded us down the Hampstead-road two and two, that she was walking with a stately step at the head of Polygamy and Mahomedanism. I believe that a mysterious and terrible joy with which the contemplation of Miss Griffin, in this unconscious state, inspired us, and a grim sense prevalent among us that there was a dreadful power in our knowledge of what Miss Griffin (who knew all things that could be learnt out of book) didn't know, were the mainspring of the preservation of our secret. It was wonderfully kept, but was once upon the verge of self-betrayal. The danger and escape occurred upon a Sunday. We were all ten ranged in a conspicuous part of the gallery at church, with Miss Griffin at our head—as we were every Sunday—advertising the establishment in an unsecular sort of way—when the description of Solomon in his domestic glory happened to be read. The moment that monarch was thus referred to, conscience whispered me, "Thou, too, Haroun!" The officiating minister had a cast in his eye, and it assisted conscience by giving him the appearance of reading personally at me. A crimson blush, attended by a fearful perspiration, suffused my features. The Grand Vizier became more dead than alive, and the whole Seraglio reddened as if the sunset of Bagdad shone direct upon their lovely faces. At this portentous time the awful Griffin rose, and balefully surveyed the children of Islam. My own impression was, that Church and State had entered into a conspiracy with Miss Griffin to expose us, and that we should all be put into white sheets, and exhibited in the centre aisle. But, so Westerly—if I may be allowed the expression as opposite to Eastern associations—was Miss Griffin's sense of rectitude, that she merely suspected Apples, and we were saved.

I have called the Seraglio, united. Upon the question, solely, whether the Commander of the Faithful durst exercise a right of kissing in that sanctuary of the palace, were its peerless inmates divided. Zobeide asserted a counter-right in the Favourite to scratch, and the fair Circassian put her face, for refuge, into a green baize bag, originally designed for books. On the other hand, a young antelope of transcendant beauty from the fruitful plains of Camden-town (whence she had been brought, by traders, in the half-yearly caravan that crossed the intermediate desert after the holidays), held more liberal opinions, but stipulated for limiting the benefit of them to that dog, and son of a dog, the Grand Vizier—who had no rights, and was not in question. At length, the difficulty was compromised by the installation of a very youthful slave as Deputy. She, raised upon a stool, officially received upon her cheeks the salutes intended by the gracious Haroun for other Sultanas, and was privately rewarded from the coffers of the Ladies of the Hareem.

And now it was, at the full height of enjoyment of my bliss, that I became heavily troubled. I began to think of my mother, and what she would say to my taking home at Midsummer eight of the most beautiful of the daughters of men, but all unexpected. I thought of the number of beds we made up at our house, of my father's income, and of the baker, and my despondency redoubled. The Seraglio and malicious Vizier, divining the cause of their Lord's unhappiness, did their utmost to augment it. They professed unbounded fidelity, and declared that they would live and die with him. Reduced to the utmost wretchedness by these protestations of attachment, I lay awake, for hours at a time, ruminating on my frightful lot. In my despair, I think I might have taken an early opportunity of falling on my knees before Miss Griffin, avowing my resemblance to Solomon, and praying to be dealt with according to the outraged laws of my country, if an unthought-of means of escape had not opened before me.

One day, we were out walking, two and two—on which occasion the Vizier had his usual instructions to take note of the boy at the turnpike, and if he profanely gazed (which he always did) at the beauties of the Hareem, to have him bow-strung in the course of the night—and it happened that our hearts were veiled in gloom. An unaccountable action on the part of the antelope had plunged the State into disgrace. That charmer, on the representation that the previous day was her birthday, and that vast treasures had been sent in a hamper for its celebration (both baseless assertions), had secretly but most pressingly invited thirty-five neighbouring princes and princesses to a ball and supper: with a special stipulation that they were "not to be fetched till twelve." This wandering of the antelope's fancy, led to the surprising arrival at Miss Griffin's door, in divers equipages and under various escorts, of a great company in full dress, who were deposited on the top step in a flush of high expectancy, and who were dismissed in tears. At the beginning of the double knocks attendant on these ceremonies, the antelope had retired to a back attic, and bolted herself in; and at every new arrival, Miss Griffin had gone so much more and more distracted, that at last she had been seen to tear her front. Ultimate capitulation on the part of the offender, had been followed by solitude in the linen-closet, bread and water and a lecture to all, of vindictive length, in which Miss Griffin had used expressions: Firstly, "I believe you all of you knew of it"; Secondly, "Every one of you is as wicked as another"; Thirdly, "A pack of little wretches."

Under these circumstances, we were walking drearily along; and I especially, with my Moosulmaun responsibilities heavy on me, was in a very low state of mind; when a strange man accosted Miss Griffin, and, after walking on at her side for a little while and talking with her, looked at me. Supposing him to be a minion of the law, and that my hour was come, I instantly ran away, with the general purpose of making for Egypt.

The whole Seraglio cried out, when they saw me making off as fast as my legs would carry me (I had an impression that the first turning on the left, and round by the public-house, would be the shortest way to the Pyramids), Miss Griffin screamed after me, the faithless Vizier ran after me, and the boy at the turnpike dodged me into a corner, like a sheep, and cut me off. Nobody scolded me when I was taken and brought back; Miss Griffin only said, with a stunning gentleness, This was very curious! Why had I run away when the gentleman looked at me?

If I had had any breath to answer with, I dare say I should have made no answer; having no breath, I certainly made none. Miss Griffin and the strange man took me between them, and walked me back to the palace in a sort of state; but not at all (as I couldn't help feeling, with astonishment), in culprit state.

When we got there, we went into a room by ourselves, and Miss Griffin called in to her assistance, Mesrour, chief of the dusky guards of the Hareem. Mesrour, on being whispered to, began to shed tears.

"Bless you, my precious!" said that officer, turning to me; "your pa's took bitter bad!"

I asked, with a fluttered heart, "Is he very ill?"

"Lord temper the wind to you, my lamb!" said the good Mesrour, kneeling down, that I might have a comforting shoulder for my head to rest on, "your pa's dead!"

Haroun Alraschid took to flight at the words; the Seraglio vanished; from that moment, I never again saw one of the eight of the fairest of the daughters of men.

I was taken home, and there was Debt at home as well as Death, and we had a sale there. My own little bed was so superciliously looked upon by a Power unknown to me, hazily called "The Trade," that a brass coal-scuttle, a roasting-jack, and a birdcage, were obliged to be put into it to make a Lot of it, and then it went for a song. So I heard mentioned, and I wondered what song, and thought what a dismal song it must have been to sing!

Then, I was sent to a great, cold, bare school of big boys; where everything to eat and wear was thick and clumpy, without being enough; where everybody, large and small, was cruel; where the boys knew all about the sale, before I got there, and asked me what I had fetched, and who had bought me, and hooted at me, "Going, going, gone!" I never whispered in that wretched place that I had been Haroun, or had had a Seraglio: for, I knew that if I mentioned my reverses, I should be so worried, that I should have to drown myself in the muddy pond near the playground, which looked like the beer.

Ah me, ah me! No other ghost has haunted the boy's room, my friends, since I have occupied it, than the ghost of my own childhood, the ghost of my own innocence, the ghost of my own airy belief. Many a time have I pursued the phantom: never with this man's stride of mine to come up with it, never with these man's hands of mine to touch it, never more to this man's heart of mine to hold it in its purity. And here you see me working out, as cheerfully and thankfully as I may, my doom of shaving in the glass a constant change of customers, and of lying down and rising up with the skeleton allotted to me for my mortal companion.

A MESSAGE FROM THE SEA

[1860]

CHAPTER I

THE VILLAGE

"AND a mighty sing'lar and pretty place it is, as ever I saw in all the days of my life!" said Captain Jorgan, looking up at it.

Captain Jorgan had to look high to look at it, for the village was built sheer up the face of a steep and lofty cliff. There was no road in it, there was no wheeled vehicle in it, there was not a level yard in it. From the sea-beach to the cliff-top two irregular rows of white houses, placed opposite to one another, and twisting here and there, and there and here, rose, like the sides of a long succession of stages of crooked ladders, and you climbed up the village or climbed down the village by the staves between, some six feet wide or so, and made of sharp irregular stones. The old pack-saddle, long laid aside in most parts of England as one of the appendages of its infancy, flourished here intact. Strings of pack-horses and pack-donkeys toiled slowly up the staves of the ladders, bearing fish, and coal, and such other cargo as was unshipping at the pier from the dancing fleet of village boats, and from two or three little coasting traders. As the beasts of burden ascended laden, or descended light, they got so lost at intervals in the floating clouds of village smoke, that they seemed to dive down some of the village chimneys, and come to the surface again far off, high above others. No two houses in the village were alike, in chimney, size, shape, door, window, gable, roof-tree, anything. The sides of the ladders were musical with water, running clear and bright. The staves were musical with the clattering feet of the pack-horses and pack-donkeys, and the voices of the fishermen urging them up, mingled with the voices of the fishermen's wives and their many children. The pier was musical with the wash of the sea, the creaking of capstans and windlasses, and the airy fluttering of little vanes and sails. The rough, sea-bleached boulders of which the pier was made, and the whiter boulders of the shore, were brown with drying nets. The red-brown cliffs, richly wooded to their extremest verge, had their softened and beautiful forms reflected in the bluest water, under the clear North Devonshire sky of a November day without a cloud. The village itself was so steeped in autumnal foliage, from the houses lying on the pier to the topmost round of the topmost ladder, that one might ave fancied it was out a bird's-nesting, and was (as indeed it was) a wonderful climber. And mentioning birds, the place was not without some music from them too; for the rook was very busy on the higher levels, and the gull with his flapping wings was fishing in the bay, and the lusty little robin was hopping among the great stone blocks and iron rings of the breakwater, fearless in the faith of his ancestors, and the Children in the Wood.

Thus it came to pass that Captain Jorgan, sitting balancing himself on the pier-wall, struck his leg with his open hand, as some men do when they are pleased—and as he always did when he was pleased—and said,—

"A mighty sing'lar and pretty place it is, as ever I saw in all the days of my life!"

Captain Jorgan had not been through the village, but had come down to the pier by a winding side-road, to have a preliminary look at it from the level of his own natural element. He had seen many things and places, and had stowed them all away in a shrewd intellect and a vigorous memory. He was an American born, was Captain Jorgan,—a New Englander,—but he was a citizen of the world, and a combination of most of the best qualities of most of its best countries.

For Captain Jorgan to sit anywhere in his long-skirted blue coat and blue trousers, without holding converse with everybody within speaking distance, was a sheer impossibility. So the captain fell to talking with the fishermen, and to asking them knowing questions about the fishery, and the tides, and the currents, and the race of water off that point yonder, and what you kept in your eye, and got into a line with what else when you ran into the little harbour; and other nautical profundities. Among the men who exchanged ideas with the captain was a young fellow, who exactly hit his fancy,—a young fisherman of two or three and twenty, in the rough sea-dress of his craft, with a brown face, dark curling hair, and bright, modest eyes under his Sou'wester hat, and with a frank, but simple and retiring manner, which the captain found uncommonly taking. "I'd bet a thousand dollars," said the captain to himself, "that your father was an honest man!"

"Might you be married now?" asked the captain, when he had had some talk with this new acquaintance.

"Not yet."

"Going to be?" said the captain.

"I hope so."

The captain's keen glance followed the slightest possible turn of the dark eye, and the slightest possible tilt of the Sou'wester hat. The captain then slapped both his legs, and said to himself,—

"Never knew such a good thing in all my life! There's his sweetheart looking over the wall!"

There was a very pretty girl looking over the wall, from a little platform of cottage, vine, and fushsia; and she certainly did not look as if the presence of this young fisherman in the landscape made it any the less sunny and hopeful for her.

Captain Jorgan, having doubled himself up to laugh with that hearty good-nature which is quite exultant in the innocent happiness of other people, had undoubled himself, and was going to start a new subject, when there appeared coming down the lower ladders of stones, a man whom he hailed as "Tom Pettifer Ho!" Tom Pettifer Ho, responded with alacrity, and in speedy course descended on the pier.

"Afraid of a sun-stroke in England in November, Tom, that you wear your tropical hat, strongly paid outside and paper-lined inside, here?" said the captain, eyeing it.

"It's as well to be on the safe side, Sir," replied Tom.

"Safe side!" repeated the captain, laughing. "You'd guard against a sun-stroke, with that old hat, in an Ice Pack. Wa'al! What have you made out at the Post-office?"

"It is the Post-office, Sir."

"What's the Post-office?" said the captain.

"The name, Sir. The name keeps the Post-office."

"A coincidence!" said the captain. "A lucky hit! Show me where it is. Good-bye, shipmates, for the present! I shall come and have another look at you, afore I leave, this afternoon."

This was addressed to all there, but especially the young fisherman; so all there acknowledged it, but especially the young fisherman. "He's a sailor!" said one to another, as they looked after the captain moving away. That he was; and so outspeaking was the sailor in him, that although his dress had nothing nautical about it, with the single exception of its colour, but was a suit of a shore-going shape and form, too long in the sleeves and too short in the legs, and too unaccommodating everywhere, terminating earthward in a pair of Wellington boots, and surmounted by a tall, stiff hat, which no mortal could have worn at sea in any wind under heaven; nevertheless, a glimpse of his sagacious, weather-beaten face, or his strong, brown hand, would have established the captain's calling. Whereas Mr. Pettifer—a man of a certain plump neatness, with a curly whisker, and elaborately nautical in a jacket, and shoes, and all things correspondent—looked no more like a seaman, beside, beside Captain Jorgan, than he looked like a sea-serpent.

The two climbed high up the village,—which had the most arbitrary turns and twists in it, so that the cobbler's house came dead across the ladder, and to have held a reasonable course, you must have gone through his house, and through him too, as he sat at his work between two little windows, with one eye microscopically on the geological formation of that part of Devonshire, and the other telescopically on the open sea,—the two climbed high up the village, and stopped before a quaint little house, on which was painted, "MRS. RAYBROCK, DRAPER"; and also "POST-OFFICE." Before it, ran a rill of murmuring water, and access to it was gained by a little plank-bridge.

"Here's the name," said Captain Jorgan, "sure enough. You can come in if you like, Tom."

The captain opened the door, and passed into an odd little shop about six feet high, with a great variety of beams and bumps in the ceiling, and, besides the principal window giving on the ladder of stones, a purblind little window of a single pane of glass, peeping out of an abutting corner at the sun-lighted ocean, and winking at its brightness.

"How do you do, ma'am?" said the captain. "I am very glad to see you. I have come a long way to see you."

"*Have* you, Sir? Then I am sure I am very glad to see *you*, though I don't know you from Adam."

Thus a comely elderly woman, short of stature, plump of form, sparkling and dark of eye, who, perfectly clean and neat herself, stood in the midst of her perfectly clean and neat arrangements, and surveyed Captain Jorgan with smiling curiosity. "Ah! but you are a sailor, Sir," she added, almost immediately, and with a slight movement of her hands, that was not very unlike wringing them; "then you are heartily welcome."

"Thank'ee, ma'am," said the captain, "I don't know what it is, I am sure, that brings out the salt in me, but everybody seems to see it on the crown of my hat and the collar of my coat. Yes, ma'am, I am in that way of life."

"And the other gentleman, too," said Mrs. Raybrock.

"Well now, ma'am," said the captain, glancing shrewdly at the other gentleman, "you are that nigh right, that he goes to sea,—if that makes him a sailor. This is my steward, ma'am, Tom Pettifer; he's been a'most all trades you could name, in the course of his life,—would have bought all your chairs and tables once, if you had wished to sell 'em,—but now he's my steward. My name's Jorgan, and I'm a shipowner, and I sail my own and my partner's ships, and have done so this five-and-twenty year. According to custom I am called Captain Jorgan, but I am no more a captain, bless your heart! than you are."

"Perhaps you'll come into my parlour, Sir, and take a chair?" said Mrs. Raybrock.

"Ex-actly what I was going to propose myself, ma'am. After you."

Thus replying, and enjoining Tom to give an eye to the shop, Captain Jorgan followed Mrs. Raybrock into the little, low back-room,—decorated with divers plants in pots, tea-trays, old china teapots, and punch-bowls,—which was at once the private sitting-room of the Raybrock family and the inner cabinet of the post-office of the village of Steepways.

"Now, ma'am," said the captain, "it don't signify a cent to you where I was born, except——" But here the shadow of some one entering fell upon the captain's figure, and he broke off to double himself up, slap both his legs, and ejaculate. "Never knew such a thing in all my life! Here he is again! How are you?"

These words referred to the young fellow who had so taken Captain Jorgan's fancy down at the pier. To make it all quite complete he came in accompanied by the sweetheart whom the captain had detected looking over the wall. A prettier sweetheart the sun could not have shone upon that shining day. As she stood before the captain with her rosy lips just parted in surprise, her brown eyes a little wider open that was usual from the same cause, and her breathing a little quickened by the ascent (and possibly by some mysterious hurry and flurry at the parlour door, in which the captain had observed her face to be for a moment totally eclipsed by the Sou'wester hat), she looked so charming, that the captain felt himself under a moral obligation to slap both his legs again. She was very simply dressed, with no other ornament than an autumnal flower in her bosom. She wore neither hat nor bonnet, but merely a scarf or kerchief, folded squarely back over the head, to keep the sun off,—according to a fashion that may be sometimes seen in the more genial parts of England as well as of Italy, and which is probably the first fashion of head-dress that came into the world when grasses and leaves went out.

"In my country," said the captain, rising to give her his chair, and dexterously sliding it close to another chair on which the young fisherman must necessarily establish himself,—"in my country we should call Devonshire beauty first-rate!"

Whenever a frank manner is offensive, it is because it is strained or feigned; for there may be quite as much intolerable affectation in plainness as in mincing nicety. All that the captain said and did was honestly according to his nature; and his nature was open nature and good nature; therefore, when he paid this little compliment, and expressed with a sparkle or two of his knowing eye, "I see how it is, and nothing could be better," he had established a delicate confidence on that subject with the family.

"I was saying to your worthy mother," said the captain to the young man, after again introducing himself by name and occupation —"I was saying to your mother (and you're very like her) that it didn't signify where I was born, except that I was raised on question-asking ground, where the babies as soon as ever they come into the world, inquire of their mothers, 'Neow, how old may *you* be, and wa'at air you a goin' to name me?'—which is a fact," Here he slapped his leg. "Such being the case, I may be excused for asking you if your name's Alfred?"

"Yes, Sir, my name is Alfred," returned the young man.

"I am not a conjuror," pursued the captain, "and don't think me so, or I shall right soon undeceive you. Likewise don't think, if you please, though I *do* come from that country of the babies, that I am asking questions for question-asking's sake, for I am not. Somebody belonging to you went to sea?"

"My elder brother, Hugh," returned the young man. He said it in an altered and lower voice, and glanced at his mother, who raised her hands hurriedly, and put them together across her black gown, and looked eagerly at the visitor.

"No! For God's sake, don't think that!" said the captain, in a solemn way; "I bring no good tidings of him."

There was a silence, and the mother turned her face to the fire and put her hand between it and her eyes. The young fisherman slightly motioned toward the window, and the captain, looking in that direction, saw a young widow, sitting at a neighbouring window across a little garden, engaged in needlework, with a young child sleeping on her bosom. The silence continued until the captain asked of Alfred,—

"How long is it since it happened?"

"He shipped for his last voyage better than three years ago."

"Ship struck upon some reef or rock, as I take it," said the captain, "and all hands lost?"

"Yes."

"Wa'al!" said the captain, after a shorter silence, "Here I sit who may come to the same end, like enough. He holds the seas in the hollow of His hand. We must all strike somewhere and go down. Our comfort, then, for ourselves and one another is to have done our duty. I'd wager your brother did his!"

"He did!" answered the young fisherman, "If ever man strove faithfully on all occasions to do his duty, my brother did. My brother was not a quick man (anything but that), but he was a faithful, true, and just man. We were the sons of only a small tradesman in this county, Sir; yet our father was as watchful of his good name as if he had been a king."

"A precious sight more so, I hope,—bearing in mind the general run of that class of crittur," said the captain. "But I interrupt."

"My brother considered that our father left the good name to us, to keep clear and true."

"Your brother considered right," said the captain; "and you couldn't take care of a better legacy. But again I interrupt."

"No, for I have nothing more to say. We know that Hugh lived well for the good name, and we feel certain that he died well for the good name. And now it has come into my keeping. And that's all."

"Well spoken!" cried the captain. "Well spoken, young man! Concerning the manner of your brother's death"—by this time the captain had released the hand he had shaken, and sat with his own broad, brown hands spread out on his knees, and spoke aside,— "concerning the manner of your brother's death, it may be that I have some information to give you; though it may not be, for I am far from sure. Can we have a little talk alone?"

The young man rose; but not before the captain's quick eye had noticed that, on the pretty sweetheart's turning to the window to greet the young widow with a nod and a wave of the hand, the young widow had held up to her the needlework on which she was engaged, with a patient and pleasant smile. So the captain said, being on his legs,—

"What might she be making now?"

"What is Margaret making, Kitty?" asked the young fisherman,— with one of his arms apparently mislaid somewhere.

As Kitty only blushed in reply, the captain doubled himself up as far as he could, standing, and said, with a slap of his leg,—

"In my country we should call it wedding-clothes. Fact! We should, I do assure you."

But it seemed to strike the captain in another light too; for his laugh was not a long one, and he added, in quite a gentle tone,—

"And it's very pretty, my dear, to see her—poor young thing, with her fatherless child upon her bosom—giving up her thoughts to your home and your happiness. It's very pretty, my dear, and it's very good. May your marriage be more prosperous than hers, and be a comfort to her too. May the blessed sun see you all happy together, in possession of the good name, long after I have done ploughing the great salt field that is never sown!"

Kitty answered very earnestly, "O! Thank you, Sir, with all my heart!" And, in her loving little way, kissed her hand to him, and possibly by implication to the young fisherman, too, as the latter held the parlour-door open for the captain to pass out.

CHAPTER II

THE MONEY

"THE stairs are very narrow, Sir," said Alfred Raybrock to Captain Jorgan.

"Like my cabin-stairs," returned the captain, "on many a voyage."

"And they are rather inconvenient for the head."

"If my head can't take care of itself by this time, after all the knocking about the world it has had," replied the captain, as unconcernedly as if he had no connexion with it, "it's not worth looking after."

Thus they came into the young fisherman's bedroom, which was as perfectly neat and clean as the shop and parlour below; though it was but a little place with a sliding window, and a phrenological ceiling expressive of all the peculiarities of the house-roof. Here the captain sat down on the foot of the bed, and glancing at a dreadful libel on Kitty which ornamented the wall,—the production of some wandering limner, whom the captain secretly admired as having studied portraiture from the figure-heads of ships,—motioned to the young man to take the rush-chair on the other side of the small, round table. That done, the captain put his hand in the deep breast-pocket of his long-skirted blue coat, and took out of it a strong square case-bottle,—not a large bottle, but such as may be seen in any ordinary ship's medicine-chest. Setting this bottle on the table without removing his hand from it, Captain Jorgan then spake as follows:—

"In my last voyage homeward-bound," said the captain, "and that's the voyage off of which I now come straight, I encountered such weather off the Horn as is not very often met with, even there. I have rounded that stormy Cape pretty often, and I believe I first beat about there in the identical storms that blew the Devil's horns and tail off, and led to the horns being worked up into toothpicks for the plantation overseers in my country, who may be seen (if you travel down South, or away West, fur enough) picking their teeth with 'em, while the whips, made of the tail, flog hard. In this last voyage, homeward-bound for Liverpool from South America, I say to you, my young friend, it blew. Whole measures! No half measures, nor making believe to blow; it blew! Now I warn't blown clean out of the water into the sky,—though I expected to be even that,—but I was blown clean out of my course; and when at last it fell calm, it fell dead calm, and a strong current set one way, day and night, night and day, and I drifted—drifted—drifted—out of all the ordinary tracks and courses of ships, and drifted yet, and yet drifted. It behooves a man who takes charge of fellow-critturs' lives, never to rest from making himself master of his calling. I never did rest, and consequently I knew pretty well ('specially looking over the side in the dead calm of that strong current) what dangers to expect, and what precautions to take against 'em. In short, we were driving head on to an island. There was no island in the chart, and, therefore, you may say it was ill-manners in the island to be there; I don't dispute its bad breeding, but there it was. Thanks be to Heaven, I was as ready for the island as the island was ready for me. I made it out myself from the masthead, and I got enough way upon her in good time to keep her off. I ordered a boat to be lowered and manned, and went in that boat myself to explore the island. There was a reef outside it, and, floating in a corner of the smooth water within the reef, was a heap of sea-weed, and entangled in that sea-weed was this bottle."

Here the captain took his hand from the bottle for a moment, that the young fisherman might direct a wondering glance at it; and then replaced his hand and went on:—

"If ever you come—or even if ever you don't come—to a desert place, use you your eyes and your spy-glass well; for the smallest thing you see may prove of use to you, and may have some information or some warning in it. That's the principle on which I came to see this bottle. I picked up the bottle and ran the boat alongside the island, and made fast and went ashore armed, with a part of my boat's crew. We found that every scrap of vegetation on the island (I give it you as my opinion, but scant and scrubby at the best of times) had been consumed by fire. As we were making our way, cautiously and toilsomely, over the pulverised embers, one of my people sank into the earth breast-high. He turned pale, and 'Haul me out smart, shipmates,' says he, 'for my feet are among bones.' We soon got him on his legs again, and then we dug up the spot, and we found that the man was right, and that his feet had been among bones. More than that, they were human bones; though whether the remains of one man, or of two or three men, what with calcination and ashes, and what with a poor practical knowledge of anatomy, I can't undertake to say. We examined the whole island and made out nothing else,

save and except that, from its opposite side, I sighted a considerable
tract of land, which land I was able to identify, and according to the
bearings of which (not to trouble you with my log) I took a fresh
departure. When I got aboard again I opened the bottle, which was
oilskin-covered as you see, and glass-stoppered as you see. Inside of
it," pursued the captain, suiting his action to his words, "I found
this little crumpled, folded paper, just as you see. Outside of it was
written, as you see, these words: '*Whoever finds this, is solemnly entreated by the dead to convey it unread to Alfred Raybrock, Steepways
North Devon, England.*' A sacred charge," said the captain, concluding
his narrative, "and, Alfred Raybrock, there it is!"

"This is my poor brother's writing!"

"I suppose so," said Captain Jorgan. "I'll take a look out of this
little window while you read it."

"Pray no, Sir! I should be hurt. My brother couldn't know it would
fall into such hands as yours."

The captain sat down again on the foot of the bed, and the young
man opened the folded paper with a trembling hand, and spread it
on the table. The ragged paper, evidently creased and torn both before and after being written on, was much blotted and stained, and
the ink had faded and run, and many words were wanting. What the
captain and the young fisherman made out together, after much re-
reading and much humouring of the folds of the paper, is given below.

The young fishermen had become more and more agitated, as the
writing had become clearer to him. He now left it lying before the
captain, over whose shoulder he had been reading it, and dropping
into his former seat, leaned forward on the table and laid his face in
his hands.

"What, man," urged the captain, "don't give in! Be up and doing
like a man!"

"It is selfish, I know,—but doing what, doing what?" cried the
young fisherman, in complete despair, and stamping his sea-boot on
the ground.

"Doing what?" returned the captain. "Something! I'd go down to
the little breakwater below yonder, and take a wrench at one of the
salt-rusted iron rings there, and either wrench it up by the roots or
wrench my teeth out of my head, sooner than I'd do nothing. Nothing!" ejaculated the captain. "Any fool or fainting heart can do
that, and nothing can come of nothing,—which was pretended to be
found out, I believe, by one of them Latin critters," said the captain
with the deepest disdain; "as if Adam hadn't found it out, afore ever
he so much as named the beasts!"

Yet the captain saw, in spite of his bold words, that there was some
greater reason than he yet understood for the young man's distress.
And he eyed him with a sympathising curiosity.

"Come, come!" continued the captain. "Speak out. What is it,
boy!"

"You have seen how beautiful she is, Sir," said the young man,
looking up for the moment, with a flushed face and rumpled hair.

"Did any man ever say she warn't beautiful?" retorted the captain. "If so, go and lick him."

The young man laughed fretfully in spite of himself, and said, "It's not that, it's not that."

"Wa'al, then, what is it?" said the captain in a more soothing tone.

The young fisherman mournfully composed himself to tell the captain what it was, and began: "We were to have been married next Monday week——"

"Were to have been!" interrupted Captain Jorgan, "And are to be? Hey?"

Young Raybrock shook his head, and traced out with his fore-finger the words, "*poor father's five hundred pounds*," in the written paper.

"Go along," said the captain. "Five hundred pounds? Yes?"

"That sum of money," pursued the young fisherman, entering with the greatest earnestness on his demonstration, while the captain eyed him with equal earnestness, "was all my late father possessed. When he died, he owed no man more than he left means to pay, but he had been able to lay by only five hundred pounds."

"Five hundred pounds," repeated the captain. "Yes?"

"In his lifetime, years before, he had expressly laid the money aside to leave to my mother,—like to settle upon her, if I make myself understood."

"Yes?"

"He had risked it once—my father put down in writing at that time, respecting the money—and was resolved never to risk it again."

"Not a spec'lator," said the captain. "My country wouldn't have suited him. Yes?"

"My mother has never touched the money till now. And now it was to have been laid out, this very next week, in buying me a handsome share in our neighbouring fishery here, to settle me in life with Kitty."

The captain's face fell, and he passed and repassed his sun-browned right hand over his thin hair, in a discomfited manner.

"Kitty's father has no more than enough to live on, even in the sparing way in which we live about here. He is a kind of bailiff or steward of manor rights here, and they are not much, and it is but a poor little office. He was better off once, and Kitty must never marry to mere drudgery and hard living."

The captain still sat stroking his thin hair, and looking at the young fisherman.

"I am as certain that my father had no knowledge that any one was wronged as to this money, or that any restitution ought to be made, as I am certain that the sun now shines. But, after this solemn warning from my brother's grave in the sea, that the money is Stolen Money," said Young Raybrock, forcing himself to the utterance of the words, "can I doubt it? Can I touch it?"

"About not doubting, I ain't so sure," observed the captain; "but about not touching—no—I don't think you can."

"See then," said Young Raybrook, "why I am so grieved. Think of Kitty. Think what I have got to tell her!"

His heart quite failed him again when he had come round to that, and he once more beat his sea-boot softly on the floor. But not for long; he soon began again, in a quietly resolute tone.

"However! Enough of that! You spoke some brave words to me just now, Captain Jorgan, and they shall not be spoken in vain. I have got to do something. What I have got to do, before all other things, is to trace out the meaning of this paper, for the sake of the Good Name that has no one else to put it right. And still for the sake of the Good Name, and my father's memory, not a word of this writing must be breathed to my mother, or to Kitty, or to any human creature. You agree in this?"

"I don't know what they'll think of us below," said the captain, "but for certain I can't oppose it. Now, as to tracing. How will you do?"

They both, as by consent, bent over the paper again, and again carefully puzzled out the whole of the writing.

"I make out that this would stand, if all the writing was here, 'Inquire among the old men living there, for'—some one. Most like, you'll go to this village named here?" said the captain, musing, with his finger on the name.

"Yes! And Mr. Tregarthen is a Cornishman, and—to be sure!—comes from Lanrean."

"Does he?" said the captain quietly. "As I ain't acquainted with him, who may *he* be?"

"Mr. Tregarthen is Kitty's father."

"Ay, ay!" cried the captain. "Now you speak! Tregarthen knows this village of Lanrean, then?"

"Beyond all doubt he does. I have often heard him mention it, as being his native place. He knows it well."

"Stop half a moment," said the captain. "We want a name here. You could ask Tregarthen (or if you couldn't I could) what names of old men he remembers in his time in those diggings? Hey?"

"I can go straight to his cottage, and ask him now."

"Take me with you," said the captain, rising in a solid way that had a most comfortable reliability in it, "and just a word more first. I have knocked about harder than you, and have got along further than you. I have had, all my sea-going life long, to keep my wits polished bright with acid and friction, like the brass cases of the ship's instruments. I'll keep you company on this expedition. Now you don't live by talking any more than I do. Clench that hand of yours in this hand of mine, and that's a speech on both sides."

Captain Jorgan took command of the expedition with that hearty shake. He at once refolded the paper exactly as before, replaced it in the bottle, put the stopper in, put the oilskin over the stopper confided the whole to Young Raybrock's keeping, and led the way downstairs.

But it was harder navigation below-stairs than above. The instant they set foot in the parlour the quick, womanly eye detected that there was something wrong. Kitty exclaimed, frightened, as she ran to her lover's side, "Alfred! What's the matter?" Mrs. Raybrock cried out to the captain, "Gracious! what have you done to my son to change him like this all in a minute?" And the young widow—who was there with her work upon her arm—was at first so agitated that she frightened the little girl she held in her hand, who hid her face in her mother's skirts and screamed. The captain, conscious of being held responsible for this domestic change, contemplated it with quite a guilty expression of countenance, and looked to the young fisherman to come to his rescue.

"Kitty, darling," said Young Raybrock, "Kitty, dearest love, I must go away to Lanrean, and I don't know where else or how much further, this very day. Worse than that—our marriage, Kitty, must be put off, and I don't know for how long."

Kitty stared at him, in doubt and wonder and in anger, and pushed him from her with her hand.

"Put off?" cried Mrs. Raybrock. "The marriage put off? And you going to Lanrean! Why, in the name of the dear Lord?"

"Mother dear, I can't say why; I must not say why. It would be dishonourable and undutiful to say why."

"Dishonourable and undutiful?" returned the dame. "And is there nothing dishonourable or undutiful in the boy's breaking the heart of his own plighted love, and his mother's heart too, for the sake of the dark secrets and counsels of a wicked stranger? Why did you ever come here?" she apostrophised the innocent captain. "Who wanted you? Where did you come from? Why couldn't you rest in your own bad place, wherever it is, instead of disturbing the peace of quiet unoffending folk like us?"

"And what," sobbed the poor little Kitty, "have I ever done to you, you hard and cruel captain, that you should come and serve me so?"

And then they both began to weep most pitifully, while the captain could only look from the one to the other, and lay hold of himself by the coat collar.

"Margaret," said the poor young fisherman, on his knees at Kitty's feet, while Kitty kept both her hands before her tearful face, to shut out the traitor from her view,—but kept her fingers wide asunder and looked at him all the time,—"Margaret, you have suffered so much, so uncomplainingly, and are always so careful and considerate! Do take my part, for poor Hugh's sake!"

The quiet Margaret was not appealed to in vain. "I will, Alfred," she returned, "and I do. I wish this gentleman had never come near us;" whereupon the captain laid hold of himself the tighter; "but I take your part for all that. I am sure you have some strong reason and some sufficient reason for what you do, strange as it is, and even for not saying why you do it, strange as that is. And, Kitty darling, you are bound to think so more than any one, for true love believes everything, and bears everything, and trusts everything. And, mother dear, you are bound to think so too, for you know you have been blest with good sons, whose word was always as good as their oath, and who were brought up in as true a sense of honour as any gentleman in this land. And I am sure you have no more call, mother, to doubt your living son than to doubt your dead son; and for the sake of the dear dead, I stand up for the dear living."

"Wa'al now," the captain struck in, with enthusiasm, "this I say, That whether your opinions flatter me or not, you are a young woman of sense, and spirit, and feeling; and I'd sooner have you by my side, in the hour of danger, than a good half of the men I've ever fallen in with—or fallen out with, ayther."

Margaret did not return the captain's compliment, or appear fully to reciprocate his good opinion, but she applied herself to the consolation of Kitty, and of Kitty's mother-in-law that was to have been next Monday week, and soon restored the parlour to a quiet condition.

"Kitty, my darling," said the young fisherman, "I must go to your father to entreat him still to trust me in spite of this wretched change and mystery, and to ask him for some directions concerning Lanrean. Will you come home? Will you come with me, Kitty?"

Kitty answered not a word, but rose sobbing, with the end of her simple head-dress at her eyes. Captain Jorgan followed the lovers out, quite sheepishly, pausing in the shop to give an instruction to Mr. Pettifer.

"Here, Tom!" said the captain, in a low voice, "Here's something in your line. Here's an old lady poorly and low in her spirits. Cheer her up a bit, Tom. Cheer 'em all up."

Mr. Pettifer, with a brisk nod of intelligence, immediately assumed his steward face, and went with his quiet, helpful, steward step into the parlour, where the captain had the great satisfaction of seeing him, through the glass door, take the child in his arms (who offered no objection), and bend over Mrs. Raybrock, administering soft words of consolation.

"Though what he finds to say, unless he's telling her that 't'll soon be over, or that most people is so at first, or that it'll do her good afterwards, I cannot imaginate!" was the captain's reflection as he followed the lovers.

He had not far to follow them, since it was but a short descent down the stony ways to the cottage of Kitty's father. But short as the distance was, it was long enough to enable the captain to observe that he was fast becoming the village Ogre; for there was not a woman standing working at her door, or a fisherman coming up or going down, who saw Young Raybrock unhappy and little Kitty in tears, but he or she instantly darted a suspicious and indignant glance at the captain, as the foreigner who must somehow be responsible for this unusual spectacle. Consequently, when they came into Tregarthen's little garden,—which formed the platform from which the captain had seen Kitty peeping over the wall,—the captain brought to, and stood off and on at the gate, while Kitty hurried to hide her tears in her own room, and Alfred spoke with her father, who was working in the garden. He was a rather infirm man, but could scarcely be called old yet, with an agreeable face and a promising air of making the best of things. The conversation began on his side with great cheerfulness and good humour, but soon became distrustful, and soon angry. That was the captain's cue for striking both into the conversation and the garden.

"Morning, Sir!" said Captain Jorgan. "How do you do?"

"The gentleman I am going away with," said the young fisherman to Tregarthen.

"O!" returned Kitty's father, surveying the unfortunate captain with a look of extreme disfavour. "I confess that I can't say I am glad to see you."

"No," said the captain, "and, to admit the truth, that seems to be the general opinion in these parts. But don't be hasty; you may think better of me by-and-by."

"I hope so," observed Tregarthen.

"Wa'al, I hope so," observed the captain, quite at his ease; "more than that, I believe so,—though you don't. Now, Mr. Tregarthen, you don't want to exchange words of mistrust with me; and if you did, you couldn't, because I wouldn't. You and I are old enough to know better than to judge against experience from surfaces and appearances; and if you haven't lived to find out the evil and injustice of such judgments, you are a lucky man."

The other seemed to shrink under this remark, and replied, "Sir, I *have* lived to feel it deeply."

"Wa'al." said the captain, mollified, "then I've made a good cast without knowing it. Now, Tregarthen, there stands the lover of your only child, and here stand I who know his secret. I warrant it a righteous secret, and none of his making, though bound to be of his keeping. I want to help him out with it, and tewwards that end we ask you to favour us with the names of two or three old residents in the village of Lanrean. As I am taking out my pocket-book and pencil to put the names down, I may as well observe to you that this, wrote atop of the first page here, is my name and address: 'Silas Jonas Jorgan, Salem, Massachusetts, United States.' If ever you take it in your head to run over any morning, I shall be glad to welcome you. Now, what may be the spelling of these said names?"

"There was an elderly man," said Tregarthen, "named David Polreath. He may be dead."

"Wa'al," said the captain, cheerfully, "if Polreath's dead and buried, and can be made of any service to us, Polreath won't object to our digging of him up. Polreath's down, anyhow."

"There was another named Penrewen. I don't know his Christian name."

"Never mind his Chris'en name," said the captain. "Penrewen, for short."

"There was another named John Tredgear."

"And a pleasant-sounding name, too," said the captain; "John Tredgear's booked."

"I can recall no other except old Parvis."

"One of old Parvis's fam'ly I reckon," said the captain, "kept a dry-goods store in New York city, and realised a handsome competency by burning his house to ashes. Same name, anyhow. David Polreath, Unchris'en Penrewen, John Tredgear, and old Arson Parvis."

"I cannot recall any others at the moment."

"Thank'ee," said the captain. "And so, Tregarthen, hoping for your good opinion yet, and likewise for the fair Devonshire Flower's, your daughter's, I give you my hand, Sir, and wish you good-day."

Young Raybrock accompanied him disconsolately; for there was no Kitty at the window when he looked up, no Kitty in the garden when he shut the gate, no Kitty gazing after them along the stony ways when they began to climb back.

"Now I tell you what," said the captain. "Not being at present calc'lated to promote harmony in your family, I won't come in. You go and get your dinner at home, and I'll get mine at the little hotel. Let our hour of meeting be two o'clock, and you'll find me smoking a cigar in the sun afore the hotel door. Tell Tom Pettifer, my steward, to consider himself on duty, and to look after your people till we come back; you'll find he'll have made himself useful to 'em already, and will be quite acceptable."

All was done as Captain Jorgan directed. Punctually at two o'clock the young fisherman appeared with his knapsack at his back; and punctually at two o'clock the captain jerked away the last feather-end of his cigar.

"Let me carry your baggage, Captain Jorgan; I can easily take it with mine."

"Thank'ee," said the captain. "I'll carry it myself. It's only a comb."

They climbed out of the village, and paused among the trees and fern on the summit of the hill above, to take breath, and to look down at the beautiful sea. Suddenly the captain gave his leg a resounding slap, and cried, "Never knew such a right thing in all my life!"—and ran away.

The cause of this abrupt retirement on the part of the captain was little Kitty among the trees. The captain went out of sight and waited, and kept out of sight and waited, until it occurred to him to beguile the time with another cigar. He lighted it, and smoked it out, and still he was out of sight, and waiting. He stole within sight at last, and saw the lovers, with their arms entwined and their bent heads touching, moving slowly among the trees. It was the golden time of the afternoon then, and the captain said to himself, "Golden sun, golden sea, golden sails, golden leaves, golden love, golden youth,—a golden state of things altogether!"

Nevertheless the Captain found it necessary to hail his young companion before going out of sight again. In a few moments more he came up and they began their journey.

"That still young woman with the fatherless child," said Captain Jorgan, as they fell into step, "didn't throw her words away; but good honest words are never thrown away. And now that I am conveying you off from that tender little thing that loves, and relies, and hopes, I feel just as if I was the snarling crittur in the picters, with the tight legs, the long nose, and the feather in his cap, the tips of whose moustaches get up near to his eyes the wickeder he gets."

The young fisherman knew nothing of Mephistopheles; but he smiled when the captain stopped to double himself up and slap his leg, and they went along in right good-fellowship.*

CHAPTER V

THE RESTITUTION

CAPTAIN JORGAN, up and out betimes, had put the whole village of Lanrean under an amicable cross-examination, and was returning to

---

* NOTE.—The third and fourth chapters of this Christmas number were not by Mr. Dickens. After the first and second he did not resume the pen until the chapter entitled the "*Restitution*," here numbered as the fifth. For the two intervening chapters the reader is referred to the number as republished in the Volume of the *Nine Christmas numbers of All the Year Round.*

the King Arthur's Arms to breakfast, none the wiser for his trouble, when he beheld the young fisherman advancing to meet him, accompanied by a stranger. A glance at this stranger assured the captain that he could be no other than the Seafaring Man; and the captain was about to hail him as a fellow-craftsman, when the two stood still and silent before the captain, and the captain stood still, silent, and wondering before them.

"Why, what's this?" cried the captain, when at last he broke the silence. "You two are alike. You two are much alike! What's this?"

Not a word was answered on the other side, until after the seafaring brother had got hold of the captain's right hand and the fisherman brother had got hold of the captain's left hand; and if ever the captain had had his fill of handshaking, from his birth to that hour, he had it then. And presently up and spoke the two brothers, one at a time, two at a time, two dozen at a time for the bewilderment into which they plunged the captain, until he gradually had Hugh Raybrock's deliverance made clear to him, and also unravelled the fact that the person referred to in the half-obliterated paper was Tregarthen himself.

"Formerly, dear Captain Jorgan," said Alfred, "of Lanrean, you recollect? Kitty and her father came to live at Steepways after Hugh shipped on his last voyage."

"Ay, ay!" cried the captain, fetching a breath. "*Now* you have me in tow. Then your brother here don't know his sister-in-law that is to be so much as by name?"

"Never saw her, never heard of her!"

"Ay, ay, ay!" cried the captain. "Why then we every one go back together—paper, writer, and all—and take Tregarthen into the secret we kept from him?"

"Surely," said Alfred, "we can't help it now. We must go through with our duty."

"Not a doubt," returned the captain. "Give me an arm apiece, and let us set this ship-shape."

So walking up and down in the shrill wind on the wild moor, while the neglected breakfast cooled within, the captain and the brothers settled their course of action.

It was that they should all proceed by the quickest means they could secure to Barnstaple, and there look over the father's books and papers in the lawyer's keeping; as Hugh had proposed to himself to do if ever he reached home. That, enlightened or unenlightened, they should then return to Steepways and go straight to Mr. Tregarthen, and tell him all they knew, and see what came of it, and act accordingly. Lastly, that when they got there they should enter the village with all precautions against Hugh's being recognised by any chance; and that to the captain should be consigned the task of preparing his wife and mother for his restoration to this life.

"For you see," quoth Captain Jorgan, touching the last head, "it requires caution anyway, great joys being as dangerous as great griefs, if not more dangerous, as being more uncommon (and therefore ess provided against) in this round world of ours. And besides, I should like to free my name with the ladies, and take you home again at your brightest and luckiest; so don't let's throw away a chance of success."

The captain was highly lauded by the brothers for his kind interest and foresight.

"And now stop!" said the captain, coming to a standstill, and looking from one brother to the other, with quite a new rigging of wrinkles about each eye; "you are of opinion," to the elder, "that you are ra'ather slow?"

"I assure you I am very slow," said the honest Hugh.

"Wa'al," replied the captain, "I assure *you* that to the best of my belief I am ra'ather smart. Now a slow man ain't good at quick business, is he?"

That was clear to both.

"You," said the captain, turning to the younger brother, "are a little in love; ain't you?"

"Not a little, Captain Jorgan."

"Much or little, you're sort preoccupied; ain't you?"

It was impossible to be denied.

"And a sort preoccupied man ain't good at quick business, is he?" said the captain.

Equally clear on all sides.

"Now," said the captain, "I ain't in love myself, and I've made many a smart run across the ocean, and I should like to carry on and go ahead with this affair of yours and make a run slick through it. Shall I try? Will you hand it over to me?"

They were both delighted to do so, and thanked him heartily.

"Good," said the captain, taking out his watch. "This is half-past eight A.M., Friday morning. I'll jot that down, and we'll compute how many hours we've been out when we run into your mother's post-office. There! The entry's made, and now we go ahead."

They went ahead so well that before the Barnstaple lawyer's office was open next morning, the captain was sitting whistling on the step of the door, waiting for the clerk to come down the street with his key and open it. But instead of the clerk there came the master, with whom the captain fraternised on the spot to an extent that utterly confounded him.

As he personally knew both Hugh and Alfred, there was no difficulty in obtaining immediate access to such of the father's papers as were in his keeping. These were chiefly old letters and cash accounts; from which the captain, with a shrewdness and dispatch that left the lawyer far behind, established with perfect clearness, by noon, the following particulars:—

That one Lawrence Clissold had borrowed of the deceased, at a time when he was a thriving young tradesman in the town of Barnstaple, the sum of five hundred pounds. That he had borrowed it on the written statement that it was to be laid out in furtherance of a speculation which he expected would raise him to independence; he being, at the time of writing that letter, no more than a clerk in the house of Dringworth Brothers, America-square, London. That the money was borrowed for a stipulated period; but that, when the term was out, the aforesaid speculation failed, and Clissold was without means of repayment. That, hereupon, he had written to his creditor, in no very persuasive terms, vaguely requesting further time. That the creditor had refused this concession, declaring that he could not afford delay. That Clissold then paid the debt, accompanying the remittance of the money with an angry letter describing it as having been advanced by a relative to save him from ruin. That, in acknowledging the receipt, Raybrock had cautioned Clissold to seek to borrow money of him no more, as he would never so risk money again.

Before the lawyer the captain said never a word in reference to these discoveries. But when the papers had been put back in their box, and he and his two companions were well out of the office, his right leg suffered for it, and he said,—

"So far this run's begun with a fair wind and a prosperous; for don't you see that all this agrees with that dutiful trust in his father maintained by the slow member of the Raybrock family?"

Whether the brothers had seen it before or no, they saw it now. Not that the captain gave them much time to contemplate the state of things at their ease, for he instantly whipped them into a chaise again, and bore them off to Steepways. Although the afternoon was but just beginning to decline when they reached it, and it was broad daylight, still they had no difficulty, by dint of muffling the returned sailor up, and ascending the village rather than descending it, in reaching Tregarthen's cottage unobserved. Kitty was not visible, and they surprised Tregarthen sitting writing in the small bay-window of his little room.

"Sir," said the captain, instantly shaking hands with him, pen and all, "I'm glad to see you, Sir. How do you do, Sir? I told you you'd think better of me by-and-by, and I congratulate you on going to do it."

Here the captain's eye fell on Tom Pettifer Ho, engaged in preparing some cookery at the fire.

"That crittur," said the captain, smiting his leg, "is a born steward, and never ought to have been in any other way of life. Stop where you are, Tom, and make yourself useful. Now, Tregarthen, I'm going to try a chair."

Accordingly the captain drew one close to him, and went on:—

"This loving member of the Raybrock family you know, Sir. This slow member of the same family you don't know, Sir. Wa'al, these two are brothers,—fact! Hugh's come to life again, and here he stands. Now see here, my friend! You don't want to be told that he was cast away, but you do want to be told (for there's a purpose in it) that he was cast away with another man. That man by name was Lawrence Clissold."

At the mention of this name Tregarthen started and changed colour. "What's the matter?" said the captain.

"He was a fellow-clerk of mine thirty—five-and-thirty—years ago."

"True," said the captain, immediately catching at the clue: "Dringworth Brothers, America-square, London City."

The other started again, nodded, and said, "That was the house."

"Now," pursued the captain, "between those two men cast away there arose a mystery concerning the round sum of five hundred pound."

Again Tregarthen started, changing colour. Again the captain said, "What's the matter?"

As Tregarthen only answered, "Please to go on," the captain recounted, very tersely and plainly, the nature of Clissold's wanderings on the barren island, as he had condensed them in his mind from the seafaring man. Tregarthen became greatly agitated during this recital, and at length exclaimed,—

"Clissold was the man who ruined me! I have suspected it for many a long year, and now I know it."

"And how," said the captain, drawing his chair still closer to Tregarthen, and clapping his hand upon his shoulder,—"how may you know it?"

"When we were fellow clerks," replied Tregarthen, "in that London house, it was one of my duties to enter daily in a certain book an account of the sums received that day by the firm, and afterwards paid into the bankers'. One memorable day,—a Wednesday, the black day of my life,—among the sums I so entered was one of five hundred pounds."

"I begin to make it out," said the captain. "Yes?"

"It was one of Clissold's duties to copy from this entry a memorandum of the sums which the clerk employed to go to the bankers' paid in there. It was my duty to hand the money to Clissold; it was Clissold's to hand it to the clerk, with that memorandum of his writing. On that Wednesday I entered a sum of five hundred pounds received. I handed that sum, as I handed the other sums in the day's entry, to Clissold. I was absolutely certain of it at the time; I have been absolutely certain of it ever since. A sum of five hundred pounds was afterward found by the house to have been that day wanting from the bag, from Clissold's memorandum, and from the entries in my book. Clissold, being questioned, stood upon his perfect clearness in the matter, and emphatically declared that he asked no better than to be tested by 'Tregarthen's book.' My book was examined, and the entry of five hundred pounds was not there."

"How not there," said the captain, "when you made it yourself?"

Tregarthen continued:—

"I was then questioned. Had I made the entry? Certainly I had. The house produced my book, and it was not there. I could not deny my book; I could not deny my writing. I knew there must be forgery by some one; but the writing was wonderfully like mine, and I could impeach no one if the house could not. I was required to pay the money back. I did so; and I left the house, almost broken-hearted, rather than remain there,—even if I could have done so,—with a dark shadow of suspicion always on me. I returned to my native place, Lanrean, and remained there, clerk to a mine, until I was appointed to my little post here.

"I well remember," said the captain, "that I told you that if you had no experience of ill judgments on deceiving appearances, you were a lucky man. You went hurt at that, and I see why. I'm sorry."

"Thus it is," said Tregarthen. "Of my own innocence I have of course been sure; it has been at once my comfort and my trial. Of Clissold I have always had suspicions almost amounting to certainty; but they have never been confirmed until now. For my daughter's sake and for my own I have carried this subject in my own heart, as the only secret of my life, and have long believed that it would die with me."

"Wa'al, my good Sir," said the captain cordially, "the present question is, and will be long, I hope, concerning living, and not dying. Now, here are our two honest friends, the loving Raybrock and the slow. Here they stand, agreed on one point, on which I'd back 'em round the world, and right across it from north to south, and then again from east to west, and through it, from your deepest Cornish mine to China. It is, that they will never use this same so-often-mentioned sum of money, and that restitution of it must be made to you. These two, the loving member and the slow, for the sake of the right and of their father's memory, will have it ready for you to-morrow. Take it, and ease their minds and mine, and end a most unfort'-nate transaction."

Tregarthen took the captain by the hand, and gave his hand to each of the young men, but positively and finally answered No. He said, they trusted to his word, and he was glad of it, and at rest in his mind; but there was no proof, and the money must remain as it was. All were very earnest over this; and earnestness in men, when they are right and true, is so impressive, that Mr. Pettifer deserted his cookery and looked on quite moved.

"And so," said the captain, "so we come—as that lawyer-crittur over yonder where we were this morning might—to mere proof; do we? We must have it; must we? How? From this Clissold's wanderings, and from what you say, it ain't hard to make out that there was a neat forgery of your writing committed by the too-smart rowdy that was grease and ashes when I made his acquaintance, and a substitution of a forged leaf in your book for a real and true leaf torn out. Now was that real and true leaf then and there destroyed? No, —for says he, in his drunken way, he slipped it into a crack in his own desk, because you came into the office before there was time to burn it, and could never get back to it arterwards. Wait a bit. Where is that desk now? Do you consider it likely to be in America-square, London City?"

Tregarthen shook his head.

"The house has not, for years, transacted business in that place. I have heard of it, and read of it, as removed, enlarged, every way ltered. Things alter so fast in these times."

"You think so," returned the captain, with compassion; "but you
hould come over and see *me* afore you talk about *that*. Wa'al, now.
his desk, this paper,—this paper, this desk," said the captain,
uminating and walking about, and looking, in his uneasy abstrac-
ion, into Mr. Pettifer's hat on a table, among other things. "This
esk, this paper,—this paper, this desk," the captain continued,
ausing and roaming about the room, "I'd give——"

However, he gave nothing, but took up his steward's hat instead,
nd stood looking into it, as if he had just come into church. After
hat he roamed again, and again said, "This desk, belonging to this
ouse of Dringworth Brothers, America-square, London City——"

Mr. Pettifer, still strangely moved, and now more moved than
efore, cut the captain off as he backed across the room and bespake
im thus:—

"Captain Jorgan, I have been wishful to engage your attention,
ut I couldn't do it. I am unwilling to interrupt Captain Jorgan, but
must do it. *I* know something about that house."

The captain stood stock-still and looked at him,—with his (Mr.
Pettifer's) hat under his arm.

"You're aware," pursued his steward, "that I was once in the
roking business, Captain Jorgan?"

"I was aware," said the captain, "that you had failed in that
alling, and in half the businesses going, Tom."

"Not quite so, Captain Jorgan; but I ailed in the broking business.
. was partners with my brother, Sir. There was a sale of old office
urniture at Dringworth Brothers' when the house was moved from
America-square, and me and my brother made what we call in the
rade a Deal there, Sir. And I'll make bold to say, Sir, that the only
hing I ever had from my brother, or from any relation,—for my
elations have mostly taken property from me instead of giving me
any,—was an old desk we bought at that same sale, with a crack in it.
My brother wouldn't have given me even that, when we broke
partnership, if it had been worth anything."

"Where is that desk now?" said the captain.

"Well, Captain Jorgan," replied the steward, "I couldn't say for
certain where it is now; but when I saw it last,—which was last time
we were outward bound,—it was at a very nice lady's at Wapping,
along with a little chest of mine which was detained for a small
matter of a bill owing."

The captain, instead of paying that rapt attention to his steward
which was rendered by the other three persons present, went to church
again, in respect of the steward's hat. And a most especially agitated
and memorable face the captain produced from it, after a short pause.

"Now, Tom," said the captain, "I spoke to you, when we first came
here, respecting your constitutional weakness on the subject of sun-
stroke."

"You did, Sir."

"Will my slow friend," said the captain, "lend me his arm, or I

shall sink right back'ards into this blessed steward's cookery? Now
Tom," pursued the captain, when the required assistance was given
"on your oath as a steward, didn't you take that desk to pieces t
make a better one of it, and put it together fresh,—or something o
the kind?"

"On my oath I did, Sir," replied the steward.

"And by the blessing of Heaven, my friends, one and all," crie
the captain, radiant with joy,—"of the Heaven that put it into th
Tom Pettifer's head to take so much care of his head against th
bright sun,—he lined his hat with the original leaf in Tregarthen'
writing,—and here it is!"

With that the captain, to the utter destruction of Mr. Pettifer
favourite hat, produced the book-leaf, very much worn, but sti
legible, and gave both his legs such tremendous slaps that they wer
heard far off in the bay, and never accounted for.

"A quarter past five P.M.," said the captain, pulling out his watch
"and that's thirty-three hours and a quarter in all, and a pritty run!

How they were all overpowered with delight and triumph; how th
money was restored, then and there, to Tregarthen; how Tregarthen
then and there, gave it all to his daughter; how the captain under
took to go to Dringworth Brothers and re-establish the reputatio
of their forgotten old clerk; how Kitty came in, and was nearly tor
to pieces, and the marriage was reappointed, needs not to be told
Nor how she and the young fisherman went home to the post-offic
to prepare the way for the captain's coming, by declaring him to b
the mightiest of men, who had made all their fortunes,—and the
dutifully withdrew together, in order that he might have the do
mestic coast entirely to himself. How he availed himself of it is al
that remains to tell.

Deeply delighted with his trust, and putting his heart into it, h
raised the latch of the post-office parlour where Mrs. Raybrock an
the young widow sat, and said,—

"May I come in?"

"Sure you may, Captain Jorgan!" replied the old lady. "And goo
reason you have to be free of the house, though you have not bee
too well used in it by some who ought to have known better. I asl
your pardon."

"No you don't, ma'am," said the Captain, "for I won't let you
Wa'al, to be sure!"

By this time he had taken a chair on the hearth between them.

"Never felt such an evil spirit in the whole course of my life. There
I tell you! I could a'most have cut my own connexion. Like the deale
in my country, away West, who when he had let himself be outdone
in a bargain, said to himself, 'Now I tell you what! I'll never speal
to you again.' And he never did, but joined a settlement of oysters
and translated the multiplication table into their language,—whicl
is a fact that can be proved. If you doubt it, mention it to any oyste
you come across, and see if he'll have the face to contradict it."

He took the child from her mother's lap and set it on his knee.

"Not a bit afraid of me now, you see. Knows I am fond of small people. I have a child, and she's a girl, and I sing to her sometimes."

"What do you sing?" asked Margaret.

"Not a long song, my dear.

"Silas Jorgan
Played the organ.

hat's about all. And sometimes I tell her stories,—stories of sailors upposed to be lost, and recovered after all hope was abandoned." Here the captain musingly went back to his song,—

"Silas Jorgan
Played the organ;"

peating it with his eyes on the fire, as he softly danced the child on his knee. For he felt that Margaret had stopped working.

"Yes," said the captain, still looking at the fire, "I make up stories and tell 'em to that child. Stories of shipwreck on desert islands, and long delay in getting back to civilised lands. It is to stories the like of that, mostly, that

"Silas Jorgan
Plays the organ."

There was no light in the room but the light of the fire; for the shades of night were on the village, and the stars had begun to peep out of the sky one by one, as the houses of the village peeped out from among the foliage when the night departed. The captain felt that Margaret's eyes were upon him, and thought it discreetest to keep his own eyes on the fire.

"Yes; I make 'em up," said the captain. "I make up stories of brothers brought together by the good providence of GOD,—of sons brought back to mothers, husbands brought back to wives, fathers raised from the deep, for little children like herself."

Margaret's touch was on his arm, and he could not choose but look round now. Next moment her hand moved imploringly to his breast, and she was on her knees before him,—supporting the mother, who was also kneeling.

"What's the matter?" said the captain. "What's the matter?

"Silas Jorgan
Played the——"

Their looks and tears were too much for him, and he could not finish the song, short as it was.

"Mistress Margaret, you have borne ill fortune well. Could you bear good fortune equally well, if it was to come?"

"I hope so. I thankfully and humbly and earnestly hope so!"

"Wa'al, my dear," said the captain, "p'r'aps it has come. He's— don't be frightened—shall I say the word——"

"Alive?"

"Yes!"

The thanks they fervently addressed to Heaven were again too much for the captain, who openly took out his handkerchief and dried his eyes.

"He's no further off," resumed the captain, "than my country Indeed, he's no further off than his own native country. To tell yo the truth, he's no further off than Falmouth. Indeed, I doubt if he' quite so fur. Indeed, if you was sure you could bear it nicely, and was to do no more than whistle for him——"

The captain's trust was discharged. A rush came, and they were all together again.

This was a fine opportunity for Tom Pettifer to appear with a tumbler of cold water, and he presently appeared with it, and ad ministered it to the ladies; at the same time soothing them, and com posing their dresses, exactly as if they had been passengers crossing the Channel. The extent to which the captain slapped his legs, when Mr. Pettifer acquitted himself of this act of stewardship, could have been thoroughly appreciated by no one but himself; inasmuch as he must have slapped them black and blue, and they must have smarted tremendously.

He couldn't stay for the wedding, having a few appointments to keep at the irreconcilable distance of about four thousand miles. So next morning all the village cheered him up to the level ground above and there he shook hands with a complete Census of its population and invited the whole, without exception, to come and stay severa months with him at Salem, Mass., U.S. And there as he stood on the spot where he had seen that little golden picture of love and parting and from which he could that morning contemplate another golden picture with a vista of golden years in it, little Kitty put her arms around his neck, and kissed him on both his bronzed cheeks, and laid her pretty face upon his storm-beaten breast, in sight of all,—ashamed to have called such a noble captain names. And there the captain waved his hat over his head three final times; and there he was last seen, going away accompanied by Tom Pettifer Ho, and carrying his hands in his pockets. And there, before that ground was softened with the fallen leaves of three more summers, a rosy little boy took his first unsteady run to a fair young mother's breast, and the name of that infant fisherman was Jorgan Raybrock.

TOM TIDDLER'S GROUND

IN THREE CHAPTERS *

[1861]

CHAPTER I

PICKING UP SOOT AND CINDERS

"AND why Tom Tiddler's ground?" asked the Traveller.

"Because he scatters halfpence to Tramps and such-like," returned the Landlord, "and of course they pick 'em up. And this being done on his own land (which it *is* his own land, you observe, and were his family's before him), why it is but regarding the halfpence as gold and silver, and turning the ownership of the property a bit round your finger, and there you have the name of the children's game complete. And it's appropriate too," said the Landlord, with his favourite action of stooping a little, to look across the table out of window at vacancy, under the window-blind which was half drawn down. "Leastwise it has been so considered by many gentlemen which have partook of chops and tea in the present humble parlour."

The Traveller was partaking of chops and tea in the present humble parlour, and the Landlord's shot was fired obliquely at him.

"And you call him a Hermit?" said the Traveller.

"They call him such," returned the Landlord, evading personal responsibility; "he is in general so considered."

"What *is* a Hermit?" asked the Traveller.

"What is it?" repeated the Landlord, drawing his hand across his chin.

"Yes, what is it?"

The Landlord stooped again, to get a more comprehensive view of vacancy under the window-blind, and—with an asphyxiated appearance on him as one unaccustomed to definition—made no answer.

"I'll tell you what I suppose it to be," said the Traveller. "An abominably dirty thing."

"Mr. Mopes is dirty, it cannot be denied," said the Landlord.

"Intolerably conceited."

"Mr. Mopes is vain of the life he leads, some do say," replied the Landlord, as another concession.

* The original has seven chapters; but those not printed here were not written by Mr. Dickens.

213

"A slothful, unsavoury, nasty reversal of the laws of huma
nature," said the Traveller; "and for the sake of GOD'S workin
world and its wholesomeness, both moral and physical, I would pu
the thing on the treadmill (if I had my way) wherever I found it
whether on a pillar, or in a hole; whether on Tom Tiddler's ground
or the Pope of Rome's ground, or a Hindoo fakeer's ground, or an
other ground."

"I don't know about putting Mr. Mopes on the treadmill," said th
Landlord, shaking his head very seriously. "There ain't a doubt bu
what he has got landed property."

"How far may it be to this said Tom Tiddler's ground?" asked th
Traveller.

"Put it at five mile," returned the Landlord.

"Well! When I have done my breakfast," said the Traveller, "I'
go there. I came over here this morning, to find it out and see it."

"Many does," observed the Landlord.

The conversation passed, in the Midsummer weather of no remot
year of grace, down among the pleasant dales and trout-streams of
green English county. No matter what county. Enough that you ma
hunt there, shoot there, fish there, traverse long grass-grown Roma
roads there, open ancient burrows there, see many a square mil
of richly cultivated land there, and hold Arcadian talk with a bol
peasantry, their country's pride, who will tell you (if you want t
know) how pastoral housekeeping is done on nine shillings a week.

Mr. Traveller sat at his breakfast in the little sanded parlour of th
Peal of Bells village alehouse, with the dew and dust of an early wall
upon his shoes—an early walk by road and meadow and coppice, tha
had sprinkled him bountifully with little blades of grass, and scrap
of new hay, and with leaves both young and old, and with other suc
fragrant tokens of the freshness and wealth of summer. The windov
through which the landlord had concentrated his gaze upon vacanc
was shaded, because the morning sun was hot and bright on th
village street. The village street was like most other village streets
wide for its height, silent for its size, and drowsy in the dullest degree
The quietest little dwellings with the largest of window-shutters (t
shut up Nothing as carefully as if it were the Mint, or the Bank o
England) had called in the Doctor's house so suddenly, that his bras
door-plate and three stories stood among them as conspicuous an
different as the Doctor himself in his broadcloth, among the smock
frocks of his patients. The village residences seemed to have gone t
law with a similar absence of consideration, for a score of weak littl
lath-and-plaster cabins clung in confusion about the Attorney's red
brick house, which, with glaring doorsteps and a most terrific scraper
seemed to serve all manner of ejectments upon them. They were a
various as labourers—high-shouldered, wry-necked, one-eyed, goggle
eyed, squinting, bow-legged, knock-kneed, rheumatic, crazy. Som
of the small tradesmen's houses, such as the crockery-shop and th
harness-maker's, had a Cyclops window in the middle of the gable
within an inch or two of its apex, suggesting that some forlorn rura

entice must wriggle himself into that apartment horizontally,
hen he retired to rest, after the manner of the worm. So bountiful
its abundance was the surrounding country, and so lean and scant
e village, that one might have thought the village had sown and
anted everything it once possessed, to convert the same into crops.
his would account for the bareness of the little shops, the bareness
the few boards and trestles designed for market purposes in a
rner of the street, the bareness of the obsolete Inn and Inn Yard,
ith the omnibus inscription "Excise Office" not yet faded out from
e gateway, as indicating the very last thing that poverty could get
d of. This would also account for the determined abandonment of
e village by one stray dog, fast lessening in the perspective where
e white posts and the pond were, and would explain his conduct
a the hypothesis that he was going (through the act of suicide) to
nvert himself into manure, and become a part proprietor in turnips
mangold-wurzel.

Mr. Traveller having finished his breakfast and paid his moderate
ore, walked out to the threshold of the Peal of Bells, and, thence
rected by the pointing finger of his host, betook himself towards
e ruined hermitage of Mr. Mopes the hermit.

For, Mr. Mopes, by suffering everything about him to go to ruin,
d by dressing himself in a blanket and skewer, and by steeping
mself in soot and grease and other nastiness, had acquired great
nown in all that country-side—far greater renown than he could
er have won for himself, if his career had been that of any ordinary
ristian, or decent Hottentot. He had even blanketed and skewered
d sooted and greased himself into the London papers. And it was
rious to find, as Mr. Traveller found by stopping for a new direc-
on at this farmhouse or at that cottage as he went along, with how
uch accuracy the morbid Mopes had counted on the weakness of
s neighbours to embellish him. A mist of home-brewed marvel and
mance surrounded Mopes, in which (as in all fogs) the real propor-
ons of the real object were extravagantly heightened. He had mur-
red his beautiful beloved in a fit of jealousy and was doing penance ;
e had made a vow under the influence of grief; he had made a vow
nder the influence of a fatal accident; he had made a vow under the
fluence of religion; he had made a vow under the influence of drink;
e had made a vow under the influence of disappointment; he had
ever made any vow, but "had got led into it" by the possession of
mighty and most awful secret; he was enormously rich, he was
upendously charitable, he was profoundly learned, he saw spectres,
e knew and could do all kinds of wonders. Some said he went out
ery night, and was met by terrified wayfarers stalking along dark
ads, others said he never went out, some knew his penance to be
early expired, others had positive information that his seclusion
as not a penance at all, and would never expire but with himself.
ven, as to the easy facts of how old he was, or how long he had held
erminous occupation of his blanket and skewer, no consistent infor-
ation was to be got, from those who must know if they would. He

was represented as being all the ages between five-and-twenty an
sixty, and as having been a hermit seven years, twelve, twenty
thirty,—though twenty, on the whole, appeared the favourite term

"Well, well!" said Mr. Traveller. "At any rate, let us see what
real live Hermit looks like."

So, Mr. Traveller went on, and on, and on, until he came to Tor
Tiddler's ground.

It was a nook in a rustic by-road, which the genius of Mopes ha
laid waste as completely, as if he had been born an Emperor and
Conqueror. Its centre object was a dwelling-house, sufficientl
substantial, all the window-glass of which had been long ago abolishe
by the surprising genius of Mopes, and all the windows of which wer
barred across with rough-split logs of trees nailed over them on th
outside. A rickyard, hip-high in vegetable rankness and ruin, con
tained outbuildings, from which the thatch had lightly flutter
away, on all the winds of all the seasons of the year, and from whic
the planks and beams had heavily dropped and rotted. The frosts an
damps of winter, and the heats of summer, had warped what wrec
remained, so that not a post or a board retained the position it wa
meant to hold, but everything was twisted from its purpose, like it
owner, and degraded and debased. In this homestead of the sluggarc
behind the ruined hedge, and sinking away among the ruined gras
and the nettles, were the last perishing fragments of certain ricks
which had gradually mildewed and collapsed, until they looked lik
mounds of rotten honeycomb, or dirty sponge. Tom Tiddler's groun
could even show its ruined water; for, there was a slimy pond int
which a tree or two had fallen—one soppy trunk and branches la
across it then—which in its accumulation of stagnant weed, and in it
black decomposition, and in all its foulness and filth, was almos
comforting, regarded as the only water that could have reflecte
the shameful place without seeming polluted by that low office.

Mr. Traveller looked all around him on Tom Tiddler's ground, an
his glance at last encountered a dusky Tinker lying among the weed
and rank grass, in the shade of the dwelling-house. A rough walking
staff lay on the ground by his side, and his head rested on a smal
wallet. He met Mr. Traveller's eye without lifting up his head
merely depressing his chin a little (for he was lying on his back) to ge
a better view of him.

"Good day!" said Mr. Traveller.

"Same to you, if you like it," returned the Tinker.

"Don't *you* like it? It's a very fine day."

"I ain't partickler in weather," returned the Tinker, with a yawn

Mr. Traveller had walked up to where he lay, and was looking
down at him. "This is a curious place," said Mr. Traveller.

"Ay, I suppose so!" returned the Tinker. "Tom Tiddler's ground
they call this."

"Are you well acquainted with it?"

"Never saw it afore to-day," said the Tinker, with another yawn
"and don't care if I never see it again. There was a man here just now

old me what it was called. If you want to see Tom himself, you must go in at that gate." He faintly indicated with his chin a little mean ruin of a wooden gate at the side of the house.

"Have you seen Tom?"

"No, and I ain't partickler to see him. I can see a dirty man anywhere."

"He does not live in the house, then?" said Mr. Traveller, casting his eyes upon the house anew.

"The man said," returned the Tinker, rather irritably,—"him as was here just now,—'this what you're lying on, mate, is Tom Tiddler's ground. And if you want to see Tom,' he says, 'you must go in at that gate.' The man come out at that gate himself, and he ought to know."

"Certainly," said Mr. Traveller.

"Though, perhaps," exclaimed the Tinker, so struck by the brightness of his own idea, that it had the electric effect upon him of causing him to lift up his head an inch or so, "perhaps he was a liar! He told some rum'uns—him as was here just now did, about this place of Tom's. He says—him as was here just now—'When Tom shut up the house, mate, to go to rack, the beds was left, all made, like as if somebody was a going to sleep in every bed. And if you was to walk through the bedrooms now, you'd see the ragged mouldy bedclothes a heaving and a heaving like seas. And a heaving and a heaving with what?' he says. 'Why, with the rats under 'em.'"

"I wish I had seen that man," Mr. Traveller remarked.

"You'd have been welcome to see him instead of me seeing him," growled the Tinker; "for he was a long-winded one."

Not without a sense of injury in the remembrance, the Tinker gloomily closed his eyes. Mr. Traveller, deeming the Tinker a short-winded one, from whom no further breath of information was to be derived, betook himself to the gate.

Swung upon its rusty hinges, it admitted him into a yard in which there was nothing to be seen but an outhouse attached to the ruined building, with a barred window in it. As there were traces of many recent footsteps under this window, and as it was a low window, and unglazed, Mr. Traveller made bold to peep within the bars. And there to be sure he had a real live Hermit before him, and could judge how the real dead Hermits used to look.

He was lying on a bank of soot and cinders, on the floor, in front of a rusty fireplace. There was nothing else in the dark little kitchen, or scullery, or whatever his den had been originally used as, but a table with a litter of old bottles on it. A rat made a clatter among these bottles, jumped down, and ran over the real live Hermit on his way to his hole, or the man in *his* hole would not have been so easily discernible. Tickled in the face by the rat's tail, the owner of Tom Tiddler's ground opened his eyes, saw Mr. Traveller, started up, and sprang to the window.

"Humph!" thought Mr. Traveller, retiring a pace or two from the bars. "A compound of Newgate, Bedlam, a Debtor's Prison in the

worst time, a chimney-sweep, a mudlark, and the Noble Savage! .
nice old family, the Hermit family. Hah!''

Mr. Traveller thought this, as he silently confronted the soot
object in the blanket and skewer (in sober truth it wore nothing else
with the matted hair and the staring eyes. Further, Mr. Travelle
thought, as the eye surveyed him with a very obvious curiosity i
ascertaining the effect they produced, ''Vanity, vanity, vanity
Verily, all is vanity!''

''What is your name, Sir, and where do you come from?'' asked M
Mopes the Hermit—with an air of authority, but in the ordinar
human speech of one who has been to school.

Mr. Traveller answered the inquiries.

''Did you come here, Sir, to see *me?*''

''I did. I heard of you, and I came to see you.—I know you like t
be seen.'' Mr. Traveller coolly threw the last words in, as a matter c
course, to forestall an affectation of resentment or objection that h
saw rising beneath the grease and grime of the face. They had thei
effect.

''So,'' said the Hermit, after a momentary silence, unclasping th
bars by which he had previously held, and seating himself behin
them on the ledge of the window, with his bare legs and feet crouche
up, ''you know I like to be seen?''

Mr. Traveller looked about him for something to sit on, anc
observing a billet of wood in the corner, brought in near the windov
Deliberately seating himself upon it, he answered, ''Just so.''

Each looked at the other, and each appeared to take some pair
to get the measure of the other.

''Then you have come to ask me why I lead this life,'' said th
Hermit, frowning in a stormy manner. ''I never tell that to an
human being. I will not be asked that.''

''Certainly you will not be asked that by me,'' said Mr. Travelle
''for I have not the slightest desire to know.''

''You are an uncouth man,'' said Mr. Mopes the Hermit.

''You are another,'' said Mr. Traveller.

The Hermit, who was plainly in the habit of overawing his visitor
with the novelty of his filth and his blanket and skewer, glared at hi
present visitor in some discomfiture and surprise: as if he had take
aim at him with a sure gun, and his piece had missed fire.

''Why do you come here at all?'' he asked, after a pause.

''Upon my life,'' said Mr. Traveller, ''I was made to ask myself tha
very question only a few minutes ago—by a Tinker too.''

As he glanced towards the gate in saying it, the Hermit glanced i
that direction likewise.

''Yes. He is lying on his back in the sunlight outside,'' said M
Traveller, as if he had been asked concerning the man, ''and he won'
come in; for he says—and really very reasonably—'What should
come in for? I can see a dirty man anywhere.' ''

''You are an insolent person. Go away from my premises. Go!''
said the Hermit, in an imperious and angry tone.

"Come, come!" returned Mr. Traveller, quite undisturbed. "This is little too much. You are not going to call yourself clean? Look at our legs. And as to these being your premises—they are in far too disgraceful a condition to claim any privilege of ownership, or anything else.

The Hermit bounced down from his window-ledge, and cast himself on his bed of soot and cinders.

"I am not going," said Mr. Traveller, glancing in after him; "you won't get rid of me in that way. You had better come and talk."

"I won't talk," said the Hermit, flouncing round to get his back towards the window.

"Then I will," said Mr. Traveller. "Why should you take it ill that I have no curiosity to know why you live this highly absurd and highly indecent life? When I contemplate a man in a state of disease, surely there is no moral obligation on me to be anxious to know how he took it."

After a short silence, the Hermit bounced up again, and came back to the barred window.

"What? You are not gone?" he said, affecting to have supposed that he was.

"Nor going," Mr. Traveller replied; "I design to pass this summer day here."

"How dare you come, Sir, upon my premises——" the Hermit was returning, when his visitor interrupted him.

"Really, you know, you must *not* talk about your premises. I cannot allow such a place as this to be dignified with the name of premises."

"How dare you," said the Hermit, shaking his bars, "come in at my gate, to taunt me with being in a diseased state?"

"Why, Lord bless my soul," returned the other, very composedly, "you have not the face to say that you are in a wholesome state? Do allow me again to call your attention to your legs. Scrape yourself anywhere—with anything—and then tell me you are in a wholesome state. The fact is, Mr. Mopes, that you are not only a Nuisance——"

"A Nuisance?" repeated the Hermit, fiercely.

"What is a place in this obscene state of dilapidation but a Nuisance? What is a man in your obscene state of dilapidation but a Nuisance? Then, as you very well know, you cannot do without an audience, and your audience is a Nuisance. You attract all the disreputable vagabonds and prowlers within ten miles around, by exhibiting yourself to them in that objectionable blanket, and by throwing copper money among them, and giving them drink out of those very dirty jars and bottles that I see in there (their stomachs need be strong!); and in short," said Mr. Traveller, summing up in a quietly and comfortably settled manner, "you are a Nuisance, and this kennel is a Nuisance, and the audience that you cannot possibly dispense with is a Nuisance, and the Nuisance is not merely a local Nuisance, because it is a general Nuisance to know that there *can be* such a Nuisance left in civilisation so very long after its time."

"Will you go away? I have a gun in here," said the Hermit.

"Pooh!"

"I *have!*"

"Now, I put it to you. Did I say you had not? And as to goin‹
away, didn't I say I am not going away? You have made me forge‹
where I was. I now remember that I was remarking on your conduc‹
being a Nuisance. Moreover, it is in the last and lowest degree in
consequent foolishness and weakness."

"Weakness?" echoes the Hermit.

"Weakness," said Mr. Traveller, with his former comfortabl‹
settled final air.

"I weak, you fool?" cried the Hermit, "I, who have held to m‹
purpose, and my diet, and my only bed there, all these years?"

"The more the years, the weaker you," returned Mr. Travelle‹
"Though the years are not so many as folks say, and as you willingl‹
take credit for. The crust upon your face is thick and dark, M‹
Mopes, but I can see enough of you through it, to see that you ar‹
still a young man."

"Inconsequent foolishness is lunacy, I suppose?" said the Hermi‹

"I suppose it is very like it," answered Mr. Traveller.

"Do I converse like a lunatic?"

"One of us two must have a strong presumption against him c‹
being one, whether or no. Either the clean and decorously clad ma‹
or the dirty and indecorously clad man. I don't say which."

"Why, you self-sufficient bear," said the Hermit, "not a day passe‹
but I am justified in my purpose by the conversations I hold here: no‹
a day passes but I am shown, by everything I hear and see here, ho‹
right and strong I am in holding my purpose."

Mr. Traveller, lounging easily on his billet of wood, took out ‹
pocket pipe and began to fill it. "Now, that a man," he said, appealin‹
to the summer sky as he did so, "that a man—even behind bars, in ‹
blanket and skewer—should tell me that he can see, from day to da‹
any orders or conditions of men, women, or children, who can by an‹
possibility teach him that it is anything but the miserablest drivellin‹
for a human creature to quarrel with his social nature—not to go s‹
far as to say, to renounce his common human decency, for that is a‹
extreme case; or who can teach him that he can in any wise separat‹
himself from his kind and the habits of his kind, without becoming ‹
deteriorated spectacle calculated to give the Devil (and perhaps th‹
monkeys) pleasure,—is something wonderful! I repeat," said M‹
Traveller, beginning to smoke, "the unreasoning hardihood of it i‹
something wonderful—even in a man with the dirt upon him an incl‹
or two thick—behind bars—in a blanket and skewer!"

The Hermit looked at him irresolutely, and retired to his soot an‹
cinders and lay down, and got up again and came to the bars, an‹
again looked at him irresolutely, and finally said with sharpness‹
"I don't like tobacco."

"I don't like dirt," rejoined Mr. Traveller; "tobacco is an excellen‹
disinfectant. We shall both be the better for my pipe. It is my in‹

ention to sit here through this summer day, until that blessed
ummer sun sinks low in the west, and to show you what a poor
reature you are, through the lips of every chance wayfarer who may
ome in at your gate."

"What do you mean?" inquired the Hermit, with a furious air.

"I mean that yonder is your gate, and there are you, and here am
; I mean that I know it to be a moral impossibility that any person
an stray in at that gate from any point of the compass, with any
ort of experience, gained at first hand, or derived from another, that
an confute and justify you."

"You are an arrogant and boastful hero," said the Hermit. "You
hink yourself profoundly wise."

"Bah!" returned Mr. Traveller, quietly smoking. "There is little
visdom in knowing that every man must be up and doing, and that all
nankind are made dependent on one another."

"You have companions outside," said the Hermit. "I am not to be
mposed upon by your assumed confidence in the people who may
nter."

"A depraved distrust," returned the visitor, compassionately
aising his eyebrows, "of course belongs to your state. I can't help
hat."

"Do you mean to tell me you have no confederates?"

"I mean to tell you nothing but what I have told you. What I have
told you is, that it is a moral impossibility that any son or daughter
f Adam can stand on this ground that I put my foot on, or on any
ground that mortal treads, and gainsay the healthy tenure on which
ve hold our existence."

"Which is," sneered the Hermit, "according to you——"

"Which is," returned the other, "according to Eternal Providence,
that we must arise and wash our faces and do our gregarious work
and act and re-act on one another, leaving only the idiot and the
palsied to sit blinking in the corner. Come!" apostrophising the gate.
'Open Sesame! Show his eyes and grieve his heart! I don't care who
comes, for I know what must come of it!"

With that, he faced round a little on his billet of wood towards the
gate; and Mr. Mopes, the Hermit, after two or three ridiculous
bounces of indecision at his bed and back again, submitted to what
he could not help himself against, and coiled himself on his window-
ledge, holding to his bars and looking out rather anxiously.

CHAPTER VI

PICKING UP MISS KIMMEENS

THE day was by this time waning, when the gate again opened, and,
with the brilliant golden light that streamed from the declining sun
and touched the very bars of the sooty creature's den, there passed

in a little child; a little girl with beautiful bright hair. She wore a
plain straw hat, had a door-key in her hand, and tripped towards Mr
Traveller as if she were pleased to see him and were going to repose
some childish confidence in him, when she caught sight of the figur
behind the bars, and started back in terror.

"Don't be alarmed, darling!" said Mr. Traveller, taking her by th
hand.

"Oh, but I don't like it!" urged the shrinking child; "it's dreadful."

"Well! I don't like it either," said Mr. Traveller.

"Who has put it there?" asked the little girl. "Does it bite?"

"No,—only barks. But can't you make up your mind to see it
my dear?" For she was covering her eyes.

"O no no no!" returned the child. "I cannot bear to look at it!"

Mr. Traveller turned his head towards his friend in there, as mucl
as to ask him how he liked that instance of his success, and then tool
the child out at the still open gate, and stood talking to her for som
half an hour in the mellow sunlight. At length he returned, encour
aging her as she held his arm with both her hands; and laying hi
protecting hand upon her head and smoothing her pretty hair, he
addressed his friend behind the bars as follows:

Miss Pupford's establishment for six young ladies of tender years
is an establishment of a compact nature, an establishment in
miniature, quite a pocket establishment. Miss Pupford, Miss Pup
ford's assistant with the Parisian accent, Miss Pupford's cook, and
Miss Pupford's housemaid, complete what Miss Pupford calls the
educational and domestic staff of her Lilliputian College.

Miss Pupford is one of the most amiable of her sex; it necessarily
follows that she possesses a sweet temper, and would own to the
possession of a great deal of sentiment if she considered it quite
reconcilable with her duty to parents. Deeming it not in the bond
Miss Pupford keeps it as far out of sight as she can—which (God bles
her!) is not very far.

Miss Pupford's assistant with the Parisian accent, may be regarded
as in some sort an inspired lady, for she never conversed with a
Parisian, and was never out of England—except once in the pleasure
boat Lively, in the foreign waters that ebb and flow two miles of
Margate at high water. Even under those geographically favourable
circumstances for the acquisition of the French language in its utmost
politeness and purity, Miss Pupford's assistant did not fully profit by
the opportunity; for the pleasure-boat, Lively, so strongly asserted its
title to its name on that occasion, that she was reduced to the con
dition of lying in the bottom of the boat pickling in brine—as if she
were being salted down for the use of the Navy—undergoing at the
same time great mental alarm, corporeal distress, and clear-starching
derangement.

When Miss Pupford and her assistant first foregathered, is not
known to men, or pupils. But, it was long ago. A belief would have
established itself among pupils that the two once went to schoo

ogether, were it not for the difficulty and audacity of imagining Miss
Pupford born without mittens, and without a front, and without a
bit of gold wire among her front teeth, and without little dabs of
powder on her neat little face and nose. Indeed, whenever Miss
Pupford gives a little lecture on the mythology of the misguided
heathens (always carefully excluding Cupid from recognition), and
tells how Minerva sprang, perfectly equipped, from the brain of
Jupiter, she is half supposed to hint, "So I myself came into the
world, completely up in Pinnock, Mangnall, Tables, and the use of
the Globes."

Howbeit, Miss Pupford and Miss Pupford's assistant are old old
friends. And it is thought by pupils that, after pupils are gone to bed,
they even call one another by their christian names in the quiet little
parlour. For, once upon a time on a thunderous afternoon, when Miss
Pupford fainted away without notice, Miss Pupford's assistant (never
heard, before or since, to address her otherwise than as Miss Pupford)
ran to her, crying out "My dearest Euphemia!" And Euphemia is
Miss Pupford's christian name on the sampler (date picked out)
hanging up in the College-hall, where the two peacocks, terrified to
death by some German text that is waddling down hill after them out
of a cottage, are scuttling away to hide their profiles in two immense
bean-stalks growing out of flower-pots.

Also, there is a notion latent among pupils, that Miss Pupford was
once in love, and that the beloved object still moves upon this ball.
Also, that he is a public character, and a personage of vast consequence. Also, that Miss Pupford's assistant knows all about it. For,
sometimes of an afternoon when Miss Pupford has been reading the
paper through her little gold eye-glass (it is necessary to read it on
the spot, as the boy calls for it, with ill-conditioned punctuality, in
an hour), she has become agitated, and has said to her assistant
"G!" Then Miss Pupford's assistant has gone to Miss Pupford, and
Miss Pupford has pointed out, with her eye-glass, G in the paper,
and then Miss Pupford's assistant has read about G, and has shown
sympathy. So stimulated has the pupil-mind been in its time to
curiosity on the subject of G, that once under temporary circumstances favourable to the bold sally, one fearless pupil did actually
obtain possession of the paper and range all over it in search of G,
who had been discovered therein by Miss Pupford not ten minutes
before. But no G could be identified, except one capital offender,
who had been executed in a state of great hardihood, and it was
not to be supposed that Miss Pupford could ever have loved *him*.
Besides, he couldn't be always being executed. Besides, he got into
the paper again, alive, within a month.

On the whole, it is suspected by the pupil-mind that G. is a short
chubby old gentleman, with little black sealing-wax boots up to his
knees, whom a sharply observant pupil, Miss Linx, when she once
went to Tunbridge Wells with Miss Pupford for the holidays, reported
on her return (privately and confidentially) to have seen come caper-
ing up to Miss Pupford on the Promenade, and to have detected in the

act of squeezing Miss Pupford's hand, and to have heard pronounc
the words, "Cruel Euphemia, ever thine!"—or something like tha
Miss Linx hazarded a guess that he might be House of Commons, c
Money Market, or Court Circular, or Fashionable Movements; whic
would account for his getting into the paper so often. But, it wა
fatally objected by the pupil-mind, that none of those notabiliti
could possibly be spelt with a G.

There are other occasions closely watched and perfectly compre
hended by the pupil-mind, when Miss Pupford imparts with myster
to her assistant that there is special excitement in the morning pape
These occasions are, when Miss Pupford finds an old pupil comin
out under the head of Births, or Marriages. Affectionate tears an
invariably seen in Miss Pupford's meek little eyes when this is th
case; and the pupil-mind, perceiving that its order has distinguishe
itself—though the fact is never mentioneed by Miss Pupford—
becomes elevated, and feels that it likewise is reserved for greatness

Miss Pupford's assistant with the Parisian accent has a little mor
bone than Miss Pupford, but is of the same trim orderly diminutiv
cast, and, from long contemplation, admiration, and imitation c
Miss Pupford, has grown like her. Being entirely devoted to Mis
Pupford, and having a pretty talent for pencil-drawing, she onc
made a portrait of that lady: which was so instantly identified an
hailed by the pupils, that it was done on stone at five shilling
Surely the softest and milkiest stone that ever was quarried, receive
that likeness of Miss Pupford! The lines of her placid little nose are s
undecided in it that strangers to the work of art are observed to b
exceedingly perplexed as to where the nose goes to, and involuntaril
feel their own noses in a disconcerted manner. Miss Pupford bein
represented in a state of dejection at an open window, ruminatin
over a bowl of goldfish, the pupil-mind has settled that the bowl wa
presented by G, and that he wreathed the bowl with flowers of sou
and that Miss Pupford is depicted as waiting for him on a memorabl
occasion when he was behind his time.

The approach of the last Midsummer holidays had a particula
interest for the pupil-mind, by reason of its knowing that Mis
Pupford was bidden, on the second day of those holidays, to th
nuptials of a former pupil. As it was impossible to conceal the fact—
so extensive were the dressmaking preparations—Miss Pupfor
openly announced it. But, she held it due to parents to make th
announcement with an air of gentle melancholy, as if marriage wer
(as indeed it exceptionally has been) rather a calamity. With an air c
softened resignation and pity, therefore, Miss Pupford went on wit
her preparations: and meanwhile no pupil ever went upstairs, c
came down, without peeping in at the door of Miss Pupford's bed
room (when Miss Pupford wasn't there), and bringing back som
surprising intelligence concerning the bonnet.

The extensive preparations being completed on the day before th
holidays, an unanimous entreaty was preferred to Miss Pupford b
the pupil-mind—finding expression through Miss Pupford's assistan

—that she would deign to appear in all her splendour. Miss Pupford consenting, presented a lovely spectacle. And although the oldest pupil was barely thirteen, every one of the six became in two minutes perfect in the shape, cut, colour, price, and quality, of every article Miss Pupford wore.

Thus delightfully ushered in, the holidays began. Five of the six pupils kissed little Kitty Kimmeens twenty times over (round total, one hundred times, for she was very popular), and so went home. Miss Kitty Kimmeens remained behind, for her relations and friends were all in India, far away. A self-helpful steady little child is Miss Kitty Kimmeens, a dimpled child too, and a loving.

So, the great marriage-day came, and Miss Pupford, quite as much fluttered as any bride could be (G! thought Miss Kitty Kimmeens), went away, splendid to behold, in the carriage that was sent for her. But not Miss Pupford only went away, for Miss Pupford's assistant went away with her, on a dutiful visit to an aged uncle—though surely the venerable gentleman couldn't live in the gallery of the church where the marriage was to be, thought Miss Kitty Kimmeens —and yet Miss Pupford's assistant had let it out that she was going there. Where the cook was going, didn't appear, but she generally conveyed to Miss Kimmeens that she was bound, rather against her will, on a pilgrimage to perform some pious office that rendered new ribbons necessary to her best bonnet, and also sandals to her shoes.

"So you see," said the housemaid, when they were all gone, "there's nobody left in the house but you and me, Miss Kimmeens."

"Nobody else," said Miss Kitty Kimmeens, shaking her curls a little sadly. "Nobody!"

"And you wouldn't like your Bella to go too; would you, Miss Kimmeens?" said the housemaid. (She being Bella.)

"N—no," answered little Miss Kimmeens.

"Your poor Bella is forced to stay with you, whether she likes it or not; ain't she, Miss Kimmeens?"

"*Don't* you like it?" inquired Kitty.

"Why, you're such a darling, Miss, that it would be unkind of your Bella to make objections. Yet my brother-in-law has been took unexpected bad by this morning's post. And your poor Bella is much attached to him, letting alone her favourite sister, Miss Kimmeens."

"Is he very ill?" asked little Kitty.

"Your poor Bella has her fears so, Miss Kimmeens," returned the housemaid, with her apron at her eyes. "It was but his inside, it is true, but it might mount, and the doctor said that if it mounted he wouldn't answer." Here the housemaid was so overcome that Kitty administered the only comfort she had ready: which was a kiss.

"If it hadn't been for disappointing Cook, dear Miss Kimmeens," said the housemaid, "your Bella would have asked her to stay with you. For Cook is sweet company, Miss Kimmeens, much more so than your own poor Bella."

"But you are very nice, Bella."

"Your Bella could wish to be so, Miss Kimmeens," returned the

housemaid, "but she knows full well that it do not lay in her powe
this day."

With which despondent conviction, the housemaid drew a heavy
sigh, and shook her head, and dropped it on one side.

"If it had been anyways right to disappoint Cook," she pursued, i
a contemplative and abstracted manner, "it might have been so easy
done! I could have got to my brother-in-law's, and had the best par
of the day there, and got back, long before our ladies come home a
night, and neither the one nor the other of them need never hav
known it. Not that Miss Pupford would at all object, but that i
might put her out, being tenderhearted. Hows'ever, your own poo
Bella, Miss Kimmeens," said the housemaid, rousing herself, "i
forced to stay with you, and you're a precious love, if not a liberty.'

"Bella," said little Kitty, after a short silence.

"Call your own poor Bella, *your* Bella, dear," the housemai
besought her.

"My Bella, then."

"Bless your considerate heart!" said the housemaid.

"If you would not mind leaving me, I should not mind being left.
am not afraid to stay in the house alone. And you need not be uneas
on my account, for I would be very careful to do no harm."

"O! As to harm, you more than sweetest, if not a liberty," ex
claimed the housemaid, in a rapture, "your Bella could trust yo
anywhere, being so steady, and so answerable. The oldest hea
in this house (me and Cook says), but for its bright hair, i
Miss Kimmeens. But no, I will not leave you; for you would thin
your Bella unkind."

"But if you are my Bella, you *must* go," returned the child.

"Must I?" said the housemaid, rising, on the whole with alacrity
"What must be, must be, Miss Kimmeens. Your own poor Bella act
according, though unwilling. But go or stay, your own poor Bell
loves you, Miss Kimmeens."

It was certainly go, and not stay, for within five minutes Mis
Kimmeens's own poor Bella—so much improved in point of spirits a
to have grown almost sanguine on the subject of her brother-in-law—
went her way, in apparel that seemed to have been expressly prepare
for some festive occasion. Such are the changes of this fleeting world
and so short sighted are we poor mortals!

When the house door closed with a bang and a shake, it seemed t
Miss Kimmeens to be a very heavy house door, shutting her up in
wilderness of a house. But, Miss Kimmeens being, as before stated, o
a self-reliant and methodical character, presently began to parcel ou
the long summer-day before her.

And first she thought she would go all over the house, to make quit
sure that nobody with a great-coat on and a carving-knife in it, ha
got under one of the beds or into one of the cupboards. Not that sh
had ever before been troubled by the image of anybody armed with
great-coat and a carving-knife, but that it seemed to have been shake
into existence by the shake and bang of the great street door, rever

perating through the solitary house. So, little Miss Kimmeens looked under the five empty beds of the five departed pupils, and looked under her own bed, and looked under Miss Pupford's bed, and looked under Miss Pupford's assistant's bed. And when she had done this, and was making the tour of the cupboards, the disagreeable thought came into her young head, What a very alarming thing it would be to find somebody with a mask on like Guy Fawkes, hiding bolt upright in a corner and pretending not to be alive! However, Miss Kimmeens having finished her inspection without making any such uncomfortable discovery, sat down in her tidy little manner to needlework, and began stitching away at a great rate.

The silence all about her soon grew very oppressive, and the more so because of the odd inconsistency that the more silent it was, the more noises there were. The noise of her own needle and thread as she stitched, was infinitely louder in her ears than the stitching of all six pupils, and of Miss Pupford, and of Miss Pupford's assistant, all stitching away at once on a highly emulative afternoon. Then, the school-room clock conducted itself in a way in which it had never conducted itself before—fell lame, somehow, and yet persisted in running on as hard and as loud as it could: the consequence of which behaviour was, that it staggered among the minutes in a state of the greatest confusion, and knocked them about in all directions without appearing to get on with its regular work. Perhaps this alarmed the stairs: but be that as it might, they began to creak in a most unusual manner, and then the furniture began to crack, and then poor little Miss Kimmeens, not liking the furtive aspect of things in general, began to sing as she stitched. But, it was not her own voice that she heard—it was somebody else making believe to be Kitty, and singing excessively flat, without any heart—so as that would never mend matters, he left off again.

By and by, the stitching became so palpable a failure that Miss Kitty Kimmeens folded her work neatly, and put it away in its box, and gave it up, Then the question arose about reading. But no; the book that was so delightful when there was somebody she loved for her eyes to fall on when they rose from the page, had not more heart in it than her own singing now. The book went to its shelf as the needlework had gone to its box, and, since something *must* be done—thought the child, "I'll go put my room to rights."

She shared her room with her dearest little friend among the other five pupils, and why then should she now conceive a lurking dread of the little friend's bedstead? But she did. There was a stealthy air about its innocent white curtains, and there were even dark hints of a dead girl lying under the coverlet. The great want of human company, the great need of a human face, began now to express itself in the facility with which the furniture put on strange exaggerated resemblances to human looks. A chair with a menacing frown was horribly out of temper in a corner; a most vicious chest of drawers snarled at her from between the windows. It was no relief to escape from those monsters to the looking-glass, for the reflection said, "What? Is that you all

alone there? How you stare!" And the background was all a grea
void stare as well.

The day dragged on, dragging Kitty with it very slowly by the hai
of her head, until it was time to eat. There were good provisions in th
pantry, but their right flavour and relish had evaporated with th
five pupils, and Miss Pupford, and Miss Pupford's assistant, and th
cook and housemaid. Where was the use of laying the cloth symmetr
cally for one small guest, who had gone on ever since the mornin
growing smaller and smaller, while the empty house had gone o
swelling larger and larger? The very Grace came out wrong, for wh
were "we" who were going to receive and be thankful? So, Mis
Kimmeens was *not* thankful, and found herself taking her dinner i
very slovenly style—gobbling it up, in short, rather after the manne
of the lower animals, not to particularise the pigs.

But, this was by no means the worst of the change wrought out i
the naturally lovely and cheery little creature as the solitary da
wore on. She began to brood and be suspicious. She discovered tha
she was full of wrongs and injuries. All the people she knew, go
tainted by her lonely thoughts and turned bad.

It was all very well for papa, a widower in India, to send her hom
to be educated, and to pay a handsome round sum every year for he
to Miss Pupford, and to write charming letters to his darling littl
daughter; but what did he care for her being left by herself, when h
was (as no doubt he always was) enjoying himself, in company fror
morning till night? Perhaps he only sent her here, after all, to get he
out of the way. It looked like it—looked like it to-day, that is, for sh
had never dreamed of such a thing before.

And this old pupil who was being married. It was insupportabl
conceited and selfish in the old pupil to be married. She was very vair
and very glad to show off; but it was highly probable that she wasn'
pretty; and even if she were pretty (which Miss Kimmeens now totall
denied), she had no business to be married; and, even if marriage wer
conceded, she had no business to ask Miss Pupford to her wedding
As to Miss Pupford, she was too old to go to any wedding. She ough
to know that. She had much better attend to her business. She ha
thought she looked nice in the morning, but she didn't look nice. Sh
was a stupid old thing. G was another stupid old thing. Miss Pupford
assistant was another. They were all stupid old things together.

More than that: it began to be obvious that this was a plot. The
had said to one another, "Never mind Kitty: you get off, and I'll ge
off; and we'll leave Kitty to look after herself. Who cares for *her*?
To be sure they were right in that question; for who *did* care for he
a poor little lonely thing against whom they all planned and plotted
Nobody, nobody! Here Kitty sobbed.

At all other times she was the pet of the whole house, and loved he
five companions in return with a child's tenderest and most ingenu
ous attachment; but now, the five companions put on ugly colours
and appeared for the first time under a sullen cloud. There they were
all at their homes that day, being made much of, being taken ou

eing spoilt and made disagreeable, and caring nothing for her. It
vas like their artful selfishness always to tell her when they came
back, under pretence of confidence and friendship, all those details
about where they had been, and what they had done and seen, and
iow often they had said, "O! If we had only darling little Kitty here!"
Iere indeed; I dare say! When they came back after the holidays,
hey were used to being received by Kitty, and to saying that coming
o Kitty was like coming to another home. Very well then, why did
hey go away? If they meant it, why did they go away? Let them
answer that. But they didn't mean it, and couldn't answer that, and
hey didn't tell the truth, and people who didn't tell the truth were
hateful. When they came back next time, they should be received
n a new manner; they should be avoided and shunned.

And there, the while she sat all alone revolving how ill she was
used, and how much better she was than the people who were not
alone, the wedding breakfast was going on: no question of it! With
a nasty great bride-cake, and with those ridiculous orange-flowers,
and with that conceited bride, and that hideous bridegroom, and
those heartless bridesmaids, and Miss Pupford stuck up at the
table! They thought they were enjoying themselves, but it would
come home to them one day to have thought so. They would all be
dead in a few years, let them enjoy themselves ever so much. It was
a religious comfort to know that.

It was such a comfort to know it, that little Miss Kitty Kimmeens
suddenly sprang from the chair in which she had been musing in a
corner, and cried out, "O those envious thoughts are not mine, O this
wicked creature isn't me! Help me! somebody! I go wrong, alone by
my weak self! Help me, anybody!"

"—Miss Kimmeens is not a professed philosopher, Sir," said Mr.
Traveller, presenting her at the barred window, and smoothing her
shining hair, "but I apprehend there was some tincture of philosophy
in her words and in the prompt action with which she followed them.
That action was, to emerge from her unnatural solitude, and look
abroad for wholesome sympathy, to bestow and to receive. Her footsteps strayed to this gate, bringing her here by chance, as an opposite
contrast to you. The child came out, Sir. If you have the wisdom to
learn from a child (but I doubt it, for that requires more wisdom than
one in your condition would seem to possess), you cannot do better
than imitate the child, and come out too—from that very demoralis-
ing hutch of yours."

CHAPTER VII

PICKING UP THE TINKER

IT was now sunset. The Hermit had betaken himself to his bed of
cinders half an hour ago, and lying on it in his blanket and skewer
with his back to the window, took not the smallest heed of the appeal
addressed to him.

All that had been said for the last two hours, had been said to a tinkling accompaniment performed by the Tinker, who had got to work upon some villager's pot or kettle, and was working briskly outside. This music still continuing, seemed to put it into Mr Traveller's mind to have another word or two with the Tinker. So, holding Miss Kimmeens (with whom he was now on the most friendly terms) by the hand, he went out at the gate to where the Tinker was seated at his work on the patch of grass on the opposite side of the road, with his wallet of tools open before him, and his little fire smoking.

"I am glad to see you employed," said Mr. Traveller.

"I am glad to *be* employed," returned the Tinker, looking up as he put the finishing touches to his job. "But why are you glad?"

"I thought you were a lazy fellow when I saw you this morning."

"I was only disgusted," said the Tinker.

"Do you mean with the fine weather?"

"With the fine weather?" repeated the Tinker, staring.

"You told me you were not particular as to weather, and I thought——"

"Ha, ha! How should such as me get on, if we *was* particular as to weather? We must take it as it comes, and make the best of it. There's something good in all weathers. If it don't happen to be good for my work to-day, it's good for some other man's to-day, and will come round to me to-morrow. We must all live."

"Pray, shake hands," said Mr. Traveller.

"Take care, Sir," was the Tinker's caution, as he reached up his hand in surprise; "the black comes off."

"I am glad of it," said Mr. Traveller. " I have been for several hours among other black that does not come off."

"You are speaking of Tom in there?"

"Yes."

"Well now," said the Tinker, blowing the dust off his job: which was finished. "Ain't it enough to disgust a pig, if he could give his mind to it?"

"If he could give his mind to it," returned the other, smiling, "the probability is that he wouldn't be a pig."

"There you clench the nail," returned the Tinker. "Then what's to be said for Tom?"

"Truly, very little."

"Truly nothing you mean, Sir," said the Tinker, as he put away his tools.

" A better answer, and (I freely acknowledge) my meaning. I infer that he was the cause of your disgust?"

"Why, look'ee here, Sir," said the Tinker, rising to his feet, and wiping his face on the corner of his black apron energetically; "I leave you to judge!—I ask you!—Last night I has a job that needs to be done in the night, and I works all night. Well, there's nothing in that. But this morning I comes along this road here, looking for a sunny and soft spot to sleep in, and I sees this desolation and ruination. I've lived myself in desolation and ruination; I knows many a fellow-creetur that's forced to live life long in desolation and ruination; and I sits me down and takes pity on it, as I casts my eyes about. Then comes up the long-winded one as I told you of, from that gate, and spins himself out like a silkworm concerning the Donkey (if my Donkey at home will excuse me) as has made it all—made it of his own choice! And tells me, if you please, of his likewise choosing to go ragged and naked, and grimy—maskerading, mountebanking, in what is the real hard lot of thousands and thousands! Why, then I say it's unbearable and nonsensical a piece of inconsistency, and I'm disgusted. I'm ashamed and disgusted!''

"I wish you would come and look at him," said Mr. Traveller, clapping the Tinker on the shoulder.

"Not I, Sir," he rejoined. "*I* ain't agoing to flatter him up by looking at him."

"But he is asleep."

"Are you sure he is asleep?" asked the Tinker, with an unwilling air, as he shouldered his wallet.

"Sure."

"Then I'll look at him for a quarter of a minute," said the Tinker, "since you so much wish it; but not a moment longer."

They all three went back across the road; and, through the barred window, by the dying glow of the sunset coming in at the gate—which the child held open for its admission—he could be pretty clearly discerned lying on his bed.

"You see him?" asked Mr. Traveller.

"Yes," returned the Tinker, "and he's worse than I thought him."

Mr. Traveller then whispered in few words what he had done since morning; and asked the Tinker what he thought of that?

"I think," returned the Tinker, as he turned from the window, "that you've wasted a day on him."

"I think so too; though not, I hope, upon myself. Do you happen to be going anywhere near the Peal of Bells?"

"That's my direct way, Sir," said the Tinker.

"I invite you to supper there. And as I learn from this young lady that she goes some three-quarters of a mile in the same direction, we will drop her on the road, and we will spare time to keep her company at her garden gate until her own Bella comes home."

So, Mr. Traveller, and the child, and the Tinker, went along very amicably in the sweet-scented evening; and the moral with which the Tinker dismissed the subject was, that he said in his trade that metal that rotted for want of use, had better be left to rot, and couldn't rot too soon, considering how much true metal rotted from over-use and hard service.

SOMEBODY'S LUGGAGE

IN FOUR CHAPTERS

[1862]

CHAPTER I

HIS LEAVING IT TILL CALLED FOR

THE writer of these humble lines being a Waiter, and having come of a family of Waiters, and owning at the present time five brothers who are all Waiters, and likewise an only sister who is a Waitress, would wish to offer a few words respecting his calling; first having the pleasure of hereby in a friendly manner offering the Dedication of the same unto JOSEPH, much respected Head Waiter at the Slamjam Coffeehouse, London, E.C., than which an individual more eminently deserving of the name of man, or a more amenable honour to his own head and heart, whether considered in the light of a Waiter or regarded as a human being, do not exist.

In case confusion should arise in the public mind (which it is open to confusion on many subjects) respecting what is meant or implied by the term Waiter, the present humble lines would wish to offer an explanation. It may not be generally known that the person as goes out to wait is *not* a Waiter. It may not be generally known that the hand, as is called in extra, at the Freemason's Tavern, or the London, or the Albion, or otherwise, is *not* a Waiter. Such hands may be took on for Public Dinners by the bushel (and you may know them by their breathing with difficulty when in attendance, and taking away the bottle ere yet it is half out); but such are *not* Waiters. For you cannot lay down the tailoring, or the shoemaking, or the brokering, or the green-grocering, or the pictorial-periodicalling, or the second-hand wardrobe, or the small fancy businesses,—you cannot lay down those lines of life at your will and pleasure by the half-day or evening, and take up Waitering. You may suppose you can, but you cannot; or you may go so far as to say you do, but you do not. Nor yet can you lay down the gentleman's-service when stimulated by prolonged imcompatibility on the part of Cooks (and here it may be remarked that Cooking and Incompatibility will be mostly found united), and take up Waitering. It has been ascertained that what a gentleman will sit meek under at home, he will not bear out of doors, at the Slamjam or any similar establishment. Then, what is the

232

nference to be drawn respecting true Waitering? You must be bred to it. You must be born to it.

Would you know how born to it, Fair Reader,—if of the adorable female sex? Then learn from the biographical experience of one that is a Waiter in the sixty-first year of his age.

You were conveyed,—ere yet your dawning powers were otherwise developed than to harbour vacancy in your inside,—you were conveyed, by surreptitious means, into a pantry adjoining the Admiral Nelson, Civic and General Dining Rooms, there to receive by stealth that healthful sustenance which is the pride and boast of the British female constitution. Your mother was married to your father (himself a distant Waiter) in the profoundest secrecy; for a Waitress known to be married would ruin the best of businesses,—it is the same as on the stage. Hence your being smuggled into the pantry, and that—to add to the infliction—by an unwilling grandmother. Under the combined influence of the smells of roast and boiled, and soup, and gas, and malt liquors, you partook of your earliest nourishment; your unwilling grandmother sitting prepared to catch you when your mother was called and dropped you; your grandmother's shawl ever ready to stifle your natural complainings; your innocent mind surrounded by uncongenial cruets, dirty plates, dish-covers, and cold gravy; your mother calling down the pipe for veals and porks, instead of soothing you with nursery rhymes. Under these untoward circumstances you were early weaned. Your unwilling grandmother, ever growing more unwilling as your food assimilated less, then contracted habits of shaking you till your system curdled, and your food would not assimilate at all. At length she was no longer spared, and could have been thankfully spared much sooner. When your brothers began to appear in succession, your mother retired, left off her smart dressing (she had previously been a smart dresser), and her dark ringlets (which had previously been flowing), and haunted your father late of nights, lying in wait for him, through all weathers, up the shabby court which led to the back door of the Royal Old Dust-Bin (said to have been so named by George the Fourth), where your father was Head. But the Dust-Bin was going down then, and your father took but little,—excepting from a liquid point of view. Your mother's object in those visits was of a housekeeping character, and you was set on to whistle your father out. Sometimes he came out, but generally not. Come or not come, however, all that part of his existence which was unconnected with open Waitering was kept a close secret, and was acknowledged by your mother to be a close secret, and you and your mother flitted about the court, close secrets both of you, and would scarcely have confessed under torture that you knew your father, or that your father had any name than Dick (which wasn't his name, though he was never known by any other), or that he had kith or kin or chick or child. Perhaps the attraction of this mystery, combined with your father's having a damp compartment to himself, behind a leaky cistern, at the Dust-bin,—a sort of a cellar compartment, with a sink in it, and a smell, and a plate-rack, and a bottle-rack, and three windows that didn't match each other, or anything else, and no daylight,—caused your young mind to feel convinced that you must grow up to be a Waiter too; but you did feel convinced of it, and so did all your brothers, down to your sister. Every one of you felt convinced that you was born to the Waitering. At this stage of your career, what was your feelings one day when your father came home to your mother in open broad daylight,—of itself an act of Madness on the part of a Waiter,—and took to his bed (leastwise, your mother and family's bed), with a statement that his eyes were devilled kidneys. Physicians being in vain, your father expired, after repeating at intervals for a day and a night, when gleams of reason and old business fitfully illuminated his being, "Two and two is five. And three is sixpence." Interred in the parochial department of the neighbouring churchyard, and accompanied to the grave by as many Waiters of long standing as could spare the morning time from their soiled glasses (namely, one), your bereaved form was attired in a white neckankecher, and you was took on from motives of benevolence at the George and Gridiron, theatrical and supper. Here, supporting nature on what you found in the plates (which was as it happened, and but too often thoughtlessly, immersed in mustard), and on what you found in the glasses (which rarely went beyond driblets and lemon), by night you dropped asleep standing, till you was cuffed awake, and by day was set to polishing every individual article in the coffee-room. Your couch being saw-dust; your counterpane being ashes of cigars. Here, frequently hiding a heavy heart under the smart tie of your white neckankercher (or correctly speaking lower down and more to the left), you picked up the rudiments of knowledge from an extra, by the name of Bishops, and by calling plate-washer, and gradually elevating your mind with chalk on the back of the corner-box partition, until such time as you used the inkstand when it was out of hand, attained to manhood, and to be the Waiter that you find yourself.

I could wish here to offer a few respectful words on behalf of the calling so long the calling of my self and family, and the public interest in which is but too often very limited. We are not generally understood. No, we are not. Allowance enough is not made for us. For, say that we ever show a little drooping listlessness of spirits, or what might be termed indifference or apathy. Put it to yourself what would your own state of mind be, if you was one of an enormous family every member of which except you was always greedy, and in a hurry. Put it to yourself that you was regularly replete with animal food at the slack hours of one in the day and again at nine P.M., and that the repleter you was, the more voracious all your fellow-creatures came in. Put it to yourself that it was your business, when your digestion was well on, to take a personal interest and sympathy in a hundred gentlemen fresh and fresh (say, for the sake of argument, only a hundred), whose imaginations was given up to grease and fat and gravy and melted butter, and abandoned to questioning you about cuts of this, and dishes of that,—each of 'em going on as if him and you and the bill of fare was alone in the world. Then look what you are expected to know. You are never out, but they seem to think you regularly attend everywhere. "What's this, Christopher, that I hear about the smashed Excursion Train?"— "How are they doing at the Italian Opera, Christopher?"—"Christopher, what are the real particulars of this business at the Yorkshire Bank?" Similarly a ministry gives me more trouble than it gives the Queen. As to Lord Palmerston, the constant and wearing connexion into which I have been brought with his lordship during the last few years is deserving of a pension. Then look at the Hypocrites we are made and the lies (white, I hope) that are forced upon us! Why must a sedentary-pursuited Waiter be considered to be a judge of horse-flesh, and to have a most tremendous interest in horse-training and racing? Yet it would be half our little incomes out of our pockets if we didn't take on to have those sporting tastes. It is the same (inconceivable why!) with Farming. Shooting, equally so. I am sure that so regular as the months of August, September, and October come round, I am ashamed of myself in my own private bosom for the way in which I make believe to care whether or not the grouse is strong on the wing, (much their wings, or drumsticks either, signifies to me, uncooked!), and whether the partridges is plentiful among the turnips, and whether the peasants is shy or bold, or anything else you please to mention. Yet you may see me, or any other Waiter of my standing, holding by on the back of the box, and leaning over a gentleman with his purse out and his bill before him, discussing these points in a confidential tone of voice, as if my happiness in life entirely depended on 'em.

I have mentioned our little incomes. Look at the most unreasonable point of all, and the point on which the greatest injustice is done us! Whether it is owing to our always carrying so much change in our right-hand trousers-pocket, and so many half-pence in our coat-tails, or whether it is human nature (which I were loth to believe), what is meant by the everlasting fable that Head Waiters is rich? How did that fable get into circulation? Who first put it about, and what are the facts to establish the unblushing statement? Come forth, thou slanderer, and refer the public to the Waiter's will in Doctors' Commons supporting thy malignant hiss! Yet it is so commonly dwelt upon—especially by the screws who give Waiters the least— that denial is vain: and we are obliged, for our credit's sake, to carry our heads as if we were going into a business, when of the two we are much more likely to go into a union. There was formerly a screw as frequented the Slamjam ere yet the present writer had quitted that establishment on a question of tea-ing his assistant staff out of his own pocket, which screw carried the taunt to its bitterest height. Never soaring above threepence, and as often as not grovelling on the earth a penny lower, he yet represented the present writer as a large holder of Consols, a lender of money on mortgage, a Capitalist. He has been overheard to dilate to other customers on the allegation

that the present writer put out thousands of pounds at interest in
Distilleries and Breweries. "Well, Christopher," he would say (having
grovelled his lowest on the earth, half a moment before), "looking out
for a House to open, eh? Can't find a business to be disposed of on a
scale as is up to your resources, humph?" To such a dizzy precipice
of falsehood has this misrepresentation taken wing, that the well
known and highly respected OLD CHARLES, long eminent at the West
Country Hotel, and by some considered the Father of the Waitering
found himself under the obligation to fall into it through so many
years that his own wife (for he had an unbeknown old lady in that
capacity towards himself) believed it! And what was the consequence?
When he was borne to his grave on the shoulders of six picked Waiters
with six more for change, six more acting as pall-bearers, all keeping
step in a pouring shower without a dry eye visible, and a concourse
only inferior to Royalty, his pantry and lodgings was equally ran-
sacked high and low for property, and none was found! How could it
be found, when, beyond his last monthly collection of walking-sticks
umbrellas, and pocket-handkerchiefs (which happened to have been
not yet disposed of, though he had ever been through life punctual
in clearing off his collections by the month), there was no property
existing? Such, however, is the force of this universal libel, that the
widow of Old Charles, at the present hour an inmate of the Almshouses
of the Cork-Cutters' Company, in Blue Anchor-road (identified sitting
at the door of one of 'em, in a clean cap and a Windsor arm-chair
only last Monday), expects John's hoarded wealth to be found hourly
Nay, ere yet he had succumbed to the grisly dart, and when his
portrait was painted in oils life-size, by subscription of the fre-
quenters of the West Country, to hang over the coffee-room chimney
piece, there were not wanting those who contended that what is
termed the accessories of such a portrait ought to be the Bank of
England out of the window, and a strong-box on the table. And but
for better regulated minds contending for a bottle and screw and the
attitude of drawing,—and carrying their point,—it would have been
so handed down to posterity.

I am now brought to the title of the present remarks. Having, I
hope without offence to any quarter, offered such observations as I
felt it my duty to offer, in a free country which has ever dominated
the seas, on the general subject, I will now proceed to wait on the
particular question.

At a momentous period of my life, when I was off, so far as concerned notice given, with a House that shall be nameless,—for the
question on which I took my departing stand was a fixed charge for
waiters, and no House as commits itself to that eminently un-English
act of more than foolishness and baseness shall be advertised by
me,—I repeat, at a momentous crisis, when I was off with a House
too mean for mention, and not yet on with that to which I have ever
since had the honour of being attached in the capacity of Head,* I

* Its name and address at length, with other full particulars, all editorially
struck out.

was casting about what to do next. Then it were that proposals were made to me on behalf of my present establishment. Stipulations were necessary on my part, emendations were necessary on my part: in the end, ratifications ensued on both sides, and I entered on a new career.

We are a bed business, and a coffee-room business. We are not a general dining business, nor do we wish it. In consequence, when diners drop in, we know what to give 'em as will keep 'em away another time. We are a Private Room or Family business also; but coffee-room principal. Me and the Directory and the Writing Materials and cetrer occupy a place to ourselves—a place fended off up a step or two at the end of the coffee-room, in what I call the good old-fashioned style. The good old-fashioned style is, that whatever you want, down to a wafer, you must be olely and solely dependent on the Head Waiter for. You must put yourself a new-born Child into his hands. There is no other way in which a business untinged with Continental Vice can be conducted. (It were bootless to add, that if languages is required to be jabbered and English is not good enough, both families and gentlemen had better go somewhere else.)

When I began to settle down in this right-principled and well-conducted House, I noticed, under the bed in No. 24 B (which it is up a angle off the staircase, and usually put off upon the lowly-minded), a heap of things in a corner. I asked our Head Chambermaid in the course of the day,

"What are them things in 24 B?"

To which she answered with a careless air,

"Somebody's Luggage."

Regarding her with a eye not free from severity, I says.

"Whose Luggage?"

Evading my eye, she replied,

"Lor! How should *I* know!"

—Being, it may be right to mention, a female of some pertness, though acquainted with her business.

A Head Waiter must be either Head or Tail. He must be at one extremity or the other of the social scale. He cannot be at the waist of it, or anywhere else but the extremities. It is for him to decide which of the extremities.

On the eventful occasion under consideration, I give Mrs. Pratchett so distinctly to understand my decision, that I broke her spirit as towards myself, then and there, and for good. Let not inconsistency be suspected on account of my mentioning Mrs. Pratchett as "Mrs.," and having formerly remarked that a waitress must not be married. Readers are respectfully requested to notice that Mrs. Pratchett was not a waitress, but a chambermaid. Now a chambermaid *may* be married; if Head, generally is married,—or says so. It comes to the same thing as expressing what is customary. (N.B. Mr. Pratchett is in Australia, and his address there is "the Bush.")

Having took Mrs. Pratchett down as many pegs as was essential to the future happiness of all parties, I requested her to explain herself.

"For instance," I says, to give her a little encouragement, "who is Somebody?"

"I give you my sacred honour, Mr. Christopher," answers Pratchett, "that I haven't the faintest notion."

But for the manner in which she settled her cap-strings, I should have doubted this; but in respect of positiveness it was hardly to be discriminated from an affidavit.

"Then you never saw him?" I followed her up with.

"Nor yet," said Mrs. Pratchett, shutting her eyes and making as if she had just took a pill of unusual circumference,—which gave a remarkable force to her denial,—"nor yet any servant in this house. All have been changed, Mr. Christopher, within five year, and Somebody left his Luggage her before then."

Inquiry of Miss Martin yielded (in the language of the Bard of A. 1.) "confirmation strong." So it had really and truly happened. Miss Martin is the young lady at the bar as makes out our bills; and though higher than I could wish considering her station, is perfectly well-behaved.

Farther investigation led to the disclosure that there was a bill against this Luggage to the amount of two sixteen six. The luggage had been lying under the bedstead of 24 B over six year. The bedstead is a four-poster, with a deal of old hanging and valance, and is, as I once said, probably connected with more than 24 Bs,—which I remember my hearers was pleased to laugh at, at the time.

I don't know why,—when DO we know why?—but this Luggage laid heavy on my mind. I fell a wondering about Somebody, and what he had got and been up to. I couldn't satisfy my thoughts why he should leave so much luggage against so small a bill. For I had the Luggage out within a day or two and turned it over, and the following were the items:—A black portmanteau, a black bag, a desk, a dressing-case, a brown-paper parcel, a hat-box, and an umbrella strapped to a walking-stick. It was all very dusty and fluey. I had our porter up to get under the bed and fetch it out; and thought he habitually wallows in dust,—swims in it from morning to night, and wears a close-fitting waistcoat with black calimanco sleeves for the purpose,—it made him sneeze again, and his throat was that hot with it that it was obliged to be cooled with a drink of Allsopp's draft.

The Luggage so got the better of me, that instead of having it put back when it was well dusted and washed with a wet cloth,— previous to which it was so covered with feathers that you might have thought it was turning into poultry, and would by and by begin to Lay,—I say, instead of having it put back, I had it carried into one of my places downstairs. There from time to time I stared at it and stared at it, till it seemed to grow big and grow little, and come forward at me and retreat again, and go through all manner of performances resembling intoxication. When this had lasted weeks,— I may say months, and not be far out,—I one day thought of asking Miss Martin for the particulars of the Two sixteen six total. She was

so obliging as to extract it from the books,—it dating before her
time,—and here follows a true copy:

Coffee-Room. 1856.	No. 4.	£	s.	d.
Feb. 2d,	Pen and Paper	0	0	6
	Port Negus	0	2	0
	Ditto	0	2	0
	Pen and Paper	0	0	6
	Tumbler broken	0	2	6
	Brandy	0	2	0
	Pen and paper	0	0	6
	Anchovy toast	0	2	6
	Pen and paper	0	0	6
	Bed	0	3	0
Feb. 3d,	Pen and paper	0	0	6
	Breakfast	0	2	6
	,, Broiled ham	0	2	0
	,, Eggs	0	1	0
	,, Watercresses	0	1	0
	Breakfast—Shrimps	0	1	0
	Pen and paper	0	0	6
	Blotting-paper	0	0	6
	Messenger to Paternoster-row and back	0	1	6
	Again, when No Answer	0	1	6
	Brandy 2s., Devilled Pork chop 2s.	0	4	0
	Pens and paper	0	1	0
	Messenger to Albemarle-street and back	0	1	0
	Again (detained), when No Answer	0	1	6
	Salt-cellar broken	0	3	6
	Large Liqueur-glass Orange Brandy	0	1	6
	Dinner, Soup, Fish, Joint, and bird	0	7	6
	Bottle old East India Brown	0	8	0
	Pen and paper	0	0	6
		£2	16	6

Mem.: January 1st, 1857. He went out after dinner, directing
Luggage to be ready when he called for it. Never called.

So far from throwing a light upon the subject, this bill appeared to
me, if I may so express my doubts, to involve it in a yet more lurid
halo. Speculating it over with the Mistress, she informed me that the
luggage had been advertised in the Master's time as being to be sold
after such and such a day to pay expenses, but no farther steps had
been taken. (I may here remark, that the Mistress is a widow in her
fourth year. The Master was possessed of one of those unfortunate
constitutions in which Spirits turns to Water, and rises in the ill-
starred Victim.)

My speculating it over, not then, but repeatedly, sometimes with

the Mistress, sometimes with one, sometimes with another, led up to
the Mistress's saying to me,—whether at first in joke or in earnest, or
half joke and half earnest, it matters not:

"Christopher, I am going to make you a handsome offer."

(If this should meet her eye—a lovely blue,—may she not take it
ill my mentioning that if I had been eight or ten year younger, I
would have done as much by her! That is, I would have made her a
offer. It is for others than me to denominate it a handsome one.)

"Christopher, I am going to make you a handsome offer."

"Put a name to it, ma'am."

"Look here, Christopher. Run over the articles of Somebody's
Luggage. You've got it all by heart, I know."

"A black portmanteau, ma'am, a black bag, a desk, a dressing-
case, a brown-paper parcel, a hat-box, and an umbrella strapped to
a walking-stick."

"All just as they were left. Nothing opened, nothing tampered
with."

"You are right, ma'am. All locked but the brown-paper parcel, and
that sealed."

The Mistress was leaning on Miss Martin's desk at the bar-window,
and she taps the open book that lays upon the desk,—she has a
pretty-made hand to be sure,—and bobs her head over it and laughs.

"Come," says she, "Christopher. Pay me Somebody's bill, and you
shall have Somebody's Luggage."

I rather took to the idea from the first moment; but,

"I mayn't be worth the money," I objected, seeming to hold back.

"That's a Lottery," says the Mistress, folding her arms upon the
book,—it ain't her hands alone that's pretty made, the observation
extends right up her arms. "Won't you venture two pound
sixteen shillings and sixpence in the Lottery? Why, there's no
blanks!" says the Mistress, laughing and bobbing her head again,
"you *must* win. If you lose, you must win! All prizes in this Lottery!
Draw a blank and, remember, Gentlemen-Sportsmen, you'll still be
entitled to a black portmanteau, a black bag, a desk, a dressing-
case, a sheet of brown paper, a hat-box, and an umbrella strapped to
a walking-stick!"

To make short of it, Miss Martin come round me, and Mrs. Pratchett come round me, and the Mistress she was completely round me
already, and all the women in the house come round me, and if it had
been Sixteen two instead of Two sixteen, I should have thought
myself well out of it. For what can you do when they do come round
you?

So I paid the money—down—and such a laughing as there was
among 'em! But I turned the tables on 'em regularly, when I said:

"My family name is Blue-Beard. I'm going to open Somebody's
Luggage all alone in the Secret Chamber, and not a female eye
catches sight of the contents!"

Whether I thought proper to have the firmness to keep to this,
don't signify, or whether any female eye, and if any, how many, was

really present when the opening of the Luggage came off. Somebody's Luggage is the question at present: Nobody's eyes, nor yet noses.

What I still look at most, in connexion with the Luggage, is the extraordinary quantity of writing-paper, and all written on! And not our paper neither,—not the paper charged in the bill, for we know our paper,—so he must have been always at it. And he had crumpled up this writing of his, everywhere, in every part and parcel of his luggage. There was writing in his dressing-case, writing in his boots, writing among his shaving-tackle, writing in his hat-box, writing folded away down among the very whalebones of his umbrella.

His clothes wasn't bad, what there was of 'em. His dressing-case was poor,—not a particle of silver stopper,—bottle apertures with nothing in 'em, like empty little dog-kennels,—and a most searching description of tooth-powder diffusing itself around, as under a deluded mistake that all the chinks in the fittings was divisions in teeth. His clothes I parted with, well enough, to a second-hand dealer not far from St. Clement's Danes, in the Strand,—him as the officers in the Army mostly dispose of their uniforms to, when hard pressed with debts of honour, if I may judge from their coats and epaulets diversifying the window with their backs towards the public. The same party bought in one lot the portmanteau, the bag, the desk, the dressing-case, the hat-box, the umbrella, strap, and walking-stick. On my remarking that I should have thought those articles not quite in his line, he said: "No more ith a man'th grandmother, Mithter Chrithtopher; but if any man will bring hith grandmother here, and offer her at a fair trifle below what the'll feth with good luck when the'th thcoured and turned—I'll buy her!"

These transactions brought me home, and, indeed, more than home, for they left a goodish profit on the original investments. And now there remained the writings; and the writings I particular wish to bring under the candid attention of the reader.

I wish to do so without postponement, for this reason. This is to say, namely, viz. i.e., as follows, thus:—Before I proceed to recount the mental sufferings of which I became the prey in consequence of the writings, and before following up that harrowing tale with a statement of the wonderful and impressive catastrophe, as thrilling in its nature as unlooked for in any other capacity, which crowned the ole and filled the cup of unexpectedness to overflowing, the writings themselves ought to stand forth to view. Therefore it is that they now come next. One word to introduce them, and I lay down my pen (I hope, my unassuming pen) until I take it up to trace the gloomy sequel of a mind with something on it.

He was a smeary writer, and wrote a dreadful bad hand. Utterly regardless of ink, he lavished it on every undeserving object,—on his clothes, his desk, his hat, the handle of his tooth-brush, his umbrella. Ink was found freely on the coffee-room carpet by No. 4 table, and two blots was on his restless couch. A reference to the document I have given entire will show that on the morning of the third of February, eighteen fifty-six, he procured his no less than fifth pen and

paper. To whatever deplorable act of ungovernable composition he
immolated those materials obtained from the bar, there is no doubt
that the fatal deed was committed in bed, and that it left its
evidences but too plainly, long afterwards, upon the pillow-case.

He had put no Headings to any of his writings. Alas! Was he
likely to have a Heading without a Head, and where was *his* Head
when he took such things into it? In some cases, such as his Boots, he
would appear to have hid the writings; thereby involving his
style in greater obscurity. But his boots was at least pairs,—and no
two of his writings can put in any claim to be so regarded. Here
follows (not to give more specimens) what was found in—

CHAPTER II

HIS BOOTS

"Eh! well then, Monsieur Mutuel! What do I know, what can I say?
I assure you that he calls himself Monsieur The Englishman."

"Pardon. But I think it is impossible," said Monsieur Mutuel,—a
spectacled, snuffy, stooping old gentleman in carpet shoes and a
cloth cap with a peaked shade, a loose blue frock-coat reaching to his
heels, a large limp white shirt-frill, and cravat to correspond,—that
is to say, white was the natural colour of his linen on Sundays, but it
toned down with the week.

"It is," repeated Monsieur Mutuel, his amiable old walnut-shell
countenance very walnut-shelly indeed as he smiled and blinked in
the bright morning sunlight,—"it is, my cherished Madame Bouclet,
I think, impossible!"

"Hey!" (with a little vexed cry and a great many tosses of her
head.) "But it is not impossible that you are a Pig!" retorted Madame
Bouclet, a compact little woman of thirty-five or so. "See then,—
look there,—read! 'On the second floor Monsieur L'Anglais.' Is it not
so?"

"It is so," said Monsieur Mutuel.

"Good. Continue your morning walk. Get out!" Madame Bouclet
dismissed him with a lively snap of her fingers.

The morning walk of Monsieur Mutuel was in the brightest patch
that the sun made in the Grande Place of a dull old fortified French
town. The manner of his morning walk was with his hand crossed
behind him; an umbrella, in figure the express image of himself
always in one hand; a snuff-box in the other. Thus, with the shuffling
gait of the Elephant (who really does deal with the very worst
trousers-maker employed by the Zoological world, and who appeared
to have recommended him to Monsieur Mutuel), the old gentleman
sunned himself daily when the sun was to be had—of course, at the
same time sunning a red ribbon at his button-hole; for he was not an
ancient Frenchman?

Being told by one of the angelic sex to continue his morning walk and get out, Monsieur Mutuel laughed a walnut-shell laugh, pulled off his cap at arm's length with the hand that contained his snuff-box, kept it off for a considerable period after he had parted from Madame Bouclet, and continued his morning walk and got out, like a man of gallantry as he was.

The documentary evidence to which Madame Bouclet had referred Monsieur Mutuel was the list of her lodgers, sweetly written forth by her own Nephew and Bookkeeper, who held the pen of an Angel, and posted up at the side of her gateway, for the information of the Police: "Au second, M. L'Anglais, Propriétaire." On the second floor, Mr. The Englishman, man of property. So it stood; nothing could be plainer.

Madame Bouclet now traced the line with her forefinger, as it were to confirm and settle herself in her parting snap at Monsieur Mutuel, and so placing her right hand on her hip with a defiant air, as if nothing should ever tempt her to unsnap that snap, strolled out into the Place to glance at the windows of Mr. The Englishman. That worthy happening to be looking out of the window at moment, Madame Bouclet gave him a graceful salutation with her head, looked to the right and looked to the left to account to him for her being there, considered for a moment, like one who accounted to herself for somebody she had expected not being there, and re-entered her own gateway. Madame Bouclet let all her house giving on the Place in furnished flats or floors, and lived up the yard behind in company with Monsieur Bouclet her husband (great at billiards), an inherited brewing business, several fowls, two carts, a nephew, a little dog in a big kennel, a grape-vine, a counting-house, four horses, a married sister (with a share in the brewing business), the husband and two children of the married sister, a parrot, a drum (performed on by the little boy of the married sister), two billeted soldiers, a quantity of pigeons, a fife (played by the nephew in a ravishing manner), several domestics and supernumeraries, a perpetual flavour of coffee and soup, a terrific range of artificial rocks and wooden precipices at least four feet high, a small fountain, and a half-dozen large sunflowers.

Now the Englishman, in taking his Appartement,—or, as one might say on our side of the Channel, his set of chambers,—had given his name, correct to the letter, LANGLEY. But as he had a British way of not opening his mouth very wide on foreign soil, except at meals, the Brewery had been able to make nothing of it but L'Anglais. So Mr. The Englishman he had become and he re-mained.

"Never saw such people," muttered Mr. The Englishman! as he now looked out of window. "Never did, in my life!"

This was true enough, for he had never before been out of his own country,—a right little island, a tight little island, a bright little island, a show-fight little island, and full of merit of all sorts; but not the whole round world.

"These chaps," said Mr. The Englishman to himself, as his eyes rolled over the Place, sprinkled with military here and there, "are no more like soldiers—" Nothing being sufficiently strong for the end of his sentence, he left it unended.

This again (from the point of view of his experience) was strictly correct; for though there was a great agglomeration of soldiers in the town and neighbouring country, you might have held a grand Review and Field-day of them every one, and looked in vain among them all for a soldier choking behind his foolish stock, or a soldier lamed by his ill-fitting shoes, or a soldier deprived of the use of his limbs by straps and buttons, or a soldier elaborately forced to be self-helpless in all the small affairs of life. A swarm of brisk, bright, active, bustling, handy, odd, skirmishing, fellows, able to turn cleverly at anything, from a siege to soup, from great guns to needles and thread, from the broadsword exercise to slicing an onion, from making war to making omelets, was all you would have found.

What a swarm! From the Great Place under the eye of Mr. The Englishman, where a few awkward squads from the last conscription were doing the goose-step,—some members of those squads still as to their bodies, in the chrysalis peasant-state of Blouse, and only military butterflies as to their regimentally-clothed legs—from the Great Place, away outside the fortifications, and away for miles along the dusty roads, soldiers swarmed. All day long, upon the grass-grown ramparts of the town, practising soldiers trumpeted and bugled; all day long, down in angles of dry trenches, practising soldiers drummed and drummed. Every forenoon, soldiers burst out of the great barracks into the sandy gymnasium-ground hard by, and flew over the wooden horse, and hung on to flying ropes, and dangled upside-down between parallel bars, and shot themselves off wooden platforms,—splashes, sparks, coruscations, showers of soldiers. At every corner of the town-wall, every guard-house, every gateway, every sentry-box, every drawbridge, every reedy ditch, and rushy dike, soldiers, soldiers, soldiers. And the town being pretty well all wall, guard-house, gateway, sentry-box, drawbridge, reedy ditch, and rushy dike, the town was pretty well all soldiers.

What would the sleepy old town have been without the soldiers, seeing that even with them, it had so overslept itself as to have slept its echoes hoarse, its defensive bars and locks and bolts and chains all rusty, and its ditches stagnant! From the days when VAUBAN engineered it to that perplexing extent that to look at it was like being knocked on the head with it, the stranger becoming stunned and stertorous under the shock of its incomprehensibility,—from the days when VAUBAN made it the express incorporation of every substantive and adjective in the art of military engineering, and not only twisted you into it and twisted you out if it, to the right, to the left, opposite, under here, over there, in the dark, in the dirt, by the gateway, archway, covered way, dry way, wet way, fosse, portcullis, drawbridge, sluice, squat tower, pierced wall, and heavy battery, but likewise took a fortifying dive under the neighbouring country, and came to the surface three or four miles off, blowing out incomprehensible mounds and batteries among the quiet crops of chicory and beet-root,—from those days to these the town had been asleep, and dust and rust and must had settled on its drowsy Arsenals and Magazines, and grass had grown up in its silent streets.

On market-days alone, its Great Place suddenly leaped out of bed. On market-days, some friendly enchanter struck his staff upon the stones of the Great Place, and instantly arose the liveliest booths and stalls, and sittings and standings, and a pleasant hum of chaffering and huckstering from many hundreds of tongues, and a pleasant, though peculiar, blending of colours,—white caps, blue blouses, and green vegetables,—and at last the Knight destined for the adventure seemed to have come in earnest, and all the Vaubanois sprang up awake. And now, by long, low-lying avenues of trees, jolting in white-hooded donkey-cart, and on donkey-back and in tumbril and wagon, and cart and cabriolet, and afoot with barrow and burden,— and along the dikes and ditches and canals, in little peak-prowed country boats,—came peasant-men and women in flocks and crowds, bringing articles for sale. And here you had boots and shoes, and sweetmeats and stuffs to wear, and here (in the cool shade of the Town-hall) you had milk and cream and butter and cheese, and here you had fruits, and onions and carrots and all things needful for your soup, and here you had poultry and flowers and protesting pigs, and here new shovels, axes, spades, and billhooks for your farming work, and here huge mounds of bread, and here your unground grain in sacks, and here your children's dolls, and here the cake-seller, announcing his wares by the beat and roll of drum. And hark! fanfaronade of trumpets, and here into the Great Place, resplendent in an open carriage, with four gorgeously-attired servitors up behind, playing horns, drums, and cymbals, rolled "the Daughter of a Physician" in massive golden chains and earrings, and blue-feathered hat, shaded from the admiring sun by two immense umbrellas of artificial roses, to dispense (from motives of philanthropy) that small and pleasant dose which had cured so many thousands! Toothache, earache, headache, heartache, stomachache, debility, nervousness, fits, fainting, fever, ague, all equally cured by the small and pleasant dose of the great Physician's great daughter! The process was this,—she, the Daughter of a Physician, proprietress of the superb equipage you now admired with its confirmatory blasts of trumpet, drum, and cymbal, told you so: On the first day after taking the small and pleasant dose, you would feel no particular influence beyond a most harmonious sensation of indescribable and irresistible joy; on the second day you would be so astonishingly better that you would think yourself changed into somebody else; on the third day you would be entirely free from your disorder, whatever its nature and however long you had had it, and would seek out the Physician's Daughter to throw yourself at her feet, kiss the hem of her garment, and buy as many more of the small and pleasant doses as by the sale of all your few effects you could obtain; but she would be inaccessible, —gone for herbs to the Pyramids of Egypt,—and you would be (though cured) reduced to despair! Thus would the Physician's daughter drive her trade (and briskly too), and thus would the buying and selling and mingling of tongues and colours continue, until the changing sunlight, leaving the Physician's Daughter in the shadow of high roofs, admonished her to jolt out westward, with a departing effect of gleam and glitter on the splendid equipage and brazen blast. And now the enchanter struck his staff upon the stones of the Great Place once more, and down went the booths, the sittings and standings and vanished merchandise, and with it the barrows, donkeys, donkey-carts, and tumbrils, and all other things on wheels and feet, except the slow scavengers with unwieldy carts and meagre horses clearing up the rubbish, assisted by the sleek town pigeons, better plumped out than on non-market days. While there was yet an hour or two to wane before the autumn sunset, the loiterer outside town-gate and drawbridge, and postern and double-ditch, would see the last white-hooded cart lessening in the avenue of lengthening shadows of trees, or the last country boat, paddled by the last market-woman on her way home, showing black upon the reddening long, low, narrow dike between him and the mill; and as the paddle-parted scum and weed closed over the boat's track, he might be comfortably sure that its sluggish rest would be troubled no more until next market-day.

As it was not one of the Great Place's days for getting out of bed, when Mr. The Englishman looked down at the young soldiers practising the goose-step there, his mind was left at liberty to take a military turn.

"These fellows are billeted everywhere about," said he; "and to see them lighting the people's fires, boiling the people's pots, minding the people's babies, rocking the people's cradles, washing the people's greens, and making themselves generally useful, in every sort of un-military way, is most ridiculous! Never saw such a set of fellows,—never did in my life!"

All perfectly true again. Was there not Private Valentine in that very house, acting as sole housemaid, valet, cook, steward, and nurse, in the family of his captain, Monsieur le Capitaine de la Cour,—cleaning the floors, making the beds, doing the marketing, dressing the captain, dressing the dinners, dressing the salads, and dressing the baby, all with equal readiness? Or, to put him aside, he being in loyal attendance on his Chief, was there not Private Hyppolite, billeted at the Perfumer's two hundred yards off, who, when not on duty, volunteered to keep shop while the fair Perfumeress stepped out to speak to a neighbour or so, and laughingly sold soap with his war-sword girded on him? Was there not Emile, billeted at the Clock-maker's, perpetually turning to of an evening, with his coat off, winding up the stock? Was there not Eugene, billeted at the Tinman's, cultivating, pipe in mouth, a garden four feet square, for the Tinman, in the little court, behind the shop, and extorting the fruits of the earth

rom the same, on his knees, with the sweat of his brow? Not to multiply examples, was there not Baptiste, billeted on the poor Water-
carrier, at that very instant sitting on the pavement in the sunlight,
with his martial legs asunder and one of the Water-carrier's spare
pails between them, which (to the delight and glory of the heart of
the Water-carrier coming across the Place from the fountain, yoked
and burdened) he was painting bright-green outside and bright-red
within? Or, to go no farther than the Barber's at the very next door,
was there not Corporal Théophile——

"No," said Mr. The Englishman, glancing down at the Barber's,
"he is not there at present. There's the child, though."

A mere mite of a girl stood on the steps of the Barber's shop, looking across the Place. A mere baby, one might call her, dressed in the
close white linen cap which small French country children wear (like
the children in Dutch pictures), and in a frock of homespun blue, that
had no shape except where it was tied round her little fat throat. So
that, being naturally short and round all over, she looked, behind,
as if she had been cut off at her natural waist, and had had her head
neatly fitted on it.

"There's the child, though."

To judge from the way in which the dimpled hand was rubbing the
eyes, the eyes had been closed in a nap, and were newly opened. But
they seemed to be looking so intently across the Place, that the
Englishman looked in the same direction.

"O!" said he presently "I thought as much. The Corporal's there."

The Corporal, a smart figure of a man of thirty, perhaps a thought
under the middle size, but very neatly made,—a sunburnt Corporal
with a brown peaked beard,—faced about at the moment, addressing
voluble words of instruction to the squad in hand. Nothing was amiss
or awry about the Corporal. A lithe and nimble Corporal, quite complete, from the sparkling dark eyes under his knowing uniform cap
to his sparkling white gaiters. The very image and presentment of
a Corporal of his country's army, in the line of his shoulders, the line
of his waist, the broadest line of his Bloomer trousers, and their
narrowest line at the calf of his leg.

Mr. The Englishman looked on, and the child looked on, and the
Corporal looked on (but the last-named at his men), until the drill
ended a few minutes afterwards, and the military sprinkling dried up
directly, and was gone. Then said Mr. The Englishman to himself,
"Look here! By George!" And the Corporal, dancing towards the
Barber's with his arms wide open, caught up the child, held her over
his head in a flying attitude, caught her down again, kissed her, and
made off with her into the Barber's house.

Now Mr. The Englishman had had a quarrel with his erring and
disobedient and disowned daughter, and there was a child in that
case too. Had not his daughter been a child, and had she not taken
angel-flights above his head as this child had flown above the
Corporal's?

"He's a"—National Participled—"fool!" said the Englishman,

and shut his window.

But the windows of the house of Memory, and the windows of the house of Mercy, are not so easily closed as windows of glass and wood. They fly open unexpectedly; they rattle in the night; they must be nailed up. Mr. The Englishman had tried nailing them, but had not driven the nails quite home. So he passed but a disturbed evening and a worse night.

By nature a good-tempered man? No; very little gentleness, confounding the quality with weakness. Fierce and wrathful when crossed? Very, and stupendously unreasonable. Moody? Exceedingly so. Vindictive? well; he *had* had scowling thoughts that he would formally curse his daughter, as he had seen it done on the stage. But remembering that the real Heaven is some paces removed from the mock one in the great chandelier of the Theatre, he had given that up.

And he had come abroad to be rid of his repudiated daughter for the rest of his life. And here he was.

At bottom, it was for this reason, more than for any other, that Mr. The Englishman took it extremely ill that Corporal Théophile should be so devoted to little Bebelle, the child at the Barber's shop. In an unlucky moment he had chanced to say to himself, "Why, confound the fellow, he is not her father!" There was a sharp sting in the speech which ran into him suddenly, and put him in a worse mood. So he had National Participled the unconscious Corporal with the hearty emphasis, and had made up his mind to think no more about such a mountebank.

But it came to pass that the Corporal was not to be dismissed. If he had known the most delicate fibres of the Englishman's mind, instead of knowing nothing on earth about him, and if he had been the most obstinate Corporal in the Grand Army of France, instead of being the most obliging, he could not have planted himself with more determined immovability plump in the midst of all the Englishman's thoughts. Not only so, but he seemed to be always in his view. Mr. The Englishman had but to look out of window, to look upon the Corporal with little Bebelle. He had but to go for a walk, and there was the Corporal walking with Bebelle. He had but to come home again, disgusted, and the Corporal and Bebelle were at home before him. If he looked out at his back windows early in the morning, the Corporal was in the Barber's back yard, washing and dressing and brushing Bebelle. If he took refuge at his front windows, the Corporal brought his breakfast out into the Place, and shared it there with Bebelle. Always Corporal and always Bebelle. Never Corporal without Bebelle. Never Bebelle without Corporal.

Mr. The Englishman was not particularly strong in the French language as a means of oral communication, though he read it very well. It is with languages as with people,—when you only know them by sight, you are apt to mistake them; you must be on speaking terms before you can be said to have established an acquaintance.

For this reason, Mr. The Englishman had to gird up his loins considerably before he could bring himself to the point of exchanging

"The Corporal, dancing towards the Barber's
with his arms wide open, caught up the child."

leas with Madame Bouclet on the subject of this Corporal and this
ebelle. But Madame Bouclet looking in apologetically one morning
o remark, that, O Heaven! she was in a state of desolation because
ne lamp-maker had not sent home that lamp confided to him to
epair, but that truly he was a lamp-maker against whom the whole
orld shrieked out, Mr. The Englishman seized the occasion.

"Madame, that baby——"

"Pardon, monsieur. That lamp."

"No, no, that little girl."

"But, pardon!" said Madame Bouclet, angling for a clew, "one
annot light a little girl, or send her to be repaired?"

"The little girl—at the house of the barber."

"Ah-h-h!" cried Madame Bouclet, suddenly catching the idea with
er delicate little line and rod. "Little Bebelle? Yes, yes, yes! And
er friend the Corporal? Yes, yes, yes, yes! So genteel of him,—is it
ot?"

"He is not——?"

"Not at all; not at all! He is not one of her relations. Not at all!"

"Why, then he——"

"Perfectly!" cried Madame Bouclet, "you are right, monsieur. It
s so genteel of him. The less relation, the more genteel. As you say."

"Is she——?"

"The child of the barber?" Madame Bouclet whisked up her skil-
ul little line and rod again. "Not at all, not at all! She is the child of
—in a word, of no one."

"The wife of the barber, then——?"

"Indubitably. As you say. The wife of the barber receives a small
tipend to take care of her. So much by the month. Eh, then! It is
vithout doubt very little, for we are all poor here."

"You are not poor, madame?"

"As to my lodgers," replied Madame Bouclet, with a smiling and
a gracious bend of her head, "no. As to all things else, so-so."

"You flatter me, madame."

"Monsieur, it is you who flatter me in living here."

Certain fishy gasps on Mr. The Englishman's part, denoting that
ne was about to resume his subject under difficulties, Madame Bouclet
observed him closely, and whisked up her delicate line and rod again
vith triumphant success.

"O no, monsieur, certainly not. The wife of the barber is not cruel
.o the poor child, but she is careless. Her health is delicate, and she
.its all day, looking out at window. Consequently, when the Corporal
irst came, the poor little Bebelle was much neglected."

"It is a curious——" began Mr. The Englishman.

"Name? That Bebelle? Again you are right, monsieur. But it is a
playful name for Gabrielle."

"And so the child is a mere fancy of the Corporal's?" said Mr. The
Englishman, in a gruffly disparaging tone of voice.

"Eh, well!" returned Madame Bouclet, with a pleading shrug:
one must love something. Human nature is weak."

("Devilish weak," muttered the Englishman, in his own language.

"And the Corporal," pursued Madame Bouclet, "being billeted a the barber's,—where he will probably remain a long time, for he i attached to the General,—and finding the poor unowned child i need of being loved, and finding himself in need of loving,—why there you have it all, you see!"

Mr. The Englishman accepted this interpretation of the matte with an indifferent grace, and observed to himself, in an injured manner, when he was again alone: "I shouldn't mind it so much, i these people were not such a"—National Participled—"sentimenta people!"

There was a Cemetery outside the town, and it happened ill for the reputation of the Vaubanois, in this sentimental connexion, that he took a walk there that same afternoon. To be sure there were som wonderful things in it (from the Englishman's point of view), and o a certainty in all Britain you would have found nothing like it. No to mention the fanciful flourishes of hearts and crosses in wood and iron, that were planted all over the place, making it look very like a Firework-ground, where a most splendid pyrotechnic display migh be expected after dark, there were so many wreaths upon the graves embroidered, as it might be, "To my mother," "To my daughter," "To my father," "To my brother," "To my sister," "To my friend," and those many wreaths were in so many stages of elaboration and decay, from the wreath of yesterday, all fresh colour and brigh beads, to the wreath of last year, a poor mouldering wisp of straw There were so many little gardens and grottoes made upon graves in so many tastes, with plants and shells and plaster figures and porcelain pitchers, and so many odds and ends! There were so many tributes of remembrance hanging up, not to be discriminated by the closest inspection from little round waiters, whereon were depicted in glowing hues either a lady or a gentleman with a white pocket handkerchief out of all proportion, leaning, in a state of the mos faultless mourning and most profound affliction, on the most archi tectural and gorgeous urn! There were so many surviving wives wh had put their names on the tombs of their deceased husbands, with a blank for the date of their own departure from this weary world; and there were so many surviving husbands who had rendered the sam homage to their deceased wives; and out of the number there mus have been so many who had long ago married again! In fine, ther was so much in the place that would have seemed mere frippery to a stranger, save for the consideration that the lightest paper flowe that lay upon the poorest heap of earth was never touched by a rud hand, but perished there, a sacred thing!

"Nothing of the solemnity of Death here," Mr. The Englishman had been going to say, when this last consideration touched him with a mild appeal, and on the whole he walked out without saying it "But these people are," he insisted, by way of compensation, when he was well outside the gate, "they are so"—Participled—"senti mental!"

His way back lay by the military gymnasium-ground. And there he passed the Corporal glibly instructing young soldiers how to swing themselves over rapid and deep water-courses on their way to Glory, by means of a rope, and himself deftly plunging off a platform, and flying a hundred feet or two, as an encouragement to them to begin. And there he also passed, perched on a crowning eminence (probably by the Corporal's careful hands) the small Bebelle, with her round eyes wide open, surveying the proceeding like a wondering sort of blue and white bird.

"If that child was to die," this was his reflection as he turned his back and went his way,—"and it would almost serve the fellow right for making such a fool of himself,—I suppose we should have *him* sticking up a wreath and a waiter in that fantastic burying-ground."

Nevertheless, after another early morning or two of looking out of window, he strolled down into the Place, when the Corporal and Bebelle were walking there, and touching his hat to the Corporal (an immense achievement), wished him Good-day.

"Good-day, monsieur."

"This is a rather pretty child you have here," said Mr. The Englishman, taking her chin in his hand, and looking down into her astonished blue eyes.

"Monsieur, she is a very pretty child," returned the Corporal, with a stress on his polite correction of the phrase.

"And good?" said the Englishman.

"And very good. Poor little thing!"

"Hah!" The Englishman stooped down and patted her cheek, not without awkwardness, as if he were going too far in his conciliation. "And what is this medal round your neck, my little one?"

Bebelle having no other reply on her lips than her chubby right fist, the Corporal offered his services as interpreter.

"Monsieur demands, what is this, Bebelle?"

"It is the Holy Virgin," said Bebelle.

"And who gave it you?" asked the Englishman.

"Théophile."

"And who is Théophile?"

Bebelle broke into a laugh, laughed merrily and heartily, clapped her chubby hands, and beat her little feet on the stone pavement of the Place.

"He doesn't know Théophile! Why, he doesn't know any one! He doesn't know anything!" Then, sensible of a small solecism in her manners, Bebelle twisted her right hand in a leg of the Corporal's Bloomer trousers, and, laying her cheek against the place, kissed it.

"Monsieur Théophile, I believe?" said the Englishman to the Corporal.

"It is I, monsieur."

"Permit me." Mr. The Englishman shook him heartily by the hand and turned away. But he took it mighty ill that old Monsieur Mutuel in his patch of sunlight, upon whom he came as he turned, should pull

off his cap to him with a look of pleased approval. And he muttered
in his own tongue, as he returned the salutation, "Well, walnut-shell
And what business is it of *yours?*"

Mr. The Englishman went on for many weeks passing but disturbe
evenings and worse nights, and constantly experiencing that thos
aforesaid windows in the houses of Memory and Mercy rattled afte
dark, and that he had very imperfectly nailed them up. Likewise, h
went on for many weeks daily improving the acquaintance of th
Corporal and Bebelle. That is to say, he took Bebelle by the chin, an
the Corporal by the hand, and offered Bebelle sous and the Corpora
cigars, and even got the length of changing pipes with the Corpora
and kissing Bebelle. But he did it all in a shamefaced way, an
always took it extremely ill that Monsieur Mutuel in his patch o
sunlight should note what he did. Whenever that seemed to be th
case, he always growled in his own tongue, "There you are again
walnut-shell! What business is it of *yours?*"

In a word, it had become the occupation of Mr. The Englishman'
life to look after the Corporal and little Bebelle, and to resent ol
Monsieur Mutuel's looking after *him.* An occupation only varied b
a fire in the town one windy night, and much passing of water
buckets from hand to hand (in which the Englishman rendered goo
service), and much beating of drums,—when all of a sudden th
Corporal disappeared.

Next, all of a sudden, Bebelle disappeared.

She had been visible a few days later than the Corporal,—sadl
deteriorated as to washing and brushing,—but she had not spoke
when addressed by Mr. The Englishman, and had looked scared an
had run away. And now it would seem that she had run away fo
good. And there lay the Great Place under the windows, bare an
barren.

In his shamefaced and constrained way, Mr. The Englishman aske
no question of any one, but watched from his front windows an
watched from his back windows, and lingered about the Place, an
peeped in at the Barber's shop, and did all this and much more wit
a whistling and tune-humming pretence of not missing anything
until one afternoon when Monsieur Mutuel's patch of sunlight wa
in shadow, and when, according to all rule and precedent, he had n
right whatever to bring his red ribbon out of doors, behold here h
was, advancing with his cap already in his hand twelve paces off!

Mr. The Englishman had got as far into his usual objurgation as
"What bu—si—" when he checked himself.

"Ah, it is sad, it is sad! Hélas, it is unhappy, it is sad!" Thus ol
Monsieur Mutuel, shaking his grey head.

"What busin—at least, I would say, what do you mean, Monsieu
Mutuel?"

"Our Corporal. Hélas, our dear Corporal!"

"What has happened to him?"

"You have not heard?"

"No."

"At the fire. But he was so brave, so ready. Ah, too brave, too ready!"

"May the Devil carry you away!" the Englishman broke in impatiently; "I beg your pardon,—I mean me,—I am not accustomed to speak French,—go on, will you?"

"And a falling beam——"

"Good God!" exclaimed the Englishman. "It was a private soldier who was killed?"

"No. A Corporal, the same Corporal, our dear Corporal. Beloved by all his comrades. The funeral ceremony was touching,—penetrating. Monsieur The Englishman, your eyes fill with tears."

"What bu—si——"

"Monsieur The Englishman, I honour those emotions. I salute you with profound respect. I will not obtrude myself upon your noble heart."

Monsieur Mutuel,—a gentleman in every thread of his cloudy linen, under whose wrinkled hand every grain in the quarter of an ounce of poor snuff in his poor little tin box became a gentleman's property,—Monsieur Mutuel passed on, with his cap in his hand.

"I little thought," said the Englishman, after walking for several minutes, and more than once blowing his nose, "when I was looking round that cemetery—I'll go there!"

Straight he went there, and when he came within the gate he paused, considering whether he should ask at the lodge for some direction to the grave. But he was less than ever in a mood for asking questions, and he thought, "I shall see something on it to know it by."

In search of the Corporal's grave he went softly on, up this walk and down that, peering in, among the crosses and hearts and columns and obelisks and tombstones, for a recently disturbed spot. It troubled him now to think how many dead there were in the cemetery,—he had not thought them a tenth part so numerous before,—and after he had walked and sought for some time, he said to himself, as he struck down a new vista of tombs, "I might suppose that every one was dead but I."

Not every one. A live child was lying on the ground asleep. Truly he had found something on the Corporal's grave to know it by, and the something was Bebelle.

With such a loving will had the dead soldier's comrades worked at his resting-place, that it was already a neat garden. On the green turf of the garden Bebelle lay sleeping, with her cheek touching it. A plain, unpainted little wooden Cross was planted in the turf, and her short arm embraced this little Cross, as it had many a time embraced the Corporal's neck. They had put a tiny flag (the flag of France) at his head, and a laurel garland.

Mr. The Englishman took off his hat, and stood for a while silent. Then, covering his head again, he bent down on one knee, and softly roused the child.

"Bebelle! My little one!"

Opening her eyes, on which the tears were still wet, Bebelle was at first frightened; but seeing who it was, she suffered him to take her in his arms, looking steadfastly at him.

"You must not lie here, my little one. You must come with me.'

"No, no. I can't leave Théophile. I want the good dear Théophile.

"We will go and seek him, Bebelle. We will go and look for him i England. We will go and look for him at my daughter's, Bebelle."

"Shall we find him there?"

"We shall find the best part of him there. Come with me, poo forlorn little one. Heaven is my witness," said the Englishman, in low voice, as, before he rose, he touched the turf above the gent Corporal's breast, "that I thankfully accept this trust!"

It was a long way for the child to have come unaided. She was soo asleep again, with her embrace transferred to the Englishman's necl He looked at her worn shoes, and her galled feet, and her tired face and believed that she had come there every day.

He was leaving the grave with the slumbering Bebelle in h arms, when he stopped, looked wistfully down at it, and looked wist fully at the other graves around. "It is the innocent custom of th people," said Mr. The Englishman, with hesitation. "I think I shoul like to do it. No one sees."

Careful not to wake Bebelle as he went, he repaired to the lodg where such little tokens of remembrance were sold, and bought tw wreaths. One, blue and white and glistening silver, "To my friend' one of a soberer red and black and yellow, "To my friend." Wit these he went back to the grave, and so down on one knee agair Touching the child's lips with the brighter wreath, he guided her han to hang it on the Cross; then hung his own wreath there. After all, th wreaths were not far out of keeping with the little garden. To m friend. To my friend.

Mr. The Englishman took it very ill when he looked round a stree corner into the Great Place, carrying Bebelle in his arms, that ol Mutuel should be there airing his red ribbon. He took a world o pains to dodge the worthy Mutuel, and devoted a surprising amoun of time and trouble to skulking into his own lodging like a ma pursued by Justice. Safely arrived there at last, he made Bebelle' toilet with as accurate a remembrance as he could bring to bear upo: that work of the way in which he had often seen the poor Corpora make it, and having given her to eat and drink, laid her down on hi own bed. Then he slipped out into the Barber's shop, and after brief interview with the Barber's wife, and a brief recourse to hi purse and card-case, came back again with the whole of Bebelle' personal property in such a very little bundle that it was quite los under his arm.

As it was irreconcilable with his whole course and character tha he should carry Bebelle off in state, or receive any compliments o congratulations on that feat, he devoted the next day to getting hi two portmanteaus out of the house by artfulness and stealth, and t comporting himself in every particular as if he were going to ru: away,—except, indeed, that he paid his few debts in the town, an prepared a letter to leave for Madame Bouclet, enclosing a sufficien

ιm of money in lieu of notice. A railway train would come through
midnight, and by that train he would take away Bebelle to look for
héophile in England and at his forgiven daughter's.

At midnight, on a moonlight night, Mr. The Englishman came
eeping forth like a harmless assassin, with Bebelle on his breast
.stead of a dagger. Quiet the Great Place, and quiet the never-
irring streets; closed the cafés; huddled together motionless their
lliard-balls; drowsy the guard or sentinel on duty here and there;
lled for the time, by sleep, even the insatiate appetite of the Office
f Town-dues.

Mr. The Englishman left the Place behind, and left the streets
ehind, and left the civilian-inhabited town behind, and descended
ʌwn among the military works of Vauban, hemming all in. As the
ιadow of the first heavy arch and postern fell upon him and was left
ehind, as the shadow of the second heavy arch and postern fell
ρon him and was left behind, as his hollow tramp over the first
rawbridge was succeeded by a gentler sound, as his hollow tramp
ver the second drawbridge was succeeded by a gentler sound, as he
vercame the stagnant ditches one by one, and passed out where the
owing waters were and where the moonlight, so the dark shades
nd the hollow sounds and the unwholesomely locked currents of his
ɔul were vanquished and set free. See to it, Vaubans of your own
earts, who gird them in with triple walls and ditches, and with bolt
nd chain and bar and lifted bridge,—raze those fortifications, and
ιy them level with the all-absorbing dust, before the night cometh
ɣhen no hand can work!

All went prosperously, and he got into an empty carriage in the
rain, where he could lay Bebelle on the seat over against him, as on
couch, and cover her from head to foot with his mantle. He had
ust drawn himself up from perfecting this arrangement, and had
ust leaned back in his own seat contemplating it with great satis-
action, when he became aware of a curious appearance at the open
arriage window,—a ghostly little tin box floating up in the moon-
ight, and hovering there.

He leaned forward, and put out his hand. Down among the rails
nd wheels and ashes, Monsieur Mutuel, red ribbon and all!

"Excuse me, Monsieur The Englishman," said Monsieur Mutuel,
ιolding up his box at arm's length, the carriage being so high and he
o low; "but I shall reverence the little box for ever, if your so gener-
ɔus hand will take a pinch from it at parting."

Mr. The Englishman reached out of the window before complying,
nd—without asking the old fellow what business it was of his—
ιhook hands and said, " Adieu! God bless you!"

"And Mr. The Englishman, God bless *you*!" cried Madame Bouclet,
vho was also there among the rails and wheels and ashes. "And God
vill bless you in the happiness of the protected child now with you.
And God will bless you in your own child at home. And God will
ɔless you in your own remembrances. And this from me!"

He had barely time to catch a bouquet from her hand, when the

train was flying through the night. Round the paper that enfold
it was bravely written (doubtless by the nephew who held the pen
an Angel), "Homage to the friend of the friendless."

"Not bad people, Bebelle!" said Mr. The Englishman, softly draw
ing the mantle a little from her sleeping face, that he might kiss i
"though they are so——."

Too "sentimental" himself at the moment to be able to get out tha
word, he added nothing but a sob, and travelled for some mile
through the moonlight, with his hand before his eyes.

CHAPTER III

HIS BROWN-PAPER PARCEL

My works are well known. I am a young man in the Art line. Yo
have seen my works many a time, though it's fifty thousand to one
you have seen me. You say you don't want to see me? You say you
interest is in my works, and not in me? Don't be too sure about tha
Stop a bit.

Let us have it down in black and white at the first go off, so tha
there may be no unpleasantness or wrangling afterwards. And this
looked over by a friend of mine, a ticket writer, that is up to litera
ture. I am a young man in the Art line—in the Fine-Art line. Yo
have seen my works over and over again, and you have been curiou
about me, and you think you have seen me. Now, as a safe rule, yo
never have seen me, and you never do see me, and you never wil
see me. I think that's plainly put—and it's what knocks me over.

If there's a blighted public character going, I am the party.

It has been remarked by a certain (or an uncertain) philosophe
that the world knows nothing of its greatest men. He might have pu
it plainer if he had thrown his eye in my direction. He might hav
put it, that while the world knows something of them that apparentl
go in and win, it knows nothing of them that really go in and don'
win. There it is again in another form—and that's what knocks m
over.

Not that it's only myself that suffers from injustice, but that I an
more alive to my own injuries than to any other man's. Being, as
have mentioned, in the Fine-Art line, and not the Philanthropic line
I openly admit it. As to company in injury, I have company enough
Who are you passing every day at your Competitive Excruciations
The fortunate candidates whose heads and livers you have turned
upside down for life? Not you. You are really passing the Crammer
and Coaches. If your principle is right, why don't you turn out to
morrow morning with the keys of your cities on velvet cushions, you
musicians playing, and your flags flying, and read addresses to th
Crammers and Coaches on your bended knees, beseeching them t
come out and govern you? Then, again, as to your public business o

ll sorts, your Financial statements and your Budgets; the Public nows much, truly, about the real doers of all that! Your Nobles nd Right Honourables are first-rate men? Yes, and so is a goose a rst-rate bird. But I'll tell you this about the goose;—you'll find his atural flavour disappointing, without stuffing.

Perhaps I am soured by not being popular? But suppose I AM opular. Suppose my works never fail to attract. Suppose that, hether they are exhibited by natural light or by artificial, they evitably draw the public. Then no doubt they are preserved in some ollection? No, they are not; they are not preserved in any Collection. opyright? No, nor yet copyright. Anyhow they must be some- here? Wrong again, for they are often nowhere.

Says you, "At all events, you are in a moody state of mind, my iend." My answer is, I have described myself as a public character ith a blight upon him—which fully accounts for the curdling of the ilk in *that* cocoa-nut.

Those that are acquainted with London are aware of a locality on he Surrey side of the river Thames, called the Obelisk, or, more enerally, the Obstacle. Those that are not acquainted with London ill also be aware of it, now that I have named it. My lodging is not ar from that locality. I am a young man of that easy disposition, hat I lie abed till it's absolutely necessary to get up and earn some- hing, and then I lie abed again till I have spent it.

It was on an occasion when I had had to turn to with a view to ictuals, that I found myself walking along the Waterloo Road, one vening after dark, accompanied by an acquaintance and fellow- odger in the gas-fitting way of life. He is very good company, having vorked at the theatres, and indeed, he has a theatrical turn himself, nd wishes to be brought out in the character of Othello; but whether n account of his regular work always blacking his face and hands nore or less, I cannot say.

"Tom," he says, "what a mystery hangs over you!"

"Yes, Mr. Click"—the rest of the house generally give him his ame, as being first, front, carpeted all over, his own furniture, and f not mahogany, an out-and-out imitation—"yes, Mr. Click, a nystery does hang over me."

"Makes you low, you see, don't it?" says he, eyeing me sideways.

"Why, yes, Mr. Click, there are circumstances connected with it hat have," I yielded to a sigh, "a lowering effect."

"Gives you a touch of the misanthrope too, don't it?" says he. 'Well, I'll tell you what. If I was you, I'd shake it off."

"If I was you, I would, Mr. Click; but, if you was me, you vouldn't."

"Ah!" says he, "there's something in that."

When we had walked a little further, he took it up again by :ouching me on the chest.

"You see, Tom, it seems to me as if, in the words of the poet who wrote the domestic drama of The Stranger, you had a silent sorrow :here."

"I have, Mr. Click."

"I hope, Tom," lowering his voice in a friendly way, "it isn't coining, or smashing?"

"No, Mr. Click. Don't be uneasy."

"Not yet forg——" Mr. Click checked himself, and added, "counterfeiting anything, for instance?"

"No, Mr. Click. I am lawfully in the Art line—Fine-Art line—but I can say no more."

"Ah! Under a species of star? A kind of malignant spell? A sort of a gloomy destiny? A cankerworm pegging away at your vitals in secret, as well as I make it out?" said Mr. Click, eyeing me with some admiration.

I told Mr. Click that was about it, if we came to particulars; and I thought he appeared rather proud of me.

Our conversation had brought us to a crowd of people, the greater part struggling for a front place from which to see something on the pavement, which proved to be various designs executed in coloured chalks on the pavement stones, lighted by two candles stuck in mud sconces. The subjects consisted of a fine fresh salmon's head and shoulders, supposed to have been recently sent home from the fishmonger's; a moonlight night at sea (in a circle); dead game; scrollwork; the head of a hoary hermit engaged in devout contemplation; the head of a pointer smoking a pipe; and a cherubim, his flesh creased as in infancy, going on a horizontal errand against the wind. All these subjects appeared to me to be exquisitely done.

On his knees on one side of this gallery, a shabby person of modest appearance who shivered dreadfully (though it wasn't at all cold), was engaged in blowing the chalk-dust off the moon, toning the outline of the back of the hermit's head with a bit of leather, and fattening the down-stroke of a letter or two in the writing. I have forgotten to mention that writing formed a part of the composition, and that it also—as it appeared to me—was exquisitely done. It ran as follows, in fine round characters: "An honest man is the noblest work of God. 1 2 3 4 5 6 7 8 9 0. £ s. d. Employment in an office is humbly requested. Honour the Queen. Hunger is a o 9 8 7 6 5 4 3 2 1 sharp thorn. Chip chop, cherry chop, fol de rol de ri do. Astronomy and mathematics. I do this to support my family."

Murmurs of admiration at the exceeding beauty of this performance went about among the crowd. The artist, having finished his touching (and having spoilt those places), took his seat on the pavement, with his knees crouched up very nigh his chin; and halfpence began to rattle in.

"A pity to see a man of that talent brought so low; ain't it?" said one of the crowd to me.

"What he might have done in the coach-painting, or housedecorating!" said another man, who took up the first speaker because I did not.

"Why, he writes—alone—like the Lord Chancellor!" said another man.

"Better," said another. "I know *his* writing. *He* couldn't support is family this way."

Then, a woman noticed the natural fluffiness of the hermit's hair, nd another woman, her friend, mentioned of the salmon's gills that ou could almost see him gasp. Then, an elderly country gentleman tepped forward and asked the modest man how he executed his vork? And the modest man took some scraps of brown paper with olours in 'em out of his pockets, and showed them. Then a fair-omplexioned donkey, with sandy hair and spectacles, asked if the ermit was a portrait? To which the modest man, casting a sorrowful lance upon it, replied that it was, to a certain extent, a recollection f his father. This caused a boy to yelp out, "Is the Pinter a smoking he pipe your mother?" who was immediately shoved out of view by , sympathetic carpenter with his basket of tools at his back.

At every fresh question or remark the crowd leaned forward more agerly and dropped the halfpence more freely, and the modest man athered them up more meekly. At last, another elderly gentleman ame to the front, and gave the artist his card, to come to his office o-morrow, and get some copying to do. The card was accompanied y sixpence, and the artist was profoundly grateful, and, before he ut the card in his hat, read it several times by the light of his andles to fix the address well in his mind, in case he should lose it. The crowd was deeply interested by this last incident, and a man in he second row with a gruff voice growled to the artist, "You've got a hance in life now, ain't you?" The artist answered (sniffing in a very ow-spirited way, however), "I'm thankful to hope so." Upon which here was a general chorus of "*You* are all right," and the halfpence lackened very decidedly.

I felt myself pulled away by the arm, and Mr. Click and I stood lone at the corner of the next crossing.

"Why, Tom," said Mr. Click, "what a horrid expression of face you've got!"

"Have I?" says I.

"Have you?" says Mr. Click. "Why, you looked as if you would have his blood?"

"Whose blood?"

"The artist's."

"The artist's?" I repeated. And I laughed, frantically, wildly, gloomily, incoherently, disagreeably. I am sensible that I did. I know I did.

Mr. Click stared at me in a scared sort of a way, but said nothing until we had walked a street's length. He then stopped short, and said, with excitement on the part of his forefinger:

"Thomas, I find it necessary to be plain with you. I don't like the envious man. I have identified the cankerworm that's pegging away at *your* vitals, and it's envy, Thomas."

"Is it?" says I.

"Yes, it is," says he. "Thomas, beware of envy. It is the green-eyed monster, which never did and never will improve each shining hour,

but quite the reverse. I dread the envious man, Thomas. I confess
that I am afraid of the envious man, when he is so envious as you
are. Whilst you contemplated the works of a gifted rival, and whilst
you heard that rival's praises, and especially whilst you met his
humble glance as he put that card away, your countenance was so
malevolent as to be terrific. Thomas, I have heard of the envy of
them that follows the Fine-Art line, but I never believed it could be
what yours is. I wish you well, but I take my leave of you. And if
you should ever get into trouble through knifeing — or say, garotting
—a brother artist, as I believe you will, don't call me to character,
Thomas, or I shall be forced to injure your case."

Mr. Click parted from me with those words, and we broke off our
acquaintance.

I became enamoured. Her name was Henrietta. Contending with
my easy disposition, I frequently got up to go after her. She also
dwelt in the neighbourhood of the Obstacle, and I did fondly hope
that no other would interpose in the way of our union.

To say that Henrietta was volatile is but to say that she was
woman. To say that she was in the bonnet-trimming is feebly to
express the taste which reigned predominant in her own.

She consented to walk with me. Let me do her the justice to say
that she did so upon trial. "I am not," said Henrietta, "as yet
prepared to regard you, Thomas, in any other light than as a friend;
but as a friend I am willing to walk with you, on the understanding
that softer sentiments may flow."

We walked.

Under the influence of Henrietta's beguilements, I now got out of
bed daily. I pursued my calling with an industry before unknown,
and it cannot fail to have been observed at that period, by those most
familiar with the streets of London, that there was a larger supply.
But hold! The time is not yet come!

One evening in October I was walking with Henrietta, enjoying
the cool breezes wafted over Vauxhall Bridge. After several slow
turns, Henrietta gaped frequently (so inseparable from woman is the
love of excitement), and said, "Let's go home by Grosvenor Place,
Piccadilly, and Waterloo"—localities, I may state for the information of the stranger and the foreigner, well known in London, and the
last a Bridge.

"No. Not by Piccadilly, Henrietta," said I.

"And why not Piccadilly, for goodness' sake?" said Henrietta.

Could I tell her? Could I confess to the gloomy presentiment that
overshadowed me? Could I make myself intelligible to her? No.

"I don't like Piccadilly, Henrietta."

"But I do," said she. "It's dark now, and the long rows of lamps
in Piccadilly after dark are beautiful. I *will* go to Piccadilly!"

Of course we went. It was a pleasant night, and there were
numbers of people in the streets. It was a brisk night, but not too
cold, and not damp. Let me darkly observe, it was the best of all
nights—FOR THE PURPOSE.

As we passed the garden wall of the Royal Palace, going up Gros-
enor Place, Henrietta murmured:

"I wish I was a Queen!"

"Why so, Henrietta?"

"I would make *you* Something," said she, and crossed her two
ands on my arm, and turned away her head.

Judging from this that the softer sentiments alluded to above had
egun to flow, I adapted my conduct to that belief. Thus happily we
assed on into the detested thoroughfare of Piccadilly. On the right
f that thoroughfare is a row of trees, the railing of the Green Park,
nd a fine broad eligible piece of pavement.

"Oh my!" cried Henrietta presently. "There's been an accident!"

I looked to the left, and said, "Where, Henrietta?"

"Not there, stupid!" said she. "Over by the Park railings. Where
he crowd is. Oh no, it's not an accident, it's something else to look
at! What's them lights?"

She referred to two lights twinkling low amongst the legs of the
assemblage: two candles on the pavement.

"Oh, do come along!" cried Henrietta, skipping across the road
with me. I hung back, but in vain. "Do let's look!"

Again, designs upon the pavement. Centre compartment, Mount
Vesuvius going it (in a circle), supported by four oval compartments,
severally representing a ship in heavy weather, a shoulder of mutton
attended by two cucumbers, a golden harvest with distant cottage
of proprietor, and a knife and fork after nature; above the centre
compartment a bunch of grapes, and over the whole a rainbow. The
whole, as it appeared to me, exquisitely done.

The person in attendance on these works of art was in all respects,
shabbiness excepted, unlike the former personage. His whole appearance and manner denoted briskness. Though threadbare, he expressed
to the crowd that poverty had not subdued his spirit, or tinged with
any sense of shame this honest effort to turn his talents to some
account. The writing which formed part of his composition was
conceived in a similarly cheerful tone. It breathed the following sentiments: "The writer is poor, but not despondent. To a British 1 2 3 4 5
6 7 8 9 0 Public he £ s. d. appeals. Honour to our brave Army! And
also 0 9 8 7 6 5 4 3 2 1 to our gallant Navy. BRITONS STRIKE the A B
C D E F G writer in common chalks would be grateful for any suitable
employment HOME! HURRAH!" The whole of this writing appeared
to me to be exquisitely done.

But this man, in one respect like the last, though seemingly hard
at it with a great show of brown paper and rubbers, was only really
fattening the down-stroke of a letter here and there, or blowing the
loose chalk off the rainbow, or toning the outside edge of the shoulder
of mutton. Though he did this with the greatest confidence, he hid it
(as it struck me) in so ignorant a manner, and so spoilt everything he
touched, that when he began upon the purple smoke from the chimney of the distant cottage of the proprietor of the golden harvest
(which smoke was beautifully soft), I found myself saying aloud,

without considering of it:

"Let that alone, will you?"

"Halloa!" said the man next me in the crowd, jerking me rough
from him with his elbow, "why didn't you send a telegram? If we ha
known you was coming, we'd have provided something better f
you. You understand the man's work better than he does himse
don't you? Have you made your will? You're too clever to live long.

"Don't be hard upon the gentleman, Sir," said the person i
attendance on the works of art, with a twinkle in his eye as h
looked at me; "he may chance to be an artist himself. If so, Sir, h
will have a fellow-feeling with me, Sir, when I"—he adapted h
action to his words as he went on, and gave a smart slap of his hand
between each touch, working himself all the time about and abou
the composition—"when I lighten the bloom of my grapes—shade o
the orange in my rainbow—dot the i of my Britons—throw a yello
light into my cow-cum-ber—insinuate another morsel of fat into m
shoulder of mutton—dart another zigzag flash of lightning at m
ship in distress!"

He seemed to do this so neatly, and was so nimble about it, tha
the halfpence came flying in.

"Thanks, generous public, thanks!" said the professor. "You wi
stimulate me to further exertions! My name will be found in the li
of British Painters yet. I shall do better than this, with encourage
ment. I shall indeed."

"You never can do better than that bunch of grapes," sai
Henrietta. "Oh, Thomas, them grapes!"

"Not better than *that*, lady? I hope for the time when I shall pair
anything but your own bright eyes and lips equal to life."

"(Thomas, did you ever?) But it must take a long time, Sir," sai
Henrietta, blushing, "to paint equal to that."

"I was prenticed to it, Miss," said the young man, smartly touch
ing up the composition—"prenticed to it in the caves of Spain an
Portingale, ever so long and two year over."

There was a laugh from the crowd; and a new man who had worke
himself in next me, said, "He's a smart chap, too, ain't he?"

"And what a eye!" exclaimed Henrietta softly.

"Ah! He need have a eye," said the man.

"Ah! He just need," was murmured among the crowd.

"He couldn't come that 'ere burning mountain without a eye,
said the man. He had got himself accepted as an authority, somehow
and everybody looked at his finger as it pointed out Vesuvius. "T
come that effect in a general illumination would require a eye; bu
to come it with two dips—why, it's enough to blind him!"

That impostor, pretending not to have heard what was said, no
winked to any extent with both eyes at once, as if the strain upon hi
sight was too much, and threw back his long hair—it was very long—
as if to cool his fevered brow. I was watching him doing it, whe
Henrietta suddenly whispered, "Oh, Thomas, how horrid you look!
and pulled me out by the arm.

Remembering Mr. Click's words, I was confused when I retorted,
"What do you mean by horrid?"

"Oh, gracious! Why, you looked," said Henrietta, "as if you would
have his blood."

I was going to answer, "So I would, for twopence——from his
nose," when I checked myself and remained silent.

We returned home in silence. Every step of the way, the softer
sentiments that had flowed, ebbed twenty mile an hour. Adapting
my conduct to the ebbing, as I had done to the flowing, I let my arm
drop limp, so as she could scarcely keep hold of it, and I wished her
such a cold good night at parting, that I keep within the bounds of
truth when I characterise it as a Rasper.

In the course of the next day I received the following document:

"Henrietta informs Thomas that my eyes are open to you. I must
ever wish you well, but walking and us is separated by an unfarmable
abyss. One so malignant to superiority—Oh that look at him!—can
never never conduct

"HENRIETTA.

"P.S.—To the altar."

Yielding to the easiness of my disposition, I went to bed for a week,
after receiving this letter. During the whole of such time, London was
bereft of the usual fruits of my labour. When I resumed it, I found
that Henrietta was married to the artist of Piccadilly.

Did I say to the artist? What fell words were those, expressive of
what a galling hollowness, of what a bitter mockery! I—I—I—am
the artist. I was the real artist of Piccadilly, I was the real artist of
the Waterloo Road, I am the only artist of all those pavement-
subjects which daily and nightly arouse your admiration. I do 'em,
and I let 'em out. The man you behold with the papers of chalks and
the rubbers, touching up the down strokes of the writing and shading
off the salmon, the man you give the credit to, the man you give the
money to, hires—yes! and I live to tell it!—hires those works of art
of me, and brings nothing to 'em but the candles.

Such is genius in a commercial country. I am not up to the shivering,
I am not up to the liveliness, I am not up to the wanting-employment-
in-an-office move; I am only up to originating and executing the work.
In consequence of which you never see me; you think you see me
when you see somebody else, and that somebody else is a mere
Commercial character. The one seen by self and Mr. Click in the
Waterloo Road can only write a single word, and that I taught him,
and it's MULTIPLICATION—which you may see him execute upside
down, because he can't do it the natural way. The one seen by self
and Henrietta by the Green Park railings can just smear into existence the two ends of a rainbow, with his cuff and a rubber—if very
hard put upon making a show—but he could no more come the arch
of the rainbow, to save his life, than he could come the moonlight,

fish, volcano, shipwreck, mutton, hermit, or any of my most cele
brated effects.

To conclude as I began: if there's a blighted public character going
I am the party. And often as you have seen, do see, and will see, my
Works, it's fifty thousand to one if you'll ever see me, unless, when
the candles are burnt down and the Commercial character is gone,
you should happen to notice a neglected young man perseveringly
rubbing out the last traces of the pictures, so that nobody can renew
the same. That's me.

CHAPTER IV

HIS WONDERFUL END

IT will have been, ere now, perceived that I sold the foregoing writings.
From the fact of their being printed in these pages, the inference will,
ere now, have been drawn by the reader (may I add, the gentle
reader?) that I sold them to One who never yet——*

Having parted with the writings on most satisfactory terms,—for,
in opening negotiations with the present Journal, was I not placing
myself in the hands of One of whom it may be said, in the words of
Another,†—I resumed my usual functions. But I too soon discovered
that peace of mind had fled from a brow which, up to that time,
Time had merely took the hair off, leaving an unruffled expanse
within.

It were superfluous to veil it,—the brow to which I allude is my
own.

Yes, over that brow uneasiness gathered like the sable wing of the
fabled bird, as—as no doubt will be easily indentified by all right-
minded individuals. If not, I am unable, on the spur of the moment
to enter into particulars of him. The reflection that the writings must
now inevitably get into print, and that He might yet live and meet
with them, sat like the Hag of Night upon my jaded form. The elasticity of my spirits departed. Fruitless was the Bottle, whether Wine
or Medicine. I had recourse to both, and the effect of both upon my
system was witheringly lowering.

In this state of depression, into which I subsided when I first began
to revolve what could I ever say if He—the unknown—was to appear
in the Coffee-room and demand reparation, I one forenoon in this
last November received a turn that appeared to be given me by the
finger of Fate and Conscience, hand in hand. I was alone in the Coffee-
room, and had just poked the fire into a blaze, and was standing with
my back to it, trying whether heat would penetrate with soothing
influence to the Voice within, when a young man in a cap, of an intelligent countenance, though requiring his hair cut, stood before me.

* The remainder of this complimentary parenthesis editorially struck out.
† The remainder of this complimentary sentence editorially struck out.

"Mr. Christopher, the Head Waiter?"

"The same."

The young man shook his hair out of his vision,—which it impeded,—took a packet from his breast, and handing it over to me, said, with his eye (or did I dream?) fixed with a lambent meaning on me, "THE PROOFS."

Although I smelt my coat-tails singeing at the fire, I had not the power to withdraw them. The young man put the packet in my faltering grasp, and repeated,—let me do him the justice to add, with civility:

"THE PROOFS. A. Y. R."

With those words he departed.

A. Y. R.? And You Remember. Was that his meaning? At Your Risk. Were the letters short for *that* reminder? Anticipate Your Retribution. Did they stand for *that* warning? Out-dacious Youth Repent? But no; for that, a O was happily wanting, and the vowel here was a A.

I opened the packet, and found that its contents were the foregoing writings printed just as the reader (may I add the discerning reader?) peruses them. In vain was the reassuring whisper,—A. Y. R., All the Year Round,—it could not cancel the Proofs. Too appropriate name. The Proofs of my having sold the Writings.

My wretchedness daily increased. I had not thought of the risk I ran, and the defying publicity I put my head into, until all was done, and all was in print. Give up the money to be off the bargain and prevent the publication, I could not. My family was down in the world, Christmas was coming on, a brother in the hospital and a sister in the rheumatics could not be entirely neglected. And it was not only ins in the family that had told on the resources of one unaided Waitering; outs were not wanting. A brother out of a situation, and another brother out of money to meet an acceptance, and another brother out of his mind, and another brother out at New York (not the same, though it might appear so), had really and truly brought me to a stand till I could turn myself round. I got worse and worse in my meditations, constantly reflecting "The Proofs," and reflecting that when Christmas drew nearer, and the Proofs were published, there could be no safety from hour to hour but that He might confront me in the Coffee-room, and in the face of day and his country demand his rights.

The impressive and unlooked-for catastrophe towards which I dimly pointed the reader (shall I add, the highly intellectual reader?) in my first remarks now rapidly approaches.

It was November still, but the last echoes of the Guy Foxes had long ceased to reverberate. We was slack,—several joints under our average mark, and wine, of course, proportionate. So slack had we become at last, that Beds Nos. 26, 27, 28, and 31, having took their six o'clock dinners, and dozed over their respective pints, had drove away in their respective Hansoms for their respective Night Mail-trains and left us empty.

I had took the evening paper to No. 6 table,—which is warm an
most to be preferred,—and, lost in the all-absorbing topics of the da
had dropped into a slumber. I was recalled to consciousness by th
well-known intimation, "Waiter!" and replying, "Sir!" found
gentleman standing at No. 4 table. The reader (shall I add, the obse
vant reader?) will please to notice the locality of the gentleman,—
No. 4 *table.*

He had one of the new-fangled uncollapsible bags in his han
(which I am against, for I don't see why you shouldn't collaps
while you are about it, as your fathers collapsed before you), and h
said:

"I want to dine, waiter. I shall sleep here to-night."

"Very good, Sir. What will you take for dinner, Sir?"

"Soup, bit of codfish, oyster sauce, and the joint."

"Thank you, Sir."

I rang the chambermaid's bell; and Mrs. Pratchett marched i
according to custom, demurely carrying a lighted flat candle befor
her, as if she was one of a long public procession, all the othe
members of which was invisible.

In the meanwhile the gentleman had gone up to the mantelpiece
right in front of the fire, and had laid his forehead against the mante
piece (which it is a low one, and brought him into the attitude of leap
frog), and had heaved a tremenjous sigh. His hair was long and light
ish; and when he laid his forehead against the mantelpiece, his hai
all fell in a dusty fluff together over his eyes; and when he now turne
round and lifted up his head again, it all fell in a dusty fluff togethe
over his ears. This give him a wild appearance, similar to a blaste
heath.

"O! The chambermaid. Ah!" He was turning something in hi
mind. "To be sure. Yes. I won't go upstairs now, if you will take m
bag. It will be enough for the present to know my number,—Ca
you give me 24 B?"

(O Conscience, what a Adder art thou!)

Mrs. Pratchett allotted him the room, and took his bag to it. H
then went back before the fire, and fell a biting his nails.

"Waiter!" biting between the words, "give me," bite, "pen an
paper; and in five minutes," bite, "let me have, if you please," bite
"a," bite, "Messenger."

Unmindful of his waning soup, he wrote and sent off six note
before he touched his dinner. Three were City; three West-end. Th
City letters were to Cornhill, Ludgate-hill, and Farringdon-street
The West-End letters were to Great Marlborough-street, New Bur
lington-street, and Piccadilly. Everybody was systematically denie
at every one of the six places, and there was not a vestige of any
answer. Our light porter whispered to me, when he came back wit
that report, "All Booksellers."

But before then he had cleared off his dinner, and his bottle o
wine. He now—mark the concurrence with the document formerly
given in full!—knocked a plate of biscuits off the table with hi

gitated elber (but without breakage), and demanded boiling brandy-
and-water.

Now fully convinced that it was Himself, I perspired with the
utmost freedom. When he become flushed with the heated stimulant
referred to, he again demanded pen and paper, and passed the succeeding two hours in producing a manuscript which he put in place
were when completed. He then went up to bed, attended by Mrs.
Pratchett. Mrs. Pratchett (who was aware of my emotions) told me,
in coming down, that she had noticed his eye rolling into every
corner of the passages and staircase, as if in search of his Luggage,
and that, looking back as she shut the door of 24 B, she perceived
him with his coat already thrown off immersing himself bodily
under the bedstead, like a chimley-sweep before the application of
machinery.

The next day—I forbear the horrors of that night—was a very
foggy day in our part of London, insomuch that it was necessary to
light the Coffee-room gas. We was still alone, and no feverish words
of mine can do justice to the fitfulness of his appearance as he sat at
No. 4 table, increased by there being something wrong with the meter.

Having again ordered his dinner, he went out, and was out for the
best part of two hours. Inquiring on his return whether any of the
answers had arrived, and receiving an unqualified negative, his
instant call was for Mulligatawny, the Cayenne Pepper, and Orange
Brandy.

Feeling that the mortal struggle was now at hand, I also felt that
I must be equal to him, and with that view resolved that whatever
he took I would take. Behind my partition, but keeping my eye on
him over the curtain, I therefore operated on Mulligatawny, Cayenne
Pepper, and Orange Brandy. And at a later period of the day, when
he again said, "Orange Brandy," I said so too, in a lower tone, to
George, my Second Lieutenant (my First was absent on leave) who
acts between me and the bar.

Throughout that awful day he walked about the Coffee-room continually. Often he came close up to my partition, and then his eye
rolled within, too evidently in search of any signs of his Luggage.
Half-past six came, and I laid his cloth. He ordered a bottle of Old
Brown. I likewise ordered a bottle of Old Brown. He drank his. I
drank mine (as nearly as my duties would permit) glass for glass
against his. He topped with coffee and a small glass. I topped with
coffee and a small glass. He dozed. I dozed. At last, "Waiter!"—and
he ordered his bill. The moment was now at hand when we two must
be locked in the deadly grapple.

Swift as the arrow from the bow, I had formed my resolution; in
other words, I had hammered it out between nine and nine. It was,
that I would be the first to open up the subject with a full acknow-
edgment, and would offer any gradual settlement within my power.
He paid his bill (doing what was right by attendance) with his eye
rolling about him to the last for any tokens of his Luggage. One only
time our gaze then met, with the lustrous fixedness (I believe I am

correct in imputing that character to it?) of the well-known Basilis.
The decisive moment had arrived.

With a tolerable steady hand, though with humility, I laid T
Proofs before him.

"Gracious Heavens!" he cries out, leaping up, and catching hol
of his chair. "What's this? Print!"

"Sir," I replied, in a calming voice, and bending forward. '
humbly acknowledge to being the unfortunate cause of it. But I hop
Sir, that when you have heard the circumstances explained, and th
innocence of my intentions——"

To my amazement, I was stopped short by his catching me in bot
his arms, and pressing me to his breast-bone; where I must confes
to my face (and particular, nose) having undergone some temporar
vexation from his wearing his coat buttoned high up, and his buttor
being uncommon hard.

"Ha, ha, ha!" he cried, releasing me with a wild laugh, and grasp
ing my hand. "What is your name, my Benefactor?"

"My name, Sir" (I was crumpled, and puzzled to make him out
"is Christopher; and I hope, Sir, that, as such, when you've hear
my ex——"

"In print!" he exclaims again, dashing the proofs over and ove
as if he was bathing in them. "In print!! O Christopher! Philanthro
pist! Nothing can recompense you,—but what sum of money woul
be acceptable to you?"

I had drawn a step back from him, or I should have suffered fror
his buttons again.

"Sir, I assure you, I have been already well paid, and——"

"No, no, Christopher! Don't talk like that! What sum of mone
would be acceptable to you, Christopher? Would you find twent
pounds acceptable, Christopher?"

However great my surprise, I naturally found words to say, "Si
I am not aware that the man was ever yet born without more tha
the average amount of water on the brain, as would *not* find twent
pounds acceptable. But—extremely obliged to you, Sir, I'm sure;
for he had tumbled it out of his purse and crammed it in my hand i
two bank-notes; "but I could wish to know, Sir, if not intruding, ho
I have merited this liberality?"

"Know then, my Christopher," he says, "that from boyhood'
hour I have unremittingly and unavailingly endeavoured to get int
print. Know, Christopher, that all the Booksellers alive—and severa
dead—have refused to put me into print. Know, Christopher, tha
I have written unprinted Reams. But they shall be read to you, m
friend and brother. You sometimes have a holiday?"

Seeing the great danger I was in, I had the presence of mind t
answer, "Never!" To make it more final, I added, "Never! Not fron
the cradle to the grave."

"Well," says he, thinking no more about that, and chuckling a
his proofs again. "But I am in print! The first flight of ambitio
emanating from my father's lowly cot is realised at length! The

golden bow,"—he was getting on—"struck by the magic hand, has emitted a complete and perfect sound! When did this happen, my Christopher?"

"Which happen, Sir?"

"This," he held it out at arm's length to admire it—"this Per-rint."

When I had given him my detailed account of it, he grasped me by the hand again, and said:

"Dear Christopher, it should be gratifying to you to know that you are an instrument in the hands of Destiny. Because you *are*."

A passing Something of a melancholy cast put it into my head to shake it, and to say, "Perhaps we all are."

"I don't mean that," he answered; "I don't take that wide range; I confine myself to the special case. Observe me well, my Christopher! Hopeless of getting rid, through any effort of my own, of any of the manuscripts among my Luggage,—all of which, send them where I would, were always coming back to me,—it is now some seven years since I left that Luggage here, on the desperate chance, either that the too, too faithful manuscripts would come back to me no more, or that some one less accursed than I might give them to the world. You follow me, my Christopher?"

"Pretty well, Sir." I followed him so far as to judge that he had a weak head, and that the Orange, the Boiling, and Old Brown combined was beginning to tell. (The Old Brown, being heady, is best adapted to seasoned cases.)

"Years elapsed, and those compositions slumbered in dust. At length, Destiny, choosing her agent from all mankind, sent You here, Christopher, and lo! the Casket was burst asunder, and the Giant was free!"

He made hay of his hair after he said this, and he stood a-tiptoe.

"But," he reminded himself in a state of excitement, "we must sit up all night, my Christopher. I must correct these Proofs for the press. Fill all the inkstands, and bring me several new pens."

He smeared himself and he smeared the Proofs, the night through, to that degree that when Sol gave him warning to depart (in a four-wheeler), few could have said which was them, and which was him, and which was blots. His last instructions was, that I should instantly run and take his corrections to the office of the present Journal. I did so. They most likely will not appear in print, for I noticed a message being brought round from Beauford Printing House, while I was a throwing this concluding statement on paper, that the ole resources of that establishment was unable to make out what they meant. Upon which a certain gentleman in company, as I will not more particularly name,—but of whom it will be sufficient to remark standing on the broad basis of a wave-girt isle, that whether we regard him in the light of,—* laughed, and put the corrections in the fire.

* The remainder of this complimentary parenthesis editorially struck out.

NOTE.—Mr. Dickens partly contributed to another of the chapters, entitled "His Umbrella"; but for this the reader is referred to the number as republished in a collected volume—the *Nine Christmas numbers of All the Year Round*.

MRS. LIRRIPER'S LODGINGS

IN TWO CHAPTERS

[1863]

CHAPTER I

HOW MRS. LIRRIPER CARRIED ON THE BUSINESS

WHOEVER would begin to be worried with letting Lodgings that wasn't a lone woman with a living to get is a thing inconceivable to me, my dear; excuse the familiarity, but it comes natural to me in my own little room, when wishing to open my mind to those that I can trust, and I should be truly thankful if they were all mankind but such is not so, for have but a Furnished bill in the window and your watch on the mantelpiece, and farewell to it if you turn your back for but a second, however gentlemanly the manners; nor is being of your own sex any safeguard, as I have reason, in the form of sugar-tongs to know, for that lady (and a fine woman she was) got me to run for a glass of water, on the plea of going to be confined, which certainly turned out true, but it was in the Station-house.

Number Eighty-one Norfolk Street, Strand—situated midway between the City and St. James's, and within five minutes' walk of the principal places of public amusement—is my address. I have rented this house many years, as the parish rate-books will testify, and I could wish my landlord was as alive to the fact as I am myself but no, bless you, not a half a pound of paint to save his life, nor so much, my dear, as a tile upon the roof, though on your bended knees.

My dear, you never have found Number Eighty-one Norfolk Street Strand advertised in Bradshaw's *Railway Guide,* and with the blessing of Heaven you never will or shall so find it. Some there are who do not think it lowering themselves to make their names that cheap, and even going the lengths of a portrait of a house not like it, with a blot in every window and a coach and four at the door, but what will suit Wozenham's lower down on the other side of the way will not suit me, Miss Wozenham having her opinions and me having mine, though when it comes to systematic underbidding capable of being proved on oath in a court of justice and taking the form of "If Mrs. Lirriper names eighteen shillings a week, I name fifteen and six," it then comes to a settlement between yourself and your conscience, supposing for the sake of argument your name to be Wozen am, which I am well aware it is not or my opinion of you would be greatly lowered, and as to airy bedrooms and a night-porter in constant attendance the less said the better, the bedrooms being stuffy and the porter stuff.

It is forty years ago since me and my poor Lirriper got married at St. Clement's Danes, where I now have a sitting in a very pleasant pew with genteel company and my own hassock, and being partial to evening service not too crowded. My poor Lirriper was a handsome figure of a man, with a beaming eye and a voice as mellow as a musical instrument made of honey and steel, but he had ever been a free liver, being in the commercial travelling line and travelling what he called a limekiln road—"a dry road, Emma my dear," my poor Lirriper says to me, "where I have to lay the dust with one drink or another all day long and half the night, and it wears me, Emma"—and this led to his running through a good deal and might have run through the turnpike too when that dreadful horse that never would stand still for a single instant set off, but for its being night and the gate shut, and consequently took his wheel, my poor Lirriper and the gig smashed to atoms and never spoke afterwards. He was a handsome figure of a man, and a man with a jovial heart and a sweet temper; but if they had come up then they never could have given you the mellowness of his voice, and indeed I consider photographs wanting in mellowness as a general rule and making you look like a new-ploughed field.

My poor Lirriper being behindhand with the world and being buried at Hatfield church in Hertfordshire, not that it was his native place but that he had a liking for the Salisbury Arms where we went upon our wedding-day and passed as happy a fortnight as ever happy was, I went round to the creditors and I say "Gentlemen I am acquainted with the fact that I am not answerable for my late husband's debts but I wish to pay them for I am his lawful wife and his good name is dear to me. I am going into the Lodgings gentlemen as a business and if I prosper every farthing that my late husband owed shall be paid for the sake of the love I bore him, by this right hand." It took a long time to do but it was done, and the silver cream-jug which is between ourselves and the bed and the mattress in my room upstairs (or it would have found legs so sure as ever the Furnished bill was up) being presented by the gentlemen engraved "To Mrs. Lirriper a mark of grateful respect for her honourable conduct" gave me a turn which was too much for my feelings, till Mr. Betley which at that time had the parlours and loved his joke says "Cheer up Mrs. Lirriper, you should feel as if it was only your christening and they were your godfathers and godmothers which did promise for you." And it brought me round, and I don't mind confessing to you my dear that I then put a sandwich and a drop of sherry in a little basket and went down to Hatfield churchyard outside the coach and kissed my hand and laid it with a kind of proud and swelling love on my husband's grave, though bless you it had taken me so long to clear his name that my wedding-ring was worn quite fine and smooth when I laid it on the green waving grass.

I am an old woman now and my good looks are gone but that' me my dear over the plate-warmer and considered like in the time when you used to pay two guineas on ivory and took your chanc pretty much how you came out, which made you very careful hov you left it about afterwards because people were turned so red an uncomfortable by mostly guessing it was somebody else quit different, and there was once a certain person that had put his money in a hop business that came in one morning to pay his rent and hi respects being the second floor that would have taken it down from its hook and put it in his breast-pocket—you understand my dear— for the L, he says of the original—only there was no mellowness in *his* voice and I wouldn't let him, but his opinion of it you may gathe from his saying to it "Speak to me Emma!" which was far from a rational observation no doubt but still a tribute to its being a like ness, and I think myself it *was* like me when I was young and wor that sort of stays.

But it was about the Lodgings that I was intending to hold fort] and certainly I ought to know something of the business having been in it so long, for it was early in the second year of my married lif that I lost my poor Lirriper and I set up at Islington directly after wards and afterwards came here, being two houses and eight-and-thirty years and some losses and a deal of experience.

Girls are your first trial after fixtures and they try you even wors than what I call the Wandering Christians, though why *they* should roam the earth looking for bills and then coming in and viewing the apartments and stickling about terms and never at all wantin them or dreaming of taking them being already provided, is a mystery I should be thankful to have explained if by any miracle i could be. It's wonderful they live so long and thrive on it but suppose the exercise makes it healthy, knocking so much and going from house to house and up and down stairs all day, and then thei pretending to be so particular and punctual is a most astonishing thing, looking at their watches and saying "Could you give me the refusal of the rooms till twenty minutes past eleven the day afte to-morrow in the forenoon, and supposing it to be considered essentia by my friend from the country could there be a small iron bedstead put in the little room upon the stairs?" Why when I was new to i my dear I used to consider before I promised and to make my mind anxious with calculations and to get quite wearied out with dis appointments, but now I says "Certainly by all means" well knowing it's a Wandering Christian and I shall hear no more about it, indeed by this time I know most of the Wandering Christians by sight as well as they know me, it being the habit of each individual revolving round London in that capacity to come back about twice a year and it's very remarkable that it runs in families and the children grow up to it, but even were it otherwise I should no sooner hear o the friend from the country which is a certain sign than I should nod and say to myself You're a Wandering Christian, though whether they are (as I *have* heard) persons of small property with a taste for regular employment and frequent change of scene I cannot undertake to tell you.

Girls as I was beginning to remark are one of your first and your lasting troubles, being like your teeth which begin with convulsions and never cease tormenting you from the time you cut them till they cut you, and then you don't want to part with them which seems hard but we must all succumb or buy artificial, and even where you get a will nine times out of ten you'll get a dirty face with it and naturally lodgers do not like good society to be shown in with a smear of black across the nose or a smudgy eyebrow. Where they pick the black up is a mystery I cannot solve, as in the case of the willingest girl that ever came into a house half-starved poor thing, a girl so willing that I called her Willing Sophy down upon her knees scrubbing early and late and ever cheerful but always smiling with a black face. And I says to Sophy, "Now Sophy my good girl have a regular day for your stoves and keep the width of the Airy between yourself and the blacking and do not brush your hair with the bottoms of the saucepans and do not meddle with the snuffs of the candles and it stands to reason that it can no longer be" yet there it was and always on her nose, which turning up and being broad at the end seemed to boast of it and caused warning from a steady gentleman and excellent lodger with breakfast by the week but a little irritable and use of a sitting-room when required, his words being "Mrs. Lirriper I have arrived at the point of admitting that the Black is a man and a brother, but only in a natural form and when it can't be got off." Well consequently I put poor Sophy on to other work and forbid her answering the door or answering a bell on any account but she was so unfortunately willing that nothing would stop her flying up the kitchen-stairs whenever a bell was heard to tingle. I put it to her "O Sophy Sophy for goodness' goodness' sake where does it come from?" To which that poor unlucky willing mortal bursting out crying to see me so vexed replied "I took a deal of black into me ma'am when I was a small child being much neglected and I think it must be, that it works out," so it continuing to work out of that poor thing and not having another fault to find with her I says "Sophy what do you seriously think of my helping you away to New South Wales where it might not be noticed?" Nor did I ever repent the money which was well spent, for she married the ship's cook on the voyage (himself a Mulotter) and did well and lived happy, and so far as ever I heard it was *not* noticed in a new state of society to her dying day.

In what way Miss Wozenham lower down on the other side of the way reconciled it to her feelings as a lady (which she is not) to entice Mary Anne Perkinsop from my service is best known to herself, I do not know and I do not wish to know how opinions are formed at Wozenham's on any point. But Mary Anne Perkinsop although I behaved handsomely to her and she behaved unhandsomely to me was worth her weight in gold as overawing lodgers without driving them away, for lodgers would be far more sparing of their bells with Mary Anne than I ever knew them to be with Maid or Mistress, which is a great triumph especially when accompanied with a cast in the eye and a bag of bones, but it was the steadiness of her way with them through her father's having failed in Pork. It was Mary Anne's looking so respectable in her person and being so strict in her spirits that conquered the tea-and-sugarest gentleman (for he weighed them both in a pair of scales every morning) that I have ever had to deal with and no lamb grew meeker, still it afterwards came round to me that Miss Wozenham happening to pass and seeing Mary Anne take in the milk of a milkman that made free in a rosy-faced way (I think no worse of him) with every girl in the street but was quite frozen up like the statue at Charing-cross by her, saw Mary Anne's value in the lodging business and went as high as one pound per quarter more, consequently Mary Anne with not a word betwixt us says "If *you* will provide yourself Mrs. Lirriper in a month from this day *I* have already done the same," which hurt me and I said so, and she then hurt me more by insinuating that her father having failed in Pork had laid her open to it.

My dear I do assure you it's a harassing thing to know what kind of girls to give the preference to, for if they are lively they get bell'd off their legs and if they are sluggish you suffer from it yourself in complaints and if they are sparkling-eyed they get made love to, and if they are smart in their persons they try on your Lodgers' bonnets and if they are musical I defy you to keep them away from bands and organs, and allowing for any difference you like in their heads their heads will be always out of window just the same. And then what the gentlemen like in girls the ladies don't, which is fruitful hot water for all parties, and then there's temper though such a temper as Caroline Maxey's I hope not often. A good-looking black-eyed girl was Caroline and a comely-made girl to your cost when she did break out and laid about her, as took place first and last through a new-married couple come to see London in the first floor and the lady very high and it *was* supposed not liking the good looks of Caroline having none of her own to spare, but anyhow she did try Caroline though that was no excuse. So one afternoon Caroline comes down into the kitchen flushed and flashing, and she says to me "Mrs. Lirriper that woman in the first has aggravated me past bearing," I says "Caroline keep your temper," Caroline says with a curdling laugh "Keep my temper? You're right Mrs. Lirriper, so I will. Capital D her!" bursts out Caroline (you might have struck me into the centre of the earth with a feather when she said it) "I'll give her a touch of the temper that *I* keep!" Caroline downs with her hair my dear, screeches and rushes upstairs, I following as fast as my trembling legs could bear me, but before I got into the room the dinner-cloth and pink-and-white service all dragged off upon the floor with a crash and the new-married couple on their backs in the fire-grate, him with the shovel and tongs and a dish of cucumber across him and a mercy it was summer-time. "Caroline" I says "be calm," but she catches off my cap and tears it in her teeth as she passes me, then pounces on the new-married lady makes her a bundle of ribbons takes her by the two ears and knocks the back of her head upon the carpet Murder screaming all the time Policeman running down the street and Wozenham's windows (judge of my feelings when I came to know it) thrown up and Miss Wozenham calling out from the balcony with crocodile's tears "It's Mrs. Lirriper been overcharging somebody to madness—she'll be murdered—I always thought so—Pleeseman save her!" My dear four of them and Caroline behind the chiffoniere attacking with the poker and when disarmed prize-fighting with her double fists, and down and up and up and down and dreadful! But I couldn't bear to see the poor young creature roughly handled and her hair torn when they got the better of her, and I says "Gentlemen Policemen pray remember that her sex is the sex of your mothers and sisters and your sweethearts, and God bless them and you!" And there she was sitting down on the ground handcuffed, taking breath against the skirting-board and them cool with their coats in strips, and all she says was "Mrs. Lirriper I'm sorry as ever I touched *you*, for you're a kind motherly old thing," and it made me think that I had often wished I had been a mother indeed and how would my heart have felt if I had been the mother of that girl! Well you know it turned out at the Police-office that she had done it before, and she had her clothes away and was sent to prison, and when she was to come out I trotted off to the gate in the evening with just a morsel of jelly in that little basket of mine to give her a mite of strength to face the world again, and there I met with a very decent mother waiting for her son through bad company and a stubborn one he was with his half-boots not laced. So out came Caroline and I says "Caroline come along with me and sit down under the wall where it's retired and eat a little trifle that I have brought with me to do you good," and she throws her arms round my neck and says sobbing "O why were you never a mother when there are such mothers as there are?" she says, and in half a minute more she begins to laugh and says "Did I really tear your cap to shreds?" and when I told her "You certainly did so Caroline" she laughed again and said while she patted my face "Then why do you wear such queer old caps you dear old thing? If you hadn't worn such queer old caps I don't think I should have done it even then." Fancy the girl! Nothing could get out of her what she was going to do except O she would do well enough, and we parted she being very thankful and kissing my hands, and I nevermore saw or heard of that girl, except that I shall always believe that a very genteel cap which was brought anonymous to me one Saturday night in an oil-skin basket by a most impertinent young sparrow of a monkey whistling with dirty shoes on the clean steps and playing the harp on the Airy railings with a hoop-stick came from Caroline.

What you lay yourself open to my dear in the way of being the object of uncharitable suspicions when you go into the Lodging business I have not the words to tell you, but never was I so dishonourable as to have two keys nor would I willingly think it even of Miss Wozenham lower down on the other side of the way sincerely hoping that it may not be, though doubtless at the same time money cannot come from nowhere and it is not reason to suppose that Bradshaws put it in for love be it blotty as it may. It *is* a hardship hurting to the feelings that Lodgers open their minds so wide to the idea that you are trying to get the better of them and shut their minds so close to the idea that they are trying to get the better of you, but as Major Jackman says to me "I know the ways of this circular world Mrs. Lirriper, and that's one of 'em all round it" and many is the little ruffle in my mind that the Major has smoothed, for he is a clever man who has seen much. Dear dear, thirteen years have passed though it seems but yesterday since I was sitting with my glasses on at the open front parlour window one evening in August (the parlours being then vacant) reading yesterday's paper my eyes for print being poor though still I am thankful to say a long sight at a distance, when I hear a gentleman come posting across the road and up the street in a dreadful rage talking to himself in a fury and d'ing and c'ing somebody. "By George!" says he out loud and clutching his walking-stick, "I'll go to Mrs. Lirriper's. Which IS Mrs. Lirriper's?" Then looking round and seeing me he flourishes his hat right off his head as if I had been the queen and he says, "Excuse the intrusion madam, but pray madam can you tell me at what number in this street there resides a well-known and much-respected lady by the name of Lirriper?" A little flustered though I must say gratified I took off my glasses and courtesied and said "Sir, Mrs. Lirriper is your humble servant." "Astonishing!" says he. "A million pardons! Madam, may I ask you to have the kindness to direct one of your domestics to open the door to a gentleman in search of apartments, by the name of Jackman?" I had never heard the name but a politer gentleman I never hope to see, for says he "Madam I am shocked at your opening the door yourself to no worthier a fellow than Jemmy Jackman. After you madam. I never precede a lady." Then he comes into the parlours and he sniffs, and he says "Hah! These are parlours! Not musty cupboards" he says "but parlours, and no smell of coal-sacks." Now my dear it having been remarked by some inimical to the whole neighbourhood that it always smells of coal-sacks which might prove a drawback to Lodgers if encouraged, I says to the Major gently though firmly that I think he is referring to Arundel or Surrey or Howard but not Norfolk. "Madam" says he "I refer to Wozenham's lower down over the way—madam you can form no notion what Wozenham's is—madam it is a vast coal-sack, and Miss Wozenham has the principles and manners of a female heaver—madam from the manner in which I have heard her mention you I know she has no appreciation of a lady, and from the manner in which she has conducted herself towards me I know she has no appreciation of a gentleman—madam my name is Jackman—should you require any other reference than what I have already said, I name the Bank of

_ngland—perhaps you know it!'' Such was the beginning of the
_Iajor's occupying the parlours and from that hour to this the same
_nd a most obliging Lodger and punctual in all respects except one
_regular which I need not particularly specify, but made up for by
_is being a protection and at all times ready to fill in the papers of
_he Assessed Taxes and Juries and that, and once collared a young
_aan with the drawing-room clock under his coat, and once on the
_arapets with his own hands and blankets put out the kitchen
_himney and afterwards attending the summons made a most
_loquent speech against the Parish before the magistrates and saved
_he engine, and ever quite the gentleman though passionate. And
_ertainly Miss Wozenham's detaining the trunks and umbrella was
_ot in a liberal spirit though it may have been according to her rights
_1 law or an act _I_ would myself have stooped to, the Major being so
_1uch the gentleman that though he is far from tall he seems almost
_o when he has his shirt-frill out and his frock-coat on and his hat
_rith the curly brims, and in what service he was I cannot truly tell
_ou my dear whether Militia or Foreign, for I never heard him even
_ame himself as Major but always simple ''Jemmy Jackman'' and
_nce soon after he came when I felt it my duty to let him know that
_Iiss Wozenham had put it about that he was no Major and I took
_he liberty of adding ''which you are Sir'' his words were ''Madam at
_ny rate I am not a Minor, and sufficient for the day is the evil
_hereof'' which cannot be denied to be the sacred truth, nor yet his
_1ilitary ways of having his boots with only the dirt brushed off
_aken to him in the front parlour every morning on a clean plate and
_arnishing them himself with a little sponge and a saucer and a
_vhistle in a whisper so sure as ever his breakfast is ended, and so
_eat his ways that it never soils his linen which is scrupulous though
_nore in quality than quantity, neither that nor his mustachios which
_o the best of my belief are done at the same time and which are as
_lack and shining as his boots, his head of hair being a lovely white.

It was the third year nearly up of the Major's being in the parlours
_hat early one morning in the month of February when Parliament
_vas coming on and you may therefore suppose a number of im-
_oostors were about ready to take hold of anything they could get,
_, gentleman and a lady from the country came in to view the Second,
_ind I well remember that I had been looking out of window and had
_vatched them and the heavy sleet driving down the street together
_ooking for bills. I did not quite take to the face of the gentleman
_hough he was good-looking too but the lady was a very pretty young
_hing and delicate, and it seemed too rough for her to be out at all
_hough she had only come from the Adelphi Hotel which would not
_iave been much above a quarter of a mile if the weather had been
_ess severe. Now it did so happen my dear that I had been forced to
_out five shillings weekly additional on the Second in consequence of
_, loss from running away full dressed as if going out to a dinner-
_oarty, which was very artful and had made me rather suspicious
_aking it along with Parliament, so when the gentleman proposed

three months certain and the money in advance and leave them reserved to renew on the same terms for six months more, I says I was not quite certain but that I might have engaged myself to another party but would step downstairs and look into it if they would take a seat. They took a seat and I went down to the handle of the Major's door that I had already began to consult finding it a great blessing, and I knew by his whistling in a whisper that he was varnishing his boots which was generally considered private, however he kindly calls out "If it's you, madam, come in," and I went in and told him.

"Well, madam," says the Major rubbing his nose—as I did fear at the moment with the black sponge but it was only his knuckle he being always neat and dexterous with his fingers—"well, madam I suppose you would be glad of the money?"

I was delicate of saying "Yes" too out, for a little extra colour rose into the Major's cheeks and there was irregularity which I will now particularly specify in a quarter which I will not name.

"I am of opinion, madam," says the Major, "that when money is ready for you—when it is ready for you, Mrs. Lirriper—you ought to take it. What is there against it, madam, in this case upstairs?"

"I really cannot say there is anything against it, Sir, still I thought I would consult you."

"You said a newly-married couple, I think, madam?" says the Major.

I says "Ye-es. Evidently. And indeed the young lady mentioned to me in a casual way that she had not been married many months."

The Major rubbed his nose again and stirred the varnish round and round in its little saucer with his piece of sponge and took to his whistling in a whisper for a few moments. Then he says "You would call it a Good Let, Madam?"

"O certainly a Good Let Sir."

"Say they renew for the additional six months. Would it put you about very much madam if—if the worst was to come to the worst?" said the Major.

"Well I hardly know," I says to the Major. "It depends upon circumstances. Would you object Sir for instance?"

"I?" says the Major. "Object? Jemmy Jackman? Mrs. Lirriper close with the proposal."

So I went upstairs and accepted, and they came in next day which was Saturday and the Major was so good as to draw up a Memorandum of an agreement in a beautiful round hand and expressions that sounded to me equally legal and military, and Mr. Edson signed it on the Monday morning and the Major called upon Mr. Edson on the Tuesday and Mr. Edson called upon the Major on the Wednesday and the Second and the parlours were as friendly as could be wished

The three months paid for had run out and we had got without any fresh overtures as to payment into May my dear, when there came an obligation upon Mr. Edson to go a business expedition right across the Isle of Man, which fell quite unexpected upon that pretty

ittle thing and is not a place that according to my views is particu-
arly in the way to anywhere at any time but that may be a matter
of opinion. So short a notice was it that he was to go next day, and
dreadfully she cried poor pretty, and I am sure I cried too when I
saw her on the cold pavement in the sharp east wind—it being a very
backward spring that year—taking a last leave of him with her
pretty bright hair blowing this way and that and her arms clinging
round his neck and him saying "There there there. Now let me go
Peggy." And by that time it was plain that what the Major had been
so accommodating as to say he would not object to happening in the
house, would happen in it, and I told her as much when he was gone
while I comforted her with my arm up the staircase, for I says "You
will soon have others to keep up for my pretty and you must think
of that."

His letter never came when it ought to have come and what she
went through morning after morning when the postman brought
none for her the very postman himself compassionated when she ran
down to the door, and yet we cannot wonder at its being calculated
to blunt the feelings to have all the trouble of other people's letters
and none of the pleasure and doing it oftener in the mud and mizzle
than not and at a rate of wages more resembling Little Britain than
Great. But at last one morning when she was too poorly to come
running downstairs he says to me with a pleased look in his face that
made me next to love the man in his uniform coat though he was
dripping wet "I have taken you first in the street this morning Mrs.
Lirriper, for here's the one for Mrs. Edson." I went up to her bedroom
with it as fast as ever I could go, and she sat up in bed when she saw
it and kissed it and tore it open and then a blank stare came upon
her. "It's very short!" she says lifting her large eyes to my face.
"O Mrs. Lirriper it's very short!" I says "My dear Mrs. Edson no
doubt that's because your husband hadn't time to write more just
at that time." "No doubt, no doubt," says she, and puts her two
hands on her face and turns round in her bed.

I shut her softly in and I crept downstairs and I tapped at the
Major's door, and when the Major having his thin slices of bacon in
his own Dutch oven saw me he came out of his chair and put me
down on the sofa. "Hush!" says he, "I see something's the matter.
Don't speak—take time." I says "O Major I'm afraid there's cruel
work upstairs." "Yes yes," says he "I had begun to be afraid of it—
take time." And then in opposition to his own words he rages out
frightfully, and says "I shall never forgive myself madam, that I,
Jemmy Jackman, didn't see it all that morning—didn't go straight
upstairs when my boot-sponge was in my hand—didn't force it
down his throat—and choke him dead with it on the spot!"

The Major and me agreed when we came to ourselves that just at
present we could do no more than take on to suspect nothing and
use our best endeavours to keep that poor young creature quiet, and
what I ever should have done without the Major when it got about
among the organ-men that quiet was our object is unknown, for he

made lion and tiger war upon them to that degree that without seeing it I could not have believed it was in any gentleman to have such a power of bursting out with fire-irons walking-sticks water-jugs coals potatoes off his table the very hat off his head, and at the same time so furious in foreign languages that they would stand with their handles half-turned fixed like the Sleeping Ugly—for I cannot say Beauty.

Even to see the postman come near the house now gave me such a fear that it was a reprieve when he went by, but in about another ten days or a fortnight he says again, "Here's one for Mrs. Edson.— Is she pretty well?" "She is pretty well postman, but not well enough to rise so early as she used" which was so far gospel-truth.

I carried the letter in to the Major at his breakfast and I says tottering "Major I have not the courage to take it up to her."

"It's an ill-looking villain of a letter," says the Major.

"I have not the courage Major" I says again in a tremble "to take it up to her."

After seeming lost in consideration for some moments the Major says, raising his head as if something new and useful had occurred to his mind "Mrs. Lirriper, I shall never forgive myself that I, Jemmy Jackman, didn't go straight upstairs that morning when my boot-sponge was in my hand—and force it down his throat—and choke him dead with it."

"Major" I says a little hasty "you didn't do it which is a blessing, for it would have done no good and I think your sponge was better employed on your own honourable boots."

So we got to be rational, and planned that I should tap at her bedroom door and lay the letter on the mat outside and wait on the upper landing for what might happen, and never was gunpowder cannon-balls or shells or rockets more dreaded than that dreadful letter was by me as I took it to the second floor.

A terrible loud scream sounded through the house the minute after she had opened it, and I found her on the floor lying as if her life was gone. My dear I never looked at the face of the letter which was lying open by her, for there was no occasion.

Everything I needed to bring her round the Major brought up with his own hands, besides running out to the chemist's for what was not in the house and likewise having the fiercest of all his many skirmishes with a musical instrument representing a ball-room I do not know in what particular country and company waltzing in and out at folding-doors with rolling eyes. When after a long time I saw her coming to, I slipped on the landing till I heard her cry, and then I went in and says cheerily "Mrs. Edson you're not well my dear and it's not to be wondered at," as if I had not been in before. Whether she believed or disbelieved I cannot say and it would signify nothing if I could, but I stayed by her for hours and then she God ever blesses me! and says she will try to rest for her head is bad.

"Major," I whispers, looking in at the parlours, "I beg and pray of you don't go out."

The Major whispers, "Madam, trust me I will do no such a thing. How is she?"

I says "Major the good Lord above us only knows what burns and rages in her poor mind. I left her sitting at her window. I am going to sit at mine."

It came on afternoon and it came on evening. Norfolk is a delightful street to lodge in—provided you don't go lower down—but of a summer evening when the dust and waste paper lie in it and stray children play in it and a kind of a gritty calm and bake settles on it and a peal of church-bells is practising in the neighbourhood it is a trifle dull, and never have I seen it since at such a time and never shall I see it evermore at such a time without seeing the dull June evening when that forlorn young creature sat at her open corner window on the Second and me at my open corner window (the other corner) on the Third. Something merciful, something wiser and better far than my own self, had moved me while it was yet light to sit in my bonnet and shawl, and as the shadows fell and the tide rose I could sometimes—when I put out my head and looked at her window below—see that she leaned out a little looking down the street. It was just settling dark when I saw *her* in the street.

So fearful of losing sight of her that it almost stops my breath while I tell it, I went downstairs faster than I ever moved in all my life and only tapped with my hand at the Major's door in passing it and slipping out. She was gone already. I made the same speed down the street and when I came to the corner of Howard-street I saw that she had turned it and was there plain before me going towards the west. O with what a thankful heart I saw her going along!

She was quite unacquainted with London and had very seldom been out for more than an airing in our own street where she knew two or three little children belonging to neighbours and had sometimes stood among them at the street looking at the water. She must be going at hazard I knew, still she kept the bye-streets quite correctly as long as they would serve her, and then turned up into the Strand. But at every corner I could see her head turned one way, and that way was always the river way.

It may have been only the darkness and quiet of the Adelphi that caused her to strike into it but she struck into it much as readily as if she had set out to go there, which perhaps was the case. She went straight down to the Terrace and along it and looked over the iron rail, and I often woke afterwards in my own bed with the horror of seeing her do it. The desertion of the wharf below and the flowing of the high water there seemed to settle her purpose. She looked about as if to make out the way down, and she struck out the right way or the wrong way—I don't know which, for I don't know the place before or since—and I followed her the way she went.

It was noticeable that all this time she never once looked back. But there was now a great change in the manner of her going, and instead of going at a steady quick walk with her arms folded before her,—among the dark dismal arches she went in a wild way with her

arms opened wide, as if they were wings and she was flying to he
death.

We were on the wharf and she stopped. I stopped. I saw her hand
at her bonnet-strings, and I rushed between her and the brink an
took her round the waist with both my arms. She might hav
drowned me, I felt then, but she could never have got quit of me.

Down to that moment my mind had been all in a maze and no
half an idea had I had in it what I should say to her, but the instant
I touched her it came to me like magic and I had my natural voic
and my senses and even almost my breath.

"Mrs. Edson!" I says "My dear! Take care. However did you los
your way and stumble on a dangerous place like this? Why you mus
have come here by the most perplexing streets in all London. N
wonder you are lost, I'm sure. And this place too! Why I though
nobody ever got here, except me to order my coals and the Major i
the parlours to smoke his cigar!"—for I saw that blessed man clos
by, pretending to it.

"Hah—Hah—Hum!" coughs the Major.

"And good gracious me" I says, "why here he is!"

"Halloa! who goes there?" says the Major in a military manner

"Well!" I says, "if this don't beat everything! Don't you know u
Major Jackman?"

"Halloa!" says the Major. "Who calls on Jemmy Jackman?" (and
more out of breath he was, and did it less like life than I should have
expected).

"Why here's Mrs. Edson Major" I says, "strolling out to cool he
poor head which has been very bad, has missed her way and got lost
and Goodness knows where she might have got to but for me coming
here to drop an order into my coal merchant's letter-box and you
coming here to smoke your cigar!—And you really are not wel
enough my dear" I says to her "to be half so far from home withou
me.—And your arm will be very acceptable I am sure Major" I say:
to him "and I know she may lean upon it as heavy as she likes.'
And now we had both got her—thanks be Above!—one on each side

She was all in a cold shiver and she so continued till I laid her or
her own bed, and up to the early morning she held me by the hand
and moaned and moaned "O wicked, wicked, wicked!" But when
at last I made believe to droop my head and be overpowered with a
dead sleep, I heard that poor young creature give such touching and
such humble thanks for being preserved from taking her own life in
her madness that I thought I should have cried my eyes out on the
counterpane and I knew she was safe.

Being well enough to do and able to afford it, me and the Major
laid our little plans next day while she was asleep worn out, and so I
says to her as soon as I could do it nicely: "Mrs. Edson my dear, when
Mr. Edson paid me the rent for these farther six months——"

She gave a start and I felt her large eyes look at me, but I went on
with it and with my needlework.

"—I can't say that I am quite sure I dated the receipt right uld you let me look at it?"

She laid her frozen cold hand upon mine and she looked through me
hen I was forced to look up from my needlework, but I had taken
e precaution of having on my spectacles.

"I have no receipt" says she.

"Ah! Then he has got it" I says in a careless way. "It's of no great
nsequence. A receipt's a receipt."

From that time she always had hold of my hand when I could
are it which was generally only when I read to her, for of course
e and me had our bits of needlework to plod at and neither of us
as very handy at those little things, though I am still rather proud
my share in them too considering. And though she took to all I
ad to her, I used to fancy that next to what was taught upon the
ount she took most of all to His gentle compassion for us poor
omen and to His young life and to how His mother was proud of Him
d treasured His sayings in her heart. She had a grateful look in her
es that never never will be out of mine until they are closed
my last sleep, and when I chanced to look at her without thinking
f it I would always meet that look, and she would often offer me her
embling lip to kiss, much more like a little affectionate half-broken-
earted child than ever I can imagine any grown person.

One time the trembling of this poor lip was so strong and her tears
n down so fast that I thought she was going to tell me all her woe,
I takes her two hands in mine and I says:

"No my dear not now, you had best not try to do it now. Wait for
etter times when you have got over this and are strong, and then
ou shall tell me whatever you will. Shall it be agreed?"

With our hands still joined she nodded her head many times, and
e lifted my hands and put them to her lips and to her bosom.

"Only one word now my dear" I says. "Is there any one?"

She looked inquiringly "Any one?"

"That I can go to?"

She shook her head.

"No one that I can bring?"

She shook her head.

"No one is wanted by *me* my dear. Now that may be considered
ast and gone."

Not much more than a week afterwards—for this was far on in the
ime of our being so together—I was bending over at her bedside with
y ear down to her lips, by turns listening for her breath and looking
or a sign of life in her face. At last it came in a solemn way—not in a
lash but like a kind of pale faint light brought very slow to the face.

She said something to me that had no sound in it, but I saw she
sked me:

"Is this death?"

And I says:

"Poor dear poor dear, I think it is."

Knowing somehow that she wanted me to move her weak right
and, I took it and laid it on her breast and then folded her other

hand upon it, and she prayed a good good prayer and I joined in i
poor me though there were no words spoke. Then I brought the baby
in its wrappers from where it lay, and I says:

"My dear this is sent to a childless old woman. This is for me to
take care of."

The trembling lip was put up towards my face for the last time
and I dearly kissed it.

"Yes my dear," I says. "Please God! Me and the Major."

I don't know how to tell it right, but I saw her soul brighten and
leap up, and get free and fly away in the grateful look.

* * * * * *

So this is the why and wherefore of its coming to pass my dea
that we called him Jemmy, being after the Major his own godfathe
with Lirriper for a surname being after myself, and never was a dea
child such a brightening thing in a Lodgings or such a playmate to hi
grandmother as Jemmy to this house and me, and always good and
minding what he was told (upon the whole) and soothing for the tem
per and making everything pleasanter except when he grew old
enough to drop his cap down Wozenham's Airy and they wouldn'
hand it up to him, and being worked into a state I put on my bes
bonnet and gloves and parasol with the child in my hand and I say
"Miss Wozenham I little thought ever to have entered *your* house bu
unless my grandson's cap is instantly restored, the laws of thi
country regulating the property of the Subject shall at length decide
betwixt yourself and me, cost what it may." With a sneer upon he
face which did strike me I must say as being expressive of two key
but it may have been a mistake and if there is any doubt let Mis
Wozenham have the full benefit of it as is but right, she rang the bel
and she says "Jane, is there a street-child's old cap down our Airy?'
I says "Miss Wozenham before your housemaid answers that question
you must allow me to inform you to your face that my grandson i
not a street-child and is *not* in the habit of wearing old caps. In fact'
I says "Miss Wozenham I am far from sure that my grandson's cap
may not be newer than your own" which was perfectly savage in me
her lace being the commonest machine-make washed and torn besides
but I had been put into a state to begin with fomented by impertin
ence. Miss Wozenham says red in the face "Jane you heard my
question, is there any child's cap down our Airy?" "Yes ma'am'
says Jane "I think I did see some such rubbish a-lying there." "Then'
says Miss Wozenham "let these visitors out, and then throw up tha
worthless article out of my premises." But here the child who had
been staring at Miss Wozenham with all his eyes and more, frowns
down his little eyebrows purses up his little mouth puts his chubby
legs far apart turns his little dimpled fists round and round slowly
over one another like a little coffee-mill, and says to her "Oo impdent
to mi Gran, me tut oor hi!" "O!" says Miss Wozenham looking down
scornfully at the Mite "this is not a street-child is it not? Really!" I
bursts out laughing and I says "Miss Wozenham if this ain't a pretty
sight to you I don't envy your feelings and I wish you good-day

'emmy come along with Gran." And I was still in the best of humours though his cap came flying up into the street as if it had been just turned on out of the water-plug, and I went home laughing all the way, all owing to that dear boy.

The miles and miles that me and the Major have travelled with 'emmy in the dusk between the lights are not to be calculated, 'emmy driving on the coach-box which is the Major's brass-bound writing-desk on the table, me inside in the easy-chair and the Major Guard up behind with a brown-paper horn doing it really wonderful. I do assure you my dear that sometimes when I have taken a few winks in my place inside the coach and have come half awake by the lashing light of the fire and have heard that precious pet driving and the Major blowing up behind to have the change of horses ready when we got to the Inn, I have half believed we were on the old North Road that my poor Lirriper knew so well. Then to see that child and the Major both wrapped up getting down to warm their feet and going stamping about and having glasses of ale out of the paper match-boxes on the chimney-piece is to see the Major enjoying it fully as much as the child I am very sure, and it's equal to any play when Coachee opens the coach-door to look in at me inside and say "Wery past that 'tage.—'Prightened old lady?"

But what my inexpressible feelings were when we lost that child can only be compared to the Major's which were not a shade better, through his straying out at five years old and eleven o'clock in the forenoon and never heard of by word or sign or deed till half-past nine at night, when the Major had gone to the Editor of the *Times* newspaper to put in an advertisement, which came out next day four-and-twenty hours after he was found, and which I mean always carefully to keep in my lavender drawer as the first printed account of him. The more the day got on, the more I got distracted and the Major too and both of us made worse by the composed ways of the police though very civil and obliging and what I must call their obstinacy in not entertaining the idea that he was stolen. "We mostly find mum" says the sergeant who came round to comfort me, which he didn't at all and he had been one of the private constables in Caroline's time to which he referred in his opening words when he said "Don't give way to uneasiness in your mind mum, it'll all come as right as my nose did when I got the same barked by that young woman in your second floor"—says this sergeant, "we mostly find mum as people ain't over-anxious to have what I may call second-hand children. You'll get him back mum." "O but my dear good Sir" I says clasping my hands and wringing them and clasping them again "he is such an uncommon child!" "Yes mum" says the sergeant, "we mostly find that too mum. The question is what his clothes were worth." "His clothes," I says "were not worth much Sir for he had only got his playing-dress on, but the dear child!—" "All right mum" says the sergeant. "*You*'ll get him back mum. And even if he'd had his best clothes on, it wouldn't come to worse than his being found wrapped up in a cabbage-leaf, a shivering in a lane." His words pierced my heart like daggers and daggers, and me and the Major ran in and out like wild things all day long till the Major returning from his interview with the Editor of the *Times* at night rushes into my little room hysterical and squeezes my hand and wipes his eyes and says "Joy joy—officer in plain clothes came up on the steps as I was letting myself in—compose your feelings—Jemmy's found." Consequently I fainted away and when I came to, embraced the legs of the officer in plain clothes who seemed to be taking a kind of a quiet inventory in his mind of the property in my little room with brown whiskers and I says "Blessings on you Sir where is the Darling?" and he says "In Kennington Station House." I was dropping at his feet Stone at the image of that Innocence in cells with murderers when he adds "He followed the Monkey." I says deeming it slang language "O Sir explain for a loving grandmother what Monkey!" He says "Him in the spangled cap with the strap under the chin, as won't keep on—him as sweeps the crossings on a round table and don't want to draw his sabre more than he can help". Then I understood it all and most thankfully thanked him, and me and the Major and him drove over to Kennington and there we found our boy lying quite comfortable before a blazing fire having sweetly played himself to sleep upon a small accordion nothing like so big as a flat iron which they had been so kind to lend him for the purpose and which it appeared had been stopped upon a very young person.

My dear the system upon which the Major commenced and as I may say perfected Jemmy's learning when he was so small that if the dear was on the other side of the table you had to look under it instead of over it to see him with his mother's own bright hair in beautiful curls, is a thing that ought to be known to the Throne and Lords and Commons and then might obtain some promotion for the Major which he well deserves and would be none the worse for (speaking between friends) L. S. D.-ically. When the Major first undertook his learning he says to me:

"I'm going madam," he says "to make our child a Calculating Boy."

"Major," I says, "you terrify me and may do the pet a permanent injury you would never forgive yourself."

"Madam," says the Major, "next to my regret that when I had my boot-sponge in my hand, I didn't choke that scoundrel with it—on the spot——"

"There! For Gracious' sake," I interrupts, "let his conscience fine him without sponges."

"—I say next to that regret, madam," says the Major "would be the regret with which my breast," which he tapped, "would be surcharged if this fine mind was not early cultivated. But mark me madam," says the Major holding up his forefinger "cultivated on a principle that will make it a delight."

"Major" I says "I will be candid with you and tell you openly that if ever I find the dear child fall off in his appetite I shall know it is his calculations and shall put a stop to them at two minutes' notice Or if I find them mounting to his head" I says, "or striking anyway

ld to his stomach or leading to anything approaching flabbiness in
s legs, the result will be the same, but Major you are a clever man
d have seen much and you love the child and are his own godfather,
d if you feel a confidence in trying try."

"Spoken madam" says the Major "like Emma Lirriper. All I have
ask, madam, is that you will leave my godson and myself to make
week or two's preparations for surprising you, and that you will
ve me leave to have up and down any small articles not actually in
e that I may require from the kitchen."

"From the kitchen Major?" I says half feeling as if he had a mind
cook the child.

"From the kitchen" says the Major, and smiles and swells, and at
e same time looks taller.

So I passed my word and the Major and the dear boy were shut up
gether for half an hour at a time through a certain while, and never
uld I hear anything going on betwixt them but talking and laugh-
g and Jemmy clapping his hands and screaming out numbers, so I
ys to myself "it has not armed him yet" nor could I on examining
e dear find any signs of it anywhere about him which was likewise
great relief. At last one day Jemmy brings me a card in joke in the
ajor's neat writing "The Messrs. Jemmy Jackman" for we had
ven him the Major's other name too "request the honour of Mrs.
irriper's company at the Jackman Institution in the front parlour
is evening at five, military time, to witness a few slight feats of
ementary arithmetic." And if you'll believe me there in the front
rlour at five punctual to the moment was the Major behind the
mbroke table with both leaves up and a lot of things from the
tchen tidily set out on old newspapers spread atop of it, and there
as the Mite stood up on a chair with his rosy cheeks flushing and
s eyes sparkling clusters of diamonds.

"Now Gran," says he, " oo tit down and don't oo touch ler poople'"
-for he saw with every one of those diamonds of his that I was going
give him a squeeze.

"Very well Sir" I says "I am obedient in this good company I am
re." And I sits down in the easy-chair that was put for me, shaking
y sides.

But picture my admiration when the Major going on almost as
uick as if he was conjuring sets out all the articles he names, and
ys "Three saucepans, an Italian iron, a handbell, a toasting-fork, a
utmeg-grater, four potlids, a spice-box, two egg-cups, and a chopping
ard—how many?" and when that Mite instantly cries "Fifteen,
it down tive and carry ler 'toppin-board" and then claps his hands
raws up his legs and dances on his chair.

My dear with the same astonishing ease and correctness him and
e Major added up the tables chairs and sofy, the picters fenders and
re-irons their own selves me and the cat and the eyes in Miss
ozenham's head, and when ever the sum was done Young Roses
nd Diamonds claps his hands and draws up his legs and dances on
is chair.

The pride of the Major! ("*Here's* a mind ma'am!" he says to m
behind his hand.)

Then he says aloud, "We now come to the next elementary rule,-
which is called——"

"Umtraction!" cries Jemmy.

"Right," says the Major. "We have here a toasting-fork, a potat
in its natural state, two potlids, one egg-cup, a wooden spoon, an
two skewers, from which it is necessary for commercial purposes t
subtract a sprat-gridiron, a small pickle jar, two lemons, one peppe
castor, a blackbeetle-trap, and a knob of the dresser-drawer,—wha
remains?"

"Toatin-fork!" cries Jemmy.

"In numbers how many?" says the Major.

"One!" cries Jemmy.

("*Here's* a boy, ma'am!" says the Major to me behind his hand.)

Then the Major goes on:

"We now approach the next elementary rule,—which is entitle
——"

"Tickleication" cries Jemmy.

"Correct" says the Major.

But my dear to relate to you in detail the way in which the
multiplied fourteen sticks of firewood by two bits of ginger and
larding-needle, or divided pretty well everything else there was o
the table by the heater of the Italian iron and a chamber candlestic
and got a lemon over, would make my head spin round and roun
and round as it did at the time. So I says "if you'll excuse m
addressing the chair Professor Jackman I think the period of th
lecture has now arrived when it becomes necessary that I shoul
take a good hug of this young scholar." Upon which Jemmy calls ou
from his station on the chair, "Gran oo open oor arms and me'
make a 'pring into 'em." So I opened my arms to him as I ha
opened my sorrowful heart when his poor young mother lay a dying
and he had his jump and we had a good long hug together and th
Major prouder than any peacock says to me behind his hand, "Yo
need not let him know it madam" (which I certainly need not for th
Major was quite audible) "but he IS a boy!"

In this way Jemmy grew and grew and went to day-school an
continued under the Major too, and in summer we were as happy a
the days were long, and in winter we were as happy as the day
were short and there seemed to rest a Blessing on the Lodgings fo
they as good as Let themselves and would have done it if there ha
been twice the accommodation, when sore and hard against my wi
I one day says to the Major:

"Major you know what I am going to break to you. Our boy mus
go to a boarding-school."

It was a sad sight to see the Major's countenance drop, and
pitied the good soul with all my heart.

"Yes Major," I says, "though he is as popular with the Lodgers a
you are yourself and though he is to you and me what only you an

me know, still it is in the course of things and Life is made of partings and we must part with our Pet."

Bold as I spoke, I saw two Majors and half-a-dozen fireplaces, and when the poor Major put one of his neat bright-varnished boots upon the fender and his elbow on his knee and his head upon his hand and rocked himself a little to and fro, I was dreadfully cut up.

"But," says I clearing my throat, "you have so well prepared him Major—he has had such a Tutor in you—that he will have none of the first drudgery to go through. And he is so clever besides that he'll soon make his way to the front rank."

"He is a boy" says the Major—having sniffed—"that has not his like on the face of the earth."

"True as you say Major, and it is not for us merely for our own sakes to do anything to keep him back from being a credit and an ornament wherever he goes and perhaps even rising to be a great man, is it Major? He will have all my little savings when my work is done (being all the world to me) and we must try to make him a wise man and a good man, mustn't we Major?"

"Madam" says the Major rising "Jemmy Jackman is becoming an older file than I was aware of, and you put him to shame. You are thoroughly right madam. You are simply and undeniably right.—And if you'll excuse me, I'll take a walk."

So the Major being gone out and Jemmy being at home, I got the child into my little room here and I stood him by my chair and I took his mother's own curls in my hand and I spoke to him loving and serious. And when I had reminded the darling how that he was now in his tenth year and when I had said to him about his getting on in life pretty much what I had said to the Major I broke to him how that we must have this same parting, and there I was forced to stop for there I saw of a sudden the well-remembered lip with its tremble, and it so brought back that time! But with the spirit that was in him he controlled it soon and he says gravely nodding through his tears, "I understand Gran—I know it *must* be, Gran,—go on Gran, don't be afraid of *me*." And when I had said all that ever I could think of, he turned his bright steady face to mine and he says just a little broken here and there "You shall see Gran that I can be a man and that I can do anything that is grateful and loving to you—and if I don't grow up to be what you would like to have me—I hope it will be—because I shall die." And with that he sat down by me and I went on to tell him of the school of which I had excellent recommendations and where it was and how many scholars and what games they played as I had heard and what length of holidays, to all of which he listened bright and clear. And so it came that at last he says "And now dear Gran let me kneel down here where I have been used to say my prayers and let me fold my face for just a minute in your gown and let me cry, for you have been more than father—more than mother—more than brothers sisters friends—to me!" And so he did cry and I too and we were both much the better for it.

From that time forth he was true to his word and ever blithe and ready, and even when me and the Major took him down into Lincoln-shire he was far the gayest of the party though for sure and certain he might easily have been that, but he really was and put life into us only when it came to the last Good-bye, he says with a wistful look, "You wouldn't have me not really sorry would you Gran?" and when I says "No dear, Lord forbid!" he says "I am glad of that!" and ran in out of sight.

But now that the child was gone out of the Lodgings the Major fell into a regularly moping state. It was taken notice of by all the Lodgers that the Major moped. He hadn't even the same air of being rather tall that he used to have, and if he varnished his boots with a single gleam of interest it was as much as he did.

One evening the Major came into my little room to take a cup of tea and a morsel of buttered toast and to read Jemmy's newest letter which had arrived that afternoon (by the very same postman more than middle-aged upon the Beat now), and the letter raising him up a little I says to the Major:

"Major you mustn't get into a moping way."

The Major shook his head. "Jemmy Jackman madam," he says with a deep sigh, "is an older file than I thought him."

"Moping is not the way to grow younger Major."

"My dear madam," says the Major, "is there *any* way of growing younger?"

Feeling that the Major was getting rather the best of that point I made a diversion to another.

"Thirteen years! Thir-teen years! Many Lodgers have come and gone, in the thirteen years that you have lived in the parlours Major."

"Hah!" says the Major warming. "Many madam, many."

" And I should say you have been familiar with them all?"

"As a rule (with its exceptions like all rules) my dear madam" says the Major, "they have honoured me with their acquaintance, and not unfrequently with their confidence."

Watching the Major as he drooped his white head and stroked his black mustachios and moped again, a thought which I think must have been going about looking for an owner somewhere dropped into my old noddle if you will excuse the expression.

"The walls of my Lodgings" I says in a casual way—for my dear it is of no use going straight at a man who mopes—"might have something to tell if they could tell it."

The Major neither moved nor said anything but I saw he was attending with his shoulders my dear—attending with his shoulders to what I said. In fact I saw that his shoulders were struck by it.

"The dear boy was always fond of story books" I went on, like as if I was talking to myself. "I am sure this house—his own home—might write a story or two for his reading one day or another."

The Major's shoulders gave a dip and a curve and his head came up in his shirt-collar. The Major's head came up in his shirt-collar as

I hadn't seen it come up since Jemmy went to school.

"It is unquestionable that in intervals of cribbage and a friendly rubber, my dear madam," says the Major, "and also over what used to be called in my young times—in the salad days of Jemmy Jackman—the social glass, I have exchanged many a reminiscence with your Lodgers."

My remark was—I confess I made it with the deepest and artfullest of intentions—"I wish our dear boy had heard them!"

"Are you serious madam?" asks the Major starting and turning full round.

"Why not Major?"

"Madam" says the Major, turning up one of his cuffs, "they shall be written for him."

"Ah! Now you speak" I says giving my hands a pleased clap. "Now you are in a way out of moping Major!"

"Between this and my holidays—I mean the dear boy's" says the Major turning up his other cuff, "a good deal may be done towards it."

"Major you are a clever man and you have seen much and not a doubt of it."

"I'll begin," says the Major looking as tall as ever he did, "to-morrow."

My dear the Major was another man in three days and he was himself again in a week and he wrote and wrote and wrote with his pen scratching like rats behind the wainscot, and whether he had many grounds to go upon or whether he did at all romance I cannot tell you, but what he has written is in the left-hand glass closet of the little bookcase close behind you.

CHAPTER II

HOW THE PARLOURS ADDED A FEW WORDS

I HAVE the honour of presenting myself by the name of Jackman. I esteem it a proud privilege to go down to posterity through the instrumentality of the most remarkable boy that ever lived,—by the name of JEMMY JACKMAN LIRRIPER,—and of my worthy and most highly respected friend, Mrs. Emma Lirriper, of Eighty-one, Norfolk Street, Strand, in the County of Middlesex, in the United Kingdom of Great Britain and Ireland.

It is not for me to express the rapture with which we received that dear and eminently remarkable boy, on the occurrence of his first Christmas holidays. Suffice it to observe that when he came flying into the house with two splendid prizes (Arithmetic, and Exemplary Conduct), Mrs. Lirriper and myself embraced with emotion, and instantly took him to the Play, where we were all three admirably entertained.

Nor is it to render homage to the virtues of the best of her good and honoured sex—whom, in deference to her unassuming worth, I will only here designate by the initials E.L.—that I add this record to the bundle of papers with which our, in a most distinguished degree, remarkable boy has expressed himself delighted, before reconsigning the same to the left-hand glass closet of Mrs. Lirriper's little book-case.

Neither is it to obtrude the name of the old original superannuated obscure Jemmy Jackman, once (to his degradation) of Wozenham's, long (to his elevation) of Lirriper's. If I could be consciously guilty of that piece of bad taste, it would indeed be a work of supererogation, now that the name is borne by JEMMY JACKMAN LIRRIPER.

No, I take up my humble pen to register a little record of our strikingly remarkable boy, which my poor capacity regards as presenting a pleasant little picture of the dear boy's mind. The picture may be interesting to himself when he is a man.

Our first reunited Christmas-day was the most delightful one we have ever passed together. Jemmy was never silent for five minutes, except in church-time. He talked as we sat by the fire, he talked when we were out walking, he talked as we sat by the fire again, he talked incessantly at dinner, though he made a dinner almost as remarkable as himself. It was the spring of happiness in his fresh young heart flowing and flowing, and it fertilised (if I may be allowed so bold a figure) my much-esteemed friend, and J. J. the present writer.

There were only we three. We dined in my esteemed friend's little room, and our entertainment was perfect. But everything in the establishment is, in neatness, order, and comfort, always perfect. After dinner our boy slipped away to his old stool at my esteemed friend's knee, and there, with his hot chestnuts and his glass of brown sherry (really, a most excellent wine!) on a chair for a table, his face outshone the apples in the dish.

We talked of these jottings of mine, which Jemmy had read through and through by that time; and so it came about that my esteemed friend remarked, as she sat smoothing Jemmy's curls:

"And as you belong to the house too, Jemmy,—and so much more than the Lodgers, having been born in it,—why, your story ought to be added to the rest, I think, one of these days."

Jemmy's eyes sparkled at this, and he said, "So *I* think, Gran."

Then he sat looking at the fire, and then he began to laugh in a sort of confidence with the fire, and then he said, folding his arms across my esteemed friend's lap, and raising his bright face to hers: "Would you like to hear a boy's story, Gran?"

"Of all things," replied my esteemed friend.

"Would you, godfather?"

"Of all things," I too replied.

"Well, then," said Jemmy, "I'll tell you one."

Here our indisputably remarkable boy gave himself a hug, and laughed again, musically, at the idea of his coming out in that new

ne. Then he once more took the fire into the same sort of confidence
s before, and began:

"Once upon a time, When pigs drank wine, And monkeys
hewed tobaccer, 'Twas neither in your time nor mine, But that's no
hacker——"

"Bless the child!" cried my esteemed friend, "what's amiss with
is brain?"

"It's poetry, Gran," returned Jemmy, shouting with laughter.
We always begin stories that way at school."

"Gave me quite a turn, Major," said my esteemed friend, fanning
herself with a plate. "Thought he was light-headed!"

"In those remarkable times, Gran and godfather, there was once a
boy,—not me, you know."

"No, no," says my respected friend, "not you. Not him, Major, you
understand?"

"No, no," says I.

"And he went to school in Rutlandshire——"

"Why not Lincolnshire?" says my respected friend.

"Why not, you dear old Gran? Because *I* go to school in Lincoln-
shire, don't I?"

"Ah, to be sure!" says my respected friend. "And it's not Jemmy,
you understand, Major?"

"No, no," says I.

"Well!" our boy proceeded, hugging himself comfortably, and
laughing merrily (again in confidence with the fire), before he again
looked up in Mrs. Lirriper's face, "and so he was tremendously in
love with his schoolmaster's daughter, and she was the most beautiful creature that ever was seen, and she had brown eyes, and she had
brown hair all curling beautifully, and she had a delicious voice, and
she was delicious altogether, and her name was Seraphina."

"What the name of *your* schoolmaster's daughter, Jemmy?" asks
my respected friend.

"Polly!" replied Jemmy, pointing his forefinger at her. "There
now! Caught you! Ha, ha, ha!"

When he and my respected friend had had a laugh and a hug
together, our admittedly remarkable boy resumed with a great
relish:

"Well! And so he loved her. And so he thought about her, and
dreamed about her, and made her presents of oranges and nuts, and
would have made her presents of pearls and diamonds if he could
have afforded it out of his pocket-money, but he couldn't. And so her
father—O, he WAS a Tartar! Keeping the boys up to the mark,
holding examinations once a month, lecturing upon all sorts of
subjects at all sorts of times, and knowing everything in the world
out of book. And so this boy——"

"Had he any name?" asked my respected friend.

"No, he hadn't, Gran. Ha, ha! There now! Caught you again!"

After this, they had another laugh and another hug, and then our
boy went on.

"Well! And so this boy, he had a friend about as old as himself
the same school, and his name (for He *had* a name, as it happene
was—let me remember—was Bobbo."

"Not Bob," says my respected friend.

"Of course not," says Jemmy. "What made you think it wa
Gran? Well! And so this friend was the cleverest and bravest an
best-looking and most generous of all the friends that ever were, an
so he was in love with Seraphina's sister, and so Seraphina's sist
was in love with him, and so they all grew up."

"Bless us!" says my respected friend. "They were very sudde
about it."

"So they all grew up," our boy repeated, laughing heartily, "an
Bobbo and this boy went away together on horseback to seek the
fortunes, and they partly got their horses by favour, and partly in
bargain; that is to say they had saved up between them seven an
fourpence, and the two horses, being Arabs, were worth more, on
the man said he would take that, to favour them. Well! And so the
made their fortunes and came prancing back to the school, with the
pockets full of gold, enough to last for ever. And so they rang at th
parents' and visitors' bell (not the back gate), and when the bell wa
answered they proclaimed 'The same as if it was scarlet fever! Ever
boy goes home for an indefinite period!' And then there was grea
hurrahing, and then they kissed Seraphina and her sister,—each h
own love, and not the other's on any account,—and then they ordere
the Tartar into instant confinement."

"Poor man!" said my respected friend.

"Into instant confinement, Gran," repeated Jemmy, trying t
look severe and roaring with laughter; "and he was to have nothin
to eat but the boys' dinners, and was to drink half a cask of their bee
every day. And so then the preparations were made for the tw
weddings, and there were hampers, and potted things, and swee
things, and nuts, and postage-stamps, and all manner of things. An
so they were so jolly, that they let the Tartar out, and he was joll
too."

"I am glad they let him out," says my respected friend, "becaus
he had only done his duty."

"O, but hadn't he overdone it, though!" cried Jemmy. "Wel
And so then this boy mounted his horse, with his bride in his arm
and cantered away, and cantered on and on till he came to
certain place where he had a certain Gran and a certain godfather,-
not you two, you know."

"No, no," we both said.

"And there he was received with great rejoicings, and he filled th
cupboard and the bookcase with gold, and he showered it out on h
Gran and his godfather because they were the two kindest an
dearest people that ever lived in this world. And so while they wer
sitting up to their knees in gold, a knocking was heard at the stree
door, and who should it be but Bobbo, also on horseback with h
bride in his arms, and what had he come to say but that he woul

take (at double rent) all the Lodgings for ever, that were not wanted by this boy and this Gran and this godfather, and that they would all live together, and all be happy! And so they were, and so it never ended!"

"And was there no quarrelling?" asked my respected friend, as Jemmy sat upon her lap and hugged her.

"No! Nobody ever quarrelled."

"And did the money never melt away?"

"No! Nobody could ever spend it all."

"And did none of them ever grow older?"

"No! Nobody ever grew older after that."

"And did none of them ever die?"

"Oh, no, no, no, Gran!" exclaimed our dear boy, laying his cheek upon her breast, and drawing her closer to him. "Nobody ever died."

"Ah, Major, Major!" says my respected friend, smiling benignly upon me, "this beats our stories. Let us end with the Boy's story, Major, for the Boy's story is the best that is ever told!"

In submission to which request on the part of the best of women, I have here noted it down as faithfully as my best abilities, coupled with my best intentions, would admit, subscribing it with my name,

J. JACKMAN.

THE PARLOURS.
MRS. LIRRIPER'S LODGINGS.

MRS. LIRRIPER'S LEGACY

IN TWO CHAPTERS

[1864]

CHAPTER I

MRS. LIRRIPER RELATES HOW SHE WENT ON, AND WENT OVER

AH! It's pleasant to drop into my own easy-chair my dear though a little palpitating what with trotting upstairs and what with trotting down, and why kitchen stairs should all be corner stairs is for the builders to justify though I do not think they fully understand their trade and never did, else why the sameness and why not more conveniences and fewer draughts and likewise making a practice of laying the plaster on too thick I am well convinced which holds the damp, and as to chimney-pots putting them on by guesswork like hats at a party and no more knowing what their effect will be upon the smoke bless you than I do if so much, except that it will mostly be either to send it down your throat in a straight form or to give it a twist before it goes there. And what I says speaking as I find of those new metal chimneys all manner of shapes (there's a row of 'em at Miss Wozenham's lodging-house lower down on the other side of the way) is that they only work your smoke into artificial patterns for you before you swallow it and that I'd quite as soon swallow mine plain, the flavour being the same, not to mention the conceit of putting up signs on the top of your house to show the forms in which you take your smoke into your inside.

Being here before your eyes my dear in my own easy-chair in my own quiet room in my own Lodging-House Number Eighty-one Norfolk Street Strand London situated midway between the city and St. James's—if anything is where it used to be with these hotels calling themselves Limited but called unlimited by Major Jackman rising up everywhere and rising up into flagstaffs where they can't go any higher, but my mind of those monsters is give me a landlord's or landlady's wholesome face when I come off a journey and not a brass plate with an electrified number clicking out of it which it's not in nature can be glad to see me and to which I don't want to be hoisted like molasses at the Docks and left there telegraphing for help with the most ingenious instruments but quite in vain—being here my dear I have no call to mention that I am still in the Lodgings

s a business hoping to die in the same and if agreeable to the clergy
artly read over at Saint Clement's Danes and concluded in Hatfield
hurchyard when lying once again by my poor Lirriper ashes to
shes and dust to dust.

Neither should I tell you any news my dear in telling you that the
Major is still a fixture in the Parlours quite as much so as the roof of
he house, and that Jemmy is of boys the best and brightest and has
ver had kept from him the cruel story of his poor pretty young
nother Mrs. Edson being deserted in the second floor and dying in
ny arms, fully believing that I am his born Gran and him an orphan,
hough what with engineering since he took a taste for it and him and
he Major making Locomotives out of parasols broken iron pots and
otton-reels and them absolutely a getting off the line and falling
ver the table and injuring the passengers almost equal to the
riginals it really is quite wonderful. And when I says to the Major,
'Major can't you by *any* means give us a communication with the
guard?" the Major says quite huffy, "No madam it's not to be done,"
and when I says, "Why not?" the Major says, "That is between us
vho are in the Railway Interest madam and our friend the Right
Honourable Vice-President of the Board of Trade" and if you'll
pelieve me my dear the Major wrote to Jemmy at school to consult
aim on the answer I should have before I could get even that amount
of unsatisfactoriness out of the man, the reason being that when we
irst began with the little model and the working signals beautiful and
perfect (being in general as wrong as the real) and when I says
laughing "What appointment am I to hold in this undertaking
gentlemen?" Jemmy hugs me round the neck and tells me dancing,
'You shall be the Public Gran" and consequently they put upon me
ust as much as ever they like and I sit a growling in my easy-chair.

My dear whether it is that a grown man as clever as the Major
cannot give half his heart and mind to anything—even a plaything—
out must get into right down earnest with it, whether it is so or
vhether it is not so I do not undertake to say, but Jemmy is far outdone by the serious and believing ways of the Major in the management of the United Grand Junction Lirriper and Jackman Great
Norfolk Parlour Line, "For" says my Jemmy with the sparkling eyes
when it was christened, "we must have a whole mouthful of name
Gran or our dear old Public" and there the young rogue kissed me,
'won't stump up." So, the Public took the shares—ten at ninepence,
and immediately when that was spent twelve Preference to one-and-
sixpence—and they were all signed by Jemmy and countersigned by
the Major, and between ourselves much better worth the money than
some shares I have paid for in my time. In the same holidays the line
was made and worked and opened and ran excursions and had
collisions and burst its boilers and all sorts of accidents and offences
all most regular correct and pretty. The sense of responsibility entertained by the Major as a military style of station-master my dear
starting the down train behind time and ringing one of those little
bells that you buy with the little coal-scuttles off the tray round the

man's neck in the street did him honour, but noticing the Major of a
night when he is writing out his monthly report to Jemmy at school
of the state of the Rolling Stock and the Permanent Way and all the
rest of it (the whole kept upon the Major's sideboard and dusted with
his own hands every morning before varnishing his boots) I notice him
as full of thought and care as full can be and frowning in a fearful
manner, but indeed the Major does nothing by halves as witness his
great delight in going out surveying with Jemmy when he has
Jemmy to go with, carrying a chain and a measuring-tape and driving I don't know what improvements right through Westminster
Abbey and fully believed in the streets to be knocking everything
upside down by Act of Parliament. As please Heaven will come to pass
when Jemmy takes to that as a profession!

Mentioning my poor Lirriper brings into my head his own youngest
brother the Doctor though Doctor of what I am sure it would be hard
to say unless Liquor, for neither Physic nor Music nor yet Law does
Joshua Lirriper know a morsel of except continually being summoned
to the County Court and having orders made upon him which he runs
away from, and once was taken in the passage of this very house with
an umbrella up and the Major's hat on, giving his name with the door-
mat round him as Sir Johnson Jones, K.C.B. in spectacles residing at
the Horse Guards. On which occasion he had got into the house not a
minute before, through the girl letting him on the mat when he sent
in a piece of paper twisted more like one of those spills for lighting
candles than a note, offering me the choice between thirty shillings in
hand and his brains on the premises marked immediate and waiting
for an answer. My dear it gave me such a dreadful turn to think of
the brains of my poor dear Lirriper's own flesh and blood flying about
the new oilcloth however unworthy to be so assisted, that I went out
of my room here to ask him what he would take once for all not to do
it for life when I found him in the custody of two gentlemen that I
should have judged to be in the feather-bed trade if they had not
announced the law, so fluffy were their personal appearance. "Bring
your chains, Sir," says Joshua to the littlest of the two in the biggest
hat, "rivet on my fetters!" Imagine my feelings when I pictered him
clanking up Norfolk-street in irons and Miss Wozenham looking out
of window! "Gentlemen," I says all of a tremble and ready to drop
"please to bring him into Major Jackman's apartments." So they
brought him into the Parlours, and when the Major spies his own
curly-brimmed hat on him which Joshua Lirriper had whipped off its
Peg in the passage for a military disguise he goes into such a tearing
passion that he tips it off his head with his hand and kicks it up to
the ceiling with his foot where it grazed long afterwards. "Major" I
says "be cool and advise me what to do with Joshua my dead and
gone Lirriper's own youngest brother." "Madam" says the Major
"my advice is that you board and lodge him in a Powder Mill, with a
handsome gratuity to the proprietor when exploded." "Major" I
says "as a Christian you cannot mean your words." "Madam" says
the Major "by the Lord I do!" and indeed the Major besides being

ith all his merits a very passionate man for his size had a bad
pinion of Joshua on account of former troubles even unattended by
berties taken with his apparel. When Joshua Lirriper hears this
onversation betwixt us he turns upon the littlest one with the
iggest hat and says "Come Sir! Remove me to my vile dungeon.
Vhere is my mouldy straw?" My dear at the picter of him rising in
ny mind dressed almost entirely in padlocks like Baron Trenck in
emmy's book I was so overcome that I burst into tears and I says to
he Major, "Major take my keys and settle with these gentlemen or I
hall never know a happy minute more," which was done several
imes both before and since, but still I must remember that Joshua
Lirriper has his good feelings and shows them in being always so
roubled in his mind when he cannot wear mourning for his brother.
Many a long year have I left off my widow's mourning not being
vishful to intrude, but the tender point in Joshua that I cannot help
a little yielding to is when he writes "One single sovereign would
nable me to wear a decent suit of mourning for my much-loved
orother. I vowed at the time of his lamented death that I would ever
vear sables in memory of him but Alas how short-sighted is man,
How keep that vow when penniless!" It says a good deal for the
strength of his feelings that he couldn't have been seven year old
vhen my poor Lirriper died and to have kept to it ever since is highly
creditable. But we know there's good in all of us,—if we only knew
vhere it was in some of us,—and though it was far from delicate in
Joshua to work upon the dear child's feelings when first sent to school
and write down into Lincolnshire for his pocket-money by return of
post and got it, still he is my poor Lirriper's own youngest brother
and mightn't have meant not paying his bill at the Salisbury Arms
when his affection took him down to stay a fortnight at Hatfield
churchyard and might have meant to keep sober but for bad company. Consequently if the Major had played on him with the garden-
engine which he got privately into his room without my knowing of
it, I think that much as I should have regretted it there would have
been words betwixt the Major and me. Therefore my dear though he
played on Mr. Buffle by mistake being hot in his head, and though it
might have been misrepresented down at Wozenham's into not being
ready for Mr. Buffle in other respects he being the Assessed Taxes,
still I do not so much regret it as perhaps I ought. And whether
Joshua Lirriper will yet do well in life I cannot say, but I did hear of
his coming out at a Private Theatre in the character of a Bandit
without receiving any offers afterwards from the regular managers.

Mentioning Mr. Buffle gives an instance of there being good in
persons where good is not expected, for it cannot be denied that Mr.
Buffle's manners when engaged in his business were not agreeable.
To collect is one thing, and to look about as if suspicious of the goods
being gradually removing in the dead of the night by a back door is
another, over taxing you have no control but suspecting is voluntary.
Allowances too must ever be made for a gentleman of the Major's
warmth not relishing being spoke to with a pen in the mouth, and

while I do not know that it is more irritable to my own feelings to have a low-crowned hat with a broad brim kept on indoors than any other hat still I can appreciate the Major's, besides which without bearing malice or vengeance the Major is a man that scores up arrear as his habit always was with Joshua Lirriper. So at last my dear the Major lay in wait for Mr. Buffle and it worried me a good deal. Mr Buffle gives his rap of two sharp knocks one day and the Major bounces to the door. "Collector has called for two quarters' Assessed Taxes" says Mr. Buffle. "They are ready for him" says the Major and brings him in here. But on the way Mr. Buffle looks about him in his usual suspicious manner and the Major fires and asks him "Do you see a Ghost Sir?" "No Sir" says Mr. Buffle. "Because I have before noticed you" says the Major "apparently looking for a spectre very hard beneath the roof of my respected friend. When you find that supernatural agent, be so good as point him out Sir." Mr. Buffle stares at the Major and then nods at me. "Mrs. Lirriper Sir" says the Major going off into a perfect steam and introducing me with his hand "Pleasure of knowing her" says Mr. Buffle. "A—hum!—Jemmy Jackman Sir!" says the Major introducing himself. "Honour of knowing you by sight" says Mr. Buffle. "Jemmy Jackman Sir" says the Major wagging his head sideways in a sort of obstinate fury "presents to you his esteemed friend that lady Mrs. Emma Lirriper of Eighty-one Norfolk Street Strand London in the County of Middlesex in the United Kingdom of Great Britain and Ireland. Upon which occasion Sir," says the Major, "Jemmy Jackman takes your hat off." Mr. Buffle looks at his hat where the Major drops it on the floor, and he picks it up and puts it on again. "Sir" says the Major very red and looking him full in the face "there are two quarters of the Gallantry Taxes due and the Collector has called." Upon which if you can believe my words my dear the Major drops Mr. Buffle's hat off again "This——" Mr. Buffle begins very angry with his pen in his mouth, when the Major steaming more and more says "Take your bit out Sir! Or by the whole infernal system of Taxation of this country and every individual figure in the National Debt, I'll get upon your back and ride you like a horse!" which it's my belief he would have done and even actually jerking his neat little legs ready for a spring as it was. "This," says Mr. Buffle without his pen "is an assault and I'll have the law of you." "Sir" replies the Major "if you are a man of honour, your Collector of whatever may be due on the Honourable Assessment by applying to Major Jackman at the Parlours Mrs. Lirriper's Lodgings, may obtain what he wants in full at any moment."

When the Major glared at Mr. Buffle with those meaning words my dear I literally gasped for a teaspoonful of salvolatile in a wineglass of water, and I says "Pray let it go no farther gentlemen I beg and beseech you!" But the Major could be got to do nothing else but snort long after Mr. Buffle was gone, and the effect it had upon my whole mass of blood when on the next day of Mr. Buffle's rounds the Major spruced himself up and went humming a tune up and down the street with one eye almost obliterated by his hat there are not expressions in Johnson's dictionary to state. But I safely put the street door on the jar and got behind the Major's blinds with my shawl on and my mind made up the moment I saw danger to rush out screeching till my voice failed me and catch the Major round the neck till my strength went and have all parties bound. I had not been behind the blinds a quarter of an hour when I saw Mr. Buffle approaching with his Collecting-books in his hand. The Major likewise saw him approaching and hummed louder and himself approached. They met before the Airy railings. The Major takes off his hat at arm's length and says "Mr. Buffle I believe?" Mr. Buffle takes off *his* hat at arm's length and says "That is my name Sir." Says the Major "Have you any commands for me, Mr. Buffle?" Says Mr. Buffle "Not any Sir." Then my dear both of 'em bowed very low and haughty and parted, and whenever Mr. Buffle made his rounds in future him and the Major always met and bowed before the Airy railings, putting me much in mind of Hamlet and the other gentleman in mourning before killing one another, though I could have wished the other gentleman had done it fairer and even if less polite no poison.

Mr. Buffle's family were not liked in this neighbourhood, for when you are a householder my dear you'll find it does not come by nature to like the Assessed, and it was considered besides that a one-horse pheayton ought not to have elevated Mrs. Buffle to that height especially when purloined from the Taxes which I myself did consider uncharitable. But they were *not* liked and there was that domestic unhappiness in the family in consequence of their both being very hard with Miss Buffle and one another on account of Miss Buffle's favouring Mr. Buffle's articled young gentleman, that it *was* whispered that Miss Buffle would go either into a consumption or a convent she being so very thin and off her appetite and two close-shaved gentlemen with white bands round their necks peeping round the corner whenever she went out in waistcoats resembling black pinafores. So things stood towards Mr. Buffle when one night I was woke by a frightful noise and a smell of burning, and going to my bedroom window saw the whole street in a glow. Fortunately we had two sets empty just then and before I could hurry on some clothes I heard the Major hammering at the attics' doors and calling out "Dress yourselves!—Fire! Don't be frightened!—Fire! Collect your presence of mind!—Fire! All right—Fire!" most tremenjously. As I opened my bedroom door the Major came tumbling in over himself and me, and caught me in his arms. "Major" I says breathless "where is it?" "I don't know dearest madam" says the Major—"Fire! Jemmy Jackman will defend you to the last drop of his blood—Fire! If the dear boy was at home what a treat this would be for him—Fire!" and altogether very collected and bold except that he couldn't say a single sentence without shaking me to the very centre with roaring Fire. We ran down to the drawing-room and put our heads out of window, and the Major calls to an unfeeling young monkey, scampering by be joyful and ready to split "Where is it?—Fire!" The monkey answers without stopping "O here's a lark! Old Buffle's been setting his house alight to prevent its being found out that he boned the Taxes. Hurrah! Fire!" And then the sparks came flying up and the smoke came pouring down and the crackling of flames and spatting of water and banging of engines and hacking of axes and breaking of glass and knocking at doors and the shouting and crying and hurrying and the heat and altogether gave me a dreadful palpitation. "Don't be frightened dearest madam," says the Major, "——Fire! There's nothing to be alarmed at——Fire! Don't open the street door till I come back——Fire! I'll go and see if I can be of any service——Fire! You're quite composed and comfortable ain't you?——Fire, Fire, Fire!" It was in vain for me to hold the man and tell him he'd be galloped to death by the engines——pumped to death by his over-exertions——wet-feeted to death by the slop and mess——flattened to death when the roofs fell in——his spirit was up and he went scampering off after the young monkey with all the breath he had and none to spare, and me and the girls huddled together at the parlour windows looking at the dreadful flames above the houses over the way, Mr. Buffle's being round the corner. Presently what should we see but some people running down the street straight to our door, and then the Major directing operations in the busiest way, and then some more people and then—— carried in a chair similar to Guy Fawkes——Mr. Buffle in a blanket!

My dear the Major has Mr. Buffle brought up our steps and whisked into the parlour and carted out on the sofy, and then he and all the rest of them without so much as a word burst away again full speed, leaving the impression of a vision except for Mr. Buffle awful in his blanket with his eyes a rolling. In a twinkling they all burst back again with Mrs. Buffle in another blanket, which whisked in and carted out on the sofy they all burst off again and all burst back again with Miss Buffle in another blanket, which again whisked in and carted out they all burst off again and all burst back again with Mr. Buffle's articled young gentleman in another blanket——him a holding round the necks of two men carrying him by the legs, similar to the picter of the disgraceful creetur who has lost the fight (but where the chair I do not know) and his hair having the appearance of newly played upon. When all four of a row, the Major rubs his hands and whispers me with what little hoarseness he can get together, "If our dear remarkable boy was only at home what a delightful treat this would be for him!"

My dear we made them some hot tea and toast and some hot brandy-and-water with a little comfortable nutmeg in it, and at first they were scared and low in their spirits but being fully insured got sociable. And the first use Mr. Buffle made of his tongue was to call the Major his Preserver and his best of friends and to say "My for ever dearest Sir let me make you known to Mrs. Buffle" which also addressed him as her Preserver and her best of friends and was fully as cordial as the blanket would admit of. Also Miss Buffle. The articled young gentleman's head was a little light and he sat a moaning "Robina is reduced to cinders, Robina is reduced to cinders!" Which

ent more to the heart on account of his having got wrapped in his
lanket as if he was looking out of a violinceller case, until Mr.
uffle says "Robina speak to him!" Miss Buffle says "Dear George!"
nd but for the Major's pouring down brandy-and-water on the
nstant which caused a catching in his throat owing to the nutmeg
nd a violent fit of coughing it might have proved too much for his
rength. When the articled young gentleman got the better of it
Mr. Buffle leaned up against Mrs. Buffle being two bundles, a little
hile in confidence, and then says with tears in his eyes which the
Major noticing wiped, "We have not been an united family, let us
fter this danger become so, take her George." The young gentleman
ould not put his arm out far to do it, but his spoken expressions were
ery beautiful though of a wandering class. And I do not know that I
ver had a much pleasanter meal than the breakfast we took together
fter we had all dozed, when Miss Buffle made tea very sweetly in
uite the Roman style as depicted formerly at Covent Garden
heatre and when the whole family was most agreeable, as they have
ver proved since that night when the Major stood at the foot of the
ire-Escape and claimed them as they came down——the young gentle-
an head-foremost, which accounts. And though I do not say that
e should be less liable to think ill of one another if strictly limited
o blankets, still I do say that we might most of us come to a better
nderstanding if we kept one another less at a distance.

Why there's Wozenham's lower down on the other side of the street.
had a feeling of much soreness several years respecting what I must
till ever call Miss Wozenham's systematic underbidding and the
keness of the house in Bradshaw having far too many windows and
most umbrageous and outrageous Oak which never yet was seen
Norfolk-street nor yet a carriage and four at Wozenham's door,
hich it would have been far more to Bradshaw's credit to have
rawn a cab. This frame of mind continued bitter down to the very
fternoon in January last when one of my girls, Sally Rairyganoo
hich I still suspect of Irish extraction though family represented
ambridge, else why abscond with a bricklayer of the Limerick per-
uasion and be married in pattens not waiting till his black eye was
ecently got round with all the company fourteen in number and one
orse fighting outside on the roof of the vehicle,——I repeat my dear my
l-regulated state of mind towards Miss Wozenham continued down
o the very afternoon of January last past when Sally Rairyganoo
ame banging (I can use no milder expression) into my room with a
imp which may be Cambridge and may not, and said "Hurroo
issis! Miss Wozenham's sold up!" My dear when I had it thrown in
y face and conscience that the girl Sally had reason to think I could
e glad of the ruin of a fellow-creeter, I burst into tears and dropped
ack in my chair and I says "I am ashamed of myself!"

Well! I tried to settle to my tea but I could not do it what with
hinking of Miss Wozenham and her distresses. It was a wretched
ight and I went up to a front window and looked over at Wozen-
am's and as well as I could make it out down the street in the fog it

was the dismallest of the dismal and not a light to be seen. So at last says to myself "This will not do," and I puts on my oldest bonnet an shawl not wishing Miss Wozenham to be reminded of my best at suc a time, and lo and behold you I goes over to Wozenham's and knock " Miss Wozenham at home?" I says turning my head when I hear the door go. And then I saw it was Miss Wozenham herself who ha opened it and sadly worn she was poor thing and her eyes all swelle and swelled with crying. "Miss Wozenham" I says "it is several year since there was a little unpleasantness betwixt us on the subject c my grandson's cap being down your Airy. I have overlooked it an I hope you have done the same." "Yes Mrs. Lirriper" she says in surprise "I have." "Then my dear" I says "I should be glad to com in and speak a word to you." Upon my calling her my dear Mis Wozenham breaks out a crying most pitiful, and a not unfeelin elderly person that might have been better shaved in a nightcap wit a hat over it offering a polite apology for the mumps having worke themselves into his constitution, and also for sending home to h wife on the bellows which was in his hand as a writing-desk, looks ou of the back parlour and says "The lady wants a word of comfort" an goes in again. So I was able to say quite natural "Wants a word c comfort does she Sir? Then please the pigs she shall have it!" An Miss Wozenham and me we go into the front room with a wretche light that seemed to have been crying too and was sputtering ou and I says "Now my dear, tell me all," and she wrings her hands an says "O Mrs. Lirriper that man is in possession here, and I have not friend in the world who is able to help me with a shilling."

It doesn't signify a bit what a talkative old body like me said t Miss Wozenham when she said that, and so I'll tell you instead m dear that I'd have given thirty shillings to have taken her over to tea only I durstn't on account of the Major. Not you see but what I kne I could draw the Major out like thread and wind him round my finge on most subjects and perhaps even on that if I was to set myself to i but him and me had so often belied Miss Wozenham to one anothe that I was shamefaced, and I knew she had offended his pride an never mine, and likewise I felt timid that that Rairyganoo gi might make things awkward. So I says "My dear if you could giv me a cup of tea to clear my muddle of a head I should better unde stand your affairs." And we had the tea and the affairs too and afte all it was but forty pound, and—— There! she's as industrious an straight a creeter as ever lived and has paid back half of it alread and where's the use of saying more, particularly when it ain't t point? For the point is that when she was a kissing my hands an holding them in hers and kissing them again and blessing blessir blessing, I cheered up at last and I says "Why what a waddling o goose I have been my dear to take you for something so very diffe ent!" "Ah but I too" says she "how have I mistaken you!" "Con for goodness' sake tell me" I says "what you thought of me?" "O says she "I thought you had no feeling for such a hard hand-t mouth life as mine, and were rolling in affluence." I says shaking m sides (and very glad to do it for I had been a choking quite long enough) "Only look at my figure my dear and give me your opinion whether if I was in affluence I should be likely to roll in it?" That did it! We got as merry as grigs (whatever *they* are, if you happen to know my dear—*I* don't) and I went home to my blessed home as happy and as thankful as could be. But before I make an end of it, think even of my having misunderstood the Major! Yes! For next forenoon the Major came into my little room with his brushed hat in his hand and he begins "My dearest madam——" and then put his face in his hat as if he had just come into church. As I sat all in a maze he came out of his hat and began again, "My esteemed and be-loved friend——" and then went into his hat again. "Major," I cries out frightened "has anything happened to our darling boy?" "No, no, no" says the Major "but Miss Wozenham has been here this morning to make her excuses to me, and by the Lord I can't get over what she told me." "Hoity, toity Major," I says "you don't know yet that I was afraid of you last night and didn't think half as well of you as I ought! So come out of church Major and forgive me like a dear old friend and I'll never do so any more." And I leave you to judge my dear whether I ever did or will. And how affecting to think of Miss Wozenham out of her small income and her losses doing so much for her poor old father, and keeping a brother that had had the misfor-tune to soften his brain against the hard mathematics as neat as a new pin in the three back represented to lodgers as a lumber-room and consuming a whole shoulder of mutton whenever provided!

And now my dear I really am a going to tell you about my Legacy if you're inclined to favour me with your attention, and I did fully intend to have come straight to it only one thing does so bring up another. It was the month of June and the day before Midsummer Day when my girl Winifred Madgers—she was what is termed a Plymouth Sister, and the Plymouth Brother that made away with her was quite right, for a tidier young woman for a wife never came into a house and afterwards called with the beautifullest Plymouth Twins—it was the day before Midsummer Day when Winifred Mad-gers comes and says to me "A gentleman from the Consul's wishes particular to speak to Mrs. Lirriper." If you'll believe me my dear the Consols at the bank where I have a little matter for Jemmy got into my head, and I says "Good gracious I hope he ain't had any dreadful fall!" Says Winifred "He don't look as if he had ma'am." And I says "Show him in."

The gentleman came in dark and with his hair cropped what I should consider too close, and he says very polite "Madame Lirr-wiper!" I says "Yes, Sir. Take a chair." "I come," says he "frrwom the Frrwench Consul's." So I saw at once that it wasn't the Bank of England. "We have rrweceived," says the gentleman turning his r's very curious and skilful, "frrwom the Mairrwie at Sens, a communica-tion which I will have the honour to rrwead. Madame Lirrwiper understands Frrwench?" "O dear no Sir!" says I. "Madame Lirriper don't understand anything of the sort." "It matters not," says the gentleman, "I will trrwanslate."

With that my dear the gentleman after reading something about a Department and a Marie (which Lord forgive me I supposed till the Major came home was Mary, and never was I more puzzled than to think how that young woman came to have so much to do with it) translated a lot with the most obliging pains, and it came to this:— That in the town of Sens in France an unknown Englishman lay a dying. That he was speechless and without motion. That in his lodging there was a gold watch and a purse containing such and such money and a trunk containing such and such clothes, but no passport and no papers, except that on his table was a pack of cards and that he had written in pencil on the back of the ace of hearts: "To the authorities. When I am dead, pray send what is left, as a last Legacy, to Mrs. Lirriper Eighty-one Norfolk Street Strand London." When the gentleman had explained all this, which seemed to be drawn up much more methodical than I should have given the French credit for, not at that time knowing the nation, he put the document into my hand. And much the wiser I was for that you may be sure, except that it had the look of being made out upon grocery paper and was stamped all over with eagles.

"Does Madame Lirrwiper" says the gentleman, "believe she rrwecognises her unfortunate compatrrwiot?"

You may imagine the flurry it put me into my dear to be talked to about my compatriots.

I says "Excuse me. Would you have the kindness Sir to make your language as simple as you can?"

"This Englishman unhappy, at the point of death. This compatrrwiot afflicted," says the gentleman.

"Thank you, Sir," I says "I understand you now. No Sir I have not the least idea who this can be."

"Has Madame Lirrwiper no son, no nephew, no godson, no frrwiend, no acquaintance of any kind in Frrwance?"

"To my certain knowledge," says I "no relation or friend, and to the best of my belief no acquaintance."

"Pardon me. You take Locataires?" says the gentleman.

My dear fully believing he was offering me something with his obliging foreign manners,—snuff for anything I knew,—I gave a little bend of my head and I says if you'll credit it, "No I thank you. I have not contracted the habit."

The gentleman looks perplexed and says "Lodgers!"

"Oh!" says I laughing. "Bless the man! Why yes to be sure!"

"May it not be a former lodger?" says the gentleman. "Some lodger that you pardoned some rrwent? You have pardoned lodgers some rrwent?"

"Hem! It has happened Sir " says I, "but I assure you I can call to mind no gentleman of that description that this is at all likely to be."

In short my dear, we could make nothing of it, and the gentleman noted down what I said and went away. But he left me the paper of which he had two with him, and when the Major came in I says to the

Major as I put it in his hand "Major here's Old Moore's Almanac with the hieroglyphic complete, for your opinion."

It took the Major a little longer to read than I should have thought, judging from the copious flow with which he seemed to be gifted when attacking the organ-men, but at last he got through it, and stood a gazing at me in amazement.

"Major," I says "you're paralysed."

"Madam " says the Major, "Jemmy Jackman is doubled up."

Now it did so happen that the Major had been out to get a little information about railroads and steamboats, as our boy was coming home for his Midsummer holidays next day and we were going to take him somewhere for a treat and a change. So while the Major stood a gazing it came into my head to say to him "Major I wish you'd go and look at some of your books and maps, and see whereabouts this same town of Sens is in France."

The Major he roused himself and he went into the Parlours and he poked about a little, and he came back to me and he says "Sens my dearest madam is seventy-odd miles south of Paris."

With what I may truly call a desperate effort "Major," I says "we'll go there with our blessed boy."

If ever the Major was beside himself it was at the thoughts of that journey. All day long he was like the wild man of the woods after meeting with an advertisement in the papers telling him something to his advantage, and early next morning hours before Jemmy could possibly come home he was outside in the street ready to call out to him that we was all a going to France. Young Rosycheeks you may believe was as wild as the Major, and they did carry on to that degree that I says "If you two children ain't more orderly I'll pack you both off to bed." And then they fell to cleaning up the Major's telescope to see France with, and went out and bought a leather bag with a snap to hang round Jemmy, and him to carry the money like a little Fortunatus with his purse.

If I hadn't passed my word and raised their hopes, I doubt if I could have gone through with the undertaking but it was too late to go back now. So on the second day after Midsummer Day we went off by the morning mail. And when we came to the sea which I had never seen but once in my life and that when my poor Lirriper was courting me, the freshness of it and the deepness and the airiness and to think that it had been rolling ever since and that it was always a rolling and so few of us minding, made me feel quite serious. But I felt happy too and so did Jemmy and the Major and not much motion on the whole, though me with a swimming in the head and a sinking but able to take notice that the foreign insides appear to be constructed hollower than the English, leading to much more tremenjous noises when bad sailors.

But my dear the blueness and the lightness and the coloured look of everything and the very sentry-boxes striped and the shining rattling drums and the little soldiers with their waists and tidy gaiters, when we got across to the Continent—it made me feel as if I

don't know what—as if the atmosphere had been lifted off me. And
as to lunch why bless you if I kept a man-cook and two kitchen-
maids I couldn't get it done for twice the money, and no injured
young woman a glaring at you and grudging you and acknowledging
your patronage by wishing that your food might choke you, but so
civil and so hot and attentive and every way comfortable except
Jemmy pouring wine down his throat by tumblers-full and me expecting to see him drop under the table.

And the way in which Jemmy spoke his French was a real charm.
It was often wanted of him, for whenever anybody spoke a syllable
to me I says "Non-comprenny, you're very kind, but it's no use—Now
Jemmy!" and then Jemmy he fires away at 'em lovely, the only
thing wanting in Jemmy's French being as it appeared to me that he
hardly ever understood a word of what they said to him which made
it scarcely of the use it might have been though in other respects a
perfect Native and regarding the Major's fluency I should have been
of the opinion judging French by English that there might have been
a greater choice of words in the language though still I must admit
that if I hadn't known him when he asked a military gentleman in a
grey cloak what o'clock it was I should have took him for a Frenchman born.

Before going on to look after my Legacy we were to make one
regular day in Paris, and I leave you to judge my dear what a day
that was with Jemmy and the Major and the telescope and me and the
prowling young man at the inn door (but very civil too) that went
along with us to show the sights. All along the railway to Paris
Jemmy and the Major had been frightening me to death by stooping
down on the platforms at stations to inspect the engines underneath
their mechanical stomachs, and by creeping in and out I don't know
where all, to find improvements for the United Grand Junction
Parlour, but when we got out into the brilliant streets on a bright
morning they gave up all their London improvements as a bad job
and gave their minds to Paris. Says the prowling young man to me
"Will I speak Inglis No?" So I says "If you can young man I shall
take it as a favour," but after half-an-hour of it when I fully believed
the man had gone mad and me too I says "Be so good as fall back on
your French, Sir," knowing that then I shouldn't have the agonies of
trying to understand him, which was a happy release. Not that I lost
much more than the rest either, for I generally noticed that when he
had described something very long indeed and I says to Jemmy
"What does he say Jemmy?" Jemmy says looking with vengeance in
his eye. "He is so jolly indistinct!" and that when he had described
it longer all over again and I says to Jemmy "Well Jemmy what's it
all about?" Jemmy says "He says the building was repaired in
seventeen hundred and four, Gran."

Wherever that prowling young man formed his prowling habits I
cannot be expected to know, but the way in which he went round the
corner while we had our breakfasts and was there again when we
swallowed the last crumb was most marvellous, and just the same at

inner and at night, prowling equally at the theatre and the inn gateway and the shop doors when we bought a trifle or two and everywhere else but troubled with a tendency to spit. And of Paris I can
tell you no more my dear than that it's town and country both in one,
and carved stone and long streets of high houses and gardens and
fountains and statues and trees and gold, and immensely big soldiers
and immensely little soldiers and the pleasantest nurses with the
whitest caps a playing at skipping-rope with the bunchiest babies in
the flattest caps, and clean table-cloths spread everywhere for dinner
and people sitting out of doors smoking and sipping all day long and
little plays being acted in the open air for little people and every shop
complete and elegant room, and everybody seeming to play at
everything in this world. And as to the sparkling lights my dear after
dark, glittering high up and low down and on before and on behind
and all round, and the crowd of theatres and the crowd of people and
the crowd of all sorts, it's pure enchantment. And pretty well the
only thing that grated on me was that whether you pay your fare at
the railway or whether you change your money at a money-dealer's
or whether you take your ticket at the theatre, the lady or gentleman is caged up (I suppose by government) behind the strongest iron
bars having more of a Zoological appearance than a free country.

Well to be sure when I did after all get my precious bones to bed
that night, and my Young Rogue came in to kiss me and asks
What do you think of this lovely lovely Paris, Gran?" I says
Jemmy I feel as if it was beautiful fireworks being let off in my
head." And very cool and refreshing the pleasant country was next
day when we went on to look after my Legacy, and rested me much
and did me a deal of good.

So at length and at last my dear we come to Sens, a pretty little
town with a great two-towered cathedral and the rooks flying in and
out of the loopholes and another tower atop of one of the towers like
sort of a stone pulpit. In which pulpit with the birds skimming
below him if you'll believe me, I saw a speck while I was resting at
the inn before dinner which they made signs to me was Jemmy and
which really was. I had been a fancying as I sat in the balcony of the
hotel that an Angel might light there and call down to the people to
be good, but I little thought what Jemmy all unknown to himself was
calling down from that high place to some one in the town.

The pleasantest-situated inn my dear! Right under the two towers,
with their shadows a changing upon it all day like a kind of a sundial,
and country people driving in and out of the courtyard in carts and
hooded cabriolets and such like, and a market outside in front of the
cathedral, and all so quaint and like a picter. The Major and me
agreed that whatever came of my Legacy this was the place to stay
at for our holiday, and we also agreed that our dear boy had best not
be checked in his joy that night by the sight of the Englishman if he
was still alive, but that we would go together and alone. For you are
to understand that the Major not feeling himself quite equal in his
mind to the height to which Jemmy had climbed, had come back to

me and left him with the Guide.

So after dinner when Jemmy had set off to see the river, the Majo
went down to the Mairie, and presently came back with a militar
character in a sword and spurs and a cocked hat and a yellow shou
der-belt and long tags about him that he must have found incon
venient. And the Major says "The Englishman still lies in the sam
state dearest madam. This gentleman will conduct us to his lodging.
Upon which the military character pulled off his cocked hat to me
and I took notice that he had shaved his forehead in imitation o
Napoleon Bonaparte but not like.

We went out at the courtyard gate and past the great doors of the
cathedral and down a narrow High-street where the people wen
sitting chatting at their shop doors and the children were at play
The military character went in front and he stopped at a pork-sho
with a little statue of a pig sitting up, in the window, and a privat
door that a donkey was looking out of.

When the donkey saw the military character he came slipping ou
on the pavement to turn round and then clattered along the passag
into a back yard. So the coast being clear, the Major and me wen
conducted up the common stair and into the front room on the
second, a bare room with a red tiled floor and the outside lattio
blinds pulled close to darken it. As the military character opened the
blinds I saw the tower where I had seen Jemmy, darkening as the
sun got low, and I turned to the bed by the wall and saw the English
man.

It was some kind of brain fever he had had, and his hair was a
gone, and some wetted folded linen lay upon his head. I looked at hin
very attentive as he lay there all wasted away with his eyes closed
and I says to the Major:

"I never saw this face before."

The Major looked at him very attentive too, and he says:

"*I* never saw his face before."

When the Major explained our words to the military characte:
that gentleman shrugged his shoulders and showed the Major the
card on which it was written about the Legacy for me. It had bee
written with a weak and trembling hand in bed, and I knew no mor
of the writing than of the face. Neither did the Major.

Though lying there alone, the poor creetur was as well taken car
of as could be hoped, and would have been quite unconscious of an
one's sitting by him then. I got the Major to say that we were no
going away at present and that I would come back to-morrow an
watch a bit by the bedside. But I got him to add—and I shook m
head hard to make it stronger—"We agree that we never saw the
face before."

Our boy was greatly surprised when we told him sitting out in the
balcony in the starlight, and he ran over some of those stories o
former Lodgers, of the Major's putting down, and asked wasn't i
possible that it might be this lodger or that lodger. It was not possible
and we went to bed.

In the morning just at breakfast-time the military character came jingling round, and said that the doctor thought from the signs he saw there might be some rally before the end. So I says to the Major and Jemmy, "You two boys go and enjoy yourselves, and I'll take my Prayer Book and go sit by the bed." So I went, and I sat there some hours, reading a prayer for him poor soul now and then, and it was quite on in the day when he moved his hand.

He had been so still, that the moment he moved I knew of it, and I pulled off my spectacles and laid down my book and rose and looked at him. From moving one hand he began to move both, and then his action was the action of a person groping in the dark. Long after his eyes had opened, there was a film over them and he still felt for his way out into light. But by slow degrees his sight cleared and his hands stopped. He saw the ceiling, he saw the wall, he saw me. As his sight cleared, mine cleared too, and when at last we looked in one another's faces, I started back and I cries passionately:

"O you wicked wicked man! Your sin has found you out!"

For I knew him, the moment life looked out of his eyes, to be Mr. Edson, Jemmy's father who had so cruelly deserted Jemmy's young unmarried mother who had died in my arms, poor tender creetur, and left Jemmy to me.

"You cruel wicked man! You bad black traitor!"

With the little strength he had, he made an attempt to turn over on his wretched face to hide it. His arm dropped out of the bed and his head with it, and there he lay before me crushed in body and in mind. Surely the miserablest sight under the summer sun!

"O blessed Heaven," I says a crying, "teach me what to say to this broken mortal! I am a poor sinful creetur, and the Judgment is not mine."

As I lifted my eyes up to the clear bright sky, I saw the high tower where Jemmy had stood above the birds, seeing that very window; and the last look of that poor pretty young mother when her soul brightened and got free, seemed to shine down from it.

"O man, man, man!" I says, and I went on my knees beside the bed; "if your heart is rent asunder and you are truly penitent for what you did, Our Saviour will have mercy on you yet!"

As I leaned my face against the bed, his feeble hand could just move itself enough to touch me. I hope the touch was penitent. It tried to hold my dress and keep hold, but the fingers were too weak to close.

I lifted him back upon the pillows and I says to him:

"Can you hear me?"

He looked yes.

"Do you know me?"

He looked yes, even yet more plainly.

"I am not here alone. The Major is with me. You recollect the Major?"

Yes. That is to say he made out yes, in the same way as before.

"And even the Major and I are not alone. My grandson—his godson—is with us. Do you hear? My grandson."

The fingers made another trial to catch at my sleeve, but could only creep near it and fall.

"Do you know who my grandson is?"

Yes.

"I pitied and loved his lonely mother. When his mother lay a dying I said to her, 'My dear, this baby is sent to a childless old woman.' He has been my pride and joy ever since. I love him as dearly as if he had drunk from my breast. Do you ask to see my grandson before you die?"

Yes.

"Show me, when I leave off speaking, if you correctly understand what I say. He has been kept unacquainted with the story of his birth. He has no knowledge of it. No suspicion of it. If I bring him here to the side of this bed, he will suppose you to be a perfect stranger.   It is more than I can do to keep from him the knowledge that there is such wrong and misery in the world; but that it was ever so near him in his innocent cradle I have kept from him, and I do keep from him, and I ever will keep from him, for his mother's sake, and for his own,"

He showed me that he distinctly understood, the tears fell from his eyes.

"Now rest, and you shall see him."

So I got him a little wine and some brandy, and I put things straight about his bed. But I began to be troubled in my mind lest Jemmy and the Major might be too long of coming back. What with this occupation for my thoughts and hands, I didn't hear a foot upon the stairs, and was startled when I saw the Major stopped short in the middle of the room by the eyes of the man upon the bed, and knowing him then, as I had known him a little while ago.

There was anger in the Major's face, and there was horror and repugnance and I don't know what. So I went up to him and I led him to the bedside, and when I clasped my hands and lifted them up, the Major did the like.

"O Lord" I says "Thou knowest what we two saw together of the sufferings and sorrows of that young creetur now with Thee. If this dying man is truly penitent, we two together humbly pray Thee to have mercy on him!"

The Major says "Amen!" and then after a little stop I whispers him, "Dear old friend fetch our beloved boy." And the Major, so clever as to have got to understand it all without being told a word, went away and brought him.

Never never never shall I forget the fair bright face of our boy when he stood at the foot of the bed, looking at his unknown father. And O so like his dear young mother then!

"Jemmy," I says, "I have found out all about this poor gentleman who is so ill, and he did lodge in the old house once. And as he wants to see all belonging to it, now that he is passing away, I sent for you."

"Ah poor man!" says Jemmy stepping forward and touching one

f his hands with great gentleness. "My heart melts for him. Poor,
oor man!"

The eyes that were so soon to close for ever turned to me, and I was
ot that strong in the pride of my strength and I could resist them.

"My darling boy, there is a reason in the secret history of this
llow-creetur lying as the best and worst of us must all lie one day,
hich I think would ease his spirit in his last hour if you would lay
our cheek against his forehead and say, 'May God forgive you!'"

"O Gran," says Jemmy with a full heart "I am not worthy!" But
e leaned down and did it. Then the faltering fingers made out to
atch hold of my sleeve at last, and I believe he was a-trying to kiss
ne when he died.

*　　*　　*　　*　　*　　*　　*

There my dear! There you have the story of my Legacy in full, and
's worth ten times the trouble I have spent upon it if you are pleased
o like it.

You might suppose that it set us against the little French town of
ens, but no we didn't find that. I found myself that I never looked up
t the high tower atop of the other tower, but the days came back again
hen that fair young creetur with her pretty bright hair trusted in
ne like a mother, and the recollection made the place so peaceful to
ne as I can't express. And every soul about the hotel down to the
igeons in the courtyard made friends with Jemmy and the Major,
nd went lumbering away with them on all sorts of expeditions in all
orts of vehicles drawn by rampagious cart-horses—with heads and
ithout,—mud for paint and ropes for harness,—and every new friend
ressed in blue like a butcher, and every new horse standing on his
ind legs wanting to devour and consume every other horse, and
very man that had a whip to crack crack-crack-crack-crack-cracking
t as if it was a schoolboy with his first. As to the Major my dear that
nan lived the greater part of his time with a little tumbler in one
and and a bottle of small wine in the other, and whenever he saw
nybody else with a little tumbler, no matter who it was,—the
nilitary character with the tags, or the inn-servants at their supper
n the courtyard, or townspeople a chatting on a bench, or country
eople a starting home after Market,—down rushes the Major to
link his glass against their glasses and cry,—Hola! Vive Somebody!
r Vive Something! as if he was beside himself. And though I could
ot quite approve of the Major's doing it, still the ways of the world
arying according to the different parts of it, and dancing at all in
he open Square with a lady that kept a barber's shop my opinion is
hat the Major was right to dance his best and to lead off with a
ower that I did not think was in him, though I was a little uneasy at
he Barricading sound of the cries that were set up by the other
ancers and the rest of the company, until when I says "What are
hey ever calling out Jemmy?" Jemmy says, "They're calling out
Gran, Bravo the Military English! Bravo the Military English!"
vhich was very gratifying to my feelings as a Briton and became the
name the Major was known by.

But every evening at a regular time we all three sat out in the balcony of the hotel at the end of the courtyard, looking up at the golden and rosy light as it changed on the great towers, and looking at the shadows of the towers as they changed on all about us ourselves included, and what do you think we did there? My dear, if Jemmy hadn't brought some other of those stories of the Major's taking down from the telling of former lodgers at Eighty-one Norfolk-street, and if he didn't bring 'em out with this speech :

"Here you are Gran! Here you are godfather! More of 'em! I'll read. And though you wrote 'em for me, godfather, I know you won't disapprove of my making 'em over to Gran; will you?"

"No, my dear boy," says the Major. "Everything we have is hers and we are hers."

"Hers ever affectionately and devotedly J. Jackman, and J. Jackman Lirriper," cries the Young Rogue giving me a close hug. "Very well then godfather. Look here. As Gran is in the Legacy way just now, I shall make these stories a part of Gran's Legacy. I'll leave 'em to her. What do you say godfather?"

"Hip hip Hurrah!" says the Major.

"Very well then," cries Jemmy all in a bustle. "Vive the Military English! Vive the Lady Lirriper! Vive the Jemmy Jackman Ditto! Vive the Legacy! Now, you look out, Gran. And you'll look out, godfather. I'll read! And I'll tell you what I'll do besides. On the last night of our holiday here when we are all packed and going away I'll top up with something of my own."

"Mind you do, Sir," says I.

CHAPTER II

MRS. LIRRIPER RELATES HOW JEMMY TOPPED UP

WELL my dear and so the evening readings of those jottings of the Major's brought us round at last to the evening when we were all packed and going away next day, and I do assure you that by that time though it was deliciously comfortable to look forward to the dear old house in Norfolk-street again, I had formed quite a high opinion of the French nation and had noticed them to be much more homely and domestic in their families and far more simple and amiable in their lives than I had ever been led to expect, and it did strike me between ourselves that in one particular they might be imitated to advantage by another nation which I will not mention, and that is in the courage with which they take their little enjoyments on little means and with little things and don't let solemn big-wigs stare them out of countenance or speechify them dull, of which said solemn big-wigs I have ever had the one opinion that I wish they were all made comfortable separately in coppers with the lids on and never let out any more.

"Now young man," I says to Jemmy when we brought our chairs

to the balcony that last evening, "you please to remember who was 'top up.' "

"All right Gran," says Jemmy. "I am the illustrious personage."

But he looked so serious after he had made me that light answer, that the Major raised his eyebrows at me and I raised mine at the Major.

"Gran and godfather," says Jemmy, "you can hardly think how much my mind has run on Mr. Edson's death."

It gave me a little check. "Ah! it was a sad scene my love " I says, and sad remembrances came back stronger than merry. But this" says after a little silence, to rouse myself and the Major and Jemmy together, "is not topping up. Tell us your story my dear."

"I will," says Jemmy.

"What is that date Sir?" says I. "Once upon a time when pigs drank wine?"

"No Gran," says Jemmy, still serious; "once upon a time when the French drank wine."

Again I glanced at the Major, and the Major glanced at me.

"In short, Gran and godfather," says Jemmy, looking up, "the date is this time, and I'm going to tell you Mr. Edson's story."

The flutter that it threw me into. The change of colour on the part of the Major!

"That is to say, you understand," our bright-eyed boy says, "I am going to give you my version of it. I shall not ask whether it's right or not, firstly because you said you knew very little about it, Gran, and secondly because what little you did know was a secret."

I folded my hands in my lap and I never took my eyes off Jemmy as he went running on.

"The unfortunate gentleman" Jemmy commences, "who is the object of our present narrative was the son of Somebody, and was born Somewhere, and chose a profession Somehow. It is not with those parts of his career that we have to deal; but with his early attachment to a young and beautiful lady."

I thought I should have dropped. I durstn't look at the Major; but knew what his state was, without looking at him.

"The father of our ill-starred hero " says Jemmy, copying as it seemed to me the style of some of his story-books, "was a worldly man who entertained ambitious views for his only son and who firmly set his face against the contemplated alliance with a virtuous but penniless orphan. Indeed he went so far as roundly to assure our hero that unless he weaned his thoughts from the object of his devoted affection, he would disinherit him. At the same time, he proposed as a suitable match the daughter of a neighbouring gentleman of a good estate, who was neither ill-favoured nor unamiable, and whose eligibility in a pecuniary point of view could not be disputed. But young Mr. Edson, true to the first, and only love that had inflamed his breast, rejected all considerations of self-advancement, and, appreciating his father's anger in a respectful letter, ran away with her."

My dear I had begun to take a turn for the better, but when
come to running away I began to take another turn for the worse.

"The lovers," says Jemmy "fled to London and were united at t]
altar of Saint Clement's Danes. And it is at this period of their simp
but touching story that we find them inmates of the dwelling of
highly-respected and beloved lady of the name of Gran, residi
within a hundred miles of Norfolk-street."

I felt that we were almost safe now, I felt that the dear boy had
suspicion of the bitter truth, and I looked at the Major for the fi
time and drew a long breath. The Major gave me a nod.

"Our hero's father" Jemmy goes on "proving implacable a
carrying his threat into unrelenting execution, the struggles of t]
young couple in London were severe, and would have been far mc
so, but for their good angel's having conducted them to the abode
Mrs. Gran; who, divining their poverty (in spite of their endeavou
to conceal it from her), by a thousand delicate arts smoothed the
rough way, and alleviated the sharpness of their first distress."

Here Jemmy took one of my hands in one of his, and began a mar
ing the turns of his history by making me give a beat from time
time upon his other hand.

"After a while, they left the house of Mrs. Gran, and pursued the
fortunes through a variety of successes and failures elsewhere. But
all reverses, whether for good or evil, the words of Mr. Edson to t]
fair young partner of his life were, 'Unchanging Love and Tru
will carry us through all!'"

My hand trembled in the dear boy's, those words so wofully unli
the fact.

"Unchanging Love and Truth" says Jemmy over again, as if]
had a proud kind of a noble pleasure in it, "will carry us through al
Those were his words. And so they fought their way, poor but galla
and happy, until Mrs. Edson gave birth to a child."

"A daughter," I says.

"No," says Jemmy, "a son. And the father was so proud of it th
he could hardly bear it out of his sight. But a dark cloud oversprea
the scene. Mrs. Edson sickened, drooped, and died.

"Ah! Sickened, drooped, and died!" I says.

"And so Mr. Edson's only comfort, only hope on earth, and on
stimulus to action, was his darling boy. As the child grew older,]
grew so like his mother that he was her living picture. It used to ma]
him wonder why his father cried when he kissed him. But u
happily he was like his mother in constitution as well as in face, an
he died too before he had grown out of childhood. Then Mr. Edso
who had good abilities, in his forlornness and despair, threw them a
to the winds. He became apathetic, reckless, lost. Little by little l
sank down, down, down, down, until at last he almost lived (I thin]
by gaming. And so sickness overtook him in the town of Sens i
France, and he lay down to die. But now that he laid him down whe
all was done, and looked back upon the green Past beyond the tin
when he had covered it with ashes, he thought gratefully of the goo

Mrs. Gran long lost sight of, who had been so kind to him and his young wife in the early days of their marriage, and he left the little hat he had as a last Legacy to her. And she, being brought to see him, at first no more knew him than she would know from seeing the ruin of a Greek or Roman Temple, what it used to be before it fell; but at length she remembered him. And then he told her, with tears, of his regret for the misspent part of his life, and besought her to think as mildly of it as she could, because it was the poor fallen Angel of his unchanging Love and Constancy after all. And because she had her grandson with her, and he fancied that his own boy, if he had lived, might have grown to be something like him, he asked her to let him touch his forehead with his cheek and say certain parting words."

Jemmy's voice sank low when it got to that, and tears filled my eyes, and filled the Major's.

"You little Conjurer " I says, "how did you ever make it all out? Go in and write it every word down, for it's a wonder."

Which Jemmy did, and I have repeated it to you my dear from his writing.

Then the Major took my hand and kissed it, and said, "Dearest madam all has prospered with us."

"Ah Major," I says drying my eyes, "we needn't have been afraid. We might have known it. Treachery don't come natural to beaming youth; but trust and pity, love and constancy,—they do, thank God !"

DOCTOR MARIGOLD

IN THREE CHAPTERS

[1865]

CHAPTER I

TO BE TAKEN IMMEDIATELY

I AM a Cheap Jack, and my own father's name was Willum Marigold.
It was in his lifetime supposed by some that his name was William,
but my own father always consistently said, No, it was Willum. On
which point I content myself with looking at the argument this way.
If a man is not allowed to know his own name in a free country; how
much is he allowed to know in a land of slavery? As to looking at the
argument through the medium of the Register, Willum Marigold come
into the world before Registers come up much,—and went out of it
too. They wouldn't have been greatly in his line neither, if they had
chanced to come up before him.

I was born on the Queen's highway, but it was the King's at that
time. A doctor was fetched to my own mother by my own father,
when it took place in a common; and in consequence of his being a
very kind gentleman, and accepting no fee but a tea-tray, I was
named Doctor, out of gratitude and compliment to him. There you
have me. Doctor Marigold.

I am at present a middle-aged man of a broadish build, in cords,
leggings, and a sleeved waistcoat the strings of which is always gone
behind. Repair them how you will, they go like fiddle-strings. You
have been to the theatre, and you have seen one of the wiolin-players
screw up his wiolin, after listening to it as if it had been whispering
the secret to him that it feared it was out of order, and then you have
heard it snap. That's as exactly similar to my waistcoat as a waistcoat and a wiolin can be like one another.

I am partial to a white hat, and I like a shawl round my neck wore
loose and easy. Sitting down is my favourite posture. If I have a taste
in point of personal jewelry, it is mother-of-pearl buttons. There
you have me again, as large as life.

The doctor having accepted a tea-tray, you'll guess that my father
was a Cheap Jack before me. You are right. He was. It was a pretty
tray. It represented a large lady going along a serpentining up-hill
gravel-walk, to attend a little church. Two swans had likewise come

tray with the same intentions. When I call her a large lady, I don't
ean in point of breadth, for there she fell below my views, but she
ore than made it up in heighth; her heighth and slimness was—in
ort THE heighth of both.

I often saw that tray, after I was the innocently smiling cause (or
ore like screeching one) of the doctor's standing it up on a table
gainst the wall in his consulting-room. Whenever my own father and
other were in that part of the country I used to put my head (I have
eard my own mother say it was flaxen curls at that time, though you
ouldn't know an old hearth-broom from it now till you come to the
andle, and found it wasn't me) in at the doctor's door, and the
octor was always glad to see me, and said, "Aha, my brother
ractitioner! Come in, little M.D. How are your inclinations as to
xpence?"

You can't go on for ever, you'll find, nor yet could my father nor
et my mother. If you don't go off as a whole when you are about
ae, you're liable to go off in part, and two to one your head's the
art. Gradually my father went off his, and my mother went off hers.
: was in a harmless way, but it put out the family where I boarded
aem. The old couple, though retired, got to be wholly and solely
evoted to the Cheap Jack business, and were always selling the
mily off. Whenever the cloth was laid for dinner, my father began
ttling the plates and dishes, as we do in our line when we put up
ockery for a bid, only he had lost the trick of it, and mostly let 'em
rop and broke 'em. As the old lady had been used to sit in the cart
ad hand the articles out one by one to the old gentleman on the
otboard to sell, just in the same way she handed him every item of
ae family's property, and they disposed of it in their own imagina-
ons from morning to night. At last the old gentleman, lying bed-
dden in the same room with the old lady, cries out in the old patter,
aent, after having been silent for two days and nights: "Now here,
y jolly companions every one—which the Nightingale club in a
llage was held, At the sign of the Cabbage and Shears, Where the
ngers no doubt would have greatly excelled, But for want of taste,
oices, and ears,—now, here, my jolly companions every one, is a
orking model of a used-up old Cheap Jack, without a tooth in his
ead, and with a pain in every bone: so like life that it would be just
s good if it wasn't better, just as bad if it wasn't worse, and just as
ew if it wasn't worn out. Bid for the working model of the old
heap Jack, who has drunk more gunpowder-tea with the ladies in
is time than would blow the lid off a washerwoman's copper, and
arry it as many thousands of miles higher than the moon as naught
ix naught, divided by the national debt, carry nothing to the poor-
ates, three under, and two over. Now, my hearts of oak and men of
raw, what do you say for the lot? Two shillings, a shilling, tenpence,
ghtpence, sixpence, fourpence. Twopence? Who said twopence?
he gentleman in the scarecrow's hat? I am ashamed of the gentle-
aan in the scarecrow's hat. I really am ashamed of him for his want
f public spirit. Now I'll tell you what I'll do with you. Come! I'll

throw you in a working model of a old woman that was married
the old Cheap Jack so long ago that upon my word and honour
took place in Noah's Ark, before the Unicorn could get in to forb
the banns by blowing a tune upon his horn. There now! Com
What do you say for both! I'll tell you what I'll do with you. I don
bear you malice for being so backward. Here! If you make me a b:
that'll only reflect a little credit on your town, I'll throw you in
warming-pan for nothing, and lend you a toasting-fork for lif
Now come; what do you say after that splendid offer? Say two poun
say thirty shillings, say a pound, say ten shillngs, say five, sa
two and six? You don't say even two and six? You say two an
three? No. You shan't have the lot for two and three. I'd sooner gi
it to you, if you was good-looking enough. Here! Missis! Chuck th
old man and woman into the cart, put the horse to, and drive 'e
away and bury 'em!" Such were the last words of Willum Marigol
my own father, and they were carried out, by him and by his wif
my own mother, on one and the same day, as I ought to know
having followed as mourner.

My father had been a lovely one in his time at the Cheap Jac
work, as his dying observations went to prove. But I top him.
don't say it because it's myself, but because it has been universall
acknowledged by all that has had the means of comparison. I hav
worked at it. I have measured myself against other public speaker
—Members of Parliament, Platforms, Pulpits, Counsel learned i
the law,—and where I have found 'em good, I have took a bit
imagination from 'em, and where I have found 'em bad, I have le
'em alone. Now I'll tell you what. I mean to go down into my grav
declaring that of all the callings ill used in Great Britain, the Chea
Jack calling is the worst used. Why ain't we a profession? Why ain
we endowed with privileges? Why are we forced to take out a haw
ker's licence, when no such thing is expected of the political hawkers
Where's the difference betwixt us? Except that we are Cheap Jack
and they are Dear Jacks, I don't see any difference but what's in ou
favour.

For look here! Say it's election time. I am on the foot-board of m
cart in the market-place, on a Saturday night. I put up a genera
miscellaneous lot. I say: "Now here, my free and independer
woters, I'm a going to give you such a chance as you never had in a
your born days, nor yet the days preceding. Now I'll show you wha
I am a going to do with you. Here's a pair of razors that'll shav
you closer than the Board of Guardians; here's a flat-iron worth it
weight in gold; here's a frying-pan artificially flavoured with essenc
of beefsteaks to that degree that you've only got for the rest of you
lives to fry bread and dripping in it and there you are replete wit
animal food; here's a genuine chronometer watch in such a solid silve
case that you may knock at the door with it when you come hom
late from a social meeting, and rouse your wife and family, and sav
up your knocker for the postman; and here's half-a-dozen dinne
plates that you may play the cymbals with to charm the baby whe

it's fractious. Stop! I'll throw you in another article, and I'll give you that, and it's a rolling-pin; and if the baby can only get it well into its mouth when its teeth is coming and rub the gums once with it, they'll come through double, in a fit of laughter equal to being tickled. Stop again! I'll throw you in another article, because I don't like the looks of you, for you haven't the appearance of buyers unless I lose by you, and because I'd rather lose than not take money to-night, and that's a looking-glass in which you may see how ugly you look when you don't bid. What do you say now? Come. Do you say a pound? Not you, for you haven't got it. Do you say ten shillings? Not you, for you owe more to the tallyman. Well then, I'll tell you what I'll do with you. I'll heap 'em all on the footboard of the cart,—there they are! razors, flat-iron, frying-pan, chronometer watch, dinner plates, rolling-pin, and looking-glass,—take 'em all away for four shillings, and I'll give you sixpence for your trouble!" This is me the Cheap Jack. But on the Monday morning, in the same market-place, comes the Dear Jack on the hustings—*his* cart— and what does *he* say? "Now my free and independent woters, I am a going to give you such a chance" (he begins just like me) "as you never had in all your born days, and that's the chance of sending Myself to Parliament. Now I'll tell you what I am a going to do for you. Here's the interests of the magnificent town promoted above all the rest of the civilised and uncivilised earth. Here's your railways carried, and your neighbour's railways jockeyed. Here's all your sons in the Post-office. Here's Britannia smiling on you. Here's the eyes of Europe on you. Here's uniwersal prosperity for you, repletion of animal food, golden cornfields, gladsome homesteads, and rounds of applause from your own hearts, all in one lot, and that's myself. Will you take me as I stand? You won't? Well, then, I'll tell you what I'll do with you. Come now! I'll throw you in anything you ask for. There! Church-rates, abolition of church-rates, more malt tax, no malt tax, uniwersal education to the highest mark, or uniwersal ignorance to the lowest, total abolition of flogging in the army or a dozen for every private once a month all round. Wrongs of Men or Rights of Women—only say which it shall be, take 'em or leave 'em, and I'm of your opinion altogether, and the lot's your own on your own terms. There! You won't take it yet! Well, then, I'll tell you what I'll do with you. Come! You *are* such free and independent woters, and I *am* so proud of you,—you *are* such a noble and enlightened constituency, and I *am* so ambitious of the honour and dignity of being your member, which is by far the highest level to which the wings of the human mind can soar,—that I'll tell you what I'll do with you. I'll throw you in all the public-houses in your magnificent town for nothing. Will that content you? It won't? You won't take the lot yet? Well, then, before I put the horse in and drive away, and make the offer to the next most magnificent town that can be discovered, I'll tell you what I'll do. Take the lot, and I'll drop two thousand pound in the streets of your magnificent town for them to pick up that can. Not enough? Now look here. This is the very furthest that I'm a going to. I'll make it two thousand five hundred. And still you won't? Here, missis! Put the horse—no, stop half a moment, I shouldn't like to turn my back upon you neither for a trifle, I'll make it two thousand seven hundred and fifty pound. There! Take the lot on your own terms, and I'll count out two thousand seven hundred and fifty pound on the footboard of the cart, to be dropped in the streets of your magnificent town for them to pick up that can. What do you say? Come now! You won't do better, and you may do worse. You take it? Hooray! Sold again, and got the seat!"

These Dear Jacks soap the people shameful, but we Cheap Jacks don't. We tell 'em the truth about themselves to their faces, and scorn to court 'em. As to wenturesomeness in the way of puffing up the lots, the Dear Jack beats us hollow. It is considered in the Cheap Jack calling, that better patter can be made out of a gun than any article we put up from the cart except a pair of spectacles. I often hold forth about a gun for a quarter of an hour, and feel as if I need never leave off. But when I tell 'em what the gun can do, and what the gun has brought down, I never go half so far as the Dear Jacks do when they make speeches in praise of *their* guns—their great guns that set 'em on to do it. Besides, I'm in business for myself: I ain't sent down into the market-place to order, as they are. Besides, again, my guns don't know what I say in their laudation, and their guns do, and the whole concern of 'em have reason to be sick and ashamed all round. These are some of my arguments for declaring that the Cheap Jack calling is treated ill in Great Britain, and for turning warm when I think of the other Jacks in question setting themselves up to pretend to look down upon it.

I courted my wife from the footboard of the cart. I did indeed. She was a Suffolk young woman, and it was in Ipswich market-place right opposite the corn-chandler's shop. I had noticed her up at a window last Saturday that was, appreciating highly. I had took to her, and I had said to myself, "If not already disposed of, I'll have that lot." Next Saturday that come, I pitched the cart on the same pitch, and I was in very high feather indeed, keeping 'em laughing the whole of the time, and getting off the goods briskly. At last I took out of my waistcoat pocket a small lot wrapped in soft paper, and I put it this way (looking up at the window where she was). "Now here, my blooming English maidens, is an article, the last article of the present evening's sale, which I offer to only you, the lovely Suffolk Dumplings biling over with beauty, and I won't take a bid of a thousand pounds for from any man alive. Now what is it? Why, I'll tell you what it is. It's made of fine gold, and it's not broke, though there's a hole in the middle of it, and it's stronger than any fetter that ever was forged, though it's smaller than any finger in my set of ten. Why ten? Because, when my parents made over my property to me, I tell you true, there was twelve sheets, twelve towels, twelve table-cloths, twelve knives, twelve forks, twelve tablespoons, and twelve tea-spoons, but my set of fingers was two short of a dozen, and could never since be matched. Now what else is it? Come, I'll tell you. It's a hoop of solid gold, wrapped in a silver curl-paper, that I myself took off the shining locks of the ever-beautiful old lady of Threadneedle-street, London city; I wouldn't tell you so if I hadn't the paper to show, or you mightn't believe it even of me. Now what else is it? It's a man-trap and a handcuff, the parish stocks and leg-lock, all in gold and all in one. Now what else is it? It's a wedding-ring. Now I'll tell you what I'm a going to do with it. I'm not a going to offer this lot for money; but I mean to give it to the next of you beauties that laughs, and I'll pay her a visit to-morrow morning at exactly half after nine o'clock as the chimes go, and I'll take her out for a walk to put up the banns." *She* laughed, and got the ring handed up to her. When I called in the morning, she says, "O dear! It's never you, and you never mean it?" "It's ever me," says I, "and I am ever yours, and I ever mean it." So we got married after being put up three times—which by the bye, is quite in the Cheap Jack way again, and shows once more how the Cheap Jack customs pervade society.

She wasn't a bad wife, but she had a temper. If she could have parted with that one article at a sacrifice, I wouldn't have swopped her away in exchange for any other woman in England. Not that I ever did swop her away, for we lived together till she died, and that was thirteen year. Now, my lords and ladies and gentlefolks all, I'll let you into a secret, though you won't believe it. Thirteen year of temper in a Palace would try the worst of you, but thirteen year of temper in a Cart would try the best of you. You are kept so very close to it in a cart, you see. There's thousands of couples among you getting on like sweet ile upon a whetstone in houses five and six pairs of stairs high, that would go to the Divorce Court in a cart. Whether the jolting makes it worse, I don't undertake to decide; but in a cart it does come home to you, and stick to you. Wiolence in a cart is *so* wiolent, and aggrawation in a cart is *so* aggrawating.

We might have had such a pleasant life! A roomy cart, with the large goods hung outside, and the bed slung underneath it when on the road, an iron pot and a kettle, a fireplace for the cold weather, a chimney for the smoke, a hanging-shelf and a cupboard, a dog and a horse. What more do you want? You draw off upon a bit of turf in a green lane or by the roadside, you hobble your old horse and turn him grazing, you light your fire upon the ashes of the last visitors, you cook your stew, and you wouldn't call the Emperor of France your father. But have a temper in the cart, flinging language and the hardest goods in stock at you, and where are you then? Put a name to your feelings.

My dog knew as well when she was on the turn as I did. Before she broke out, he would give a howl, and bolt. How he knew it, was a mystery to me; but the sure and certain knowledge of it would wake him up out of his soundest sleep, and he would give a howl, and bolt. At such times I wished I was him.

The worst of it was, we had a daughter born to us, and I love children with all my heart. When she was in her furies she beat the child. This got to be so shocking, as the child got to be four or five year old, that I have many a time gone on with my whip over my shoulder, at the old horse's head, sobbing and crying worse than ever little Sophy did. For how could I prevent it? Such a thing is not to be tried with such a temper—in a cart—without coming to a fight. It's in the natural size and formation of a cart to bring it to a fight. And then the poor child got worse terrified than before, as well as worse hurt generally, and her mother made complaints to the next people we lighted on, and the word went round, "Here's a wretch of a Cheap Jack been a beating his wife."

Little Sophy was such a brave child! She grew to be quite devoted to her poor father, though he could do so little to help her. She had a wonderful quantity of shining dark hair, all curling natural about her. It is quite astonishing to me now, that I didn't go tearing mad when I used to see her run from her mother before the cart, and her mother catch her by this hair, and pull her down by it, and beat her.

Such a brave child I said she was! Ah! with reason.

"Don't you mind next time, father dear," she would whisper to me, with her little face still flushed, and her bright eyes still wet; "if I don't cry out, you may know I am not much hurt. And even if I do cry out, it will be only to get mother to let go and leave off." What I have seen the little spirit bear—for me—without crying out!

Yet in other respects her mother took great care of her. Her clothes were always clean and neat, and her mother was never tired of working at 'em. Such is the inconsistency in things. Our being down in the marsh country in unhealthy weather, I consider the cause of Sophy's taking bad low fever; but however she took it, once she got it she turned away from her mother for evermore, and nothing would persuade her to be touched by her mother's hand. She would shiver and say, "No, no, no," when it was offered at, and would hide her face on my shoulder, and hold me tighter round the neck.

The Cheap Jack business had been worse than ever I had known it, what with one thing and what with another (and not least with railroads, which will cut it all to pieces, I expect, at last), and I was run dry of money. For which reason, one night at that period of little Sophy's being so bad, either we must have come to a dead-lock for victuals and drink, or I must have pitched the cart as I did.

I couldn't get the dear child to lie down or leave go of me, and indeed I hadn't the heart to try, so I stepped out on the footboard with her holding round my neck. They all set up a laugh when they see us, and one chuckle-headed Joskin (that I hated for it) made the bidding, "Tuppence for her!"

"Now, you country boobies," says I, feeling as if my heart was a heavy weight at the end of a broken sashline, "I give you notice that I am a going to charm the money out of your pockets, and to give you so much more than your money's worth that you'll only persuade yourselves to draw your Saturday night's wages ever again arterwards by the hopes of meeting me to lay 'em out with, which you

ver will, and why not? Because I've made my fortune by selling
y goods on a large scale for seventy-five per cent. less than
give for 'em, and I am consequently to be elevated to the House of
eers next week, by the title of the Duke of Cheap and Markis
ackaloorul. Now let's know what you want to-night, and you shall
ave it. But first of all, shall I tell you why I have got this little girl
und my neck? You don't want to know? Then you shall. She
elongs to the Fairies. She's a fortune-teller. She can tell me all about
ou in a whisper, and can put me up to whether you're going to buy
lot or leave it. Now do you want a saw? No, she says you don't,
cause you're too clumsy to use one. Else here's a saw which would
e a lifelong blessing to a handy man, at four shillings, at three and
x, at three, at two and six, at two, at eighteen-pence. But none
you shall have it at any price, on account of your well-known
vkwardness, which would make it manslaughter. The same objec-
on applies to this set of three planes which I won't let you have
either, so don't bid for 'em. Now I am a going to ask her what you
want." (Then I whispered, "Your head burns so, that I am afraid
hurts you bad, my pet," and she answered, without opening her
eavy eyes, "Just a little, father.") "O! This little fortune-teller says
's a memorandum-book you want. Then why didn't you mention
? Here it is. Look at it. Two hundred super-fine hot-pressed wire-
ove pages—if you don't believe me, count 'em—ready ruled for
our expenses, an everlastingly pointed pencil to put 'em down with,
double-bladed penknife to scratch 'em out with, a book of printed
bles to calculate your income with, and a camp-stool to sit down
pon while you give your mind to it! Stop! And an umbrella to keep
e moon off when you give your mind to it on a pitch-dark night.
ow I won't ask you how much for the lot, but how little? How little
e you thinking of? Don't be ashamed to mention it, because my
rtune-teller knows already." (Then making believe to whisper, I
issed her, and she kissed me.) "Why, she says you are thinking of as
ttle as three and threepence! I couldn't have believed it, even of
ou, unless she told me. Three and threepence! And a set of printed
bles in the lot that'll calculate your income up to forty thousand
year! With an income of forty thousand a year, you grudge three
nd sixpence. Well, then, I'll tell you my opinion. I so despise the
reepence, that I'd sooner take three shillings. There. For three
illings, three shillings, three shillings! Gone. Hand 'em over to the
icky man."

As there had been no bid at all, everybody looked about and
rinned at everybody, while I touched little Sophy's face and asked
er if she felt faint, or giddy. "Not very, father. It will soon be over."
hen turning from the pretty patient eyes, which were opened now,
nd seeing nothing but grins across my lighted grease-pot, I went on
gain in my Cheap Jack style. "Where's the butcher!" (My sorrowful
ye had just caught sight of a fat young butcher on the outside of the
rowd.) "She says the good luck is the butcher's. Where is he?"
veryody handed on the blushing butcher to the front, and there

was a roar, and the butcher felt himself obliged to put his hand in h
pocket, and take the lot. The party so picked out, in general, does fe
obliged to take the lot—good four times out of six. Then we ha
another lot, the counterpart of that one, and sold it sixpence cheape
which is always very much enjoyed. Then we had the spectacles. I
ain't a special profitable lot, but I put 'em on, and I see what th
Chancellor of the Exchequer is going to take off the taxes, and I se
what the sweetheart of the young woman in the shawl is doing a
home, and I see what the Bishops has got for dinner, and a deal mor
that seldom fails to fetch 'em up in their spirits; and the better thei
spirits, the better their bids. Then we had the ladies' lot,—the tea
pot, tea-caddy, glass sugar-basin, half a dozen spoons, and caudle
cup—and all the time I was making similar excuses to give a look o
two and say a word or two to my poor child. It was while the secon
ladies' lot was holding 'em enchained that I felt her lift herself a littl
on my shoulder, to look across the dark street. "What troubles you
darling?" "Nothing troubles me, father. I am not at all trouble
But don't I see a pretty churchyard over there?" "Yes, my dear.
"Kiss me twice, dear father, and lay me down to rest upon tha
churchyard grass so soft and green." I staggered back into the car
with her head dropped on my shoulder, and I says to her mothe
"Quick. Shut the door! Don't let those laughing people see!
"What's the matter?" she cries. "O woman, woman," I tells he
"you'll never catch my little Sophy by her hair again, for she ha
flown away from you!"

Maybe those were harder words than I meant 'em; but from tha
time forth my wife took to brooding, and would sit in the cart o
walk beside it, hours at a stretch, with her arms crossed, and he
eyes looking on the ground. When her furies took her (which wa
rather seldomer than before) they took her in a new way, and sh
banged herself about to that extent that I was forced to hold he
She got none the better for a little drink now and then, and throug
some years I used to wonder, as I plodded along at the old horse'
head, whether there was many carts upon the road that held so muc
dreariness as mine, for all my being looked up to as the King of th
Cheap Jacks. So sad our lives went on till one summer evening, when
as we were coming into Exeter, out of the farther West of England
we saw a woman beating a child in a cruel manner, who screamed
"Don't beat me! O mother, mother, mother!" Then my wife stoppe
her ears, and ran away like a wild thing, and next day she was foun
in the river.

Me and my dog were all the company left in the cart now; and th
dog learned to give a short bark when they wouldn't bid, and to giv
another and a nod of his head when I asked him, "Who said half a
crown? Are you the gentleman, Sir, that offered half a crown?"
He attained to an immense height of popularity, and I shall alway
believe taught himself entirely out of his own head to growl at any
person in the crowd that bid as low as sixpence. But he got to be wel
on in years, and one night when I was conwulsing York with the

spectacles, he took a convulsion on his own account upon the very footboard by me, and it finished him.

Being naturally of a tender turn, I had dreadful lonely feelings on me arter this. I conquered 'em at selling times, having a reputation to keep (not to mention keeping myself), but they got me down in private, and rolled upon me. That's often the way with us public characters. See us on the footboard, and you'd give pretty well anything you possess to be us. See us off the footboard, and you'd add a trifle to be off your bargain. It was under these circumstances that I come acquainted with a giant. I might have been too high to fall into conversation with him, had it not been for my lonely feelings. For the general rule is, going round the country, to draw the line at dressing up. When a man can't trust his getting a living to his undisguised abilities, you consider him below your sort. And this giant when on view figured as a Roman.

He was a languid young man, which I attribute to the distance betwixt his extremities. He had a little head and less in it, he had weak eyes and weak knees, and altogether you couldn't look at him without feeling that there was greatly too much of him both for his joints and his mind. But he was an amiable though timid young man (his mother let him out, and spent the money), and we come acquainted when he was walking to ease the horse betwixt two fairs. He was called Rinaldo di Velasco, his name being Pickleson.

This giant, otherwise Pickleson, mentioned to me under the seal of confidence that, beyond his being a burden to himself, his life was made a burden to him by the cruelty of his master towards a step-daughter who was deaf and dumb. Her mother was dead, and she had no living soul to take her part, and was used most hard. She travelled with his master's caravan only because there was nowhere to leave her, and this giant, otherwise Pickleson, did go so far as to believe that his master often tried to lose her. He was such a very languid young man, that I don't know how long it didn't take him to get this story out, but it passed through his defective circulation to his top extremity in course of time.

When I heard this account from the giant, otherwise Pickleson, and likewise that the poor girl had beautiful long dark hair, and was often pulled down by it and beaten, I couldn't see the giant through what stood in my eyes. Having wiped 'em, I gave him sixpence (for he was kept as short as he was long), and he laid it out in two three-penn'orths of gin-and-water, which so brisked him up, that he sang the Favourite Comic of Shivery Shakey, ain't it cold?—a popular effect which his master had tried every other means to get out of him as a Roman wholly in vain.

His master's name was Mim, a wery hoarse man, and I knew him to speak to. I went to that Fair as a mere civilian, leaving the cart outside the town, and I looked about the back of the Vans while the performing was going on, and at last, sitting dozing against a muddy cart-wheel, I came upon the poor girl who was deaf and dumb. At the first look I might almost have judged that she had escaped from the Wild Beast Show; but at the second I thought better of her, and thought that if she was more cared for and more kindly used she would be like my child. She was just the same age that my own daughter would have been, if her pretty head had not fell down upon my shoulder that unfortunate night.

To cut it short, I spoke confidential to Mim while he was beating the gong outside betwixt two lots of Pickleson's publics, and I put it to him, "She lies heavy on your own hands; what'll you take for her?" Mim was a most ferocious swearer. Suppressing that part of his reply which was much the longest part, his reply was, "A pair of braces." "Now I'll tell you," says I, "what I'm a going to do with you. I'm a going to fetch you half-a-dozen pair of the pimest braces in the cart, and then to take her away with me." Says Mim (again ferocious), "I'll believe it when I've got the goods, and no sooner." I made all the haste I could, lest he should think twice of it, and the bargain was completed, which Pickleson he was thereby so relieved in his mind that he come out at his little back door, longways like a serpent, and give us Shivery Shakey in a whisper among the wheels at parting.

It was happy days for both of us when Sophy and me began to travel in the cart. I at once give her the name of Sophy, to put her ever towards me in the attitude of my own daughter. We soon made out to begin to understand one another, through the goodness of the Heavens, when she knowed that I meant true and kind by her. In a very little time she was wonderful fond of me. You have no idea what it is to have anybody wonderful fond of you, unless you have been got down and rolled upon by the lonely feelings that I have mentioned as having once got the better of me.

You'd have laughed—or the reverse—it's according to your disposition—if you could have seen me trying to teach Sophy. At first I was helped—you'd never guess by what—milestones. I got some large alphabets in a box, all the letters separate on bits of bone, and saying we was going to WINDSOR, I gave her those letters in that order, and then at every milestone I showed her those same letters in that same order again, and pointed towards the abode of royalty. Another time I give her CART, and then chalked the same upon the cart. Another time I give her DOCTOR MARIGOLD, and hung a corresponding inscription outside my waistcoat. People that met us might stare a bit and laugh, but what did *I* care, if she caught the idea? She caught it after long patience and trouble, and then we did begin to get on swimmingly, I believe you! At first she was a little given to consider me the cart, and the cart the abode of royalty, but that soon wore off.

We had our signs, too, and they was hundreds in number. Sometimes she would sit looking at me and considering hard how to communicate with me about something fresh,—how to ask me what she wanted explained,—and then she was (or I thought she was; what does it signify?) so like my child with those years added to her, that I half-believed it was herself, trying to tell me where she had been to

in the skies, and what she had seen since that unhappy night
en she flied away. She had a pretty face, and now that there was
one to drag at her bright dark hair, and it was all in order, there
s a something touching in her looks that made the cart most
aceful and most quiet, though not at all melancholy. [N.B. In the
eap Jack patter, we generally sound it lemonjolly, and it gets a
ugh.]

The way she learnt to understand any look of mine was truly sur-
ising. When I sold of a night, she would sit in the cart unseen by
em outside, and would give a eager look into my eyes when I looked
, and would hand me straight the precise article or articles I
nted. And then she would clap her hands, and laugh for joy.
d as for me, seeing her so bright, and remembering what she was
en I first lighted on her, starved and beaten and ragged, leaning
eep against the muddy cartwheel, it give me such heart that I
ined a greater heighth of reputation than ever, and I put Pickleson
wn (by the name of Mim's Travelling Giant otherwise Pickleson)
r a fypunnote in my will.

This happiness went on in the cart till she was sixteen year old.
y which time I began to feel not satisfied that I had done my
ole duty to her, and to consider that she ought to have better
aching than I could give her. It drew a many tears on both sides
en I commenced explaining my views to her; but what's right is
ght, and you can't neither by tears nor laughter do away with its
aracter.

So I took her hand in mine, and I went with her one day to the
eaf and Dumb establishment in London, and when the gentleman
me to speak to us, I says to him: "Now I'll tell you what I'll do
th you, Sir. I am nothing but a Cheap Jack, but of late years I
ve laid by for a rainy day notwithstanding. This is my only
ughter (adopted), and you can't produce a deafer nor a dumber.
ach her the most that can be taught her in the shortest separation
at can be named,—state the figure for it,—and I am game to put
e money down. I won't bate you a single farthing, Sir, but I'll put
wn the money here and now, and I'll thankfully throw you in a
und to take it. There!" The gentleman smiled, and then, "Well,
ell," says he, "I must first know what she has learned already.
ow do you communicate with her?" Then I showed him, and she
rote in printed writing many names of things and so forth; and we
ld some sprightly conversation, Sophy and me, about a little story
a book which the gentleman showed her, and which she was able
read. "This is most extraordinary," says the gentleman; "is it
ssible that you have been her only teacher?" "I have been her only
acher, Sir," I says, "besides herself." "Then," says the gentleman,
d more acceptable words was never spoken to me, "you're a clever
llow, and a good fellow." This he makes known to Sophy, who
sses his hands, clasps her own, and laughs and cries upon it.

We saw the gentleman four times in all, and when he took down
y name and asked how in the world it ever chanced to be Doctor,

it come out that he was own nephew by the sister's side, if you
believe me, to the very Doctor that I was called after. This made o
footing still easier, and he says to me:

"Now, Marigold, tell me what more do you want your adopte
daughter to know?"

"I want her, Sir, to be cut off from the world as little as can b
considering her deprivations, and therefore to be able to read wha
ever is wrote with perfect ease and pleasure."

"My good fellow," urges the gentleman, opening his eyes wid
"why I can't do that myself!"

I took his joke, and gave him a laugh (knowing by experien
how flat you fall without it), and I mended my words accordingl

"What do you mean to do with her afterwards?" asks the gentl
man, with a sort of a doubtful eye. "To take her about the country:

"In the cart, Sir, but only in the cart. She will live a private lif
you understand, in the cart. I should never think of bringing h
infirmities before the public. I wouldn't make a show of her for ar
money."

The gentleman nodded, and seemed to approve.

"Well," says he, "can you part with her for two years?"

"To do her that good,—yes, Sir."

"There's another question," says the gentleman, looking towar
her,—"can she part with you for two years?"

I don't know that it was a harder matter of itself (for the oth
was hard enough to me), but it was harder to get over. Howeve
she was pacified to it at last, and the separation betwixt us w
settled. How it cut up both of us when it took place, and when I le
her at the door in the dark of an evening, I don't tell. But I kno
this; remembering that night, I shall never pass that same establis
ment without a heartache and a swelling in the throat; and I couldn
put you up the best of lots in sight of it with my usual spirit,—n
not even the gun, nor the pair of spectacles,—for five hundred poun
reward from the Secretary of State for the Home Department, an
throw in the honour of putting my legs under his mahogany arte
wards.

Still, the loneliness that followed in the cart was not the old lon
liness, because there was a term put to it, however long to look fo
ward to; and because I could think, when I was anyways down, tha
she belonged to me and I belonged to her. Always planning for he
coming back, I bought in a few months' time another cart and wha
do you think I planned to do with it. I'll tell you. I planned to fit
up with shelves and books for her reading, and to have a seat in
where I could sit and see her read, and think that I had been her firs
teacher. Not hurrying over the job, I had the fittings knocked to
gether in contriving ways under my own inspection, and here was he
bed in a berth with curtain, and there was her reading table, and her
was her writing-desk, and elsewhere was her books in rows upon row
picters and no picters, bindings and no bindings, gilt-edged and plai
just as I could pick 'em up for her in lots up and down the country

orth and South and West and East, Winds liked best and winds liked
ast, Here and there and gone astray, Over the hills and far away.
nd when I had got together pretty well as many books as the cart
ould neatly hold, a new scheme come into my head, which, as it
rned out, kept my time and attention a good deal employed, and
elped me over the two years' stile.

Without being of an awaricious temper, I like to be the owner of
ings. I shouldn't wish, for instance, to go partners with yourself in
e Cheap Jack cart. It's not that I mistrust you, but that I'd rather
now it was mine. Similarly, very likely you'd rather know it was
ours. Well! A kind of a jealousy began to creep into my mind when
reflected that all those books would have been read by other people
ng before they was read by her. It seemed to take away from her
eing the owner of 'em like. In this way, the question got into my
ead Couldn't I have a book new-made express for her, which she
ould be the first to read?

It pleased me, that thought did; and as I never was a man to let a
ought sleep (you must wake up the whole family of thoughts you've
ot and burn their nightcaps, or you won't do in the Cheap Jack line).
set to work at it. Considering that I was in the habit of changing so
uch about the country, and that I should have to find out a literary
naracter here to make a deal with, and another literary character
ere to make a deal with, as opportunities presented, I hit on the
lan that this same book should be a general miscellaneous lot,—like
he razors, flat-iron, chronometer watch, dinner plates, rolling-pin,
nd looking-glass,—and shouldn't be offered as a single indiwidual
rticle, like the spectacles or the gun. When I had come to that con-
lusion, I came to another, which shall likewise be yours.

Often had I regretted that she never had heard me on the footboard,
nd that she never could hear me. It ain't that *I* am vain, but that *you*
on't like to put your own light under a bushel. What's the worth of
our reputation, if you can't convey the reason for it to the person
ou most wish to value it? Now I'll put it to you. Is it worth sixpence,
ppence, fourpence, threepence, twopence, a penny, a halfpenny, a
arthing? No, it ain't. Not worth a farthing. Very well, then. My
onclusion was that I would begin her book with some account of
ayself. So that, through reading a specimen or two of me on the foot-
oard, she might form an idea of my merits there. I was aware that
couldn't do myself justice. A man can't write his eye (at least *I*
on't know how to), nor yet can a man write his voice, nor the rate of
is talk, nor the quickness of his action, nor his general spicy way.
3ut he can write his turns of speech, when he is a public speaker,—
nd indeed I have heard that he very often does, before he speaks 'em.

Well! Having formed that resolution, then come the question of a
ame. How did I hammer that hot iron into shape? This way. The
nost difficult explanation I had ever had with her was, how I come to
e called Doctor, and yet was no Doctor. After all, I felt that I had
ailed of getting it correctly into her mind, with my utmost pains.
3ut trusting to her improvement in the two years, I thought that I

might trust to her understanding it when she should come to read
as put down by my own hand. Then I thought I would try a joke wit
her and watch how it took, by which of itself I might fully judge of h
understanding it. We had first discovered the mistake we had dropp
into, through her having asked me to prescribe for her when she ha
supposed me to be a Doctor in a medical point of view; so thinks
"Now if I give this book the name of my Prescriptions, and if sh
catches the idea that my only Prescriptions are for her amusemer
and interest,—to make her laugh in a pleasant way, or to make he
cry in a pleasant way,—it will be a delightful proof to both of us tha
we have got over our difficulty." It fell out to absolute perfectio
For when she saw the book, as I had it got up,—the printed an
pressed book,—lying on her desk in her cart, and saw the titl
DOCTOR MARIGOLD'S PRESCRIPTIONS, she looked at me for a momer
with astonishment, then fluttered the leaves, then broke out a laugh
ing in the charmingest way, then felt her pulse and shook her head
then turned the pages pretending to read them most attentive, an
then kissed the book to me, and put it to her bosom with both he
hands. I never was better pleased in all my life!

But let me not anticipate. (I take that expression out of a lot c
romances I bought for her. I never opened a single one of 'em—an
I have opened many—but I found the romancer saying "let me no
anticipate." Which being so, I wonder why he did anticipate, or wh
asked him to it.) Let me not, I say, anticipate. This same book too
up all my spare time. It was no play to get the other articles togethe
in the general miscellaneous lot, but when it come to my own article
There! I couldn't have believed the blotting, nor yet the buckling t
at it, nor the patience over it. Which again is like the footboard
The public have no idea.

At last it was done, and the two years' time was gone after all th
other time before it, and where it's all gone to, who knows? The new
cart was finished,—yellow outside, relieved with wermilion and bras
fittings,—the old horse was put in it, a new 'un and a boy being lai
on for the Cheap Jack cart, and I cleaned myself up to go and fetc
her. Bright cold weather it was, cart-chimneys smoking, carts pitche
private on a piece of waste ground over at Wandsworth, where yo
may see 'em from the Sou'western Railway when not upon the road
(Look out of the right-hand window going down.)

"Marigold," says the gentleman, giving his hand hearty, "I am
very glad to see you."

"Yet I have my doubts, Sir," says I, "if you can be half as glad t
see me as I am to see you."

"The time has appeared so long,—has it, Marigold?"

"I won't say that, Sir, considering its real length; but——"

"What a start, my good fellow!"

'Ah! I should think it was! Grown such a woman, so pretty, so
intelligent, so expressive! I knew then that she must be really like my
child, or I could never have known her, standing quiet by the door.'

"You are affected," says the gentleman in a kindly manner.

"I feel, Sir," says I, "that I am but a rough chap in a sleeved waistcoat."

"I feel," says the gentleman, "that it was you who raised her from misery and degradation, and brought her into communication with her kind. But why do we converse alone together, when we can converse so well with her? Address her in your own way."

"I am such a rough chap in a sleeved waistcoat, Sir," says I, "and she is such a graceful woman, and she stands so quiet at the door!"

"Try if she moves at the old sign," says the gentleman.

They had got it up together o' purpose to please me! For when I give her the old sign, she rushed to my feet, and dropped upon her knees, holding up her hands to me with pouring tears of love and joy; and when I took her hands and lifted her, she clasped me round the neck, and lay there; and I don't know what a fool I didn't make of myself, until we all three settled down into talking without sound, as if there was a something soft and pleasant spread over the whole world for us.

[A portion is here omitted from the text, having reference to the sketches contributed by other writers; but the reader will be pleased to have what follows retained in a note:

"Now I'll tell you what I am a-going to do with you. I am a-going to offer you the general miscellaneous lot, her own book, never read by anybody else but me, added to and completed by me after her first reading of it, eight-and-forty printed pages, six-and-ninety columns, Whiting's own work, Beaufort House to wit, thrown off by the steam-engine, best of paper, beautiful green wrapper, folded like clean linen come home from the clear-starcher's, and so exquisitely stitched that, regarded as a piece of needlework alone, it's better than the sampler of a seamstress undergoing a Competitive examination for Starvation before the Civil Service Commissioners—and I offer the lot for what? For eight pound? Not so much. For six pound? Less. For four pound. Why, I hardly expect you to believe me, but that's the sum. Four pound! The stitching alone cost half as much again. Here's forty-eight original pages, ninety-six original columns, for four pound. You want more for the money? take it. Three whole pages of advertisements of thrilling interest thrown in for nothing. Read 'em and believe 'em. More? My best wishes for your merry Christmases and your happy New Years, your long lives and your true prosperities. Worth twenty pound good if they are delivered as I send them. Remember! Here's a final prescription added, "To be taken for life," which will tell you how the cart broke down, and where the journey ended. You think Four Pound too much; And still you think so? Come! I'll tell you what then. Say Four Pence, and keep the secret."]

CHAPTER II

TO BE TAKEN WITH A GRAIN OF SALT

I HAVE always noticed a prevalent want of courage, even among persons of superior intelligence and culture, as to imparting their own psychological experiences when those have been of a strange sort. Almost all men are afraid that what they could relate in such wise would find no parallel or response in a listener's internal life, and might be suspected or laughed at. A truthful traveller, who should have seen some extraordinary creature in the likeness of a sea-serpent, would have no fear of mentioning it; but the same traveller, having had some singular presentiment, impulse, vagary of thought, vision (so called), dream, or other remarkable mental impression, would hesitate considerably before he would own to it. To this reticence I attribute much of the obscurity in which such subjects are involved. We do not habitually communicate our experiences of these subjective things as we do our experiences of objective creation. The consequence is, that the general stock of experience in this regard appears exceptional, and really is so, in respect of being miserably imperfect.

In what I am going to relate, I have no intention of setting up, opposing, or supporting, any theory whatever. I know the history of the Bookseller of Berlin, I have studied the case of the wife of a late Astronomer Royal as related by Sir David Brewster, and I have followed the minutest details of a much more remarkable case of Spectral Illusion occurring within my private circle of friends. It may be necessary to state as to this last, that the sufferer (a lady) was in no degree, however distant, related to me. A mistaken assumption on that head might suggest an explanation of a part of my own case,— but only a part,—which would be wholly without foundation. It cannot be referred to my inheritance of any developed peculiarity, nor had I ever before any at all similar experience, nor have I ever had any at all similar experience since.

It does not signify how many years ago, or how few, a certain murder was committed in England, which attracted great attention. We hear more than enough of murderers as they rise in succession to their atrocious eminence, and I would bury the memory of this particular brute, if I could, as his body was buried, in Newgate Jail. I purposely abstain from giving any direct clew to the criminal's individuality.

When the murder was first discovered, no suspicion fell—or I ought rather to say, for I cannot be too precise in my facts, it was nowhere publicly hinted that any suspicion fell—on the man who was afterwards brought to trial. As no reference was at that time made to him in the newspapers, it is obviously impossible that any description of him can at that time have been given in the newspapers. It is essential that this fact be remembered.

Unfolding at breakfast my morning paper, containing the account
that first discovery, I found it to be deeply interesting, and I read
with close attention. I read it twice, if not three times. The discov-
y had been made in a bedroom, and, when I laid down the paper, I
as aware of a flash—rush—flow—I do not know what to call it,—no
ord I can find is satisfactorily descriptive,—in which I seemed to
e that bedroom passing through my room, like a picture impossibly
ainted on a running river. Though almost instantaneous in its
assing, it was perfectly clear; so clear that I distinctly, and with a
nse of relief, observed the absence of the dead body from the bed.

It was in no romantic place that I had this curious sensation, but
chambers in Piccadilly, very near to the corner of St. James's-street.
: was entirely new to me. I was in my easy-chair at the moment, and
e sensation was accompanied with a peculiar shiver which started
e chair from its position. (But it is to be noted that the chair ran
sily on castors.) I went to one of the windows (there are two in the
om, and the room is on the second floor) to refresh my eyes with the
oving objects down in Piccadilly. It was a bright autumn morning,
d the street was sparkling and cheerful. The wind was high. As I
oked out, it brought down from the Park a quantity of fallen leaves,
hich a gust took, and whirled into a spiral pillar. As the pillar fell
d the leaves dispersed, I saw two men on the opposite side of the
ay, going from West to East. They were one behind the other. The
remost man often looked back over his shoulder. The second man
llowed him, at a distance of some thirty paces, with his right
and menacingly raised. First, the singularity and steadiness of
is threatening gesture in so public a thoroughfare attracted my
tention; and next, the more remarkable circumstance that nobody
eded it. Both men threaded their way among the other passengers
ith a smoothness hardly consistent even with the action of walking
1 a pavement; and no single creature, that I could see, gave them
ace, touched them, or looked after them. In passing before my
indows, they both stared up at me. I saw their two faces very dis-
nctly, and I knew that I could recognise them anywhere. Not that I
onsciously noticed anything very remarkable in either face, except
at the man who went first had an unusually lowering appearance,
d that the face of the man who followed him was of the colour of
npure wax.

I am a bachelor, and my valet and his wife constitute my whole
stablishment. My occupation is in a certain Branch Bank, and I
ish that my duties as head of a Department were as light as they are
opularly supposed to be. They kept me in town that autumn, when
stood in need of change. I was not ill, but I was not well. My reader
to make the most that can be reasonably made of my feeling jaded,
aving a depressing sense upon me of a monotonous life, and being
slightly dyspeptic." I am assured by my renowned doctor that my
al state of health at that time justifies no stronger description, and
quote his own from his written answer to my request for it.

As the circumstances of the murder, gradually unravelling, took

stronger and stronger possession of the public mind, I kept the
away from mine by knowing as little about them as was possible
the midst of the universal excitement. But I knew that a verdict
Wilful Murder had been found against the suspected murderer, a
that he had been committed to Newgate for trial. I also knew th
his trial had been postponed over one Sessions of the Centr
Criminal Court, on the ground of general prejudice and want of tin
for the preparation of the defence. I may further have known, but
believe I did not, when, or about when, the Sessions to which his tri
stood postponed would come on.

My sitting-room, bedroom, and dressing-room, are all on one floc
With the last there is no communication but through the bedroo
True, there is a door in it, once communicating with the staircas
but a part of the fitting of my bath has been,—and had then been f
some years—fixed across it. At the same period, and as a part of tl
same arrangement, the door had been nailed up and canvased over.

I was standing in my bedroom late one night, giving some dire
tions to my servant before he went to bed. My face was towards tl
only available door of communication with the dressing-room, and
was closed. My servant's back was towards that door. While I w
speaking to him, I saw it open, and a man look in, who very earnest
and mysteriously beckoned to me. That man was the man who ha
gone second of the two along Piccadilly, and whose face was tl
colour of impure wax.

The figure, having beckoned, drew back, and closed the doc
With no longer pause than was made by my crossing the bedroom,
opened the dressing-room door, and looked in. I had a lighted cand
already in my hand. I felt no inward expectation of seeing the figure
the dressing-room, and I did not see it there.

Conscious that my servant stood amazed, I turned round to hir
and said: "Derrick, could you believe that in my cool senses I fancie
I saw a——" As I there laid my hand upon his breast, with a sudde
start he trembled violently, and said, "O Lord, yes, Sir! A dead ma
beckoning!"

Now I do not believe that this John Derrick, my trusty and attache
servant for more than twenty years, had any impression whatev
of having seen any such figure, until I touched him. The change
him was so startling, when I touched him, that I fully believe
derived his impression in some occult manner from me at tha
instant.

I bade John Derrick bring some brandy, and I gave him a drar
and was glad to take one myself. Of what had preceded that night
phenomenon, I told him not a single word. Reflecting on it, I w
absolutely certain that I had never seen that face before, except o
the one occasion in Piccadilly. Comparing its expression when bec
oning at the door with its expression when it had stared up at me as
stood at my window, I came to the conclusion that on the first occ
sion it had sought to fasten itself upon my memory, and that on tl
second occasion it had made sure of being immediately remembere

I was not very comfortable that night, though I felt a certainty, difficult to explain, that the figure would not return. At daylight I fell into a heavy sleep, from which I was awakened by John Derrick's coming to my bedside with a paper in his hand.

This paper, it appeared, had been the subject of an altercation at the door between its bearer and my servant. It was a summons to me to serve upon a Jury at the forthcoming Sessions of the Central Criminal Court at the Old Bailey. I had never before been summoned on such a Jury, as John Derrick well knew. He believed—I am not certain at this hour whether with reason or otherwise—that that class of Jurors were customarily chosen on a lower qualification than mine, and he had at first refused to accept the summons. The man who served it had taken the matter very coolly. He had said that my attendance or non-attendance was nothing to him; there the summons was; and I should deal with it at my own peril, and not at his.

For a day or two I was undecided whether to respond to this call, or take no notice of it. I was not conscious of the slightest mysterious bias, influence, or attraction, one way or other. Of that I am as strictly sure as of every other statement that I make here. Ultimately I decided, as a break in the monotony of my life, that I would go.

The appointed morning was a raw morning in the month of November. There was a dense brown fog in Piccadilly, and it became positively black and in the last degree oppressive East of Temple Bar. I found the passages and staircases of the Court-House flaringly lighted with gas, and the Court itself similarly illuminated. I *think* that, until I was conducted by officers into the Old Court and saw its crowded state, I did not know that the Murderer was to be tried that day. I *think* that, until I was so helped into the Old Court with considerable difficulty, I did not know into which of the two Courts sitting my summons would take me. But this must not be received as a positive assertion, for I am not completely satisfied in my mind on either point.

I took my seat in the place appropriated to Jurors in waiting, and I looked about the Court as well as I could through the cloud of fog and breath that was heavy in it. I noticed the black vapour hanging like a murky curtain outside the great windows, and I noticed the stifled sound of wheels on the straw or tan that was littered in the street; also, the hum of the people gathered there, which a shrill whistle, or a louder song or hail than the rest, occasionally pierced. Soon afterwards the Judges, two in number, entered, and took their seats. The buzz in the Court was awfully hushed. The direction was given to put the Murderer to the bar. He appeared there. And in that same instant I recognised in him the first of the two men who had gone down Piccadilly.

If my name had been called then, I doubt if I could have answered to it audibly. But it was called about sixth or eighth in the panel, and I was by that time able to say "Here!" Now, observe. As I stepped into the box, the prisoner, who had been looking on attentively, but with no sign of concern, became violently agitated, and beckoned to his

attorney. The prisoner's wish to challenge me was so manifest, that
it occasioned a pause, during which the attorney, with his hand upon
the dock, whispered with his client, and shook his head. I afterwards
had it from that gentleman, that the prisoner's first affrighted words
to him were, *"At all hazards, challenge that man!"* But that, as he
would give no reason for it, and admitted that he had not even known
my name until he heard it called and I appeared, it was not done.

Both on the ground already explained, that I wish to avoid reviving
the unwholesome memory of that Murderer, and also because a detailed account of his long trial is by no means indispensable to my
narrative, I shall confine myself to such incidents in the ten days and
nights during which we, the Jury, were kept together, as directly
bear on my own curious personal experience. It is in that, and not in
the Murderer, that I seek to interest my reader. It is to that, and not
to a page of the Newgate Calendar, that I beg attention.

I was chosen Foreman of the Jury. On the second morning of the
trial, after evidence had been taken for two hours (I heard the church
clocks strike), happening to cast my eyes over my brother jurymen,
I found an inexplicable difficulty in counting them. I counted them
several times, yet always with the same difficulty. In short, I made
them one too many.

I touched the brother juryman whose place was next me, and I
whispered to him, "Oblige me by counting us." He looked surprised
by the request, but turned his head and counted. "Why," says he,
suddenly, "we are Thirt—; but no, it's not possible. No. We are
twelve."

According to my counting that day, we were always right in detail,
but in the gross we were always one too many. There was no appearance—no figure—to account for it; but I had now an inward fore-
shadowing of the figure that was surely coming.

The Jury were housed at the London Tavern. We all slept in one
large room on separate tables, and we were constantly in the charge
and under the eye of the officer sworn to hold us in safe-keeping. I
see no reason for suppressing the real name of that officer. He was
intelligent, highly polite, and obliging, and (I was glad to hear) much
respected in the City. He had an agreeable presence, good eyes,
enviable black whiskers, and a fine sonorous voice. His name was
Mr. Harker.

When we turned into our twelve beds at night, Mr. Harker's bed
was drawn across the door. On the night of the second day, not being
disposed to lie down, and seeing Mr. Harker sitting on his bed, I went
and sat beside him, and offered him a pinch of snuff. As Mr. Harker's
hand touched mine in taking it from my box, a peculiar shiver crossed
him, and he said, "Who is this?"

Following Mr. Harker's eyes, and looking along the room, I saw
again the figure I expected,—the second of the two men who had
gone down Piccadilly. I rose, and advanced a few steps; then stopped,
and looked round at Mr. Harker. He was quite unconcerned, laughed,
and said in a pleasant way, "I thought for a moment we had a thir-

teenth juryman, without a bed. But I see it is the moonlight."

Making no revelation to Mr. Harker, but inviting him to take a walk with me to the end of the room, I watched what the figure did. It stood for a few moments by the bedside of each of my eleven brother jurymen, close to the pillow. It always went to the right-hand side of the bed, and always passed out crossing the foot of the next bed. It seemed, from the action of the head, merely to look down pensively at each recumbent figure. It took no notice of me, or of my bed, which was that nearest to Mr. Harker's. It seemed to go out where the moonlight came in, through a high window, as by an aërial flight of stairs.

Next morning at breakfast, it appeared that everybody present had dreamed of the murdered man last night, except myself, and Mr. Harker.

I now felt convinced that the second man who had gone down Piccadilly was the murdered man (so to speak), as if it had been borne into my comprehension by his immediate testimony. But even this took place, and in a manner for which I was not at all prepared.

On the fifth day of the trial, when the case for the prosecution was drawing to a close, a miniature of the murdered man, missing from his bedroom upon the discovery of the deed, and afterwards found in a hiding-place where the Murderer had been seen digging, was put in evidence. Having been identified by the witness under examination, it was handed up to the Bench, and thence handed down to be inspected by the Jury. As an officer in a black gown was making his way with it across to me, the figure of the second man who had gone down Piccadilly impetuously started from the crowd, caught the miniature from the officer, and gave it to me with his own hands, at the same time saying, in a low and hollow tone,—before I saw the miniature, which was in a locket,—"*I was younger then, and my face was not then drained of blood.*" It also came between me and the brother juryman to whom I would have given the miniature, and between him and the brother juryman to whom he would have given it, and so passed it on through the whole of our number, and back into my possession. Not one of them, however, detected this.

At table, and generally when we were shut up together in Mr. Harker's custody, we had from the first naturally discussed the day's proceedings a good deal. On that fifth day, the case for the prosecution being closed, and we having that side of the question in a completed shape before us, our discussion was more animated and serious. Among our number was a vestry-man,—the densest idiot I have ever seen at large,—who met the plainest evidence with the most preposterous objections, and who was sided with by two flabby parochial parasites; all the three impanelled from a district so delivered over to Fever that they ought to have been upon their own trial for five hundred Murders. When these mischievous blockheads were at their loudest, which was towards midnight, while some of us were already preparing for bed, I again saw the murdered man. He stood grimly behind them, beckoning to me. On my going towards them, and striking into the conversation, he immediately retired. This was the beginning of a separate series of appearances, confined to that long room in which *we* were confined. Whenever a knot of my brother jurymen laid their heads together, I saw the head of the murdered man among theirs. Whenever their comparison of notes was going against him, he would solemnly and irresistibly beckon to me.

It will be borne in mind that down to the production of the miniature, on the fifth day of the trial, I had never seen the Appearance in Court. Three changes occurred now that we entered on the case for the defence. Two of them I will mention together, first. The figure was now in Court continually, and it never there addressed itself to me, but always to the person who was speaking at the time. For instance: the throat of the murdered man had been cut straight across. In the opening speech for the defence, it was suggested that the deceased might have cut his own throat. At that very moment, the figure, with its throat in the dreadful condition referred to (this it had concealed before), stood at the speaker's elbow, motioning across and across its windpipe, now with the right hand, now with the left, vigorously suggesting to the speaker himself the impossibility of such a wound having been self-inflicted by either hand. For another instance: a witness to character, a woman, deposed to the prisoner's being the most amiable of mankind. The figure at that instant stood on the floor before her, looking her full in the face, and pointing out the prisoner's evil countenance with an extended arm and an outstretched finger.

The third change now to be added impressed me strongly as the most marked and striking of all. I do not theorise upon it; I accurately state it, and there leave it. Although the Appearance was not itself perceived by those whom it addressed, its coming close to such persons was invariably attended by some trepidation or disturbance on their part. It seemed to me as if it were prevented, by laws to which I was not amenable, from fully revealing itself to others, and yet as if it could invisibly, dumbly, and darkly overshadow their minds. When the leading counsel for the defence suggested that hypothesis of suicide, and the figure stood at the learned gentleman's elbow, frightfully sawing at its severed throat, it is undeniable that the counsel faltered in his speech, lost for a few seconds the thread of his ingenious discourse, wiped his forehead with his handkerchief, and turned extremely pale. When the witness to character was confronted by the Appearance, her eyes most certainly did follow the direction of its pointed finger, and rest in great hesitation and trouble upon the prisoner's face. Two additional illustrations will suffice. On the eighth day of the trial, after a pause which was every day made early in the afternoon for a few minutes' rest and refreshment, I came back into court with the rest of the Jury some little time before the return of the Judges. Standing up in the box and looking about me, I thought the figure was not there, until, chancing to raise my eyes to the gallery, I saw it bending forward, and leaning over a very decent woman, as if to assure itself whether the Judges had resumed their seats or not.

ımediately afterwards that woman screamed, fainted, and was rried out. So with the venerable, sagacious, and patient Judge who nducted the trial. When the case was over, and he settled himself d his papers to sum up, the murdered man, entering by the Judges' ›or, advanced to his Lordship's desk, and looked eagerly over his ›oulder at the pages of his notes which he was turning. A change me over his Lordship's face; his hand stopped; the peculiar shiver, at I knew so well, passed over him; he faltered, "Excuse me, ntlemen, for a few moments. I am somewhat oppressed by the tiated air"; and did not recover until he had drunk a glass of water.

Through all the monotony of six of those interminable ten days,— e same Judges and others on the bench, the same Murderer in the ›ck, the same lawyers at the table, the same tones of question and swer rising to the roof of the Court, the same scratching of the ıdge's pen, the same ushers going in and out, the same lights kindled the same hour when there had been any natural light of day, the me foggy curtain outside the great windows when it was foggy, the me rain pattering and dripping when it was rainy, the same foot-ırks of turnkeys and prisoner day after day on the same sawdust, e same keys locking and unlocking the same heavy doors,—through . the wearisome monotony which made me feel as if I had been ›reman of the Jury for a vast period of time, and Piccadilly had ›urished coevally with Babylon, the murdered man never lost one ıce of his distinctness in my eyes, nor was he at any moment less stinct than anybody else. I must not omit, as a matter of fact, that ıever once saw the Appearance which I call by the name of the ırdered man look at the Murderer. Again and again I wondered, ¸hy does he not?" But he never did.

Nor did he look at me, after the production of the miniature, until e last closing minutes of the trial arrived. We retired to consider, at ¸en minutes before ten at night. The idiotic vestryman and his two ›ochial parasites gave us so much trouble that we twice returned to Court to beg to have certain extracts from the Judge's notes re-ıd. Nine of us had not the smallest doubt about those passages, ither, I believe, had any one in Court; the dunderheaded trium-rate, however, having no idea but obstruction, disputed them for at very reason. At length we prevailed, and finally the Jury re-rned into Court at ten minutes past twelve.

The murdered man at that time stood directly opposite the Jury-x, on the other side of the Court. As I took my place, his eyes rested me with great attention; he seemed satisfied, and slowly shook a ›at grey veil, which he carried on his arm for the first time, over ; head and whole form. As I gave in our verdict, "Guilty," the veil llapsed, all was gone, and his place was empty.

The Murderer, being asked by the Judge, according to usage, ıether he had anything to say before sentence of Death should be ssed upon him, indistinctly muttered something which was scribed in the leading newspapers of the following day as "a few mbling, incoherent, and half-audible words, in which he was

understood to complain that he had not had a fair trial, because th
Foreman of the Jury was prepossessed against him." The remarkab
declaration that he really made was this: "*My Lord, I knew I was*
doomed man, when the Foreman of my Jury came into the box. My Lord,
knew he would never let me off, because, before I was taken, he someho
got to my bedside in the night, woke me, and put a rope round my neck.

CHAPTER III

TO BE TAKEN FOR LIFE

So every item of my plan was crowned with success. Our reunited li
was more than all that we had looked forward to. Content and joy wei
with us as the wheels of the two carts went round, and the san
stopped with us when the two carts stopped. I was as pleased and
proud as a Pug-Dog with his muzzle black-leaded for a evening part
and his tail extra curled by machinery.

But I had left something out of my calculations. Now, what had
left out? To help you to guess I'll say, a figure. Come. Make a gue
and guess right. Nought? No. Nine? No. Eight? No. Seven? N
Six? No. Five? No. Four? No. Three? No. Two? No. One? No. No
I'll tell you what I'll do with you. I'll say it's another sort of figu
altogether. There. Why then, says you, it's a mortal figure. No, n
yet a mortal figure. By such means you get yourself penned into
corner, and you can't help guessing a *immortal* figure. That's abo
it. Why didn't you say so sooner?

Yes. It was a immortal figure that I had altogether left out of n
calculations. Neither man's, nor woman's, but a child's. Girl's
boy's? Boy's. "I, says the sparrow, with my bow and arrow." Now yo
have got it.

We were down at Lancaster, and I had done two nights more tha
fair average business (though I cannot in honour recommend them
a quick audience) in the open square there, near the end of the stre
where Mr. Sly's Kings' Arms and Royal Hotel stands. Mim's trave
ling giant, otherwise Pickleson, happened at the self-same time to I
trying it on in the town. The genteel lay was adopted with him. N
hint of a van. Green baize alcove leading up to Pickleson in a Auctic
Room. Printed poster, "Free list suspended, with the exception
that proud boast of an enlightened country, a free press. Schoc
admitted by private arrangement. Nothing to raise a blush in t
cheek of youth or shock the most fastidious." Mim swearing mc
horrible and terrific, in a pink calico pay-place at the slackness of t
public. Serious handbill in the shops, importing that it was all b
impossible to come to a right understanding of the history of Dav
without seeing Pickleson.

I went to the Auction Room in question, and I found it entire
empty of everything but echoes and mouldiness, with the sing

xception of Pickleson on a piece of red drugget. This suited my
urpose, as I wanted a private and confidential word with him, which
vas: "Pickleson. Owing much happiness to you, I put you in my will
or a fypunnote; but, to save trouble, here's fourpunten down, which
nay equally suit your views, and let us so conclude the transaction."
Pickleson, who up to that remark had had the dejected appearance of
a long Roman rushlight that couldn't anyhow get lighted, brightened
up at his top extremity, and made his acknowledgments in a way
which (for him) was parliamentary eloquence. He likewise did add,
hat, having ceased to draw as a Roman, Mim had made proposals for
his going in as a conwerted Indian Giant worked upon by the Dairy-
nan's Daughter. This, Pickleson, having no acquaintance with the
fact named after that young woman, and not being willing to couple
ag with his serious views, had declined to do, thereby leading to
vords and the total stoppage of the unfortunate young man's beer.
All of which, during the whole of the interview, was confirmed by the
ferocious growling of Mim down below in the pay-place, which shook
he giant like a leaf.

But what was to the present point in the remarks of the travelling
iant, otherwise Pickleson, was this: "Doctor Marigold,"—I give his
words without a hope of conweying their feebleness,—"who is the
trange young man that hangs about your carts?"—"The strange
young *man*?" I gives him back, thinking that he meant her, and his
anguid circulation had dropped a syllable. "Doctor," he returns,
with a pathos calculated to draw a tear from even a manly eye, "I am
weak, but not so weak yet as that I don't know my words. I repeat
hem, Doctor. The strange young man." It then appeared that Pickle-
on, being forced to stretch his legs (not that they wanted it) only
t times when he couldn't be seen for nothing, to wit in the dead of
he night and towards daybreak, had twice seen hanging about my
arts, in that same town of Lancaster where I had been only two
nights, this same unknown young man.

It put me rather out of sorts. What it meant as to particulars I no
nore foreboded then than you forebode now, but it put me rather out
of sorts. Howsoever, I made light of it to Pickleson, and I took leave
of Pickleson, advising him to spend his legacy in getting up his
tamina, and to continue to stand by his religion. Towards morning I
kept a look out for the strange young man. He was well dressed and
well looking. He loitered very nigh my carts, watching them like as if
he was taking care of them, and soon after daybreak turned and went
away. I sent a hail after him, but he never started or looked round, or
ook the smallest notice.

We left Lancaster within an hour or two, on our way towards
Carlisle. Next morning, at daybreak, I looked out again for the strange
young man. I did not see him. But next morning I looked out again,
and there he was once more. I sent another hail after him, but as
before he gave not the slightest sign of being anyways disturbed.
This put a thought into my head. Acting on it I watched him in
different manners and at different times not necessary to enter into,

till I found that this strange young man was deaf and dumb.

The discovery turned me over, because I knew that a part of tha establishment where she had been was allotted to young men (som of them well off) and I thought to myself, "If she favours him, wher am I? and where is all that I have worked and planned for?" Hopin —I must confess to the selfishness—that she might *not* favour him, set myself to find out. At last I was by accident present at a meetin between them in the open air, looking on leaning behind a fir-tre without their knowing of it. It was a moving meeting for all th three parties concerned. I knew every syllable that passed betwee them as well as they did. I listened with my eyes, which had come t be as quick and true with deaf and dumb conversation as my ear with the talk of people that can speak. He was a-going out to Chin as clerk in a merchant's house, which his father had been before him He was in circumstances to keep a wife, and he wanted her to marr him and go along with him. She persisted, no. He asked if she didn' love him. Yes, she loved him dearly, dearly; but she could neve disappoint her beloved, good, noble, generous, and I don't-know what-all father (meaning me, the Cheap Jack in the sleeved waist coat), and she would stay with him, Heaven bless him! though it wa to break her heart. Then she cried most bitterly, and that made u my mind.

While my mind had been in an unsettled state about her favourin this young man, I had felt that unreasonable towards Pickleson, tha it was well for him he had got his legacy down. For I often thought "If it hadn't been for this same weak-minded giant, I might neve have come to trouble my head and wex my soul about the youn man." But, once that I knew she loved him,—once that I had seen he weep for him,—it was a different thing. I made it right in my min with Pickleson on the spot, and I shook myself together to do wha was right by all.

She had left the young man by that time (for it took a few minute to get me thoroughly well shook together), and the young man wa leaning against another of the fir-trees,—of which there was a cluster —with his face upon his arm. I touched him on the back. Looking u and seeing me, he says, in our deaf-and-dumb talk, "Do not b angry."

"I am not angry, good boy. I am your friend. Come with me."

I left him at the foot of the steps of the Library Cart, and I wen up alone. She was drying her eyes.

"You have been crying, my dear."

"Yes, father."

"Why?"

"A headache."

"Not a heartache?"

"I said a headache, father."

"Doctor Marigold must prescribe for that headache."

She took up the book of my Prescriptions, and held it up with forced smile; but seeing me keep still and look earnest, she softly lai own again, and her eyes were very attentive.

"The Prescription is not there, Sophy."

"Where is it?"

"Here, my dear."

I brought her young husband in, and I put her hand in his, and my only farther words to both of them were these: "Doctor Marigold's last Prescription. To be taken for life." After which I bolted.

When the wedding came off, I mounted a coat (blue, and bright buttons), for the first and last time in all my days, and I gave Sophy away with my own hand. There were only us three and the gentleman who had had charge of her for those two years. I gave the wedding dinner of four in the Library Cart. Pigeon-pie, a leg of pickled pork, a pair of fowls, and suitable garden stuff. The best of drinks. I give them a speech, and the gentleman give us a speech, and all our jokes told, and the whole went off like a sky-rocket. In the course of the entertainment I explained to Sophy that I should keep the Library Cart as my travelling-cart when not upon the road, and that I should keep all her books for her just as they stood, till she come back to claim them. So she went to China with her young husband, and it was a parting sorrowful and heavy, and I got the boy I had another service; and so of old, when my child and wife were gone, I went plodding along alone, with my whip over my shoulder, at the old horse's head.

Sophy wrote me many letters, and I wrote her many letters. About the end of the first year she sent me one in an unsteady hand: "Dearest father, not a week ago I had a darling little daughter, but I am so well that they let me write these words to you. Dearest and best father, I hope my child may not be deaf and dumb, but I do not yet know." When I wrote back, I hinted the question; but as Sophy never answered that question, I felt it to be a sad one, and I never repeated it. For a long time our letters were regular, but then they got irregular, through Sophy's husband being moved to another station, and through my being always on the move. But we were in one another's thoughts, I was equally sure, letters or no letters.

Five years, odd months, had gone since Sophy went away. I was still the King of the Cheap Jacks, and at a greater height of popularity than ever. I had had a first-rate autumn of it, and on the twenty-third of December, one thousand eight hundred and sixty-four, I found myself at Uxbridge, Middlesex, clean sold out. So I jogged up to London with the old horse, light and easy, to have my Christmas-eve and Christmas-day alone by the fire in the Library Cart, and then to buy a regular new stock of goods all round, to sell 'em again and get the money.

I am a neat hand at cookery, and I'll tell you what I knocked up for my Christmas-eve dinner in the Library Cart. I knocked up a beefsteak-pudding for one, with two kidneys, a dozen oysters, and a couple of mushrooms thrown in. It's a pudding to put a man in good humour with everything, except the two bottom buttons of his waistcoat. Having relished that pudding and cleared away, I turned the lamp low, and sat down by the light of the fire, watching it as it shone upon the backs of Sophy's books.

Sophy's books so brought up Sophy's self, that I saw her touchi
face quite plainly, before I dropped off dozing by the fire. This m
be a reason why Sophy, with her deaf-and-dumb child in her arr
seemed to stand silent by me all through my nap. I was on the roa
off the road, in all sorts of places, North and South and West a
East, Winds liked best and winds liked least, Here and there a
gone astray, Over the hills and far away, and still she stood silent
me, with her silent child in her arms. Even when I woke with a sta
she seemed to vanish, as if she had stood by me in that very place or
a single instant before.

I had started at a real sound, and the sound was on the steps of t
cart. It was the light hurried tread of a child, coming clambering u
That tread of a child had once been so familiar to me, that for hal
moment I believed I was a-going to see a little ghost.

But the touch of a real child was laid upon the outer handle of t
door, and the handle turned, and the door opened a little way, and
real child peeped in. A bright little comely girl with large dark ey

Looking full at me, the tiny creature took off her mite of a stra
hat, and a quantity of dark curls fell all about her face. Then s
opened her lips, and said in a pretty voice,

"Grandfather!"

"Ah, my God!" I cries out. "She can speak!"

"Yes, dear grandfather. And I am to ask you whether there w
ever any one that I remind you of?"

In a moment Sophy was round my neck, as well as the child, a
her husband was a-wringing my hand with his face hid, and we all h
to shake ourselves together before we could get over it. And when
did begin to get over it, and I saw the pretty child a-talking, pleas
and quick and eager and busy, to her mother, in the signs that I h
first taught her mother, the happy and yet pitying tears fell rolli
down my face.

MUGBY JUNCTION

IN FOUR CHAPTERS

[1866]

CHAPTER I

BARBOX BROTHERS

I

uard! What place is this?"

'Mugby Junction, Sir."

'A windy place!"

'Yes, it mostly is, Sir."

'And looks comfortless indeed!"

'Yes, it generally does, Sir."

'Is it a rainy night still?"

'Pours, Sir."

'Open the door. I'll get out."

'You'll have, Sir," said the guard, glistening with drops of wet, d looking at the tearful face of his watch by the light of his lantern the traveller descended, "three minutes here."

'More, I think.—For I am not going on."

'Thought you had a through ticket, Sir?"

'So I have, but I shall sacrifice the rest of it. I want my luggage."

'Please to come to the van and point it out, Sir. Be good enough to k very sharp, Sir. Not a moment to spare."

The guard hurried to the luggage van, and the traveller hurried er him. The guard got into it, and the traveller looked into it.

'Those two large black portmanteaus in the corner where your light nes. Those are mine."

'Name upon 'em, Sir?"

'Barbox Brothers."

'Stand clear, Sir, if you please. One. Two. Right!" Lamp waved. nal lights ahead already changing. Shriek from engine. Train le.

'Mugby Junction!" said the traveller, pulling up the woollen ffler round his throat with both hands. "At past three o'clock of a pestuous morning! So!"

He spoke to himself. There was no one else to speak to. Perhaps, ugh there had been any one else to speak to, he would have pre-

ferred to speak to himself. Speaking to himself he spoke to a m
within five years of fifty either way, who had turned grey too so
like a neglected fire; a man of pondering habit, brooding carriage
the head, and suppressed internal voice; a man with many indicatio
on him of having been much alone.

He stood unnoticed on the dreary platform, except by the rain a
by the wind. Those two vigilant assailants made a rush at him. "Ve
well," said he, yielding. "It signifies nothing to me to what quarte
turn my face."

Thus, at Mugby Junction, at past three o'clock of a tempestuo
morning, the traveller went where the weather drove him.

Not but what he could make a stand when he was so minded, f
coming to the end of the roofed shelter (it is of considerable extent
Mugby Junction), and looking out upon the dark night, with a
darker spirit-wing of storm beating its wild way through it, he fac
about, and held his own as ruggedly in the difficult direction as he h
held it in the easier one. Thus, with a steady step, the traveller we
up and down, up and down, up and down seeking nothing and find
it.

A place replete with shadowy shapes, this Mugby Junction in
black hours of the four-and-twenty. Mysterious goods trains, cover
with palls and gliding on like vast weird funerals, conveying the
selves guiltily away from the presence of the few lighted lamps, a
their freight had come to a secret and unlawful end. Half-miles
coal pursuing in a Detective manner, following when they le
stopping when they stop, backing when they back. Red-hot emb
showering out upon the ground, down this dark avenue, and down
other, as if torturing fires were being raked clear; concurrent
shrieks and groans and grinds invading the ear, as if the tortur
were at the height of their suffering. Iron-barred cages full of cat
jangling by midway, the drooping beasts with horns entangled, e
frozen with terror, and mouths too: at least they have long icicles
what seem so) hanging from their lips. Unknown languages in
air, conspiring in red, green, and white characters. An earthqua
accompanied with thunder and lightning, going up express to Lond
Now, all quiet, all rusty, wind and rain in possession, lamps ext
guished, Mugby Junction dead and indistinct, with its robe drawn o
its head, like Cæsar.

Now, too, as the belated traveller plodded up and down, a sha
owy train went by in the gloom which was no other than the train
a life. From whatsoever intangible deep cutting or dark tunnel
emerged, here it came, unsummoned and unannounced, steali
upon him, and passing away into obscurity. Here mournfully went
a child who had never had a childhood or known a parent, inseparat
from a youth with a bitter sense of his namelessness, coupled to
man the enforced business of whose best years had been distaste
and oppressive, linked to an ungrateful friend, dragging after him
woman once beloved. Attendant, with many a clank and wrenc
were lumbering cares, dark meditations, huge dim disappointmen

ionotonous years, a long jarring line of the discords of a solitary and
nhappy existence.

"—Yours, Sir?"

The traveller recalled his eyes from the waste into which they had
een staring, and fell back a step or so under the abruptness, and
erhaps the chance appropriateness, of the question.

"Oh! My thoughts were not here for the moment. Yes. Yes. Those
wo portmanteaus are mine. Are you a Porter?"

"On Porter's wages, Sir. But I am Lamps."

The traveller looked a little confused.

"Who did you say you are?"

"Lamps, Sir," showing an oily cloth in his hand, as further ex-
lanation.

"Surely, surely. Is there any hotel or tavern here?"

"Not exactly here, Sir. There is a Refreshment Room here, but
——" Lamps, with a mighty serious look, gave his head a warning
oll that plainly added—"but it's a blessed circumstance for you that
t's not open."

"You couldn't recommend it, I see, if it was available?"

"Ask your pardon, Sir. If it was——?"

"Open?"

"It ain't my place, as a paid servant of the company, to give my
pinion on any of the company's toepics,"—he pronounced it more
ke toothpicks,—"beyond lamp-ile and cottons," returned Lamps
n a confidential tone; "but, speaking as a man, I wouldn't recom-
nend my father (if he was to come to life again) to go and try how
e'd be treated at the Refreshment Room. Not speaking as a man,
o, I would *not*."

The traveller nodded conviction. "I suppose I can put up in the
own? There is a town here?" For the traveller (though a stay-at-
ome compared with most travellers) had been, like many others,
arried on the steam winds and the iron tides through that Junction
efore without having ever, as one might say, gone ashore there.

"Oh yes, there's a town, Sir! Anyways, there's town enough to put
p in. "But," following the glance of the other at his luggage, "this
s a very dead time of the night with us, Sir. The deadest time. I
ight a'most call it our deadest and buriedest time."

"No porters about?"

"Well, Sir, you see," returned Lamps, confidential again, "they
n general goes off with the gas. That's how it is. And they seem to
ave overlooked you, through your walking to the furder end of the
latform. But, in about twelve minutes or so, she may be up."

"Who may be up?"

"The three forty-two, Sir. She goes off in a sidin' till the Up X
asses, and then she"—here an air of hopeful vagueness pervaded
amps—"does all as lays in her power."

"I doubt if I comprehend the arrangement."

"I doubt if anybody do, Sir. She's a Parliamentary, Sir. And, you
ee, a Parliamentary, or a Skirmishun——"

"Do you mean an Excursion?"

"That's it, Sir.—A Parliamentary or a Skirmishun, she mostl *doos* go off into a sidin'. But, when she *can* get a chance, she's whistle out of it, and she's whistled up into doin' all as,"—Lamps agai wore the air of a highly sanguine man who hoped for the best,—"a as lays in her power."

He then explained that porters on duty, being required to be i attendance on the Parliamentary matron in question, would doubt less turn up with the gas. In the meantime, if the gentleman woul not very much object to the smell of lamp-oil, and would accept th warmth of his little room —— The gentleman, being by this time ver cold, instantly closed with the proposal.

A greasy little cabin it was, suggestive, to the sense of smell, of cabin in a Whaler. But there was a bright fire burning in its rust grate, and on the floor there stood a wooden stand of newly trimme and lighted lamps, ready for carriage service. They made a brigh show, and their light, and the warmth, accounted for the popularit of the room, as borne witness to by many impressions of velvetee trousers on a form by the fire, and many rounded smears and smudge of stooping velveteen shoulders on the adjacent wall. Various untid shelves accommodated a quantity of lamps and oil-cans, and also fragrant collection of what looked like the pocket-handkerchiefs c the whole lamp family.

As Barbox Brothers (so to call the traveller on the warranty of hi luggage) took his seat upon the form, and warmed his now unglove hands at the fire, he glanced aside at a little deal desk, much blotte with ink, which his elbow touched. Upon it were some scraps of coars paper, and a superannuated steel pen in very reduced and gritt circumstances.

From glancing at the scraps of paper, he turned involuntarily t his host, and said, with some roughness:

"Why, you are never a poet, man?"

Lamps had certainly not the conventional appearance of one, a he stood modestly rubbing his squab nose with a handkerchief s exceedingly oily, that he might have been in the act of mistakin himself for one of his charges. He was a spare man of about th Barbox Brothers' time of life, with his features whimsically draw upward as if they were attracted by the roots of his hair. He had peculiarly shining transparent complexion, probably occasioned b constant oleaginous application; and his attractive hair, being cu short, and being grizzled, and standing straight up on end as if it i its turn were attracted by some invisible magnet above it, the to of his head was not very unlike a lamp-wick.

"But, to be sure, it's no business of mine," said Barbox Brothers "That was an impertinent observation on my part. Be what yo like."

"Some people, Sir," remarked Lamps in a tone of apology, "ar sometimes what they don't like."

"Nobody knows that better than I do," sighed the other. "I hav een what I don't like, all my life."

"When I first took, Sir," resumed Lamps, "to composing little omic-Songs like——"

Barbox Brothers eyed him with great disfavour.

"——To composing little Comic-Songs-like—and what was more ard—to singing 'em afterwards," said Lamps, "it went against the rain at that time, it did indeed."

Something that was not all oil here shining in Lamps's eye, Barbox rothers withdrew his own a little disconcerted, looked at the fire, nd put a foot on the top bar. "Why did you do it, then?" he asked ter a short pause; abruptly enough, but in a softer tone. "If you idn't want to do it, why did you do it? Where did you sing them? ublic-house?"

To which Mr. Lamps returned the curious reply: "Bedside."

At this moment, while the traveller looked at him for elucidation, ugby Junction started suddenly, trembled violently, and opened s gas eyes. "She's got up!" Lamps announced, excited. "What lays her power is sometimes more, and sometimes less; but it's laid in er power to get up to-night, by George!"

The legend "Barbox Brothers," in large white letters on two black urfaces, was very soon afterwards trundling on a truck through a lent street, and, when the owner of the legend had shivered on the avement half an hour, what time the porter's knocks at the Inn oor knocked up the whole town first, and the Inn last, he groped his ay into the close air of a shut-up house, and so groped between the neets of a shut-up bed that seemed to have been expressly refriger- ted for him when last made.

II

"You remember me, Young Jackson?"

"What do I remember if not you? You are my first remembrance. was you who told me that was my name. It was you who told me at on every twentieth of December my life had a penitential anni- ersary in it called a birthday. I suppose the last communication as truer than the first!"

"What am I like, Young Jackson?"

"You are like a blight all through the year to me. You hard-lined, in-lipped, repressive, changeless woman with a wax mask on. You re like the Devil to me; most of all when you teach me religious ings, for you make me abhor them."

"You remember me, Mr. Young Jackson?" In another voice from nother quarter.

"Most gratefully, Sir. You were the ray of hope and prospering mbition in my life. When I attended your course, I believed that I nould come to be a great healer, and I felt almost happy—even nough I was still the one boarder in the house with that horrible task, and ate and drank in silence and constraint with the mask be- nre me, every day. As I had done every, every, every day, through my school-time and from my earliest recollection."

"What am I like, Mr. Young Jackson?"

"You are like a Superior Being to me. You are like Nature beginning to reveal herself to me. I hear you again, as one of the hushed
crowd of young men kindling under the power of your presence and
knowledge, and you bring into my eyes the only exultant tears that
ever stood in them."

"You remember Me, Mr. Young Jackson?" In a grating voice from
quite another quarter.

"Too well. You made your ghostly appearance in my life one day,
and announced that its course was to be suddenly and wholly changed
You showed me which was my wearisome seat in the Galley of Barbox
Brothers. (When *they* were, if they ever were, is unknown to me
there was nothing of them but the name when I bent to the oar.) You
told me what I was to do, and what to be paid; you told me afterwards, at intervals of years, when I was to sign for the Firm, when
I became a partner, when I became the Firm. I know no more of it
or of myself."

"What am I like, Mr. Young Jackson?"

"You are like my father, I sometimes think. You are hard enough
and cold enough so to have brought up an acknowledged son. I see
your scanty figure, your close brown suit, and your tight brown wig
but you, too, wear a wax mask to your death. You never by a chance
remove it—it never by a chance falls off—and I know no more of
you."

Throughout this dialogue, the traveller spoke to himself at his
window in the morning, as he had spoken to himself at the Junction
overnight. And as he had then looked in the darkness, a man who
had turned grey too soon, like a neglected fire so he now looked in
the sunlight, an ashier grey, like a fire which the brightness of the
sun put out.

The firm of Barbox Brothers had been some offshoot or irregular
branch of the Public Notary and bill-broking tree. It had gained for
itself a griping reputation before the days of Young Jackson, and the
reputation had stuck to it and to him. As he had imperceptibly come
into possession of the dim den up in the corner of a court off Lombard
Street, on whose grimy windows the inscription Barbox Brothers had
for many long years daily interposed itself between him and the sky
so he had insensibly found himself a personage held in chronic distrust
whom it was essential to screw tight to every transaction in which
he engaged, whose word was never to be taken without his attested
bond, whom all dealers with openly set up guards and wards against
This character had come upon him through no act of his own. It
was as if the original Barbox had stretched himself down upon the
office floor, and had thither caused to be conveyed Young Jackson
in his sleep, and had there effected a metempsychosis and exchange
of persons with him. The discovery—aided in its turn by the deceit
of the only woman he had ever loved, and the deceit of the only
friend he had ever made; who eloped from him to be married together

-the discovery, so followed up, completed what his earliest rearing
ad begun. He shrank, abashed, within the form of Barbox, and
'ted up his head and heart no more.

But he did at last effect one great release in his condition. He broke
ie oar he had plied so long, and he scuttled and sank the galley. He
'evented the gradual retirement of an old conventional business
om him, by taking the initiative and retiring from it. With enough
» live on (though, after all, with not too much), he obliterated the
'm of Barbox Brothers from the pages of the Post-Office Directory
id the face of the earth, leaving nothing of it but its name on two
ortmanteaus.

"For one must have some name in going about, for people to
ck up," he explained to Mugby High Street, through the Inn
indow, "and that name at least was real once. Whereas, Young
ackson!—Not to mention its being a sadly satirical misnomer for
ld Jackson."

He took up his hat and walked out just in time to see, passing along
i the opposite side of the way, a velveteen man, carrying his day's
nner in a small bundle that might have been larger without sus-
cion of gluttony, and pelting away towards the Junction at a great
ice.

"There's Lamps!" said Barbox Brothers. "And by-the-bye——"
Ridiculous, surely, that a man so serious, so self-contained, and
ot yet three days emancipated from a routine of drudgery, should
and rubbing his chin in the street, in a brown study about Comic
ongs.

"Bedside?" said Barbox Brothers testily. "Sings them at the bed-
de? Why at the bedside, unless he goes to bed drunk? Does, I
iouldn't wonder. But it's no business of mine. Let me see. Mugby
inction, Mugby Junction. Where shall I go next? As it came into
y head last night when I woke from an uneasy sleep in the carriage
id found myself here, I can go anywhere from here. Where shall I
o? I'll go and look at the Junction by daylight. There's no hurry,
id I may like the look of one Line better than another."

But there were so many Lines. Gazing down upon them from a
ridge at the Junction, it was as if the concentrating Companies
irmed a great Industrial Exhibition of the works of extraordinary
round spiders that spun iron. And then so many of the Lines went
ich wonderful ways, so crossing and curving among one another,
iat the eye lost them. And then some of them appeared to start
ith the fixed intention of going five hundred miles, and all of a
idden gave it up at an insignificant barrier, or turned off into a
orkshop. And then others, like intoxicated men, went a little way
ery straight, and surprisingly slued round and came back again.
nd then others were so chock-full of trucks of coal, others were so
locked with trucks of casks, others were so gorged with trucks of
allast, others were so set apart for wheeled objects like immense
on cotton-reels; while others were so bright and clear, and others
ere so delivered over to rust and ashes and idle wheelbarrows out

of work, with their legs in the air (looking much like their maste
on strike), that there was no beginning, middle, or end to the bewil
erment.

Barbox Brothers stood puzzled on the bridge, passing his rig
hand across the lines on his forehead, which multiplied while I
looked down, as if the railway Lines were getting themselves phot
graphed on that sensitive plate. Then was heard a distant ringin
of bells and blowing of whistles. Then, puppet-looking heads of me
popped out of boxes in perspective, and popped in again. Then, pr
digious wooden razors, set up on end, began shaving the atmospher
Then, several locomotive engines in several directions began to screa
and be agitated. Then, along one avenue a train came in. Then, alon
another two trains appeared that didn't come in, but stopped wit
out. Then, bits of trains broke off. Then, a struggling horse becam
involved with them. Then, the locomotives shared the bits of train
and ran away with the whole.

"I have not made my next move much clearer by this. No hurr
No need to make up my mind to-day, or to-morrow, nor yet the da
after. I'll take a walk."

It fell out somehow (perhaps he meant it should) that the wa
tended to the platform at which he had alighted, and to Lamps
room. But Lamps was not in his room. A pair of velveteen shoulde
were adapting themselves to one of the impressions on the wall l
Lamps's fireplace, but otherwise the room was void. In passing bac
to get out of the station again, he learnt the cause of this vacan
by catching sight of Lamps on the opposite line of railway, skippir
along the top of a train, from carriage to carriage, and catchir
lighted namesakes thrown up to him by a coadjutor.

"He is busy. He has not much time for composing or singing Com
Songs this morning, I take it."

The direction he pursued now was into the country, keeping ver
near to the side of one great Line of railway, and within easy view o
others. "I have half a mind," he said, glancing around, "to settle th
question from this point, by saying, 'I'll take this set of rails, or tha
or t'other, and stick to it.' They separate themselves from the cor
fusion, out here, and go their ways."

Ascending a gentle hill of some extent, he came to a few cottage
There, looking about him as a very reserved man might who ha
never looked about him in his life before, he saw some six or eigh
young children come merrily trooping and whooping from one of th
cottages, and disperse. But not until they had all turned at the litt
garden-gate, and kissed their hands to a face at the upper windov
a low window enough, although the upper, for the cottage had but
story of one room above the ground.

Now, that the children should do this was nothing; but that the
should do this to a face lying on the sill of the open window, turne
towards them in horizontal position, and apparently only a face, wa
something noticeable. He looked up at the window again. Could onl
see a very fragile, though a very bright face, lying on one cheek o

; window-sill. The delicate smiling face of a girl or woman. Framed
long bright brown hair, round which was tied a light blue band or
et, passing under the chin.

He walked on, turned back, passed the window again, shyly
anced up again. No change. He struck off by a winding branch-
ad at the top of the hill —which he must otherwise have descended
kept the cottages in view, worked his way round at a distance so
to come out once more into the main road, and be obliged to
ss the cottages again. The face still lay on the window-sill, but
t so much inclined towards him. And now there were a pair of
licate hands too. They had the action of performing on some
usical instrument, and yet it produced no sound that reached his
rs.

"Mugby Junction must be the maddest place in England," said
arbox Brothers, pursuing his way down the hill. "The first thing I
id here is a Railway Porter who composes comic songs to sing at
s bedside. The second thing I find here is a face, and a pair of hands
aying a musical instrument that *don't* play!"

The day was a fine bright day in the early beginning of November,
ie air was clear and inspiriting, and the landscape was rich in beauti-
il colours. The prevailing colours in the court off Lombard Street,
ondon city, had been few and sombre. Sometimes, when the
eather elsewhere was very bright indeed, the dwellers in those tents
njoyed a pepper-and-salt-coloured day or two, but their atmos-
here's usual wear was slate or snuff-coloured.

He relished his walk so well that he repeated it next day. He was
little earlier at the cottage than on the day before, and he could
ear the children upstairs singing to a regular measure, and clap-
ing out the time with their hands.

"Still, there is no sound of any musical instrument," he said,
istening at the corner, "and yet I saw the performing hands again as
came by. What are the children singing? Why, good Lord, they can
iever be singing the multiplication table?"

They were though, and with infinite enjoyment. The mysterious
ace had a voice attached to it, which occasionally led or set the
children right. Its musical cheerfulness was delightful. The measure
it length stopped, and was succeeded by a murmuring of young
voices, and then by a short song which he made out to be about the
current month of the year, and about what work it yielded to the
abourers in the fields and farmyards. Then there was a stir of little
feet, and the children came trooping and whooping out, as on the
previous day. And again, as on the previous day, they all turned at
the garden-gate, and kissed their hands—evidently to the face on
the window-sill, though Barbox Brothers from his retired post of
disadvantage at the corner could not see it.

But, as the children dispersed, he cut off one small straggler—a
brown-faced boy with flaxen hair—and said to him:

"Come here, little one. Tell me, whose house is that?"

The child, with one swarthy arm held up across his eyes, half in

shyness and half ready for defence, said from behind the inside of l
elbow:

"Phœbe's."

"And who," said Barbox Brothers, quite as much embarrassed l
his part in the dialogue as the child could possibly be by his, '
Phœbe?"

To which the child made answer: "Why, Phœbe, of course."

The small but sharp observer had eyed his questioner closely, a
had taken his moral measure. He lowered his guard, and rather a
sumed a tone with him: as having discovered him to be an unaccu
tomed person in the art of polite conversation.

"Phœbe," said the child, "can't be anybody else but Phœbe. C
she?"

"No, I suppose not."

"Well," returned the child, "then why did you ask me?"

Deeming it prudent to shift his ground, Barbox Brothers took
a new position.

"What do you do there? Up there in that room where the op
window is. What do you do there?"

"Cool," said the child.

"Eh?"

"Co-o-ol," the child repeated in a louder voice, lengthening out t
word with a fixed look and great emphasis, as much as to sa
"What's the use of your having grown up, if you're such a donk
as not to understand me?"

"Ah! School, school," said Barbox Brothers. "Yes, yes, yes. A
Phœbe teaches you?"

The child nodded.

"Good boy."

"Tound it out, have you?" said the child.

"Yes, I have found it out. What would you do with twopence,
I gave it you?"

"Pend it."

The knock-down promptitude of this reply leaving him not a l
to stand upon, Barbox Brothers produced the twopence with gre
lameness, and withdrew in a state of humiliation.

But, seeing the face on the window-sill as he passed the cotta
he acknowledged its presence there with a gesture, which was no
nod, not a bow, not a removal of his hat from his head, but wa
diffident compromise between or struggle with all three. The eyes
the face seemed amused, or cheered, or both, and the lips modes
said: "Good day to you, Sir."

"I find I must stick for a time to Mugby Junction," said Barb
Brothers with much gravity, after once more stopping on his retu
road to look at the Lines where they went their several ways
quietly. "I can't make up my mind yet which iron road to take.
fact, I must get a little accustomed to the Junction before I c
decide."

So, he announced at the Inn that he was "going to stay on for t

resent," and improved his acquaintance with the Junction that
ight, and again next morning, and again next night and morning:
ping down to the station, mingling with the people there, looking
bout him down all the avenues of railway, and beginning to take an
nterest in the incomings and outgoings of the trains. At first, he
ften put his head into Lamps's little room, but he never found
amps there. A pair or two of velveteen shoulders he usually found
ere, stooping over the fire, sometimes in connexion with a clasped
nife and a piece of bread and meat; but the answer to his inquiry,
Where's Lamps?" was, either that he was "t'other side the line,"
r, that it was his off-time, or (in the latter case) his own personal
ntroduction to another Lamps who was not his lamps. However, he
as not so desperately set upon seeing Lamps now, but he bore the
isappointment. Nor did he so wholly devote himself to his severe
pplication to the study of Mugby Junction as to neglect exercise.
n the contrary, he took a walk every day, and always the same walk.
ut the weather turned cold and wet again, and the window was
ever open.

III

At length, after a lapse of some days, there came another streak of
ne bright hardy autumn weather. It was a Saturday. The window
as open, and the children were gone. Not surprising, this, for he had
atiently watched and waited at the corner until they *were* gone.

"Good day," he said to the face; absolutely getting his hat clear
ff his head this time.

"Good day to you, Sir."

"I am glad you have a fine sky again to look at."

"Thank you, Sir. It is kind of you."

"You are an invalid, I fear?"

"No, Sir. I have very good health."

"But are you not always lying down?"

"Oh yes, I am always lying down, because I cannot sit up! But I
m not an invalid."

The laughing eyes seemed highly to enjoy his great mistake.

"Would you mind taking the trouble to come in, Sir? There is a
eautiful view from this window. And you would see that I am not
t all ill—being so good as to care."

It was said to help him, as he stood irresolute, but evidently desir-
ng to enter, with his diffident hand on the latch of the garden-gate.
t did help him, and he went in.

The room upstairs was a very clean white room with a low roof.
ts only inmate lay on a couch that brought her face to a level with
ne window. The couch was white too; and her simple dress or wrapper
eing light blue, like the band around her hair, she had an ethereal
ok, and a fanciful appearance of lying among clouds. He felt that
ne instinctively perceived him to be by habit a downcast taciturn
an; it was another help to him to have established that understand-

ing so easily, and got it over.

There was an awkward constraint upon him, nevertheless, as he touched her hand, and took a chair at the side of her couch.

"I see now," he began, not at all fluently, "how you occupy your hand. Only seeing you from the path outside, I thought you were playing upon something."

She was engaged in very nimbly and dexterously making lace. A lace-pillow lay upon her breast; and the quick movements and change of her hands upon it, as she worked, had given them the action he had misinterpreted.

"That is curious," she answered with a bright smile. "For I often fancy, myself, that I play tunes while I am at work."

"Have you any musical knowledge?"

She shook her head.

"I think I could pick out tunes, if I had any instrument, which could be made as handy to me as my lace-pillow. But I dare say I deceive myself. At all events, I shall never know."

"You have a musical voice. Excuse me; I have heard you sing."

"With the children?" she answered, slightly colouring. "Oh yes, I sing with the dear children, if it can be called singing."

Barbox Brothers glanced at the two small forms in the room, and hazarded the speculation that she was fond of children, and that she was learned in new systems of teaching them?

"Very fond of them," she said, shaking her head again; "but I know nothing of teaching, beyond the interest I have in it, and the pleasure it gives me when they learn. Perhaps your overhearing my little scholars sing some of their lessons has led you so far astray as to think me a grand teacher? Ah! I thought so! No, I have only read and been told about that system. It seemed so pretty and pleasant, and to treat them so like the merry Robins they are, that I took up with it in my little way. You don't need to be told what a very little way mine is, Sir," she added with a glance at the small forms and round the room.

All this time her hands were busy at her lace-pillow. As they still continued so, and as there was a kind of substitute for conversation in the click and play of its pegs, Barbox Brothers took the opportunity of observing her. He guessed her to be thirty. The charm of her transparent face and large bright brown eyes was, not that they were passively resigned, but that they were actively and thoroughly cheerful. Even her busy hands, which of their own thinness alone might have besought compassion, plied their task with a gay courage that made mere compassion an unjustifiable assumption of superiority, and an impertinence.

He saw her eyes in the act of rising towards his, and he directed his towards the prospect, saying: "Beautiful, indeed!"

"Most beautiful, Sir. I have sometimes had a fancy that I would like to sit up, for once, only to try how it looks to an erect head. But what a foolish fancy that would be to encourage! It cannot look more lovely to any one than it does to me."

Her eyes were turned to it, as she spoke, with a most delighted admiration and enjoyment. There was not a trace in it of any sense of deprivation.

"And those threads of railway, with their puffs of smoke and steam hanging places so fast, make it so lively for me," she went on. "I think of the number of people who *can* go where they wish, on their business, or their pleasure; I remember that the puffs make signs to me that they are actually going while I look; and that enlivens the prospect with abundance of company, if I want company. There is the great Junction, too. I don't see it under the foot of the hill, but can very often hear it, and I always know it is there. It seems to join me, in a way, to I don't know how many places and things that I shall never see."

With an abashed kind of idea that it might have already joined himself to something he had never seen, he said constrainedly: "Just so."

"And so you see, Sir," pursued Phœbe, "I am not the invalid you thought me, and I am very well off indeed."

"You have a happy disposition," said Barbox Brothers: perhaps with a slight excusatory touch for his own disposition.

"Ah! But you should know my father," she replied. "His is the happy disposition!—Don't mind, Sir!" For his reserve took the alarm at a step upon the stairs, and he distrusted that he would be set down for a troublesome intruder. "This is my father coming."

The door opened, and the father paused there.

"Why, Lamps!" exclaimed Barbox Brothers, starting from his chair. "How do you DO, Lamps?"

To which Lamps responded: "The gentleman for Nowhere! How do you DO, Sir?"

And they shook hands, to the greatest admiration and surprise of Lamps's daughter.

"I have looked you up half-a-dozen times since that night," said Barbox Brothers, "but have never found you."

"So I've heerd on, Sir, so I've heerd on," returned Lamps. "It's our being noticed so often down at the Junction, without taking any train, that has begun to get you the name among us of the gentleman for Nowhere. No offence in my having called you by it when took by surprise, I hope, Sir?"

"None at all. It's as good a name for me as any other you could call me by. But may I ask you a question in the corner here?"

Lamps suffered himself to be led aside from his daughter's couch by one of the buttons of his velveteen jacket.

"Is this the bedside where you sing your songs?"

Lamps nodded.

The gentleman for Nowhere clapped him on the shoulder, and they faced about again.

"Upon my word, my dear," said Lamps then to his daughter, looking from her to her visitor, "it is such an amaze to me, to find you brought acquainted with this gentleman, that I must (if this gentle-

255*

man will excuse me) take a rounder."

Mr. Lamps demonstrated in action what this meant, by pullin
out his oily handkerchief rolled up in the form of a ball, and givin
himself an elaborate smear, from behind the right ear, up the cheek
across the forehead, and down the other cheek to behind his left ear
After this operation he shone exceedingly.

"It's according to my custom when particular warmed up by any
agitation, Sir," he offered by way of apology. "And really, I an
throwed into that state of amaze by finding you brought acquainte
with Phœbe, that I—that I think I will, if you'll excuse me, tak
another rounder." Which he did, seeming to be greatly restored by
it.

They were now both standing by the side of her couch, and sh
was working at her lace-pillow. "Your daughter tells me," sai
Barbox Brothers, still in a half-reluctant shamefaced way, "that sh
never sits up."

"No, Sir, nor never has done. You see, her mother (who died whe
she was a year and two months old) was subject to very bad fits an
as she had never mentioned to me that she *was* subject to fits, the
couldn't be guarded against. Consequently, she dropped the bab
when took, and this happened."

"It was very wrong of her," said Barbox Brothers with a knitte
brow, "to marry you, making a secret of her infirmity."

"Well, Sir!" pleaded Lamps in behalf of the long-deceased. "Yo
see, Phœbe and me, we have talked that over too. And Lord bless us
Such a number on us has our infirmities, what with fits, and wha
with misfits, of one sort and another, that if we confessed to 'em al
before we got married, most of us might never get married."

"Might not that be for the better?"

"Not in this case, Sir," said Phœbe, giving her hand to her fathe

"No, not in this case, Sir," said her father, patting it between hi
own.

"You correct me," returned Barbox Brothers with a blush; "an
I must look so like a Brute, that at all events it would be superfluou
in me to confess to *that* infirmity. I wish you would tell me a littl
more about yourselves. I hardly know how to ask it of you, for I an
conscious that I have a bad stiff manner, a dull discouraging wa
with me, but I wish you would."

"With all our hearts, Sir," returned Lamps gaily for both. "An
first of all, that you may know my name——"

"Stay!" interposed the visitor with a slight flush. "What signifie
your name? Lamps is name enough for me. I like it. It is bright an
expressive. What do I want more?"

"Why, to be sure, Sir," returned Lamps. "I have in general n
other name down at the Junction; but I thought, on account of you
being here as a first-class single, in a private character, that yo
might——"

The visitor waved the thought away with his hand, and Lamp
acknowledged the mark of confidence by taking another rounder.

"You are hard-worked, I take for granted?" said Barbox Brothers, when the subject of the rounder came out of it much dirtier than he went into it.

Lamps was beginning, "Not particular so"—when his daughter took him up.

"Oh yes, Sir, he is very hard-worked. Fourteen, fifteen, eighteen hours a day. Sometimes twenty-four hours at a time."

"And you," said Barbox Brothers, "what with your school, Phœbe, and what with your lace-making——"

"But my school is a pleasure to me," she interrupted, opening her brown eyes wider, as if surprised to find him so obtuse. "I began it when I was but a child, because it brought me and other children into company, don't you see? *That* was not work. I carry it on still, because it keeps children about me. *That* is not work. I do it as love, not as work. Then my lace-pillow;" her busy hands had stopped, as if her argument required all her cheerful earnestness, but now went on again at the name; "it goes with my thoughts when I think, and it goes with my tunes when I hum any, and *that's* not work. Why, you yourself thought it was music, you know, Sir. And so it is to me."

"Everything is!" cried Lamps radiantly. "Everything is music to her, Sir."

"My father is, at any rate," said Phœbe, exultingly pointing her thin forefinger at him. "There is more music in my father than there is in a brass band."

"I say! My dear! It's very fillyillially done, you know; but your are flattering your father," he protested, sparkling.

"No, I am not, Sir, I assure you. No, I am not. If you could hear my father sing, you would know I am not. But you never will hear him sing, because he never sings to any one but me. However tired he is, he always sings to me when he comes home. When I lay here long ago, quite a poor little broken doll, he used to sing to me. More than that, he used to make songs, bringing in whatever little jokes we had between us. More than that, he often does so to this day. Oh! I'll tell of you, father, as the gentleman has asked about you. He is a poet, Sir."

"I shouldn't wish the gentleman, my dear," observed Lamps, for the moment turning grave, "to carry away that opinion of your father, because it might look as if I was given to asking the stars in a molloncolly manner what they was up to. Which I wouldn't at once waste the time, and take the liberty, my dear."

"My father," resumed Phœbe, amending her text, "is always on the bright side, and the good side. You told me, just now, I had a happy disposition. How can I help it?"

"Well; but, my dear," returned Lamps argumentatively, "how can *I* help it? Put it to yourself, Sir. Look at her. Always as you see her now. Always working—and after all, Sir, for but a very few shillings a week—always contented, always lively, always interested in others, of all sorts. I said, this moment, she was always as you see her now. So she is, with a difference that comes to much the same. For, when it is my Sunday off and the morning bells have done ringing, I hear the prayers and thanks read in the touchingest way, and I have the hymns sung to me—so soft, Sir, that you couldn't hear 'em out of this room —in notes that seem to me, I am sure, to come from heaven and go back to it."

It might have been merely through the association of these words with their sacredly quiet time, or it might have been through the larger association of the words with the Redeemer's presence beside the bedridden; but here her dexterous fingers came to a stop on the lace-pillow, and clasped themselves around his neck as he bent down. There was great natural sensibility in both father and daughter, the visitor could easily see; but each made it, for the other's sake, retiring, not demonstrative; and perfect cheerfulness, intuitive or acquired, was either the first or second nature of both. In a very few moments Lamps was taking another rounder with his comical features beaming, while Phœbe's laughing eyes (just glistening a speck or so upon their lashes) were again directed by turns to him, and to her work, and to Barbox Brothers.

"When my father, Sir," she said brightly, "tells you about my being interested in other people, even though they know nothing about me—which, by-the-bye, I told you myself—you ought to know how that comes about. That's my father's doing."

"No, it isn't!" he protested.

"Don't you believe him, Sir; yes it is. He tells me of everything he sees down at his work. You would be surprised what a quantity he gets together for me every day. He looks into the carriages, and tells me how the ladies are dressed—so that I know all the fashions! He looks into the carriages and tells me what pairs of lovers he sees, and what new-married couples on their wedding trip—so that I know all about that! He collects chance newspapers and books—so that I have plenty to read! He tells me about the sick people who are travelling to try to get better—so that I know all about them! In short, as I began by saying, he tells me everything he sees and makes out down at his work, and you can't think what a quantity he does see and make out."

"As to collecting newspapers and books, my dear," said Lamps, "it's clear I can have no merit in that, because they're not my perquisites. You see, Sir, it's this way: A Guard, he'll say to me, 'Hallo, here you are, Lamps. I've saved this paper for your daughter. How is she going on?' A Head Porter, he'll say to me, 'Here catch hold, Lamps. Here's a couple of wollumes for your daughter. Is she pretty much where she were?' And that's what makes it doubly welcome, you see. If she had a thousand pound in a box, they wouldn't trouble themselves about her; but being what she is—that is, you understand," Lamps added somewhat hurriedly, "not having a thousand pound in a box—they take thought for her. And as concerning the young pairs, married and unmarried, it's only natural I should bring home what little I can about *them*, seeing that there's not a Couple of either sort in the neighbourhood that don't come of their own accord to confide in Phœbe."

She raised her eyes triumphantly to Barbox Brothers as she said: "Indeed, Sir, that is true. If I could have got up and gone to church, I don't know how often I should have been a bridesmaid. But, if I could have done that, some girls in love might have been jealous of me, and, as it is, no girl is jealous of me. And my pillow would not have been half as ready to put the piece of cake under, as I always find it," she added, turning her face on it with a light sigh, and a smile at her father.

The arrival of a little girl, the biggest of the scholars, now led to an understanding on the part of Barbox Brothers, that she was the domestic of the cottage, and had come to take active measures in it, attended by a pail that might have extinguished her, and a broom three times her height. He therefore rose to take his leave, and took it; saying that, if Phœbe had no objection, he would come again.

He had muttered that he would come "in the course of his walks." The course of his walks must have been highly favourable to his return, for he returned after an interval of a single day.

"You thought you would never see me any more, I suppose?" he said to Phœbe as he touched her hand, and sat down by her couch.

"Why should I think so?" was her surprised rejoinder.

"I took it for granted you would mistrust me."

"For granted, Sir? Have you been so much mistrusted?"

"I think I am justified in answering yes. But I may have mistrusted, too, on my part. No matter just now. We were speaking of the Junction last time. I have passed hours there since the day before yesterday."

"Are you now the gentleman for Somewhere?" she asked with a smile.

"Certainly for Somewhere; but I don't yet know Where. You would never guess what I am travelling from. Shall I tell you? I am travelling from my birthday."

Her hands stopped in her work, and she looked at him with incredulous astonishment.

"Yes," said Barbox Brothers, not quite easy in his chair, "from my birthday. I am, to myself, an unintelligible book with the earlier chapters all torn out, and thrown away. My childhood had no grace of childhood, my youth had no charm of youth, and what can be expected from such a lost beginning?" His eyes meeting hers as they were addressed intently to him, something seemed to stir within his breast, whispering: "Was this bed a place for the graces of childhood and the charms of youth to take to kindly? Oh, shame, shame!"

"It is a disease with me," said Barbox Brothers, checking himself, and making as though he had a difficulty in swallowing something, "to go wrong about that. I don't know how I came to speak of that. I hope it is because of an old misplaced confidence in one of your sex involving an old bitter treachery. I don't know. I am all wrong together."

Her hands quietly and slowly resumed their work. Glancing at her, he saw that her eyes were thoughtfully following them.

"I am travelling from my birthday," he resumed, "because it has always been a dreary day to me. My first free birthday coming round some five or six weeks hence, I am travelling to put its predecessors far behind me, and to try to crush the day—or, at all events, put it out of my sight—by heaping new objects on it."

As he paused, she looked at him; but only shook her head as being quite at a loss.

"This is unintelligible to your happy disposition," he pursued, abiding by his former phrase as if there were some lingering virtue of self-defence in it. "I knew it would be, and am glad it is. However, on this travel of mine (in which I mean to pass the rest of my days, having abandoned all thought of a fixed home), I stopped, as you have heard from your father, at the Junction here. The extent of its ramifications quite confused me as to whither I should go, *from* here. I have not yet settled, being still perplexed among so many roads. What do you think I mean to do? How many of the branching roads can you see from your window?"

Looking out, full of interest, she answered, "Seven."

"Seven," said Barbox Brothers, watching her with a grave smile. "Well! I propose to myself at once to reduce the gross number to those very seven, and gradually to fine them down to one—the most promising for me—and to take that."

"But, how will you know, Sir, which *is* the most promising?" she asked, with her brightened eyes roving over the view.

"Ah!" said Barbox Brothers with another grave smile, and considerably improving in his ease of speech. "To be sure. In this way. Where your father can pick up so much every day for a good purpose, I may once and again pick up a little for an indifferent purpose. The gentleman for Nowhere must become still better known at the Junction. He shall continue to explore it, until he attaches something that he has seen, heard, or found out, at the head of each of the seven roads, to the road itself. And so his choice of a road shall be determined by his choice among his discoveries."

Her hands still busy, she again glanced at the prospect, as if it comprehended something that had not been in it before, and laughed as if it yielded her new pleasure.

"But I must not forget," said Barbox Brothers, "(having got so far) to ask a favour. I want your help in this expedient of mine. I want to bring you what I pick up at the heads of the seven roads that you lie here looking out at, and to compare notes with you about it. May I? They say two heads are better than one. I should say myself that probably depends upon the heads concerned. But I am quite sure, though we are so newly acquainted, that your head and your father's have found out better things, Phœbe, than ever mine of itself discovered."

She gave him her sympathetic right hand, in perfect rapture with his proposal, and eagerly and gratefully thanked him.

"That's well!" said Barbox Brothers. "Again I must not forget (having got so far) to ask a favour. Will you shut your eyes?"

Laughing playfully at the strange nature of the request, she did so.

"Keep them shut," said Barbox Brothers, going softly to the door and coming back. "You are on your honour, mind, not to open your eyes until I tell you that you may?"

"Yes! On my honour."

"Good. May I take your lace-pillow from you for a minute?"

Still laughing and wondering, she removed her hands from it, and he put it aside.

"Tell me. Did you see the puffs of smoke and steam made by the morning fast-train yesterday on road number seven from here?"

"Behind the elm-trees and the spire?"

"That's the road," said Barbox Brothers, directing his eyes towards it.

"Yes. I watched them melt away."

"Anything unusual in what they expressed?"

"No!" she answered merrily.

"Not complimentary to me, for I was in that train. I went—don't open your eyes—to fetch you this, from the great ingenious town. It is not half so large as your lace-pillow, and lies easily and lightly in its place. These little keys are like the keys of a miniature piano, and you supply the air required with your left hand. May you pick out delightful music from it, my dear! For the present—you can open your eyes now—good-bye!"

In his embarrassed way, he closed the door upon himself, and only saw, in doing so, that she ecstatically took the present to her bosom and caressed it. The glimpse gladdened his heart, and yet saddened it; for so might she, if her youth had flourished in its natural course, have taken to her breast that day the slumbering music of her own child's voice.

CHAPTER II

BARBOX BROTHERS AND CO.

WITH good-will and earnest purpose, the gentleman for Nowhere began, on the very next day, his researches at the heads of the seven roads. The results of his researches, as he and Phœbe afterwards set them down in fair writing, hold their due places in this voracious chronicle. But they occupied a much longer time in the getting together than they ever will in the perusal. And this is probably the case with most reading matter, except when it is of that highly beneficial kind (for Posterity) which is "thrown off in a few moments of leisure" by the superior poetic geniuses who scorn to take prose pains.

It must be admitted, however, that Barbox by no means hurried himself. His heart being in his work of good-nature, he revelled in it. There was the joy, too (it was a true joy to him), of sometimes sitting

by, listening to Phœbe as she picked out more and more discourse
from her musical instrument, and as her natural taste and ear refined
daily upon her first discoveries. Besides being a pleasure, this was an
occupation, and in the course of weeks it consumed hours. It resulted
that his dreaded birthday was close upon him before he had troubled
himself any more about it.

The matter was made more pressing by the unforeseen circumstance that the councils held (at which Mr. Lamps, beaming most
brilliantly, on a few rare occasions assisted) respecting the road to be
selected were, after all, in nowise assisted by his investigations. For,
he had connected this interest with this road, or that interest with the
other, but could deduce no reason from it for giving any road the
preference. Consequently when the last council was holden, that part
of the business stood, in the end, exactly where it had stood in the
beginning.

"But, Sir," remarked Phœbe, "we have only six roads after all.
Is the seventh dumb?"

"The seventh road? Oh!" said Barbox Brothers, rubbing his chin.
"That is the road I took, you know, when I went to get your little
present. That is *its* story, Phœbe."

"Would you mind taking that road again, Sir?" she asked with
hesitation.

"Not in the least; it is a great high-road after all."

"I should like you to take it," returned Phœbe with a persuasive
smile, "for the love of that little present which must ever be so dear
to me. I should like you to take it, because that road can never be
again like any other road to me. I should like you to take it, in remembrance of you having done me so much good: of your having
made me so much happier! If you leave me by the road you travelled
when you went to do me this great kindness," sounding a faint chord
as she spoke, "I shall feel, lying here watching at my window, as if it
must conduct you to a prosperous end, and bring you back some day."

"It shall be done, my dear; it shall be done."

So at last the gentleman for Nowhere took a ticket for Somewhere,
and his destination was the great ingenious town.

He had loitered so long about the Junction that it was the eight-
eenth of December when he left it. "High time," he reflected, as he
seated himself in the train, "that I started in earnest! Only one clear
day remains between me and the day I am running away from. I'll
push onward for the hill-country to-morrow. I'll go to Wales."

It was with some pains that he placed before himself the undeniable advantages to be gained in the way of novel occupation for his
senses from misty mountains, swollen streams, rain, cold, a wild
seashore, and rugged roads. And yet he scarcely made them out as
distinctly as he could have wished. Whether the poor girl, in spite of
her new resource, her music, would have any feeling of loneliness
upon her now—just at first—that she had not had before; whether she
saw those very puffs of steam and smoke that he saw, as he sat in the
train thinking of her; whether her face would have any pensive

shadow on it as they died out of the distant view from her window;
whether, in telling him he had done her so much good, she had not
unconsciously corrected his old moody bemoaning of his station in
life, by setting him thinking that a man might be a great healer, if he
would, and yet not be a great doctor; these and other similar meditations got between him and his Welsh picture. There was within him,
too, that dull sense of vacuity which follows separation from an
object of interest, and cessation of a pleasant pursuit; and this sense,
being quite new to him, made him restless. Further, in losing Mugby
Junction, he had found himself again; and he was not the more
enamoured of himself for having lately passed his time in better
company.

But surely here, not far ahead, must be the great ingenious town.
This crashing and clashing that the train was undergoing, and this
coupling on to it of a multitude of new echoes, could mean nothing
less than approach to the great station. It did mean nothing less.
After some stormy flashes of town lightning, in the way of swift
revelations of red brick blocks of houses, high red brick chimney-
shafts, vistas of red brick railway arches, tongues of fire, blocks of
smoke, valleys of canal, and hills of coal, there came the thundering in
at the journey's end.

Having seen his portmanteaus safely housed in the hotel he chose,
and having appointed his dinner hour, Barbox Brothers went out for
a walk in the busy streets. And now it began to be suspected by him
that Mugby Junction was a Junction of many branches, invisible as
well as visible, and had joined him to an endless number of by-ways.
For, whereas he would, but a little while ago, have walked these
streets blindly brooding, he now had eyes and thoughts for a new
external world. How the many toiling people lived, and loved, and
died ; how wonderful it was to consider the various trainings of eye
and hand, the nice distinctions of sight and touch, that separated
them into classes of workers, and even into classes of workers at sub-
divisions of one complete whole which combined their many intelli-
gences and forces, though of itself but some cheap object of use or
ornament in common life ; how good it was to know that such
assembling in a multitude on their part, and such contribution of
their several dexterities towards a civilising end, did not deteriorate
them as it was the fashion of the supercilious Mayflies of humanity
to pretend, but engendered among them a self-respect, and yet a
modest desire to be much wiser than they were (the first evinced in
their well-balanced bearing and manner of speech when he stopped to
ask a question; the second, in the announcements of their popular
studies and amusements on the public walls); these considerations,
and a host of such, made his walk a memorable one. "I too am but a
little part of a great whole," he began to think; "and to be serviceable
to myself and others, or to be happy, I must cast my interest into,
and draw it out of, the common stock."

Although he had arrived at his journey's end for the day by noon,
he had since insensibly walked about the town so far and so long that

the lamplighters were now at their work in the streets, and the shop
were sparkling up brilliantly. Thus reminded to turn towards hi
quarters, he was in the act of doing so, when a very little hand crep
into his, and a very little voice said:

"Oh! if you please, I am lost!"

He looked down, and saw a very little fair-haired girl.

"Yes," she said, confirming her words with a serious nod. "I ar
indeed. I am lost!"

Greatly perplexed, he stopped, looked about him for help, descrie
none, and said, bending low:

"Where do you live, my child?"

"I don't know where I live," she returned. "I am lost."

"What is your name?"

"Polly."

"What is your other name?"

The reply was prompt, but unintelligible.

Imitating the sound as he caught it, he hazarded the gues
"Trivits."

"Oh no!" said the child, shaking her head. "Nothing like that."

"Say it again, little one."

An unpromising business. For this time it had quite a differen
sound.

He made the venture, "Paddens?"

"Oh no!" said the child. "Nothing like that."

"Once more. Let us try it again, dear."

A most hopeless business. This time it swelled into four syllable
"It can't be Tappitarver?" said Barbox Brothers, rubbing his hea
with his hat in discomfiture.

"No! It ain't," the child quietly assented.

On her trying this unfortunate name once more, with extra
ordinary efforts at distinctness, it swelled into eight syllables at leas

"Ah! I think," said Barbox Brothers with a desperate air of resigna
tion, "that we had better give it up."

"But I am lost," said the child, nestling her little hand more close
in his, "and you'll take care of me, won't you?"

If ever a man were disconcerted by division between compassio
on the one hand, and the very imbecility of irresolution on the othe
here the man was. "Lost!" he repeated, looking down at the chilc
"I am sure *I* am. What is to be done?"

"Where do *you* live?" asked the child, looking up at him wistfully

"Over there," he answered, pointing vaguely in the direction of hi
hotel.

"Hadn't we better go there?" said the child.

"Really," he replied, "I don't know but what we had."

So they set off, hand-in-hand. He, through comparison of himse
against his little companion, with a clumsy feeling on him as if l
had just developed into a foolish giant. She, clearly elevated in he
own tiny opinion by having got him so neatly out of his embarras
ment.

"We are going to have dinner when we get there, I suppose?" id Polly.

"Well," he rejoined, "I—— Yes, I suppose we are."

"Do you like your dinner?" asked the child.

"Why, on the whole," said Barbox Brothers, "yes, I think I do."

"I do mine," said Polly. "Have you any brothers and sisters?"

"No. Have you?"

"Mine are dead."

"Oh!" said Barbox Brothers. With that absurd sense of un-ieldiness of mind and body weighing him down, he would have not 1own how to pursue the conversation beyond this curt rejoinder, it that the child was always ready for him.

"What," she asked, turning her soft hand coaxingly in his, "are bu going to do to amuse me after dinner?"

"Upon my soul, Polly," exclaimed Barbox Brothers, very much at loss, "I have not the slightest idea!"

"Then I tell you what," said Polly. "Have you got any cards at bur house?"

"Plenty," said Barbox Brothers in a boastful vein.

"Very well. Then I'll build houses, and you shall look at me. You ustn't blow, you know."

"Oh no," said Barbox Brothers. "No, no, no. No blowing. Blowing's ot fair."

He flattered himself that he had said this pretty well for an idiotic ionster; but the child, instantly perceiving the awkwardness of his ttempt to adapt himself to her level, utterly destroyed his hopeful pinion of himself by saying compassionately: "What a funny man bu are!"

Feeling, after this melancholy failure, as if he every minute grew igger and heavier in person, and weaker in mind, Barbox gave imself up for a bad job. No giant ever submitted more meekly to be d in triumph by all-conquering Jack than he to be bound in avery to Polly.

"Do you know any stories?" she asked him.

He was reduced to the humiliating confession: "No."

"What a dunce you must be, mustn't you?" said Polly.

He was reduced to the humiliating confession: "Yes."

"Would you like me to teach you a story? But you must remember , you know, and be able to tell it right to somebody else afterwards."

He professed that it would afford him the highest mental gratifica-on to be taught a story, and that he would humbly endeavour to :tain it in his mind. Whereupon Polly, giving her hand a new little irn in his, expressive of settling down for enjoyment, commenced long romance, of which every relishing clause began with the words: So this," or, "And so this." As, "So this boy"; or, "So this fairy"; r, "And so this pie was four yards round, and two yards and a uarter deep." The interest of the romance was derived from the inter-ention of this fairy to punish this boy for having a greedy appetite. o achieve which purpose, this fairy made this pie, and this boy ate

and ate and ate, and his cheeks swelled and swelled and swelled
There were many tributary circumstances, but the forcible interes
culminated in the total consumption of this pie, and the bursting o
this boy. Truly he was a fine sight, Barbox Brothers, with seriou
attentive face, and ear bent down, much jostled on the pavements o
the busy town, but afraid of losing a single incident of the epic, les
he should be examined in it by-and-by, and found deficient.

Thus they arrived at the hotel. And there he had to say at the ba
and said awkwardly enough: "I have found a little girl!"

The whole establishment turned out to look at the little girl. N
body knew her; nobody could make out her name, as she set it fort
—except one chambermaid, who said it was Constantinople—whic
it wasn't.

"I will dine with my young friend in a private room," said Barbo
Brothers to the hotel authorities, "and perhaps you will be so goo
as to let the police know that the pretty baby is here. I suppose sh
is sure to be inquired for soon, if she has not been already. Com
along, Polly."

Perfectly at ease and peace, Polly came along, but, finding th
stairs rather stiff work, was carried up by Barbox Brothers. Th
dinner was a most transcendent success, and the Barbox sheepisl
ness, under Polly's directions how to mince her meat for her, an
how to diffuse gravy over the plate with a liberal and equal hand
was another fine sight.

"And now," said Polly, "while we are at dinner, you be good, an
tell me that story I taught you."

With the tremors of a Civil Service examination upon him, an
very uncertain indeed, not only as to the epoch at which the pi
appeared in history; but also as to the measurements of that indis
pensable fact, Barbox Brothers made a shaky beginning, but unde
encouragement did very fairly. There was a want of breadth observ
able in his rendering of the cheeks, as well as the appetite, of the boy
and there was a certain tameness in his fairy, referable to an under
current of desire to account for her. Still, as the first lumbering per
formance of a good-humoured monster, it passed muster.

"I told you to be good," said Polly, "and you are good, ain
you?"

"I hope so," replied Barbox Brothers.

Such was his deference that Polly, elevated on a platform of sof
cushions in a chair at his right hand, encouraged him with a pat o
two on the face from the greasy bowl of her spoon, and even with
gracious kiss. In getting on her feet upon her chair, however, to giv
him this last reward, she toppled forward among the dishes, an
caused him to exclaim, as he effected her rescue: "Gracious Angels
Whew! I thought we were in the fire, Polly!"

"What a coward you are, ain't you?" said Polly when replaced.

"Yes, I am rather nervous," he replied. "Whew! Don't, Polly
Don't flourish your spoon, or you'll go over sideways. Don't tilt u
your legs when you laugh, Polly, or you'll go over backwards. Whew

lly, Polly, Polly," said Barbox Brothers, nearly succumbing to
spair, "we are environed with dangers!"
Indeed, he could descry no security from the pitfalls that were
wning for Polly, but in proposing to her, after dinner, to sit upon
low stool. "I will, if you will," said Polly. So, as peace of mind
ould go before all, he begged the waiter to wheel aside the table,
ing a pack of cards, a couple of footstools, and a screen, and close
Polly and himself before the fire, as it were in a snug room within
e room. Then, finest sight of all, was Barbox Brothers on his foot-
ool, with a pint decanter on the rug, contemplating Polly as she
ilt successfully, and growing blue in the face with holding his
eath, lest he should blow the house down.

"How you stare, don't you?" said Polly in a houseless pause.
Detected in the ignoble fact, he felt obliged to admit, apologetic-
ly: "I am afraid I was looking rather hard at you, Polly."

"Why do you stare?" asked Polly.

"I cannot," he murmured to himself, "recall why,—I don't know,
lly."

"You must be a simpleton to do things and not know why,
ustn't you?" said Polly.

In spite of which reproof, he looked at the child again intently,
she bent her head over her card structure, her rich curls shading
r face. "It is impossible," he thought, "that I can ever have seen
is pretty baby before. Can I have dreamed of her? In some sorrow-
l dream?"

He could make nothing of it. So he went into the building trade
a journeyman under Polly, and they built three stories high, four
ories high; even five.

"I say! Who do you think is coming?" asked Polly, rubbing her
es after tea.

He guessed: "The waiter?"

"No," said Polly, "the dustman. I am getting sleepy."

A new embarrassment for Barbox Brothers!

"I don't think I am going to be fetched to-night," said Polly.
What do you think?"

He thought not, either. After another quarter of an hour, the dust-
an not merely impending, but actually arriving, recourse was had
the Constantinopolitan chambermaid: who cheerily undertook
at the child should sleep in a comfortable and wholesome room,
iich she herself would share.

"And I know you will be careful, won't you," said Barbox Brothers,
a new fear dawned upon him, "that she don't fall out of bed?"

Polly found this so highly entertaining that she was under the
cessity of clutching him round the neck with both arms as he sat
his footstool picking up the cards and rocking him to and fro, with
r dimpled chin on his shoulder.

"Oh, what a coward you are, ain't you?" said Polly. "Do *you* fall
t of bed?"

"N—not generally, Polly."

"No more do I."

With that, Polly gave him a reassuring hug or two to keep hi
going, and then giving that confiding mite of a hand of hers to h
swallowed up in the hand of the Constantinopolitan chambermai
trotted off, chattering, without a vestige of anxiety.

He looked after her, had the screen removed and the table an
chairs replaced, and still looked after her. He paced the room f
half an hour. "A most engaging little creature, but it's not that.
most winning little voice, but it's not that. That has much to do wi
it, but there is something more. How can it be that I seem to kno
this child? What was it she imperfectly recalled to me when I fe
her touch in the street, and, looking down at her, saw her lookin
up at me?"

"Mr. Jackson!"

With a start he turned towards the sound of the subdued voice, an
saw his answer standing at the door.

"Oh, Mr. Jackson, do not be severe with me! Speak a word
encouragement to me, I beseech you."

"You are Polly's mother."

"Yes."

Yes. Polly herself might come to this, one day. As you see what t
rose was in its faded leaves; as you see what the summer growth
the woods was in their wintry branches; so Polly might be traced, o
day, in a careworn woman like this, with her hair turned grey. Befo
him were the ashes of a dead fire that had once burned bright. Th
was the woman he had loved. This was the woman he had lost. Su
had been the constancy of his imagination to her, so had Time spar
her under its withholding, that now, seeing how roughly the inexo
able hand had struck her, his soul was filled with pity and amazeme

He led her to a chair, and stood leaning on a corner of the chimne
piece, with his head resting on his hand, and his face half averte

"Did you see me in the street, and show me to your child?"
asked.

"Yes."

"Is the little creature, then, a party to deceit?"

"I hope there is no deceit. I said to her, 'We have lost our wa
and I must try to find mine by myself. Go to that gentleman, and t
him you are lost. You shall be fetched by-and-by.' Perhaps you ha
not thought how very young she is?"

"She is very self-reliant."

"Perhaps because she is so young."

He asked, after a short pause, "Why did you do this?"

"Oh, Mr. Jackson, do you ask me? In the hope that you might s
something in my innocent child to soften your heart towards m
Not only towards me, but towards my husband."

He suddenly turned about, and walked to the opposite end of t
room. He came back again with a slower step, and resumed h
former attitude, saying:

"I thought you had emigrated to America?"

"We did. But life went ill with us there, and we came back."

"Do you live in this town?"

"Yes. I am a daily teacher of music here. My husband is a book-eeper."

"Are you—forgive my asking—poor?"

"We earn enough for our wants. That is not our distress. My usband is very, very ill of a lingering disorder. He will never ecover——"

"You check yourself. If it is for want of the encouraging word you poke of, take it from me. I cannot forget the old time, Beatrice."

"God bless you!" she replied with a burst of tears, and gave him er trembling hand.

"Compose yourself. I cannot be composed if you are not, for to see ou weep distresses me beyond expression. Speak freely to me. rust me."

She shaded her face with her veil, and after a little while spoke almly. Her voice had the ring of Polly's.

"It is not that my husband's mind is at all impaired by his bodily uffering, for I assure you that is not the case. But in his weakness, nd in his knowledge that he is incurably ill, he cannot overcome the scendancy of one idea. It preys upon him, embitters every moment f his painful life, and will shorten it."

She stopping, he said again: "Speak freely to me. Trust me."

"We have had five children before this darling, and they all lie in heir little graves. He believes that they have withered away under curse, and that it will blight this child like the rest."

"Under what curse?"

"Both I and he have it on our conscience that we tried you very eavily, and I do not know but that, if I were as ill as he, I might uffer in my mind as he does. This is the constant burden:—'I believe, Beatrice, I was the only friend that Mr. Jackson ever cared to make, hough I was so much his junior. The more influence he acquired in he business, the higher he advanced me, and I was alone in his rivate confidence. I came between him and you, and I took you rom him. We were both secret, and the blow fell when he was wholly nprepared. The anguish it caused a man so compressed must have een terrible; the wrath it awakened inappeasable. So, a curse came o be invoked on our poor pretty little flowers, and they fall.'"

"And you, Beatrice," he asked, when she had ceased to speak, and here had been a silence afterwards, "how say you?"

"Until within these few weeks I was afraid of you and I believed hat you would never, never forgive."

"Until within these few weeks," he repeated. "Have you changed our opinion of me within these few weeks?"

"Yes."

"For what reason?"

"I was getting some pieces of music in a shop in this town, when, o my terror, you came in. As I veiled my face and stood in the dark nd of the shop, I heard you explain that you wanted a musical

instrument for a bedridden girl. Your voice and manner were s◦
softened, you showed such interest in its selection, you took it away
yourself with so much tenderness of care and pleasure, that I knew
you were a man with a most gentle heart. Oh, Mr. Jackson, Mr
Jackson, if you could have felt the refreshing rain of tears that
followed for me!''

Was Phœbe playing at that moment on her distant couch? He
seemed to hear her.

"I inquired in the shop where you lived, but could get no informa
tion. As I had heard you say that you were going back by the nex◦
train (but you did not say where), I resolved to visit the station a◦
about that time of day, as often as I could, between my lessons, or
the chance of seeing you again. I have been there very often, but saw
you no more until to-day. You were meditating as you walked the
street, but the calm expression of your face emboldened me to sen◦
my child to you. And when I saw you bend your head to speak
tenderly to her, I prayed to GOD to forgive me for having ever
brought a sorrow on it. I now pray to you to forgive me, and to for
give my husband. I was very young, he was young too, and, in the
ignorant hardihood of such a time of life, we don't know what we d◦
to those who have undergone more discipline. You generous man
You good man! So to raise me up and make nothing of my crim◦
against you!''—for he would not see her on her knees, and soothe◦
her as a kind father might have soothed an erring daughter—"than◦
you, bless you, thank you!''

When he next spoke, it was after having drawn aside the window
curtain and looked out awhile. Then he only said:

"Is Polly asleep?''

"Yes. As I came in, I met her going away upstairs, and put her t◦
bed myself.''

"Leave her with me for to-morrow, Beatrice, and write me you◦
address on this leaf of my pocket-book. In the evening I will brin◦
her home to you—and to her father.''

* * * * * *

"Hallo!'' cried Polly, putting her saucy sunny face in at the doo◦
next morning when breakfast was ready: "I thought I was fetche◦
last night?''

"So you were, Polly, but I asked leave to keep you here for th◦
day, and to take you home in the evening.''

"Upon my word!'' said Polly. "You are very cool, ain't you?''

However, Polly seemed to think it a good idea, and added:

"I suppose I must give you a kiss, though you *are* cool.''

The kiss given and taken, they sat down to breakfast in a highly
conversational tone.

"Of course, you are going to amuse me?'' said Polly.

"Oh! of course!'' said Barbox Brothers.

In the pleasurable height of her anticipations, Polly found i◦
indispensable to put down her piece of toast, cross one of her littl◦

t knees over the other, and bring her little fat right hand down into
er left hand with a business-like slap. After this gathering of herself
ogether, Polly, by that time a mere heap of dimples, asked in a
wheedling manner:

"What are you going to do, you dear old thing?"

"Why, I was thinking," said Barbox Brothers, "—but are you fond
f horses, Polly?"

"Ponies, I am," said Polly, "especially when their tails are long.
But horses—n—no—too big, you know."

"Well," pursued Barbox Brothers, in a spirit of grave mysterious
confidence adapted to the importance of the consultation, "I did see
esterday, Polly, on the walls, pictures of two long-tailed ponies,
peckled all over——"

"No, no, NO!" cried Polly, in an ecstatic desire to linger on the
charming details. "Not speckled all over!"

"Speckled all over. Which ponies jump through hoops——"

"No, no, NO!" cried Polly as before. "They never jump through
oops!"

"Yes, they do. Oh, I assure you they do! And eat pie in pina-
ores——"

"Ponies eating pie in pinafores!" said Polly. "What a story-teller
ou are, ain't you?"

"Upon my honour. —And fire off guns."

(Polly hardly seemed to see the force of the ponies resorting to
re-arms.)

"And I was thinking," pursued the exemplary Barbox, "that if you
nd I were to go to the circus where these ponies are, it would do our
onstitutions good."

"Does that mean amuse us?" inquired Polly. "What long words
ou do use, don't you?"

Apologetic for having wandered out of his depth, he replied:

"That means amuse us. That is exactly what it means. There are
many other wonders besides the ponies, and we shall see them all.
Ladies and gentlemen in spangled dresses, and elephants and lions
nd tigers."

Polly became observant of the teapot, with a curled-up nose
ndicating some uneasiness of mind.

"They never get out, of course," she remarked as a mere truism.

"The elephants and lions and tigers? Oh, dear no!"

"Oh, dear no!" said Polly. "And of course nobody's afraid of the
onies shooting anybody."

"Not the least in the world."

"No, no, not the least in the world," said Polly.

"I was also thinking," proceeded Barbox, "that if we were to look
n at the toy-shop, to choose a doll——"

"Not dressed!" cried Polly with a clap of her hands. "No, no, NO,
ot dressed!"

"Full-dressed. Together with a house, and all the things necessary
or house-keeping——"

Polly gave a little scream, and seemed in danger of falling into a swoon of bliss.

"What a darling you are!" she languidly exclaimed, leaning back in her chair. "Come and be hugged, or I must come and hug you."

This resplendent programme was carried into execution with the utmost rigour of the law. It being essential to make the purchase of the doll its first feature—or that lady would have lost the ponies—the toy-shop expedition took precedence. Polly in the magic warehouse with a doll as large as herself under each arm, and a neat assortment of some twenty more on view upon the counter, did indeed present a spectacle of indecision not quite compatible with unalloyed happiness, but the light cloud passed. The lovely specimen oftenest chosen oftenest rejected, and finally abided by, was of Circassian descent, possessing as much boldness of beauty as was reconcilable with extreme feebleness of mouth, and combining a sky-blue silk pelisse with rose-coloured satin trousers, and a black velvet hat: which this fair stranger to our northern shores would seem to have founded on the portraits of the late Duchess of Kent. The name this distinguished foreigner brought with her from beneath the glowing skies of a sunny clime was (on Polly's authority) Miss Melluka, and the costly nature of her outfit as a housekeeper, from the Barbox coffers, may be inferred from the two facts that her silver tea-spoons were as large as her kitchen poker, and that the proportions of her watch exceeded those of her frying-pan. Miss Melluka was graciously pleased to express her entire approbation of the Circus, and so was Polly; for the ponies *were* speckled, and brought down nobody when they fired, and the savagery of the wild beasts appeared to be mere smoke—which article, in fact, they did produce in large quantities from their insides. The Barbox absorption in the general subject throughout the realisation of the delights was again a sight to see, nor was it less worthy to behold at dinner, when he drank to Miss Melluka, tied stiff in a chair opposite to Polly (the fair Circassian possessing an unbendable spine), and even induced the waiter to assist in carrying out with due decorum the prevailing glorious idea. To wind up, there came the agreeable fever of getting Miss Melluka and all her wardrobe and rich possessions into a fly with Polly, to be taken home. But, by that time Polly had become unable to look upon such accumulated joys with waking eyes, and had withdrawn her consciousness into the wonderful Paradise of a child's sleep. "Sleep, Polly, sleep," said Barbox Brothers, as her head dropped on his shoulder; "you shall not fall out of this bed easily, at any rate!"

What rustling piece of paper he took from his pocket, and carefully folded into the bosom of Polly's frock, shall not be mentioned. He said nothing about it, and nothing shall be said about it. They drove to a modest suburb of the great ingenious town and stopped at the fore-court of a small house. "Do not wake the child," said Barbox Brothers softly to the driver; "I will carry her in as she is."

Greeting the light at the opened door which was held by Polly's mother, Polly's bearer passed on with mother and child into a ground floor room. There, stretched on a sofa, lay a sick man, sorely wasted, who covered his eyes with his emaciated hands.

"Tresham," said Barbox in a kindly voice, "I have brought you back your Polly, fast asleep. Give me your hand, and tell me you are better."

The sick man reached forth his right hand, and bowed his head over the hand into which it was taken, and kissed it. "Thank you, thank you! I may say that I am well and happy."

"That's brave," said Barbox. "Tresham, I have a fancy——Can you make room for me beside you here?"

He sat down on the sofa as he said the words, cherishing the plump peachy cheek that lay uppermost on his shoulder.

"I have a fancy, Tresham (I am getting quite an old fellow now, you know, and old fellows may take fancies into their heads sometimes), to give up Polly, having found her, to no one but you. Will you take her from me?"

As the father held out his arms for the child, each of the two men looked steadily at the other.

"She is very dear to you, Tresham?"

"Unutterably dear."

"God bless her! It is not much, Polly," he continued, turning his eyes upon her peaceful face as he apostrophized her, "it is not much, Polly, for a blind and sinful man to invoke a blessing on something so far better than himself as a little child is; but it would be much—much upon his cruel head, and much upon his guilty soul—if he could be so wicked as to invoke a curse. He had better have a millstone round his neck, and be cast into the deepest sea. Live and thrive, my pretty baby!" Here he kissed her. "Live and prosper, and become in time the mother of other little children, like the Angels who behold The Father's Face!"

He kissed her again, gave her up gently to both her parents, and went out.

But he went not to Wales. No, he never went to Wales. He went straightway for another stroll about the town, and he looked in upon the people at their work, and at their play, here, there, and everywhere, and where not. For he was Barbox Brothers and Co. now, and had taken thousands of partners into the solitary firm.

He had at length got back to his hotel room, and was standing before his fire refreshing himself with a glass of hot drink which he had stood upon the chimneypiece, when he heard the town clocks striking, and referring to his watch, found the evening to have so slipped away, that they were striking twelve. As he put up his watch again, his eyes met those of his reflection in the chimney-glass.

"Why, it's your birthday already," he said, smiling. "You are looking very well. I wish you many happy returns of the day."

He had never before bestowed that wish upon himself. "By Jupiter!" he discovered, "it alters the whole case of running away from one's birthday! It's a thing to explain to Phœbe. Besides, here is quite a long story to tell her, that has sprung out of the road with no story. I'll go back instead of going on. I'll go back by my friend Lamps's Up X presently."

He went back to Mugby Junction, and, in point of fact, he established himself at Mugby Junction. It was the convenient place to live in, for brightening Phœbe's life. It was the convenient place to live in, for having her taught music by Beatrice. It was the convenient place to live in, for occasionally borrowing Polly. It was the convenient place to live in, for being joined at will to all sorts of agreeable places and persons. So, he became settled there, and, his house standing in an elevated situation, it is noteworthy of him in conclusion, as Polly herself might (nor irreverently) have put it:

> "There was an Old Barbox who lived on a hill,
> And if he ain't gone, he lives there still."

HERE FOLLOWS THE SUBSTANCE OF WHAT WAS SEEN, HEARD, OR OTHERWISE PICKED UP, BY THE GENTLEMAN FOR NOWHERE, IN HIS CAREFUL STUDY OF THE JUNCTION.

CHAPTER III

MAIN LINE: THE BOY AT MUGBY

I AM the boy at Mugby. That's about what I am.

You don't know what I mean? What a pity! But I think you do. I think you must. Look here. I am the boy at what is called The Refreshment Room at Mugby Junction, and what's proudest boast is, that it never yet refreshed a mortal being.

Up in a corner of the Down Refreshment Room at Mugby Junction in the height of twenty-seven cross draughts (I've often counted 'em while they brush the First-Class hair twenty-seven ways), behind the bottles, among the glasses, bounded on the nor'west by the beer, stood pretty far to the right of a metallic object that's at times the tea-urn and at times the soup-tureen, according to the nature of the last twang imparted to its contents which are the same groundwork, fended off from the traveller by a barrier of stale sponge-cakes erected atop of the counter, and lastly exposed sideways to the glare of Our Missis's eye—you ask a Boy so sitiwated, next time you stop in a hurry at Mugby, for anything to drink; you take particular notice that he'll try to seem not to hear you, that he'll appear in a absent manner to survey the Line through a transparent medium composed of your head and body and that he won't serve you as long as you can possibly bear it. That's me.

What a lark it is! We are the Model Establishment, we are, at Mugby. Other Refreshment Rooms send their imperfect young ladies up to be finished off by Our Missis. For some of the young ladies, when they're new to the business, come into it mild! Ah! Our Missis,

he soon takes that out of 'em. Why, I originally come into the busi-
ess meek myself. But Our Missis, she soon took that out of *me*.

What a delightful lark it is! I look upon us Refreshmenters as
ckipying the only proudly independent footing on the Line. There's
'apers, for instance,—my honourable friend, if he will allow me to
all him so,—him as belongs to Smith's bookstall. Why, he no more
ares to be up to our Refreshmenting games than he dares to jump
top of a locomotive with her steam at full pressure, and cut away
pon her alone, driving himself, at limited mail-speed. Papers, he'd
et his head punched at every compartment, first, second, and third,
he whole length of a train, if he was to ventur to imitate my demean-
ur. It's the same with the porters, the same with the guards, the
ame with the ticket clerks, the same the whole way up to the secre-
ary, traffic-manager, or very chairman. There ain't a one among 'em
n the nobly independent footing we are. Did you ever catch one of
iem, when you wanted anything of him, making a system of sur-
eying the Line through a transparent medium composed of your
ead and body? I should hope not.

You should see our Bandolining Room at Mugby Junction. It's led
o by the door behind the counter, which you'll notice usually stands
jar, and it's the room where Our Missis and our young ladies Ban-
olines their hair. You should see 'em at it, betwixt trains, Bando-
ning away, as if they were anointing themselves for the combat.
Vhen you're telegraphed, you should see their noses all a-going up
vith scorn, as if it was a part of the working of the same Cooke and
Vheatstone electrical machinery. You should hear Our Missis give
he word. "Here comes the Beast to be Fed!" and then you should see
em indignantly skipping across the Line, from the Up to the Down,
r Wicer Warsaw, and begin to pitch the stale pastry into the plates,
nd chuck the sawdust sangwiches under the glass covers, and get
ut the—ha, ha, ha!—the sherry,—O my eye, my eye!—for your
Refreshment.

It's only in the Isle of the Brave and Land of the Free (by which, of
ourse, I mean to say Britannia) that Refreshmenting is so effective,
o 'olesome, so constitutional a check upon the public. There was a
'oreigner, which having politely, with his hat off, beseeched our
oung ladies and Our Missis for "a leetel gloss hoff prarndee," and
aaving had the Line surveyed through him by all and no other
cknowledgment, was a proceeding at last to help himself, as seems
o be the custom in his own country, when Our Missis, with her hair
lmost a-coming un-Bandolined with rage, and her eyes omitting
parks, flew at him, cotched the decanter out of his hand, and said,
'Put it down! I won't allow that!" The foreigner turned pale,
tepped back with his arms stretched out in front of him, his hands
lasped, and his shoulders riz, and exclaimed: "Ah! Is it possible,
his! That these disdaineous females and this ferocious old woman
re placed here by the administration, not only to empoison the
oyagers, but to affront them! Great Heaven! How arrives it? The
English people. Or is he then a slave? Or idiot?" Another time, a

merry, wideawake American gent had tried the sawdust and spit it
out, and had tried the Sherry and spit that out, and had tried in
vain to sustain exhausted natur upon Butter-Scotch, and had been
rather extra Bandolined and Line-surveyed through, when, as the
bell was ringing and he paid Our Missis, he says, very loud and good-
tempered: "I tell Yew what 'tis ma'arm. I la'af. Theer! I la'af.
Dew. I oughter ha' seen most things, for I hail from the Onlimited
side of the Atlantic Ocean, and I haive travelled right slick over the
Limited, head on through Jeerusalemm and the East, and likeways
France and Italy, Europe Old World, and am now upon the track to
the Chief Europian Village; but such an Institution as Yew, and
Yewer young ladies, and Yewer fixin's solid and liquid, afore the
glorious Tarnal I never did see yet! And if I hain't found the eighth
wonder of monarchical Creation, in finding Yew, and Yewer young
ladies, and Yewer fixin's solid and liquid, all as aforesaid, established
in a country where the people air not absolute Loo-naticks, I am
Extra Double Darned with a Nip and Frizzle to the innermostest grit!
Wheerfur—Theer!—I la'af! I Dew, ma'arm. I la'af!" And so he
went, stamping and shaking his sides, along the platform all the way
to his own compartment.

I think it was her standing up agin the Foreigner as giv' Our Missis
the idea of going over to France, and droring a comparison betwixt
Refreshmenting as followed among the frog-eaters, and Refreshmenting as triumphant in the Isle of the Brave and Land of the Free
(by which, of course, I mean to say agin, Britannia). Our young
ladies, Miss Whiff, Miss Piff, and Mrs. Sniff, was unanimous opposed
to her going; for, as they says to Our Missis one and all, it is well
beknown to the hends of the herth as no other nation except Britain
has a idea of anythink, but above all of business. Why then should
you tire yourself to prove what is already proved? Our Missis
however (being a teazer at all pints) stood out grim obstinate, and
got a return pass by South-eastern Tidal, to go right through, if such
should be her dispositions, to Marseilles.

Sniff is husband to Mrs. Sniff, and is a regular insignificant cove.
He looks arter the sawdust department in a back room, and is sometimes, when we are very hard put to it, led behind the counter with
a corkscrew; but never when it can be helped, his demeanour towards the public being disgusting servile. How Mrs. Sniff ever come
so far to lower herself as to marry him, I don't know; but I suppose
he does, and I should think he wished he didn't, for he leads a awful
life. Mrs. Sniff couldn't be much harder with him if he was public.
Similarly, Miss Whiff and Miss Piff, taking the tone of Mrs. Sniff,
they shoulder Sniff about when he *is* let in with a corkscrew, and they
whisk things out of his hands when in his servility he is a-going to
let the public have 'em, and they snap him up when in the crawling
baseness of his spriit he is a-going to answer a public question, and
they drore more tears into his eyes than ever the mustard does which
he all day long lays on to the sawdust. (But it ain't strong.) Once
when Sniff had the repulsiveness to reach across to get the milk-po

hand over for a baby, I see Our Missis in her rage catch him by
oth his shoulders, and spin him into the Bandolining Room.

But Mrs. Sniff,—how different! She's the one! She's the one as
ou'll notice to be always looking another way from you, when you
ok at her. She's the one with the small waist buckled in tight in
ont, and with the lace cuffs at her wrists, which she puts on the
dge of the counter before her, and stands a-smoothing while the
iblic foams. This smoothing the cuffs and looking another way
hile the public foams is the last accomplishment taught to the
oung ladies as come to Mugby to be finished by Our Missis; and it's
ways taught by Mrs. Sniff.

When Our Missis went away upon her journey, Mrs. Sniff was left
charge. She did hold the public in check most beautiful! In all my
me, I never see half so many cups of tea given without milk to
ople as wanted it with, nor half so many cups of tea with milk
ven to people as wanted it without. When foaming ensued, Mrs.
iiff would say: "Then you'd better settle it among yourselves, and
ange with one another." It was a most highly delicious lark. I
joyed the Refreshmenting business more than ever, and was so
ad I had took to it when young.

Our Missis returned. It got circulated among the young ladies, and
as it might be penetrated to me through the crevices of the Bando-
ing Room, that she had Orrors to reveal, if revelations so contemp-
ble could be dignified with the name. Agitation become awakened.
xcitement was up to the stirrups. Expectation stood a-tiptoe. At
ngth it was put forth that on our slacked evening in the week, and
our slackest time of that evening betwixt trains, Our Missis would
ve her views of foreign Refreshmenting, in the Bandolining Room.

It was arranged tasteful for the purpose. The Bandolining table
d glass was hid in a corner, a armchair was elevated on a packing-
se for Our Missis's ockypation, a table and a tumbler of water (no
erry in it, thankee) was placed beside it. Two of the pupils, the
ason being autumn, and hollyhocks and dahlias being in, orna-
ented the wall with three devices in those flowers. On one might be
ad, "MAY ALBION NEVER LEARN"; on another, "KEEP THE PUBLIC
OWN"; on another, "OUR REFRESHMENTING CHARTER." The whole
d a beautiful appearance, with which the beauty of the sentiments
rresponded.

On Our Missis's brow was wrote Severity, as she ascended the
tal platform. (Not that that was anythink new.) Miss Whiff and
iss Piff sat at her feet. Three chairs from the Waiting Room might
ve been perceived by a average eye, in front of her, on which the
upils was accommodated. Behind them a very close observer
ight have discerned a Boy. Myself.

"Where," said Our Missis, glancing gloomily around, "is Sniff?"

"I thought it better," answered Mrs. Sniff, "that he should not be
t to come in. He is such an Ass."

"No doubt," assented Our Missis. "But for that reason is it not
esirable to improve his mind?"

"Oh, nothing will ever improve *him*," said Mrs. Sniff.

"However," pursued Our Missis, "call him in, Ezekiel."

I called him in. The appearance of the low-minded cove wa[s] hailed with disapprobation from all sides, on account of his havin[g] brought his corkscrew with him. He pleaded "the force of habit."

"The force!" said Mrs. Sniff. "Don't let us have you talking abou[t] force, for Gracious' sake. There! Do stand still where you are, wit[h] your back against the wall."

He is a smiling piece of vacancy, and he smiled in the mean way i[n] which he will even smile at the public if he gets a chance (languag[e] can say no meaner of him), and he stood upright near the door wit[h] the back of his head agin the wall, as if he was a-waiting for som[e] body to come and measure his heighth for the Army.

"I should not enter, ladies," says Our Missis, "on the revoltin[g] disclosures I am about to make, if it was not in the hope that the[y] will cause you to be yet more implacable in the exercise of the powe[r] you wield in a constitutional country, and yet more devoted to th[e] constitutional motto which I see before me,"—it was behind her, bu[t] the words sounded better so,—" 'May Albion never learn!' "

Here the pupils as had made the motto admired it, and crie[d] "Hear! Hear! Hear!" Sniff, showing an inclination to join in choru[s] got himself frowned down by every brow.

"The baseness of the French," pursued Our Missis, "as displaye[d] in the fawning nature of their Refreshmenting, equals, if not sur[-] passes, anythink as was ever heard of the baseness of the celebrate[d] Bonaparte."

Miss Whiff, Miss Piff, and me, we drored a heavy breath, equal t[o] saying, "We thought as much!" Miss Whiff and Miss Piff seeming t[o] object to my droring mine along with theirs, I drored another t[o] aggravate 'em.

"Shall I be believed," says Our Missis, with flashing eyes, "when [I] tell you that no sooner had I set my foot upon that treacherou[s] shore——"

Here Sniff, either bursting out mad, or thinking aloud, says, in [a] low voice: "Feet. Plural, you know."

The cowering that come upon him when he was spurned by a[ll] eyes, added to his being beneath contempt, was sufficient punish[-] ment for a cove so grovelling. In the midst of a silence rendered mor[e] impressive by the turned-up female noses with which it was pervade[d] Our Missis went on:

"Shall I be believed when I tell you, that no sooner had I landed," this word with a killing look at Sniff, "on that treacherous shor[e] than I was ushered into a Refreshment Room where there were—I d[o] not exaggerate—actually eatable things to eat?"

A groan burst from the ladies. I not only did myself the honour [of] jining, but also of lengthening it out.

"Where there were," Our Missis added, "not only eatable things t[o] eat, but also drinkable things to drink?"

A murmur, swelling almost into a scream, ariz. Miss Piff, tremblin[g] ith indignation, called out, "Name!"

"I *will* name," said Our Missis. "There was roast fowls, hot and
old; there was smoking roast veal surrounded with browned pota-
oes; there was hot soup with (again I ask shall I be credited?)
othing bitter in it, and no flour to choke off the consumer; there
as a variety of cold dishes set off with jelly; there was salad; there
as—mark me! *fresh* pastry, and that of a light construction; there
as a luscious show of fruit; there was bottles and decanters of sound
nall wine, of every size, and adapted to every pocket; the same
dious statement will apply to brandy; and these were set out upon
ie counter so that all could help themselves."

Our Missis's lips so quivered, that Mrs. Sniff, though scarcely less
onvulsed than she were, got up and held the tumbler to them.

"This," proceeds Our Missis, "was my first unconstitutional
xperience. Well would it have been if it had been my last and worst.
ut no. As I proceeded farther into that enslaved and ignorant land,
s aspect became more hideous. I need not explain to this assembly
ie ingredients and formation of the British Refreshment sang-
'ich?''

Universal laughter,—except from Sniff, who, as sangwich-cutter,
took his head in a state of the utmost dejection as he stood with it
gin the wall.

"Well!" said Our Missis, with dilated nostrils. "Take a fresh,
risp, long, crusty penny loaf made of the whitest and best flour. Cut
longwise through the middle. Insert a fair and nicely fitting slice of
am. Tie a smart piece of ribbon round the middle of the whole to
ind it together. Add at one end a neat wrapper of clean white paper
y which to hold it. And the universal French Refreshment sangwich
usts on your disgusted vision."

A cry of "Shame!" from all—except Sniff, which rubbed his
tomach with a soothing hand.

"I need not," said Our Missis, "explain to this assembly the usual
ormation and fitting of the British Refreshment Room?"

No, no, and laughter. Sniff agin shaking his head in low spirits agin
ie wall.

Well," said Our Missis, "what would you say to a general decora-
on of everythink, to hangings (sometimes elegant), to easy velvet
urniture, to abundance of little tables, to abundance of little seats,
o brisk bright waiters, to great convenience, to a pervading cleanli-
ess and tastefulness positively addressing the public, and making
ie Beast thinking itself worth the pains?"

Contemptuous fury on the part of all the ladies. Mrs. Sniff looking
s if she wanted somebody to hold her, and everybody else looking as
they'd rayther not.

"Three times," said Our Missis, working herself into a truly
errimenjious state,—"three times did I see these shameful things,
nly between the coast and Paris, and not counting either: at
azebrouche, at Arras, at Amiens. But worse remains. Tell me, what
ould you call a person who should propose in England that there

should be kept, say at our own model Mugby Junction, pretty baskets, each holding an assorted cold lunch and dessert for one each at a certain fixed price, and each within a passenger's power to take away, to empty in the carriage at perfect leisure, and to return at another station fifty or a hundred miles farther on?''

There was disagreement what such a person should be called. Whether revolutionist, atheist, Bright (I said him), or Un-English. Miss Piff screeched her shrill opinion last, in the words: "A malignant maniac!"

"I adopt," says Our Missis, "the brand set upon such a person by the righteous indignation of my friend Miss Piff. A malignant maniac. Know, then, that that malignant maniac has sprung from the congenial soil of France, and that his malignant madness was in unchecked action on this same part of my journey."

I noticed that Sniff was a-rubbing his hands, and that Mrs. Sniff had got her eye upon him. But I did not take more particular notice owing to the excited state in which the young ladies was, and to feeling myself called upon to keep it up with a howl.

"On my experience south of Paris," said Our Missis, in a deep tone, "I will not expatiate. Too loathsome were the task! But fancy this. Fancy a guard coming round, with the train at full speed, to inquire how many for dinner. Fancy his telegraphing forward the number of dinners. Fancy every one expected, and the table elegantly laid for the complete party. Fancy a charming dinner, in a charming room, and the head-cook, concerned for the honour of every dish, superintending in his clean white jacket and cap. Fancy the Beast travelling six hundred miles on end, very fast, and with great punctuality, yet being taught to expect all this to be done for it!"

A spirited chorus of "The Beast!"

I noticed that Sniff was agin a-rubbing his stomach with a soothing hand, and that he had drored up one leg. But agin I didn't take particular notice, looking on myself as called upon to stimulate public feeling. It being a lark besides.

"Putting everything together," said Our Missis, "French Refreshmenting comes to this, and oh, it comes to a nice total! First: eatable things to eat, and drinkable things to drink."

A groan from the young ladies, kep' up by me.

"Second: convenience, and even elegance."

Another groan from the young ladies, kep' up by me.

"Third: moderate charges."

This time a groan from me, kep' up by the young ladies.

"Fourth:—and here," says Our Missis, "I claim your angriest sympathy,—attention, common civility, nay, even politeness!"

Me and the young ladies regularly raging mad all together.

"And I cannot in conclusion," says Our Missis, with her spitefullest sneer, "give you a completer pictur of that despicable nation (after what I have related), than assuring you that they wouldn't bear our constitutional ways and noble independence at Mugby

Junction, for a single month, and that they would return us to the right-about and put another system in our places, and soon as look at us; perhaps sooner, for I do not believe they have the good taste to care to look at us twice."

The swelling tumult was arrested in its rise. Sniff, bore away by his servile disposition, had drored up his leg with a higher and a higher relish, and was now discovered to be waving his corkscrew over his head. It was at this moment that Mrs. Sniff, who had kep' her eye upon him like the fabled obelisk, descended on her victim. Our Missis followed them both out, and cries was heard in the sawdust department.

You come into the Down Refreshment Room, at the Junction, making believe you don't know me, and I'll pint you out with my right thumb over my shoulder which is Our Missis, and which is Miss Whiff, and which is Miss Piff, and which is Mrs. Sniff. But you won't get a chance to see Sniff, because he disappeared that night. Whether he perished, tore to pieces, I cannot say; but his corkscrew alone remains, to bear witness to the servility of his disposition.

CHAPTER IV

NO. I BRANCH LINE: THE SIGNAL-MAN

"Halloa! Below there!"

When he heard a voice thus calling to him, he was standing at the door of his box, with a flag in his hand, furled round its short pole. One would have thought, considering the nature of the ground, that he could not have doubted from what quarter the voice came; but instead of looking up to where I stood on the top of the steep cutting nearly over his head, he turned himself about, and looked down the Line. There was something remarkable in his manner of doing so, though I could not have said for my life what. But I know it was remarkable enough to attract my notice, even though his figure was foreshortened and shadowed, down to the deep trench, and mine was high above him, so steeped in the glow of an angry sunset, that I had shaded my eyes with my hand before I saw him at all.

"Halloa! Below!"

From looking down the Line, he turned himself about again, and, raising his eyes, saw my figure high above him.

"Is there any path by which I can come down and speak to you?"

He looked up at me without replying, and I looked down at him without pressing him too soon with a repetition of my idle question. Just then there came a vague vibration in the earth and air, quickly changing into a violent pulsation, and an oncoming rush that caused me to start back, as though it had force to draw me down. When such vapour as rose to my height from this rapid train had passed me, and was skimming away over the landscape, I looked down again, and saw him refurling the flag he had shown while the train went by.

I repeated my inquiry. After a pause, during which he seemed to regard me with fixed attention, he motioned with his rolled-up flag towards a point on my level, some two or three hundred yards distant. I called down to him, "All right!" and made for that point. There, by dint of looking closely about me, I found a rough zigzag descending path notched out, which I followed.

The cutting was extremely deep, and unusually precipitate. It was made through a clammy stone, that became oozier and wetter as I went down. For these reasons, I found the way long enough to give me time to recall a singular air of reluctance or compulsion with which he had pointed out the path.

When I came down low enough upon the zigzag descent to see him again, I saw that he was standing between the rails on the way by which the train had lately passed, in an attitude as if he were waiting for me to appear. He had his left hand at his chin, and that left elbow rested on his right hand, crossed over his breast. His attitude was one of such expectation and watchfulness that I stopped a moment, wondering at it.

I resumed my downward way, and stepping out upon the level of the railroad, and drawing nearer to him, saw that he was a dark sallow man, with a dark beard and rather heavy eyebrows. His post was in as solitary and dismal a place as ever I saw. On either side, a dripping-wet wall of jagged stone, excluding all view but a strip of sky; the perspective one way only a crooked prolongation of this great dungeon; the shorter perspective in the other direction terminating in a gloomy red light, and the gloomier entrance to a black tunnel, in whose massive architecture there was a barbarous, depressing, and forbidding air. So little sunlight ever found its way to this spot, that it had an earthy, deadly smell; and so much cold wind rushed through it, that it struck chill to me, as if I had left the natural world.

Before he stirred, I was near enough to him to have touched him. Not even then removing his eyes from mine, he stepped back one step, and lifted his hand.

This was a lonesome post to occupy (I said), and it had riveted my attention when I looked down from up yonder. A visitor was a rarity, I should suppose; not an unwelcome rarity, I hoped? In me, he merely saw a man, who had been shut up within narrow limits all his life, and who, being at last set free, had a newly-awakened interest in these great works. To such purpose I spoke to him; but I am far from sure of the terms I used; for, besides that I am not happy in opening any conversation, there was something in the man that daunted me.

He directed a most curious look towards the red light near the tunnel's mouth, and looked all about it, as if something were missing from it, and then looked at me.

That light was part of his charge? Was it not?

He answered in a low voice,—"Don't you know it is?"

The monstrous thought came into my mind, as I perused the fixed eyes and the saturnine face, that this was a spirit, not a man. I have speculated since, whether there may have been infection in his mind.

In my turn, I stepped back. But in making the action, I detected in his eyes some latent fear of me. This put the monstrous thought to flight.

"You look at me," I said, forcing a smile, "as if you had a dread of me."

"I was doubtful," he returned, "whether I had seen you before."

"Where?"

He pointed to the red light he had looked at.

"There?" I said.

Intently watchful of me, he replied (but without sound), "Yes."

"My good fellow, what should I do there? However, be that as it may, I never was there, you may swear."

"I think I may," he rejoined. "Yes; I am sure I may."

His manner cleared, like my own. He replied to my remarks with readiness, and in well-chosen words. Had he much to do there? Yes; that was to say, he had enough responsibility to bear; but exactness and watchfulness were what was required of him, and of actual work—manual labour—he had next to none. To change that signal, to trim those lights, and to turn this iron handle now and then, was all he had to do under that head. Regarding those many long and lonely hours of which I seemed to make so much, he could only say that the routine of his life had shaped itself into that form, and he had grown used to it. He had taught himself a language down here,—if only to know it by sight, and to have formed his own crude ideas of its pronunciation, could be called learning it. He had also worked at fractions and decimals, and tried a little algebra; but he was, and had been as a boy, a poor hand at figures. Was it necessary for him when on duty always to remain in that channel of damp air, and could he never rise into the sunshine from between those high stone walls? Why, that depended upon times and circumstances. Under some conditions there would be less upon the Line than under others, and the same held good as to certain hours of the day and night. In bright weather, he did choose occasions for getting a little above these lower shadows; but, being at all times liable to be called by his electric bell, and at such times listening for it with redoubled anxiety, the relief was less than I would suppose.

He took me into his box, where there was a fire, a desk for an official book in which he had to make certain entries, a telegraphic instrument with its dial, face, and needles, and the little bell of which he had spoken. On my trusting that he would excuse the remark that he had been well educated, and (I hoped I might say without offence), perhaps educated above that station, he observed that instances of slight incongruity in such wise would rarely be found wanting among large bodies of men; that he had heard it was so in workhouses, in the police force, even in that last desperate resource,

the army; and that he knew it was so, more or less, in any grea
railway staff. He had been, when young (if I could believe it, sittin;
in that hut,—he scarcely could), a student of natural philosophy
and had attended lectures; but he had run wild, misused his oppor
tunities, gone down, and never risen again. He had no complaint to
offer about that. He had made his bed, and he lay upon it. It was far
too late to make another.

All that I have here condensed he said in a quiet manner, with
his grave dark regards divided between me and the fire. He threw
in the word, "Sir," from time to time, and especially when he referred
to his youth,—as though to request me to understand that he claimed
to be nothing but what I found him. He was several times interrupted
by the little bell, and had to read off messages, and send replies
Once he had to stand without the door, and display a flag as a train
passed, and make some verbal communication to the driver. In the
discharge of his duties, I observed him to be remarkably exact and
vigilant, breaking off his discourse at a syllable, and remaining silent
until what he had to do was done.

In a word, I should have set this man down as one of the safest
of men to be employed in that capacity, but for the circumstance
that while he was speaking to me he twice broke off with a fallen
colour, turned his face towards the little bell when it did NOT ring
opened the door of the hut (which was kept shut to exclude the unhealthy damp), and looked out towards the red light near the mouth
of the tunnel. On both of those occasions, he came back to the fire
with the inexplicable air upon him which I had remarked, without
being able to define, when we were so far asunder.

Said I, when I rose to leave him, "You almost make me think that
I have met with a contented man."

(I am afraid I must acknowledge that I said it to lead him on.)

"I believe I used to be so," he rejoined, in the low voice in which
he had first spoken; "but I am troubled, Sir, I am troubled."

He would have recalled the words if he could. He had said them,
however, and I took them up quickly.

"With what? What is your trouble?"

"It is very difficult to impart, Sir. It is very, very difficult to speak
of. If ever you make me another visit, I will try to tell you."

"But I expressly intend to make you another visit. Say, when shall
it be?"

"I go off early in the morning and I shall be on again at ten
to-morrow night, Sir."

"I will come at eleven."

He thanked me, and went out at the door with me. "I'll show my
white light, Sir," he said, in his peculiar low voice, "till you have
found the way up. When you have found it, don't call out! And when
you are at the top, don't call out!"

His manner seemed to make the place strike colder to me, but I
said no more than, "Very well."

"And when you come down to-morrow night, don't call out! Let ne ask you a parting question. What made you cry, 'Halloa! Below here!' to-night?"

"Heaven knows," said I. "I cried something to that effect——"

"Not to that effect, Sir. Those were the very words. I know them well."

"Admit those were the very words. I said them no doubt, because saw you below."

"For no other reason?"

"What other reason could I possibly have?"

"You had no feeling that they were conveyed to you in any supernatural way?"

"No."

He wished me good night, and held up his light. I walked by the side of the down Line of rails (with a very disagreeable sensation of a rain coming behind me) until I found the path. It was easier to mount than to descend, and I got back to my inn without any adventure.

Punctual to my appointment, I placed my foot on the first notch of the zigzag next night, as the distant clocks were striking eleven. He was waiting for me at the bottom, with his white light on. "I have not called out," I said, when we came close together; "may I speak now?" "By all means, Sir." "Good night, then, and here's my hand." "Good night, Sir, and here's mine." With that we walked side by side to his box, entered it, closed the door, and sat down by the fire.

"I have made up my mind, Sir," he began, bending forward as soon as we were seated, and speaking in a tone but a little above a whisper, "that you shall not have to ask me twice what troubles me. I took you for some one else yesterday evening. That troubles me."

"That mistake?"

"No. That some one else."

"Who is it?"

"I don't know."

"Like me?"

"I don't know. I never saw the face. The left arm is across the face, and the right arm is waved,—violently waved. This way."

I followed his action with my eyes, and it was the action of an arm gesticulating with the utmost passion and vehemence, "For God's sake, clear the way!"

"One moonlight night," said the man, "I was sitting here, when I heard a voice cry, 'Halloa! Below there!' I started up, looked from that door, and saw this Some one else standing by the red light near the tunnel, waving as I just now showed you. The voice seemed hoarse with shouting, and it cried, 'Look out! Look out!' And then again, 'Halloa! Below there! Look out!' I caught up my lamp, turned it on red, and ran towards the figure, calling, 'What's wrong? What has happened? Where?' It stood just outside the blackness of the tunnel. I advanced so close upon it that I wondered at its keeping the sleeve across its eyes. I ran right up at it, and had my hand stretched out to pull the sleeve away, when it was gone."

"Into the tunnel?" said I.

"No. I ran on into the tunnel, five hundred yards. I stopped, an
held my lamp above my head, and saw the figures of the measure
distance, and saw the wet stains stealing down the walls and tricklin
through the arch. I ran out again faster than I had run in (for I ha
a mortal abhorrence of the place upon me), and I looked all roun
the red light with my own red light, and I went up the iron ladder t
the gallery atop of it, and I came down again, and ran back here
I telegraphed both ways. 'An alarm has been given. Is anythin
wrong?' The answer came back, both ways, 'All well.' "

Resisting the slow touch of a frozen finger tracing out my spine
I showed him how that this figure must be a deception of his sense o
sight; and how that figures, originating in disease of the delicat
nerves that minister to the functions of the eye, were known to hav
often troubled patients, some of whom had become conscious of th
nature of their affliction, and had even proved it by experiment
upon themselves. "As to an imaginary cry," said I, "do but listen
for a moment to the wind in this unnatural valley while we speak
so low, and to the wild harp it makes of the telegraph wires."

That was all very well, he returned, after we had sat listening for a
while, and he ought to know something of the wind and the wires,—
he who so often passed long winter nights there, alone and watching
But he would beg to remark that he had not finished.

I asked his pardon, and he slowly added these words, touching my
arm,—

"Within six hours after the Appearance, the memorable acciden
on this Line happened, and within ten hours the dead and wounded
were brought along through the tunnel over the spot where the figure
had stood."

A disagreeable shudder crept over me, but I did my best against
it. It was not to be denied, I rejoined, that this was a remarkable
coincidence, calculated deeply to impress his mind. But it was un
questionable that remarkable coincidences did continually occur
and they must be taken into account in dealing with such a subject
Though to be sure I must admit, I added (for I thought I saw that he
was going to bring the objection to bear upon me), men of common
sense did not allow much for coincidences in making the ordinary
calculations of life.

He again begged to remark that he had not finished.

I again begged his pardon for being betrayed into interruptions

"This," he said, again laying his hand upon my arm, and glancing
over his shoulder with hollow eyes, "was just a year ago. Six or
seven months passed, and I had recovered from the surprise and
shock, when one morning, as the day was breaking, I, standing at
the door, looked towards the red light, and saw the spectre again."
He stopped, with a fixed look at me.

"Did it cry out?"

"No. It was silent."

"Did it wave its arm?"

"No. It leaned against the shaft of light, with both hands before he face. Like this."

Once more I followed his action with my eyes. It was an action of mourning. I have seen such an attitude in stone figures on tombs.

"Did you go up to it?"

"I came in and sat down, partly to collect my thoughts, partly because it had turned me faint. When I went to the door again, daylight was above me, and the ghost was gone."

"But nothing followed? Nothing came of this?"

He touched me on the arm with his forefinger twice or thrice, giving a ghastly nod each time :—

"That very day, as a train came out of the tunnel, I noticed, at a carriage window on my side, what looked like a confusion of hands and heads, and something waved. I saw it just in time to signal the driver, Stop! He shut off, and put his brake on, but the train drifted past here a hundred and fifty yards or more. I ran after it, and, as I went along, heard terrible screams and cries. A beautiful young lady had died instantaneously in one of the compartments, and was brought in here, and laid down on this floor between us."

Involuntarily I pushed my chair back, as I looked from the boards at which he pointed to himself.

"True, Sir. True. Precisely as it happened, so I tell it you."

I could think of nothing to say, to any purpose, and my mouth was very dry. The wind and the wires took up the story with a long lamenting wail.

He resumed. "Now, Sir, mark this, and judge how my mind is troubled. The spectre came back a week ago. Ever since, it has been there, now and again, by fits and starts."

"At the light?"

"At the Danger-light."

"What does it seem to do?"

He repeated if possible with increased passion and vehemence, that former gesticulation of "For God's sake, clear the way!"

Then he went on. "I have no peace or rest for it. It calls to me, for many minutes together, in an agonised manner, 'Below there! Look out!' It stands waving to me. It rings my little bell——"

I caught at that. "Did it ring your bell yesterday evening when I was here, and you went to the door?"

"Twice."

"Why, see," said I, "how your imagination misleads you. My eyes were on the bell, and my ears were open to the bell, and if I am a living man, it did NOT ring at those times. No, nor at any other time, except when it was rung in the natural course of physical things by the station communicating with you."

He shook his head. "I have never made a mistake as to that yet, Sir. I have never confused the spectre's ring with the man's. The ghost's ring is a strange vibration in the bell that it derives from nothing else, and I have not asserted that the bell stirs to the eye. I don't wonder that you failed to hear it. But I heard it."

"And did the spectre seem to be there, when you looked out?"

"It was there."

"Both times?"

He repeated firmly: "Both times."

"Will you come to the door with me, and look for it now?"

He bit his under lip as though he were somewhat unwilling, b[ut] arose. I opened the door, and stood on the step, while he stood in th[e] doorway. There was the Danger-light. There was the dismal mouth [of] the tunnel. There were the high, wet stone walls of the cuttin[g.] There were the stars above them.

"Do you see it?" I asked him, taking particular note of his fac[e.] His eyes were prominent and strained, but not very much more s[o,] perhaps, than my own had been when I had directed them earnestl[y] towards the same spot.

"No," he answered. "It is not there."

"Agreed," said I.

We went in again, shut the door, and resumed our seats. I wa[s] thinking how best to improve this advantage, if it might be calle[d] one, when he took up the conversation in such a matter-of-cours[e] way, so assuming that there could be no serious question of fac[t] between us, that I felt myself placed in the weakest of positions.

"By this time you will fully understand, Sir," he said, "that wha[t] troubles me so dreadfully is the question, What does the spectre mean?"

I was not sure, I told him, that I did fully understand.

"What is its warning against?" he said, ruminating, with his eye[s] on the fire, and only by times turning them on me. "What is th[e] danger? Where is the danger? There is danger overhanging some[-] where on the Line. Some dreadful calamity will happen. It is not t[o] be doubted this third time, after what has gone before. But surel[y] this is a cruel haunting of *me*. What can *I* do?"

He pulled out his handkerchief, and wiped the drops from hi[s] heated forehead.

"If I telegraph Danger, on either side of me, or on both, I can giv[e] no reason for it," he went on, wiping the palms of his hands. "[I] should get into trouble, and do no good. They would think I wa[s] mad. This is the way it would work,—Message: 'Danger! Take care!' Answer: 'What Danger? Where?' Message: 'Don't know. But, fo[r] God's sake, take care!' They would displace me. What else coul[d] they do?"

His pain of mind was most pitiable to see. It was the menta[l] torture of a conscientious man, oppressed beyond endurance by a[n] unintelligible responsibility involving life.

"When it first stood under the Danger-light," he went on, puttin[g] his dark hair back from his head, and drawing his hands outwar[d] across and across his temples in an extremity of feverish distress "why not tell me where that accident was to happen,—if it mus[t] happen? Why not tell me how it could be averted,—if it could hav[e] been averted? When on its second coming it hid its face, why not tel[l] me, instead, 'She is going to die. Let them keep her at home'? If i[f] me, on those two occasions, only to show me that its warnings ere true, and so to prepare me for the third, why not warn me ainly now? And I, Lord help me! A mere poor signal-man on this ilitary station! Why not go to somebody with credit to be believed id power to act?"

When I saw him in this state, I saw that for the poor man's sake, s well as for the public safety, what I had to do for the time was to impose his mind. Therefore, setting aside all question of reality or inreality between us, I represented to him that whoever thoroughly ischarged his duty must do well, and that at least it was his comfort hat he understood his duty, though he did not understand these onfounding Appearances. In this effort I succeeded far better than i the attempt to reason him out of his conviction. He became calm; the ccupations incidental to his post as the night advanced began to make irger demands on his attention: and I left him at two in the morning. had offered to stay through the night, but he would not hear of it.

That I more than once looked back at the red light as I ascended he pathway, that I did not like the red light, and that I should have lept but poorly if my bed had been under it, I see no reason to con- eal. Nor did I like the two sequences of the accident and the dead girl. I see no reason to conceal that either.

But what ran most in my thoughts was the consideration how ought I to act, having become the recipient of this disclosure? I had proved the man to be intelligent, vigilant, painstaking, and exact; but how long might he remain so, in his state of mind? Though in a subordinate position, still he held a most important trust, and would I (for instance) like to stake my own life on the chances of his con- tinuing to execute it with precision?

Unable to overcome a feeling that there would be something treacherous in my communicating what he had told me to his superiors in the Company, without first being plain with himself and proposing a middle course to him, I ultimately resolved to offer to accompany him (otherwise keeping his secret for the present) to the wisest medical practitioner we could hear of in those parts, and to take his opinion. A change in his time of duty would come round next night, he had apprised me, and he would be off an hour or two after sunrise, and on again soon after sunset. I had appointed to return accordingly.

Next evening was a lovely evening, and I walked out early to enjoy it. The sun was not yet quite down when I traversed the field- path near the top of the deep cutting. I would extend my walk for an hour, I said to myself, half an hour on and half an hour back, and it would then be time to go to my signal-man's box.

Before pursuing my stroll, I stepped to the brink, and mechanically looked down, from the point from which I had first seen him. I cannot describe the thrill that seized upon me, when, close at the mouth of the tunnel, I saw the appearance of a man, with his left sleeve across his eyes, passionately waving his right arm.

The nameless horror that oppressed me passed in a moment,

for in a moment I saw that this appearance of a man was a m:
indeed, and that there was a little group of other men, standing at
short distance, to whom he seemed to be rehearsing the gesture I
made. The Danger-light was not yet lighted. Against its shaft,
little low hut, entirely new to me, had been made of some woode
supports and tarpaulin. It looked no bigger than a bed.

With an irresistible sense that something was wrong,—with
flashing self-reproachful fear that fatal mischief had come of m
leaving the man there, and causing no one to be sent to overlook o
correct what he did,—I descended the notched path with all th
speed I could make.

"What is the matter?" I asked the men.

"Signal-man killed this morning, Sir."

"Not the man belonging to that box?"

"Yes, Sir."

"Not the man I know?"

"You will recognise him, Sir, if you knew him," said the man who
spoke for the others, solemnly uncovering his own head, and raising
an end of the tarpaulin, "for his face is quite composed."

"O, how did this happen, how did this happen?" I asked, turning
from one to another as the hut closed in again.

"He was cut down by an engine, Sir. No man in England knew
his work better. But somehow he was not clear of the outer rail.
It was just at broad day. He had struck the light, and had the lamp
in his hand. As the engine came out of the tunnel, his back was
towards her, and she cut him down. That man drove her, and was
showing how it happened. Show the gentleman, Tom."

The man, who wore a rough dark dress, stepped back to his
former place at the mouth of the tunnel.

"Coming round the curve in the tunnel, Sir," he said, "I saw him
at the end, like as if I saw him down a perspective-glass. There was
no time to check speed, and I knew him to be very careful. As he
didn't seem to take heed of the whistle, I shut it off when we were
running down upon him, and called to him as loud as I could call."

"What did you say?"

"I said, 'Below there! Look out! Look out! For God's sake, clear
the way!'"

I started.

"Ah! it was a dreadful time, Sir. I never left off calling to him. I
put this arm before my eyes not to see, and I waved this arm to the
last; but it was no use."

Without prolonging the narrative to dwell on any one of its curious
circumstances more than on any other, I may, in closing it, point out
the coincidence that the warning of the Engine-Driver included, not
only the words which the unfortunate Signal-man had repeated to
me as haunting him, but also the words which I myself—not he—
had attached, and that only in my own mind, to the gesticulation he
had imitated.

NO THOROUGHFARE

[1867]

[This was written by Mr. Wilkie Collins conjointly with Mr. Dickens; the only rtions furnished exclusively by Mr. Dickens being the "Overture" and the hird Act"; Mr. Collins contributing to acts first and fourth, and writing the ole of the second.]

THE OVERTURE

AY of the month and year, November the thirtieth, one thousand ght hundred and thirty-five. London Time by the great clock of int Paul's, ten at night. All the lesser London churches strain their etallic throats. Some, flippantly begin before the heavy bell of the eat cathedral; some, tardily begin three, four, half-a-dozen, strokes hind it; all are in sufficiently near accord, to leave a resonance in e air, as if the winged father who devours his children, had made sounding sweep with his gigantic scythe in flying over the city.

What is this clock lower than most of the rest, and nearer to the r, that lags so far behind to-night as to strike into the vibration one? This is the clock of the Hospital for Foundling Children. Time as, when the Foundlings were received without question in a cradle t the gate. Time is, when inquiries are made respecting them, and ey are taken as by favour from the mothers who relinquish all atural knowledge of them and claim to them for evermore.

The moon is at the full, and the night is fair with light clouds. The ay has been otherwise than fair, for slush and mud, thickened with he droppings of heavy fog, lie black in the streets. The veiled lady ho flutters up and down near the postern-gate of the Hospital for oundling Children has need to be well shod to-night.

She flutters to and fro, avoiding the stand of hackney-coaches, and ften pausing in the shadow of the western end of the great quad-angle wall, with her face turned towards the gate. As above her there s the purity of the moonlit sky, and below her there are the defile-ments of the pavements, so may she, haply, be divided in her mind etween two vistas of reflection or experience. As her footprints rossing and recrossing one another have made a labyrinth in the nire, so may her track in life have involved itself in an intricate and nravellable tangle.

The postern-gate of the Hospital for Foundling Children opens, nd a young woman comes out. The lady stands aside, observes losely, sees that the gate is quietly closed again from within, and ollows the young woman.

Two or three streets have been traversed in silence before she, following close behind the object of her attention, stretches out her hand and touches her. Then the young woman stops and looks round startled.

"You touched me last night, and, when I turned my head, you would not speak. Why do you follow me like a silent ghost?"

"It was not," returned the lady, in a low voice, "that I would not speak, but that I could not when I tried."

"What do you want of me? I have never done you any harm?"

"Never."

"Do I know you?"

"No."

"Then what can you want of me?"

"Here are two guineas in this paper. Take my poor little present, and I will tell you."

Into the young woman's face, which is honest and comely, comes a flush as she replies: "There is neither grown person nor child in all the large establishment that I belong to, who hasn't a good word for Sally. I am Sally. Could I be so well thought of, if I was to be bought?"

"I do not mean to buy you; I mean only to reward you very slightly."

Sally firmly, but not ungently, closes and puts back the offering hand. "If there is anything I can do for you, ma'am, that I will not do for its own sake, you are much mistaken in me if you think that I will do it for money. What is it you want?"

"You are one of the nurses or attendants at the Hospital; I saw you leave to-night and last night."

"Yes, I am. I am Sally."

"There is a pleasant patience in your face which makes me believe that very young children would take readily to you."

"God bless 'em! So they do."

The lady lifts her veil, and shows a face no older than the nurse's. A face far more refined and capable than hers, but wild and worn with sorrow.

"I am the miserable mother of a baby lately received under your care. I have a prayer to make to you."

Instinctively respecting the confidence which has drawn aside the veil, Sally—whose ways are all ways of simplicity and spontaneity—replaces it, and begins to cry.

"You will listen to my prayer?" the lady urges. "You will not be deaf to the agonised entreaty of such a broken suppliant as I am?"

"O dear, dear, dear!" cries Sally. "What shall I say, or can I say? Don't talk of prayers. Prayers are to be put up to the Good Father of All, and not to nurses and such. And there! I am only to hold my place for half a year longer, till another young woman can be trained up to it. I am going to be married. I shouldn't have been out last night, and I shouldn't have been out to-night, but that my Dick (he is the young man I am going to be married to) lies ill, and I help his mother and sister to watch him. Don't take on so, don't take on so!"

"O good Sally, dear Sally," moans the lady, catching at her dress ntreatingly. "As you are hopeful, and I am hopeless; as a fair way 1 life is before you, which can never, never, be before me; as you an aspire to become a respected wife, and as you can aspire to become proud mother, as you are a living loving woman, and must die; for GOD's sake hear my distracted petition!"

"Deary, deary, deary ME!" cries Sally, her desperation culminating n the pronoun, "what am I ever to do? And there! See how you turn ny own words back upon me. I tell you I am going to be married, on purpose to make it clearer to you that I am going to leave, and herefore couldn't help you if I would, Poor Thing, and you make it seem to my own self as if I was cruel in going to be married and *not* nelping you. It ain't kind. Now, is it kind, Poor Thing?"

"Sally! Hear me, my dear. My entreaty is for no help in the future. It applies to what is past. It is only to be told in two words."

"There! This is worse and worse," cries Sally, "supposing that I understand what two words you mean."

"You do understand. What are the names they have given my poor baby? I ask no more than that. I have read of the customs of the place. He has been christened in the chapel, and registered by some surname in the book. He was received last Monday evening. What have they called him?"

Down upon her knees in the foul mud of the by-way into which they have strayed—an empty street without a thoroughfare giving on the dark gardens of the Hospital—the lady would drop in her passionate entreaty, but that Sally prevents her.

"Don't! Don't! You make me feel as if I was setting myself up to be good. Let me look in your pretty face again. Put your two hands in mine. Now, promise. You will never ask me anything more than the two words?"

"Never! Never!"

"You will never put them to a bad use, if I say them?"

"Never! Never!"

"Walter Wilding."

The lady lays her face upon the nurse's breast, draws her close in her embrace with both arms, murmurs a blessing and the words, "Kiss him for me!" and is gone.

Day of the month and year, the first Sunday in October, one thousand eight hundred and forty-seven. London Time by the great clock of Saint Paul's, half-past one in the afternoon. The clock of the Hospital for Foundling Children is well up with the Cathedral to-day. Service in the chapel is over, and the Foundling children are at dinner. There are numerous lookers-on at the dinner, as the custom is. There are two or three governors, whole families from the congregation, smaller groups of both sexes, individual stragglers of various degrees. The bright autumnal sun strikes freshly into the wards; and the heavy-framed windows through which it shines, and the panelled walls on which it strikes, are such windows and such walls as pervade

Hogarth's pictures. The girls' refectory (including that of the younger children) is the principal attraction. Neat attendants silently glide about the orderly and silent tables; the lookers-on move or stop as the fancy takes them; comments in whispers on face such a number from such a window are not unfrequent; many of the faces are of a character to fix attention. Some of the visitors from the outside public are accustomed visitors. They have established a speaking acquaintance with the occupants of particular seats at the tables and halt at those points to bend down and say a word or two. It is no disparagement to their kindness that those points are generally points where personal attractions are. The monotony of the long spacious rooms and the double lines of faces is agreeably relieved by these incidents, although so slight.

A veiled lady, who has no companion, goes among the company. It would seem that curiosity and opportunity have never brought her there before. She has the air of being a little troubled by the sight, and, as she goes the length of the tables, it is with a hesitating step and an uneasy manner. At length she comes to the refectory of the boys. They are so much less popular than the girls that it is bare of visitors when she looks in at the doorway.

But just within the doorway, chances to stand, inspecting, an elderly female attendant: some order of matron or housekeeper. To whom the lady addresses natural questions: As, how many boys? At what age are they usually put out in life? Do they often take a fancy to the sea? So, lower and lower in tone until the lady puts the question: "Which is Walter Wilding?"

Attendant's head shaken. Against the rules.

"You know which is Walter Wilding?"

So keenly does the attendant feel the closeness with which the lady's eyes examine her face, that she keeps her own eyes fast upon the floor, lest by wandering in the right direction they should betray her.

"I know which is Walter Wilding, but it is not my place, ma'am, to tell names to visitors."

"But you can show me without telling me."

The lady's hand moves quietly to the attendant's hand. Pause and silence.

"I am going to pass round the tables," says the lady's interlocutor, without seeming to address her. "Follow me with your eyes. The boy that I stop at and speak to, will not matter to you. But the boy that I touch, will be Walter Wilding. Say nothing more to me, and move a little away."

Quickly acting on the hint, the lady passes on into the room, and looks about her. After a few moments, the attendant, in a staid official way, walks down outside the line of tables commencing on her left hand. She goes the whole length of the line, turns, and comes back on the inside. Very slightly glancing in the lady's direction, she stops, bends forward, and speaks. The boy whom she addresses, lifts his head and replies. Good humouredly and easily, as she listens to what he says, she lays her hand upon the shoulder of the next boy on his right. That the action may be well noted, she keeps her hand on the shoulder while speaking in return, and pats it twice or thrice before moving away. She completes her tour of the tables, touching no one else, and passes out by a door at the opposite end of the long room.

Dinner is done, and the lady, too, walks down outside the line of tables commencing on her left hand, goes the whole length of the line, turns, and comes back on the inside. Other people have strolled in, fortunately for her, and stand sprinkled about. She lifts her veil, and, stopping at the touched boy, asks how old he is?

"I am twelve, ma'am," he answers, with his bright eyes fixed on hers.

"Are you well and happy?"

"Yes, ma'am."

"May you take these sweetmeats from my hand?"

"If you please to give them to me."

In stooping low for the purpose, the lady touches the boy's face with her forehead and with her hair. Then, lowering her veil again, she passes on, and passes out without looking back.

ACT I

THE CURTAIN RISES

IN a court-yard in the City of London, which was No Thoroughfare either for vehicles or foot-passengers; a court-yard diverging from a steep, a slippery, and a winding street connecting Tower-street with the Middlesex shore of the Thames; stood the place of business of Wilding and Co., Wine Merchants. Probably as a jocose acknowledgment of the obstructive character of this main approach, the point nearest to its base at which one could take the river (if so inodorously minded) bore the appellation Break-Neck-Stairs. The court-yard itself had likewise been descriptively entitled in old time, Cripple Corner.

Years before the year one thousand eight hundred and sixty-one, people had left off taking boat at Break-Neck-Stairs, and watermen had ceased to ply there. The slimy little causeway had dropped into the river by a slow process of suicide, and two or three stumps of piles and a rusty iron mooring-ring were all that remained of the departed Break-Neck glories. Sometimes, indeed, a laden coal barge would bump itself into the place, and certain laborious heavers, seemingly mud-engendered, would arise, deliver the cargo in the neighbourhood, shove off, and vanish; but at most times the only commerce of Break-Neck-Stairs arose out of the conveyance of casks and bottles, both full and empty, both to and from the cellars of Wilding and Co., Wine Merchants. Even that commerce was but occasional, and through three-fourths of its rising tides the dirty indecorous drab of a river would come solitarily oozing and lapping at the rusty ring, as if it had heard of the Doge and the Adriatic, and wanted to be married to the great conserver of its filthiness, the Right Honourable the Lord Mayor.

Some two hundred and fifty yards on the right, up the opposite hill (approaching it from the low ground of Break-Neck-Stairs) was Cripple Corner. There was a pump in Cripple Corner, there was a tree in Cripple Corner. All Cripple Corner belonged to Wilding and Co., Wine Merchants. Their cellars burrowed under it, their mansion towered over it. It really had been a mansion in the days when merchants inhabited the City, and had a ceremonious shelter to the doorway without visible support, like the sounding-board over an old pulpit. It had also a number of long narrow strips of window, so disposed in its grave brick front as to render it symmetrically ugly. It had also, on its roof, a cupola with a bell in it.

"When a man at five-and-twenty can put his hat on, and can say 'this hat covers the owner of this property and of the business which is transacted on this property,' I consider, Mr. Bintrey, that, without being boastful, he may be allowed to be deeply thankful. I don't know how it may appear to you, but so it appears to me."

Thus Mr. Walter Wilding to his man of law, in his own counting-house; taking his hat down from its peg to suit the action to the word, and hanging it up again when he had done so, not to overstep the modesty of nature.

An innocent, open-speaking, unused-looking man, Mr. Walter Wilding, with a remarkably pink and white complexion, and a figure much too bulky for so young a man, though of a good stature. With crispy curling brown hair, and amiable bright blue eyes. An extremely communicative man: a man with whom loquacity was the irrestrainable outpouring of contentment and gratitude. Mr. Bintrey, on the other hand, a cautious man, with twinkling beads of eyes in a large overhanging bald head, who inwardly but intensely enjoyed the comicality of openness of speech, or hand, or heart.

"Yes," said Mr. Bintrey. "Yes. Ha, ha!"

A decanter, two wine-glasses, and a plate of biscuits, stood on the desk.

"You like this forty-five-year-old port wine?" said Mr. Wilding.

"Like it?" repeated Mr. Bintrey. "Rather, Sir!"

"It's from the best corner of our best forty-five-year-old bin," said Mr. Wilding.

"Thank you, Sir," said Mr. Bintrey. "It's most excellent."

He laughed again, as he held up his glass and ogled it, at the highly ludicrous idea of giving away such wine.

"And now," said Wilding, with a childish enjoyment in the discussion of affairs, "I think we have got everything straight, Mr. Bintrey."

"Everything straight," said Bintrey.

"A partner secured——"

"Partner secured," said Bintrey.

"A housekeeper advertised for——"

"Housekeeper advertised for," said Bintrey, "'apply personally at Cripple Corner, Great Tower-street, from ten to twelve'—to-morrow, by-the-bye."

"My late dear mother's affairs wound up——"

"Wound up," said Bintrey.

"And all charges paid,"

"And all charges paid," said Bintrey, with a chuckle: probably occasioned by the droll circumstance that they had been paid without a haggle.

"The mention of my late dear mother," Mr. Wilding continued, his eyes filling with tears and his pocket-handkerchief drying them, "unmans me still, Mr. Bintrey. You know how I loved her; you (her lawyer) know how she loved me. The utmost love of mother and child was cherished between us, and we never experienced one moment's division or unhappiness from the time when she took me under her care. Thirteen years in all! Thirteen years under my late dear mother's care, Mr. Bintrey, and eight of them her confidentially acknowledged son! You know the story, Mr. Bintrey, who but you, Sir!" Mr. Wilding sobbed and dried his eyes, without attempt at concealment, during these remarks.

Mr. Bintrey enjoyed his comical port, and said, after rolling it in his mouth: "I know the story."

"My late dear mother, Mr. Bintrey," pursued the wine-merchant, "had been deeply deceived, and had cruelly suffered. But on that subject my late dear mother's lips were for ever sealed. By whom deceived, or under what circumstances, Heaven only knows. My late dear mother never betrayed her betrayer."

"She had made up her mind," said Mr. Bintrey, again turning his wine on his palate, "and she could hold her peace." An amused twinkle in his eyes pretty plainly added—"A devilish deal better than *you* ever will!"

"'Honour,'" said Mr. Wilding, sobbing as he quoted from the Commandments, "'thy father and thy mother, that thy days may be long in the land.' When I was in the Foundling, Mr. Bintrey, I was at such a loss how to do it, that I apprehended my days would be short in the land. But I afterwards came to honour my mother deeply, profoundly. And I honour and revere her memory. For seven happy years, Mr. Bintrey," pursued Wilding, still with the same innocent catching in his breath, and the same unabashed tears, "did my excellent mother article me to my predecessors in this business, Pebbleson Nephew. Her affectionate forethought likewise apprenticed me to the Vintners' Company and made me in time a free Vintner, and—and—everything else that the best of mothers could desire. When I came of age, she bestowed her inherited share in this business upon me; it was her money that afterwards bought out Pebbleson Nephew, and painted in Wilding and Co., it was she who left me everything she possessed, but the mourning ring you wear. And yet, Mr. Bintrey, with a fresh burst of honest affection, "she is no more. It is little over half a year since she came into the Corner to read on that door-post with her own eyes, WILDING AND CO., WINE MERCHANTS. And yet she is no more!"

"Sad. But the common lot, Mr. Wilding," observed Bintrey. "At some time or other we must all be no more." He placed the forty-five-year-old port wine in the universal condition, with a relishing sigh.

"So now, Mr. Bintrey," pursued Wilding, putting away his pocket-handkerchief, and smoothing his eyelids with his fingers, "now that I can no longer show my love and honour for the dear parent to whom my heart was mysteriously turned by Nature when she first spoke to me, a strange lady, I sitting at our Sunday dinner-table in the Foundling, I can at least show that I am not ashamed of having been a Foundling, and that I, who never knew a father of my own, wish to be a father to all in my employment. Therefore," continued Wilding, becoming enthusiastic in his loquacity, "therefore, I want a thoroughly good housekeeper to undertake this dwelling-house of Wilding and Co., Wine Merchants, Cripple Corner, so that I may restore in it some of the old relations betwixt employer and employed! So that I may live in it on the spot where my money is made! So that I may daily sit at the head of the table at which the people in my employment eat together, and may eat of the same roast and boiled, and drink of the same beer! So that the people in my employment may lodge under the same roof with me! So that we may one and all——I beg your pardon, Mr. Bintrey, but that old singing in my head has suddenly come on, and I shall feel obliged if you will lead me to the pump."

Alarmed by the excessive pinkness of his client, Mr. Bintrey lost not a moment in leading him forth into the court-yard. It was easily done; for the counting-house in which they talked together opened on to it, at one side of the dwelling-house. There the attorney pumped with a will, obedient to a sign from the client, and the client laved his head and face with both hands, and took a hearty drink. After these remedies, he declared himself much better.

"Don't let your good feelings excite you," said Bintrey, as they returned to the counting-house, and Mr. Wilding dried himself on a jack-towel behind an inner door.

"No, no. I won't," he returned, looking out of the towel. "I won't. I have not been confused, have I?"

"Not at all. Perfectly clear."

"Where did I leave off, Mr. Bintrey?"

"Well, you left off—but I wouldn't excite myself, if I was you, by taking it up again just yet."

"I'll take care. I'll take care. The singing in my head, came on at where, Mr. Bintrey?"

"At roast, and boiled, and beer," answered the lawyer, prompting, "lodging under the same roof—and one and all——"

"Ah! And one and all singing in the head together——"

"Do you know, I really *would not* let my good feelings excite me, if I was you," hinted the lawyer again, anxiously. "Try some more pump."

"No occasion, no occasion. All right, Mr. Bintrey. And one and all forming a kind of family! You see, Mr. Bintrey, I was not used in my childhood to that sort of individual existence which most individuals have led, more or less, in their childhood. After that time I became absorbed in my late dear mother. Having lost her, I find that I am more fit for being one of a body than one by myself. To be that, and at the same time to do my duty to those dependent on me, and attach them to me, has a patriarchal and pleasant air about it. I don't know how it may appear to you, Mr. Bintrey, but so it appears to me."

"It is not I who am all-important in the case, but you," returned Bintrey. "Consequently, how it may appear to me is of very small importance."

"It appears to *me*," said Mr. Wilding, in a glow, "hopeful, useful, delightful!"

"Do you know," hinted the lawyer again, "I really would not ex——"

"I am not going to. Then there's Handel."

"There's who?" asked Bintrey.

"Handel, Mozart, Haydn, Kent, Purcell, Doctor Arne, Greene, Mendelssohn. I know the choruses to those anthems by heart. Foundling Chapel Collection. Why shouldn't we learn them together?"

"Who learn them together?" asked the lawyer, rather shortly.

"Employer and employed."

"Ay, ay," returned Bintrey, mollified; as if he had half expected the answer to be, Lawyer and client. "That's another thing."

"Not another thing, Mr. Bintrey! The same thing. A part of the bond among us. We will form a choir in some quiet church near the Corner here, and, having sung together of a Sunday with a relish, we will come home and take an early dinner together with a relish. The object that I have at heart now is, to get this system well in action without delay, so that my new partner may find it founded when he enters on his partnership."

"All good be with it!" exclaimed Bintrey, rising. "May it prosper! Is Joey Ladle to take a share in Handel, Mozart, Haydn, Kent, Purcell, Doctor Arne, Greene, and Mendelssohn?"

"I hope so."

"I wish them all well out of it," returned Bintrey, with much heartiness. "Good-bye, Sir."

They shook hands and parted. Then (first knocking with his knuckles for leave) entered to Mr. Wilding from a door of communication between his private counting-house and that in which his clerks sat, the Head Cellarman of the cellars of Wilding and Co., Wine Merchants, and the erst Head Cellarman of the cellars of Pebbleson Nephew. The Joey Ladle in question. A slow and ponderous man, of the drayman order of human architecture, dressed in a corrugated suit and bibbed apron, apparently a composite of door-mat and rhinoceros-hide.

"Respecting this same boarding and lodging, Young Master Wilding," said he.

"Yes, Joey?"

"Speaking for myself, Young Master Wilding—and I never did speak and I never do speak for no one else—*I* don't want no boarding nor yet no lodging. But if you wish to board me and to lodge me, take me. I can peck as well as most men. Where I peck ain't so high a object with me as What I peck. Nor even so high a object with me as How Much I peck. Is all to live in the house, Young Master Wilding? The two other cellarmen, the three porters, the two 'prentices, and the odd men?"

"Yes. I hope we shall all be an united family, Joey."

"Ah!" said Joey. "I hope they may be."

"They? Rather say we, Joey."

Joey Ladle shook his head. "Don't look to me to make we on it, Young Master Wilding, not at my time of life and under the circumstances which has formed my disposition. I have said to Pebbleson Nephew many a time, when they have said to me, 'Put a livelier face upon it, Joey'—I have said to them, 'Gentlemen, it is all wery well for you that has been accustomed to take your wine into your systems by the conwivial channel of your throttles, to put a lively face upon it; but,' I says, 'I have been accustomed to take *my* wine in at the pores of the skin, and, took that way, it acts different. It acts depressing. It's one thing, gentlemen,' I says to Pebbleson Nephew, 'to charge your glasses in a dining-room with a Hip Hurrah and a Jolly Companions Every One, and it's another thing to be charged yourself, through the pores, in a low dark cellar and a mouldy atmosphere. It makes all the difference betwixt bubbles and wapours,' I tells Pebbleson Nephew. And so it do. I've been a cellarman my life through, with my mind fully given to the business. What's the consequence? I'm as muddled a man as lives—you won't find a muddleder man than me—nor yet you won't find my equal in molloncolly. Sing of Filling the bumper fair, Every drop you sprinkle, O'er the brow of care, Smooths away a wrinkle? Yes. P'r'aps so. But try filling yourself through the pores, underground, when you don't want to it!"

"I am sorry to hear this, Joey. I had even thought that you might join a singing-class in the house."

"Me, Sir? No, no, Young Master Wilding, you won't catch Joey Ladle muddling the Armony. A pecking-machine, Sir, is all that I am capable of proving myself, out of my cellars; but that you're welcome to, if you think it's worth your while to keep such a thing on your premises."

"I do, Joey."

"Say no more, Sir. The Business's word is my law. And you're a going to take Young Master George Vendale partner into the old Business?"

"I am, Joey."

"More changes, you see! But don't change the name of the Firm again. Don't do it, Young Master Wilding. It was bad luck enough to make it Yourself and Co. Better by far have left it Pebbleson Nephew that good luck always stuck to. You should never change luck when it's good, Sir."

"At all events, I have no intention of changing the name of the House again, Joey."

"Glad to hear it, and wish you good-day, Young Master Wilding. But you had better by half," muttered Joey Ladle inaudibly, as he closed the door and shook his head, "have let the name alone from the first. You had better by half have followed the luck instead of crossing it."

ENTER THE HOUSEKEEPER

The wine-merchant sat in his dining-room next morning, to receive the personal applicants for the vacant post in his establishment. It was an old-fashioned wainscoted room; the panels ornamented with festoons of flowers carved in wood; with an oaken floor, a well-worn Turkey carpet, and dark mahogany furniture, all of which had seen service and polish under Pebbleson Nephew. The great sideboard had assisted at many business-dinners given by Pebbleson Nephew to their connexion, on the principle of throwing sprats overboard to catch whales; and Pebbleson Nephew's comprehensive three-sided plate-warmer, made to fit the whole front of the large fireplace, kept watch beneath it over a sarcophagus-shaped cellaret that had in its time held many a dozen of Pebbleson Nephew's wine. But the little rubicund old bachelor with a pigtail, whose portrait was over the sideboard (and who could easily be identified as decidedly Pebbleson and decidedly not Nephew), had retired into another sarcophagus, and the plate-warmer had grown as cold as he. So, the golden and black griffins that supported the candelabra, with black balls in their mouths at the end of gilded chains, looked as if in their old age they had lost all heart for playing at ball, and were dolefully exhibiting their chains in the Missionary line of inquiry whether they had not earned emancipation by this time, and were not griffins and brothers.

Such a Columbus of a morning was the summer morning, that it discovered Cripple Corner. The light and warmth pierced in at the open windows, and irradiated the picture of a lady hanging over the chimneypiece, the only other decoration of the walls.

"My mother at five-and-twenty," said Mr. Wilding to himself, as his eyes enthusiastically followed the light to the portrait's face, "I hang up here, in order that visitors may admire my mother in the bloom of her youth and beauty. My mother at fifty I hang in the seclusion of my own chamber, as a remembrance sacred to me. O! It's you, Jarvis!"

These latter words he addressed to a clerk who had tapped at the door, and now looked in.

"Yes, Sir. I merely wished to mention that it's gone ten, Sir, and that there are several females in the Counting-house."

"Dear me!" said the wine-merchant, deepening in the pink of his complexion and whitening in the white, "are there several? So many as several? I had better begin before there are more. I'll see them one by one, Jarvis, in the order of their arrival."

Hastily entrenching himself in his easy-chair at the table behind a great inkstand, having first placed a chair on the other side of the table opposite his own seat, Mr. Wilding entered on his task with considerable trepidation.

He ran the gauntlet that must be run on any such occasion. There were the usual species of profoundly unsympathetic women, and the usual species of much too sympathetic women. There were buccaneering widows who came to seize him, and who griped umbrellas under their arms, as if each umbrella were he, and each griper had got him. There were towering maiden ladies who had seen better days, and who came armed with clerical testimonials to their theology, as if he were Saint Peter with his keys. There were gentle maiden ladies who came to marry him. There were professional housekeepers, like non-commissioned officers, who put him through his domestic exercise, instead of submitting themselves to catechism. There were languid invalids, to whom salary was not so much an object as the comforts of a private hospital. There were sensitive creatures who burst into tears on being addressed, and had to be restored with glasses of cold water. There were some respondents who came two together, a highly promising one and a wholly unpromising one: of whom the promising one answered all questions charmingly, until it would at last appear that she was not a candidate at all, but only the friend of the unpromising one, who had glowered in absolute silence and apparent injury.

At last, when the good wine-merchant's simple heart was failing him, there entered an applicant quite different from all the rest. A woman, perhaps fifty, but looking younger, with a face remarkable for placid cheerfulness, and a manner no less remarkable for its quiet expression of equability of temper. Nothing in her dress could have been changed to her advantage. Nothing in the noiseless self-possession of her manner could have been changed to her advantage. Nothing could have been in better unison with both, than her voice when she answered the question: "What name shall I have the pleasure of noting down?" with the words, "My name is Sarah Goldstraw. Mrs. Goldstraw. My husband has been dead many years, and we had no family."

Half-a-dozen questions had scarcely extracted as much to the purpose from any one else. The voice dwelt so agreeably on Mr. Wilding's ear as he made his note, that he was rather long about it. When he looked up again, Mrs. Goldstraw's glance had naturally gone round the room, and now returned to him from the chimney-piece. Its expression was one of frank readiness to be questioned, and to answer straight.

"You will excuse my asking you a few questions?" said the modest wine-merchant.

"O, surely, Sir. Or I should have no business here."

"Have you filled the station of housekeeper before?"

"Only once. I have lived with the same widow lady for twelve years. Ever since I lost my husband. She was an invalid, and is lately dead; which is the occasion of my now wearing black."

"I do not doubt that she has left you the best credentials?" said Mr. Wilding.

"I hope I may say, the very best. I thought it would save trouble, Sir, if I wrote down the name and address of her representatives, and brought it with me." Laying a card on the table.

"You singularly remind me, Mrs. Goldstraw," said Wilding, taking the card beside him, "of a manner and tone of voice that I was once acquainted with. Not of an individual—I feel sure of that, though I cannot recall what it is I have in my mind—but of a general bearing. I ought to add, it was a kind and pleasant one."

She smiled, as she rejoined: "At least, I am very glad of that, Sir."

"Yes," said the wine-merchant, thoughtfully repeating his last phrase, with a momentary glance at his future housekeeper, "it was a kind and pleasant one. But that is the most I can make of it. Memory is sometimes like a half-forgotten dream. I don't know how it may appear to you, Mrs. Goldstraw, but so it appears to me."

Probably it appeared to Mrs. Goldstraw in a similar light, for she quietly assented to the proposition. Mr. Wilding then offered to put himself at once in communication with the gentleman named upon the card: a firm of proctors in Doctors' Commons. To this, Mrs. Goldstraw thankfully assented. Doctors' Commons not being far off, Mr. Wilding suggested the feasibility of Mrs. Goldstraw's looking in again, say in three hours' time. Mrs. Goldstraw readily undertook to do so. In fine, the result of Mr. Wilding's inquiries being eminently satisfactory, Mrs. Goldstraw was that afternoon engaged (on her own perfectly fair terms) to come to-morrow and set up her rest as housekeeper in Cripple Corner.

THE HOUSEKEEPER SPEAKS

On the next day Mrs. Goldstraw arrived, to enter on her domestic duties.

Having settled herself in her own room, without troubling the servants, and without wasting time, the new housekeeper announced herself as waiting to be favoured with any instructions which her master might wish to give her. The wine-merchant received Mrs. Goldstraw in the dining-room, in which he had seen her on the previous day; and, the usual preliminary civilities having passed on either side, the two sat down to take counsel together on the affairs of the house.

"About the meals, Sir?" said Mrs. Goldstraw. "Have I a large, or small, number to provide for?"

"If I can carry out a certain old-fashioned plan of mine," replied Mr. Wilding, "you will have a large number to provide for. I am a

lonely single man, Mrs. Goldstraw; and I hope to live with all th
persons in my employment as if they were members of my family
Until that time comes, you will only have me, and the new partne
whom I expect immediately, to provide for. What my partner'
habits may be, I cannot yet say. But I may describe myself as a ma
of regular hours, with an invariable appetite that you may depen
upon to an ounce."

"About breakfast, Sir?" asked Mrs. Goldstraw. "Is there anythin,
particular——?"

She hesitated, and left the sentence unfinished. Her eyes turne
slowly away from her master, and looked towards the chimney
piece. If she had been a less excellent and experienced housekeepe
Mr. Wilding might have fancied that her attention was beginning t
wander at the very outset of the interview.

"Eight o'clock is my breakfast-hour," he resumed. "It is one of m
virtues to be never tired of broiled bacon, and it is one of my vices t
be habitually suspicious of the freshness of eggs." Mrs. Goldstrav
looked back at him, still a little divided between her master'
chimneypiece and her master. "I take tea," Mr. Wilding went on
"and I am perhaps rather nervous and fidgety about drinking it
within a certain time after it is made. If my tea stands to
long——"

He hesitated, on his side, and left the sentence unfinished. If h
had not been engaged in discussing a subject of such paramoun
interest to himself as his breakfast, Mrs. Goldstraw might hav
fancied that his attention was beginning to wander at the very outse
of the interview.

"If your tea stands too long, Sir——?" said the housekeepe
politely taking up her master's lost thread.

"If my tea stands too long," repeated the wine-merchant mechan
ically, his mind getting farther and farther away from his breakfast
and his eyes fixing themselves more and more inquiringly on hi
housekeeper's face. "If my tea——Dear, dear me, Mrs. Goldstraw
what *is* the manner and tone of voice that you remind me of? I
strikes me even more strongly to-day, than it did when I saw yo
yesterday. What can it be?"

"What can it be?" repeated Mrs. Goldstraw.

She said the words, evidently thinking while she spoke them o
something else. The wine-merchant, still looking at her inquiringly
observed that her eyes wandered towards the chimneypiece onc
more. They fixed on the portrait of his mother, which hung there
and looked at it with that slight contraction of the brow whicl
accompanies a scarcely conscious effort of memory. Mr. Wildin;
remarked:

"My late dear mother, when she was five-and-twenty."

Mrs. Goldstraw thanked him with a movement of the head fo
being at the pains to explain the picture, and said, with a cleared
brow, that it was the portrait of a very beautiful lady.

Mr. Wilding, falling back into his former perplexity, tried onc

ore to recover that lost recollection, associated so closely, and yet
) undiscoverably, with his new housekeeper's voice and manner.

"Excuse my asking you a question which has nothing to do with
e or my breakfast," he said. "May I inquire if you have ever
:cupied any other situation than the situation of housekeeper?"

"O yes, Sir. I began life as one of the nurses at the Foundling."

"Why, that's it!" cried the wine-merchant, pushing back his
1air. "By heaven! Their manner is the manner you remind me of!"
In an astonished look at him, Mrs. Goldstraw changed colour,
1ecked herself, turned her eyes upon the ground, and sat still and
lent.

"What is the matter?" said Mr. Wilding.

"Do I understand that you were in the Foundling, Sir?"

"Certainly. I am not ashamed to own it."

"Under the name you now bear?"

"Under the name of Walter Wilding."

"And the lady——?" Mrs. Goldstraw stopped short with a look at
1e portrait which was now unmistakably a look of alarm.

"You mean my mother," interrupted Mr. Wilding.

"Your—mother," repeated the housekeeper, a little constrainedly,
:emoved you from the Foundling? At what age, Sir?"

"At between eleven and twelve years old. It's quite a romantic
lventure, Mrs. Goldstraw."

He told the story of the lady having spoken to him, while he sat at
inner with the other boys in the Foundling, and of all that had
•llowed in his innocently communicative way. "My poor mother
>uld never have discovered me," he added, "if she had not met with
1e of the matrons who pitied her. The matron consented to touch
1e boy whose name was 'Walter Wilding' as she went round the
inner-tables—and so my mother discovered me again after having
arted from me as an infant at the Foundling doors."

At those words Mrs. Goldstraw's hand, resting on the table,
:ropped helplessly into her lap. She sat, looking at her new master,
ith a face that had turned deadly pale, and with eyes that expressed
1 utterable dismay.

"What does this mean?" asked the wine-merchant. "Stop!" he
ied."Is there something else in the past time which I ought to
ssociate with you? I remember my mother telling me of another
erson at the Foundling, to whose kindness she owed a debt of
:ratitude. When she first parted with me, as an infant, one of the
urses informed her of the name that had been given to me in the
.stitution. You were that nurse?"

"God forgive me, Sir—I was that nurse!"

"God forgive you?"

"We had better get back, Sir (if I may make so bold as to say so),
> my duties in the house," said Mrs. Goldstraw. "Your breakfast-
>ur is eight. Do you lunch, or dine, in the middle of the day?"

The excessive pinkness which Mr. Bintrey had noticed in his
ient's face began to appear there once more. Mr. Wilding put his

hand to his head, and mastered some momentary confusion in tha
quarter, before he spoke again.

"Mrs. Goldstraw," he said, "you are concealing something fro
me!"

The housekeeper obstinately repeated, "Please to favour me, Si
by saying whether you lunch, or dine, in the middle of the day?"

"I don't know what I do in the middle of the day. I can't ent
into my household affairs, Mrs. Goldstraw, till I know why yo
regret an act of kindness to my mother, which she always spoke
gratefully to the end of her life. You are not doing me a service b
your silence. You are agitating me, you are alarming me, you ar
bringing on the singing in my head."

His hand went up to his head again, and the pink in his fac
deepened by a shade or two.

"It's hard, Sir, on just entering your service," said the housekeepe
"to say what may cost me the loss of your good-will. Please t
remember, end how it may, that I only speak because you hav
insisted on my speaking, and because I see that I am alarming yo
by my silence. When I told the poor lady, whose portrait you hav
got there, the name by which her infant was christened in th
Foundling, I allowed myself to forget my duty, and dreadful con
sequences, I am afraid, have followed from it. I'll tell you the trut
as plainly as I can. A few months from the time when I had informe
the lady of her baby's name, there came to our institution in th
country another lady (a stranger), whose object was to adopt one c
our children. She brought the needful permission with her, and afte
looking at a great many of the children, without being able to mak
up her mind, she took a sudden fancy to one of the babies—a boy—
under my care. Try, pray try, to compose yourself, Sir! It's no us
disguising it any longer. The child the stranger took away was th
child of that lady whose portrait hangs there!"

Mr. Wilding started to his feet. "Impossible!" he cried out
vehemently. "What are you talking about? What absurd story ar
you telling me now? There's her portrait! Haven't I told you s
already? The portrait of my mother!"

"When that unhappy lady removed you from the Foundling, i
after years," said Mrs. Goldstraw, gently, "she was the victim, an
you were the victim, Sir, of a dreadful mistake."

He dropped back into his chair. "The room goes round with me,"
he said. "My head! my head!" The housekeeper rose in alarm, an
opened the windows. Before she could get to the door to call fo
help, a sudden burst of tears relieved the oppression which had a
first almost appeared to threaten his life. He signed entreatingly t
Mrs. Goldstraw not to leave him. She waited until the paroxysm o
weeping had worn itself out. He raised his head as he recovered him
self, and looked at her with the angry unreasoning suspicion of a
weak man.

"Mistake?" he said, wildly repeating her last word. "How do
know you are not mistaken yourself?"

"There is no hope that I am mistaken, Sir. I will tell you why,
when you are better fit to hear it."

"Now! now!"

The tone in which he spoke warned Mrs. Goldstraw that it would
cruel kindness to let him comfort himself a moment longer with
the vain hope that she might be wrong. A few words more would end
and those few words she determined to speak.

"I have told you," she said, "that the child of the lady whose
portrait hangs there, was adopted in its infancy, and taken away by
stranger. I am as certain of what I say as that I am now sitting
here, obliged to distress you, Sir, sorely against my will. Please to
carry your mind on, now, to about three months after that time. I
was then at the Foundling, in London, waiting to take some children
our Institution in the country. There was a question that day
about naming an infant—a boy—who had just been received. We
generally named them out of the Directory. On this occasion, one of
the gentlemen who managed the Hospital happened to be looking
over the Register. He noticed that the name of the baby who had
been adopted ('Walter Wilding') was scratched out—for the reason
course, that the child had been removed for good from our care.
'Here's a name to let,' he said. 'Give it to the new foundling who has
been received to-day.' The name was given, and the child was
christened. You, Sir, were that child."

The wine-merchant's head dropped on his breast. "I was that
child!" he said to himself, trying helplessly to fix the idea in his
mind. "I was that child."

"Not very long after you had been received into the Institution,
Sir," pursued Mrs. Goldstraw, "I left my situation there, to be
married. If you will remember that, and if you can give your mind to
you will see for yourself how the mistake happened. Between
eleven and twelve years passed before the lady, whom you have
believed to be your mother, returned to the Foundling, to find her
son, and to remove him to her own home. The lady only knew that
her infant had been called 'Walter Wilding.' The matron who took
pity on her, could but point out the only 'Walter Wilding' known in
the Institution. I, who might have set the matter right, was far
away from the Foundling and all that belonged to it. There was
nothing—there was really nothing that could prevent this terrible
mistake from taking place. I feel for you—I do indeed, Sir! You
must think—and with reason—that it was in an evil hour that I
came here (innocently enough, I'm sure), to apply for your housekeeper's place. I feel as if I was to blame—I feel as if I ought to
have had more self-command. If I had only been able to keep my
face from showing you what that portrait and what your own words
put into my mind, you need never, to your dying day, have known
that you know now."

Mr. Wilding looked up suddenly. The inbred honesty of the man
rose in protest against the housekeeper's last words. His mind seemed
steady itself, for the moment, under the shock that had fallen on it.

"Do you mean to say that you would have concealed this from m
if you could?" he exclaimed.

"I hope I should always tell the truth, Sir, if I was asked," sai
Mrs. Goldstraw. "And I know it is better for *me* that I should no
have a secret of this sort weighing on my mind. But is it better fo
you? What use can it serve now——?"

"What use? Why, good Lord! if your story is true——"

"Should I have told it, Sir, as I am now situated, if it had no
been true?"

"I beg your pardon," said the wine-merchant. "You must mak
allowance for me. This dreadful discovery is something I can't realis
even yet. We loved each other so dearly—I felt so fondly that I wa
her son. She died, Mrs. Goldstraw, in my arms—she died blessing m
as only a mother *could* have blessed me. And now, after all these year
to be told she was *not* my mother! O me, O me! I don't know what
am saying!" he cried, as the impulse of self-control under which h
had spoken a moment since, flickered, and died out. "It was not thi
dreadful grief—it was something else that I had it in my mind t
speak of. Yes, yes. You surprised me—you wounded me just now
You talked as if you would have hidden this from me, if you coul
Don't talk in that way again. It would have been a crime to hav
hidden it. You mean well, I know. I don't want to distress you—yo
are a kind-hearted woman. But you don't remember what m
position is. She left me all that I possess, in the firm persuasion tha
I was her son. I am not her son. I have taken the place, I hav
innocently got the inheritance of another man. He must be found
How do I know he is not at this moment in misery, without bread t
eat? He must be found! My only hope of bearing up against th
shock that has fallen on me, is the hope of doing something whic
she would have approved. You must know more, Mrs. Goldstraw
than you have told me yet. Who was the stranger who adopted th
child? You must have heard the lady's name?"

"I never heard it, Sir. I have never seen her, or heard of her, since.

"Did she say nothing when she took the child away? Search you
memory. She must have said something."

"Only one thing, Sir, that I can remember. It was a miserably ba
season, that year; and many of the children were suffering from i
When she took the baby away, the lady said to me, laughing, 'Don'
be alarmed about his health. He will be brought up in a bette
climate than this—I am going to take him to Switzerland.' "

"To Switzerland? What part of Switzerland?"

"She didn't say, Sir."

"Only that faint clue!" said Mr. Wilding. "And a quarter of
century has passed since the child was taken away! What am
to do?"

"I hope you won't take offence at my freedom, Sir," said Mrs
Goldstraw; "but why should you distress yourself about what is to b
done? He may not be alive now, for anything you know. And, if he i
alive, it's not likely he can be in any distress. The lady who adopte

im was a bred-and-born lady—it was easy to see that. And she must
ave satisfied them at the Foundling that she could provide for the
hild, or they would never have let her take him away. If I was in
our place, Sir—please to excuse my saying so—I should comfort
nyself with remembering that I had loved that poor lady whose por-
rait you have got there—truly loved her as my mother, and that she
ad truly loved me as her son. All she gave to you, she gave for the
ake of that love. It never altered while she lived and it won't alter,
'm sure, as long as *you* live. How can you have a better right, Sir, to
keep what you have got than that?"

Mr. Wilding's immovable honesty saw the fallacy in his housekeeper's point of view at a glance.

"You don't understand me," he said. "It's *because* I loved her that
I feel it a duty—a sacred duty—to do justice to her son. If he is a
living man, I must find him: for my own sake, as well as for his. I
shall break down under this dreadful trial, unless I employ myself—
actively, instantly employ myself—in doing what my conscience tells
me ought to be done. I must speak to my lawyer; I must set my lawyer at work before I sleep to-night." He approached a tube in the wall
of the room, and called down through it to the office below. "Leave
me for a little, Mrs. Goldstraw," he resumed; "I shall be more composed, I shall be better able to speak to you later in the day. We
shall get on well—I hope we shall get on well together—in spite of
what has happened. It isn't your fault; I know it isn't your fault.
There! there! shake hands; and—and do the best you can in the
house—I can't talk about it now."

The door opened as Mrs. Goldstraw advanced towards it; and Mr.
Jarvis appeared.

"Send for Mr. Bintrey," said the wine-merchant. "Say I want to
see him directly."

The clerk unconsciously suspended the execution of the order, by
announcing "Mr. Vendale," and showing in the new partner in the
firm of Wilding and Co.

"Pray excuse me for one moment, George Vendale," said Wilding.
"I have a word to say to Jarvis. Send for Mr. Bintrey," he repeated—
"send at once."

Mr. Jarvis laid a letter on the table before he left the room.

"From our correspondents at Neuchâtel, I think, Sir. The letter
has got the Swiss postmark."

NEW CHARACTERS ON THE SCENE

The words, "The Swiss Postmark," following so soon upon the
housekeeper's reference to Switzerland, wrought Mr. Wilding's agitation to such a remarkable height, that his new partner could not
decently make a pretence of letting it pass unnoticed.

"Wilding," he asked hurriedly, and yet stopping short and glancing around as if for some visible cause of his state of mind: "what is
the matter?"

"My good George Vendale," returned the wine-merchant, giving
his hand with an appealing look, rather as if he wanted help to get
over some obstacle, than as if he gave it in welcome or salutation
"my good George Vendale, so much is the matter, that I shall never
be myself again. It is impossible that I can ever be myself again. For
in fact, I am not myself."

The new partner, a brown-cheeked handsome fellow, of about his
own age, with a quick determined eye and an impulsive manner
retorted with natural astonishment: "Not yourself?"

"Not what I supposed myself to be," said Wilding.

"What, in the name of wonder, *did* you suppose yourself to be that
you are not?" was the rejoinder, delivered with a cheerful frankness
inviting confidence from a more reticent man. "I may ask without
impertinence, now that we are partners."

"There again!" cried Wilding, leaning back in his chair, with a lost
look at the other. "Partners! I had no right to come into this business
It was never meant for me. My mother never meant it should be
mine. I mean, his mother meant it should be his—if I mean anything
—or if I am anybody."

"Come, come," urged his partner, after a moment's pause, and
taking possession of him with that calm confidence which inspires a
strong nature when it honestly desires to aid a weak one. "Whatever
has gone wrong, has gone wrong through no fault of yours, I am very
sure. I was not in this counting-house with you, under the old *régime*
for three years, to doubt you, Wilding. We were not younger men
than we are, together, for that. Let me begin our partnership by
being a serviceable partner, and setting right whatever is wrong
Has that letter anything to do with it?"

"Hah!" said Wilding, with his hand to his temple. "There again
My head! I was forgetting the coincidence. The Swiss postmark."

"At a second glance I see that the letter is unopened, so it is not
very likely to have much to do with the matter," said Vendale, with
comforting composure. "Is it for you, or for us?"

"For us," said Wilding.

"Suppose I open it and read it aloud, to get it out of our way?"

"Thank you, thank you."

"The letter is only from our champagne-making friends, the house
at Neuchâtel. 'Dear Sir. We are in receipt of yours of the 28th ult.
informing us that you have taken your Mr. Vendale into partnership
whereon we beg you to receive the assurance of our felicitations
Permit us to embrace the occasion of specially commending to you
M. Jules Obenreizer.' Impossible!"

Wilding looked up in quick apprehension, and cried, "Eh?"

"Impossible sort of name," returned his partner, slightly—

"Obenreizer. '—Of specially commending to you M. Jules Oben
reizer, of Soho-square, London (north side), henceforth fully accred
ited as our agent, and who has already had the honour of making the
acquaintance of your Mr. Vendale, in his (said M. Obenreizer's
native country, Switzerland.' To be sure! pooh pooh, what have I

been thinking of! I remember now; 'when travelling with his niece.'"

"With his——?" Vendale had so slurred the last word, that Wilding had not heard it.

"When travelling with his Niece. Obenreizer's Niece," said Vendale, in a somewhat superfluously lucid manner. "Niece of Obenreizer. (I met them in my first Swiss tour, travelled a little with them, and lost them for two years; met them again, my Swiss tour before last, and have lost them ever since.) Obenreizer. Niece of Obenreizer. To be sure! Possible sort of name, after all! 'M. Obenreizer is in possession of our absolute confidence, and we do not doubt you will esteem his merits.' Duly signed by the House, 'Defresnier et Cⁱᵉ.' Very well. I undertake to see M. Obenreizer presently, and clear him out of the way. That clears the Swiss postmark out of the way. So now, my dear Wilding, tell me what I can clear out of *your* way, and I'll find a way to clear it."

More than ready and grateful to be thus taken charge of, the honest wine-merchant wrung his partner's hand, and, beginning his tale by pathetically declaring himself an Impostor, told it.

"It was on this matter, no doubt, that you were sending for Bintrey when I came in?" said his partner, after reflecting.

"It was."

"He has experience and a shrewd head; I shall be anxious to know his opinion. It is bold and hazardous in me to give you mine before I know his, but I am not good at holding back. Plainly, then, I do not see these circumstances as you see them. I do not see your position as you see it. As to your being an Impostor, my dear Wilding, that is simply absurd, because no man can be that without being a consenting party to an imposition. Clearly you never were so. As to your enrichment by the lady who believed you to be her son, and whom you were forced to believe, on her showing, to be your mother, consider whether that did not arise out of the personal relations between you. You gradually became much attached to her; she gradually became much attached to you. It was on you, personally you, as I see the case, that she conferred these worldly advantages; it was from her, personally her, that you took them."

"She supposed me," objected Wilding, shaking his head, "to have a natural claim upon her, which I had not."

"I must admit that," replied his partner, "to be true. But if she had made the discovery that you have made, six months before she died, do you think it would have cancelled the years you were together, and the tenderness that each of you had conceived for the other, each on increasing knowledge of the other?"

"What I think," said Wilding, simply but stoutly holding to the bare fact, "can no more change the truth than it can bring down the sky. The truth is that I stand possessed of what was meant for another man."

"He may be dead," said Vendale.

"He may be alive," said Wilding. "And if he is alive, have I not—innocently, I grant you innocently—robbed him of enough? Have I

not robbed him of all the happy time that I enjoyed in his stead?
Have I not robbed him of the exquisite delight that filled my soul
when that dear lady," stretching his hand towards the picture, "told
me she was my mother? Have I not robbed him of all the care she
lavished on me? Have I not even robbed him of all the devotion and
duty that I so proudly gave to her? Therefore it is that I ask myself,
George Vendale, and I ask you, where is he? What has become of
him?"

"Who can tell?"

"I must try to find out who can tell. I must institute inquiries. I
must never desist from prosecuting inquiries. I will live upon the
interest of my share—I ought to say his share—in this business, and
will lay up the rest for him. When I find him, I may perhaps throw
myself upon his generosity; but I will yield up all to him. I will, I
swear. As I loved and honoured her," said Wilding, reverently
kissing his hand towards the picture, and then covering his eyes with
it. "As I loved and honoured her, and have a world of reasons to be
grateful to her!" And so broke down again.

His partner rose from the chair he had occupied, and stood beside
him with a hand softly laid upon his shoulder. "Walter, I knew you
before to-day to be an upright man, with a pure conscience and a
fine heart. It is very fortunate for me that I have the privilege to
travel on in life so near to so trustworthy a man. I am thankful for it.
Use me as your right hand, and rely upon me to the death. Don't
think the worse of me if I protest to you that my uppermost feeling
at present is a confused, you may call it an unreasonable, one. I feel far
more pity for the lady and for you, because you did not stand in your
supposed relations, than I can feel for the unknown man (if he ever
became a man), because he was unconsciously displaced. You have
done well in sending for Mr. Bintrey. What I think will be a part of
his advice, I know is the whole of mine. Do not move a step in this
serious matter precipitately. The secret must be kept among us
with great strictness, for to part with it lightly would be to invite
fraudulent claims, to encourage a host of knaves, to let loose a flood
of perjury and plotting. I have no more to say now, Walter, than to
remind you that you sold me a share in your business, expressly to
save yourself from more work than your present health is fit for,
and that I bought it expressly to do work, and mean to do it."

With these words, and a parting grip of his partner's shoulder that
gave them the best emphasis they could have had, George Vendale
betook himself presently to the counting-house, and presently afterwards to the address of M. Jules Obenreizer.

As he turned into Soho-square, and directed his steps towards its
north side, a deepened colour shot across his sun-browned face, which
Wilding, if he had been a better observer, or had been less occupied
with his own trouble, might have noticed when his partner read aloud
a certain passage in their Swiss correspondent's letter, which he had
not read so distinctly as the rest.

A curious colony of mountaineers has long been enclosed within that small flat London district of Soho. Swiss watchmakers, Swiss silver-chasers, Swiss jewellers, Swiss importers of Swiss musical boxes and Swiss toys of various kinds, draw close together there. Swiss professors of music, painting, and languages; Swiss artificers in steady work; Swiss couriers, and other Swiss servants chronically out of place; industrious Swiss laundresses and clear-starchers; mysteriously existing Swiss of both sexes; Swiss creditable and Swiss discreditable; Swiss to be trusted by all means, and Swiss to be trusted by no means; these divers Swiss particles are attracted to a centre in the district of Soho. Shabby Swiss eating-houses, coffee-houses, and lodging-houses, Swiss drinks and dishes, Swiss service for Sundays, and Swiss schools for week-days, are all to be found there. Even the native-born English taverns drive a sort of broken-English trade; announcing in their windows Swiss whets and drams, and sheltering in their bars Swiss skirmishes of love and animosity on most nights in the year.

When the new partner in Wilding and Co. rang the bell of a door bearing the blunt inscription OBENREIZER on a brass plate—the inner door of a substantial house, whose ground story was devoted to the sale of Swiss clocks—he passed at once into domestic Switzerland. A white-tiled stove for winter-time filled the fireplace of the room into which he was shown, the room's bare floor was laid together in a neat pattern of several ordinary woods, the room had a prevalent air of surface bareness and much scrubbing; and the little square of flowery carpet by the sofa, and the velvet chimneyboard with its capacious clock and vases of artificial flowers, contended with that tone, as if, in bringing out the whole effect, a Parisian had adapted a dairy to domestic purposes.

Mimic water was dropping off a mill-wheel under the clock. The visitor had not stood before it, following it with his eyes, a minute, when M. Obenreizer, at his elbow, startled him by saying, in very good English, very slightly clipped: "How do you do? So glad!"

"I beg your pardon. I didn't hear you come in."

"Not at all! Sit, please."

Releasing his visitor's two arms, which he had lightly pinioned at the elbows by way of embrace, M. Obenreizer also sat, remarking, with a smile: "You are well? So glad!" and touching his elbows again.

"I don't know," said Vendale, after exchange of salutations, "whether you may yet have heard of me from your House at Neu-châtel?"

"Ah yes!"

"In connexion with Wilding and Co.?"

"Ah, surely!"

"Is it not odd that I should come to you, in London here, as one of the Firm of Wilding and Co., to pay the Firm's respects?"

"Not at all! What did I always observe when we were on the mountains? We call them vast; but the world is so little. So little is the world, that one cannot keep away from persons. There are so few persons in the world, that they continually cross and re-cross. So very little is the world, that one cannot get rid of a person. Not," touching his elbows again, with an ingratiatory smile, "that one would desire to get rid of you."

"I hope not, M. Obenreizer."

"Please call me, in your country, Mr. I call myself so, for I love your country. If I *could* be English! But I am born. And you? Though descended from so fine a family, you have had the condescension to come into trade? Stop though. Wines? Is it trade in England or profession? Not fine art?"

"Mr. Obenreizer," returned Vendale, somewhat out of countenance, "I was but a silly young fellow, just of age, when I first had the pleasure of travelling with you, and when you and I and Mademoiselle your niece—who is well?"

"Thank you. Who is well."

"—Shared some slight glacier dangers together. If, with a boy's vanity, I rather vaunted my family, I hope I did so as a kind of introduction of myself. It was very weak, and in very bad taste; but perhaps you know our English proverb, 'Live and Learn.' "

"You make too much of it," returned the Swiss. "And what the devil! After all, yours *was* a fine family."

George Vendale's laugh betrayed a little vexation as he rejoined: "Well! I was strongly attached to my parents, and when we first travelled together, Mr. Obenreizer, I was in the first flush of coming into what my father and mother left me. So I hope it may have been, after all, more youthful openness of speech and heart than boastfulness."

"All openness of speech and heart! No boastfulness!" cried Obenreizer. "You tax yourself too heavily. You tax yourself, my faith! as if you was your Government taxing you! Besides, it commenced with me. I remember, that evening in the boat upon the lake, floating among the reflections of the mountains and valleys, the crags and pine woods, which were my earliest remembrance, I drew a word-picture of my sordid childhood. Of our poor hut, by the waterfall which my mother showed to travellers; of the cow-shed where I slept with the cow; of my idiot half-brother always sitting at the door, or limping down the Pass to beg; of my half-sister always spinning, and resting her enormous goître on a great stone; of my being a famished naked little wretch of two or three years, when they were men and women with hard hands to beat me, I, the only child of my father's second marriage—if it even was a marriage. What more natural than for you to compare notes with me, and say, 'We are as one by age; at that same time I sat upon my mother's lap in my father's carriage, rolling through the rich English streets, all luxury surrounding me, all squalid poverty kept far from me. Such is *my* earliest remembrance as opposed to yours!' "

Mr. Obenreizer was a black-haired young man of a dark complexion, through whose swarthy skin no red glow ever shone. When colour would have come into another cheek, a hardly discernible beat would come into his, as if the machinery for bringing up the ardent blood were there, but the machinery were dry. He was robustly made, well proportioned, and had handsome features. Many would have perceived that some surface change in him would have set them more at their ease with him, without being able to define what change. If his lips could have been made much thicker, and his neck much thinner, they would have found their want supplied.

But the great Obenreizer peculiarity was, that a certain nameless film would come over his eyes—apparently by the action of his own will—which would impenetrably veil, not only from those tellers of tales, but from his face at large, every expression save one of attention. It by no means followed that his attention should be wholly given to the person with whom he spoke, or even wholly bestowed on present sounds and objects. Rather, it was a comprehensive watchfulness of everything he had in his own mind, and everything that he knew to be, or suspected to be, in the minds of other men.

At this stage of the conversation, Mr. Obenreizer's film came over him.

"The object of my present visit," said Vendale, "is, I need hardly say, to assure you of the friendliness of Wilding and Co., and of the goodness of your credit with us, and of our desire to be of service to you. We hope shortly to offer you our hospitality. Things are not quite in train with us yet, for my partner, Mr. Wilding, is reorganising the domestic part of our establishment, and is interrupted by some private affairs. You don't know Mr. Wilding, I believe?"

Mr. Obenreizer did not.

"You must come together soon. He will be glad to have made your acquaintance, and I think I may predict that you will be glad to have made his. You have not been long established in London, I suppose, Mr. Obenreizer?"

"It is only now that I have undertaken this agency."

"Mademoiselle your niece—is—not married?"

"Not married."

George Vendale glanced about him, as if for any tokens of her.

"She has been in London?"

"She *is* in London."

"When, and where, might I have the honour of recalling myself to her remembrance?"

Mr. Obenreizer, discarding his film and touching his visitor's elbows as before, said lightly : "Come upstairs."

Fluttered enough by the suddenness with which the interview he had sought was coming upon him after all, George Vendale followed upstairs. In a room over the chamber he had just quitted—a room also Swiss-appointed—a young lady sat near one of three windows, working at an embroidery-frame; and an older lady sat with her face turned close to another white-tiled stove (though it was summer, and the stove was not lighted), cleaning gloves. The young lady wore an unusual quantity of fair bright hair, very prettily braided about a rather rounder white forehead than the average English type, and so her face might have been a shade—or say a light—rounder than the average English face, and her figure slightly rounder than the figure of the average English girl at nineteen. A remarkable indication of freedom and grace of limb, in her quiet attitude, and a wonderful purity and freshness of colour in her dimpled face and bright grey eyes, seemed fraught with mountain air. Switzerland too, though the general fashion of her dress was English, peeped out of the fanciful bodice she wore, and lurked in the curious clocked red stocking, and in its little silver-buckled shoe. As to the elder lady, sitting with her feet apart upon the lower brass ledge of the stove, supporting a lapful of gloves while she cleaned one stretched on her left hand, she was a true Swiss impersonation of another kind; from the breadth of her cushion-like back, and the ponderosity of her respectable legs (if the word be admissible), to the black velvet band tied tightly round her throat for the repression of a rising tendency to goître; or, higher still, to her great copper-coloured gold earrings; or, higher still, to her head-dress of black gauze stretched on wire.

"Miss Marguerite," said Obenreizer to the young lady, "do you recollect this gentleman?"

"I think," she answered, rising from her seat, surprised and a little confused: "it is Mr. Vendale?"

"I think it is," said Obenreizer, dryly. "Permit me, Mr. Vendale. Madame Dor."

The elder lady by the stove, with the glove stretched on her left hand, like a glover's sign, half got up, half looked over her broad shoulder, and wholly plumped down again and rubbed away.

"Madame Dor," said Obenreizer, smiling, "is so kind as to keep me free from stain or tear. Madame Dor humours my weakness for being always neat, and devotes her time to removing every one of my specks and spots."

Madame Dor, with the stretched glove in the air, and her eyes closely scrutinizing its palm, discovered a tough spot in Mr. Obenreizer at that instant, and rubbed hard at him. George Vendale took his seat by the embroidery-frame (having first taken the fair right hand that his entrance had checked), and glanced at the gold cross that dipped into the bodice, with something of the devotion of a pilgrim who had reached his shrine at last. Obenreizer stood in the middle of the room with his thumbs in his waistcoat-pockets, and became filmy.

"He was saying downstairs, Miss Obenreizer," observed Vendale, "that the world is so small a place, that people cannot escape one another. I have found it much too large for me since I saw you last."

"Have you travelled so far, then?" she inquired.

"Not so far, for I have only gone back to Switzerland each year; but I could have wished—and indeed I have wished very often—that the little world did not afford such opportunities for long escapes as it does. If it had been less, I might have found my fellow-travellers sooner, you know."

The pretty Marguerite coloured, and very slightly glanced in the direction of Madame Dor.

"You find us at length, Mr. Vendale. Perhaps you may lose us again."

"I trust not. The curious coincidence that has enabled me to find you, encourages me to hope not."

"What is that coincidence, Sir, if you please?" A dainty little native touch in this turn of speech, and in its tone, made it perfectly captivating, thought George Vendale, when again he noticed an instantaneous glance towards Madame Dor. A caution seemed to be conveyed in it, rapid flash though it was; so he quietly took heed of Madame Dor from that time forth.

"It is that I happen to have become a partner in a House of business in London, to which Mr. Obenreizer happens this very day to be expressly recommended: and that, too, by another house of business in Switzerland, in which (as it turns out) we both have a commercial interest. He has not told you?"

"Ah!" cried Mr. Obenreizer, striking in, filmless. "No, I had not told Miss Marguerite. The world is so small and so monotonous that a surprise is worth having in such a little jog-trot place. It is as he tells you, Miss Marguerite. He, of so fine a family, and so proudly bred, has condescended to trade. To trade! Like us poor peasants who have risen from ditches!"

A cloud crept over the fair brow, and she cast down her eyes.

"Why, it is good for trade!" pursued Obenreizer, enthusiastically. "It ennobles trade! It is the misfortune of trade, it is its vulgarity, that any low people—for example, we poor peasants—may take to it and climb by it. See you, my dear Vendale!" He spoke with great energy. "The father of Miss Marguerite, my eldest half-brother, more than two times your age or mine, if living now, wandered without shoes, almost without rags, from that wretched Pass—wandered—wandered—got to be fed with the mules and dogs at an Inn in the main valley far away—got to be Boy there—got to be Ostler—got to be Waiter—got to be Cook—got to be Landlord. As Landlord, he took me (could he take the idiot beggar his brother, or the spinning monstrosity his sister?) to put as pupil to the famous watchmaker, his neighbour and friend. His wife dies when Miss Marguerite is born. What is his will, and what are his words to me, when *he* dies, she being between girl and woman? 'All for Marguerite, except so much by the year for you. You are young, but I make her your ward, for you were of the obscurest and the poorest peasantry, and so was I, and so was her mother; we were abject peasants all, and you will remember it.' The thing is equally true of most of my countrymen, now in trade in this your London quarter of Soho. Peasants once; low-born drudging Swiss Peasants. Then how good and great for trade:" here, from having been warm, he became playfully jubilant, and touched the young wine-merchant's elbows again with his light embrace: "to be exalted by gentlemen."

"I do not think so," said Marguerite, with a flushed cheek, and a look away from the visitor, that was almost defiant. "I think it is as much exalted by us peasants."

"Fie, fie, Miss Marguerite," said Obenreizer. "You speak in proud England."

"I speak in proud earnest," she answered, quietly resuming her work, "and I am not English, but a Swiss peasant's daughter."

There was a dismissal of the subject in her words, which Vendale could not contend against. He only said in an earnest manner, "I most heartily agree with you, Miss Obenreizer, and I have already said so, as Mr. Obenreizer will bear witness," which he by no means did, "in this house."

Now, Vendale's eyes were quick eyes, and sharply watching Madame Dor by times, noted something in the broad back view of that lady. There was considerable pantomimic expression in her glove-cleaning. It had been very softly done when he spoke with Marguerite, or it had altogether stopped, like the action of a listener. When Obenreizer's peasant-speech came to an end, she rubbed most vigorously, as if applauding it. And once or twice, as the glove (which she always held before her a little above her face) turned in the air, or as this finger went down, or that went up, he even fancied that it made some telegraphic communication to Obenreizer: whose back was certainly never turned upon it, though he did not seem at all to heed it.

Vendale observed too, that in Marguerite's dismissal of the subject twice forced upon him to his misrepresentation, there was an indignant treatment of her guardian which she tried to check: as though she would have flamed out against him, but for the influence of fear. He also observed—though this was not much—that he never advanced within the distance of her at which he first placed himself: as though there were limits fixed between them. Neither had he ever spoken of her without the prefix "Miss," though whenever he uttered it, it was with the faintest trace of an air of mockery. And now it occurred to Vendale for the first time that something curious in the man, which he had never before been able to define, was definable as a certain subtle essence of mockery that eluded touch or analysis. He felt convinced that Marguerite was in some sort a prisoner as to her free-will—though she held her own against those two combined, by the force of her character, which was nevertheless inadequate to her release. To feel convinced of this, was not to feel less disposed to love her than he had always been. In a word, he was desperately in love with her, and thoroughly determined to pursue the opportunity which had opened at last.

For the present, he merely touched upon the pleasure that Wilding and Co. would soon have in entreating Miss Obenreizer to honour their establishment with her presence—a curious old place, though a bachelor house withal—and so did not protract his visit beyond such a visit's ordinary length. Going downstairs, conducted by his host, he found the Obenreizer counting-house at the back of the entrance-hall, and several shabby men in outlandish garments hanging about, whom Obenreizer put aside that he might pass, with a few words in *patois*.

"Countrymen," he explained, as he attended Vendale to the door. 'Poor compatriots. Grateful and attached, like dogs! Good-bye. To meet again. So glad!''

Two more light touches on his elbows dismissed him into the street. Sweet Marguerite at her frame, and Madame Dor's broad back at her telegraph, floated before him to Cripple Corner. On his arrival here, Wilding was closeted with Bintrey. The cellar doors happening to be open, Vendale lighted a candle in a cleft stick, and went down for a cellarous stroll. Graceful Marguerite floated before him faithfully, but Madame Dor's broad back remained outside.

The vaults were very spacious, and very old. There had been a stone crypt down there, when bygones were not bygones; some said, part of a monkish refectory; some said, of a chapel; some said, of a Pagan temple. It was all one now. Let who would make what he liked of a crumbled pillar and a broken arch or so. Old Time had made what *he* liked of it, and was quite indifferent to contradiction.

The close air, the musty smell, and the thunderous rumbling in the streets above, as being out of the routine of ordinary life, went well enough with the picture of pretty Marguerite holding her own against those two. So Vendale went on until, at a turning in the vaults, he saw a light like the light he carried.

"O! You are here, are you, Joey?"

"Oughtn't it rather to go, 'O! *You're* here, are you, Master George?' For it's my business to be here. But it ain't yourn."

"Don't grumble, Joey."

"O! *I* don't grumble," returned the Cellarman. "If anything grumbles, it's what I've took in through the pores; it ain't me. Have a care as something in *you* don't begin a grumbling, Master George. Stop here long enough for the wapours to work, and they'll be at it."

His present occupation consisted of poking his head into the bins, making measurements and mental calculations, and entering them in a rhinoceros-hide-looking note-book, like a piece of himself.

"They'll be at it," he resumed, laying the wooden rod that he measured with across two casks, entering his last calculation, and straightening his back, "trust 'em! And so you've regularly come into the business, Master George?"

"Regularly. I hope you don't object, Joey?"

"*I* don't, bless you. But Wapours objects that you're too young. You're both on you too young."

"We shall get over that objection day by day, Joey."

"Ay, Master George; but I shall day by day get over the objection that I'm too old, and so I shan't be capable of seeing much improvement in you."

The retort so tickled Joey Ladle that he grunted forth a laugh and delivered it again, grunting forth another laugh after the second edition of "improvement in you."

"But what's no laughing matter, Master George," he resumed, straightening his back once more, "is, that young Master Wilding as gone and changed the luck. Mark my words. He has changed the luck, and he'll find it out. *I* ain't been down here all my life for nothing! *I* know by what I notices down here, when it's a-going to rain, when it's a-going to hold up, when it's a-going to blow, when it's a-going to be calm. *I* know, by what I notices down here, when the luck's changed, quite as well."

"Has this growth on the roof anything to do with your divination?" asked Vendale, holding his light towards a gloomy ragged growth of dark fungus, pendent from the arches with a very disagreeable and repellent effect. "We are famous for this growth in this vault, aren't we?"

"We are, Master George," replied Joey Ladle, moving a step or two away, "and if you'll be advised by me, you'll let it alone."

Taking up the rod just now laid across the two casks, and faintly moving the languid fungus with it, Vendale asked, "Ay, indeed? Why so?"

"Why, not so much because it rises from the casks of wine, and may leave you to judge what sort of stuff a Cellarman takes into himself when he walks in the same all the days of his life, nor yet so much because at a stage of its growth it's maggots, and you'll fetch 'em down upon you," returned Joey Ladle, still keeping away, "as for another reason, Master George."

"What other reason?"

"(I wouldn't keep on touchin' it, if I was you, Sir.) I'll tell you if you'll come out of the place. First, take a look at its colour, Master George."

"I am doing so."

"Done, Sir. Now, come out of the place."

He moved away with his light, and Vendale followed with his. When Vendale came up with him, and they were going back together, Vendale, eyeing him as they walked through the arches, said: "Well, Joey? The colour."

"Is it like clotted blood, Master George?"

"Like enough, perhaps."

"More than enough, I think," muttered Joey Ladle, shaking his head solemnly.

"Well, say it is like; say it is exactly like. What then?"

"Master George, they do say——"

"Who?"

"How should I know who?" rejoined the Cellarman, apparently much exasperted by the unreasonable nature of the question. "Them! Them as says pretty well everything, you know. How should I know who They are, if you don't?"

"True. Go on."

"They do say that the man that gets by any accident a piece of that dark growth right upon his breast, will, for sure and certain, die by murder."

As Vendale laughingly stopped to meet the Cellarman's eyes, which he had fastened on his light while dreamily saying those words, he suddenly became conscious of being struck upon his own breast by a heavy hand. Instantly following with his eyes the action of the hand that struck him—which was his companion's—he saw that it had beaten off his breast a web or clot of the fungus even then floating to the ground.

For a moment he turned upon the Cellarman almost as scared a look as the Cellarman turned upon him. But in another moment they had reached the daylight at the front of the cellar-steps, and before he cheerfully sprang up them, he blew out his candle and the superstition together.

EXIT WILDING

On the morning of the next day, Wilding went out alone, after leaving a message with his clerk. "If Mr. Vendale should ask for me," he said, "or if Mr. Bintrey should call, tell them I am gone to the Foundling." All that his partner had said to him, all that his lawyer, following on the same side, could urge, had left him persisting unshaken in his own point of view. To find the lost man, whose place he had usurped, was now the paramount interest of his life, and to inquire at the Foundling was plainly to take the first step in the direction of discovery. To the Foundling, accordingly, the wine-merchant now went.

The once familiar aspect of the building was altered to him, as the look of the portrait over the chimneypiece was altered to him. His one dearest association with the place which had sheltered his childhood had been broken away from it for ever. A strange reluctance possessed him, when he stated his business at the door. His heart ached as he sat alone in the waiting-room while the Treasurer of the Institution was being sent for to see him. When the interview began, it was only by a painful effort that he could compose himself sufficiently to mention the nature of his errand.

The Treasurer listened with a face which promised all needful attention, and promised nothing more.

"We are obliged to be cautious," he said, when it came to his turn to speak, "about all inquiries which are made by strangers."

"You can hardly consider me a stranger," answered Wilding, simply. "I was one of your poor lost children here, in the bygone time."

The Treasurer politely rejoined that this circumstance inspired him with a special interest in his visitor. But he pressed, nevertheless, for that visitor's motive in making his inquiry. Without further preface, Wilding told him his motive, suppressing nothing. The Treasurer rose, and led the way into the room in which the registers of the institution were kept. "All the information which our books can give is heartily at your service," he said. "After the time that has elapsed I am afraid it is the only information we have to offer you."

The books were consulted, and the entry was found expressed as follows:—

"3d March, 1836. Adopted, and removed from the Foundling

Hospital, a male infant, named Walter Wilding. Name and condition of the person adopting the child—Mrs. Jane Ann Miller, widow. Address—Lime-Tree Lodge, Groombridge Wells. References—the Reverend John Harker, Groombridge Wells; and Messrs. Giles, Jeremie, and Giles, bankers, Lombard-street.''

"Is that all?'' asked the wine-merchant. "Had you no after-communication with Mrs. Miller?''

"None—or some reference to it must have appeared in this book.''

"May I take a copy of the entry?''

"Certainly! You are a little agitated. Let me make a copy for you.''

"My only chance, I suppose,'' said Wilding, looking sadly at the copy, "is to inquire at Mrs. Miller's residence, and to try if her references can help me?''

"That is the only chance I see at present,'' answered the Treasurer. "I heartily wish I could have been of some further assistance to you.''

With those farewell words to comfort him, Wilding set forth on the journey of investigation which began from the Foundling doors. The first stage to make for, was plainly the house of business of the bankers in Lombard-street. Two of the partners in the firm were inaccessible to chance-visitors when he asked for them. The third, after raising certain inevitable difficulties, consented to let a clerk examine the Ledger marked with the initial letter "M.'' The account of Mrs. Miller, widow, of Groombridge Wells, was found. Two long lines, in faded ink, were drawn across it; and at the bottom of the page there appeared this note: "Account closed, September 30th, 1837.''

So the first stage of the journey was reached—and so it ended in No Thoroughfare! After sending a note to Cripple Corner to inform his partner that his absence might be prolonged for some hours, Wilding took his place in the train, and started for the second stage on the journey—Mrs. Miller's residence at Groombridge Wells.

Mothers and children travelled with him; mothers and children met each other at the station; mothers and children were in the shops when he entered them to inquire for Lime-Tree Lodge. Everywhere, the nearest and dearest of human relations showed itself happily in the happy light of day. Everywhere, he was reminded of the treasured delusion from which he had been awakened so cruelly—of the lost memory which had passed from him like a reflection from a glass.

Inquiring here, inquiring there, he could hear of no such place as Lime-Tree Lodge. Passing a house-agent's office, he went in wearily, and put the question for the last time. The house-agent pointed across the street to a dreary mansion of many windows, which might have been a manufactory, but which was an hotel. "That's where Lime-Tree Lodge stood, Sir,'' said the man, "ten years ago.''

The second stage reached, and No Thoroughfare again!

But one chance was left. The clerical reference, Mr. Harker, still remained to be found. Customers coming in at the moment to occupy the house-agent's attention, Wilding went down the street, and entering a bookseller's shop, asked if he could be informed of the Reverend John Harker's present address.

The bookseller looked unaffectedly shocked and astonished, and made no answer.

Wilding repeated his question.

The bookseller took up from his counter a prim little volume in a binding of sober grey. He handed it to his visitor, open at the title-page. Wilding read:

"The martyrdom of the Reverend John Harker in New Zealand. Related by a former member of his flock."

Wilding put the book down on the counter. "I beg your pardon," he said, thinking a little, perhaps, of his own present martyrdom while he spoke. The silent bookseller acknowledged the apology by a bow. Wilding went out.

Third and last stage, and No Thoroughfare for the third and last time.

There was nothing more to be done; there was absolutely no choice but to go back to London, defeated at all points. From time to time on the return journey, the wine-merchant looked at his copy of the entry in the Foundling Register. There is one among the many forms of despair—perhaps the most pitiable of all—which persists in disguising itself as Hope. Wilding checked himself in the act of throwing the useless morsel of paper out of the carriage window. "It may lead to something yet," he thought. "While I live, I won't part with it. When I die, my executors shall find it sealed up with my will."

Now, the mention of his will set the good wine-merchant on a new track of thought, without diverting his mind from its engrossing subject. He must make his will immediately.

The application of the phrase No Thoroughfare to the case had originated with Mr. Bintrey. In their first long conference following the discovery, that sagacious personage had a hundred times repeated, with an obstructive shake of the head, "No Thoroughfare, Sir, No Thoroughfare. My belief is that there is no way out of this at this time of day, and my advice is, make yourself comfortable where you are."

In the course of the protracted consultation, a magnum of the forty-five-year-old port wine had been produced for the wetting of Mr. Bintrey's legal whistle; but the more clearly he saw his way through the wine, the more emphatically he did not see his way through the case; repeating as often as he set his glass down empty, "Mr. Wilding, No Thoroughfare. Rest and be thankful."

It is certain that the honest wine-merchant's anxiety to make a will originated in profound conscientiousness; though it is possible (and quite consistent with his rectitude) that he may unconsciously have derived some feeling of relief from the prospect of delegating his own difficulty to two other men who were to come after him. Be that as it may, he pursued his new track of thought with great ardour, and lost no time in begging George Vendale and Mr. Bintrey to meet him in Cripple Corner and share his confidence.

"Being all three assembled with closed doors," said Mr. Bintrey, addressing the new partner on the occasion, "I wish to observe, before our friend (and my client) entrusts us with his further views, that I have endorsed what I understand from him to have been your advice, Mr. Vendale, and what would be the advice of every sensible man. I have told him that he positively must keep his secret. I have spoken with Mrs. Goldstraw, both in his presence and in his absence; and if anybody is to be trusted (which is a very large IF), I think she is to be trusted to that extent. I have pointed out to our friend (and my client), that to set on foot random inquiries would not only be to raise the Devil, in the likeness of all the swindlers in the kingdom, but would also be to waste the estate. Now, you see, Mr. Vendale, our friend (and my client) does not desire to waste the estate, but, on the contrary, desires to husband it for what he considers—but I can't say I do—the rightful owner, if such rightful owner should ever be found. I am very much mistaken if he ever will be, but never mind that. Mr. Wilding and I are, at least, agreed that the estate is not to be wasted. Now, I have yielded to Mr. Wilding's desire to keep an advertisement at intervals flowing through the newspapers, cautiously inviting any person who may know anything about that adopted infant, taken from the Foundling Hospital, to come to my office; and I have pledged myself that such advertisement shall regularly appear. I have gathered from our friend (and my client) that I meet you here to-day to take his instructions, not to give him advice. I am prepared to receive his instructions, and to respect his wishes; but you will please observe that this does not imply my approval of either as a matter of professional opinion."

Thus Mr. Bintrey; talking quite as much *at* Wilding as *to* Vendale. And yet, in spite of his care for his client, he was so amused by his client's Quixotic conduct, as to eye him from time to time with twinkling eyes, in the light of a highly comical curiosity.

"Nothing," observed Wilding, "can be clearer. I only wish my head were as clear as yours, Mr. Bintrey."

"If you feel that singing in it coming on," hinted the lawyer, with an alarmed glance, "put it off.—I mean the interview."

"Not at all, I thank you," said Wilding. "What was I going to——"

"Don't excite yourself, Mr. Wilding," urged the lawyer.

"No; I *wasn't* going to," said the wine-merchant. "Mr. Bintrey and George Vendale, would you have any hesitation or objection to become my joint trustees and executors, or can you at once consent?"

"*I* consent," replied George Vendale, readily.

"*I* consent," said Bintrey, not so readily.

"Thank you both. Mr. Bintrey, my instructions for my last will and testament are short and plain. Perhaps you will now have the goodness to take them down. I leave the whole of my real and personal estate, without any exception or reservation whatsoever, to you two, my joint trustees and executors, in trust to pay over the whole to the true Walter Wilding, if he shall be found and identified within two

years after the day of my death. Failing that, in trust to you two to
pay over the whole as a benefaction and legacy to the Foundling
Hospital."

"Those are all your instructions, are they, Mr. Wilding?" demanded
Bintrey, after a blank silence, during which nobody had looked at
anybody.

"The whole."

"And as to those instructions, you have absolutely made up your
mind, Mr. Wilding?"

"Absolutely, decidedly, finally."

"It only remains," said the lawyer, with one shrug of his shoulders,
"to get them into technical and binding form, and to execute and
attest. Now, does that press? Is there any hurry about it? You are
not going to die yet, Sir."

"Mr. Bintrey," answered Wilding, gravely, "when I am going to
die is within other knowledge than yours or mine. I shall be glad to
have this matter off my mind, if you please."

"We are lawyer and client again," rejoined Bintrey, who, for the
nonce, had become almost sympathetic. "If this day week—here, at
the same hour—will suit Mr. Vendale and yourself, I will enter in my
Diary that I attend you accordingly."

The appointment was made, and in due sequence kept. The will
was formally signed, sealed, delivered, and witnessed, and was
carried off by Mr. Bintrey for safe storage among the papers of his
clients, ranged in their respective iron boxes, with their respective
owners' names outside, on iron tiers in his consulting-room, as if that
legal sanctuary were a condensed Family Vault of Clients.

With more heart than he had lately had for former subjects of
interest, Wilding then set about completing his patriarchal establishment, being much assisted not only by Mrs. Goldstraw but by
Vendale too: who, perhaps, had in his mind the giving of an Obenreizer dinner as soon as possible. Anyhow, the establishment being
reported in sound working order, the Obenreizers, Guardian and
Ward, were asked to dinner, and Madame Dor was included in the
invitation. If Vendale had been over head and ears in love before—
a phrase not to be taken as implying the faintest doubt about it—
this dinner plunged him down in love ten thousand fathoms deep.
Yet, for the life of him, he could not get one word alone with charming Marguerite. So surely as a blessed moment seemed to come,
Obenreizer, in his filmy state, would stand at Vendale's elbow, or the
broad back of Madame Dor would appear before his eyes. That
speechless matron was never seen in a front view, from the moment
of her arrival to that of her departure—except at dinner. And from
the instant of her retirement to the drawing-room, after a hearty
participation in that meal, she turned her face to the wall again.

Yet, through four or five delightful though distracting hours,
Marguerite was to be seen, Marguerite was to be heard, Marguerite
was to be occasionally touched. When they made the round of the old
dark cellars, Vendale led her by the hand; when she sang to him in

the lighted room at night, Vendale, standing by her, held her relinquished gloves, and would have bartered against them every drop of the forty-five-year-old, though it had been forty-five times forty-five years old, and its nett price forty-five times forty-five pounds per dozen. And still, when she was gone, and a great gap of an extinguisher was clapped on Cripple Corner, he tormented himself by wondering, Did she think that he admired her! Did she think that he adored her! Did she suspect that she had won him, heart and soul! Did she care to think at all about it! And so, Did she and Didn't she, up and down the gamut, and above the line and below the line, dear, dear! Poor restless heart of humanity! To think that the men who were mummies thousands of years ago, did the same, and ever found the secret how to be quiet after it!

"What do you think, George," Wilding asked him next day, "of Mr. Obenreizer? (I won't ask you what you think of Miss Obenreizer.)"

"I don't know," said Vendale, "and I never did know, what to think of him."

"He is well informed and clever," said Wilding.

"Certainly clever."

"A good musician." (He had played very well, and sung very well, overnight.)

"Unquestionably a good musician."

"And talks well."

"Yes," said George Vendale, ruminating, "and talks well. Do you know, Wilding, it oddly occurs to me, as I think about him, that he doesn't keep silence well!"

"How do you mean? He is not obtrusively talkative."

"No, and I don't mean that. But when he is silent, you can hardly help vaguely, though perhaps most unjustly, mistrusting him. Take people whom you know and like. Take any one you know and like."

"Soon done, my good fellow," said Wilding. "I take you."

"I didn't bargain for that, or foresee it," returned Vendale, laughing. "However, take me. Reflect for a moment. Is your approving knowledge of my interesting face mainly founded (however various the momentary expressions it may include) on my face when I am silent?"

"I think it is," said Wilding.

"I think so too. Now, you see, when Obenreizer speaks—in other words, when he is allowed to explain himself away—he comes out right enough; but when he has not the opportunity of explaining himself away, he comes out rather wrong. Therefore it is, that I say he does not keep silence well. And passing hastily in review such faces as I know, and don't trust, I am inclined to think, now I give my mind to it, that none of them keep silence well."

This proposition in Physiognomy being new to Wilding, he was at first slow to admit it, until asking himself the question whether Mrs. Goldstraw kept silence well, and remembering that her face in repose decidedly invited trustfulness, he was as glad as men usually are to believe what they desire to believe.

But, as he was very slow to regain his spirits or his health, his
artner, as another means of setting him up—and perhaps also with
ontingent Obenreizer views—reminded him of those musical schemes
f his in connexion with his family, and how a singing-class was to be
ormed in the house, and a Choir in a neighbouring church. The class
as established speedily, and, two or three of the people having
lready some musical knowledge, and singing tolerably, the Choir
oon followed. The latter was led, and chiefly taught, by Wilding
imself; who had hopes of converting his dependants into so many
oundlings, in respect of their capacity to sing sacred choruses.

Now, the Obenreizers being skilled musicians, it was easily brought
o pass that they should be asked to join these musical unions.
uardian and Ward consenting, or Guardian consenting for both, it
as necessarily brought to pass that Vendale's life became a life of
bsolute thraldom and enchantment. For, in the mouldy Christopher-
Wren church on Sundays, with its dearly beloved brethren assembled
nd met together, five-and-twenty strong, was not that Her voice
hat shot like light into the darkest places, thrilling the walls and
illars as though they were pieces of his heart! What time, too,
Madame Dor in a corner of the high pew, turning her back upon
verybody and everything, could not fail to be Ritualistically right
t some moment of the service; like the man whom the doctors
ecommended to get drunk once a month, and who, that he might not
verlook it, got drunk every day.

But, even those seraphic Sundays were surpassed by the Wednes-
ay concerts established for the patriarchal family. At those concerts
he would sit down to the piano and sing them, in her own tongue,
ongs of her own land, songs calling from the mountain-tops to
Vendale, "Rise above the grovelling level country; come far away
rom the crowd; pursue me as I mount higher; higher, higher, melting
nto the azure distance; rise to my supremest height of all, and love
me here!" Then would the pretty bodice, the clocked stocking, and
he silver-buckled shoe be, like the broad forehead and the bright
yes, fraught with the spring of a very chamois, until the strain was
ver.

Not even over Vendale himself did these songs of hers cast a more
otent spell than over Joey Ladle in his different way. Steadily
efusing to muddle the harmony by taking any share in it, and
vincing the supremest contempt for scales and such-like rudiments
f music—which, indeed, seldom captivate mere listeners—Joey did
t first give up the whole business for a bad job, and the whole of the
erformers for a set of howling Dervishes. But, descrying traces of
nmuddled harmony in a part song one day, he gave his two under
ellarmen faint hopes of getting on towards something in course of
me. An anthem of Handel's led to further encouragement from him:
hough he objected that that great musician must have been down in
ome of them foreign cellars pretty much, for to go and say the same
hing so many times over; which, took it in how you might, he
onsidered a certain sign of your having took it in somehow. On a

third occasion, the public appearance of Mr. Jarvis with a flute, and of an odd man with a violin, and the performance of a duet by the two, did so astonish him that, solely of his own impulse and motion he became inspired with the words, "Ann Koar!" repeatedly pronouncing them as if calling in a familiar manner for some lady who had distinguished herself in the orchestra. But this was his final testimony to the merits of his mates, for, the instrumental duet being performed at the first Wednesday concert, and being presently followed by the voice of Marguerite Obenreizer, he sat with his mouth wide open, entranced, until she had finished; when, rising in his place with much solemnity, and prefacing what he was about to say with a bow that specially included Mr. Wilding in it, he delivered himself of the gratifying sentiment: "Arter that, ye may all on ye get to bed!" And ever afterwards declined to render homage in any other words to the musical powers of the family.

Thus began a separate personal acquaintance between Marguerite Obenreizer and Joey Ladle. She laughed so heartily at his compliment, and yet was so abashed by it, that Joey made bold to say to her, after the concert was over, he hoped he wasn't so muddled in his head as to have took a liberty? She made him a gracious reply, and Joey ducked in return.

"You'll change the luck time about, Miss," said Joey, ducking again. "It's such as you in the place that can bring round the luck of the place."

"Can I? Round the luck?" she answered, in her pretty English and with a pretty wonder. "I fear I do not understand. I am so stupid."

"Young Master Wilding, Miss," Joey explained confidentially, though not much to her enlightenment, "changed the luck, afore he took in young Master George. So I say, and so they'll find. Lord Only come into the place and sing over the luck a few times, Miss, and it won't be able to help itself!"

With this, and with a whole brood of ducks, Joey backed out of the presence. But Joey being a privileged person, and even an involuntary conquest being pleasant to youth and beauty, Marguerite merrily looked out for him next time.

"Where is my Mr. Joey, please?" she asked Vendale.

So Joey was produced and shaken hands with, and that became an Institution.

Another Institution arose in this wise. Joey was a little hard of hearing. He himself said it was "Wapours," and perhaps it might have been; but whatever the cause of the effect, there the effect was upon him. On this first occasion he had been seen to sidle along the wall, with his left hand to his left ear, until he had sidled himself into a seat pretty near the singer, in which place and position he had remained, until addressing to his friends the amateurs the compliment before mentioned. It was observed on the following Wednesday that Joey's action as a Pecking Machine was impaired at dinner, and was rumoured about the table that this was explainable by his high strung expectations of Miss Obenreizer's singing, and his fears of not getting a place where he could hear every note and syllable. The rumour reaching Wilding's ears, he in his good nature called Joey to the front at night before Marguerite began. Thus the Institution came into being that on succeeding nights, Marguerite, running her hands over the keys before singing, always said to Vendale, "Where is my Mr. Joey, please?" and that Vendale always brought him forth, and stationed him near by. That he should then, when all eyes were upon him, express in his face the utmost contempt for the exertions of his friends and confidence in Marguerite alone, whom he would stand contemplating, not unlike the rhinoceros out of the spelling-book, tamed and on his hind legs, was a part of the Institution. Also that when he remained after the singing in his most ecstatic state, some bold spirit from the back should say, "What do you think of it, Joey?" and he should be goaded to reply, as having that instant conceived the retort, "Arter that, ye may all on ye get to bed!" These were other parts of the Institution.

But, the simple pleasures and small jests of Cripple Corner were not destined to have a long life. Underlying them from the first was a serious matter, which every member of the patriarchal family knew of, but which, by tacit agreement, all forbore to speak of. Mr. Wilding's health was in a bad way.

He might have overcome the shock he had sustained in the one great affection of his life, or he might have overcome his consciousness of being in the enjoyment of another man's property; but the two together were too much for him. A man haunted by twin ghosts, he became deeply depressed. The inseparable spectres sat at the board with him, ate from his platter, drank from his cup, and stood by his bedside at night. When he recalled his supposed mother's love, he felt as though he had stolen it. When he rallied a little under the respect and attachment of his dependants, he felt as though he were even fraudulent in making them happy, for that should have been the unknown man's duty and gratification.

Gradually, under the pressure of his brooding mind, his body stooped, his step lost its elasticity, his eyes were seldom lifted from the ground. He knew he could not help the deplorable mistake that had been made, but he knew he could not mend it; for the days and weeks went by and no one claimed his name or his possessions. And now there began to creep over him a cloudy consciousness of often-recurring confusion in his head. He would unaccountably lose, sometimes whole hours, sometimes a whole day and night. Once, his remembrance stopped as he sat at the head of the dinner-table, and was blank until daybreak. Another time, it stopped as he was beating time to their singing, and went on again when he and his partner were walking in the courtyard by the light of the moon, half the night later. He asked Vendale (always full of consideration, work, and help) how this was? Vendale only replied, "You have not been quite well; that's all." He looked for explanation into the faces of his people. But they would put it off with, "Glad to see you looking so much

better, Sir"; or "Hope you're doing nicely now, Sir"; in which was n~
information at all.

At length, when the partnership was but five months old, Walter
Wilding took to his bed, and his housekeeper became his nurse.

"Lying here, perhaps you will not mind my calling you Sally, Mrs
Goldstraw?" said the poor wine-merchant.

"It sounds more natural to me, Sir, than any other name, and
like it better."

"Thank you, Sally. I think, Sally, I must of late have been subjec
to fits. Is that so, Sally? Don't mind telling me now."

"It has happened, Sir."

"Ah! That is the explanation!" he quietly remarked. "M~
Obenreizer, Sally, talks of the world being so small that it is no
strange how often the same people come together, and come togethe
at various places, and in various stages of life. But it does seer
strange, Sally, that I should, as I may say, come round to th
Foundling to die."

He extended his hand to her, and she gently took it.

"You are not going to die, dear Mr. Wilding."

"So Mr. Bintrey said, but I think he was wrong. The old child
feeling is coming back upon me, Sally. The old hush and rest, as
used to fall asleep."

After an interval he said, in a placid voice, "Please kiss me, Nurse,
and, it was evident, believed himself to be lying in the old Dormitory

As she had been used to bend over the fatherless and motherles
children, Sally bent over the fatherless and motherless man, and pu
her lips to his forehead, murmuring:

"God bless you!"

"God bless you!" he replied, in the same tone.

After another interval, he opened his eyes in his own character, an
said: "Don't move me, Sally, because of what I am going to say;
lie quite easily. I think my time is come. I don't know how it ma
appear to you, Sally, but——"

Insensibility fell upon him for a few minutes; he emerged from i
once more.

"—I don't know how it may appear to you, Sally, but so it appear
to me."

When he had thus conscientiously finished his favourite sentence
his time came, and he died.

ACT II

VENDALE MAKES LOVE

THE summer and the autumn had passed. Christmas and the Ne~
Year were at hand.

As executors honestly bent on performing their duty towards th
dead, Vendale and Bintrey had held more than one anxious consulta

on on the subject of Wilding's will. The lawyer had declared, from
the first, that it was simply impossible to take any useful action in
the matter at all. The only obvious inquiries to make, in relation to
the lost man, had been made already by Wilding himself; with this
result, that time and death together had not left a trace of him
discoverable. To advertise for the claimant to the property, it would
be necessary to mention particulars—a course of proceeding which
would invite half the impostors in England to present themselves in
the character of the true Walter Wilding. "If we find a chance of
tracing the lost man, we will take it. If we don't, let us meet for
another consultation on the first anniversary of Wilding's death."
so Bintrey advised. And so, with the most earnest desire to fulfil his
dead friend's wishes, Vendale was fain to let the matter rest for the
present.

Turning from his interest in the past to his interest in the future,
Vendale still found himself confronting a doubtful prospect. Months
on months had passed since his first visit to Soho-square—and
through all that time, the one language in which he had told Marguerite that he loved her was the language of the eyes, assisted, at
convenient opportunities, by the language of the hand.

What was the obstacle in his way? The one immovable obstacle
which had been in his way from the first. No matter how fairly the
opportunities looked, Vendale's efforts to speak with Marguerite
alone ended invariably in one and the same result. Under the most
accidental circumstances, in the most innocent manner possible,
Obenreizer was always in the way.

With the last days of the old year came an unexpected chance of
spending an evening with Marguerite, which Vendale resolved should
be a chance of speaking privately to her as well. A cordial note from
Obenreizer invited him, on New Year's Day, to a little family dinner
at Soho-square. "We shall be only four," the note said. "We shall be
only two," Vendale determined, "before the evening is out!"

New Year's Day, among the English, is associated with the giving
and receiving of dinners, and with nothing more. New Year's Day,
among the foreigners, is the grand opportunity of the year for the
giving and receiving of presents. It is occasionally possible to acclima-
tise a foreign custom. In this instance Vendale felt no hesitation
about making the attempt. His one difficulty was to decide what his
New Year's gift to Marguerite should be. The defensive pride of the
peasant's daughter—morbidly sensitive to the inequality between
her social position and his—would be secretly roused against him if
he ventured on a rich offering. A gift, which a poor man's purse
might purchase, was the one gift that could be trusted to find its way
to her heart, for the giver's sake. Stoutly resisting temptation, in the
form of diamonds and rubies, Vendale bought a brooch of the
filigree-work of Genoa—the simplest and most unpretending ornament that he could find in the jeweller's shop.

He slipped his gift into Marguerite's hand as she held it out to
welcome him on the day of the dinner.

"This is your first New Year's Day in England," he said. "Will you let me help to make it like a New Year's Day at home?"

She thanked him, a little constrainedly, as she looked at the jeweller's box, uncertain what it might contain. Opening the box, and discovering the studiously simple form under which Vendale's little keepsake offered itself to her, she penetrated his motive on the spot. Her face turned on him brightly, with a look which said, "I own you have pleased and flattered me." Never had she been so charming, in Vendale's eyes, as she was at that moment. Her winter dress—a petticoat of dark silk, with a bodice of black velvet rising to her neck, and enclosing it softly in a little circle of swansdown—heightened, by all the force of contrast, the dazzling fairness of her hair and her complexion. It was only when she turned aside from him to the glass, and, taking out the brooch that she wore, put his New Year's gift in its place, that Vendale's attention wandered far enough away from her to discover the presence of other persons in the room. He now became conscious that the hands of Obenreizer were affectionately in possession of his elbows. He now heard the voice of Obenreizer thanking him for his attention to Marguerite, with the faintest possible ring of mockery in its tongue. ("Such a simple present, dear Sir! and showing such nice tact!") He now discovered, for the first time, that there was one other guest, and but one, besides himself, whom Obenreizer presented as a compatriot and friend. The friend's face was mouldy, and the friend's figure was fat. His age was suggestive of the autumnal period of human life. In the course of the evening he developed two extraordinary capacities. One was a capacity for silence; the other was a capacity for emptying bottles.

Madame Dor was not in the room. Neither was there any visible place reserved for her when they sat down to table. Obenreizer explained that it was "the good Dor's simple habit to dine always in the middle of the day. She would make her excuses later in the evening." Vendale wondered whether the good Dor had, on this occasion, varied her domestic employment from cleaning Obenreizer's gloves to cooking Obenreizer's dinner. This at least was certain—the dishes served were, one and all, as achievements in cookery, high above the reach of the rude elementary art of England. The dinner was unobtrusively perfect. As for the wine, the eyes of the speechless friend rolled over it, as in solemn ecstasy. Sometimes he said "Good!" when a bottle came in full; and sometimes he said "Ah!" when a bottle went out empty—and there his contributions to the gaiety of the evening ended.

Silence is occasionally infectious. Oppressed by private anxieties of their own, Marguerite and Vendale appeared to feel the influence of the speechless friend. The whole responsibility of keeping the talk going rested on Obenreizer's shoulders, and manfully did Obenreizer sustain it. He opened his heart in the character of an enlightened foreigner, and sang the praises of England. When other topics ran dry, he returned to this inexhaustible source, and always set the stream running again as copiously as ever. Obenreizer would have given an arm, an eye, or a leg to have been born an Englishman. Out of England there was no such institution as a home, no such thing as a fireside, no such object as a beautiful woman. His dear Miss Marguerite would excuse him, if he accounted for *her* attractions on the theory that English blood must have mixed at some former time with their obscure and unknown ancestry. Survey this English nation, and behold a tall, clean, plump, and solid people! Look at their cities! What magnificence in their public buildings! What admirable order and propriety in their streets! Admire their laws, combining the eternal principle of justice with the other eternal principle of pounds, shillings, and pence; and applying the product to all civil injuries, from an injury to a man's honour, to an injury to a man's nose! You have ruined my daughter—pounds, shillings, and pence! You have knocked me down with a blow in my face—pounds, shillings, and pence! Where was the material prosperity of such a country as *that* to stop? Obenreizer, projecting himself into the future, failed to see the end of it. Obenreizer's enthusiasm entreated permission to exhale itself, English fashion, in a toast. Here is our modest little dinner over, here is our frugal dessert on the table, and here is the admirer of England conforming to national customs, and making a speech! A toast to your white cliffs of Albion, Mr. Vendale! to your national virtues, your charming climate, and your fascinating women! to your Hearths, to your Homes, to your Habeas Corpus, and to all your other institutions! In one word—to England! Heep-heep-heep! hooray!

Obenreizer's voice had barely chanted the last note of the English cheer, the speechless friend had barely drained the last drop out of his glass, when the festive proceedings were interrupted by a modest tap at the door. A woman-servant came in, and approached her master with a little note in her hand. Obenreizer opened the note with a frown; and, after reading it with an expression of genuine annoyance, passed it on to his compatriot and friend. Vendale's spirits rose as he watched these proceedings. Had he found an ally in the annoying little note? Was the long-looked-for-chance actually coming at last?

"I am afraid there is no help for it?" said Obenreizer, addressing his fellow-countryman. "I am afraid we must go."

The speechless friend handed back the letter, shrugged his heavy shoulders, and poured himself out a last glass of wine. His fat fingers lingered fondly round the neck of the bottle. They pressed it with a little amatory squeeze at parting. His globular eyes looked dimly, as through an intervening haze, at Vendale and Marguerite. His heavy articulation laboured, and brought forth a whole sentence at a birth. "I think," he said, "I should have liked a little more wine." His breath failed him after that effort; he gasped, and walked to the door.

Obenreizer addressed himself to Vendale with an appearance of the deepest distress.

"I am so shocked, so confused, so distressed," he began. "A

misfortune has happened to one of my compatriots. He is alone
he is ignorant of your language—I and my good friend, here, have n
choice but to go and help him. What can I say in my excuse? How
can I describe my affliction at depriving myself in this way of the
honour of your company?"

He paused, evidently expecting to see Vendale take up his hat and
retire. Discerning his opportunity at last, Vendale determined to do
nothing of the kind. He met Obenreizer dexterously, with Oben
reizer's own weapons.

"Pray don't distress yourself," he said. "I'll wait here with the
greatest pleasure till you come back."

Marguerite blushed deeply, and turned away to her embroidery
frame in a corner by the window. The film showed itself in Obenreizer'
eyes, and the smile came something sourly to Obenreizer's lips. To
have told Vendale that there was no reasonable prospect of his com
ing back in good time, would have been to risk offending a man whose
favourable opinion was of solid commercial importance to him
Accepting his defeat with the best possible grace, he declared himsel
to be equally honoured and delighted by Vendale's proposal. "So
frank, so friendly, so English!" He bustled about, apparently looking
for something he wanted, disappeared for a moment through the
folding-doors communicating with the next room, came back with
his hat and coat, and protesting that he would return at the earliest
possible moment, embraced Vendale's elbows, and vanished from the
scene in company with the speechless friend.

Vendale turned to the corner by the window, in which Marguerite
had placed herself with her work. There, as if she had dropped from
the ceiling, or come up through the floor—there, in the old attitude
with her face to the stove—sat an Obstacle that had not been
foreseen, in the person of Madame Dor! She half got up, half looked
over her broad shoulder at Vendale, and plumped down again. Was
she at work? Yes. Cleaning Obenreizer's gloves, as before? No; darn
ing Obenreizer's stockings.

The case was now desperate. Two serious considerations presented
themselves to Vendale. Was it possible to put Madame Dor into the
stove? The stove wouldn't hold her. Was it possible to treat Madame
Dor, not as a living woman, but as an article of furniture? Could the
mind be brought to contemplate this respectable matron purely in
the light of a chest of drawers, with a black gauze head-dress
accidentally left on the top of it? Yes, the mind could be brought to
do that. With a comparatively trifling effort, Vendale's mind did it
As he took his place on the old-fashioned window-seat, close by
Marguerite and her embroidery, a slight movement appeared in the
chest of drawers, but no remark issued from it. Let it be remembered
that solid furniture is not easy to move, and that it has this advan
tage in consequence—there is no fear of upsetting it.

Unusually silent and unusually constrained—with the bright colour
fast fading from her face, with a feverish energy possessing her
fingers—the pretty Marguerite bent over her embroidery, and

orked as if her life depended on it. Hardly less agitated himself,
endale felt the importance of leading her very gently to the avowal
hich he was eager to make—to the other sweeter avowal still,
hich he was longing to hear. A woman's love is never to be taken by
orm; it yields insensibly to a system of gradual approach. It
entures by the roundabout way, and listens to the low voice. Vendale
d her memory back to their past meetings when they were travelling
gether in Switzerland. They revived the impressions, they recalled
e events, of the happy bygone time. Little by little, Marguerite's
onstraint vanished. She smiled, she was interested, she looked at
endale, she grew idle with her needle, she made false stitches in her
ork. Their voices sank lower and lower; their faces bent nearer and
earer to each other as they spoke. And Madame Dor? Madame Dor
ehaved like an angel. She never looked round; she never said a word;
e went on with Obenreizer's stockings. Pulling each stocking up
ght over her left arm, and holding that arm aloft from time to time,
catch the light on her work, there were moments—delicate and
describable moments—when Madame Dor appeared to be sitting
pside down, and contemplating one of her own respectable legs,
evated in the air. As the minutes wore on, these elevations followed
ch other at longer and longer intervals. Now and again, the black
auze head-dress nodded, dropped forward, recovered itself. A little
eap of stockings slid softly from Madame Dor's lap, and remained
nnoticed on the floor. A prodigious ball of worsted followed the
ockings, and rolled lazily under the table. The black gauze head-
ress nodded, dropped forward, recovered itself, nodded again,
ropped forward again, and recovered itself no more. A composite
und, partly as of the purring of an immense cat, partly as of the
laning of a soft board, rose over the hushed voices of the lovers,
d hummed at regular intervals through the room. Nature and
[adame Dor had combined together in Vendale's interests. The best
f women was asleep.

Marguerite rose to stop—not the snoring—let us say, the audible
pose of Madame Dor. Vendale laid his hand on her arm, and pressed
er back gently into her chair.

"Don't disturb her," he whispered. "I have been waiting to tell
ou a secret. Let me tell it now."

Marguerite resumed her seat. She tried to resume her needle. It
as useless; her eyes failed her; her hand failed her; she could find
othing.

"We have been talking," said Vendale, "of the happy time when
e first met, and first travelled together. I have a confession to make.
have been concealing something. When we spoke of my first visit
Switzerland, I told you of all the impressions I had brought back
ith me to England—except one. Can you guess what that one is?"

Her eyes looked steadfastly at the embroidery, and her face turned
little away from him. Signs of disturbance began to appear in her
eat velvet bodice, round the region of the brooch. She made no
ply. Vendale pressed the question without mercy.

"Can you guess what the one Swiss impression is, which I have not told you yet?"

Her face turned back towards him, and a faint smile trembled on her lips.

"An impression of the mountains, perhaps?" she said slyly.

"No; a much more precious impression than that."

"Of the lakes?"

"No. The lakes have not grown dearer and dearer in remembrance to me every day. The lakes are not associated with my happiness in the present, and my hopes in the future. Marguerite! all that make life worth having hangs, for me, on a word from your lips. Marguerite! I love you!"

Her head drooped as he took her hand. He drew her to him, and looked at her. The tears escaped from her downcast eyes, and fell slowly over her cheeks.

"O, Mr. Vendale," she said sadly, "it would have been kinder to have kept your secret. Have you forgotten the distance between us? It can never, never be!"

"There can be but one distance between us, Marguerite—a distance of your making. My love, my darling, there is no higher rank in goodness, there is no higher rank in beauty, than yours! Come! whisper the one little word which tells me you will be my wife!"

She sighed bitterly. "Think of your family," she murmured; "and think of mine!"

Vendale drew her a little nearer to him.

"If you dwell on such an obstacle as that," he said, "I shall think but one thought—I shall think I have offended you."

She started, and looked up. "O, no!" she exclaimed innocently. The instant the words passed her lips, she saw the construction that might be placed on them. Her confession had escaped her in spite of herself. A lovely flush of colour overspread her face. She made a momentary effort to disengage herself from her lover's embrace. She looked up at him entreatingly. She tried to speak. The words died on her lips in the kiss that Vendale pressed on them. "Let me go, Mr. Vendale!" she said faintly.

"Call me George."

She laid her head on his bosom. All her heart went out to him at last. "George!" she whispered.

"Say you love me!"

Her arms twined themselves gently round his neck. Her lips, timidly touching his cheek, murmured the delicious words—"I love you!"

In the moment of silence that followed, the sound of the opening and closing of the house-door came clear to them through the wintry stillness of the street.

Marguerite started to her feet.

"Let me go!" she said. "He has come back!"

She hurried from the room, and touched Madame Dor's shoulder in passing. Madame Dor woke up with a loud snort, looked first over

ne shoulder and then over the other, peered down into her lap, and
iscovered neither stockings, worsted, nor darning-needle in it. At
ne same moment, footsteps became audible ascending the stairs.
"Mon Dieu!" said Madame Dor, addressing herself to the stove, and
rembling violently. Vendale picked up the stockings and the ball,
nd huddled them all back in a heap over her shoulder. "Mon Dieu!"
aid Madame Dor, for the second time, as the avalanche of worsted
oured into her capacious lap.

The door opened, and Obenreizer came in. His first glance round
ne room showed him that Marguerite was absent.

"What!" he exclaimed, "my niece is away? My niece is not here
o entertain you in my absence? This is unpardonable. I shall bring
er back instantly."

Vendale stopped him.

"I beg you will not disturb Miss Obenreizer," he said. "You have
eturned, I see, without your friend?"

"My friend remains, and consoles our afflicted compatriot. A
eart-rending scene, Mr. Vendale! The household gods at the pawn-
roker's—the family immersed in tears. We all embraced in silence.
Iy admirable friend alone possessed his composure. He sent out,
n the spot, for a bottle of wine."

"Can I say a word to you in private, Mr. Obenreizer?"

"Assuredly." He turned to Madame Dor. "My good creature, you
re sinking for want of repose. Mr. Vendale will excuse you."

Madame Dor rose, and set forth sideways on her journey from the
tove to bed. She dropped a stocking. Vendale picked it up for her,
nd opened one of the folding-doors. She advanced a step, and
ropped three more stockings. Vendale, stooping to recover them
s before, Obenreizer interfered with profuse apologies, and with a
arning look at Madame Dor. Madame Dor acknowledged the look
y dropping the whole of the stockings in a heap, and then shuffling
way panic-stricken from the scene of disaster. Obenreizer swept up
he complete collection fiercely in both hands. "Go!" he cried, giving
is prodigious handful a preparatory swing in the air. Madame Dor
aid, "Mon Dieu," and vanished into the next room, pursued by a
hower of stockings.

"What must you think, Mr. Vendale," said Obenreizer, closing
he door, "of this deplorable intrusion of domestic details? For my-
elf, I blush at it. We are beginning the New Year as badly as possi-
le; everything has gone wrong to-night. Be seated, pray—and say,
vhat may I offer you? Shall we pay our best respects to another of
our noble English institutions? It is my study to be, what you call,
olly. I propose a grog."

Vendale declined the grog with all needful respect for that noble
nstitution.

"I wish to speak to you on a subject in which I am deeply in-
erested," he said. "You must have observed, Mr. Obenreizer, that
have, from the first, felt no ordinary admiration for your charming
iece?"

"You are very good. In my niece's name, I thank you."

"Perhaps you may have noticed, latterly, that my admiration for Miss Obenreizer has grown into a tenderer and deeper feeling——?'

"Shall we say friendship, Mr. Vendale?"

"Say love—and we shall be nearer to the truth."

Obenreizer started out of his chair. The faintly discernible beat which was his nearest approach to a change of colour, showed itself suddenly in his cheeks.

"You are Miss Obenreizer's guardian," pursued Vendale. "I ask you to confer upon me the greatest of all favours—I ask you to give me her hand in marriage."

Obenreizer dropped back into his chair. "Mr. Vendale," he said "you petrify me."

"I will wait," rejoined Vendale, "until you have recovered yourself."

"One word before I recover myself. You have said nothing about this to my niece?"

"I have opened my whole heart to your niece. And I have reason to hope——"

"What!" interposed Obenreizer. "You have made a proposal to my niece, without first asking for my authority to pay your addresses to her?" He struck his hand on the table, and lost his hold over himself for the first time in Vendale's experience of him. "Sir!' he exclaimed, indignantly, "what sort of conduct is this? As a man of honour, speaking to a man of honour, how can you justify it?"

"I can only justify it as one of our English institutions," said Vendale quietly. "You admire our English institutions. I can't honestly tell you, Mr. Obenreizer, that I regret what I have done I can only assure you that I have not acted in the matter with any intentional disrespect towards yourself. This said, may I ask you to tell me plainly what objection you see to favouring my suit?"

"I see this immense objection," answered Obenreizer, "that my niece and you are not on a social equality together. My niece is the daughter of a poor peasant; and you are the son of a gentleman. You do us an honour," he added, lowering himself again gradually to his customary polite level, "which deserves, and has, our most grateful acknowledgments. But the inequality is too glaring; the sacrifice is too great. You English are a proud people, Mr. Vendale. I have observed enough of this country to see that such a marriage as you propose would be a scandal here. Not a hand would be held out to your peasant-wife; and all your best friends would desert you."

"One moment," said Vendale, interposing on his side. "I may claim, without any great arrogance, to know more of my country people in general, and of my own friends in particular, than you do In the estimation of everybody whose opinion is worth having, my wife herself would be the one sufficient justification of my marriage. If I did not feel certain—observe, I say certain—that I am offering her a position which she can accept without so much as the shadow of a humiliation—I would never (cost me what it might) have asked her be my wife. Is there any other obstacle that you see? Have you any personal objection to me?"

Obenreizer spread out both his hands in courteous protest. "Personal objection!" he exclaimed. "Dear Sir, the bare question is painful to me."

"We are both men of business," pursued Vendale, "and you naturally expect me to satisfy you that I have the means of supporting a wife. I can explain my pecuniary position in two words. I inherit from my parents a fortune of twenty thousand pounds. In half of that sum I have only a life-interest, to which, if I die, leaving a widow, my widow succeeds. If I die, leaving children, the money itself is divided among them, as they come of age. The other half of my fortune is at my own disposal, and is invested in the wine-business. I see my way to greatly improving that business. As it stands at present I cannot state my return from my capital embarked at more than twelve hundred a year. Add the yearly value of my life-interest—and the total reaches a present annual income of fifteen hundred pounds. I have the fairest prospect of soon making it more. In the meantime, do you object to me on pecuniary grounds?"

Driven back to his last entrenchment, Obenreizer rose, and took a turn backwards and forwards in the room. For the moment, he was plainly at a loss what to say or do next.

"Before I answer that last question," he said, after a little close consideration with himself, "I beg leave to revert for a moment to Miss Marguerite. You said something just now which seemed to imply that she returns the sentiment with which you are pleased to regard her?"

"I have the inestimable happiness," said Vendale, "of knowing that she loves me."

Obenreizer stood silent for a moment, with the film over his eyes, and the faintly perceptible beat becoming visible again in his cheeks.

"If you will excuse me for a few minutes," he said, with ceremonious politeness, "I should like to have the opportunity of speaking to my niece." With those words, he bowed, and quitted the room.

Left by himself, Vendale's thoughts (as a necessary result of the interview, thus far) turned instinctively to the consideration of Obenreizer's motives. He had put obstacles in the way of the courtship; he was now putting obstacles in the way of the marriage—a marriage offering advantages which even his ingenuity could not dispute. On the face of it, his conduct was incomprehensible. What did it mean?

Seeking, under the surface, for the answer to that question—and remembering that Obenreizer was a man of about his own age; also, that Marguerite was, strictly speaking, his half-niece only—Vendale asked himself, with a lover's ready jealousy, whether he had a rival to fear, as well as a guardian to conciliate. The thought just crossed his mind, and no more. The sense of Marguerite's kiss still lingering on his cheek reminded him gently that even the jealousy of a moment was now a treason to *her*.

On reflection, it seemed most likely that a personal motive of anoth[e]
kind might suggest the true explanation of Obenreizer's conduc[t]
Marguerite's grace and beauty were precious ornaments in that litt[le]
household. They gave it a special social attraction and a speci[al]
social importance. They armed Obenreizer with a certain influenc[e]
in reserve, which he could always depend upon to make his hou[se]
attractive, and which he might always bring more or less to bear o[n]
the forwarding of his own private ends. Was he the sort of man t[o]
resign such advantages as were here implied, without obtaining th[e]
fullest possible compensation for the loss? A connexion by marriag[e]
with Vendale offered him solid advantages, beyond all doubt. B[ut]
there were hundreds of men in London with far greater pow[er]
and far wider influence than Vendale possessed. Was it possib[le]
that this man's ambition secretly looked higher than the highe[st]
prospects that could be offered to him by the alliance now propose[d]
for his niece? As the question passed through Vendale's mind, th[e]
man himself reappeared—to answer it, or not to answer it, as th[e]
event might prove.

A marked change was visible in Obenreizer when he resume[d]
his place. His manner was less assured, and there were plai[n]
traces about his mouth of recent agitation which had not been su[c]-
cessfully composed. Had he said something, referring either to Ve[n]-
dale or to himself, which had raised Marguerite's spirit, and whic[h]
had placed him, for the first time, face to face with a resolu[te]
assertion of his niece's will? It might or might not be. This only w[as]
certain—he looked like a man who had met with a repulse.

"I have spoken to my niece," he began. "I find, Mr. Vendale, th[at]
even your influence has not entirely blinded her to the social obje[c]-
tions to your proposal."

"May I ask," returned Vendale, "if that is the only result of yo[ur]
interview with Miss Obenreizer?"

A momentary flash leapt out through the Obenreizer film.

"You are master of the situation," he answered, in a tone [of]
sardonic submission. "If you insist on my admitting it, I do admit
in those words. My niece's will and mine used to be one, Mr. Vendal[e]
You have come between us, and her will is now yours. In my countr[y]
we know when we are beaten, and we submit with our best grace.
submit, with my best grace, on certain conditions. Let us revert t[o]
the statement of your pecuniary position. I have an objection to yo[u,]
my dear Sir—a most amazing, a most audacious objection, from [a]
man in my position to a man in yours."

"What is it?"

"You have honoured me by making a proposal for my niece[']
hand. For the present (with best thanks and respects), I beg t[o]
decline it."

"Why?"

"Because you are not rich enough."

The objection, as the speaker had foreseen, took Vendale completel[y]
by surprise. For the moment he was speechless.

"Your income is fifteen hundred a year," pursued Obenreizer. "In
my miserable country I should fall on my knees before your income,
and say, 'What a princely fortune!' In wealthy England, I sit as I am,
and say 'A modest independence, dear Sir; nothing more. Enough,
perhaps, for a wife in your own rank of life, who has no social prejudices to conquer. Not more than half enough for a wife who is a
meanly born foreigner, and who has all your social prejudices
against her.' Sir! if my niece is ever to marry you, she will have what
you call uphill work of it in taking her place at starting. Yes, yes;
this is not your view, but it remains, immovably remains, my view for
all that. For my niece's sake, I claim that this uphill work shall be
made as smooth as possible. Whatever material advantages she can
have to help her, ought, in common justice, to be hers. Now, tell me,
Mr. Vendale, on your fifteen hundred a year can your wife have a
house in a fashionable quarter, a footman to open her door, a butler to
wait at her table, and a carriage and horses to drive about in? I see the
answer in your face—your face says, No. Very good. Tell me one more
thing, and I have done. Take the mass of your educated, accomplished,
and lovely country-women, is it, or is it not, the fact that a lady who
has a house in a fashionable quarter, a footman to open her door, a
butler to wait at her table, and a carriage and horses to drive about
in, is a lady who has gained four steps, in female estimation, at
starting? Yes? or No?"

"Come to the point," said Vendale. "You view this question as a
question of terms. What are your terms?"

"The lowest terms, dear Sir, on which you can provide your wife
with those four steps at starting. Double your present income—
the most rigid economy cannot do it in England on less. You said
just now that you expected greatly to increase the value of your
business. To work—and increase it! I am a good devil after all! On
the day when you satisfy me, by plain proofs, that your income has
risen to three thousand a year, ask me for my niece's hand, and it is
ours."

"May I inquire if you have mentioned this arrangement to Miss
Obenreizer?"

"Certainly. She has a last little morsel of regard still left for me,
Mr. Vendale, which is not yours yet; and she accepts my terms. In
other words, she submits to be guided by her guardian's regard for her
welfare, and by her guardian's superior knowledge of the world."
He threw himself back in his chair, in firm reliance on his position, and
in full possession of his excellent temper.

Any open assertion of his own interests, in the situation in which
Vendale was now placed, seemed to be (for the present at least)
hopeless. He found himself literally left with no ground to stand on.
Whether Obenreizer's objections were the genuine product of
Obenreizer's own view of the case, or whether he was simply delaying
the marriage in the hope of ultimately breaking it off altogether—in
either of these events, any present resistance on Vendale's part
would be equally useless. There was no help for it but to yield,

making the best terms that he could on his own side.

"I protest against the conditions you impose on me," he began

"Naturally," said Obenreizer; "I dare say I should protest, mysel in your place."

"Say, however," pursued Vendale, "that I accept your terms. I that case, I must be permitted to make two stipulations on m part. In the first place, I shall expect to be allowed to see your niece

"Aha! to see my niece? and to make her in as great a hurry to b married as you are yourself? Suppose I say, No? you would see h perhaps without my permission?"

"Decidedly!"

"How delightfully frank! How exquisitely English! You shall se her, Mr. Vendale, on certain days, which we will appoint togethe What next?"

"Your objection to my income," proceeded Vendale, "has take me completely by surprise. I wish to be assured against any repet tion of that surprise. Your present views of my qualification fe marriage require me to have an income of three thousand a yea Can I be certain, in the future, as your experience of Englan enlarges, that your estimate will rise no higher?"

"In plain English," said Obenreizer, "you doubt my word?"

"Do you purpose to take *my* word for it when I inform you tha I have doubled my income?" asked Vendale. "If my memor does not deceive me, you stipulated, a minute since, for plai proofs?"

"Well played, Mr. Vendale! You combine the foreign quicknes with the English solidity. Accept my best congratulations. Accep also, my written guarantee."

He rose; seated himself at a writing-desk at a side-table, wrote few lines, and presented them to Vendale with a low bow. The er gagement was perfectly explicit, and was signed and dated wit scrupulous care.

"Are you satisfied with your guarantee?"

"I am satisfied."

"Charmed to hear it, I am sure. We had our little skirmish— we have really been wonderfully clever on both sides. For the preser our affairs are settled. I bear no malice. You bear no malice. Come Mr. Vendale, a good English shake hands."

Vendale gave his hand, a little bewildered by Obenreizer's sudde transitions from one humour to another.

"When may I expect to see Miss Obenreizer again?" he asked, a he rose to go.

"Honour me with a visit to-morrow," said Obenreizer, "and w will settle it then. Do have a grog before you go! No? Well! well we will reserve the grog till you have your three thousand a yea and are ready to be married. Aha! When will that be?"

"I made an estimate, some months since, of the capacities of m business," said Vendale. "If that estimate is correct, I shall doubl my present income——"

"And be married!" added Obenreizer.

"And be married," repeated Vendale, "within a year from this time. Good Night."

VENDALE MAKES MISCHIEF

When Vendale entered his office the next morning, the dull commercial routine at Cripple Corner met him with a new face. Marguerite had an interest in it now! The whole machinery which Wilding's death had set in motion, to realise the value of the business —the balancing of ledgers, the estimating of debts, the taking of stock, and the rest of it—was now transformed into machinery which indicated the chances for and against a speedy marriage. After looking over results, as presented by his accountant, and checking additions and subtractions, as rendered by the clerks, Vendale turned his attention to the stock-taking department next, and sent a message to the cellars, desiring to see the report.

The Cellarman's appearance, the moment he put his head in at the door of his master's private room, suggested that something very extraordinary must have happened that morning. There was an approach to alacrity in Joey Ladle's movements! There was something which actually simulated cheerfulness in Joey Ladle's face!

"What's the matter?" asked Vendale. "Anything wrong?"

"I should wish to mention one thing," answered Joey. "Young Mr. Vendale, I have never set myself up for a prophet."

"Who ever said you did?"

"No prophet, as far as I've heard tell of that profession," proceeded Joey, "ever lived principally underground. No prophet, whatever else he might take in at the pores, ever took in wine from morning to night, for a number of years together. When I said to Young Master Wilding, respecting his changing the name of the firm, that one of these days he might find he'd changed the luck of the firm—did I put myself forward as a prophet? No, I didn't. Has what I said to him come true? Yes; it has. In the time of Pebbleson Nephew, Young Mr. Vendale, no such thing was ever known as a mistake made in a consignment delivered at these doors. There's a mistake been made now. Please to remark that it happened before Miss Margaret came here. For which reason it don't go against what I've said respecting Miss Margaret singing round the luck. Read that, Sir," concluded Joey, pointing attention to a special passage in the report, with a forefinger which appeared to be in process of taking in through the pores nothing more remarkable than dirt. "It's foreign to my nature to crow over the house I serve, but I feel it a kind of a solemn duty to ask you to read that."

Vendale read as follows :—"Note, respecting the Swiss champagne. An irregularity has been discovered in the last consignment received from the firm of Defresnier and Co." Vendale stopped, and referred to a memorandum-book by his side. "That was in Mr. Wilding's time," he said. "The vintage was a particularly good one, and he

took the whole of it. The Swiss champagne has done very wel
hasn't it?"

"I don't say it's done badly," answered the Cellarman. "It ma
have got sick in our customers' bins, or it may have bust in ou
customers' hands. But I don't say it's done badly with *us*."

Vendale resumed the reading of the note: "We find the number o
the cases to be quite correct by the books. But six of them, whic
present a slight difference from the rest in the brand, have bee
opened, and have been found to contain a red wine instead of cham
pagne. The similarity in the brands, we suppose, caused a mistak
to be made in sending the consignment from Neuchâtel. The erro
has not been found to extend beyond six cases."

"Is that all!" exclaimed Vendale, tossing the note away from hin
Joey Ladle's eye followed the flying morsel of paper drearily.

"I'm glad to see you take it easy, Sir," he said. "Whatever hap
pens, it will be always a comfort to you to remember that you too
it easy at first. Sometimes one mistake leads to another. A man drop
a bit of orange-peel on the pavement by mistake, and another ma
treads on it by mistake, and there's a job at the hospital, and a part
crippled for life. I'm glad you take it easy, Sir. In Pebbleso
Nephew's time we shouldn't have taken it easy till we had seen th
end of it. Without desiring to crow over the house, Young Mi
Vendale, I wish you well through it. No offence, Sir," said the Cellai
man, opening the door to go out, and looking in again ominousl
before he shut it. "I'm muddled and molloncolly, I grant you. Bu
I'm an old servant of Pebbleson Nephew, and I wish you well throug
them six cases of red wine."

Left by himself, Vendale laughed, and took up his pen. "I may a
well send a line to Defresnier and Company," he thought, "before
forget it." He wrote at once in these terms:

"DEAR SIRS. We are taking stock, and a trifling mistake has bee
discovered in the last consignment of champagne sent by your hous
to ours. Six of the cases contain red wine—which we hereby retur
to you. The matter can easily be set right, either by your sending u
six cases of the champagne, if they can be produced, or, if not, b
your crediting us with the value of six cases on the amount last pai
(five hundred pounds) by our firm to yours. Your faithful servants
"WILDING AND CO."

This letter dispatched to the post, the subject dropped at once ou
of Vendale's mind. He had other and far more interesting matter
to think of. Later in the day he paid the visit to Obenreizer whic
had been agreed on between them. Certain evenings in the week wer
set apart which he was privileged to spend with Marguerite—always
however, in the presence of a third person. On this stipulatio
Obenreizer politely but positively insisted. The one concession h
made was to give Vendale his choice of who the third person shoul
be. Confiding in past experience, his choice fell unhesitatingly upo

he excellent woman who mended Obenreizer's stockings. On hearing
f the responsibility entrusted to her, Madame Dor's intellectual
ature burst suddenly into a new stage of development. She waited
ill Obenreizer's eye was off her—and then she looked at Vendale,
nd dimly winked.

The time passed—the happy evenings with Marguerite came and
vent. It was the tenth morning since Vendale had written to the
wiss firm, when the answer appeared on his desk, with the other
etters of the day:

"DEAR SIRS. We beg to offer our excuses for the little mistake
vhich has happened. At the same time, we regret to add that the
tatement of our error, with which you have favoured us, has led to
very unexpected discovery. The affair is a most serious one for you
nd for us. The particulars are as follows:

"Having no more champagne of the vintage last sent to you, we
made arrangements to credit your firm with the value of the six
ases, as suggested by yourself. On taking this step, certain forms
bserved in our mode of doing business necessitated a reference to
ur bankers' book, as well as to our ledger. The result is a moral
ertainty that no such remittance as you mention can have reached
ur house, and a literal certainty that no such remittance has been
aid to our account at the bank.

"It is needless, at this stage of the proceedings, to trouble you
vith details. The money has unquestionably been stolen in the course
f its transit from you to us. Certain peculiarities which we observe,
elating to the manner in which the fraud has been perpetrated, lead
s to conclude that the thief may have calculated on being able to
ay the missing sum to our bankers, before an inevitable discovery
ollowed the annual striking of our balance. This would not have
appened, in the usual course, for another three months. During
hat period, but for your letter, we might have remained perfectly
nconscious of the robbery that has been committed.

"We mention this last circumstance, as it may help to show you
hat we have to do, in this case, with no ordinary thief. Thus far we
ave not even a suspicion of who that thief is. But we believe you
vill assist us in making some advance towards discovery, by examin-
ng the receipt (forged, of course) which has no doubt purported to
ome to you from our house. Be pleased to look and see whether it is
. receipt entirely in manuscript, or whether it is a numbered and
rinted form which merely requires the filling in of the amount. The
ettlement of this apparently trivial question is, we assure you, a
natter of vital importance. Anxiously awaiting your reply, we
emain, with high esteem and consideration,

"DEFRESNIER & CIE."

Vendale had the letter on his desk, and waited a moment to steady
is mind under the shock that had fallen on it. At the time of all
thers when it was most important to him to increase the value of his

business, that business was threatened with a loss of five hundre
pounds. He thought of Marguerite, as he took the key from his pocke
and opened the iron chamber in the wall in which the books an
papers of the firm were kept.

He was still in the chamber, searching for the forged receipt, whe
he was startled by a voice speaking close behind him.

"A thousand pardons," said the voice; "I am afraid I disturb you."

He turned, and found himself face to face with Marguerite
guardian.

"I have called," pursued Obenreizer, "to know if I can be of an
use. Business of my own takes me away for some days to Mancheste
and Liverpool. Can I combine any business of yours with it? I ar
entirely at your disposal, in the character of commercial traveller fc
the firm of Wilding and Co."

"Excuse me for one moment," said Vendale; "I will speak to yo
directly." He turned round again, and continued his search amon
the papers. "You come at a time when friendly offers are more tha
usually precious to me," he resumed. "I have had very bad news th
morning from Neuchâtel."

"Bad news!" exclaimed Obenreizer. "From Defresnier and Com
pany?"

"Yes. A remittance we sent to them has been stolen. I am threat
ened with a loss of five hundred pounds. What's that?"

Turning sharply, and looking into the room for the second time
Vendale discovered his envelope-case overthrown on the floor, an
Obenreizer on his knees picking up the contents.

"All my awkwardness," said Obenreizer. "This dreadful news c
yours startled me; I stepped back——" He became too deepl
interested in collecting the scattered envelopes to finish the sentence

"Don't trouble yourself," said Vendale. "The clerk will pic
the things up."

"This dreadful news!" repeated Obenreizer, persisting in collectin
the envelopes. "This dreadful news!"

"If you will read the letter," said Vendale, "you will find I hav
exaggerated nothing. There it is, open on my desk."

He resumed his search, and in a moment more discovered th
forged receipt. It was on the numbered and printed form, describe
by the Swiss firm. Vendale made a memorandum of the number an
the date. Having replaced the receipt and locked up the iron cham
ber, he had leisure to notice Obenreizer, reading the letter in th
recess of a window at the far end of the room.

"Come to the fire," said Vendale. "You look perished with th
cold out there. I will ring for some more coals."

Obenreizer rose, and came slowly back to the desk. "Marguerit
will be as sorry to hear of this as I am," he said, kindly. "What d
you mean to do?"

"I am in the hands of Defresnier and Company," answered Ven
dale. "In my total ignorance of the circumstances, I can only d
what they recommend. The receipt which I have just found, turn

it to be the numbered and printed form. They seem to attach some
special importance to its discovery. You have had experience, when
you were in the Swiss house, of their way of doing business. Can you
guess what object they have in view?"

Obenreizer offered a suggestion.

"Suppose I examine the receipt?" he said.

"Are you ill?" asked Vendale, startled by the change in his face,
which now showed itself plainly for the first time. "Pray go to the
fire. You seem to be shivering—I hope you are not going to be ill?"

"Not I!" said Obenreizer. "Perhaps I have caught cold. Your
English climate might have spared an admirer of your English
institutions. Let me look at the receipt."

Vendale opened the iron chamber. Obenreizer took a chair, and
drew it close to the fire. He held both hands over the flames. "Let
me look at the receipt," he repeated, eagerly, as Vendale reappeared
with the paper in his hand. At the same moment a porter entered the
room with a fresh supply of coals. Vendale told him to make a good
fire. The man obeyed the order with a disastrous alacrity. As he
stepped forward and raised the scuttle, his foot caught in a fold of
the rug, and he discharged his entire cargo of coals into the grate.
The result was an instant smothering of the flame, and the production of a stream of yellow smoke, without a visible morsel of fire to
account for it.

"Imbecile!" whispered Obenreizer to himself, with a look at the
man which the man remembered for many a long day afterwards.

"Will you come into the clerks' room?" asked Vendale. "They
have a stove there."

"No, no. No matter."

Vendale handed him the receipt. Obenreizer's interest in examining it appeared to have been quenched as suddenly and as effectually
as the fire itself. He just glanced over the document, and said, "No;
I don't understand it! I am sorry to be of no use."

"I will write to Neuchâtel by to-night's post," said Vendale,
putting away the receipt for the second time. "We must wait, and
see what comes of it."

"By to-night's post," repeated Obenreizer. "Let me see. You will
get the answer in eight or nine days' time. I shall be back before that.
If I can be of any service, as commercial traveller, perhaps you will
let me know between this and then. You will send me written instructions? My best thanks. I shall be most anxious for your answer from
Neuchâtel. Who knows? It may be a mistake, my dear friend, after
all. Courage! courage! courage!" He had entered the room with no
appearance of being pressed for time. He now snatched up his hat,
and took his leave with the air of a man who had not another
moment to lose.

Left by himself, Vendale took a turn thoughtfully in the room.

His previous impression of Obenreizer was shaken by what he had
heard and seen at the interview which had just taken place. He was
disposed, for the first time, to doubt whether, in this case, he had not

been a little hasty and hard in his judgment on another man. Oben
reizer's surprise and regret, on hearing the news from Neuchâtel
bore the plainest marks of being honestly felt—not politely assumed
for the occasion. With troubles of his own to encounter, suffering, to
all appearance, from the first insidious attack of a serious illness, he
had looked and spoken like a man who really deplored the disaster
that had fallen on his friend. Hitherto Vendale had tried vainly to
alter his first opinion of Marguerite's guardian, for Marguerite's sake
All the generous instincts in his nature now combined together
and shook the evidence which had seemed unanswerable up to this
time. "Who knows?" he thought. "I may have read that man's face
wrongly, after all."

The time passed—the happy evenings with Marguerite came and
went. It was again the tenth morning since Vendale had written to
the Swiss firm; and again the answer appeared on his desk with the
other letters of the day:

"DEAR SIR. My senior partner, M. Defresnier, has been called
away, by urgent business, to Milan. In his absence (and with his full
concurrence and authority), I now write to you again on the subject
of the missing five hundred pounds.

"Your discovery that the forged receipt is executed upon one of
our numbered and printed forms has caused inexpressible surprise
and distress to my partner and to myself. At the time when your
remittance was stolen, but three keys were in existence opening the
strong-box in which our receipt-forms are invariably kept. My partner
had one key; I had the other. The third was in the possession of a
gentleman who, at that period, occupied a position of trust in our
house. We should as soon have thought of suspecting one of ourselves
as of suspecting this person. Suspicion now points at him, neverthe
less. I cannot prevail on myself to inform you who the person is, so
long as there is the shadow of a chance that he may come innocently
out of the inquiry which must now be instituted. Forgive my silence
the motive of it is good.

"The form our investigation must now take is simple enough. The
handwriting on your receipt must be compared, by competent persons
whom we have at our disposal, with certain specimens of handwriting
in our possession. I cannot send you the specimens for business
reasons, which, when you hear them, you are sure to approve. I must
beg you to send me the receipt to Neuchâtel—and, in making this
request, I must accompany it by a word of necessary warning.

"If the person, at whom suspicion now points, really proves to be
the person who has committed this forgery and theft, I have reason
to fear that circumstances may have already put him on his guard
The only evidence against him is the evidence in your hands, and he
will move heaven and earth to obtain and destroy it. I strongly urge
you not to trust the receipt to the post. Send it to me, without loss
of time, by a private hand, and choose nobody for your messenger
but a person long established in your own employment, accustomed

o travelling, capable of speaking French; a man of courage, a man
f honesty, and, above all things, a man who can be trusted to let no
tranger scrape acquaintance with him on the route. Tell no one—
bsolutely no one—but your messenger of the turn this matter has
ow taken. The safe transit of the receipt may depend on your inter-
reting *literally* the advice which I give you at the end of this letter.

"I have only to add that every possible saving of time is now of the
ast importance. More than one of our receipt-forms is missing—and
t is impossible to say what new frauds may not be committed, if we
ail to lay our hands on the thief.

"Your faithful servant,   "ROLLAND,

"(Signing for Defresnier and Cie.)"

Who was the suspected man? In Vendale's position, it seemed use-
ess to inquire.

Who was to be sent to Neuchâtel with the receipt? Men of courage
nd men of honesty were to be had at Cripple Corner for the asking.
But where was the man who was accustomed to foreign travelling,
vho could speak the French language, and who could be really relied
n to let no stranger scrape acquaintance with him on his route?
There was but one man at hand who combined all those requisites in
is own person, and that man was Vendale himself.

It was a sacrifice to leave his business; it was a greater sacrifice to
eave Marguerite. But a matter of five hundred pounds was involved
n the pending inquiry; and a literal interpretation of M. Rolland's
dvice was insisted on in terms which there was no trifling with. The
nore Vendale thought of it, the more plainly the necessity faced him,
nd said, "Go!"

As he locked up the letter with the receipt, the association of ideas
eminded him of Obenreizer. A guess at the identity of the suspected
nan looked more possible now. Obenreizer might know.

The thought had barely passed through his mind, when the door
pened, and Obenreizer entered the room.

"They told me at Soho-square you were expected back last night,"
aid Vendale, greeting him. "Have you done well in the country? Are
ou better?"

A thousand thanks. Obenreizer had done admirably well; Oben-
eizer was infinitely better. And now, what news? Any letter from
Neuchâtel?

"A very strange letter," answered Vendale. "The matter has taken
. new turn, and the letter insists—without excepting anybody—on
ny keeping our next proceedings a profound secret."

"Without excepting anybody?" repeated Obenreizer. As he said
he words, he walked away again, thoughtfully, to the window at the
ther end of the room, looked out for a moment, and suddenly came
ack to Vendale. "Surely they must have forgotten," he resumed,
or they would have excepted *me?*"

"It is Monsieur Rolland who writes," said Vendale. "And, as you
ay, he must certainly have forgotten. That view of the matter quite

escaped me. I was just wishing I had you to consult, when you came into the room. And here I am tied by a formal prohibition, which cannot possibly have been intended to include you. How very annoying!"

Obenreizer's filmy eyes fixed on Vendale attentively.

"Perhaps it is more than annoying!" he said. "I came this morning not only to hear the news, but to offer myself as messenger, negotiator —what you will. Would you believe it? I have letters which oblige me to go to Switzerland immediately. Messages, documents, anything —I could have taken them all to Defresnier and Rolland for you."

"You are the very man I wanted," returned Vendale. "I had decided, most unwillingly, on going to Neuchâtel myself, not five minutes since, because I could find no one here capable of taking my place. Let me look at the letter again."

He opened the strong room to get at the letter. Obenreizer, after first glancing round him to make sure that they were alone, followed a step or two and waited, measuring Vendale with his eye. Vendale was the tallest man, and unmistakably the strongest man also of the two. Obenreizer turned away, and warmed himself at the fire.

Meanwhile, Vendale read the last paragraph in the letter for the third time. There was the plain warning—there was the closing sentence, which insisted on a literal interpretation of it. The hand, which was leading Vendale in the dark, led him on that condition only. A large sum was at stake: a terrible suspicion remained to be verified. If he acted on his own responsibility, and if anything happened to defeat the object in view, who would be blamed? As a man of business, Vendale had but one course to follow. He locked the letter up again.

"It is most annoying," he said to Obenreizer—"it is a piece of forgetfulness on Monsieur Rolland's part which puts me to serious inconvenience, and places me in an absurdly false position towards you. What am I to do? I am acting in a very serious matter, and acting entirely in the dark. I have no choice but to be guided, not by the spirit, but by the letter of my instructions. You understand me, I am sure? You know, if I had not been fettered in this way, how gladly I should have accepted your services?"

"Say no more!" returned Obenreizer. "In your place I should have done the same. My good friend, I take no offence. I thank you for your compliment. We shall be travelling companions, at any rate," added Obenreizer. "You go, as I go, at once?"

"At once. I must speak to Marguerite first, of course!"

"Surely! surely! Speak to her this evening. Come and pick me up on the way to the station. We go together by the mail train to-night?"

"By the mail train to-night."

It was later than Vendale had anticipated when he drove up to the house in Soho-square. Business difficulties, occasioned by his sudden departure, had presented themselves by dozens. A cruelly large share of the time which he had hoped to devote to Marguerite had been aimed by duties at his office which it was impossible to neglect.

To his surprise and delight, she was alone in the drawing-room hen he entered it.

"We have only a few minutes, George," she said. "But Madame)or has been good to me—and we can have those few minutes alone." he threw her arms round his neck, and whispered eagerly, "Have ou done anything to offend Mr. Obenreizer?"

"I!" exclaimed Vendale in amazement.

"Hush!" she said, "I want to whisper it. You know the little photo- raph, I have got of you. This afternoon it happened to be on the himneypiece. He took it up and looked at it—and I saw his face in he glass. I know you have offended him! He is merciless; he is re- engeful; he is as secret as the grave. Don't go with him, George— on't go with him!"

"My own love," returned Vendale, "you are letting your fancy righten you! Obenreizer and I were never better friends than we are t this moment."

Before a word more could be said, the sudden movement of some onderous body shook the floor of the next room. The shock was)llowed by the appearance of Madame Dor. "Obenreizer!" exclaimed his excellent person in a whisper, and plumped down instantly in er regular place by the stove.

Obenreizer came in with a courier's bag strapped over his shoulder.

"Are you ready?" he asked, addressing Vendale. "Can I take any- hing for you? You have no travelling-bag. I have got one. Here is he compartment for papers, open at your service."

"Thank you," said Vendale. "I have only one paper of importance ith me; and that paper I am bound to take charge of myself. Here : is," he added, touching the breast-pocket of his coat, "and here it 1ust remain till we get to Neuchâtel."

As he said those words, Marguerite's hand caught his, and pressed t significantly. She was looking towards Obenreizer. Before Vendale ould look, in his turn, Obenreizer had wheeled round, and was taking eave of Madame Dor.

"Adieu, my charming niece!" he said, turning to Marguerite next. En route, my friend, for Neuchâtel!" He tapped Vendale lightly ver the breast-pocket of his coat, and led the way to the door.

Vendale's last look was for Marguerite. Marguerite's last words to im were, "Don't go!"

ACT III

IN THE VALLEY

T was about the middle of the month of February when Vendale and)benreizer set forth on their expedition. The winter being a hard one, he time was bad for travellers. So bad was it that these two travellers, coming to Strasbourg, found its great inns almost empty. And even the few people they did encounter in that city, who had started from England or from Paris on business journeys towards the interior of Switzerland, were turning back.

Many of the railroads in Switzerland that tourists pass easily enough now, were almost or quite impracticable then. Some were not begun; more were not completed. On such as were open, there were still large gaps of old road where communication in the winter season was often stopped; on others, there were weak points where the new work was not safe, either under conditions of severe frost, or of rapid thaw. The running of trains on this last class was not to be counted on in the worst time of the year, was contingent upon weather, or was wholly abandoned through the months considered the most dangerous.

At Strasbourg there were more travellers' stories afloat, respecting the difficulties of the way further on, than there were travellers to relate them. Many of these tales were as wild as usual; but the more modestly marvellous did derive some colour from the circumstance that people were indisputably turning back. However, as the road to Basle was open, Vendale's resolution to push on was in no wise disturbed. Obenreizer's resolution was necessarily Vendale's, seeing that he stood at bay thus desperately: He must be ruined, or must destroy the evidence that Vendale carried about him, even if he destroyed Vendale with it.

The state of mind of each of these two fellow-travellers towards the other was this. Obenreizer, encircled by impending ruin through Vendale's quickness of action, and seeing the circle narrowed every hour by Vendale's energy, hated him with the animosity of a fierce cunning lower animal. He had always had instinctive movements in his breast against him; perhaps, because of that old sore of gentleman and peasant; perhaps, because of the openness of his nature; perhaps, because of his better looks; perhaps, because of his success with Marguerite; perhaps, on all those grounds, the two last not the least. And now he saw in him, besides, the hunter who was tracking him down. Vendale, on the other hand, always contending generously against his first vague mistrust, now felt bound to contend against it more than ever: reminding himself, "He is Marguerite's guardian. We are on perfectly friendly terms; he is my companion of his own proposal, and can have no interested motive in sharing this undesirable journey." To which pleas in behalf of Obenreizer, chance added one consideration more, when they came to Basle after a journey of more than twice the average duration.

They had had a late dinner, and were alone in an inn room there, overhanging the Rhine: at that place rapid and deep, swollen and loud. Vendale lounged upon a couch, and Obenreizer walked to and fro: now, stopping at the window, looking at the crooked reflection of the town lights in the dark water (and peradventure thinking, "If I could fling him into it!"); now, resuming his walk with his eyes upon the floor.

"Where shall I rob him, if I can? Where shall I murder him, if I must?" So, as he paced the room, ran the river, ran the river, ran the river.

The burden seemed to him, at last, to be growing so plain, that he stopped; thinking it as well to suggest another burden to his companion.

"The Rhine sounds to-night," he said with a smile, "like the old waterfall at home. That waterfall which my mother showed to travellers (I told you of it once). The sound of it changed with the weather as does the sound of all falling waters and flowing waters. When I was pupil of the watchmaker, I remembered it as sometimes saying to me for whole days, 'Who are you, my little wretch? Who are you, my little wretch?' I remembered it as saying, other times, when its sound was hollow, and storm was coming up the Pass: 'Boom, boom, boom. Beat him, beat him, beat him.' Like my mother enraged—if she was my mother."

"If she was?" said Vendale, gradually changing his attitude to a sitting one. "If she was? Why do you say 'if'?"

"What do I know?" replied the other negligently, throwing up his hands and letting them fall as they would. "What would you have? I am so obscurely born, that how can I say? I was very young, and all the rest of the family were men and woman, and my so-called parents were old. Anything is possible of a case like that."

"Did you ever doubt——?"

"I told you once, I doubt the marriage of those two," he replied, throwing up his hands again, as if he were throwing the unprofitable subject away. "But here I am in Creation. I come of no fine family. What does it matter?"

"At least you are Swiss," said Vendale, after following him with his eyes to and fro.

"How do I know?" he retorted abruptly, and stopping to look back over his shoulder. "I say to you, at least you are English. How do you know?"

"By what I have been told from infancy."

"Ah! I know of myself that way."

"And," added Vendale, pursuing the thought that he could not drive back, "by my earliest recollections."

"I also. I know of myself that way—if that way satisfies."

"Does it not satisfy you?"

"It must. There is nothing like 'it must' in this little world. It must. Two short words those, but stronger than long proof or reasoning."

"You and poor Wilding were born in the same year. You were nearly of an age," said Vendale, again thoughtfully looking after him as he resumed his pacing up and down.

"Yes. Very nearly."

Could Obenreizer be the missing man? In the unknown associations of things, was there a subtler meaning than he himself thought, in that theory so often on his lips about the smallness of the world? Had the Swiss letter presenting him followed so close on Mrs. Goldstraw's revelation concerning the infant who had been taken away to Switzerland, because he was that infant grown a man? In a world where so many depths lie unsounded, it might be. The chances, or the laws—call them either—that had wrought out the revival of Vendale's own acquaintance with Obenreizer, and had ripened it into intimacy, and had brought them here together this present winter night, were hardly less curious; while read by such a light, they were seen to cohere towards the furtherance of a continuous and an intelligible purpose.

Vendale's awakened thoughts ran high while his eyes musingly followed Obenreizer pacing up and down the room, the river ever running to the tune: "Where shall I rob him, if I can? Where shall I murder him, if I must?" The secret of his dead friend was in no hazard from Vendale's lips; but just as his friend had died of its weight, so did he in his lighter succession feel the burden of the trust, and the obligation to follow any clue, however obscure. He rapidly asked himself, would he like this man to be the real Wilding? No. Argue down his mistrust as he might, he was unwilling to put such a substitute in the place of his late guileless, outspoken, childlike partner. He rapidly asked himself, would he like this man to be rich? No. He had more power than enough over Marguerite as it was, and wealth might invest him with more. Would he like this man to be Marguerite's Guardian, and yet proved to stand in no degree of relationship towards her, however disconnected and distant? No. But these were not considerations to come between him and fidelity to the dead. Let him see to it that they passed him with no other notice than the knowledge that they *had* passed him, and left him bent on the discharge of a solemn duty. And he did see to it, so soon that he followed his companion with ungrudging eyes, while he still paced the room; that companion, whom he supposed to be moodily reflecting on his own birth, and not on another man's—least of all that man's—violent Death.

The road in advance from Basle to Neuchâtel was better than had been represented. The latest weather had done it good. Drivers, both of horses and mules, had come in that evening after dark, and had reported nothing more difficult to be overcome than trials of patience, harness, wheels, axles, and whip-cord. A bargain was soon struck for a carriage and horses, to take them on in the morning, and to start before daylight.

"Do you lock your door at night when travelling?" asked Obenreizer, standing warming his hands by the wood fire in Vendale's chamber, before going to his own.

"Not I. I sleep too soundly."

"You are so sound a sleeper?" he retorted, with an admiring look. "What a blessing!"

"Anything but a blessing to the rest of the house," rejoined Vendale, "if I had to be knocked up in the morning from the outside of my bedroom door."

"I, too," said Obenreizer, "leave open my room. But let me advise you, as a Swiss who knows: always, when you travel in my country, put your papers—and, of course, your money—under your pillow. Always the same place."

"You are not complimentary to your countrymen," laughed Vendale.

"My countrymen," said Obenreizer, with that light touch of his friend's elbows by way of Good Night and benediction, "I suppose are like the majority of men. And the majority of men will take what they can get. Adieu! At four in the morning."

"Adieu! At four."

Left to himself, Vendale raked the logs together, sprinkled over them the white wood-ashes lying on the hearth, and sat down to compose his thoughts. But they still ran high on their latest theme, and the running of the river tended to agitate rather than to quiet them. As he sat thinking, what little disposition he had had to sleep departed. He felt it hopeless to lie down yet, and sat dressed by the fire. Marguerite, Wilding, Obenreizer, the business he was then upon, and a thousand hopes and doubts that had nothing to do with it, occupied his mind at once. Everything seemed to have power over him but slumber. The departed disposition to sleep kept far away.

He had sat for a long time thinking, on the hearth, when his candle burned down and its light went out. It was of little moment; there was light enough in the fire. He changed his attitude, and, leaning his arm on the chair-back, and his chin upon that hand, sat thinking still.

But he sat between the fire and the bed, and, as the fire flickered in the play of air from the fast-flowing river, his enlarged shadow fluttered on the white wall by the bedside. His attitude gave it an air, half of mourning and half of bending over the bed imploring. His eyes were observant of it, when he became troubled by the disagreeable fancy that it was like Wilding's shadow, and not his own.

A slight change of place would cause it to disappear. He made the change, and the apparition of his disturbed fancy vanished. He now sat in the shade of a little nook beside the fire, and the door of the room was before him.

It had a long cumbrous iron latch. He saw the latch slowly and softly rise. The door opened a very little, and came to again, as though only the air had moved it. But he saw that the latch was out of the hasp.

The door opened again very slowly, until it opened wide enough to admit some one. It afterwards remained still for a while, as though cautiously held open on the other side. The figure of a man then entered, with its face turned towards the bed, and stood quiet just within the door, until it said, in a low half-whisper, at the same time taking one step forward: "Vendale!"

"What now?" he answered, springing from his seat; "who is it?"

It was Obenreizer, and he uttered a cry of surprise as Vendale came upon him from that unexpected direction. "Not in bed?" he said, catching him by both shoulders with an instinctive tendency to a struggle. "Then something *is* wrong!"

"What do you mean?" said Vendale, releasing himself.

"First tell me; you are not ill?"

"Ill? No."

"I have had a bad dream about you. How is it that I see you up and dressed?"

"My good fellow, I may as well ask you how it is that I see *you* up and undressed?"

"I have told you why. I have had a bad dream about you. I tried to rest after it, but it was impossible. I could not make up my mind to stay where I was without knowing you were safe; and yet I could not make up my mind to come in here. I have been minutes hesitating at the door. It is so easy to laugh at a dream that you have not dreamed. Where is your candle?"

"Burnt out."

"I have a whole one in my room. Shall I fetch it?"

"Do so."

His room was very near, and he was absent for but a few seconds. Coming back with the candle in his hand, he kneeled down on the hearth and lighted it. As he blew with his breath a charred billet into flame for the purpose, Vendale, looking down at him, saw that his lips were white and not easy of control.

"Yes!" said Obenreizer, setting the lighted candle on the table, "it was a bad dream. Only look at me!"

His feet were bare; his red-flannel shirt was thrown back at the throat, and its sleeves were rolled above the elbows; his only other garment, a pair of under pantaloons or drawers, reaching to the ankles, fitted him close and tight. A certain lithe and savage appearance was on his figure, and his eyes were very bright.

"If there had been a wrestle with a robber, as I dreamed," said Obenreizer, "you see, I was stripped for it."

"And armed too," said Vendale, glancing at his girdle.

"A traveller's dagger, that I always carry on the road," he answered carelessly, half drawing it from its sheath with his left hand, and putting it back again. "Do you carry no such thing?"

"Nothing of the kind."

"No pistols?" said Obenreizer, glancing at the table, and from it to the untouched pillow.

"Nothing of the sort."

"You Englishmen are so confident! You wish to sleep?"

"I have wished to sleep this long time, but I can't do it."

"I neither, after the bad dream. My fire has gone the way of your candle. May I come and sit by yours? Two o'clock! It will so soon be four, that it is not worth the trouble to go to bed again."

"I shall not take the trouble to go to bed at all, now," said Vendale; "sit here and keep me company, and welcome."

Going back to his room to arrange his dress, Obenreizer soon returned in a loose cloak and slippers, and they sat down on opposite sides of the hearth. In the interval Vendale had replenished the fire from the wood-basket in his room, and Obenreizer had put upon the table a flask and cup from his.

"Common cabaret brandy, I am afraid," he said, pouring out; "bought upon the road, and not like yours from Cripple Corner. But yours is exhausted; so much the worse. A cold night, a cold time of night, a cold country, and a cold house. This may be better than nothing; try it."

Vendale took the cup, and did so.

"How do you find it?"

"It has a coarse after-flavour," said Vendale, giving back the cup with a slight shudder, "and I don't like it."

"You are right," said Obenreizer, tasting, and smacking his lips; "it *has* a coarse after-flavour, and *I* don't like it. Booh! It burns, though!" He had flung what remained in the cup upon the fire.

Each of them leaned an elbow on the table, reclined his head upon his hand, and sat looking at the flaring logs. Obenreizer remained watchful and still; but Vendale, after certain nervous twitches and starts, in one of which he rose to his feet and looked wildly about him, fell into the strangest confusion of dreams. He carried his papers in a leather case or pocket-book, in an inner breast-pocket of his buttoned travelling-coat; and whatever he dreamed of, in the lethargy that got possession of him, something importunate in these papers called him out of that dream, though he could not wake from it. He was belated on the steppes of Russia (some shadowy person gave that name to the place) with Marguerite; and yet the sensation of a hand at his breast, softly feeling the outline of the pocket-book as he lay asleep before the fire, was present to him. He was shipwrecked in an open boat at sea, and having lost his clothes, had no other covering than an old sail; and yet a creeping hand, tracing outside all the other pockets of the dress he actually wore, for papers, and finding none answer its touch, warned him to rouse himself. He was in the ancient vault at Cripple Corner, to which was transferred the very bed substantial and present in that very room at Basle; and Wilding (not dead, as he had supposed, and yet he did not wonder much) shook him, and whispered, "Look at that man! Don't you see he has risen, and is turning the pillow? Why should he turn the pillow, if not to seek those papers that are in your breast? Awake!" And yet he slept, and wandered off into other dreams.

Watchful and still, with his elbow on the table, and his head upon that hand, his companion at length said: "Vendale! We are called. Past Four!" Then, opening his eyes, he saw, turned sideways on him, the filmy face of Obenreizer.

"You have been in a heavy sleep," he said. "The fatigue of constant travelling and the cold!"

"I am broad awake now," cried Vendale, springing up, but with an unsteady footing. "Haven't you slept at all?"

"I may have dozed, but I seem to have been patiently looking at the fire. Whether or no, we must wash, and breakfast, and turn out. Past four, Vendale; past four!"

It was said in a tone to rouse him, for already he was half asleep again. In his preparation for the day, too, and at his breakfast, he was often virtually asleep while in mechanical action. It was not until the cold dark day was closing in, that he had any distincter impressions of the ride than jingling bells, bitter weather , slipping horses, frowning hill-sides, bleak woods, and a stoppage at some wayside house of entertainment, where they had passed through a cowhouse to reach the travellers' room above. He had been conscious of little more, except of Obenreizer sitting thoughtful at his side all day and eyeing him much.

But when he shook off his stupor, Obenreizer was not at his side. The carriage was stopping to bait at another wayside house; and a line of long narrow carts, laden with casks of wine, and drawn by horses with a quantity of blue collar and headgear, were baiting too. These came from the direction in which the travellers were going, and Obenreizer (not thoughtful now, but cheerful and alert) was talking with the foremost driver. As Vendale stretched his limbs, circulated his blood, and cleared off the lees of his lethargy, with a sharp run to and fro in the bracing air, the line of carts moved on: the drivers all saluting Obenreizer as they passed him.

"Who are those?" asked Vendale.

"They are our carriers—Defresnier and Company's," replied Obenreizer. "Those are our casks of wine." He was singing to himself, and lighting a cigar.

"I have been drearily dull company to-day," said Vendale, "I don't know what has been the matter with me."

"You had no sleep last night; and a kind of brain-congestion frequently comes, at first, of such cold," said Obenreizer. "I have seen it often. After all, we shall have our journey for nothing, it seems."

"How for nothing?"

"The House is at Milan. You know, we are a Wine House at Neuchâtel, and a Silk House at Milan? Well, Silk happening to press of a sudden, more than Wine, Defresnier was summoned to Milan. Rolland, the other partner, has been taken ill since his departure, and the doctors will allow him to see no one. A letter awaits you at Neuchâtel to tell you so. I have it from our chief carrier whom you saw me talking with. He was surprised to see me, and said he had that word for you if he met you. What do you do? Go back?"

"Go on," said Vendale.

"On?"

"On? Yes. Across the Alps, and down to Milan."

Obenreizer stopped in his smoking to look at Vendale, and then smoked heavily, looked up the road, looked down the road, looked down at the stones in the road at his feet.

"I have a very serious matter in charge," said Vendale; "more of these missing forms may be turned to as bad account, or worse; I am urged to lose no time in helping the House to take the thief; and nothing shall turn me back."

"No?" cried Obenreizer, taking out his cigar to smile, and giving his hand to his fellow-traveller. "Then nothing shall turn *me* back. Ho, driver! Dispatch. Quick there! Let us push on!"

They travelled through the night. There had been snow, and there was a partial thaw, and they mostly travelled at a foot-pace, and always with many stoppages to breathe the splashed and floundering horses. After an hour's broad daylight, they drew rein at the inn-door at Neuchâtel, having been some eight-and-twenty-hours in conquering some eighty English miles.

When they had hurriedly refreshed and changed, they went together to the house of business of Defresnier and Company. There they found the letter which the wine-carrier had described, enclosing the tests and comparisons of handwriting essential to the discovery of the Forger. Vendale's determination to press forward, without resting, being already taken, the only question to delay them was by what Pass could they cross the Alps? Respecting the state of the two Passes of the St. Gotthard and the Simplon, the guides and mule-drivers differed greatly; and both Passes were still far enough off, to prevent the travellers from having the benefit of any recent experience of either. Besides which, they well knew that a fall of snow might altogether change the described conditions in a single hour, even if they were correctly stated. But, on the whole, the Simplon appearing to be the hopefuller route, Vendale decided to take it. Obenreizer bore little or no part in the discussion, and scarcely spoke.

To Geneva, to Lausanne, along the level margin of the lake to Vevay, so into the winding valley between the spurs of the mountains, and into the valley of the Rhone. The sound of the carriage-wheels, as they rattled on, through the day, through the night, became as the wheels of a great clock, recording the hours. No change of weather varied the journey, after it had hardened into a sullen frost. In a sombre-yellow sky, they saw the Alpine ranges; and they saw enough of snow on nearer and much lower hill-tops and hill-sides, to sully, by contrast, the purity of lake, torrent, and waterfall, and make the villages look discoloured and dirty. But no snow fell, nor was there any snow-drift on the road. The stalking along the valley of more or less of white mist, changing on their hair and dress into icicles, was the only variety between them and the gloomy sky. And still by day, and still by night, the wheels. And still they rolled, in the hearing of one of them, to the burden, altered from the burden of the Rhine; "The time is gone for robbing him alive, and I must murder him."

They came, at length, to the poor little town of Brieg, at the foot of the Simplon. They came there after dark, but yet could see how dwarfed men's works and men became with the immense mountains towering over them. Here they must lie for the night; and here was warmth of fire, and lamp, and dinner, and wine, and after-conference resounding, with guides and drivers. No human creature had come across the Pass for four days. The snow above the snow-line was too soft for wheeled carriage, and not hard enough for sledge. There was snow in the sky. There had been snow in the sky for days past, and the marvel was that it had not fallen, and the certainty was that it must fall. No vehicle could cross. The journey might be tried on mules, or it might be tried on foot; but the best guides must be paid danger-price in either case, and that, too, whether they succeeded in taking the two travellers across, or turned for safety and brought them back.

In this discussion, Obenreizer bore no part whatever. He sat silently smoking by the fire until the room was cleared and Vendale referred to him.

"Bah! I am weary of these poor devils and their trade," he said, in reply. "Always the same story. It is the story of their trade to-day, as it was the story of their trade when I was a ragged boy. What do you and I want? We want a knapsack each, and a mountain-staff each. We want no guide; we should guide him; he would not guide us. We leave our portmanteaus here, and we cross together. We have been on the mountains together before now, and I am mountain-born, and I know this Pass—Pass!—rather High Road!—by heart. We will leave these poor devils, in pity, to trade with others; but they must not delay us to make a pretence of earning money. Which is all they mean."

Vendale, glad to be quit of the dispute, and to cut the knot; active, adventurous, bent on getting forward, and therefore very susceptible to the last hint: readily assented. Within two hours, they had purchased what they wanted for the expedition, had packed their knapsacks, and lay down to sleep.

At break of day, they found half the town collected in the narrow street to see them depart. The people talked together in groups; the guides and drivers whispered apart, and looked up at the sky; no one wished them a good journey.

As they began the ascent, a gleam of sun shone from the otherwise unaltered sky, and for a moment turned the tin spires of the town to silver.

"A good omen!" said Vendale (though it died out while he spoke). "Perhaps our example will open the Pass on this side."

"No; we shall not be followed," returned Obenreizer, looking up at the sky and back at the valley. "We shall be alone up yonder."

ON THE MOUNTAIN

The road was fair enough for stout walkers, and the air grew lighter and easier to breathe as the two ascended. But the settled gloom remained as it had remained for days back. Nature seemed to have come to a pause. The sense of hearing, no less than the sense of sight, was troubled by having to wait so long for the change, what-ever it might be, that impended. The silence was as palpable and heavy as the lowering clouds—or rather cloud, for there seemed to be but one in all the sky, and that one covering the whole of it.

Although the light was thus dismally shrouded, the prospect was not obscured. Down in the valley of the Rhone behind them, the stream could be traced through all its many windings, oppressively sombre and solemn in its one leaden hue, a colourless waste. Far and high above them, glaciers and suspended avalanches overhung the spots where they must pass, by and by; deep and dark below them on their right, were awful precipice and roaring torrent; tremendous mountains arose in every vista. The gigantic landscape, uncheered by a touch of changing light or a solitary ray of sun, was yet terribly distinct in its ferocity. The hearts of two lonely men might shrink a little, if they had to win their way for miles and hours among a legion of silent and motionless men—mere men like themselves—all looking at them with fixed and frowning front. But how much more, when the legion is of Nature's mightiest works, and the frown may turn to fury in an instant!

As they ascended, the road became gradually more rugged and difficult. But the spirits of Vendale rose as they mounted higher, leaving so much more of the road behind them, conquered. Obenreizer spoke little, and held on with a determined purpose. Both, in respect of agility and endurance, were well qualified for the expedition. Whatever the born mountaineer read in the weathertokens that was illegible to the other, he kept to himself.

"Shall we get across to-day?" asked Vendale.

"No," replied the other. "You see how much deeper the snow lies here than it lay half a league lower. The higher we mount the deeper the snow will lie. Walking is half wading even now. And the days are so short! If we get as high as the fifth Refuge, and lie to-night at the Hospice, we shall do well."

"Is there no danger of the weather rising in the night," asked Vendale, anxiously, "and snowing us up?"

"There is danger enough about us," said Obenreizer, with a cautious glance onward and upward, "to render silence our best policy. You have heard of the Bridge of the Ganther?"

"I have crossed it once."

"In the summer?"

"Yes; in the travelling season."

"Yes; but it is another thing at this season;" with a sneer, as though he were out of temper. "This is not a time of year, or a state of things, on an Alpine Pass, that you gentlemen holiday-travellers know much about."

"You are my Guide," said Vendale, good-humouredly. "I trust to you."

"I am your Guide," said Obenreizer, "and I will guide you to your journey's end. There is the Bridge before us."

They had made a turn into a desolate and dismal ravine, where the snow lay deep below them, deep above them, deep on every side. While speaking, Obenreizer stood pointing at the Bridge, and observing Vendale's face, with a very singular expression on his own.

"If I, as Guide, had sent you over there, in advance, and encouraged you to give a shout or two, you might have brought down upon yourself tons and tons and tons of snow, that would not only have struck you dead, but buried you deep, at a blow."

"No doubt," said Vendale.

"No doubt. But that is not what I have to do, as Guide. So pass silently. Or, going as we go, our indiscretion might else crush and bury *me*. Let us get on!"

There was a great accumulation of snow on the Bridge; and such enormous accumulation of snow overhung them from projecting masses of rock, that they might have been making their way through a stormy sky of white clouds. Using his staff skilfully, sounding as he went, and looking upward, with bent shoulders, as it were to resist the mere idea of a fall from above, Obenreizer softly led Vendale closely followed. They were yet in the midst of their dangerous way, when there came a mighty rush, followed by a sound as of thunder. Obenreizer clapped his hand on Vendale's mouth and pointed to the track behind them. Its aspect had been wholly changed in a moment. An avalanche had swept over it, and plunged into the torrent at the bottom of the gulf below.

Their appearance at the solitary Inn not far beyond this terrible Bridge, elicited many expressions of astonishment from the people shut up in the house. "We stay but to rest," said Obenreizer, shaking the snow from his dress at the fire. "This gentleman has very pressing occasion to get across; tell them, Vendale."

"Assuredly, I have very pressing occasion. I must cross."

"You hear, all of you. My friend has very pressing occasion to get across, and we want no advice and no help. I am as good a guide, my fellow-countrymen, as any of you. Now, give us to eat and drink."

In exactly the same way, and in nearly the same words, when it was coming on dark and they had struggled through the greatly increased difficulties of the road, and had at last reached their destination for the night, Obenreizer said to the astonished people of the Hospice, gathering about them at the fire, while they were yet in the act of getting their wet shoes off, and shaking the snow from their clothes:

"It is well to understand one another, friends all. This gentleman——"

"—Has," said Vendale, readily taking him up with a smile, "very pressing occasion to get across. Must cross."

"You hear?—has very pressing occasion to get across, must cross. We want no advice and no help. I am mountain-born, and act as Guide. Do not worry us by talking about it, but let us have supper, and wine, and bed."

All through the intense cold of the night, the same awful stillness Again at sunrise, no sunny tinge to gild or redden the snow. The same interminable waste of deathly white; the same immovable air the same monotonous gloom in the sky.

"Travellers!" a friendly voice called to them from the door, after they were afoot, knapsack on back and staff in hand, as yesterday "recollect! There are five places of shelter, near together, on the dangerous road before you; and there is the wooden cross, and there is the next Hospice. Do not stray from the track. If the *Tourmente* omes on, take shelter instantly!"

"The trade of these poor devils!" said Obenreizer to his friend, with a contemptuous backward wave of his hand towards the voice. How they stick to their trade! You Englishmen say we Swiss are mercenary. Truly, it does look like it."

They had divided between the two knapsacks such refreshments as they had been able to obtain that morning, and as they deemed it prudent to take. Obenreizer carried the wine as his share of the burden; Vendale, the bread and meat and cheese, and the flask of brandy.

They had for some time laboured upward and onward through the snow—which was now above their knees in the track, and of unknown depth elsewhere—and they were still labouring upward and onward through the most frightful part of that tremendous desolation, when snow began to fall. At first, but a few flakes descended slowly and steadily. After a little while the fall grew much denser, and suddenly it began without apparent cause to whirl itself into spiral shapes. Instantly ensuing upon this last change, an icy blast came roaring at them, and every sound and force imprisoned until now was let loose.

One of the dismal galleries through which the road is carried at that perilous point, a cave eked out by arches of great strength, was near at hand. They struggled into it, and the storm raged wildly. The noise of the wind, the noise of the water, the thundering down of displaced masses of rock and snow, the awful voices with which not only that gorge but every gorge in the whole monstrous range seemed to be suddenly endowed, the darkness as of night, the violent revolving of the snow which beat and broke it into spray and blinded them, the madness of everything around insatiate for destruction, the rapid substitution of furious violence for unnatural calm, and hosts of appalling sounds for silence: these were things, on the edge of a deep abyss, to chill the blood, though the fierce wind, made actually solid by ice and snow, had failed to chill it.

Obenreizer, walking to and fro in the gallery without ceasing, signed to Vendale to help him unbuckle his knapsack. They could see each other, but could not have heard each other speak. Vendale complying, Obenreizer produced his bottle of wine, and poured some out, motioning Vendale to take that for warmth's sake, and not brandy. Vendale again complying, Obenreizer seemed to drink after him, and the two walked backwards and forwards side by side; both well knowing that to rest or sleep would be to die.

The snow came driving heavily into the gallery by the upper end at which they would pass out of it, if they ever passed out; for greater dangers lay on the road behind them than before. The snow soon began to choke the arch. An hour more, and it lay so high as to block out half the returning daylight. But it froze hard now, as it fell, and could be clambered through or over. The violence of the mountain storm was gradually yielding to a steady snowfall. The wind still raged at intervals, but not incessantly; and when it paused, the snow fell in heavy flakes.

They might have been two hours in their frightful prison, when Obenreizer, now crunching into the mound, now creeping over it with his head bowed down and his body touching the top of the arch, made his way out. Vendale followed close upon him, but followed without clear motive or calculation. For the lethargy of Basle was creeping over him again, and mastering his senses.

How far he had followed out of the gallery, or with what obstacles he had since contended, he knew not. He became roused to the knowledge that Obenreizer had set upon him, and that they were struggling desperately in the snow. He became roused to the remembrance of what his assailant carried in a girdle. He felt for it, drew it, struck at him, struggled again, struck at him again, cast him off, and stood face to face with him.

"I promised to guide you to your journey's end," said Obenreizer, "and I have kept my promise. The journey of your life ends here. Nothing can prolong it. You are sleeping as you stand."

"You are a villain. What have you done to me?"

"You are a fool. I have drugged you. You are doubly a fool, for I drugged you once before upon the journey, to try you. You are trebly a fool, for I am the thief and forger, and in a few moments I shall take those proofs against the thief and forger from your insensible body."

The entrapped man tried to throw off the lethargy, but its fatal hold upon him was so sure that, even while he heard those words, he stupidly wondered which of them had been wounded, and whose blood it was that he saw sprinkled on the snow.

"What have I done to you," he asked, heavily and thickly, "that you should be—so base—a murderer?"

"Done to me? You would have destroyed me, but that you have come to your journey's end. Your cursed activity interposed between me, and the time I had counted on in which I might have replaced the money. Done to me? You have come in my way—not once, not twice, but again and again and again. Did I try to shake you off in the beginning, or no? You were not to be shaken off. Therefore you die here."

Vendale tried to think coherently, tried to speak coherently, tried to pick up the iron-shod staff he had let fall; failing to touch it, tried to stagger on without its aid. All in vain, all in vain! He stumbled, and fell heavily forward on the brink of the deep chasm.

Stupefied, dozing, unable to stand upon his feet, a veil before his eyes, his sense of hearing deadened, he made such a vigorous rally that, supporting himself on his hands, he saw his enemy standing calmly over him, and heard him speak.

"You call me murderer," said Obenreizer, with a grim laugh. "The name matters very little. But at least I have set my life against yours, for I am surrounded by dangers, and may never make my way out of this place. The *Tourmente* is rising again. The snow is on the whirl. I must have the papers now. Every moment has my life in it."

Obenreizer's attack on Vendale.

"Stop!" cried Vendale, in a terrible voice, staggering up with a
ast flash of fire breaking out of him, and clutching the thievish
ands at his breast, in both of his. "Stop! Stand away from me! God
less my Marguerite! Happily she will never know how I died. Stand
ff from me, and let me look at your murderous face. Let it remind
ne—of something—left to say."

The sight of him fighting so hard for his senses, and the doubt
vhether he might not for the instant be possessed by the strength of
dozen men, kept his opponent still. Wildly glaring at him, Vendale
altered out the broken words:

"It shall not be—the trust—of the dead—betrayed by me—
eputed parents—misinherited fortune—see to it!"

As his head dropped on his breast, and he stumbled on the brink of
he chasm as before, the thievish hands went once more, quick and
usy, to his breast. He made a convulsive attempt to cry "No!"
lesperately rolled himself over into the gulf; and sank away from his
nemy's touch, like a phantom in a dreadful dream.

The mountain storm raged again, and passed again. The awful
nountain-voices died away, the moon rose, and the soft and silent
now fell.

Two men and two large dogs came out at the door of the Hospice.
The men looked carefully around them, and up at the sky. The dogs
olled in the snow, and took it into their mouths, and cast it up with
heir paws.

One of the men said to the other: "We may venture now. We may
ind them in one of the five Refuges." Each fastened on his back a
asket; each took in his hand a strong spiked pole; each girded under
is arms a looped end of a stout rope, so that they were tied together.

Suddenly the dogs desisted from their gambols in the snow, stood
ooking down the ascent, put their noses up, put their noses down,
ecame greatly excited, and broke into a deep loud bay together.

The two men looked in the faces of the two dogs. The two dogs
ooked, with at least equal intelligence, in the faces of the two men.

"Au secours, then! Help! To the rescue!" cried the two men. The
wo dogs, with a glad, deep, generous bark, bounded away.

"Two more mad ones!" said the men, stricken motionless, and
ooking away in the moonlight. "Is it possible in such weather! And
ne of them a woman!"

Each of the dogs had the corner of a woman's dress in its mouth,
and drew her along. She fondled their heads as she came up, and she
ame up through the snow with an accustomed tread. Not so the
arge man with her, who was spent and winded.

"Dear guides, dear friends of travellers! I am of your country. We
seek two gentlemen crossing the Pass, who should have reached the
Hospice this evening."

"They have reached it, Ma'amselle."

"Thank Heaven! O thank Heaven!"

"But, unhappily, they have gone on again. We are setting forth to

seek them even now. We had to wait until the *Tourmente* passed. It
has been fearful up here."

"Dear guides, dear friends of travellers! Let me go with you. Let
me go with you for the love of GOD! One of those gentlemen is to be
my husband. I love him, O, so dearly. O so dearly! You see I am not
faint, you see I am not tired. I am born a peasant girl. I will show
you that I know well how to fasten myself to your ropes. I will do it
with my own hands. I will swear to be brave and good. But let me go
with you, let me go with you! If any mischance should have befallen
him, my love would find him, when nothing else could. On my
knees, dear friends of travellers! By the love your dear mothers had
for your fathers!"

The good rough fellows were moved. "After all," they murmured
to one another, "she speaks but the truth. She knows the ways of the
mountains. See how marvellously she has come here. But as to Monsieur there, Ma'amselle?"

"Dear Mr. Joey," said Marguerite, addressing him in his own
tongue, "you will remain at the house, and wait for me; will you not?"

"If I know'd which o' you two recommended it," growled Joey
Ladle, eyeing the two men with great indignation, "I'd fight you for
sixpence, and give you half-a-crown towards your expenses. No, Miss.
I'll stick by you as long as there's any sticking left in me, and I'll go
for you when I can't do better."

The state of the moon rendering it highly important that no time
should be lost, and the dogs showing signs of great uneasiness, the
two men quickly took their resolution. The rope that yoked them
together was exchanged for a longer one; the party were secured,
Marguerite second, and the Cellarman last; and they set out for the
Refuges. The actual distance of those places was nothing; the whole
five, and the next Hospice to boot, being within two miles; but the
ghastly way was whitened out and sheeted over.

They made no miss in reaching the Gallery where the two had
taken shelter. The second storm of wind and snow had so wildly
swept over it since, and their tracks were gone. But the dogs went to
and fro with their noses down, and were confident. The party stopping, however, at the further arch, where the second storm had been
especially furious, and where the drift was deep, the dogs became
troubled, and went about and about, in quest of a lost purpose.

The great abyss being known to lie on the right, they wandered too
much to the left, and had to regain the way with infinite labour
through a deep field of snow. The leader of the line had stopped it,
and was taking note of the landmarks, when one of the dogs fell to
tearing up the snow a little before them. Advancing and stooping
to look at it, thinking that some one might be overwhelmed there,
they saw that it was stained, and that the stain was red.

The other dog was now seen to look over the brink of the gulf, with
his fore legs straightened out, lest he should fall into it, and to tremble
in every limb. Then the dog who had found the stained snow joined
him, and then they ran to and fro, distressed and whining. Finally,

they both stopped on the brink together, and setting up their heads, howled dolefully.

"There is some one lying below," said Marguerite.

"I think so," said the foremost man. "Stand well inward, the two last, and let us look over."

The last man kindled two torches from his basket, and handed them forward. The leader taking one, and Marguerite the other, they looked down; now shading the torches, now moving them to the right or left, now raising them, now depressing them, as moonlight far below contended with black shadows. A piercing cry from Marguerite broke a long silence.

"My God! On a projecting point, where a wall of ice stretches forward over the torrent, I see a human form!"

"Where, Ma'amselle, where?"

"See, there! On the shelf of ice below the dogs!"

The leader, with a sickened aspect, drew inward, and they were all silent. But they were not all inactive, for Marguerite, with swift and skilful fingers, had detached both herself and him from the rope in a few seconds.

"Show me the baskets. These two are the only ropes?"

"The only ropes here, Ma'amselle; but at the Hospice——"

"If he is alive—I know it is my lover—he will be dead before you can return. Dear Guides! Blessed friends of travellers! Look at me. Watch my hands. If they falter or go wrong, make me your prisoner by force. If they are steady and go right, help me to save him!"

She girded herself with a cord under the breast and arms, she formed it into a kind of jacket, she drew it into knots, she laid its end side by side with the end of the other cord, she twisted and twined the two together, she knotted them together, she set her foot upon the knots, she strained them, she held them for the two men to strain at.

"She is inspired," they said to one another.

"By the Almighty's mercy!" she exclaimed. "You both know that I am by far the lightest here. Give me the brandy and the wine, and lower me down to him. Then go for assistance and a stronger rope. You see that when it is lowered to me—look at this about me now— I can make it fast and safe to his body. Alive or dead, I will bring him up, or die with him. I love him passionately. Can I say more?"

They turned to her companion, but he was lying senseless on the snow.

"Lower me down to him," she said, taking two little kegs they had brought, and hanging them about her, "or I will dash myself to pieces! I am a peasant, and I know no giddiness or fear; and this is nothing to me, and I passionately love him. Lower me down!"

"Ma'amselle, Ma'amselle, he must be dying or dead."

"Dying or dead, my husband's head shall lie upon my breast, or I will dash myself to pieces."

They yielded, overborne. With such precautions as their skill and the circumstances admitted, they let her slip from the summit, guiding herself down the precipitous icy wall with her hand, and they lowered down, and lowered down, and lowered down, until the cry came up: "Enough!"

"Is it really he, and is he dead?" they called down, looking over.

The cry came up: "He is insensible; but his heart beats. It beats against mine."

"How does he lie?"

The cry came up: "Upon a ledge of ice. It has thawed beneath him, and it will thaw beneath me. Hasten. If we die, I am content."

One of the two men hurried off with the dogs at such topmost speed as he could make; the other set up the lighted torches in the snow, and applied himself to recovering the Englishman. Much snow-chafing and some brandy got him on his legs, but delirious and quite unconscious where he was.

The watch remained upon the brink, and his cry went down continually: "Courage! They will soon be here. How goes it?" And the cry came up: "His heart still beats against mine. I warm him in my arms. I have cast off the rope, for the ice melts under us, and the rope would separate me from him; but I am not afraid."

The moon went down behind the mountain tops, and all the abyss lay in darkness. The cry went down: "How goes it?" The cry came up: "We are sinking lower, but his heart still beats against mine."

At length the eager barking of the dogs, and a flare of light upon the snow, proclaimed that help was coming on. Twenty or thirty men, lamps, torches, litters, ropes, blankets, wood to kindle a great fire, restoratives and stimulants, came in fast. The dogs ran from one man to another, and from this thing to that, and ran to the edge of the abyss, dumbly entreating Speed, speed, speed!

The cry went down: "Thanks to God, all is ready. How goes it?"

The cry came up: "We are sinking still, and we are deadly cold. His heart no longer beats against mine. Let no one come down, to add to our weight. Lower the rope only."

The fire was kindled high, a great glare of torches lighted the sides of the precipice, lamps were lowered, a strong rope was lowered. She could be seen passing it round him, and making it secure.

The cry came up into a deathly silence: "Raise! Softly!" They could see her diminished figure shrink, as he was swung into the air.

They gave no shout when some of them laid him on a litter, and others lowered another strong rope. The cry came again up into a deathly silence: "Raise! Softly!" But when they caught her at the brink, then they shouted, then they wept, then they gave thanks to Heaven, then they kissed her feet, then they kissed her dress, then the dogs caressed her, licked her icy hands, and with their honest faces warmed her frozen bosom!

She broke from them all, and sank over him on his litter, with both her loving hands upon the heart that stood still.

ACT IV

THE CLOCK-LOCK

THE pleasant scene was Neuchâtel; the pleasant month was April; the pleasant place was a notary's office; the pleasant person in it was the notary: a rosy, hearty, handsome old man, chief notary of Neuchâtel, known far and wide in the canton as Maître Voigt. Professionally and personally, the notary was a popular citizen. His innumerable kindnesses and his innumerable oddities had for years made him one of the recognised public characters of the pleasant Swiss town. His long brown frock-coat and his black skull-cap, were among the institutions of the place: and he carried a snuff-box which in point of size, was popularly believed to be without a parallel in Europe.

There was another person in the notary's office, not so pleasant as the notary. This was Obenreizer.

An oddly pastoral kind of office it was, and one that would never have answered in England. It stood in a neat backyard, fenced off from a pretty flower-garden. Goats browsed in the doorway, and a cow was within half-a-dozen feet of keeping company with the clerk. Maître Voigt's room was a bright and varnished little room, with panelled walls, like a toy-chamber. According to the seasons of the year, roses, sunflowers, hollyhocks, peeped in at the windows. Maître Voigt's bees hummed through the office all the summer, in at this window and out at that, taking it frequently in their day's work, as if honey were to be made from Maître Voigt's sweet disposition. A large musical box on the chimneypiece often trilled away at the Overture to Fra Diavolo, or a Selection from William Tell, with a chirruping liveliness that had to be stopped by force on the entrance of a client, and irrepressibly broke out again the moment his back was turned.

"Courage, courage, my good fellow!" said Maître Voigt, patting Obenreizer on the knee, in a fatherly and comforting way. "You will begin a new life to-morrow morning in my office here."

Obenreizer—dressed in mourning, and subdued in manner—lifted his hand, with a white handkerchief in it, to the region of his heart. "The gratitude is here," he said. "But the words to express it are not here."

"Ta-ta-ta! Don't talk to me about gratitude!" said Maître Voigt. "I hate to see a man oppressed. I see you oppressed, and I hold out my hand to you by instinct. Besides, I am not too old yet, to remember my young days. Your father sent me my first client. (It was on a question of half an acre of vineyard that seldom bore any grapes.) Do I owe nothing to your father's son? I owe him a debt of friendly obligation, and I pay it to you. That's rather neatly expressed, I think," added Maître Voigt, in high good humour with himself. "Permit me to reward my own merit with a pinch of snuff!"

Obenreizer dropped his eyes to the ground, as though he were not even worthy to see the notary take snuff.

"Do me one last favour, Sir," he said, when he raised his eyes. "Do not act on impulse. Thus far, you have only a general knowledge of my position. Hear the case for and against me, in its details, before you take me into your office. Let my claim on your benevolence be recognised by your sound reason as well as by your excellent heart. In *that* case, I may hold up my head against the bitterest of my enemies, and build myself a new reputation on the ruins of the character I have lost."

"As you will," said Maître Voigt. "You speak well, my son. You will be a fine lawyer one of these days."

"The details are not many," pursued Obenreizer. "My troubles begin with the accidental death of my late travelling companion, my lost dear friend Mr. Vendale."

"Mr. Vendale," repeated the notary. "Just so. I have heard and read of the name, several times within these two months. The name of the unfortunate English gentleman who was killed on the Simplon. When you got that scar upon your cheek and neck."

"—From my own knife," said Obenreizer, touching what must have been an ugly gash at the time of its infliction.

"From your own knife," assented the notary, "and in trying to save him. Good, good, good. That was very good. Vendale. Yes. I have several times, lately, thought it droll that I should once have had a client of that name."

"But the world, Sir," returned Obenreizer, "is so small!" Nevertheless he made a mental note that the notary had once had a client of that name.

"As I was saying, Sir, the death of that dear travelling comrade begins my troubles. What follows? I save myself. I go down to Milan. I am received with coldness by Defresnier and Company. Shortly afterwards, I am discharged by Defresnier and Company. Why? They give no reason why. I ask, do they assail my honour? No answer. I ask, what is the imputation against me? No answer. I ask, where are their proofs against me? No answer. I ask, what am I to think? The reply is, 'M. Obenreizer is free to think what he will. What M. Obenreizer thinks, is of no importance to Defresnier and Company.' And that is all."

"Perfectly. That is all," assented the notary, taking a large pinch of snuff.

"But is that enough, Sir?"

"That is not enough," said Maître Voigt. "The House of Defresnier are my fellow-townsmen—much respected, much esteemed—but the House of Defresnier must not silently destroy a man's character. You can rebut assertion. But how can you rebut silence?"

"Your sense of justice, my dear patron," answered Obenreizer, "states in a word the cruelty of the case. Does it stop there? No. For, what follows upon that?"

"True, my poor boy," said the notary, with a comforting nod or two; "your ward rebels upon that."

"Rebels is too soft a word," retorted Obenreizer. "My ward revolts om me with horror. My ward defies me. My ward withdraws herself om my authority, and takes shelter (Madame Dor with her) in the ouse of that English lawyer, Mr. Bintrey, who replies to your sumons to her to submit herself to my authority, that she will not do so."

"—And who afterwards writes," said the notary, moving his large nuff-box to look among the papers underneath it for the letter, "that e is coming to confer with me."

"Indeed?" replied Obenreizer, rather checked. "Well, Sir. Have I o legal rights?"

"Assuredly, my poor boy," returned the notary. "All but felons have heir legal rights."

"And who calls me felon?" said Obenreizer, fiercely.

"No one. Be calm under your wrongs. If the House of Defresnier vould call you felon, indeed, we should know how to deal with them."

While saying these words, he had handed Bintrey's very short etter to Obenreizer, who now read it and gave it back.

"In saying," observed Obenreizer, with recovered composure, that he is coming to confer with you, this English lawyer means hat he is coming to deny my authority over my ward."

"You think so?"

"I am sure of it. I know him. He is obstinate and contentious. You vill tell me, my dear Sir, whether my authority is unassailable, until ny ward is of age?"

"Absolutely unassailable."

"I will enforce it. I will make her submit herself to it. For," said Obenreizer, changing his angry tone to one of grateful submission, I owe it to you, Sir; to you, who have so confidingly taken an injured nan under your protection, and into your employment."

"Make your mind easy," said Maître Voigt. "No more of this now, nd no thanks! Be here to-morrow morning, before the other clerk omes—between seven and eight. You will find me in this room; nd I will myself initiate you in your work. Go away! go away! I ave letters to write. I won't hear a word more."

Dismissed with this generous abruptness, and satisfied with the avourable impression he had left on the old man's mind, Obenreizer vas at leisure to revert to the mental note he had made that Maître Voigt once had a client whose name was Vendale.

"I ought to know England well enough by this time;" so his neditations ran, as he sat on a bench in the yard; "and it is not a name I ever encountered there, except"—he looked involuntarily over his shoulder—"as his name. Is the world so small that I cannot get away from him, even now when he is dead? He confessed at the last hat he had betrayed the trust of the dead, and misinherited a fortune. And I was to see to it. And I was to stand off, that my face might emind him of it. Why my face, unless it concerned me? I am sure of his words, for they have been in my ears ever since. Can there be anyhing bearing on them, in the keeping of this old idiot? Anything to epair my fortunes, and blacken his memory? He dwelt upon my earliest remembrances, that night at Basle. Why, unless he had purpose in it?"

Maître Voigt's two largest he-goats were butting at him to butt him out of the place, as if for that disrespectful mention of their master. So he got up and left the place. But he walked alone for a long time on the border of the lake, with his head drooped in deep thought.

Between seven and eight next morning, he presented himself again at the office. He found the notary ready for him, at work on some papers which had come in on the previous evening. In a few clear words, Maître Voigt explained the routine of the office, and the duties Obenreizer would be expected to perform. It still wanted five minutes to eight, when the preliminary instructions were declared to be complete.

"I will show you over the house and the offices," said Maître Voigt; "but I must put away these papers first. They come from the municipal authorities, and they must be taken special care of."

Obenreizer saw his chance, here, of finding out the repository in which his employer's private papers were kept.

"Can't I save you the trouble, Sir?" he asked. "Can't I put those documents away under your directions?"

Maître Voigt laughed softly to himself; closed the portfolio in which the papers had been sent to him; handed it to Obenreizer.

"Suppose you try," he said. "All my papers of importance are kept yonder."

He pointed to a heavy oaken door, thickly studded with nails, at the lower end of the room. Approaching the door, with the portfolio, Obenreizer discovered, to his astonishment, that there were no means whatever of opening it from the outside. There was no handle, no bolt, no key, and (climax of passive obstruction!) no keyhole.

"There is a second door to this room?" said Obenreizer, appealing to the notary.

"No," said Maître Voigt. "Guess again."

"There is a window?"

"Nothing of the sort. The window has been bricked up. The only way in, is the way by that door. Do you give it up?" cried Maître Voigt, in high triumph. "Listen, my good fellow, and tell me if you hear nothing inside?"

Obenreizer listened for a moment, and started back from the door.

"I know!" he exclaimed. "I heard of this when I was apprenticed here at the watchmaker's. Perrin Brothers have finished their famous clock-lock at last—and you have got it?"

"Bravo!" said Maître Voigt. "The clock-lock it is! There, my son! There you have one more of what the good people of this town call 'Daddy Voigt's follies.' With all my heart! Let those laugh who win. No thief can steal my keys. No burglar can pick my lock. No power on earth, short of a battering-ram or a barrel of gunpowder, can move that door, till my little sentinel inside—my worthy friend who goes 'Tick, tick,' as I tell him—says 'Open!' The big door obeys the little Tick, Tick, and the little Tick, Tick, obeys me. That!" cried Daddy oigt, snapping his fingers, "for all the thieves in Christendom!"

"May I see it in action?" asked Obenreizer. "Pardon my curiosity, ear Sir! You know that I was once a tolerable worker in the clock ade."

"Certainly you shall see it in action," said Maître Voigt. "What is .e time now? One minute to eight. Watch, and in one minute you ill see the door open of itself."

In one minute, smoothly and slowly and silently, as if invisible ands had set it free, the heavy door opened inward, and disclosed a ark chamber beyond. On three sides, shelves filled the walls, from oor to ceiling. Arranged on the shelves, were rows upon rows of oxes made in the pretty inlaid wood-work of Switzerland, and bear-g inscribed on their fronts (for the most part in fanciful coloured tters) the names of the notary's clients.

Maître Voigt lighted a taper, and led the way into the room.

"You shall see the clock," he said proudly. "If I possess the great-t curiosity in Europe. It is only a privileged few whose eyes can ok at it. I give the privilege to your good father's son—you shall be .e of the favoured few who enter the room with me. See! here it is, a the right-hand wall at the side of the door."

"An ordinary clock," exclaimed Obenreizer. "No! Not an ordinary ock. It has only one hand."

"Aha!" said Maître Voigt. "Not an ordinary clock, my friend. No, o. That one hand goes round the dial. As I put it, so it regulates the our at which the door shall open. See! the hand points to eight. At ght the door opened, as you saw for yourself."

"Does it open more than once in the four-and-twenty hours?" sked Obenreizer.

"More than once?" repeated the notary, with great scorn. "You on't know, my good friend, Tick-Tick! He will open the door as ften as I ask him. All he wants is his directions, and he gets them ere. Look below the dial. Here is a half-circle of steel let into the wall ad here is a hand (called the regulator) that travels round it, just as y hand chooses. Notice, if you please, that there are figures to guide .e on the half-circle of steel. Figure I. means: Open once in the four-nd-twenty hours. Figure II. means: Open twice; and so on to the ad. I set the regulator every morning, after I have read my letters, nd when I know what my day's work is to be. Would you like to see .e set it now? What is to-day? Wednesday. Good! This is the day f our rifle-club; there is little business to do; I grant a half-holiday. o work here to-day, after three o'clock. Let us first put away this ortfolio of municipal papers. There! No need to trouble Tick-Tick o open the door until eight to-morrow. Good! I leave the dial-hand t eight; I put back the regulator to I.; I close the door; and closed the oor remains, past all opening by anybody, till to-morrow morning t eight."

Obenreizer's quickness instantly saw the means by which he might aake the clock-lock betray it's master's confidence, and place its aaster's papers at his disposal.

"Stop, Sir," he cried, at the moment when the notary was closin
the door. "Don't I see something moving among the boxes—on th
floor there?"

(Maître Voigt turned his back for a moment to look. In tha
moment, Obenreizer's ready hand put the regulator on, from th
figure "I." to the figure "II." Unless the notary looked again at th
half-circle of steel, the door would open at eight that evening, as we
as at eight next morning, and nobody but Obenreizer would know it

"There is nothing!" said Maître Voigt. "Your troubles have shake
your nerves, my son. Some shadow thrown by my taper; or some po
little beetle, who lives among the old lawyer's secrets, running awa
from the light. Hark! I hear your fellow-clerk in the office. To wor
to work! and build to-day the first step that leads to your new fo
tunes!"

He good-humouredly pushed Obenreizer out before him; exti
guished the taper, with a last fond glance at his clock which passe
harmlessly over the regulator beneath; and closed the oaken door.

At three, the office was shut up. The notary and everybody in th
notary's employment, with one exception, went to see the rifl
shooting. Obenreizer had pleaded that he was not in spirits for
public festival. Nobody knew what had become of him. It wa
believed that he had slipped away for a solitary walk.

The house and offices had been closed but a few minutes, when th
door of a shining wardrobe in the notary's shining room opened, an
Obenreizer stepped out. He walked to a window, unclosed the shutter
satisfied himself that he could escape unseen by way of the garde
turned back into the room, and took his place in the notary's eas
chair. He was locked up in the house, and there were five hours
wait before eight o'clock came.

He wore his way through the five hours; sometimes reading th
books and newspapers that lay on the table: sometimes thinkin
sometimes walking to and fro. Sunset came on. He closed the wi
dow-shutters before he kindled a light. The candle lighted, and th
time drawing nearer and nearer, he sat, watch in hand, with his ey
on the oaken door.

At eight, smoothly and softly and silently the door opened.

One after another, he read the names on the outer rows of boxe
No such name as Vendale! He removed the outer row, and looked a
the row behind. These were older boxes, and shabbier boxes. The fo
first that he examined, were inscribed with French and Germa
names. The fifth bore a name which was almost illegible. He broug
it out into the room, and examined it closely. There, covered thick
with time-stains and dust, was the name: "Vendale."

The key hung to the box by a string. He unlocked the box, too
out four loose papers that were in it, spread them open on the tabl
and began to read them. He had not so occupied a minute, when h
face fell from its expression of eagerness and avidity, to one of ha
gard astonishment and disappointment. But, after a little consider
tion, he copied the papers. He then replaced the papers, replaced th

box, closed the door, extinguished the candle, and stole away.

As his murderous and thievish footfall passed out of the garden, the steps of the notary and some one accompanying him stopped at the front door of the house. The lamps were lighted in the little street, and the notary had his door-key in his hand.

"Pray do not pass my house, Mr. Bintrey," he said. "Do me the honour to come in. It is one of our town half-holidays—our Tir—but my people will be back directly. It is droll that you should ask your way to the Hotel of me. Let us eat and drink before you go there."

"Thank you; not to-night," said Bintrey. "Shall I come to you at ten to-morrow?"

"I shall be enchanted, Sir, to take so early an opportunity of re-dressing the wrongs of my injured client," returned the good notary.

"Yes," retorted Bintrey; "your injured client is all very well—but—a word in your ear."

He whispered to the notary and walked off. When the notary's housekeeper came home, she found him standing at his door motionless, with the key still in his hand, and the door unopened.

OBENREIZER'S VICTORY

The scene shifts again—to the foot of the Simplon, on the Swiss side.

In one of the dreary rooms of the dreary little inn at Brieg, Mr. Bintrey and Maître Voigt sat together at a professional council of two. Mr. Bintrey was searching in his dispatch-box. Maître Voigt was looking towards a closed door, painted brown to imitate mahogany, and communicating with an inner room.

"Isn't it time he was here?" asked the notary, shifting his position, and glancing at a second door at the other end of the room, painted yellow to imitate deal.

"He *is* here," answered Bintrey, after listening for a moment.

The yellow door was opened by a waiter, and Obenreizer walked in.

After greeting Maître Voigt with a cordiality which appeared to cause the notary no little embarrassment, Obenreizer bowed with grave and distant politeness to Bintrey. "For what reason have I been brought from Neuchâtel to the foot of the mountain?" he inquired, taking the seat which the English lawyer had indicated to him.

"You shall be quite satisfied on that head before our interview is over," returned Bintrey, "For the present, permit me to suggest proceeding at once to business. There has been a correspondence, Mr. Obenreizer, between you and your niece. I am here to represent your niece."

"In other words, you, a lawyer, are here to represent an infraction of the law."

"Admirably put!" said Bintrey. "If all the people I have to deal with were only like you, what an easy profession mine would be! I am here to represent an infraction of the law—that is your point of view. I am here to make a compromise between you and your niece—that is my point of view."

"There must be two parties to a compromise," rejoined Obenreizer. "I decline, in this case, to be one of them. The law gives me authority to control my niece's actions, until she comes of age. She is not yet of age; and I claim my authority."

At this point Maître Voigt attempted to speak. Bintrey silenced him with a compassionate indulgence of tone and manner, as if he was silencing a favourite child.

"No, my worthy friend, not a word. Don't excite yourself unnecessarily; leave it to me." He turned, and addressed himself again to Obenreizer. "I can think of nothing comparable to you, Mr. Obenreizer, but granite—and even that wears out in course of time. In the interests of peace and quietness—for the sake of your own dignity—relax a little. If you will only delegate your authority to another person whom I know of, that person may be trusted never to lose sight of your niece, night or day!"

"You are wasting your time and mine," returned Obenreizer. "If my niece is not rendered up to my authority within one week from this day, I invoke the law. If you resist the law, I take her by force."

He rose to his feet as he said the last word. Maître Voigt looked round again towards the brown door which led into the inner room.

"Have some pity on the poor girl," pleaded Bintrey. "Remember how lately she lost her lover by a dreadful death! Will nothing move you?"

"Nothing."

Bintrey, in his turn, rose to his feet, and looked at Maître Voigt. Maître Voigt's hand, resting on the table, began to tremble. Maître Voigt's eyes remained fixed, as if by irresistible fascination, on the brown door. Obenreizer, suspiciously observing him, looked that way too.

"There is somebody listening in there!" he exclaimed, with a sharp backward glance at Bintrey.

"There are two people listening," answered Bintrey.

"Who are they?"

"You shall see."

With that answer, he raised his voice and spoke the next words—the two common words which are on everybody's lips, at every hour of the day: "Come in!"

The brown door opened. Supported on Marguerite's arm—his sun-burnt colour gone, his right arm bandaged and slung over his breast—Vendale stood before the murderer, a man risen from the dead.

In the moment of silence that followed, the singing of a caged bird in the courtyard outside was the one sound stirring in the room. Maître Voigt touched Bintrey, and pointed to Obenreizer. "Look at him!" said the notary, in a whisper.

The shock had paralysed every movement in the villain's body, but the movement of the blood. His face was like the face of a corpse. The one vestige of colour left in it was a livid purple streak which marked the course of the scar where his victim had wounded him on the cheek and neck. Speechless, breathless, motionless alike in eye and limb, it seemed as if, at the sight of Vendale, the death to which he had doomed Vendale had struck him where he stood.

"Somebody ought to speak to him," said Maître Voigt. "Shall I?"

Even at that moment Bintrey persisted in silencing the notary, and in keeping the lead in the proceedings to himself. Checking Maître Voigt by a gesture, he dismissed Marguerite and Vendale in these words:—"the object of your appearance here is answered," he said. "If you will withdraw for the present, it may help Mr. Obenreizer to recover himself."

It did help him. As the two passed through the door and closed it behind them, he drew a deep breath of relief. He looked round him for the chair from which he had risen, and dropped into it.

"Give him time!" pleaded Maître Voigt.

"No," said Bintrey. "I don't know what use he may make of it if I do." He turned once more to Obenreizer, and went on. "I owe it to myself," he said—"I don't admit, mind, that I owe it to *you*—to account for my appearance in these proceedings, and to state what has been done under my advice, and on my sole responsibility. Can you listen to me?"

"I can listen to you."

"Recall the time when you started from Switzerland with Mr. Vendale," Bintrey began. "You had not left England four-and-twenty hours before your niece committed an act of imprudence which not even your penetration could foresee. She followed her promised husband on his journey, without asking anybody's advice or permission, and without any better companion to protect her than a Cellarman in Mr. Vendale's employment."

"Why did she follow me on the journey? and how came the Cellarman to be the person who accompanied her?"

"She followed you on the journey," answered Bintrey, "because she suspected there had been some serious collision between you and Mr. Vendale, which had been kept secret from her; and because she rightly believed you to be capable of serving your interests, or of satisfying your enmity, at the price of a crime. As for the Cellarman, he was one, among the other people in Mr. Vendale's establishment, to whom she had applied (the moment your back was turned) to know if anything had happened between their master and you. The Cellarman alone had something to tell her. A senseless superstition and a common accident which had happened to his master, in his master's cellar, had connected Mr. Vendale in this man's mind with the idea of danger by murder. Your niece surprised him into a confession, which aggravated tenfold the terrors that possessed her. Aroused to a sense of the mischief he had done, the man, of his own accord, made the one atonement, in his power. 'If my master is in danger, Miss,' he said, 'it's my duty to follow him, too; and it's more than my duty to take care of *you*.' The two set forth together—and, for once, a superstition has had its use. It decided your niece on taking the journey; and it led the way to saving a man's life. Do you understand me, so far?"

"I understand you, so far."

"My first knowledge of the crime that you had committed," pursued Bintrey, "came to me in the form of a letter from your niece. All you need know is that her love and her courage recovered the body of your victim, and aided the after-efforts which brought him back to life. While he lay helpless at Brieg, under her care, she wrote to me to come out to him. Before starting, I informed Madame Dor that I knew Miss Obenreizer to be safe, and knew where she was. Madame Dor informed me, in return, that a letter had come for your niece, which she knew to be in your handwriting. I took possession of it, and arranged for the forwarding of any other letters which might follow. Arrived at Brieg, I found Mr. Vendale out of danger, and at once devoted myself to hastening the day of reckoning with you. Defresnier and Company turned you off on suspicion; acting on information privately supplied by me. Having stripped you of your false character, the next thing to do was to strip you of your authority over your niece. To reach this end, I not only had no scruple in digging the pitfall under your feet in the dark—I felt a certain professional pleasure in fighting you with your own weapons. By my advice the truth has been carefully concealed from you up to this day. By my advice the trap into which you have walked was set for you (you know why, now, as well as I do) in this place. There was but one certain way of shaking the devilish self-control which has hitherto made you a formidable man. That way has been tried, and (look at me as you may) that way has succeeded. The last thing that remains to be done," concluded Bintrey, producing two little slips of manuscript from his dispatch-box," is to set your niece free. You have attempted murder, and you have committed forgery and theft. We have the evidence ready against you in both cases. If you are convicted as a felon, you know as well as I do what becomes of your authority over your niece. Personally, I should have preferred taking that way out of it. But considerations are pressed on me which I am not able to resist, and this interview must end, as I have told you already, in a compromise. Sign those lines, resigning all authority over Miss Obenreizer, and pledging yourself never to be seen in England or in Switzerland again; and I will sign an indemnity which secures you against further proceedings on our part."

Obenreizer took the pen, in silence, and signed his niece's release. On receiving the indemnity in return, he rose, but made no movement to leave the room. He stood looking at Maître Voigt with a strange smile gathering at his lips, and a strange light flashing in his filmy eyes.

"What are you waiting for?" asked Bintrey.

Obenreizer pointed to the brown door. "Call them back," he answered. "I have something to say in their presence before I go."

"Say it in my presence," retorted Bintrey. "I decline to call them ack."

Obenreizer turned to Maître Voigt. "Do you remember telling me hat you once had an English client named Vendale?" he asked.

"Well," answered the notary. "And what of that?"

"Maître Voigt, your clock-lock has betrayed you."

"What do you mean?"

"I have read the letters and certificates in your client's box. I have aken copies of them. I have got the copies here. Is there, or is there ot, a reason for calling them back?"

For a moment the notary looked to and fro, between Obenreizer nd Bintrey, in helpless astonishment. Recovering himself, he drew is brother-lawyer aside, and hurriedly spoke a few words close at his ar. The face of Bintrey—after first faithfully reflecting the aston- shment on the face of Maître Voigt—suddenly altered its expression. He sprang, with the activity of a young man, to the door of the inner room, entered it, remained inside for a minute, and returned followed by Marguerite and Vendale. "Now, Mr. Obenreizer." said Bintrey, 'the last move in the game is yours. Play it."

"Before I resign my position as that young lady's guardian," said Obenreizer, "I have a secret to reveal in which she is interested. In making my disclosure, I am not claiming her attention for a narrative which she, or any other person present, is expected to take on trust. I am possessed of written proofs, copies of originals, the authenticity of which Maître Voigt himself can attest. Bear that in mind, and permit me to refer you, at starting, to a date long past—the month of February, in the year one thousand eight hundred and thirty-six."

"Mark the date, Mr. Vendale," said Bintrey.

"My first proof," said Obenreizer, taking a paper from his pocket- book. "Copy of a letter, written by an English lady (married) to her sister, a widow. The name of the person writing the letter I shall keep suppressed until I have done. The name of the person to whom the letter is written I am willing to reveal. It is addressed to 'Mrs. Jane Anne Miller, of Groombridge-wells, England.'"

Vendale started, and opened his lips to speak. Bintrey instantly stopped him, as he had stopped Maître Voigt. "No," said the pertina- cious lawyer. "Leave it to me."

Obenreizer went on:

"It is needless to trouble you with the first half of the letter," he said. "I can give the substance of it in two words. The writer's position at the time is this. She has been long living in Switzerland with her husband—obliged to live there for the sake of her husband's health. They are about to move to a new residence on the lake of Neuchâtel in a week, and they will be ready to receive Mrs. Miller as a visitor in a fortnight from that time. This said, the writer next enters into an important domestic detail. She has been childless for years—she and her husband have now no hope of children; they are lonely; they want an interest in life; they have decided on adopting a child. Here the important part of the letter begins; and here, therefore, I read it to you word for word.''

He folded back the first page of the letter and read as follows:

" * * * Will you help us, my dear sister, to realise our new project? As English people, we wish to adopt an English child. This may be done, I believe, at the Foundling: my husband's lawyers in London will tell you how. I leave the choice to you, with only these conditions attached to it—that the child is to be an infant under a year old, and is to be a boy. Will you pardon the trouble I am giving you, for my sake; and will you bring our adopted child to us, with your own children, when you come to Neuchâtel?

"I must add a word as to my husband's wishes in this matter. He is resolved to spare the child whom we make our own any future mortification and loss of self-respect which might be caused by a discovery of his true origin. He will bear my husband's name, and he will be brought up in the belief that he is really our son. His inheritance of what we have to leave will be secured to him—not only according to the laws of England in such cases, but according to the laws of Switzerland also; for we have lived so long in this country, that there is a doubt whether we may not be considered as 'domiciled' in Switzerland. The one precaution left to take is to prevent any after-discovery at the Foundling. Now, our name is a very uncommon one; and if we appear on the Register of the Institution as the persons adopting the child, there is just a chance that something might result from it. Your name, my dear, is the name of thousands of other people; and if *you* will consent to appear on the Register, there need be no fear of any discoveries in that quarter. We are moving, by the doctor's orders, to a part of Switzerland in which our circumstances are quite unknown; and you, as I understand, are about to engage a new nurse for the journey when you come to see us. Under these circumstances, the child may appear as my child, brought back to me under my sister's care. The only servant we take with us from our old home is my own maid, who can be safely trusted. As for the lawyers in England and in Switzerland, it is their profession to keep secrets—and we may feel quite easy in that direction. So there you have our harmless little conspiracy! Write by return of post, my love, and tell me you will join it." * * *

"Do you still conceal the name of the writer of that letter?" asked Vendale.

"I keep the name of the writer till the last," answered Obenreizer, "and I proceed to my second proof—a mere slip of paper this time, as you see. Memorandum given to the Swiss lawyer, who drew the documents referred to in the letter I have just read, expressed as follows:—'Adopted from the Foundling Hospital of England, 3rd March, 1836, a male infant, called, in the Institution, Walter Wilding. Person appearing on the register, as adopting the child, Mrs. Jane Anne Miller, widow, acting in this matter for her married sister, domiciled in Switzerland.' Patience!'' resumed Obenreizer, as

Vendale, breaking loose from Bintrey, started to his feet. "I shall not keep the name concealed much longer. Two more little slips of paper, and I have done, Third proof! Certificate of Doctor Ganz, still living in practice at Neuchâtel, dated July, 1838. The doctor certifies (you shall read it for yourselves directly), first, that he attended the adopted child in its infant maladies; second, that, three months before the date of the certificate, the gentleman adopting the child as his son died; third, that *on* the date of the certificate, his widow and her maid, taking the adopted child with them, left Neuchâtel on their return to England. One more link now added to this, and my chain of evidence is complete. The maid remained with her mistress till her mistress's death, only a few years since. The maid can swear to the identity of the adopted infant, from his childhood to his youth—from his youth to his manhood, as he is now. There is her address in England—and there, Mr. Vendale, is the fourth, and final proof!"

"Why do you address yourself to *me?*" said Vendale, as Obenreizer threw the written address on the table.

Obenreizer turned on him, in a sudden frenzy of triumph.

"*Because you are the man!* If my niece marries you, she marries a bastard, brought up by public charity. If my niece marries you, she marries an impostor, without name or lineage, disguised in the character of a gentleman of rank and family."

"Bravo!" cried Bintrey. "Admirably put, Mr. Obenreizer! It only wants one word more to complete it. She marries—thanks entirely to your exertions—a man who inherits a handsome fortune, and a man whose origin will make him prouder than ever of his peasant-wife. George Vendale, as brother-executors, let us congratulate each other! Our dear dead friend's last wish on earth is accomplished. We have found the lost Walter Wilding. As Mr. Obenreizer said just now—you are the man!"

The words passed by Vendale unheeded. For the moment he was conscious of but one sensation; he heard but one voice. Marguerite's hand was clasping his. Marguerite's voice was whispering to him: "I never loved you, George, as I love you now!"

THE CURTAIN FALLS

May-day. There is merry-making in Cripple Corner, the chimneys smoke, the patriarchal dining-hall is hung with garlands, and Mrs. Goldstraw, the respected housekeeper, is very busy. For, on this bright morning the young master of Cripple Corner is married to its young mistress, far away: to wit, in the little town of Brieg, in Switzerland, lying at the foot of the Simplon Pass where she saved his life.

The bells ring gaily in the little town of Brieg, and flags are stretched across the street, and rifle shots are heard, and sounding music from brass instruments. Streamer-decorated casks of wine have been rolled out under a gay awning in the public way before the Inn, and there will be free feasting and revelry. What with bells and banners, draperies hanging from windows, explosion of gunpowder, and reverberation of brass music, the little town of Brieg is all in a flutter like the hearts of its simple people.

It was a stormy night last night, and the mountains are covered with snow. But the sun is bright to-day, the sweet air is fresh, the tin spires of the little town of Brieg are burnished silver, and the Alps are ranges of far-off white cloud in a deep blue sky.

The primitive people of the little town of Brieg have built a green wood arch across the street, under which the newly married pair shall pass in triumph from the church. It is inscribed, on that side "HONOUR AND LOVE TO MARGUERITE VENDALE!" for the people are proud of her to enthusiasm. This greeting of the bride under her new name is affectionately meant as a surprise, and therefore the arrangement has been made that she, unconscious why, shall be taken to the church by a tortuous back way. A scheme not difficult to carry into execution in the crooked little town of Brieg.

So, all things are in readiness, and they are to go and come on foot. Assembled in the Inn's best chamber, festively adorned, are the bride and bridegroom, the Neuchâtel notary, the London Lawyer, Madame Dor, and a certain large mysterious Englishman, popularly known as Monsieur Zhoé-Ladelle. And behold Madame Dor, arrayed in a spotless pair of gloves of her own, with no hand in the air, but both hands clasped round the neck of the bride; to embrace whom Madame Dor has turned her broad back on the company, consistent to the last.

"Forgive me, my beautiful," pleads Madame Dor, "for that I ever was his she-cat!"

"She-cat, Madame Dor?"

"Engaged to sit watching my so-charming mouse," are the explanatory words of Madame Dor, delivered with a penitential sob.

"Why, you were our best friend! George, dearest, tell Madame Dor Was she not our best friend?"

"Undoubtedly, darling. What should we have done without her?"

"You are both so generous," cries Madame Dor, accepting consolation, and immediately relapsing. "But I commenced as a she-cat."

"Ah! But like the cat in the fairy-story, good Madame Dor," says Vendale, saluting her cheek, "you were a true woman. And, being a true woman, the sympathy of your heart was with true love."

"I don't wish to deprive Madame Dor of her share in the embraces that are going on," Mr. Bintrey put in, watch in hand, " and I don't presume to offer any objection to your having got yourselves mixed together, in the corner there, like the three Graces. I merely remark that I think it's time we were moving. What are *your* sentiments on that subject, Mr. Ladle?"

"Clear, Sir," replies Joey, with a gracious grin. "I'm clearer altogether, Sir, for having lived so many weeks upon the surface. I never was half so long upon the surface afore, and it's done me a power of good. At Cripple Corner, I was too much below it. Atop of the Simpleton, I was a deal too high above it. I've found the medium

ere, Sir. And if ever I take it in convivial, in all the rest of my
days, I mean to do it this day, to the toast of 'Bless 'em both.' "

"I, too!" says Bintrey. "And now, Monsieur Voigt, let you and me
be the two men of Marseilles, and allons, marchons, arm-in-arm!"

They go down to the door, where others are waiting for them,
and they go quietly to the church, and the happy marriage takes
place. While the ceremony is yet in progress, the notary is called out.
When it is finished, he has returned, is standing behind Vendale,
and touches him on the shoulder.

"Go to the side door, one moment, Monsieur Vendale. Alone. Leave
Madame to me."

At the side door of the church, are the same two men from the
Hospice. They are snow-stained and travel-worn. They wish him joy,
and then each lays his broad hand upon Vendale's breast, and one
says in a low voice, while the other steadfastly regards him:

"It is here, Monsieur. Your litter. The very same."

"My litter is here? Why?"

"Hush! For the sake of Madame. Your companion of that day——"

"What of him?"

The man looks at his comrade, and his comrade takes him up. Each
keeps his hand laid earnestly on Vendale's breast.

"He has been living at the first Refuge, Monsieur, for some days.
The weather was now good, now bad."

"Yes?"

"He arrived at our Hospice the day before yesterday, and, having
refreshed himself with sleep on the floor before the fire, wrapped in his
cloak, was resolute to go on, before dark, to the next Hospice. He had
a great fear of that part of the way, and thought it would be worse
to-morrow."

"Yes?"

"He went on alone. He passed the gallery when an avalanche—like
that which fell behind you near the Bridge of the Ganther——"

"Killed him?"

"We dug him out, suffocated and broken all to pieces! But,
Monsieur, as to Madame. We have brought him here on the litter, to
be buried. We must ascend the street outside. Madame must not see.
It would be an accursed thing to bring the litter through the arch
across the street, until Madame has passed through. As you descend,
we who accompany the litter will set it down on the stones of the
street the second to the right, and will stand before it. But do not
let Madame turn her head towards the street the second to the right.
There is no time to lose. Madame will be alarmed by your absence.
Adieu!"

Vendale returns to his bride, and draws her hand through his
unmaimed arm. A pretty procession awaits them at the main door of
the church. They take their station in it, and descend the street
amidst the ringing of the bells, the firing of the guns, the waving of
the flags, the playing of the music, the shouts, the smiles, and tears,
of the excited town. Heads are uncovered as she passes, hands are

kissed to her, all the people bless her. "Heaven's benediction on the dear girl! See where she goes in her youth and beauty; she who so nobly saved his life!"

Near the corner of the street the second to the right, he speaks to her, and calls her attention to the windows on the opposite side. The corner well passed, he says: "Do not look round, my darling, for a reason that I have," and turns his head. Then, looking back along the street, he sees the litter and its bearers passing up alone under the arch, as he and she and their marriage train go down towards the shining valley.

THE LAZY TOUR OF
TWO IDLE APPRENTICES

CHAPTER I

In the autumn month of September, eighteen hundred and fifty-seven, wherein these presents bear date, two idle apprentices, exhausted by the long, hot summer, and the long, hot work it had brought with it, ran away from their employer. They were bound to a highly meritorious lady (named Literature), of fair credit and repute, though, it must be acknowledged, not quite so highly esteemed in the City as she might be. This is the more remarkable, as there is nothing against the respectable lady in that quarter, but quite the contrary; her family having rendered eminent service to many famous citizens of London. It may be sufficient to name Sir William Walworth, Lord Mayor under King Richard II., at the time of Wat Tyler's insurrection, and Sir Richard Whittington: which latter distinguished man and magistrate was doubtless indebted to the lady's family for the gift of his celebrated cat. There is also strong reason to suppose that they rang the Highgate bells for him with their own hands.

The misguided young men who thus shirked their duty to the mistress from whom they had received many favours, were actuated by the low idea of making a perfectly idle trip, in any direction. They had no intention of going anywhere in particular; they wanted to see nothing, they wanted to know nothing, they wanted to learn nothing, they wanted to do nothing. They wanted only to be idle. They took to themselves (after HOGARTH), the names of Mr. Thomas Idle and Mr. Francis Goodchild; but there was not a moral pin to choose between them, and they were both idle in the last degree.

Between Francis and Thomas, however, there was this difference of character: Goodchild was laboriously idle, and would take upon himself any amount of pains and labour to assure himself that he was idle; in short, had no better idea of idleness than that it was useless industry. Thomas Idle, on the other hand, was an idler of the unmixed Irish or Neapolitan type; a passive idler, a born-and-bred idler, a consistent idler, who practised what he would have preached if he had not been too idle to preach; a one entire and perfect chrysolite of idleness.

The two idle apprentices found themselves, within a few hours of their escape, walking down into the North of England, that is to say, Thomas was lying in a meadow, looking at the railway trains as they passed over a distant viaduct—which was *his* idea of walking down into the North; while Francis was walking a mile due South against time—which was *his* idea of walking down into the North. In the meantime the day waned and the milestones remained unconquered.

"Tom," said Goodchild, "the sun is getting low. Up, and let us go forward!"

"Nay," quoth Thomas Idle, "I have not done with Annie Laurie yet." And he proceeded with that idle but popular ballad, to the effect that for the bonnie young person of that name he would "lay him doon and dee"—equivalent, in prose, to lay him down and die.

"What an ass that fellow was!" cried Goodchild, with the bitter emphasis of contempt.

"Which fellow?" asked Thomas Idle.

"The fellow in your song. Lay him doon and dee! Finely he'd show off before the girl by doing *that*. A sniveller! Why couldn't he get up, and punch somebody's head!"

"Whose?" asked Thomas Idle.

"Anybody's. Everybody's would be better than nobody's! If I fell into that state of mind about a girl, do you think I'd lay me doon and dee? No, Sir," proceeded Goodchild, with a disparaging assumption of the Scottish accent. "I'd get me oop and peetch into somebody. Wouldn't you?"

"I wouldn't have anything to do with her," yawned Thomas Idle. "Why should I take the trouble?"

"It's no trouble, Tom, to fall in love," said Goodchild, shaking his head.

"It's trouble enough to fall out of it, once you're in it," retorted Tom. "So I keep out of it altogether. It would be better for you, if you did the same."

Mr. Goodchild, who is always in love with somebody, and not unfrequently with several objects at once, made no reply. He heaved a sigh of the kind which is termed by the lower orders "a bellowser," and then, heaving Mr. Idle on his feet (who was not half so heavy as the sigh), urged him northward.

These two had sent their personal baggage on by train: only retaining each a knapsack. Idle now applied himself to constantly regretting the train, to tracking it through the intricacies of Bradshaw's Guide, and finding out where it is now—and where now—and where now—and to asking what was the use of walking, when you could ride at such a pace as that. Was it to see the country? If that was the object, look at it out of the carriage windows. There was a great deal more of it to be seen there than here. Besides, who wanted to see the country? Nobody. And again, whoever did walk? Nobody. Fellows set off to walk, but they never did it. They came back and said they did, but they didn't. Then why should he walk? He wouldn't walk. He swore it by this milestone!

It was the fifth from London, so far had they penetrated into the North. Submitting to the powerful chain of argument, Goodchild proposed a return to the Metropolis, and a falling back upon Euston

Square Terminus. Thomas assented with alacrity, and so they walked down into the North by the next morning's express, and carried their knapsacks in the luggage-van.

It was like all other expresses, as every express is and must be. It bore through the harvest country a smell like a large washing-day, and a sharp issue of steam as from a huge brazen tea-urn. The greatest power in nature and art combined, it yet glided over dangerous heights in the sight of people looking up from fields and roads, as smoothly and unreally as a light miniature plaything. Now, the engine shrieked in hysterics of such intensity, that it seemed desirable that the men who had her in charge should hold her feet, slap her hands, and bring her to; now, burrowed into tunnels with a stubborn and undemonstrative energy so confusing that the train seemed to be flying back into leagues of darkness. Here, were station after station, swallowed up by the express without stopping; here, stations where it fired itself in like a volley of cannon-balls, swooped away four country-people with nosegays, and three men of business with portmanteaus, and fired itself off again, bang, bang, bang! At long intervals were uncomfortable refreshment-rooms, made more uncomfortable by the scorn of Beauty towards Beast, the public (but to whom she never relented, as Beauty did in the story, towards the other Beast), and where sensitive stomachs were fed, with a contemptuous sharpness occasioning indigestion. Here, again, were stations with nothing going but a bell, and wonderful wooden razors set aloft on great posts, shaving the air. In these fields, the horses, sheep, and cattle were well used to the thundering meteor, and didn't mind; in those, they were all set scampering together, and a herd of pigs scoured after them. The pastoral country darkened, became coaly, became smoky, became infernal, got better, got worse, improved again, grew rugged, turned romantic; was a wood, a stream, a chain of hills, a gorge, a moor, a cathedral town, a fortified place, a waste. Now, miserable black dwellings, a black canal, and sick black towers of chimneys; now, a trim garden, where the flowers were bright and fair; now, a wilderness of hideous altars all ablaze; now, the water meadows with their fairy rings; now, the mangy patch of unlet building ground outside the stagnant town, with the larger ring where the Circus was last week. The temperature changed, the dialect changed, the people changed, faces got sharper, manner got shorter, eyes got shrewder and harder; yet all so quickly, that the spruce guard in the London uniform and silver lace, had not yet rumpled his shirt-collar, delivered half the dispatches in his shiny little pouch, or read his newspaper.

Carlisle! Idle and Goodchild had got to Carlisle. It looked congenially and delightfully idle. Something in the way of public amusement had happened last month, and something else was going to happen before Christmas; and, in the meantime there was a lecture on India for those who liked it—which Idle and Goodchild did not. Likewise, by those who liked them, there were impressions to be bought of all the vapid prints, going and gone, and of nearly all the vapid books. For those who wanted to put anything in missionary boxes, here were the boxes. For those who wanted the Reverend Mr. Podgers (artist's proofs, thirty shillings), here was Mr. Podgers to any amount. Not less gracious and abundant, Mr. Codgers also of the vineyard, but opposed to Mr. Podgers, brotherly tooth and nail. Here, were guide-books to the neighbouring antiquities, and eke the Lake country, in several dry and husky sorts; here, many physically and morally impossible heads of both sexes, for young ladies to copy, in the exercise of the art of drawing; here, further, a large impression of MR. SPURGEON, solid as to the flesh, not to say even something gross. The working young men of Carlisle were drawn up, with their hands in their pockets, across the pavements, four and six abreast, and appeared (much to the satisfaction of Mr. Idle) to have nothing else to do. The working and growing young women of Carlisle, from the age of twelve upwards, promenaded the streets in the cool of the evening, and rallied the said young men. Sometimes the young men rallied the young women, as in the case of a group gathered round an accordion-player, from among whom a young man advanced behind a young woman for whom he appeared to have a tenderness, and hinted to her that he was there and playful, by giving her (he wore clogs) a kick.

On market morning, Carlisle woke up amazingly, and became (to the two Idle Apprentices) disagreeably and reproachfully busy. There were its cattle market, its sheep market, and its pig market down by the river, with raw-boned and shock-headed Rob Roys hiding their Lowland dresses beneath heavy plaids, prowling in and out among the animals, and flavouring the air with fumes of whiskey. There was its corn market down the main street, with hum of chaffering over open sacks. There was its general market in the street too, with heather brooms on which the purple flower still flourished, and heather baskets primitive and fresh to behold. With women trying on clogs and caps at open stalls, and "Bible stalls" adjoining. With "Doctor Mantle's Dispensary for the cure of all Human Maladies and no charge for advice," and with Doctor Mantle's "Laboratory of Medical, Chemical, and Botanical Science"—both healing institutions established on one pair of trestles, one board, and one sun-blind. With the renowned phrenologist from London, begging to be favoured (at sixpence each) with the company of clients of both sexes, to whom, on examination of their heads, he would make revelations "enabling him or her to know themselves." Through all these bargains and blessings, the recruiting-sergeant watchfully elbowed his way, a thread of War in the peaceful skein. Likewise on the walls were printed hints that the Oxford Blues might not be indisposed to hear of a few fine active young men; and that whereas the standard of that distinguished corps is full six feet, "growing lads of five feet eleven" need not absolutely despair of being accepted.

Scenting the morning air more pleasantly than the buried majesty of Denmark did, Messrs. Idle and Goodchild rode away from Carlisle at eight o'clock one forenoon, bound for the village of Hesket,

Newmarket, some fourteen miles distant. Goodchild (who had already begun to doubt whether he was idle: as his way always is when he has nothing to do) had read of a certain black old Cumberland hill or mountain, called Carrock, or Carrock Fell; and had arrived at the conclusion that it would be the culminating triumph of Idleness to ascend the same. Thomas Idle, dwelling on the pains inseparable from that achievement, had expressed the strongest doubts of the expediency, and even of the sanity, of the enterprise; but Goodchild had carried his point, and they rode away.

Up hill and down hill, and twisting to the right, and twisting to the left, and with old Skiddaw (who has vaunted himself a great deal more than his merits deserve; but that is rather the way of the Lake country), dodging the apprentices in a picturesque and pleasant manner. Good, weather-proof, warm, pleasant houses, well white-limed, scantily dotting the road. Clean children coming out to look, carrying other clean children as big as themselves. Harvest still lying out and much rained upon; here and there, harvest still un-reaped. Well-cultivated gardens attached to the cottages, with plenty of produce forced out of their hard soil. Lonely nooks, and wild; but people can be born, and married, and buried in such nooks, and can live and love, and be loved, there as elsewhere, thank God! (Mr. Goodchild's remark.) By-and-by, the village. Black, coarse-stoned, rough-windowed houses; some with outer staircases, like Swiss houses; a sinuous and stony gutter winding up hill and round the corner, by the way of street. All the children running out directly. Women pausing in washing, to peep from doorways and very little windows. Such were the observations of Messrs. Idle and Goodchild, as their conveyance stopped at the village shoemaker's. Old Carrock gloomed down upon it all in a very ill-tempered state; and the rain was beginning.

The village shoemaker declined to have anything to do with Carrock. No visitors went up Carrock. No visitors came there at all. Aa' the world ganged awa' yon. The driver appealed to the Inn-keeper. The Innkeeper had two men working in the fields, and one of them should be called in, to go up Carrock as guide. Messrs. Idle and Goodchild, highly approving, entered the Innkeeper's house, to drink whiskey and eat oatcake.

The Innkeeper was not idle enough—was not idle at all, which was a great fault in him—but was a fine specimen of a north-countryman, or any kind of man. He had a ruddy cheek, a bright eye, a well-knit frame, an immense hand, a cheery outspeaking voice, and a straight, bright, broad look. He had a drawing-room, too, upstairs, which was worth a visit to the Cumberland Fells. (This was Mr. Francis Good-child's opinion, in which Mr. Thomas Idle did not concur.)

The ceiling of this drawing-room was so crossed and recrossed by beams of unequal lengths, radiating from a centre, in a corner, that it looked like a broken star-fish. The room was comfortably and solidly furnished with good mahogany and horsehair. It had a snug fireside, and a couple of well-curtained windows, looking out upon the wild country behind the house. What it most developed was, an unexpected taste for little ornaments and nick-nacks, of which it contained a most surprising number. They were not very various, consisting in great part of waxen babies with their limbs more or less mutilated, appealing on one leg to the parental affections from under little cupping glasses; but, Uncle Tom was there, in crockery, receiving theological instructions from Miss Eva, who grew out of his side like a wen, in an exceedingly rough state of profile propagandism. Engravings of Mr. Hunt's country boy, before and after his pie, were on the wall, divided by a highly-coloured nautical piece, the subject of which had all her colours (and more) flying, and was making great way through a sea of a regular pattern, like a lady's collar. A benevolent, elderly gentleman of the last century, with a powdered head, kept guard, in oil and varnish, over a most perplexing piece of furniture on a table; in appearance between a driving seat and an angular knife-box, but, when opened, a musical instrument of tinkling wires, exactly like David's harp packed for travelling. Everything became a nick-nack in this curious room. The copper tea-kettle, burnished up to the highest point of glory, took his station on a stand of his own at the greatest possible distance from the fireplace, and said: "By your leave, not a kettle, but a bijou." The Staffordshire-ware butter-dish with the cover on, got upon a little round occasional table in a window, with a worked top, and announced itself to the two chairs accidentally placed there, as an aid to polite conversation, a graceful trifle in china to be chatted over by callers, as they airily trifled away the visiting moments of a butterfly existence, in that rugged old village on the Cumberland Fells. The very footstool could not keep the floor, but got upon the sofa, and therefrom proclaimed itself, in high relief of white and liver-coloured wool, a favourite spaniel coiled up for repose. Though, truly, in spite of its bright glass eyes, the spaniel was the least successful assumption in the collection: being perfectly flat, and dismally suggestive of a recent mistake in sitting down on the part of some corpulent member of the family.

There were books, too, in this room; books on the table, books on the chimneypiece, books in an open press in the corner. Fielding was there, and Smollett was there, and Steele and Addison were there, in dispersed volumes; and there were tales of those who go down to the sea in ships, for windy nights; and there was really a choice of good books for rainy days or fine. It was so very pleasant to see these things in such a lonesome by-place—so very agreeable to find these evidences of a taste, however homely, that went beyond the beautiful cleanliness and trimness of the house—so fanciful to imagine what a wonder the room must be to the little children born in the gloomy village—what grand impressions of it those of them who became wanderers over the earth would carry away; and how, at distant ends of the world, some old voyagers would die, cherishing the belief that the finest apartment known to men was once in the Hesket-Newmarket Inn, in rare old Cumberland—it was such a charmingly lazy pursuit to entertain these rambling thoughts over the choice oatcake and the genial whiskey, that Mr. Idle and Mr. Goodchild never asked themselves how it came to pass that the men in the fields were never heard of more, how the stalwart landlord replaced them without explanation, how his dog-cart came to be waiting at the door, and how everything was arranged without the least arrangement for climbing to old Carrock's shoulders, and standing on his head.

Without a word of inquiry, therefore, the Two Idle Apprentices drifted out resignedly into a fine, soft, close, drowsy, penetrating rain; got into the landlord's light dog-cart, and rattled off through the village for the foot of Carrock. The journey at the outset was not remarkable. The Cumberland road went up and down like all other roads; the Cumberland curs burst out from backs of cottages and barked like other curs, and the Cumberland peasantry stared after the dog-cart amazedly, as long as it was in sight, like the rest of their race. The approach to the foot of the mountain resembled the approaches to the feet of most other mountains all over the world. The cultivation gradually ceased, the trees grew gradually rare, the road became gradually rougher, and the sides of the mountain looked gradually more and more lofty, and more and more difficult to get up. The dog-cart was left at a lonely farm-house. The landlord borrowed a large umbrella, and, assuming in an instant the character of the most cheerful and adventurous of guides, led the way to the ascent. Mr. Goodchild looked eagerly at the top of the mountain, and, feeling apparently that he was now going to be very lazy indeed, shone all over wonderfully to the eye, under the influence of the contentment within and the moisture without. Only in the bosom of Mr. Thomas Idle did Despondency now hold her gloomy state. He kept it a secret; but he would have given a very handsome sum, when the ascent began, to have been back again at the inn. The sides of Carrock looked fearfully steep, and the top of Carrock was hidden in mist. The rain was falling faster and faster. The knees of Mr. Idle—always weak on walking excursions—shivered and shook with fear and damp. The wet was already penetrating through the young man's outer coat to a brand-new shooting-jacket, for which he had reluctantly paid the large sum of two guineas on leaving town; he had no stimulating refreshment about him but a small packet of clammy gingerbread nuts; he had nobody to give him an arm, nobody to push him gently behind, nobody to pull him up tenderly in front, nobody to speak to who really felt the difficulties of the ascent, the dampness of the rain, the denseness of the mist, and the unutterable folly of climbing, undriven, up any steep place in the world, when there is level ground within reach to walk on instead. Was it for this that Thomas had left London? London, where there are nice short walks in level public gardens, with benches of repose set up at convenient distances for weary travellers—London, where rugged stone is humanely pounded into little lumps for the road, and intelligently shaped into smooth slabs for the pavement! No! it was not for the laborious ascent of the crags of Carrock that Idle had left his native city, and travelled to Cumberland. Never did he feel more disastrously convinced that he had committed a very grave error in judgment than when he found himself standing in the rain at the bottom of a steep mountain, and knew that the responsibility rested on his weak shoulders of actually getting to the top of it.

The honest landlord went first, the beaming Goodchild followed, the mournful Idle brought up the rear. From time to time, the two foremost members of the expedition changed places in the order of march; but the rearguard never altered his position. Up the mountain or down the mountain, in the water or out of it, over the rocks, through the bogs, skirting the heather, Mr. Thomas Idle was always the last, and was always the man who had to be looked after and waited for. At first the ascent was delusively easy, the sides of the mountain sloped gradually, and the material of which they were composed was a softy spongy turf, very tender and pleasant to walk upon. After a hundred yards or so, however, the verdant scene and the easy slope disappeared, and the rocks began. Not noble, massive rocks, standing upright, keeping a certain regularity in their positions, and possessing, now and then, flat tops to sit upon, but little irritating, comfortless rocks, littered about anyhow by Nature; treacherous, disheartening rocks of all sorts of small shapes and small sizes, bruisers of tender toes and trippers-up of wavering feet. When these impediments were passed heather and slough followed. Here the steepness of the ascent was slightly mitigated; and here the exploring party of three turned round to look at the view below them. The scene of the moorland and the fields was like a feeble water-colour drawing half sponged out. The mist was darkening, the rain was thickening, the trees were dotted about like spots of faint shadow, the division-lines which mapped out the fields were all getting blurred together, and the lonely farm-house where the dog-cart had been left, loomed spectral in the grey light like the last human dwelling at the end of the habitable world. Was this a sight worth climbing to see? Surely—surely not!

Up again—for the top of Carrock is not reached yet. The landlord just as good-tempered and obliging as he was at the bottom of the mountain. Mr. Goodchild brighter in the eyes and rosier in the face than ever; full of cheerful remarks and apt quotations; and walking with a springiness of step wonderful to behold. Mr. Idle, farther and farther in the rear, with the water squeaking in the toes of his boots, with his two-guinea shooting-jacket clinging damply to his aching sides, with his overcoat so full of rain, and standing out so pyramidically stiff, in consequence, from his shoulders downwards, that he felt as if he was walking in a gigantic extinguisher—the despairing spirit within him representing but too aptly the candle that had just been put out. Up and up and up again, till a ridge is reached and the outer edge of the mist on the summit of Carrock is darkly and drizzlingly near. Is this the top? No, nothing like the top. It is an aggravating peculiarity of all mountains, that, although they have only one top, when they are seen (as they ought always to be seen) from below, they turn out to have a perfect eruption of false tops whenever the traveller is sufficiently ill-advised to go out of his way for the purpose of ascending them. Carrock is but a trumpery little mountain of fifteen hundred feet, and it presumes to have false tops, and even precipices, as if it were Mont Blanc. No matter; Goodchild enjoys it, and will go on; and Idle, who is afraid of being left behind by himself, must follow. On entering the edge of the mist, the landlord stops, and says he hopes that it will not get any thicker. It is twenty years since he last ascended Carrock, and it is barely possible, if the mist increases, that the party may be lost on the mountain. Goodchild hears this dreadful intimation, and is not in the least impressed by it. He marches for the top that is never to be found, as if he was the Wandering Jew, bound to go on for ever, in defiance of everything. The landlord faithfully accompanies him. The two, to the dim eye of Idle, far below, look in the exaggerative mist, like a pair of friendly giants, mounting the steps of some invisible castle together. Up and up, and then down a little, and then up, and then along a strip of level ground, and then up again. The wind, a wind unknown in the happy valley, blows keen and strong; the rain-mist gets impenetrable; a dreary little cairn of stones appears. The landlord adds one to the heap, first walking all round the cairn as if he were about to perform an incantation, then dropping the stone on to the top of the heap with the gesture of a magician adding an ingredient to a cauldron in full bubble. Goodchild sits down by the cairn as if it was his study-table at home; Idle, drenched and panting, stands up with his back to the wind, ascertains distinctly that this is the top at last, looks round with all the little curiosity that is left in him, and gets, in return, a magnificent view of—Nothing!

The effect of this sublime spectacle on the minds of the exploring party is a little injured by the nature of the direct conclusion to which the sight of it points—the said conclusion being that the mountain mist has actually gathered round them, as the landlord feared it would. It now becomes imperatively necessary to settle the exact situation of the farm-house in the valley at which the dog-cart has been left, before the travellers attempt to descend. While the landlord is endeavouring to make this discovery in his own way, Mr. Goodchild plunges his hand under his wet coat, draws out a little red morocco-case, opens it, and displays to the view of his companions a neat pocket-compass. The north is found, the point at which the farm-house is situated is settled, and the descent begins. After a little downward walking, Idle (behind as usual) sees his fellow-travellers turn aside sharply—tries to follow them—loses them in the mist—is shouted after, waited for, recovered—and then finds that a halt has been ordered, partly on his account, partly for the purpose of again consulting the compass.

The point in debate is settled as before between Goodchild and the landlord, and the expedition moves on, not down the mountain, but marching straight forward round the slope of it. The difficulty of following this new route is acutely felt by Thomas Idle. He finds the hardship of walking at all greatly increased by the fatigue of moving his feet straight forward along the side of a slope, when their natural tendency, at every step, is to turn off at a right angle, and go straight down the declivity. Let the reader imagine himself to be walking along the roof of a barn, instead of up or down it, and he will have an exact idea of the pedestrian difficulty in which the travellers had now involved themselves. In ten minutes more Idle was lost in the distance again, was shouted for, waited for, recovered as before; found Goodchild repeating his observation of the compass, and remonstrated warmly against the sideway route that his companions persisted in following. It appeared to the uninstructed mind of Thomas that when three men want to get to the bottom of a mountain, their business is to walk down it; and he put this view of the case, not only with emphasis, but even with some irritability. He was answered from the scientific eminence of the compass on which his companions were mounted, that there was a frightful chasm somewhere near the foot of Carrock, called The Black Arches, into which the travellers were sure to march in the mist, if they risked continuing the descent from the place where they had now halted. Idle received this answer with the silent respect which was due to the commanders of the expedition, and followed along the roof of the barn, or rather the side of the mountain, reflecting upon the assurance which he received on starting again, that the object of the party was only to gain "a certain point," and, this haven attained, to continue the descent afterwards until the foot of Carrock was reached. Though quite unexceptionable as an abstract form of expression, the phrase "a certain point" has the disadvantage of sounding rather vaguely when it is pronounced on unknown ground, under a canopy of mist much thicker than a London fog. Nevertheless, after the compass, this phrase was all the clue the party had to hold by, and Idle clung to the extreme end of it as hopefully as he could.

More sideway walking, thicker and thicker mist, all sorts of points reached except the "certain point"; third loss of Idle, third shouts for him, third recovery of him, third consultation of compass. Mr. Goodchild draws it tenderly from his pocket, and prepares to adjust it on a stone. Something falls on the turf—it is the glass. Something else drops immediately after—it is the needle. The compass is broken, and the exploring party is lost!

It is the practice of the English portion of the human race to receive all great disasters in dead silence. Mr. Goodchild restored the useless compass to his pocket without saying a word, Mr. Idle looked at the landlord, and the landlord looked at Mr. Idle. There was nothing for it now but to go on blindfold, and trust to the chapter of chances. Accordingly, the lost travellers moved forward, still walking round the slope of the mountain, still desperately resolved to avoid the Black Arches, and to succeed in reaching the "certain point."

A quarter of an hour brought them to the brink of a ravine, at the bottom of which there flowed a muddy little stream. Here another halt was called, and another consultation took place. The landlord, still clinging pertinaciously to the idea of reaching the "point," voted for crossing the ravine, and going on round the slope of the mountain. Mr. Goodchild, to the great relief of his fellow-traveller, took another view of the case, and backed Mr. Idle's proposal to descend Carrock at once, at any hazard—the rather as the running stream was a sure guide to follow from the mountain to the valley. Accordingly, the party descended to the rugged and stony banks of the stream; and here again Thomas lost ground sadly, and fell far behind his travelling companions. Not much more than six weeks had elapsed since he had sprained one of his ankles, and he began to feel this same ankle getting rather weak when he found himself among the stones that were strewn about the running water. Goodchild and the landlord were getting farther and farther ahead of him. He saw them cross the stream and disappear round a projection on its banks. He heard them shout the moment after as a signal that they had halted and were waiting for him. Answering the shout, he mended his pace, crossed the stream where they had crossed it, and was within one step of the opposite bank, when his foot slipped on a wet stone, his weak ankle gave a twist outwards, a hot, rending, tearing pain ran through it at the same moment, and down fell the idlest of the Two Idle Apprentices, crippled in an instant.

The situation was now, in plain terms, one of absolute danger. There lay Mr. Idle writhing with pain, there was the mist as thick as ever, there was the landlord as completely lost as the strangers whom he was conducting, and there was the compass broken in Goodchild's pocket. To leave the wretched Thomas on unknown ground was plainly impossible; and to get him to walk with a badly sprained ankle seemed equally out of the question. However, Goodchild (brought back by his cry for help) bandaged the ankle with a pocket-handkerchief, and assisted by the landlord, raised the crippled Apprentice to his legs, offered him a shoulder to lean on, and exhorted him for the sake of the whole party to try if he could walk. Thomas, assisted by the shoulder on the one side, and a stick on the other, did try, with what pain and difficulty those only can imagine who have sprained an ankle and have had to tread on it afterwards. At a pace adapted to the feeble hobbling of a newly-lamed man, the lost party moved on, perfectly ignorant whether they were on the right side of the mountain or the wrong, and equally uncertain how long Idle would be able to contend with the pain in his ankle, before he gave in altogether and fell down again, unable to stir another step.

Slowly and more slowly, as the clog of crippled Thomas weighed heavily and more heavily on the march of the expedition, the lost travellers followed the windings of the stream, till they came to a faintly marked cart-track, branching off nearly at right angles, to the left. After a little consultation it was resolved to follow this dim vestige of a road in the hope that it might lead to a farm or cottage, at which Idle could be left in safety. It was now getting on towards the afternoon, and it was fast becoming more than doubtful whether the party, delayed in their progress as they now were, might not be overtaken by the darkness before the right route was found, and be condemned to pass the night on the mountain, without bit or drop to comfort them, in their wet clothes.

The cart-track grew fainter and fainter, until it was washed out altogether by another little stream, dark, turbulent, and rapid. The landlord suggested, judging by the colour of the water, that it must be flowing from one of the lead mines in the neighbourhood of Carrock; and the travellers accordingly kept by the stream for a little while, in the hope of possibly wandering towards help in that way. After walking forward about two hundred yards, they came upon a mine indeed, but a mine exhausted and abandoned; a dismal, ruinous place, with nothing but the wreck of its works and buildings left to speak for it. Here, there were a few sheep feeding. The landlord looked at them earnestly, thought he recognised the marks on them—then thought he did not—finally gave up the sheep in despair—and walked on just as ignorant of the whereabouts of the party as ever.

The march in the dark, literally as well as metaphorically in the dark, had now been continued for three-quarters of an hour from the time when the crippled Apprentice had met with his accident. Mr. Idle, with all the will to conquer the pain in his ankle, and to hobble on, found the power rapidly failing him, and felt that another ten minutes at most would find him at the end of his last physical resources. He had just made up his mind on this point, and was about to communicate the dismal result of his reflections to his companions, when the mist suddenly brightened, and begun to lift straight ahead. In another minute, the landlord, who was in advance, proclaimed that he saw a tree. Before long, other trees appeared—then a cottage —then a house beyond the cottage, and a familiar line of road rising behind it. Last of all, Carrock itself loomed darkly into view, far away to the right hand. The party had not only got down the mountain without knowing how, but had wandered away from it in the mist, without knowing why—away, far down on the very moor by which they had approached the base of Carrock that morning.

The happy lifting of the mist, and the still happier discovery that the travellers had groped their way; though by a very roundabout direction, to within a mile or so of the part of the valley in which the farm-house was situated, restored Mr. Idle's sinking spirits and reanimated his failing strength. While the landlord ran off to get the dog-cart, Thomas was assisted by Goodchild to the cottage which had been the first building seen when the darkness brightened, and was propped up against the garden wall, like an artist's lay figure waiting to be forwarded, until the dog-cart should arrive from the farm-house below. In due time—and a very long time it seemed to Mr. Idle—the rattle of wheels was heard, and the crippled Apprentice was lifted into the seat. As the dog-cart was driven back to the inn, the landlord related an anecdote which he had just heard at the farm-house, of an unhappy man who had been lost, like his two guests and himself, on Carrock: who had passed the night there alone;

who had been found the next morning, "scared and starved"; and who never went out afterwards, except on his way to the grave. Mr. Idle heard this sad story, and derived at least one useful impression from it. Bad as the pain in his ankle was, he contrived to bear it patiently, for he felt grateful that a worse accident had not befallen him in the wilds of Carrock.

CHAPTER II

THE dog-cart, with Mr. Thomas Idle and his ankle on the hanging seat behind, Mr. Francis Goodchild and the Innkeeper in front, and the rain in spouts and splashes everywhere, made the best of its way back to the little inn; the broken moor country looking like miles upon miles of Pre-Adamite sop, or the ruins of some enormous jorum of antediluvian toast-and-water. The trees dripped; the eaves of the scattered cottages dripped; the barren stone walls dividing the land, dripped; the yelping dogs dripped; carts and waggons under ill-roofed penthouses, dripped; melancholy cocks and hens perching on their shafts, or seeking shelter underneath them, dripped; Mr. Goodchild dripped; Thomas Idle dripped; the Innkeeper dripped; the mare dripped; the vast curtains of mist and cloud passed before the shadowy forms of the hills, streamed water as they were drawn across the landscape. Down such steep pitches that the mare seemed to be trotting on her head, and up such steep pitches that she seemed to have a supplementary leg in her tail, the dog-cart jolted and tilted back to the village. It was too wet for the women to look out, it was too wet even for the children to look out; all the doors and windows were closed, and the only sign of life or motion was in the rain-punctured puddles.

Whiskey and oil to Thomas Idle's ankle, and whiskey without oil to Francis Goodchild's stomach, produced an agreeable change in the systems of both; soothing Mr. Idle's pain, which was sharp before, and sweetening Mr. Goodchild's temper, which was sweet before. Portmanteaus being then opened and clothes changed, Mr. Goodchild, through having no change of outer garments but broadcloth and velvet, suddenly became a magnificent portent in the Innkeeper's house, a shining frontispiece to the fashions for the month, and a frightful anomaly in the Cumberland village.

Greatly ashamed of his splendid appearance, the conscious Goodchild quenched it as much as possible, in the shadow of Thomas Idle's ankle, and in a corner of the little covered carriage that started with them for Wigton—a most desirable carriage for any country, except for its having a flat roof and no sides; which caused the plumps of rain accumulating on the roof to play vigorous games of bagatelle into the interior all the way, and to score immensely. It was comfortable to see how the people coming back in open carts from Wigton market made no more of the rain than if it were sunshine; how the Wigton policeman taking a country walk of half-a-dozen miles (apparently for pleasure), in resplendent uniform, accepted saturation as his normal state; how clerks and schoolmasters in black, loitered along the road without umbrellas, getting varnished at every step; how the Cumberland girls, coming out to look after the Cumberland cows, shook the rain from their eyelashes and laughed it away; and how the rain continued to fall upon all, as it only does fall in hill countries.

Wigton market was over, and its bare booths were smoking with rain all down the street. Mr. Thomas Idle, melodramatically carried to the inn's first-floor, and laid upon three chairs (he should have had the sofa, if there had been one), Mr. Goodchild went to the window to take an observation of Wigton, and report what he saw to his disabled companion.

"Brother Francis, brother Francis," cried Thomas Idle. "What do you see from the turret?"

"I see," said Brother Francis, "what I hope and believe to be one of the most dismal places ever seen by eyes. I see the houses with their roofs of dull black, their stained fronts, and their dark-rimmed windows, looking as if they were all in mourning. As every little puff of wind comes down the street, I see a perfect train of rain let off along the wooden stalls in the market-place and exploded against me. I see a very big gas lamp in the centre which I know, by a secret instinct, will not be lighted to-night. I see a pump, with a trivet underneath its spout whereon to stand the vessels that are brought to be filled with water. I see a man come to pump, and he pumps very hard, but no water follows, and he strolls empty away."

"Brother Francis, brother Francis," cried Thomas Idle, "what more do you see from the turret, besides the man and the pump, and the trivet, and the houses all in mourning and the rain?"

"I see," said Brother Francis, "one, two, three, four, five, linen-drapers' shops in front of me. I see a linen-draper's shop next door to the right—and there are five more linen-drapers' shops down the corner to the left. Eleven homicidal linen-drapers' shops within a short stone's throw, each with its hands at the throats of all the rest! Over the small first-floor of one of these linen-drapers' shops appears the wonderful inscription, BANK."

"Brother Francis, brother Francis," cried Thomas Idle, "what more do you see from the turret, besides the eleven homicidal linen-drapers' shops, and the wonderful inscription, 'BANK,' on the small first-floor, and the man and the pump and the trivet and the houses all in mourning and the rain?"

"I see," said Brother Francis, "the depository for Christian Knowledge, and through the dark vapour I think I again make out Mr. Spurgeon looming heavily. Her Majesty the Queen, God bless her, printed in colours, I am sure I see. I see the *Illustrated London News* of several years ago, and I see a sweet-meat shop—which the proprietor calls a 'Salt Warehouse'—with one small female child in a cotton bonnet looking in on tiptoe, oblivious of rain. And I see a watchmaker's with only three great pale watches of a dull metal anging in his window, each in a separate pane."

"Brother Francis, brother Francis," cried Thomas Idle, "what more do you see of Wigton, besides these objects, and the man and the pump and the trivet and the houses all in mourning and the rain?"

"I see nothing more," said Brother Francis, "and there is nothing more to see, except the curlpaper bill of the theatre, which was opened and shut last week (the manager's family played all the parts), and the short, square, chinky omnibus that goes to the railway, and leads too rattling a life over the stones to hold together long. O yes! Now, I see two men with their hands in their pockets and their backs towards me."

"Brother Francis, brother Francis," cried Thomas Idle, "what do you make out from the turret, of the expression of the two men with their hands in their pockets and their backs towards you?"

"They are mysterious men," said Brother Francis, "with inscrutable backs. They keep their backs towards me with persistency. If one turns an inch in any direction, the other turns an inch in the same direction, and no more. They turn very stiffly, on a very little pivot, in the middle of the market-place. Their appearance is partly of a mining, partly of a ploughing, partly of a stable, character. They are looking at nothing—very hard. Their backs are slouched, and their legs are curved with much standing about. Their pockets are loose and dog's-eared, on account of their hands being always in them. They stand to be rained upon, without any movement of impatience or dissatisfaction, and they keep so close together that an elbow of each jostles an elbow of the other, but they never speak. They spit at times, but speak not. I see it growing darker and darker, and still I see them, sole visible population of the place, standing to be rained upon with their backs towards me, and looking at nothing very hard."

"Brother Francis, brother Francis," cried Thomas Idle, "before you draw down the blind of the turret and come in to have your head scorched by the hot gas, see if you can, and impart to me, something of the expression of those two amazing men."

"The murky shadows," said Francis Goodchild, "are gathering fast; and the wings of evening, and the wings of coal, are folding over Wigton. Still, they look at nothing very hard, with their backs towards me. Ah! Now, they turn, and I see——"

"Brother Francis, brother Francis," cried Thomas Idle, "tell me quickly what you see of the two men of Wigton!"

"I see," said Francis Goodchild, "that they have no expression at all. And now the town goes to sleep, undazzled by the large unlighted lamp in the market-place; and let no man wake it."

At the close of the next day's journey, Mr. Thomas Idle's ankle became much swollen and inflamed. There are reasons which will presently explain themselves for not publicly indicating the exact direction in which that journey lay, or the place in which it ended. It was a long day's shaking of Thomas Idle over the rough roads, and a long day's getting out and going on before the horses, and fagging up hills, and scouring down hills, on the part of Mr. Goodchild, who in the fatigues of such labours congratulated himself on attaining a high point of idleness. It was at a little town, still in Cumberland, that they halted for the night—a very little town, with the purple and brown moor close upon its one street; a curious little ancient market cross set up in the midst of it; and the town itself looking much as if it were a collection of great stones piled on end by the Druids long ago, which a few recluse people had since hollowed out for habitations

"Is there a doctor here?" asked Mr. Goodchild, on his knee, of the motherly landlady of the little Inn stopping in his examination of Mr. Idle's ankle, with the aid of a candle.

"Ey, my word!" said the landlady, glancing doubtfully at the ankle for herself; "there's Doctor Speddie."

"Is he a good Doctor?"

"Ey!" said the landlady, "I ca' him so. A' cooms efther nae doctor that I ken. Mair nor which, a's just THE doctor heer."

"Do you think he is at home?"

Her reply was, "Gang awa', Jock, and bring him."

Jock, a white-headed boy, who, under pretence of stirring up some bay salt in a basin of water for the laving of this unfortunate ankle had greatly enjoyed himself for the last ten minutes in splashing the carpet, set off promptly. A very few minutes had elapsed when he showed the Doctor in, by tumbling against the door before him and bursting it open with his head.

"Gently, Jock, gently," said the Doctor as he advanced with a quiet step. "Gentlemen, a good evening. I am sorry that my presence is required here. A slight accident, I hope? A slip and a fall? Yes, yes, yes. Carrock, indeed? Hah! Does that pain you, Sir? No doubt, it does. It is the great connecting ligament here, you see, that has been badly strained. Time and rest, Sir! They are often the recipe in greater cases," with a slight sigh, "and often the recipe in small. I can send a lotion to relieve you, but we must leave the cure to time and rest."

This he said, holding Idle's foot on his knee between his two hands, as he sat over against him. He had touched it tenderly and skilfully in explanation of what he said, and, when his careful examination was completed, softly returned it to its former horizontal position on a chair.

He spoke with a little irresolution whenever he began, but afterwards fluently. He was a tall, thin, large-boned, old gentleman, with an appearance at first sight of being hard-featured ; but, at a second glance, the mild expression of his face and some particular touches of sweetness and patience about his mouth, corrected this impression and assigned his long professional rides, by day and night, in the bleak hill-weather, as the true cause of that appearance. He stooped very little, though past seventy and very grey. His dress was more like that of a clergyman than a country doctor, being a plain black suit, and a plain white neck-kerchief tied behind like a band. His black was the worse for wear, and there were darns in his coat, and his linen was a little frayed at the hems and edges. He might have been poor—it was likely enough in that out-of-the-way spot—or he might have been a little self-forgetful and eccentric. Any one could have seen directly, that he had neither wife nor child at home. He had a scholarly air with him, and that kind of considerate humanity towards others which claimed a gentle consideration for himself. Mr. Goodchild made this study of him while he was examining the limb, and as he laid it down. Mr. Goodchild wishes to add that he considers it a very good likeness.

It came out in the course of a little conversation, that Doctor Speddie was acquainted with some friends of Thomas Idle's, and had, when a young man, passed some years in Thomas Idle's birthplace on the other side of England. Certain idle labours, the fruit of Mr. Goodchild's apprenticeship, also happened to be well known to him. The lazy travellers were thus placed on a more intimate footing with the Doctor than the casual circumstances of the meeting would of themselves have established; and when Doctor Speddie rose to go home, remarking that he would send his assistant with the lotion, Francis Goodchild said that was unnecessary, for, by the Doctor's leave, he would accompany him, and bring it back. (Having done nothing to fatigue himself for a full quarter of an hour, Francis began to fear that he was not in a state of idleness.)

Doctor Speddie politely assented to the proposition of Francis Goodchild, "as it would give him the pleasure of enjoying a few more minutes of Mr. Goodchild's society than he could otherwise have hoped for," and they went out together into the village street. The rain had nearly ceased, the clouds had broken before a cool wind from the north-east, and stars were shining from the peaceful heights beyond them.

Doctor Speddie's house was the last house in the place. Beyond it, lay the moor, all dark and lonesome. The wind moaned in a low, dull, shivering manner round the little garden, like a houseless creature that knew the winter was coming. It was exceedingly wild and solitary. "Roses," said the Doctor, when Goodchild touched some wet leaves overhanging the stone porch; "but they get cut to pieces."

The Doctor opened the door with a key he carried, and led the way into a low but pretty ample hall with rooms on either side. The door of one of these stood open, and the Doctor entered it, with a word of welcome to his guest. It, too, was a low room, half surgery and half parlour, with shelves of books and bottles against the walls, which were of a very dark hue. There was a fire in the grate, the night being damp and chill. Leaning against the chimneypiece looking down into it, stood the Doctor's Assistant.

A man of a most remarkable appearance. Much older than Mr. Goodchild had expected, for he was at least two-and-fifty; but, that was nothing. What was startling in him was his remarkable paleness. His large black eye, his sunken cheeks, his long and heavy iron-grey hair, his wasted hands, and even the attenuation of his figure, were at first forgotten in his extraordinary pallor. There was no vestige of colour in the man. When he turned his face, Francis Goodchild started as if a stone figure had looked round at him.

"Mr. Lorn," said the Doctor. "Mr. Goodchild."

The Assistant, in a distraught way—as if he had forgotten something—as if he had forgotten everything, even to his own name and himself—acknowledged the visitor's presence, and stepped further back into the shadow of the wall behind him. But, he was so pale that his face stood out in relief against the dark wall, and really could not be hidden so.

"Mr. Goodchild's friend has met with an accident, Lorn," said Doctor Speddie. "We want the lotion for a bad sprain."

A pause.

"My dear fellow, you are more than usually absent to-night. The lotion for a bad sprain."

"Ah! yes! Directly."

He was evidently relieved to turn away, and to take his white face and his wild eyes to a table in a recess among the bottles. But though he stood there, compounding the lotion with his back toward them, Goodchild could not, for many moments, withdraw his gaze from the man. When he at length did so, he found the Doctor observing him, with some trouble in his face. "He is absent," explained the Doctor, in a low voice. "Always absent. Very absent."

"Is he ill?"

"No, not ill."

"Unhappy?"

"I have my suspicions that he was," assented the Doctor, "once."

Francis Goodchild could not but observe that the Doctor accompanied these words with a benignant and protecting glance at their subject, in which there was much of the expression with which an attached father might have looked at a heavily afflicted son. Yet, that they were not father and son must have been plain to most eyes. The Assistant, on the other hand, turning presently to ask the Doctor some question, looked at him with a wan smile as if he were his whole reliance and sustainment in life.

It was in vain for the Doctor in his easy-chair, to try to lead the mind of Mr. Goodchild in the opposite easy-chair, away from what was before him. Let Mr. Goodchild do what he would to follow the Doctor, his eyes and thoughts reverted to the Assistant. The Doctor soon perceived it, and, after falling silent, and musing in a little perplexity, said:

"Lorn!"

"My dear Doctor."

"Would you go to the Inn, and apply that lotion? You will show the best way of applying it, far better than Mr. Goodchild can."

"With pleasure."

The Assistant took his hat, and passed like a shadow to the door.

"Lorn!" said the Doctor, calling after him.

He returned.

"Mr. Goodchild will keep me company till you come home. Don't hurry. Excuse my calling you back."

"It is not," said the Assistant, with his former smile, "the first time you have called me back, dear Doctor." With those words he went away.

"Mr. Goodchild," said Doctor Speddie, in a low voice, and with his former troubled expression of face, "I have seen that your attention has been concentrated on my friend."

"He fascinates me. I must apologise to you, but he has quite bewildered and mastered me."

"I find that a lonely existence and a long secret," said the Doctor, drawing his chair a little nearer to Mr. Goodchild's, "become in the course of time very heavy. I will tell you something. You may make what use you will of it, under fictitious names. I know I may trust you. I am the more inclined to confidence to-night, through having been unexpectedly led back, by the current of our conversation at the Inn, to scenes in my early life. Will you please to draw a little nearer?"

Mr. Goodchild drew a little nearer, and the Doctor went on thus: speaking, for the most part, in so cautious a voice, that the wind, though it was far from high, occasionally got the better of him.

When this present nineteenth century was younger by a good many years than it is now, a certain friend of mine, named Arthur Holliday, happened to arrive in the town of Doncaster, exactly in the middle of a race-week, or, in other words, in the middle of the month of September. He was one of those reckless, rattle-pated, open-hearted, and open-mouthed young gentlemen, who possess the gift of familiarity in its highest perfection, and who scramble carelessly along the journey of life making friends, as the phrase is, wherever they go. His father was a rich manufacturer, and had bought landed property enough in one of the midland counties to make all the born squires in his neighbourhood thoroughly envious of him. Arthur was his only son, possessor in prospect of the great estate and the great business after his father's death; well supplied with money, and not too rigidly looked after, during his father's lifetime. Report, or scandal, whichever you please, said that the old gentleman had been rather wild in his youthful days, and that, unlike most parents, he was not disposed to be violently indignant when he found that his son took after him. This may be true or not. I myself only knew the elder Mr. Holliday when he was getting on in years; and then he was as quiet and as respectable a gentleman as ever I met with.

Well, one September, as I told you, young Arthur comes to Doncaster, having decided all of a sudden, in his hare-brained way, that he would go to the races. He did not reach the town till towards the close of the evening, and he went at once to see about his dinner and bed at the principal hotel. Dinner they were ready enough to give him; but as for a bed, they laughed when he mentioned it. In the race-week at Doncaster, it is no uncommon thing for visitors who have not bespoken apartments, to pass the night in their carriages at the inn doors. As for the lower sort of strangers, I myself have often seen them, at that full time, sleeping out on the doorsteps for want of a covered place to creep under. Rich as he was, Arthur's chance of getting a night's lodging (seeing that he had not written beforehand to secure one) was more than doubtful. He tried the second hotel, and the third hotel, and two of the inferior inns after that; and was met everywhere by the same form of answer. No accommodation for the night of any sort was left. All the bright golden sovereigns in his pocket would not buy him a bed at Doncaster in the race-week.

To a young fellow of Arthur's temperament, the novelty of being turned away into the street, like a penniless vagabond, at every house where he asked for a lodging, presented itself in the light of a new and highly amusing piece of experience. He went on, with his carpet-bag in his hand, applying for a bed at every place of entertainment for travellers that he could find in Doncaster, until he wandered into he outskirts of the town. By this time, the last glimmer of twilight had faded out, the moon was rising dimly in a mist, the wind was getting cold, the clouds were gathering heavily, and there was every prospect that it was soon going to rain.

The look of the night had rather a lowering effect on young Holliday's good spirits. He began to contemplate the houseless situation in which he was placed, from the serious rather than the humorous point of view; and he looked about him, for another public-house to inquire at, with something very like downright anxiety in his mind on the subject of a lodging for the night. The suburban part of the town towards which he had now strayed was hardly lighted at all, and he could see nothing of the houses as he passed them, except that they got progressively smaller and dirtier, the farther he went. Down the winding road before him shone the dull gleam of an oil lamp, the one faint, lonely light that struggled ineffectually with the foggy darkness all round him. He resolved to go on as far as this lamp, and then, if it showed him nothing in the shape of an Inn, to return to the central part of the town and to try if he could not at least secure a chair to sit down on, through the night, at one of the principal Hotels.

As he got near the lamp, he heard voices; and, walking close under it, found that it lighted the entrance to a narrow court, on the wall of which was painted a long hand in faded flesh-colour, pointing with a lean forefinger, to this inscription :—

THE TWO ROBINS

Arthur turned into the court without hesitation, to see what The Two Robins could do for him. Four or five men were standing together round the door of the house which was at the bottom of the court, facing the entrance from the street. The men were all listening to one other man, better dressed than the rest, who was telling his audience something, in a low voice, in which they were apparently very much interested.

On entering the passage, Arthur was passed by a stranger with a knapsack in his hand, who was evidently leaving the house.

"No," said the traveller with the knapsack, turning round and addressing himself cheerfully to a fat, sly-looking, bald-headed man, with a dirty white apron on, who had followed him down the passage. "No, Mr. Landlord, I am not easily scared by trifles; but, I don't mind confessing that I can't quite stand *that*."

It occurred to young Holliday, the moment he heard these words, that the stranger had been asked an exorbitant price for a bed at The Two Robins; and that he was unable or unwilling to pay it. The moment his back was turned, Arthur, comfortably conscious of his own well-filled pockets, addressed himself in a great hurry, for fear any other benighted traveller should slip in and forestall him, to the sly-looking landlord with the dirty apron and the bald head.

"If you have got a bed to let," he said, "and if that gentleman who has just gone out won't pay your price for it, I will."

The sly landlord looked hard at Arthur.

"Will you, Sir?" he asked, in a meditative, doubtful way.

"Name your price," said young Holliday, thinking that the landlord's hesitation sprang from some boorish distrust of him. "Name your price, and I'll give you the money at once if you like?"

"Are you game for five shillings?" inquired the landlord, rubbing his stubby double chin, and looking up thoughtfully at the ceiling above him.

Arthur nearly laughed in the man's face; but thinking it prudent to control himself, offered the five shillings as seriously as he could. The sly landlord held out his hand, then suddenly drew it back again.

"You're acting all fair and above-board by me," he said: "and, before I take your money, I'll do the same by you. Look here, this is how it stands. You can have a bed all to yourself for five shillings but you can't have more than a half-share of the room it stands in. Do you see what I mean, young gentleman?"

"Of course I do," returned Arthur, a little irritably. "You mean that it is a double-bedded room, and that one of the beds is occupied?"

The landlord nodded his head, and rubbed his double chin harder than ever. Arthur hesitated, and mechanically moved back a step or two towards the door. The idea of sleeping in the same room with a total stranger, did not present an attractive prospect to him. He felt more than half inclined to drop his five shillings into his pocket, and to go out into the street once more.

"Is it yes, or no?" asked the landlord. "Settle it as quick as you can, because there's lots of people wanting a bed at Doncaster to-night, besides you."

Arthur looked towards the court, and heard the rain falling heavily in the street outside. He thought he would ask a question or two before he rashly decided on leaving the shelter of The Two Robins.

"What sort of a man is it who has got the other bed?" he inquired. "Is he a gentleman? I mean, is he a quiet, well-behaved person?"

"The quietest man I ever came across," said the landlord, rubbin
his fat hands stealthily one over the other. "As sober as a judge, an
as regular as clock-work in his habits. It hasn't struck nine, not te
minutes ago, and he's in his bed already. I don't know whether tha
comes up to your notion of a quiet man: it goes a long way ahead c
mine, I can tell you."

"Is he asleep, do you think?" asked Arthur.

"I know he's asleep," returned the landlord. "And what's more
he's gone off so fast, that I'll warrant you don't wake him. This way
Sir," said the landlord, speaking over young Holliday's shoulder, a
if he was addressing some new guest who was approaching the house

"Here you are," said Arthur, determined to be beforehand wit
the stranger, whoever he might be. "I'll take the bed." And h
handed the five shillings to the landlord, who nodded, dropped th
money carelessly into his waistcoat pocket, and lighted the candle

"Come up and see the room," said the host of The Two Robin
leading the way to the staircase quite briskly, considering how fa
he was.

They mounted to the second-floor of the house. The landlord ha
opened a door, fronting the landing, then stopped, and turned roun
to Arthur.

"It's a fair bargain, mind, on my side as well as on yours," he sai
"You give me five shillings, I give you in return a clean, comfortabl
bed; and I warrant, beforehand, that you won't be interfered with
or annoyed in any way, by the man who sleeps in the same room a
you." Saying those words, he looked hard, for a moment, in youn
Holliday's face, and then led the way into the room.

It was larger and cleaner than Arthur had expected it would be
The two beds stood parallel with each other—a space of about si
feet intervening between them. They were both of the same mediun
size, and both had the same plain white curtains, made to draw, i
necessary, all round them. The occupied bed was the bed nearest th
window. The curtains were all drawn round this, except the hal
curtain at the bottom, on the side of the bed farthest from th
window. Arthur saw the feet of the sleeping man raising the scant
clothes into a sharp little eminence, as if he was lying flat on his back
He took the candle, and advanced softly to draw the curtain—
stopped half-way, and listened for a moment—then turned to th
landlord.

"He's a very quiet sleeper," said Arthur.

"Yes," said the landlord, "very quiet."

Young Holliday advanced with the candle, and looked in at th
man cautiously.

"How pale he is!" said Arthur.

"Yes," returned the landlord, "pale enough, isn't he?"

Arthur looked closer at the man. The bedclothes were drawn up t
his chin, and they lay perfectly still over the region of his chest
Surprised and vaguely startled, as he noticed this, Arthur stoope
down closer over the stranger; looked at his ashy, parted lips

listened breathlessly for an instant; looked again at the strangely still face, and the motionless lips and chest; and turned round suddenly on the landlord, with his own cheeks as pale for the moment as the hollow cheeks of the man on the bed.

"Come here," he whispered, under his breath. "Come here, for God's sake! The man's not asleep—he is dead!"

"You have found that out sooner than I thought you would," said the landlord, composedly. "Yes, he's dead, sure enough. He died at five o'clock to-day."

"How did he die? Who is he?" asked Arthur, staggered, for a moment, by the audacious coolness of the answer.

"As to who is he," rejoined the landlord, "I know no more about him than you do. There are his books and letters and things, all sealed up in that brown-paper parcel, for the Coroner's inquest to open to-morrow or next day. He's been here a week, paying his way fairly enough, and stopping in-doors, for the most part, as if he was ailing. My girl brought him up his tea at five to-day; and as he was pouring of it out, he fell down in a faint, or a fit, or a compound of both, for anything I know. We could not bring him to—and I said he was dead. And the doctor couldn't bring him to—and the doctor said he was dead. And there he is. And the Coroner's inquest's coming as soon as it can. And that's as much as I know about it."

Arthur held the candle close to the man's lips. The flame still burnt straight up, as steadily as before. There was a moment of silence; and the rain pattered drearily through it against the panes of the window.

"If you haven't got nothing more to say to me," continued the landlord, "I suppose I may go. You don't expect your five shillings back, do you? There's the bed I promised you, clean and comfortable. There's the man I warranted not to disturb you, quiet in this world for ever. If you're frightened to stop alone with him, that's not my look out. I've kept my part of the bargain, and I mean to keep the money. I'm not Yorkshire, myself, young gentleman; but I've lived long enough in these parts to have my wits sharpened; and I shouldn't wonder if you found out the way to brighten up yours, next time you come amongst us." With these words, the landlord turned towards the door, and laughed to himself softly, in high satisfaction at his own sharpness.

Startled and shocked as he was, Arthur had by this time sufficiently recovered himself to feel indignant at the trick that had been played on him, and at the insolent manner in which the landlord exulted in it.

"Don't laugh," he said sharply, "till you are quite sure you have got the laugh against me. You shan't have the five shillings for nothing, my man. I'll keep the bed."

"Will you?" said the landlord. "Then I wish you a good night's rest." With that brief farewell, he went out, and shut the door after him.

A good night's rest! The words had hardly been spoken, the door had hardly been closed, before Arthur half-repented the hasty words that had just escaped him. Though not naturally over-sensitive, and not wanting in courage of the moral as well as the physical sort, the presence of the dead man had an instantaneously chilling effect on his mind when he found himself alone in the room—alone, and bound by his own rash words to stay there till the next morning. An older man would have thought nothing of those words, and would have acted, without reference to them, as his calmer sense suggested. But Arthur was too young to treat the ridicule, even of his inferiors, with contempt—too young not to fear the momentary humiliation of falsifying his own foolish boast, more than he feared the trial of watching out the long night in the same chamber with the dead.

"It is but a few hours," he thought to himself, "and I can get away the first thing in the morning."

He was looking towards the occupied bed as that idea passed through his mind, and the sharp angular eminence made in the clothes by the dead man's upturned feet again caught his eye. He advanced and drew the curtains, purposely abstaining, as he did so, from looking at the face of the corpse, lest he might unnerve himself at the outset by fastening some ghastly impression of it on his mind. He drew the curtain very gently, and sighed involuntarily as he closed it. "Poor fellow," he said, almost as sadly as if he had known the man. "Ah, poor fellow!"

He went next to the window. The night was black, and he could see nothing from it. The rain still pattered heavily against the glass. He inferred, from hearing it, that the window was at the back of the house; remembering that the front was sheltered from the weather by the court and the buildings over it.

While he was still standing at the window—for even the dreary rain was a relief, because of the sound it made; a relief, also, because it moved, and had some faint suggestion, in consequence, of life and companionship in it—while he was standing at the window, and looking vacantly into the black darkness outside, he heard a distant church-clock strike ten. Only ten! How was he to pass the time till the house was astir the next morning?

Under any other circumstances, he would have gone down to the public-house parlour, would have called for his grog, and would have laughed and talked with the company assembled as familiarly as if he had known them all his life. But the very thought of whiling away the time in this manner was distasteful to him. The new situation in which he was placed seemed to have altered him to himself already. Thus far, his life had been the common, trifling, prosaic, surface-life of a prosperous young man, with no troubles to conquer, and no trials to face. He had lost no relation whom he loved, no friend whom he treasured. Till this night, what share he had of the immortal inheritance that is divided amongst us all, had laid dormant within him. Till this night, Death and he had not once met, even in thought.

He took a few turns up and down the room—then stopped. The noise made by his boots on the poorly carpeted floor, jarred on his ear. He hesitated a little, and ended by taking the boots off, and walking backwards and forwards noiselessly. All desire to sleep or to rest had left him. The bare thought of lying down on the unoccupied bed instantly drew the picture on his mind of a dreadful mimicry of the position of the dead man. Who was he? What was the story of his past life? Poor he must have been, or he would not have stopped at such a place as The Two Robins Inn—and weakened, probably, by long illness, or he could hardly have died in the manner in which the landlord had described. Poor, ill, lonely,—dead in a strange place; dead, with nobody but a stranger to pity him. A sad story: truly, on the mere face of it, a very sad story.

While these thoughts were passing through his mind, he had stopped insensibly at the window, close to which stood the foot of the bed with the closed curtains. At first he looked at it absently; then he became conscious that his eyes were fixed on it; and then, a perverse desire took possession of him to do the very thing which he had resolved not to do, up to this time—to look at the dead man.

He stretched out his hand towards the curtains; but checked himself in the very act of undrawing them, turned his back sharply on the bed, and walked towards the chimneypiece, to see what things were placed on it, and to try if he could keep the dead man out of his mind in that way.

There was a pewter inkstand on the chimneypiece, with some mildewed remains of ink in the bottle. There were two coarse china ornaments of the commonest kind; and there was a square of embossed card, dirty and fly-blown, with a collection of wretched riddles printed on it, in all sorts of zigzag directions, and in variously coloured inks. He took the card, and went away, to read it, to the table on which the candle was placed; sitting down, with his back resolutely turned to the curtained bed.

He read the first riddle, the second, the third, all in one corner of the card—then turned it round impatiently to look at another. Before he could begin reading the riddles printed here, the sound of the church-clock stopped him. Eleven. He had got through an hour of the time, in the room with the dead man.

Once more he looked at the card. It was not easy to make out the letters printed on it, in consequence of the dimness of the light which the landlord had left him—a common tallow candle, furnished with a pair of heavy old-fashioned steel snuffers. Up to this time, his mind had been too much occupied to think of the light. He had left the wick of the candle unsnuffed, till it had risen higher than the flame, and had burnt into an odd penthouse shape at the top, from which morsels of the charred cotton fell off, from time to time, in little flakes. He took up the snuffers now, and trimmed the wick. The light brightened directly, and the room became less dismal.

Again he turned to the riddles; reading them doggedly and resolutely, now in one corner of the card, now in another. All his efforts, however, could not fix his attention on them. He pursued his occupation mechanically, deriving no sort of impression from what he was reading. It was as if a shadow from the curtained bed had got between his mind and the gaily printed letters—a shadow that nothing could dispel. At last, he gave up the struggle, and threw the card from him impatiently, and took to walking softly up and down the room again.

The dead man, the dead man, the *hidden* dead man on the bed! There was the one persistent idea still haunting him. Hidden? Was it only the body being there, or was it the body being there, concealed, that was preying on his mind? He stopped at the window, with that doubt in him; once more listening to the pattering rain, once more looking out into the black darkness.

Still the dead man! The darkness forced his mind back upon itself, and set his memory at work, reviving, with a painfully-vivid distinctness, the momentary impression it had received from the first sight of the corpse. Before long the face seemed to be hovering out in the middle of the darkness, confronting him through the window, with the paleness whiter, with the dreadful dull line of light between the imperfectly-closed eyelids broader than he had seen it—with the parted lips slowly dropping farther and farther away from each other—with the features growing larger and moving closer, till they seemed to fill the window and to silence the rain, and to shut out the night.

The sound of a voice, shouting below-stairs, woke him suddenly from the dream of his own distempered fancy. He recognised it as the voice of the landlord. "Shut up at twelve, Ben," he heard it say. "I'm off to bed."

He wiped away the damp that had gathered on his forehead, reasoned with himself for a little while, and resolved to shake his mind free of the ghastly counterfeit which still clung to it, by forcing himself to confront, if it was only for a moment, the solemn reality. Without allowing himself an instant to hesitate, he parted the curtains at the foot of the bed, and looked through.

There was a sad, peaceful, white face, with the awful mystery of stillness on it, laid back upon the pillow. No stir, no change there! He only looked at it for a moment before he closed the curtains again—but that moment steadied him, calmed him, restored him—mind and body—to himself.

He returned to his old occupation of walking up and down the room; persevering in it, this time, till the clock struck again. Twelve.

As the sound of the clock-bell died away, it was succeeded by the confused noise, downstairs, of the drinkers in the tap-room leaving the house. The next sound, after an interval of silence, was caused by the barring of the door, and the closing of the shutters, at the back of the Inn. Then the silence followed again, and was disturbed no more.

He was alone now—absolutely, utterly, alone with the dead man, till the next morning.

The wick of the candle wanted trimming again. He took up the snuffers—but paused suddenly on the very point of using them, and

looked attentively at the candle—then back, over his shoulder, at the
curtained bed—then again at the candle. It had been lighted, for the
first time, to show him the way upstairs, and three parts of it, at
least, were already consumed. In another hour it would be burnt out.
In another hour—unless he called at once to the man who had shut
up the Inn, for a fresh candle—he would be left in the dark.

Strongly as his mind had been affected since he had entered his
room, his unreasonable dread of encountering ridicule, and of exposing his courage to suspicion, had not altogether lost its influence over
him, even yet. He lingered irresolutely by the table, waiting till he
could prevail on himself to open the door, and call, from the landing
to the man who had shut up the Inn. In his present hesitating frame
of mind, it was a kind of relief to gain a few moments only by engaging in the trifling occupation of snuffing the candle. His hand trembled a little, and the snuffers were heavy and awkward to use. When
he closed them on the wick, he closed them a hair's breadth too low.
In an instant the candle was out, and the room was plunged in pitch
darkness.

The one impression which the absence of light immediately produced on his mind, was distrust of the curtained bed—distrust which
shaped itself into no distinct idea, but which was powerful enough, in
its very vagueness, to bind him down to his chair, to make his heart
beat fast, and to set him listening intently. No sound stirred in the
room but the familiar sound of the rain against the window, louder
and sharper now than he had heard it yet.

Still the vague distrust, the inexpressible dread possessed him, and
kept him to his chair. He had put his carpet-bag on the table, when he
first entered the room; and he now took the key from his pocket,
reached out his hand softly, opened the bag, and groped in it for his
travelling writing-case, in which he knew that there was a small store
of matches. When he had got one of the matches, he waited before
he struck it on the coarse wooden table, and listened intently again,
without knowing why. Still there was no sound in the room but the
steady, ceaseless, rattling sound of the rain.

He lighted the candle again, without another moment of delay,
and, on the instant of its burning up, the first object in the room that
his eyes sought for was the curtained bed.

Just before the light had been put out, he had looked in that direction, and had seen no change, no disarrangement of any sort, in the
folds of the closely-drawn curtains.

When he looked at the bed now, he saw, hanging over the side of it,
a long white hand.

It lay perfectly motionless, midway on the side of the bed, where
the curtain at the head and the curtain at the foot met. Nothing more
was visible. The clinging curtains hid everything but the long white
hand.

He stood looking at it unable to stir, unable to call out; feeling
nothing, knowing nothing, every faculty he possessed gathered up
and lost in the one seeing faculty. How long that first panic held him

he never could tell afterwards. It might have been only for a moment; it might have been for many minutes together. How he got to the bed—whether he ran to it headlong, or whether he approached it slowly—how he wrought himself up to unclose the curtains and look in, he never has remembered, and never will remember to his dying day. It is enough that he did go to the bed, and that he did look inside the curtains.

The man had moved. One of his arms was outside the clothes; his face was turned a little on the pillow; his eyelids were wide open. Changed as to position, and as to one of the features, the face was, otherwise, fearfully and wonderfully unaltered. The dead paleness and the dead quiet were on it still.

One glance showed Arthur this—one glance, before he flew breathlessly to the door, and alarmed the house.

The man whom the landlord called "Ben," was the first to appear on the stairs. In three words, Arthur told him what had happened, and sent him for the nearest doctor.

I, who tell you this story, was then staying with a medical friend of mine, in practice at Doncaster, taking care of his patients for him, during his absence in London; and I, for the time being, was the nearest doctor. They had sent for me from the Inn, when the stranger was taken ill in the afternoon; but I was not at home, and medical assistance was sought for elsewhere. When the man from The Two Robins rang the night-bell, I was just thinking of going to bed. Naturally enough, I did not believe a word of his story about "a dead man who had come to life again." However, I put on my hat, armed myself with one or two bottles of restorative medicine, and ran to the Inn, expecting to find nothing more remarkable, when I got there, than a patient in a fit.

My surprise at finding that the man had spoken the literal truth was almost, if not quite, equalled by my astonishment at finding myself face to face with Arthur Holliday as soon as I entered the bedroom. It was no time then for giving or seeking explanations. We just shook hands amazedly; and then I ordered everybody but Arthur out of the room, and hurried to the man on the bed.

The kitchen fire had not been long out. There was plenty of hot water in the boiler, and plenty of flannel to be had. With these, with my medicines, and with such help as Arthur could render under my direction, I dragged the man, literally, out of the jaws of death. In less than an hour from the time when I had been called in, he was alive and talking in the bed on which he had been laid out to wait for the Coroner's inquest.

You will naturally ask me, what had been the matter with him; and I might treat you, in reply, to a long theory, plentifully sprinkled with, what the children call, hard words. I prefer telling you that, in this case, cause and effect could not be satisfactorily joined together by any theory whatever. There are mysteries in life, and the condition of it, which human science has not fathomed yet; and I candidly confess to you, that, in bringing that man back to existence, I was, morally speaking, groping hap-hazard in the dark. I know (from the testimony of the doctor who attended him in the afternoon) that the vital machinery, so far as its action is appreciable by our senses, had, in this case, unquestionably stopped; and I am equally certain (seeing that I recovered him) that the vital principle was not extinct. When I add, that he had suffered from a long and complicated illness, and that his whole nervous system was utterly deranged, I have told you all I really know of the physical condition of my dead-alive patient at The Two Robins Inn.

When he "came to," as the phrase goes, he was a startling object to look at, with his colourless face, his sunken cheeks, his wild black eyes, and his long black hair. The first question he asked me about himself, when he could speak, made me suspect that I had been called in to a man in my own profession. I mentioned to him my surmise; and he told me that I was right.

He said he had come last from Paris, where he had been attached to a hospital. That he had lately returned to England, on his way to Edinburgh, to continue his studies; that he had been taken ill on the journey; and that he had stopped to rest and recover himself at Don-caster. He did not add a word about his name, or who he was: and, of course, I did not question him on the subject. All I inquired, when he ceased speaking, was what branch of the profession he intended to follow.

"Any branch," he said, bitterly, "which will put bread into the mouth of a poor man."

At this, Arthur, who had been hitherto watching him in silent curiosity, burst out impetuously in his usual good-humoured way:—

"My dear fellow!" (everybody was "my dear fellow" with Arthur) "now you have come to life again, don't begin by being downhearted about your prospects. I'll answer for it, I can help you to some capital thing in the medical line—or, if I can't, I know my father can."

The medical student looked at him steadily.

"Thank you," he said, coldly. Then added, "May I ask who your father is?"

"He's well enough known all about this part of the country," replied Arthur. "He is a great manufacturer, and his name is Holli-day."

My hand was on the man's wrist during this brief conversation. The instant the name of Holliday was pronounced I felt the pulse under my fingers flutter, stop, go on suddenly with a bound, and beat afterwards, for a minute or two, at the fever rate.

"How did you come here?" asked the stranger, quickly, excitably, passionately almost.

Arthur related briefly what had happened from the time of his first taking the bed at the inn.

"I am indebted to Mr. Holliday's son then for the help that has saved my life," said the medical student, speaking to himself, with a singular sarcasm in his voice. "Come here!"

He held out, as he spoke, his long, white, bony, right hand.

"With all my heart," said Arthur, taking the hand cordially. "I may confess it now," he continued, laughing. "Upon my honour, you almost frightened me out of my wits."

The stranger did not seem to listen. His wild black eyes were fixed with a look of eager interest on Arthur's face, and his long bony fingers kept tight hold of Arthur's hand. Young Holliday, on his side, returned the gaze, amazed and puzzled by the medical student's odd language and manners. The two faces were close together; I looked at them; and, to my amazement, I was suddenly impressed by the sense of a likeness between them—not in features, or complexion, but solely in expression. It must have been a strong likeness, or I should certainly not have found it out, for I am naturally slow at detecting resemblances between faces.

"You have saved my life," said the strange man, still looking hard in Arthur's face, still holding tightly by his hand. "If you had been my own brother, you could not have done more for me than that."

He laid a singularly strong emphasis on those three words "my own brother," and a change passed over his face as he pronounced them,—a change that no language of mine is competent to describe.

"I hope I have not done being of service to you yet," said Arthur. "I'll speak to my father, as soon as I get home."

"You seem to be fond and proud of your father," said the medical student. "I suppose, in return, he is fond and proud of you?"

"Of course, he is!" answered Arthur, laughing. "Is there anything wonderful in that? Isn't *your* father fond——"

The stranger suddenly dropped young Holliday's hand, and turned his face away.

"I beg your pardon," said Arthur. "I hope I have not unintentionally pained you. I hope you have not lost your father."

"I can't well lose what I have never had," retorted the medical student, with a harsh mocking laugh.

"What you have never had!"

The strange man suddenly caught Arthur's hand again, suddenly looked once more hard in his face.

"Yes," he said, with a repetition of the bitter laugh. "You have brought a poor devil back into the world, who has no business here. Do I astonish you? Well! I have a fancy of my own for telling you what men in my situation generally keep a secret. I have no name and no father. The merciful law of Society tells me I am Nobody's Son! Ask your father if he will be my father too, and help me on in life with the family name."

Arthur looked at me, more puzzled than ever. I signed to him to say nothing, and then laid my fingers again on the man's wrist. No! In spite of the extraordinary speech that he had just made, he was not, as I had been disposed to suspect, beginning to ge light-headed. His pulse, by this time, had fallen back to a quiet, slow beat, and his skin was moist and cool. Not a symptom of fever or agitation about him.

Finding that neither of us answered him, he turned to me, and began talking of the extraordinary nature of his case, and asking my advice about the future course of medical treatment to which he ought to subject himself. I said the matter required careful thinking over, and suggested that I should submit certain prescriptions to him the next morning. He told me to write them at once, as he would, most likely, be leaving Doncaster, in the morning, before I was up. It was quite useless to represent to him the folly and danger of such a proceeding as this. He heard me politely and patiently, but held to his resolution, without offering any reasons or any explanations, and repeated to me, that if I wished to give him a chance of seeing my prescription, I must write it at once. Hearing this, Arthur volunteered the loan of a travelling writing-case, which, he said, he had with him; and, bringing it to the bed, shook the note-paper out of the pocket of the case forthwith in his usual careless way. With the paper, there fell out on the counterpane of the bed a small packet of sticking-plaster, and a little water-colour drawing of a landscape.

The medical student took up the drawing and looked at it. His eye fell on some initials neatly written, in cypher, in one corner. He started and trembled; his pale face grew whiter than ever; his wild black eyes turned on Arthur, and looked through and through him.

"A pretty drawing," he said in a remarkably quiet tone of voice.

"Ah! and done by such a pretty girl," said Arthur. "Oh, such a pretty girl! I wish it was not a landscape—I wish it was a portrait of her!"

"You admire her very much?"

Arthur, half in jest, half in earnest, kissed his hand for answer.

"Love at first sight," he said, putting the drawing away again. "But the course of it doesn't run smooth. It's the old story. She's monopolised as usual. Trammelled by a rash engagement to some poor man who is never likely to get money enough to marry her. It was lucky I heard of it in time, or I should certainly have risked a declaration when she gave me that drawing. Here, doctor! Here is pen, ink, and paper all ready for you."

"When she gave you that drawing? Gave it. Gave it." He repeated the words slowly to himself, and suddenly closed his eyes. A momentary distortion passed across his face, and I saw one of his hands clutch up the bedclothes and squeeze them hard. I thought he was going to be ill again, and begged that there might be no more talking. He opened his eyes when I spoke, fixed them once more searchingly on Arthur, and said, slowly and distinctly, "You like her, and she likes you. The poor man may die out of your way. Who can tell that she may not give you herself as well as her drawing, after all?"

Before young Holliday could answer, he turned to me, and said in a whisper, "Now for the prescription." From that time, though he spoke to Arthur again, he never looked at him more.

When I had written the prescription, he examined it, approved of it, and then astonished us both by abruptly wishing us good night. I offered to sit up with him, and he shook his head. Arthur offered to sit up with him, and he said, shortly, with his face turned away, "No."

I insisted on having somebody left to watch him. He gave way when he found I was determined, and said he would accept the services of the waiter at the Inn.

"Thank you, both," he said, as we rose to go. "I have one last favour to ask—not of you, doctor, for I leave you to exercise your professional discretion—but of Mr. Holliday." His eyes, while he spoke, still rested steadily on me, and never once turned towards Arthur. "I beg that Mr. Holliday will not mention to any one—least of all to his father—the events that have occurred, and the words that have passed, in this room. I entreat him to bury me in his memory, as, but for him, I might have been buried in my grave. I cannot give my reasons for making this strange request. I can only implore him to grant it."

His voice faltered for the first time, and he hid his face on the pillow. Arthur, completely bewildered, gave the required pledge. I took young Holliday away with me, immediately afterwards, to the house of my friend; determining to go back to the Inn, and to see the medical student again before he had left in the morning.

I returned to the inn at eight o'clock, purposely abstaining from waking Arthur, who was sleeping off the past night's excitement on one of my friend's sofas. A suspicion had occurred to me as soon as I was alone in my bedroom, which made me resolve that Holliday and the stranger whose life he had saved should not meet again, if I could prevent it. I have already alluded to certain reports, or scandals, which I knew of, relating to the early life of Arthur's father. While I was thinking, in my bed, of what had passed at the Inn—of the change in the student's pulse when he heard the name of Holliday: of the resemblance of expression that I had discovered between his face and Arthur's, of the emphasis he had laid on those three words, "my own brother"; and of his incomprehensible acknowledgment of his own illegitimacy—while I was thinking of these things, the reports I have mentioned suddenly flew into my mind, and linked themselves fast to the chain of my previous reflections. Something within me whispered, "It is best that those two young men should not meet again." I felt it before I slept; I felt it when I woke; and I went, as I told you, alone to the Inn the next morning.

I had missed my only opportunity of seeing my nameless patient again. He had been gone nearly an hour when I inquired for him.

I have now told you everything that I know for certain, in relation to the man whom I brought back to life in the double-bedded room of the Inn at Doncaster. What I have next to add is matter for inference and surmise, and is not, strictly speaking, matter of fact.

I have to tell you, first, that the medical student turned out to be strangely and unaccountably right in assuming it as more than probable that Arthur Holliday would marry the young lady who had given him the water-colour drawing of the landscape. That marriage took place a little more than a year after the events occurred which I have just been relating. The young couple came to live in the neighbourhood in which I was then established in practice. I was present at the wedding, and was rather surprised to find that Arthur was singularly reserved with me, both before and after his marriage, on the subject of the young lady's prior engagement. He only referred to it once, when we were alone, merely telling me, on that occasion, that his wife had done all that honour and duty required of her in the matter, and that the engagement had been broken off with the full approval of her parents. I never heard more from him than this. For three years he and his wife lived together happily. At the expiration of that time, the symptoms of a serious illness first declared themselves in Mrs. Arthur Holliday. It turned out to be a long, lingering, hopeless malady. I attended her throughout. We had been great friends when she was well, and we became more attached to each other than ever when she was ill. I had many long and interesting conversations with her in the intervals when she suffered least. The result of one of these conversations I may briefly relate, leaving you to draw any inferences from it that you please.

The interview to which I refer, occurred shortly before her death. I called one evening, as usual, and found her alone, with a look in her eyes which told me that she had been crying. She only informed me at first, that she had been depressed in spirits; but, by little and little, she became more communicative, and confessed to me that she had been looking over some old letters, which had been addressed to her, before she had seen Arthur, by a man to whom she had been engaged to be married. I asked her how the engagement came to be broken off. She replied that it had not been broken off, but that it had died out in a very mysterious way. The person to whom she was engaged—her first love, she called him—was very poor, and there was no immediate prospect of their being married. He followed my profession, and went abroad to study. They had corresponded regularly, until the time when, as she believed, he had returned to England. From that period she heard no more of him. He was of a fretful, sensitive temperament; and she feared that she might have inadvertently done or said something that offended him. However that might be, he had never written to her again; and, after waiting a year, she had married Arthur. I asked when the first estrangement had begun, and found that the time at which she ceased to hear anything of her first lover exactly corresponded with the time at which I had been called in to my mysterious patient at The Two Robins Inn.

A fortnight after the conversation, she died. In course of time, Arthur married again. Of late years, he has lived principally in London, and I have seen little or nothing of him.

I have many years to pass over before I can approach to anything like a conclusion of this fragmentary narrative. And even when the later period is reached, the little that I have to say will not occupy your attention for more than a few minutes. Between six and seven years ago, the gentleman to whom I introduced you in this room, came to me, with good professional recommendations, to fill the position of my assistant. We met, not like strangers, but like friends

—the only difference between us being, that I was very much surprised to see him, and that he did not appear to be at all surprised to see me. If he was my son or my brother, I believe he could not be fonder of me than he is; but he has never volunteered any confidences since he has been here, on the subject of his past life. I saw something that was familiar to me in his face when we first met; and yet it was also something that suggested the idea of change. I had a notion once that my patient at the Inn might be a natural son of Mr. Holliday's; I had another idea that he might also have been the man who was engaged to Arthur's first wife; and I have a third idea, still clinging to me, that Mr. Lord is the only man in England who could really enlighten me, if he chose, on both those doubtful points. His hair is not black, now, and his eyes are dimmer than the piercing eyes that I remember, but, for all that, he is very like the nameless medical student of my young days—very like him. And, sometimes, when I come home late at night, and find him asleep, and wake him, he looks, in coming to, wonderfully like the stranger at Doncaster, as he raised himself in the bed on that memorable night!

The Doctor paused. Mr. Goodchild, who had been following every word that fell from his lips up to this time, leaned forward eagerly to ask a question. Before he could say a word, the latch of the door was raised, without any warning sound of footsteps in the passage outside. A long, white, bony hand appeared through the opening, gently pushing the door, which was prevented from working freely on its hinges by a fold in the carpet under it.

"That hand! Look at that hand, Doctor!" said Mr. Goodchild, touching him.

At the same moment, the Doctor looked at Mr. Goodchild, and whispered to him significantly:

"Hush! he has come back."

CHAPTER III

THE Cumberland Doctor's mention of Doncaster Races, inspired Mr. Francis Goodchild with the idea of going down to Doncaster to see the races. Doncaster being a good way off, and quite out of the way of the Idle Apprentices (if anything could be out of their way, who had no way), it necessarily followed that Francis perceived Doncaster in the race-week to be, of all possible idlenesses, the particular idleness that would completely satisfy him.

Thomas, with an enforced idleness grafted on the natural and voluntary power of his disposition, was not of this mind; objecting that a man compelled to lie on his back on a floor, a sofa, a table, a line of chairs, or anything he could get to lie upon, was not in racing condition, and that he desired nothing better than to lie where he was, enjoying himself in looking at the flies on the ceiling. But, Francis

Goodchild, who had been walking round his companion in a circuit of twelve miles for two days, and had begun to doubt whether it was reserved for him ever to be idle in his life, not only overpowered this objection, but even converted Thomas Idle to a scheme he formed (another idle inspiration), of conveying the said Thomas to the sea-coast, and putting his injured leg under a stream of salt-water.

Plunging into this happy conception headforemost, Mr. Goodchild immediately referred to the county-map, and ardently discovered that the most delicious piece of sea-coast to be found within the limits of England, Ireland, Scotland, Wales, the Isle of Man, and the Channel Islands, all summed up together, was Allonby on the coast of Cumberland. There was the coast of Scotland opposite to Allonby, said Mr. Goodchild with enthusiasm; there was a fine Scottish mountain on that Scottish coast; there were Scottish lights to be seen shining across the glorious Channel, and at Allonby itself there was every idle luxury (no doubt) that a watering-place could offer to the heart of idle man. Moreover, said Mr. Goodchild, with his finger on the map, this exquisite retreat was approached by a coach-road, from a railway-station called Aspatria—a name, in a manner, suggestive of the departed glories of Greece, associated with one of the most engaging and most famous of Greek women. On this point, Mr. Goodchild continued at intervals to breathe a vein of classic fancy and eloquence exceedingly irksome to Mr. Idle, until it appeared that the honest English pronunciation of that Cumberland country shortened Aspatria into "Spatter." After this supplementary discovery, Mr. Goodchild said no more about it.

By way of Spatter, the crippled Idle was carried, hoisted, pushed, poked, and packed, into and out of carriages, into and out of beds, into and out of tavern resting-places, until he was brought at length within sniff of the sea. And now, behold the apprentices gallantly riding into Allonby in a one-horse fly, bent upon staying in that peaceful marine valley until the turbulent Doncaster time shall come round upon the wheel, in its turn among what are in sporting registers called the "Fixtures" for the month.

"Do you see Allonby?" asked Thomas Idle.

"I don't see it yet," said Francis, looking out of window.

"It must be there," said Thomas Idle.

"I don't see it," returned Francis.

"It must be there," repeated Thomas Idle, fretfully.

"Lord bless me!" exclaimed Francis, drawing in his head, "I suppose this is it!"

"A watering-place," retorted Thomas Idle, with the pardonable sharpness of an invalid, "can't be five gentlemen in straw hats, on a form on one side of a door, and four ladies in hats and falls, on a form on another side of a door, and three geese in a dirty little brook before them, and a boy's legs hanging over a bridge (with a boy's body I suppose on the other side of the parapet), and a donkey running away. What are you talking about?"

"Allonby, gentlemen," said the most comfortable of landladies, as she opened one door of the carriage; "Allonby, gentlemen," said the most attentive of landlords, as he opened the other.

Thomas Idle yielded his arm to the ready Goodchild, and descended from the vehicle. Thomas, now just able to grope his way along, in a doubled-up condition, with the aid of two thick sticks, was no bad embodiment of Commodore Trunnion, or of one of those many gallant Admirals of the stage, who have all ample fortunes, gout, thick sticks, tempers, wards, and nephews. With this distinguished naval appearance upon him, Thomas made a crab-like progress up a clean little bulk-headed staircase, into a clean little bulk-headed room, where he slowly deposited himself on a sofa, with a stick on either hand of him, looking exceedingly grim.

"Francis," said Thomas Idle, "what do you think of this place?"

"I think," returned Mr. Goodchild, in a glowing way, "it is everything we expected."

"Hah!" said Thomas Idle.

"There is the sea," cried Mr. Goodchild, pointing out of window; "and here," pointing to the lunch on the table, "are shrimps. Let us——" here Mr. Goodchild looked out of window, as if in search of something, and looked in again,—"let us eat 'em."

The shrimps eaten and the dinner ordered, Mr. Goodchild went out to survey the watering-place. As Chorus of the Drama, without whom Thomas could make nothing of the scenery, he by-and-by returned, to have the following report screwed out of him.

In brief, it was the most delightful place ever seen.

"But," Thomas Idle asked, "where is it?"

"It's what you may call generally up and down the beach, here and there," said Mr. Goodchild, with a twist of his hand.

"Proceed," said Thomas Idle.

It was, Mr. Goodchild went on to say, in cross-examination, what you might call a primitive place. Large? No, it was not large. Who ever expected it would be large? Shape? What a question to ask! No shape. What sort of a street? Why, no street. Shops? Yes, of course (quite indignant). How many? Who ever went into a place to count the shops? Ever so many. Six? Perhaps. A library? Why, of course (indignant again). Good collection of books? Most likely—couldn't say—had seen nothing in it but a pair of scales. Any reading-room? Of course, there was a reading-room. Where? Where! why, over there. Where was over there? Why, *there*! Let Mr. Idle carry his eye to that bit of waste ground above high-water mark, where the rank grass and loose stones were most in a litter; and he would see a sort of a long ruinous brick loft, next door to a ruinous brick outhouse, which loft had a ladder outside, to get up by. That was the reading-room, and if Mr. Idle didn't like the idea of a weaver's shuttle throbbing under a reading-room, that was his look out. *He* was not to dictate, Mr. Goodchild supposed (indignant again), to the company.

"By-the-by," Thomas Idle observed; "the company?"

Well! (Mr. Goodchild went on to report) very nice company. Where were they? Why, there they were. Mr. Idle could see the tops of their hats, he supposed. What? Those nine straw hats again, five gentlemen's and four ladies'? Yes, to be sure. Mr. Goodchild hoped the company were not to be expected to wear helmets, to please Mr. Idle.

Beginning to recover his temper at about this point, Mr. Goodchild voluntarily reported that if you wanted to be primitive, you could be primitive here, and that if you wanted to be idle, you could be idle here. In the course of some days, he added, that there were three fishing-boats, but no rigging, and that there were plenty of fishermen who never fished. That they got their living entirely by looking at the ocean. What nourishment they looked out of it to support their strength, he couldn't say; but, he supposed it was some sort of Iodine. The place was full of their children, who were always upside down on the public buildings (two small bridges over the brook), and always hurting themselves or one another, so that their wailings made more continual noise in the air than could have been got in a busy place. The houses people lodged in, were nowhere in particular, and were in capital accordance with the beach; being all more or less cracked and damaged as its shells were, and all empty—as its shells were. Among them, was an edifice of destitute appearance, with a number of wall-eyed windows in it, looking desperately out to Scotland as if for help, which said it was a Bazaar (and it ought to know), and where you might buy anything you wanted—supposing what you wanted, was a little camp-stool or a child's wheelbarrow. The brook crawled or stopped between the houses and the sea, and the donkey was always running away, and when he got into the brook he was pelted out with stones, which never hit him, and which always hit some of the children who were upside down on the public buildings, and made their lamentations louder. This donkey was the public excitement of Allonby, and was probably supported at the public expense.

The foregoing descriptions, delivered in separate items, on separate days of adventurous discovery, Mr. Goodchild severally wound up, by looking out of window, looking in again, and saying, "But there is the sea, and here are the shrimps—let us eat 'em."

There were fine sunsets at Allonby when the low flat beach, with its pools of water and its dry patches, changed into long bars of silver and gold in various states of burnishing, and there were fine views—on fine days—of the Scottish coast. But, when it rained at Allonby, Allonby thrown back upon its rugged self, became a kind of place which the donkey seemed to have found out, and to have his highly sagacious reasons for wishing to bolt from. Thomas Idle observed, too, that Mr. Goodchild, with a noble show of disinterestedness, became every day more ready to walk to Maryport and back, for letters; and suspicions began to harbour in the mind of Thomas, that his friend deceived him, and that Maryport was a preferable place.

Therefore, Thomas said to Francis on a day when they had looked at the sea and eaten the shrimps, "My mind misgives me, Goodchild, that you go to Maryport, like the boy in the story-book, to ask *it* to be idle with you."

"Judge, then," returned Francis, adopting the style of the story book, "with what success. I go to a region which is a bit of water-side Bristol, with a slice of Wapping, a seasoning of Wolverhampton, and a garnish of Portsmouth, and I say, 'Will *you* come and be idle with me?' And it answers, 'No; for I am a great deal too vaporous, and a great deal too rusty, and a great deal too muddy, and a great deal too dirty altogether; and I have ships to load, and pitch and tar to boil, and iron to hammer, and steam to get up, and smoke to make, and stone to quarry, and fifty other disagreeable things to do, and can't be idle with you.' Then I go into jagged up-hill and down-hill streets, where I am in the pastrycook's shop at one moment, and next moment in savage fastnesses of moor and morass, beyond the confine of civilisation, and I say to those murky and black-dusty streets, 'Will *you* come and be idle with me?' To which they reply, 'No, we can't, indeed, for we haven't the spirits, and we are startled by the echo of your feet on the sharp pavement, and we have so many goods in our shop-windows which nobody wants, and we have so much to do for a limited public which never comes to us to be done for, that we are altogether out of sorts and can't enjoy ourselves with any one.' So I go to the Post-office, and knock at the shutter, and I say to the Post-master, 'Will *you* come and be idle with me?' To which he rejoins, 'No, I really can't, for I live, as you may see, in such a very little Post-office, and pass my life behind such a very little shutter, that my hand, when I put it out, is as the hand of a giant crammed through the window of a dwarf's house at a fair, and I am a mere Post-office anchorite in a cell much too small for him, and I can't get out, and I can't get in, and I have no space to be idle in, even if I would.' So, the boy," said Mr. Goodchild, concluding the tale, "comes back with the letters after all, and lives happy never afterwards."

But it may, not unreasonably, be asked—while Francis Goodchild was wandering hither and thither, storing his mind with perpetual observation of men and things, and sincerely believing himself to be the laziest creature in existence all the time—how did Thomas Idle, crippled and confined to the house, contrive to get through the hours of the day?

Prone on the sofa, Thomas made no attempt to get through the hours, but passively allowed the hours to get through *him*. Where other men in his situation would have read books and improved their minds, Thomas slept and rested his body. Where other men would have pondered anxiously over their future prospects, Thomas dreamed lazily of his past life. The one solitary thing he did, which most other people would have done in his place, was to resolve on making certain alterations and improvements in his mode of existence, as soon as the effects of the misfortune that had overtaken him had all passed away. Remembering that the current of his life had hitherto oozed along in one smooth stream of laziness, occasionally troubled on the surface by a slight passing ripple of industry, his present ideas on the subject of self-reform, inclined him—not as the reader may be disposed to imagine, to project schemes for a new existence of enterprise and exertion—but, on the contrary, to resolve that he would never, if he could possibly help it, be active or industrious again, throughout the whole of his future career.

It is due to Mr. Idle to relate that his mind sauntered towards this peculiar conclusion on distinct and logically-producible grounds. After reviewing, quite at his ease, and with many needful intervals of repose, the generally-placid spectacle of his past existence, he arrived at the discovery that all the great disasters which had tried his patience and equanimity in early life, had been caused by his having allowed himself to be deluded into imitating some pernicious example of activity and industry that had been set him by others. The trials to which he here alludes were three in number, and may be thus reckoned up: First, the disaster of being an unpopular and a thrashed boy at school; secondly, the disaster of falling seriously ill; thirdly, the disaster of becoming acquainted with a great bore.

The first disaster occurred after Thomas had been an idle and a popular boy at school, for some happy years. One Christmas time, he was stimulated by the evil example of a companion, whom he had always trusted and liked, to be untrue to himself, and to try for a prize at the ensuing half-yearly examination. He did try, and he got a prize,—how, he did not distinctly know at the moment, and cannot remember now. No sooner, however, had the book—Moral Hints to the Young on the Value of Time—been placed in his hands, than the first troubles of his life began. The idle boys deserted him, as a traitor to their cause. The industrious boys avoided him, as a dangerous interloper; one of their number, who had always won the prize on previous occasions, expressing just resentment at the invasion of his privileges by calling Thomas into the playground, and then and there administering to him the first sound and genuine thrashing that he had ever received in his life. Unpopular from that moment, as a beaten boy, who belonged to no side and was rejected by all parties, young Idle soon lost caste with his masters, as he had previously lost caste with his school-fellows. He had forfeited the comfortable reputation of being the one lazy member of the youthful community whom it was quite hopeless to punish. Never again did he hear the headmaster say reproachfully to an industrious boy who had committed a fault, "I might have expected this in Thomas Idle, but it is inexcusable, Sir, in you, who know better." Never more, after winning that fatal prize, did he escape the retributive imposition, or the avenging birch. From that time, the masters made him work, and the boys would not let him play. From that time, his social position steadily declined, and his life at school became a perpetual burden to him.

So, again, with the second disaster. While Thomas was lazy, he was a model of health. His first attempt at active exertion and his first suffering from severe illness are connected together by the intimate relations of cause and effect. Shortly after leaving school, he accompanied a party of friends to a cricket-field, in his natural and appropriate character of spectator only. On the ground it was discovered that the players fell short of the required number, and facile Thomas was persuaded to assist in making up the complement. At a certain appointed time, he was roused from peaceful slumber in a dry ditch, and placed before three wickets with a bat in his hand. Opposite to him, behind three more wickets, stood one of his bosom friends, filling the situation (as he was informed) of bowler. No words can describe Mr. Idle's horror and amazement, when he saw this young man—on ordinary occasions, the meekest and mildest of human beings—suddenly contract his eyebrows, compress his lips, assume the aspect of an infuriated savage, run back a few steps, then run forward, and, without the slightest previous provocation, hurl a detestably hard ball with all his might straight at Thomas's legs. Stimulated to preternatural activity of body and sharpness of eye by the instinct of self-preservation, Mr. Idle contrived, by jumping deftly aside at the right moment, and by using his bat (ridiculously narrow as it was for the purpose) as a shield, to preserve his life and limbs from the dastardly attack that had been made on both, to leave the full force of the deadly missile to strike his wicket instead of his leg; and to end the innings, so far as his side was concerned, by being immediately bowled out. Grateful for his escape, he was about to return to the dry ditch, when he was peremptorily stopped, and told that the other side was "going in," and that he was expected to "field." His conception of the whole art and mystery of "fielding," may be summed up in the three words of serious advice which he privately administered to himself on that trying occasion—avoid the ball. Fortified by this sound and salutary principle, he took his own course, impervious alike to ridicule and abuse. Whenever the ball came near him, he thought of his shins, and got out of the way immediately. "Catch it!" "Stop it!" "Pitch it up!" were cries that passed by him like the idle wind that he regarded not. He ducked under it, he jumped over it, he whisked himself away from it on either side. Never once, through the whole innings did he and the ball come together on anything approaching to intimate terms. The unnatural activity of body which was necessarily called forth for the accomplishment of this result threw Thomas Idle, for the first time in his life, into a perspiration. The perspiration, in consequence of his want of practice in the management of that particular result of bodily activity, was suddenly checked; the inevitable chill succeeded; and that, in its turn, was followed by a fever. For the first time since his birth, Mr. Idle found himself confined to his bed for many weeks together, wasted and worn by a long illness, of which his own disastrous muscular exertion had been the sole first cause.

The third occasion on which Thomas found reason to reproach himself bitterly for the mistake of having attempted to be industrious, was connected with his choice of a calling in life. Having no interest in the Church, he appropriately selected the next best profession for a lazy man in England—the Bar. Although the Benchers of the Inns of Court have lately abandoned their good old principles, and oblige their students to make some show of studying, in Mr. Idle's time no such innovation as this existed. Young men who aspired to the honourable title of barrister were, very properly, not asked to learn anything of the law, but were merely required to eat a certain number of dinners at the table of their Hall, and to pay a certain sum of money; and were called to the Bar as soon as they could prove that they had sufficiently complied with these extremely sensible regulations. Never did Thomas move more harmoniously in concert with his elders and betters than when he was qualifying himself for admission among the barristers of his native country. Never did he feel more deeply what real laziness was in all the serene majesty of its nature, than on the memorable day when he was called to the Bar, after having carefully abstained from opening his law-books during his period of probation, except to fall asleep over them. How he could ever again have become industrious, even for the shortest period, after that great reward conferred upon his idleness, quite passes his comprehension. The kind Benchers did everything they could to show him the folly of exerting himself. They wrote out his probationary exercise for him, and never expected him even to take the trouble of reading it through when it was written. They invited him, with seven other choice spirits as lazy as himself, to come and be called to the Bar, while they were sitting over their wine and fruit after dinner. They put his oaths of allegiance, and his dreadful official denunciations of the Pope and the Pretender, so gently into his mouth, that he hardly knew how the words got there. They wheeled all their chairs softly round from the table, and sat surveying the young barristers with their backs to their bottles, rather than stand up, or adjourn to hear the exercises read. And when Mr. Idle and the seven unlabouring neophytes, ranged in order, as a class, with their backs considerately placed against a screen, had begun, in rotation, to read the exercises which they had not written, even then, each Bencher, true to the great lazy principle of the whole proceeding, stopped each neophyte before he had stammered through his first line, and bowed to him, and told him politely that he was a barrister from that moment. This was all the ceremony. It was followed by a social supper, and by the presentation, in accordance with ancient custom, of a pound of sweetmeats and a bottle of Madeira, offered in the way of needful refreshment, by each grateful neophyte to each beneficent Bencher. It may seem inconceivable that Thomas should ever have forgotten the great do-nothing principle instilled by such a ceremony as this; but it is, nevertheless, true, that certain designing students of industrious habits found him out, took advantage of his easy humour, persuaded him that it was discreditable to be a barrister and to know nothing whatever about the law, and lured him, by the force of their own evil example, into a conveyancer's chambers, to make up for lost time, and to qualify himself for practice at the Bar. After a fortnight of self-delusion, the curtain fell from his eyes; he resumed his natural character, and shut up his books. But the retribution which had hitherto always followed his little casual errors of industry followed them still. He could get away from the conveyancer's chambers, but he could not get away from one of the pupils, who had taken a fancy to him,—a tall, serious, raw-boned, hard-working, disputatious pupil, with ideas of his own about reforming the Law of Real Property, who has been the scourge of Mr. Idle's existence ever since the fatal day when he fell into the mistake of attempting to study the law. Before that time his friends were all sociable idlers like himself. Since that time the burden of bearing with a hard-working young man has become part of his lot in life. Go where he will now, he can never feel certain that the raw-boned pupil is not affectionately waiting for him round a corner, to tell him a little more about the Law of Real Property. Suffer as he may under the infliction, he can never complain, for he must always remember with unavailing regret, that he has his own thoughtless industry to thank for first exposing him to the great social calamity of knowing a bore.

These events of his past life, with the significant results that they brought about, pass drowsily through Thomas Idle's memory, while he lies alone on the sofa at Allonby and elsewhere, dreaming away the time which his fellow-apprentice gets through so actively out of doors. Remembering the lesson of laziness which his past disasters teach, and bearing in mind also the fact that he is crippled in one leg because he exerted himself to go up a mountain, when he ought to have known that his proper course of conduct was to stop at the bottom of it, he holds now, and will for the future firmly continue to hold, by his new resolution never to be industrious again, on any pretence whatever, for the rest of his life. The physical results of his accident have been related in a previous chapter. The moral results now stand on record; and, with the enumeration of these, that part of the present narrative which is occupied by the Episode of The Sprained Ankle may now perhaps be considered, in all its aspects, as finished and complete.

"How do you propose that we get through this present afternoon and evening?" demanded Thomas Idle, after two or three hours of the foregoing reflections at Allonby.

Mr. Goodchild faltered, looked out of window, looked in again, and said, as he had so often said before, "There is the sea, and here are the shrimps;—let us eat 'em!"

But, the wise donkey was at that moment in the act of bolting: not with the irresolution of his previous efforts which had been wanting in sustained force of character, but with real vigour of purpose: shaking the dust off his mane and hind-feet at Allonby, and tearing away from it, as if he had nobly made up his mind that he never would be taken alive. At sight of this inspiring spectacle, which was visible from his sofa, Thomas Idle stretched his neck and dwelt upon it rapturously.

"Francis Goodchild," he then said, turning to his companion with a solemn air, "this is a delightful little Inn, excellently kept by the most comfortable of landladies and the most attentive of landlords, but——the donkey's right!"

The words, "There is the sea, and here are the——" again trembled on the lips of Goodchild, unaccompanied however by any sound.

"Let us instantly pack the portmanteaus," said Thomas Idle, "pay the bill, and order a fly out, with instructions to the driver to follow the donkey!"

Mr. Goodchild, who had only wanted encouragement to disclose the real state of his feelings, and who had been pining beneath his weary secret, now burst into tears, and confessed that he thought another day in the place would be the death of him.

So, the two idle apprentices followed the donkey until the night was far advanced. Whether he was recaptured by the town-council, or is bolting at this hour through the United Kingdom, they know not. They hope he may be still bolting; if so, their best wishes are with him.

It entered Mr. Idle's head, on the borders of Cumberland, that there could be no idler place to stay at, except by snatches of a few minutes each, than a railway station. "An intermediate station on a line—a junction—anything of that sort," Thomas suggested. Mr. Goodchild approved of the idea as eccentric, and they journeyed on and on, until they came to such a station where there was an Inn.

"Here," said Thomas, "we may be luxuriously lazy: other people will travel for us, as it were, and we shall laugh at their folly."

It was a Junction-Station, where the wooden razors before-mentioned shaved the air very often, and where the sharp electric-telegraph bell was in a very restless condition. All manner of cross-lines of rails came zig-zagging into it, like a Congress of iron vipers; and, a little way out of it, a pointsman in an elevated signal-box was constantly going through the motions of drawing immense quantities of beer at a public-house bar. In one direction, confused perspectives of embankments and arches were to be seen from the platform; in the other, the rails soon disentangled themselves into two tracks, and shot away under a bridge, and curved round a corner. Sidings were there, in which empty luggage-vans and cattle-boxes often butted against each other as if they couldn't agree; and warehouses were there, in which great quantities of goods seemed to have taken the veil (of the consistency of tarpaulin), and to have retired from the world without any hope of getting back to it. Refreshment-rooms were there; one, for the hungry and thirsty Iron Locomotives where their coke and water were ready, and of good quality, for they were dangerous to play tricks with; the other, for the hungry and thirsty human Locomotives, who might take what they could get, and whose chief consolation was provided in the form of three terrific urns or vases of white metal, containing nothing, each forming a breastwork for a defiant and apparently much-injured woman.

Established at this Station, Mr. Thomas Idle and Mr. Francis Goodchild resolved to enjoy it. But, its contrasts were very violent, and there was also an infection in it.

First, as to its contrasts. There were only two, but they were

Lethargy and Madness. The Station was either totally unconscious
or wildly raving. By day, in its unconscious state, it looked as if no
life could come to it,—as if it were all rust, dust, and ashes—as if the
last train for ever, had gone without issuing any Return-Tickets—as
if the last Engine had uttered its last shriek and burst. One awkward
shave of the air from the wooden razor, and everything changed.
Tight office-doors flew open, panels yielded, books, newspapers,
travelling-caps and wrappers broke out of brick walls, money chinked,
conveyances oppressed by nightmares of luggage came careering into
the yard, porters started up from secret places, ditto the much-
injured women, the shining bell, who lived in a little tray on stilts by
himself, flew into a man's hand and clamoured violently. The pointsman aloft in the signal-box made the motions of drawing, with some
difficulty, hogsheads of beer. Down Train! More beer! Up train!
More beer. Cross Junction Train! More beer! Cattle train! More beer.
Goods Train! Simmering, whistling, trembling, rumbling, thundering.
Trains on the whole confusion of intersecting rails, crossing one
another, bumping one another, hissing one another, backing to go
forward, tearing into distance to come close. People frantic. Exiles
seeking restoration to their native carriages, and banished to
remoter climes. More beer and more bell. Then, in a minute, the
Station relapsed into stupor as the stoker of the Cattle Train, the
last to depart, went gliding out of it, wiping the long nose of his oil-
can with a dirty pocket-handkerchief.

By night, in its unconscious state, the Station was not so much as
visible. Something in the air, like an enterprising chemist's established
in business on one of the boughs of Jack's beanstalk, was all that
could be discerned of it under the stars. In a moment it would break
out, a constellation of gas. In another moment, twenty rival chemists,
on twenty rival beanstalks, came into existence. Then, the Furies
would be seen, waving their lurid torches up and down the confused
perspectives of embankments and arches—would be heard, too,
wailing and shrieking. Then, the Station would be full of palpitating
trains, as in the day; with the heightening difference that they were
not so clearly seen as in the day, whereas the Station walls, starting
forward under the gas, like a hippopotamus's eyes, dazzled the
human locomotives with the sauce-bottle, the cheap music, the bedstead, the distorted range of buildings where the patent safes are
made, the gentleman in the rain with the registered umbrella, the
lady returning from the ball with the registered respirator, and all
their other embellishments. And now, the human locomotives, creased
as to their countenances and purblind as to their eyes, would swarm
forth in a heap, addressing themselves to the mysterious urns and the
much-injured women; while the iron locomotives, dripping fire and
water, shed their steam about plentifully, making the dull oxen in
their cages, with heads depressed, and foam hanging from their
mouths as their red looks glanced fearfully at the surrounding terrors,
seem as though they had been drinking at half-frozen waters and
were hung with icicles. Through the same steam would be caught

glimpses of their fellow-travellers, the sheep: getting their white kid faces together, away from the bars, and stuffing the interstices with trembling wool. Also, down among the wheels, of the man with the sledge-hammer, ringing the axles of the fast night-train; against whom the oxen have a misgiving that he is the man with the pole-axe who is to come by-and-by, and so the nearest of them try to get back, and get a purchase for a thrust at him through the bars. Suddenly, the bell would ring, the steam would stop with one hiss and a yell, the chemists on the beanstalks would be busy, the avenging Furies would bestir themselves, the fast night-train would melt from eye and ear, the other trains going their ways more slowly would be heard faintly rattling in the distance like old-fashioned watches running down, the sauce-bottle and the cheap music retired from view, even the bedstead went to bed, and there was no such visible thing as the Station to vex the cool wind in its blowing, or perhaps the autumn lightning, as it found out the iron rails.

The infection of the Station was this:—When it was in its raving state, the Apprentices found it impossible to be there, without labouring under the delusion that they were in a hurry. To Mr. Goodchild, whose ideas of idleness were so imperfect, this was no unpleasant hallucination, and accordingly that gentleman went through great exertions in yielding to it, and running up and down the platform, jostling everybody, under the impression that he had a highly important mission somewhere, and had not a moment to lose. But, to Thomas Idle, this contagion was so very unacceptable an incident of the situation, that he struck on the fourth day, and requested to be moved.

"This place fills me with a dreadful sensation," said Thomas, "of having something to do. Remove me, Francis."

"Where would you like to go next?" was the question of the ever-engaging Goodchild.

"I have heard there is a good old Inn at Lancaster, established in a fine old house: an Inn where they give you Bride-cake every day after dinner," said Thomas Idle. "Let us eat Bride-cake without the trouble of being married, or of knowing anybody in that ridiculous dilemma."

Mr. Goodchild, with a lover's sigh, assented. They departed from the Station in a violent hurry (for which, it is unnecessary to observe, there was not the least occasion), and were delivered at the fine old house at Lancaster, on the same night.

It is Mr. Goodchild's opinion, that if a visitor on his arrival at Lancaster could be accommodated with a pole which would push the opposite side of the street some yards farther off, it would be better for all parties. Protesting against being required to live in a trench, and obliged to speculate all day upon what the people can possibly be doing within a mysterious opposite window, which is a shop-window to look at, but not a shop-window in respect of its offering nothing for sale and declining to give any account whatever of itself, Mr. Goodchild concedes Lancaster to be a pleasant place. A place dropped in the midst of a charming landscape, a place with a fin ancient fragment of castle, a place of lovely walks, a place possessing staid old houses richly fitted with old Honduras mahogany, which has grown so dark with time that it seems to have got something of a retrospective mirror-quality into itself, and to show the visitor, in the depth of its grain, through all its polish, the hue of the wretched slaves who groaned long ago under old Lancaster merchants. And Mr. Goodchild adds that the stones of Lancaster do sometimes whisper, even yet, of rich men passed away—upon whose great prosperity some of these old doorways frowned sullen in the brightest weather—that their slave-gain turned to curses, as the Arabian Wizard's money turned to leaves, and that no good ever came of it, even unto the third and fourth generations, until it was wasted and gone.

It was a gallant sight to behold, the Sunday procession of the Lancaster elders to Church—all in black, and looking fearfully like a funeral without the Body—under the escort of Three Beadles.

"Think," said Francis, as he stood at the Inn window, admiring, "of being taken to the sacred edifice by three Beadles! I have, in my early time, been taken out of it by one Beadle; but, to be taken into it by three, O Thomas, is a distinction I shall never enjoy!"

CHAPTER IV

WHEN Mr. Goodchild had looked out of the Lancaster Inn window for two hours on end, with great perseverance, he began to entertain a misgiving that he was growing industrious. He therefore set himself next, to explore the country from the tops of all the steep hills in the neighbourhood.

He came back at dinner-time, red and glowing, to tell Thomas Idle what he had seen. Thomas, on his back reading, listened with great composure, and asked him whether he really had gone up those hills, and bothered himself with those views, and walked all those miles?

"Because I want to know," added Thomas, "what you would say of it, if you were obliged to do it?"

"It would be different, then," said Francis. "It would be work, then; now, it's play."

"Play!" replied Thomas Idle, utterly repudiating the reply. "Play! Here is a man goes systematically tearing himself to pieces, and putting himself through an incessant course of training, as if he were always under articles to fight a match for the champion's belt, and he calls it Play! Play!" exclaimed Thomas Idle, scornfully contemplating his one boot in the air. "You *can't* play. You don't know what it is. You make work of everything."

The bright Goodchild amiably smiled.

"So you do," said Thomas. "I mean it. To me you are an absolutely terrible fellow. You do nothing like another man. Where another

llow would fall into a footbath of action or emotion, you fall into a
ine. Where any other fellow would be a painted butterfly, you are a
ery dragon. Where another man would stake a sixpence, you stake
our existence. If you were to go up in a balloon, you would make for
[eaven; and if you were to dive into the depths of the earth, nothing
1ort of the other place would content you. What a fellow you are,
rancis!"

The cheerful Goodchild laughed.

"It's all very well to laugh, but I wonder you don't feel it to be
rious," said Idle. "A man who can do nothing by halves appears to
1e to be a fearful man."

"Tom, Tom," returned Goodchild, "if I can do nothing by halves,
nd be nothing by halves, it's pretty clear that you must take me as
whole, and make the best of me."

With this philosophical rejoinder, the airy Goodchild clapped Mr.
dle on the shoulder in a final manner, and they sat down to dinner.

"By-the-by," said Goodchild, "I have been over a lunatic asylum
)o, since I have been out."

"He has been," exclaimed Thomas Idle, casting up his eyes, "over
lunatic asylum! Not content with being as great an Ass as Captain
3arclay in the pedestrian way, he makes a Lunacy Commissioner of
mself—for nothing!"

"An immense place," said Goodchild, "admirable offices, very
ood arrangements, very good attendants; altogether a remarkable
lace."

"And what did you see there?" asked Mr. Idle, adapting Hamlet's
dvice to the occasion, and assuming the virtue of interest, though
e had it not.

"The usual thing," said Francis Goodchild, with a sigh. "Long
roves of blighted men-and-women-trees, interminable avenues of
opeless faces; numbers, without the slightest power of really com-
)ining for any earthly purpose; a society of human creatures who
ave nothing in common but that they have all lost the power of
)eing humanly social with one another."

"Take a glass of wine with me," said Thomas Idle, "and let *us* be
ocial."

"In one gallery, Tom," pursued Francis Goodchild, "which looked
o me about the length of the Long Walk at Windsor, more or less
—"

"Probably less," observed Thomas Idle.

"In one gallery, which was otherwise clear of patients (for they
vere all out), there was a poor little dark-chinned, meagre man, with
i perplexed brow and a pensive face, stooping low over the matting
)n the floor, and picking out with his thumb and forefinger the course
)f its fibres. The afternoon sun was slanting in at the large end-
vindow, and there were cross patches of light and shade all down the
rista, made by the unseen windows and the open doors of the little
.leeping-cells on either side. In about the centre of the perspective,
inder an arch, regardless of the pleasant weather, regardless of the

solitude, regardless of approaching footsteps, was the poor little dark-chinned, meagre man, poring over the matting. 'What are you doing there?' said my conductor, when we came to him. He looked up, and pointed to the matting. 'I wouldn't do that, I think,' said my conductor, kindly; 'if I were you, I would go and read, or I would lie down if I felt tired; but I wouldn't do that.' The patient considered a moment, and vacantly answered, 'No, Sir, I won't; I'll—I'll go and read,' and so he lamely shuffled away into one of the little rooms. I turned my head before we had gone many paces. He had already come out again, and was again poring over the matting, and tracking out its fibres with his thumb and forefinger. I stopped to look at him, and it came into my mind, that probably the course of those fibres as they plaited in and out, over and under, was the only course of thing in the whole wide world that it was left to him to understand—that his darkening intellect had narrowed down to the small cleft of light which showed him, 'This piece was twisted this way, went in here, passed under, came out there, was carried on away here to the right, where I now put my finger on it, and in this progress of events, the thing was made and came to be here.' Then, I wondered whether he looked into the matting, next, to see if it could show him anything of the process through which *he* came to be there, so strangely poring over it. Then, I thought how all of us, GOD help us! in our different ways are poring over our bits of matting, blindly enough, and what confusions and mysteries we make in the pattern. I had a sadder fellow-feeling with the little dark-chinned, meagre man, by that time, and I came away."

Mr. Idle diverting the conversation to grouse, custards, and bride-cake, Mr. Goodchild followed in the same direction. The bride-cake was as bilious and indigestible as if a real Bride had cut it, and the dinner it completed was an admirable performance.

The house was a genuine old house of a very quaint description, teeming with old carvings, and beams, and panels, and having an excellent old staircase, with a gallery or upper staircase, cut off from it by a curious fence-work of old oak, or of the old Honduras Mahogany wood. It was, and is, and will be, for many a long year to come, a remarkably picturesque house; and a certain grave mystery lurking in the depth of the old mahogany panels, as if they were so many deep pools of dark water—such, indeed, as they had been much among when they were trees—gave it a very mysterious character after nightfall.

When Mr. Goodchild and Mr. Idle had first alighted at the door, and stepped into the sombre handsome old hall, they had been received by a half-a-dozen noiseless old men in black, all dressed exactly alike, who glided up the stairs with the obliging landlord and waiter—but without appearing to get into their way, or to mind whether they did or no—and who had filed off to the right and left on the old staircase, as the guests entered their sitting-room. It was then broad, bright day. But, Mr. Goodchild had said, when their door was shut, "Who on earth are those old men?" And afterwards,

th on going out and coming in, he had noticed that there were no
d men to be seen.

Neither, had the old men, or any one of the old men, reappeared
nce. The two friends had passed a night in the house, but had seen
thing more of the old men. Mr. Goodchild, in rambling about it,
d looked along passages, and glanced in at doorways, but had en-
untered no old men; neither did it appear that any old men were,
y any member of the establishment, missed or expected.

Another odd circumstance impressed itself on their attention. It
as, that the door of their sitting-room was never left untouched for
quarter of an hour. It was opened with hesitation, opened with
nfidence, opened a little way, opened a good way,—always clapped-
again without a word of explanation. They were reading, they
ere writing, they were eating, they were drinking, they were talking,
ey were dozing; the door was always opened at an unexpected
oment, and they looked towards it, and it was clapped-to again,
nd nobody was to be seen. When this had happened fifty times or so,
r. Goodchild had said to his companion, jestingly: "I begin to think,
om, there was something wrong with those six old men."

Night had come again, and they had been writing for two or three
ours: writing, in short, a portion of the lazy notes from which these
zy sheets are taken. They had left off writing, and glasses were on
e table between them. The house was closed and quiet. Around the
ead of Thomas Idle, as he lay upon his sofa, hovered light wreaths
f fragrant smoke. The temples of Francis Goodchild, as he leaned
ack in his chair, with his two hands clasped behind his head, and
is legs crossed, were similarly decorated.

They had been discussing several idle subjects of speculation, not
mitting the strange old men, and were still so occupied, when Mr.
oodchild abruptly changed his attitude to wind up his watch. They
ere just becoming drowsy enough to be stopped in their talk by any
uch slight check. Thomas Idle, who was speaking at the moment,
aused and said, "How goes it?"

"One," said Goodchild.

As if he had ordered One old man, and the order were promptly
xecuted (truly, all orders were so, in that excellent hotel), the door
pened, and One old man stood there.

He did not come in, but stood with the door in his hand.

"One of the six, Tom, at last!" said Mr. Goodchild, in a surprised
hisper.—"Sir, your pleasure?"

"Sir, *your* pleasure?" said the One old man.

"I didn't ring."

"The bell did," said the One old man.

He said BELL, in a deep strong way, that would have expressed
he church Bell.

"I had the pleasure, I believe, of seeing you, yesterday?" said
oodchild.

"I cannot undertake to say for certain," was the grim reply of the
ne old man.

"I think you saw me? Did you not?"

"Saw *you*?" said the old man. "O yes, I saw *you*. But, I see man⟨y⟩ who never see me."

A chilled, slow, earthy, fixed old man. A cadaverous old man ⟨of⟩ measured speech. An old man who seemed as unable to wink, as ⟨if⟩ his eyelids had been nailed to his forehead. An old man whose eyes— two spots of fire—had no more motion than if they had been con⟨-⟩ nected with the back of his skull by screws driven through it, an⟨d⟩ riveted and bolted outside, among his grey hair.

The night had turned so cold, to Mr. Goodchild's sensations, tha⟨t⟩ he shivered. He remarked lightly, and half apologetically, "I thin⟨k⟩ somebody is walking over my grave."

"No," said the weird old man, "there is no one there."

Mr. Goodchild looked at Idle, but Idle lay with his head en⟨-⟩ wreathed in smoke.

"No one there?" said Goodchild.

"There is no one at your grave, I assure you," said the old man.

He had come in and shut the door, and he now sat down. He di⟨d⟩ not bend himself to sit, as other people do, but seemed to sink bol⟨t⟩ upright, as if in water, until the chair stopped him.

"My friend, Mr. Idle," said Goodchild, extremely anxious t⟨o⟩ introduce a third person into the conversation.

"I am," said the old man, without looking at him, "at Mr. Idle'⟨s⟩ service."

"If you are an old inhabitant of this place," Francis Goodchil⟨d⟩ resumed:

"Yes."

"Perhaps you can decide a point my friend and I were in doub⟨t⟩ upon, this morning. They hang condemned criminals at the Castle, ⟨I⟩ believe?"

"*I* believe so," said the old man.

"Are their faces turned towards that noble prospect?"

"Your face is turned," replied the old man, "to the Castle wall⟨.⟩ When you are tied up, you see its stones expanding and contracting violently, and a similar expansion and contraction seem to take plac⟨e⟩ in your own head and breast. Then, there is a rush of fire and a⟨n⟩ earthquake, and the Castle springs into the air, and you tumble down a precipice."

His cravat appeared to trouble him. He put his hand to his throat⟨,⟩ and moved his neck from side to side. He was an old man of a swolle⟨n⟩ character of face, and his nose was immovably hitched up on one side⟨,⟩ as if by a little hook inserted in that nostril. Mr. Goodchild felt exceedingly uncomfortable, and began to think the night was hot⟨,⟩ and not cold.

"A strong description, Sir," he observed.

"A strong sensation," the old man rejoined.

Again, Mr. Goodchild looked to Mr. Thomas Idle; but Thomas lay on his back with his face attentively turned towards the One old man, and made no sign. At this time Mr. Goodchild believed that he saw threads of fire stretch from the old man's eyes to his own, and there attach themselves. (Mr. Goodchild writes the present account of his experience, and, with the utmost solemnity, protests that he had the strongest sensation upon him of being forced to look at the old man along those two fiery films, from that moment.)

"I must tell it to you," said the old man, with a ghastly and a stony stare.

"What?" asked Francis Goodchild.

"You know where it took place. Yonder!"

Whether he pointed to the room above, or to the room below, or to any room in that old house, or to a room in some other old house in that old town, Mr. Goodchild was not, nor is, nor ever can be, sure. He was confused by the circumstance that the right forefinger of the One old man seemed to dip itself in one of the threads of fire, light itself, and make a fiery start in the air, as it pointed somewhere. Having pointed somewhere, it went out.

"You know she was a Bride," said the old man.

"I know they still send up Bride-cake," Mr. Goodchild faltered. "This is a very oppressive air."

"She was a Bride," said the old man. "She was a fair, flaxen-haired, large-eyed girl, who had no character, no purpose. A weak, credulous, incapable, helpless nothing. Not like her mother. No, no. It was her father whose character she reflected.

"Her mother had taken care to secure everything to herself, for her own life, when the father of this girl (a child at that time) died— of sheer helplessness; no other disorder—and then He renewed the acquaintance that had once subsisted between the mother and Him. He had been put aside for the flaxen-haired, large-eyed man (or nonentity) with Money. He could overlook that for Money. He wanted compensation in Money.

"So, he returned to the side of that woman the mother, made love to her again, danced attendance on her, and submitted himself to her whims. She wreaked upon him every whim she had, or could invent. He bore it. And the more he bore, the more he wanted compensation in Money, and the more he was resolved to have it.

"But, lo! Before he got it, she cheated him. In one of her imperious states, she froze, and never thawed again. She put her hands to her head one night, uttered a cry, stiffened, lay in that attitude certain hours, and died. And he had got no compensation from her in Money, yet. Blight and Murrain on her! Not a penny.

"He had hated her throughout that second pursuit, and had longed for retaliation on her. He now counterfeited her signature to an instrument, leaving all she had to leave, to her daughter—ten years old—to whom the property passed absolutely, and appointing himself the daughter's Guardian. When He slid it under the pillow of the bed on which she lay, He bent down in the deaf ear of Death, and whispered: 'Mistress Pride, I have determined a long time that, dead or alive, you must make me compensation in Money.'

"So, now there were only two left. Which two were, He, and the fair flaxen-haired, large-eyed foolish daughter, who afterwards became the Bride.

"He put her to school. In a secret, dark, oppressive, ancient house, he put her to school with a watchful and unscrupulous woman. 'My worthy lady,' he said, 'here is a mind to be formed; will you help me to form it?' She accepted the trust. For which she, too, wanted compensation in Money, and had it.

"The girl was formed in the fear of him, and in the conviction, that there was no escape from him. She was taught, from the first, to regard him as her future husband—the man who must marry her—the destiny that overshadowed her—the appointed certainty that could never be evaded. The poor fool was soft white wax in their hands, and took the impression that they put upon her. It hardened with time. It became a part of herself. Inseparable from herself, and only to be torn away from her, by tearing life away from her.

"Eleven years she had lived in the dark house and its gloomy garden. He was jealous of the very light and air getting to her, and they kept her close. He stopped the wide chimneys, shaded the little windows, left the strong-stemmed ivy to wander where it would over the house-front, the moss to accumulate on the untrimmed fruit-trees in the red-walled garden, the weeds to overrun its green and yellow walks. He surrounded her with images of sorrow and desolation. He caused her to be filled with fears of the place and of the stories that were told of it, and then on pretext of correcting them, to be left in it in solitude, or made to shrink about it in the dark. When her mind was most depressed and fullest of terrors, then, he would come out of one of the hiding-places from which he overlooked her, and present himself as her sole resource.

"Thus, by being from her childhood the one embodiment her life presented to her of power to coerce and power to relieve, power to bind and power to loose, the ascendency over her weakness was secured. She was twenty-one years and twenty-one days old, when he brought her home to the gloomy house, his half-witted, frightened, and submissive Bride of three weeks.

"He had dismissed the governess by that time—what he had left to do, he could best do alone—and they came back, upon a rainy night, to the scene of her long preparation. She turned to him upon the threshold, as the rain was dripping from the porch, and said:

" 'O Sir, it is the Death-watch ticking for me!'

" 'Well!' he answered, 'And if it were?'

" 'O Sir!' she returned to him, 'look kindly on me, and be merciful to me! I beg your pardon. I will do anything you wish, if you will only forgive me!'

"That had become the poor fool's constant song: 'I beg your pardon,' and 'Forgive me!'

"She was not worth hating; he felt nothing but contempt for her. But, she had long been in the way, and he had long been weary, and the work was near its end, and had to be worked out.

" 'You fool,' he said. 'Go up the stairs!'

"She obeyed very quickly, murmuring, 'I will do anything you wish!' When he came into the Bride's Chamber, having been a little retarded by the heavy fastenings of the great door (for they were alone in the house, and he had arranged that the people who attended on them should come and go in the day), he found her withdrawn to the furthest corner, and there standing pressed against the panelling as if she would have shrunk through it; her flaxen hair all wild about her face, and her large eyes staring at him in vague terror.

" 'What are you afraid of? Come and sit down by me.'

" 'I will do anything you wish. I beg your pardon, Sir. Forgive me!' Her monotonous tune as usual.

" 'Ellen, here is a writing that you must write out to-morrow, in your own hand. You may as well be seen by others, busily engaged upon it. When you have written it all fairly, and corrected all mistakes, call in any two people there may be about the house, and sign your name to it before them. Then, put it in your bosom to keep it safe, and when I sit here again to-morrow night, give it to me.'

" 'I will do it all, with the greatest care. I will do anything you wish.'

" 'Don't shake and tremble, then.'

" 'I will try my utmost not to do it—if you will only forgive me!'

"Next day, she sat down at her desk and did as she had been told. He often passed in and out of the room, to observe her, and always saw her slowly and laboriously writing: repeating to herself the words she copied, in appearance quite mechanically, and without caring or endeavouring to comprehend them, so that she did her task. He saw her follow the directions she had received, in all particulars; and at night, when they were alone again in the same Bride's Chamber, and he drew his chair to the hearth, she timidly approached him from her distant seat, took the paper from her bosom, and gave it into his hand.

"It secured all her possessions to him, in the event of her death. He put her before him, face to face, that he might look at her steadily; and he asked her, in so many plain words, neither fewer nor more, did he know that?

"There were spots of ink upon the bosom of her white dress, and they made her face look whiter and her eyes look larger as she nodded her head. There were spots of ink upon the hand with which she stood before him, nervously plaiting and folding her white skirts.

"He took her by the arm, and looked her, yet more closely and steadily, in the face. 'Now, die! I have done with you.'

"She shrunk, and uttered a low, suppressed cry.

" 'I am not going to kill you. I will not endanger my life for yours. Die!'

"He sat before her in the gloomy Bride's Chamber, day after day, night after night, looking the word at her when he did not utter it. As often as her large unmeaning eyes were raised from the hands in which she rocked her head, to the stern figure, sitting with crossed arms and knitted forehead, in the chair, they read in it, 'Die!' When

she dropped asleep in exhaustion, she was called back to shudderin
consciousness, by the whisper, 'Die!' When she fell upon her ol
entreaty to be pardoned, she was answered, 'Die!' When she ha
out-watched and out-suffered the long night, and the rising su
flamed into the sombre room, she heard it hailed with, 'Another day
and not dead?—Die!'

"Shut up in the deserted mansion, aloof from all mankind, an
engaged alone in such a struggle without any respite, it came to this—
that either he must die, or she. He knew it very well, and concen
trated his strength against her feebleness. Hours upon hours he hel
her by the arm when her arm was black where he held it, and bad
her Die!

"It was done, upon a windy morning, before sunrise. He compute
the time to be half-past four; but, his forgotten watch had run dowr
and he could not be sure. She had broken away from him in the night
with loud and sudden cries—the first of that kind to which she ha
given vent—and he had had to put his hands over her mouth. Sinc
then, she had been quiet in the corner of the panelling where she ha
sunk down; and he had left her, and had gone back with his folde
arms and his knitted forehead to his chair.

"Paler in the pale light, more colourless than ever in the leade
dawn, he saw her coming, trailing herself along the floor toward
him—a white wreck of hair, and dress, and wild eyes, pushing itsel
on by an irresolute and bending hand.

"'O, forgive me! I will do anything. O, Sir, pray tell me I ma
live!'

"'Die!'

"'Are you so resolved? Is there no hope for me?'

"'Die!'

"Her large eyes strained themselves with wonder and fear; wonde
and fear changed to reproach; reproach to blank nothing. It wa
done. He was not at first so sure it was done, but that the mornin
sun was hanging jewels in her hair—he saw the diamond, emerald
and ruby, glittering among it in little points, as he stood looking dow
at her—when he lifted her, and laid her on her bed.

"She was soon laid in the ground. And now they were all gone
and he had compensated himself well.

"He had a mind to travel. Not that he meant to waste his Money
for he was a pinching man and liked his Money dearly (liked nothin,
else, indeed), but, that he had grown tired of the desolate house an
wished to turn his back upon it and have done with it. But, the hous
was worth Money, and Money must not be thrown away. He deter
mined to sell it before he went. That it might look the less wretche
and bring a better price, he hired some labourers to work in th
overgrown garden; to cut out the dead wood, trim the ivy tha
dropped in heavy masses over the windows and gables, and clea
the walks in which the weeds were growing mid-leg high.

"He worked, himself, along with them. He worked later than the
did, and, one evening at dusk, was left working alone, with his bill

hook in his hand. One autumn evening, when the Bride was five weeks dead.

" 'It grows too dark to work longer,' he said to himself, 'I must give over for the night.'

"He detested the house, and was loath to enter it. He looked at the dark porch waiting for him like a tomb, and felt that it was an accursed house. Near to the porch, and near to where he stood, was a tree whose branches waved before the old bay-window of the Bride's Chamber, where it had been done. The tree swung suddenly, and made him start. It swung again, although the night was still. Looking up into it, he saw a figure among the branches.

"It was the figure of a young man. The face looked down, as his looked up; the branches cracked and swayed; the figure rapidly descended, and slid upon its feet before him. A slender youth of about her age, with long light brown hair.

" 'What thief are you?' he said, seizing the youth by the collar.

"The young man, in shaking himself free, swung him a blow with his arm across the face and throat. They closed, but the young man got from him and stepped back, crying, with great eagerness and horror, 'Don't touch me! I would as lieve be touched by the Devil!'

"He stood still, with his bill-hook in his hand, looking at the young man. For, the young man's look was the counterpart of her last look, and he had not expected ever to see that again.

" 'I am no thief. Even if I were, I would not have a coin of your wealth, if it would buy me the Indies. You murderer!'

" 'What!'

" 'I climbed it,' said the young man, pointing up into the tree, 'for the first time, nigh four years ago. I climbed it, to look at her. I saw her. I spoke to her. I have climbed it, many a time, to watch and listen for her. I was a boy, hidden among its leaves, when from that bay-window she gave me this!'

"He showed a tress of flaxen hair, tied with a mourning ribbon.

" 'Her life,' said the young man, 'was a life of mourning. She gave me this, as a token of it, and a sign that she was dead to every one but you. If I had been older, if I had seen her sooner, I might have saved her from you. But, she was fast in the web when I first climbed the tree, and what could I do then to break it!'

"In saying those words, he burst into a fit of sobbing and crying: weakly at first, then passionately.

" 'Murderer! I climbed the tree on the night when you brought her back. I heard her, from the tree, speak of the Death-watch at the door. I was three times in the tree while you were shut up with her, slowly killing her. I saw her, from the tree, lie dead upon her bed. I have watched you, from the tree, for proofs and traces of your guilt. The manner of it, is a mystery to me yet, but I will pursue you until you have rendered up your life to the hangman. You shall never, until then, be rid of me. I loved her! I can know no relenting towards you. Murderer, I loved her!'

"The youth was bareheaded, his hat having fluttered away in his descent from the tree. He moved towards the gate. He had to pass—Him—to get to it. There was breadth for two old-fashioned carriages abreast; and the youth's abhorrence, openly expressed in every feature of his face and limb of his body, and very hard to bear, had verge enough to keep itself at a distance in. He (by which I mean the other) had not stirred hand or foot, since he had stood still to look at the boy. He faced round, now, to follow him with his eyes. As the back of the bare light-brown head was turned to him, he saw a red curve stretch from his hand to it. He knew, before he threw the bill-hook, where it had alighted—I say, had alighted, and not, would alight; for, to his clear perception the thing was done before he did it. It cleft the head, and it remained there, and the boy lay on his face.

"He buried the body in the night, at the foot of the tree. As soon as it was light in the morning, he worked at turning up all the ground near the tree, and hacking and hewing at the neighbouring bushes and undergrowth. When the labourers came, there was nothing suspicious, and nothing suspected.

"But, he had, in a moment, defeated all his precautions, and destroyed the triumph of the scheme he had so long concerted, and so successfully worked out. He had got rid of the Bride, and had acquired her fortune without endangering his life; but now, for a death by which he had gained nothing, he had evermore to live with a rope around his neck.

"Beyond this, he was chained to the house of gloom and horror, which he could not endure. Being afraid to sell it or to quit it, lest discovery should be made, he was forced to live in it. He hired two old people, man and wife, for his servants; and dwelt in it, and dreaded it. His great difficulty, for a long time, was the garden. Whether he should keep it trim, whether he should suffer it to fall into its former state of neglect, what would be the least likely way of attracting attention to it?

"He took the middle course of gardening, himself, in his evening leisure, and of then calling the old serving-man to help him; but, of never letting him work there alone. And he made himself an arbour over against the tree, where he could sit and see that it was safe.

"As the seasons changed, and the tree changed, his mind perceived dangers that were always changing. In the leafy time, he perceived that the upper boughs were growing into the form of the young man —that they made the shape of him exactly, sitting in a forked branch swinging in the wind. In the time of the falling leaves, he perceived that they came down from the tree, forming tell-tale letters on the path, or that they had a tendency to heap themselves into a church-yard mound above the grave. In the winter, when the tree was bare, he perceived that the boughs swung at him the ghost of the blow the young man had given, and that they threatened him openly. In the spring, when sap was mounting in the trunk, he asked him-self, were the dried-up particles of blood mounting with it: to make out more obviously this year than last, the leaf-screened figure of the young man, swinging in the wind?

"However, he turned his Money over and over, and still over. He was in the dark trade, the gold-dust trade, and most secret trades that yielded great returns. In ten years, he had turned his Money over, so many times, that the traders and shippers who had dealings with him, absolutely did not lie—for once—when they declared that he had increased his fortune, Twelve Hundred Per Cent.

"He possessed his riches one hundred years ago, when people could be lost easily. He had heard who the youth was, from hearing of the search that was made after him; but, it died away, and the youth was forgotten.

"The annual round of changes in the tree had been repeated ten times since the night of the burial at its foot, when there was a great thunder-storm over this place. It broke at midnight, and raged until morning. The first intelligence he heard from his old serving-man that morning, was, that the tree had been struck by Lightning.

"It had been riven down the stem, in a very surprising manner, and the stem lay in two blighted shafts: one resting against the house, and one against a portion of the old red garden-wall in which its fall had made a gap. The fissure went down the tree to a little above the earth, and there stopped. There was great curiosity to see the tree, and, with most of his former fears revived, he sat in his arbour—grown quite an old man—watching the people who came to see it.

"They quickly began to come, in such dangerous numbers, that he closed his garden-gate and refused to admit any more. But, there were certain men of science who travelled from a distance to examine the tree, and, in an evil hour, he let them in—Blight and Murrain on them, let them in!

"They wanted to dig up the ruin by the roots, and closely examine it, and the earth about it. Never, while he lived! They offered money for it. They! Men of science, whom he could have bought by the gross, with a scratch of his pen! He showed them the garden-gate again, and locked and barred it.

"But they were bent on doing what they wanted to do, and they bribed the old serving-man—a thankless wretch who regularly complained when he received his wages, of being underpaid—and they stole into the garden by night with their lanterns, picks, and shovels, and fell to at the tree. He was lying in a turret-room on the other side of the house (the Bride's Chamber had been unoccupied ever since), but he soon dreamed of picks and shovels, and got up.

"He came to an upper window on that side, whence he could see their lanterns, and them, and the loose earth in a heap which he had himself disturbed and put back, when it was last turned to the air. It was found! They had that minute lighted on it. They were all bending over it. One of them said, 'The skull is fractured'; and another, 'See here the bones'; and another, 'See here the clothes'; and then the first struck in again, and said, 'A rusty bill-hook!'

"He became sensible, next day, that he was already put under a strict watch, and that he could go nowhere without being followed. Before a week was out, he was taken and laid in hold. The circumstances were gradually pieced together against him, with a desperate malignity, and an appalling ingenuity. But, see the justice of man, and how it was extended to him! He was further accused of having poisoned that girl in the Bride's Chamber. He, who had carefully and expressly avoided imperilling a hair of his head for her, and who had seen her die of her own incapacity!

"There was doubt for which of the two murders he should be first tried; but, the real one was chosen, and he was found Guilty, and cast for Death. Bloodthirsty wretches! They would have made him Guilty of anything, so set they were upon having his life.

"His money could do nothing to save him, and he was hanged. *I* am he, and I was hanged at Lancaster Castle with my face to the wall, a hundred years ago!"

At this terrific announcement, Mr. Goodchild tried to rise and cry out. But, the two fiery lines extending from the old man's eyes to his own, kept him down, and he could not utter a sound. His sense of hearing, however, was acute, and he could hear the clock strike Two. No sooner had he heard the clock strike Two, than he saw before him Two old men!

Two.

The eyes of each, connected with his eyes by two films of fire: each, exactly like the other: each, addressing him at precisely one and the same instant: each, gnashing the same teeth in the same head, with the same twitched nostril above them, and the same suffused expression around it. Two old men. Differing in nothing, equally distinct to the sight, the copy no fainter than the original, the second as real as the first.

"At what time," said the Two old men, "did you arrive at the door below?"

"At six."

"And there were Six old men on the stairs!"

Mr. Goodchild having wiped the perspiration from his brow, or tried to do it, the Two old men proceeded in one voice, and in the singular number:

"I had been anatomised, but had not yet had my skeleton put together and re-hung on an iron hook when it began to be whispered that the Bride's Chamber was haunted. It was haunted, and I was there.

"*We* were there. She and I were there. I, in the chair upon the hearth; she, a white wreck, again trailing itself towards me on the floor. But, I was the speaker no more, and the one word that she said to me from midnight until dawn was, 'Live!'

"The youth was there, likewise. In the tree outside the window. Coming and going in the moonlight, as the tree bent and gave. He has, ever since, been there, peeping in at me in my torment; revealing to me by snatches, in the pale lights and slatey shadows where he comes and goes, bareheaded—a bill-hook, standing edgewise in his hair.

"In the Bride's Chamber, every night from midnight until dawn—one month in the year excepted, as I am going to tell you—he hides in the tree, and she comes towards me on the floor; always approaching; never coming nearer; always visible as if by moonlight, whether the moon shines or no; always saying, from midnight until dawn her one word, 'Live!'

"But, in the month wherein I was forced out of this life—this present month of thirty days—the Bride's Chamber is empty and quiet. Not so my old dungeon. Not so the rooms where I was restless and afraid, ten years. Both are fitfully haunted then. At One in the morning, I am what you saw me when the clock struck that hour—One old man. At Two in the morning, I am Two old men. At Three, I am Three. By twelve at noon, I am Twelve old men, One for every hundred per cent. of old gain. Every one of the Twelve, with Twelve times my old power of suffering and agony. From that hour until Twelve at night, I, Twelve old men in anguish and fearful foreboding, wait for the coming of the executioner. At Twelve at night, I Twelve old men turned off, swing invisible outside Lancaster Castle, with Twelve faces to the wall!

"When the Bride's Chamber was first haunted, it was known to me that this punishment would never cease, until I could make its nature and my story known to two living men together. I waited for the coming of two living men together into the Bride's Chamber, years upon years. It was infused into my knowledge (of the means I am ignorant) that if two living men, with their eyes open, could be in the Bride's Chamber at One in the morning, they would see me sitting in my chair.

"At length the whispers that the room was spiritually troubled, brought two men to try the adventure. I was scarcely struck upon the hearth at midnight (I come there as if the Lightning blasted me into being), when I heard them ascending the stairs. Next, I saw them enter. One of them was a bold, gay, active man, in the prime of life, some five and forty years of age; the other, a dozen years younger. They brought provisions with them in a basket, and bottles. A young woman accompanied them, with wood and coals for the lighting of the fire. When she had lighted it, the bold, gay, active man accompanied her along the gallery outside the room, to see her safely down the staircase, and came back laughing.

"He locked the door, examined the chamber, put out the contents of the basket on the table before the fire—little recking of me, in my appointed station on the hearth, close to him—and filled the glasses, and ate and drank. His companion did the same, and was as cheerful and confident as he: though he was the leader. When they had supped, they laid pistols on the table, turned to the fire, and began to smoke their pipes of foreign make.

"They had travelled together, and had been much together, and had an abundance of subjects in common. In the midst of their talking and laughing, the younger man made a reference to the leader's being always ready for any adventure; that one, or any other. He replied in these words:

" 'Not quite so, Dick; if I am afraid of nothing else, I am afraid of myself.'

"His companion seeming to grow a little dull, asked him, in what sense? How?

" 'Why, thus,' he returned. 'Here is a Ghost to be disproved. Well! I cannot answer for what my fancy might do if I were alone here, or what tricks my senses might play with me if they had me to themselves. But, in company with another man, and especially with you, Dick, I would consent to outface all the Ghosts that were ever told of in the universe.'

" 'I had not the vanity to suppose that I was of so much importance to-night,' said the other.

" 'Of so much,' rejoined the leader, more seriously than he had spoken yet, 'that I would, for the reason I have given, on no account have undertaken to pass the night here alone.'

"It was within a few minutes of One. The head of the younger man had drooped when he made his last remark, and it drooped lower now.

" 'Keep awake, Dick!' said the leader, gaily. 'The small hours are the worst.'

"He tried, but his head drooped again.

" 'Dick!' urged the leader. 'Keep awake!'

" 'I can't,' he indistinctly muttered. 'I don't know what strange influence is stealing over me. I can't.'

"His companion looked at him with a sudden horror, and I, in my different way, felt a new horror also; for, it was on the stroke of One, and I felt that the second watcher was yielding to me, and that the curse was upon me that I must send him to sleep.

" 'Get up and walk, Dick!' cried the leader. 'Try!'

"It was in vain to go behind the slumberer's chair and shake him. One o'clock sounded, and I was present to the elder man, and he stood transfixed before me.

"To him alone, I was obliged to relate my story, without hope or benefit. To him alone, I was an awful phantom making a quite useless confession. I foresee it will ever be the same. The two living men together will never come to release me. When I appear, the senses of one of the two will be locked in sleep; he will neither see nor hear me; my communication will ever be made to a solitary listener, and will ever be unserviceable. Woe! Woe! Woe!"

As the Two old men, with these words, wrung their hands, it shot into Mr. Goodchild's mind that he was in the terrible situation of being virtually alone with the spectre, and that Mr. Idle's immovability was explained by his having been charmed asleep at One o'clock. In the terror of this sudden discovery which produced an indescribable dread, he struggled so hard to get free from the four fiery threads, that he snapped them, after he had pulled them out to a great width. Being then out of bonds, he caught up Mr. Idle from the sofa and rushed downstairs with him.

"What are you about Francis?" demanded Mr. Idle. "My bedroom is not down here. What the deuce are you carrying me at all for? I can walk with a stick now. I don't want to be carried. Put me down."

Mr. Goodchild put him down in the old hall, and looked about him wildly.

"What are you doing? Idiotically plunging at your own sex and rescuing them or perishing in the attempt?" asked Mr. Idle, in a highly petulant state.

"The One old man!" cried Mr. Goodchild, distractedly,—"and the Two old men!"

Mr. Idle deigned no other reply than "The One old woman, I think you mean," as he began hobbling his way back up the staircase, with the assistance of its broad balustrade.

"I assure you, Tom," began Mr. Goodchild, attending at his side, "that since you fell asleep——"

"Come, I like that!" said Thomas Idle, "I haven't closed an eye!"

With the peculiar sensitiveness on the subject of the disgraceful action of going to sleep out of bed, which is the lot of all mankind, Mr. Idle persisted in this declaration. The same peculiar sensitiveness impelled Mr. Goodchild, on being taxed with the same crime, to repudiate it with honourable resentment. The settlement of the question of The One old man and The Two old men was thus presently complicated, and soon made quite impracticable. Mr. Idle said it was all Bride-cake, and fragments, newly arranged, of things seen and thought about in the day. Mr. Goodchild said how could that be, when he hadn't been asleep, and what right could Mr. Idle have to say so, who had been asleep? Mr. Idle said he had never been asleep, and never did go to sleep, and that Mr. Goodchild, as a general rule, was always asleep. They consequently parted for the rest of the night, at their bedroom doors, a little ruffled. Mr. Goodchild's last words were, that he had had, in that real and tangible old sitting-room of that real and tangible old inn (he supposed Mr. Idle denied its existence?), every sensation and experience, the present record of which is now within a line or two of completion; and that he could write it out and print it every word. Mr. Idle returned that he might if he liked—and he did like, and has now done it.

CHAPTER V

Two of the many passengers by a certain late Sunday evening train, Mr. Thomas Idle and Mr. Francis Goodchild, yielded up their tickets at a little rotten platform (converted into artificial touchwood by smoke and ashes), deep in the manufacturing bosom of Yorkshire. A mysterious bosom it appeared, upon a damp, dark, Sunday night, dashed through in the train to the music of the whirling wheels, the panting of the engine, and the part-singing of hundreds of third-class excursionists, whose vocal efforts "bobbed arayound" from sacred to profane, from hymns, to our transatlantic sisters the Yankee Gal and Mairy Anne, in a remarkable way. There seemed to have been some large vocal gathering near to every lonely station on the line. No town was visible, no village was visible, no light was visible; but, a multitude got out singing, and a multitude got in singing, and the second multitude took up the hymns, and adopted our transatlantic sisters, and sang their own egregious wickedness, and of their bobbing arayound, and of how the ship it was ready and the wind it was fair, and they were bayound for the sea, Mairy Anne, until they in their turn became a getting-out-multitude, and were replaced by another getting-in multitude, who did the same. And at every station, the getting-in multitude, with an artistic reference to the completeness of their chorus, incessantly cried, as with one voice while scuffling into the carriages, "We mun aa' gang toogither!"

The singing and the multitudes had trailed off as the lonely places were left and the great towns were neared, and the way had lain as silently as a train's way ever can, over the vague black streets of the great gulf of towns, and among their branchless woods of vague black chimneys. These towns looked, in the cinderous wet, as though they had one and all been on fire and were just put out—a dreary and quenched panorama, many miles long.

Thus, Thomas and Francis got to Leeds; of which enterprising and important commercial centre it may be observed with delicacy, that you must either like it very much or not at all. Next day, the first of the Race-Week, they took train to Doncaster.

And instantly the character, both of travellers and of luggage, entirely changed, and no other business than race-business any longer existed on the face of the earth. The talk was all of horses and "John Scott." Guards whispered behind their hands to station-masters, of horses and John Scott. Men in cut-away coats and speckled cravats fastened with peculiar pins, and with the large bones of their legs developed under tight trousers, so that they should look as much as possible like horses' legs, paced up and down by twos at junction-stations, speaking low and moodily of horses and John Scott. The young clergyman in the black strait-waistcoat, who occupied the middle seat of the carriage, expounded in his peculiar pulpit-accent to the young and lovely Reverend Mrs. Crinoline, who occupied the opposite middle-seat, a few passages of rumour relative to "Oartheth, my love, and Mither John Eth-cott." A bandy vagabond, with a head like a Dutch cheese, in a fustian stable-suit, attending on a horse-box and going about the platforms with a halter hanging round his neck like a Calais burgher of the ancient period much degenerated, was courted by the best society, by reason of what he had to hint, when not engaged in eating straw, concerning "t'harses and Joon Scott." The engine-driver himself, as he applied one eye to his large stationary double-eyeglass on the engine, seemed to keep the other open, sideways, upon horses and John Scott.

Breaks and barriers at Doncaster Station to keep the crowd off;

temporary wooden avenues of ingress and egress, to help the crowd on. Forty extra porters sent down for this present blessed Race-week, and all of them making up their betting-books in the lamp-room or somewhere else, and none of them to come and touch the luggage. Travellers disgorged into an open space, a howling wilderness of idle men. All work but race-work at a stand-still; all men at a stand-still. "Ey my word! Deant ask noon 'o us to help wi' t'luggage. Bock your opinion loike a mon. Coom! Dang it, coom, t'harses and Joon Scott!" In the midst of the idle men, all the fly horses and omnibus horses of Doncaster and parts adjacent, rampant, rearing, backing, plunging, spying—apparently the result of their hearing of nothing but their own order and John Scott.

Grand Dramatic Company from London for the Race-Week. Poses Plastiques in the Grand Assembly Room up the Stable-Yard at seven and nine each evening, for the Race-Week. Grand Alliance Circus in the field beyond the bridge, for the Race-Week. Grand Exhibition of Aztec Lilliputians, important to all who want to be horrified cheap, for the Race-Week. Lodgings, grand and not grand, but all at grand prices, ranging from ten pounds to twenty, for the Grand Race-Week!

Rendered giddy enough by these things, Messieurs Idle and Good-child repaired to the quarters they had secured beforehand, and Mr. Goodchild looked down from the window into the surging street.

"By Heaven, Tom!" cried he, after contemplating it, "I am in the Lunatic Asylum again, and these are all mad people under the charge of a body of designing keepers!"

All through the Race-Week, Mr. Goodchild never divested himself of this idea. Every day he looked out of window, with something of the dread of Lemuel Gulliver looking down at men after he returned home from the horse-country; and every day he saw the Lunatics, horse-mad, betting-mad, drunken-mad, vice-mad, and the designing Keepers always after them. The idea pervaded, like the second colour in shot-silk, the whole of Mr. Goodchild's impressions. They were much as follows:

Monday, mid-day. Races not to begin until to-morrow, but all the mob-Lunatics out, crowding the pavements of the one main street of pretty and pleasant Doncaster, crowding the road, particularly crowding the outside of the Betting Rooms, whooping and shouting loudly after all passing vehicles. Frightened lunatic horses occasionally running away, with infinite clatter. All degrees of men, from peers to paupers, betting incessantly. Keepers very watchful, and taking all good chances. An awful family likeness among the Keepers, to Mr. Palmer and Mr. Thurtell. With some knowledge of expression and some acquaintance with heads (thus writes Mr. Goodchild), I never have seen anywhere, so many repetitions of one class of countenance and one character of head (both evil) as in the street at this time. Cunning, covetousness, secrecy, cold calculation, hard callousness and dire insensibility, are the uniform Keeper characteristics. Mr. Palmer passes me five times in five minutes and, as I go down the street, the back of Mr. Thurtell's skull is always going on before me.

Monday evening. Town lighted up; more Lunatics out than ever; a complete choke and stoppage of the thoroughfare outside the Betting Rooms. Keepers, having dined, pervade the Betting Rooms, and sharply snap at the moneyed Lunatics. Some Keepers flushed with drink, and some not, but all close and calculating. A vague echoing roar of "t'harses" and "t'races" always rising in the air, until midnight, at about which period it dies away in occasional drunken songs and straggling yells. But, all night, some unmannerly drinking house in the neighbourhood opens its mouth at intervals and spits out a man too drunk to be retained: who thereupon makes what uproarious protest may be left in him, and either falls asleep where he tumbles, or is carried off in custody.

Tuesday morning, at daybreak. A sudden rising, as it were out of the earth, of all the obscene creatures, who sell "correct cards of the races." They may have been coiled in corners, or sleeping on doorsteps, and, having all passed the night under the same set of circumstances, may all want to circulate their blood at the same time; but, however that may be, they spring into existence all at once and together, as though a new Cadmus had sown a race-horse's teeth. There is nobody up, to buy the cards; but the cards are madly cried. There is no patronage to quarrel for; but, they madly quarrel and fight. Conspicuous among these hyænas, as breakfast-time discloses, is a fearful creature in the general semblance of a man: shaken off his next-to-no legs by drink and devilry, bareheaded and barefooted, with a great shock of hair like a horrible broom, and nothing on him but a ragged pair of trousers and a pink glazed-calico coat—made on him—so very tight that it is as evident that he could never take it off, as that he never does. This hideous apparition, inconceivably drunk, has a terrible power of making a gong-like imitation of the braying of an ass: which feat requires that he should lay his right jaw in his begrimed right paw, double himself up, and shake his bray out of himself, with much staggering on his next to no legs, and much twirling of his horrible broom, as if it were a mop. From the present minute, when he comes in sight holding up his cards to the windows, and hoarsely proposing purchase to My Lord, Your Excellency, Colonel, the Noble Captain, and Your Honourable Worship—from the present minute until the Grand Race-Week is finished, at all hours of the morning, evening, day, and night, shall the town reverberate, at capricious intervals, to the brays of this frightful animal the Gong-donkey.

No very great racing to-day, so no very great amount of vehicles: though there is a good sprinkling, too: from farmers' carts and gigs, to carriages with post-horses and to fours-in-hand, mostly coming by the road from York, and passing on straight through the main street to the Course. A walk in the wrong direction may be a better thing for Mr. Goodchild to-day than the Course, so he walks in the wrong direction. Everybody gone to the races. Only children in the street. Grand Alliance Circus deserted; not one Star-Rider left; omnibus which forms the Pay-Place, having on separate panels Pay here for the Boxes, Pay here for the Pit, Pay here for the Gallery, hove down in a corner and locked up; nobody near the tent but the man on his knees on the grass, who is making the paper balloons for the Star young gentlemen to jump through to-night. A pleasant road, pleasantly wooded. No labourers working in the fields; all gone "t'races." The few late wenders on their way "t'races," who are yet left driving on the road, stare in amazement at the recluse who is not going "t'races." Roadside innkeeper has gone "t'races." Turnpike-man has gone "t'races." His thrifty wife, washing clothes at the toll-house door, is going "t'races" to-morrow. Perhaps there may be no one left to take the toll to-morrow; who knows? Though assuredly that would be neither turnpike-like nor Yorkshire-like. The very wind and dust seem to be hurrying "t'races," as they briskly pass the only wayfarer on the road. In the distance, the Railway-Engine, waiting at the town-end, shrieks despairingly. Nothing but the difficulty of getting off the Line, restrains that Engine from going "t'races," too, it is very clear.

At night, more Lunatics out than last night—and more Keepers. The latter very active at the Betting Rooms, the street in front of which is now impassable. Mr. Palmer as before. Mr. Thurtell as before. Unmannerly drinking-house expectorates as before. Drunken negro-melodists, Gong-donkey, and correct cards, in the night.

On Wednesday morning, the morning of the great St. Leger, it becomes apparent that there has been a great influx since yesterday, both of Lunatics and Keepers. The families of the tradesmen over the way are no longer within human ken; their places know them no more; ten, fifteen and twenty guinea-lodgers fill them. At the pastry-cook's second-floor window, a Keeper is brushing Mr. Thurtell's hair —thinking it is his own. In the wax-chandler's attic, another Keeper is putting on Mr. Palmer's braces. In the gunsmith's nursery, a Lunatic is shaving himself. In the serious stationer's best sitting-room, three Lunatics are taking a combination-breakfast, praising the (cook's) devil, and drinking neat brandy in an atmosphere of last midnight's cigars. No family sanctuary is free from our Angelic messengers—we put up at the Angel—who in the guise of extra waiters for the grand Race-Week, rattle in and out of the most secret chambers of everybody's house, with dishes and tin covers, decanters, soda-water bottle, and glasses. An hour later. Down the street and up the street, as far as eyes can see and a good deal farther, there is a dense crowd; outside the Betting Rooms it is like a great struggle at a theatre door—in the days of theatres; or at the vestibule of the Spurgeon temple—in the days of Spurgeon. An hour later. Fusing into this crowd, and somehow getting through it, are all kinds of conveyances, and all kinds of foot-passengers; carts, with brickmakers and brickmakeresses jolting up and down on planks; drags, with the needful grooms behind, sitting cross-armed in the needful manner, and slanting themselves backward from the soles of their boots at the needful angle; postboys, in the shining hats and smart jackets of the olden time, when stokers were not; beautiful Yorkshire horses, gallantly driven by their own breeders and masters. Under every pole, and every shaft, and every horse, and every wheel as it would seem, the Gong-donkey—metallically braying, when not struggling for life, or whipped out of the way.

By one o'clock, all this stir has gone out of the streets, and there is no one left in them but Francis Goodchild. Francis Goodchild will not be left in them long; for, he too is on his way "t'races."

A most beautiful sight, Francis Goodchild finds "t'races" to be, when he has left fair Doncaster behind him, and comes out on the free course, with its agreeable prospect, its quaint Red House oddly changing and turning as Francis turns, its green grass, and fresh heath. A free course and an easy one, where Francis can roll smoothly where he will, and can choose between the start, or the coming in, or the turn behind the brow of the hill, or any out-of-the-way point where he lists to see the throbbing horses straining every nerve, and making the sympathetic earth throb as they come by. Francis much delights to be, not in the Grand Stand, but where he can see it, rising against the sky with its vast tiers of little white dots of faces, and its last high rows and corners of people, looking like pins stuck into an enormous pincushion—not quite so symmetrically as his orderly eye could wish, when people change or go away. When the race is nearly run out, it is as good as the race to him to see the flutter among the pins, and the change in them from dark to light, as hats are taken off and waved. Not less full of interest, the loud anticipation of the winner's name, and the swelling, the final roar; then, the quick dropping of all the pins out of their places, the revelation of the shape of the bare pincushion, and the closing-in of the whole host of Lunatics and Keepers, in the rear of the three horses with bright-coloured riders, who have not yet quite subdued their gallop though the contest is over.

Mr. Goodchild would appear to have been by no means free from lunacy himself at "t'races," though not of the prevalent kind. He is suspected by Mr. Idle to have fallen into a dreadful state concerning a pair of little lilac gloves and a little bonnet that he saw there. Mr. Idle asserts, that he did afterwards repeat at the Angel, with an appearance of being lunatically seized, some rhapsody to the following effect: "O little lilac gloves! And O winning little bonnet, making in conjunction with her golden hair quite a Glory in the sunlight round the pretty head, why anything in the world but you and me! Why may not this day's running—of horses, to all the rest: of precious sands of life to me—be prolonged through an everlasting autumn-sunshine, without a sunset! Slave of the Lamp, or Ring, strike me yonder gallant equestrian Clerk of the Course, in the scarlet coat, motionless on the green grass for ages! Friendly Devil on Two Sticks, ten times ten thousand years, keep Blink-Bonny jibbing at the post, and let us have no start! Arab drums, powerful of old to summon Genii in the desert, sound of yourselves and raise a troop for me in the desert of my heart, which shall so enchant this dusty barouche (with a conspicuous excise-place, resembling the Collector's door-plate at a turnpike), that I, within it, loving the little lilac gloves, the winning little bonnet, and the dear unknown wearer with the golden hair, may wait by her side for ever, to see a Great St. Leger that shall never be run!''

Thursday morning. After a tremendous night of crowding, shouting, drinking-house expectoration, Gong-donkey, and correct cards. Symptoms of yesterday's gains in the way of drink, and of yesterday's losses in the way of money, abundant. Money-losses very great. As usual, nobody seems to have won; but, large losses and many losers are unquestionable facts. Both Lunatics and Keepers, in general very low. Several of both kinds look in at the chemist's while Mr. Goodchild is making a purchase there, to be "picked up." One red-eyed Lunatic, flushed, faded, and disordered, enters hurriedly and cries savagely, "Hond us a gloss of sal volatile in wather, or soom dommed thing o' thot sart!" Faces at the Betting Rooms very long, and a tendency to bite nails observable. Keepers likewise given this morning to standing about solitary, with their hands in their pockets, looking down at their boots as they fit them into cracks of the pavement, and then looking up whistling and walking away. Grand Alliance Circus out, in procession; buxom lady-member of Grand Alliance, in crimson riding-habit, fresher to look at, even in her paint under the day sky, than the cheeks of Lunatics or Keepers. Spanish Cavalier appears to have lost yesterday, and jingles his bossed bridle with disgust, as if he were paying. Reaction also apparent at the Guildhall opposite, whence certain pickpockets come out handcuffed together, with that peculiar walk which is never seen under any other circumstances—a walk expressive of going to jail, game, but still of jails being in bad state and arbitrary, and how would *you* like it if it was you instead of me, as it ought to be! Midday. Town filled as yesterday, but not so full; and emptied as yesterday, but not so empty. In the evening, Angel ordinary where every Lunatic and Keeper has his modest daily meal of turtle, venison, wine, not so crowded as yesterday, and not so noisy. At night, the theatre. More abstracted faces in it, than one ever sees at public assemblies; such faces wearing an expression which strongly reminds Mr. Goodchild of the boys at school who were "going up next," with their arithmetic or mathematics. These boys are, no doubt, going up to-morrow with *their* sums and figures. Mr. Palmer and Mr. Thurtell in the boxes O. P. Mr. Thurtell and Mr. Palmer in the boxes P. S. The firm of Thurtell, Palmer, and Thurtell, in the boxes Centre. A most odious tendency observable in these distinguished gentlemen to put vile constructions on sufficiently innocent phrases in the play, and then to applaud them in a Satyr-like manner. Behind Mr. Goodchild, with a party of other Lunatics and one Keeper to express incarnation of the thing called a "gent." A gentleman born; a gentleman manufactured. A something with a scarf round his neck, and a slipshod speech issuing from behind the scarf; more depraved, more foolish, more ignorant, more unable to believe in any noble or good thing of any kind, than the stupidest Bosjesman. The thing is but a boy in years, and is addled with drink. To do its company justice, even its company is ashamed of it, as it drawls its slang criticisms on the representation, and inflames Mr. Goodchild with a burning ardour to fling it into the pit. Its remarks are so horrible, that Mr. Goodchild, for the moment, even doubts whether that *is* a wholesome Art, which sets women apart on a high floor before such a thing as this, though as good as its own sisters, or its own mother—whom Heaven forgive for bringing it into the world! But, the consideration that a low nature must make a low world of its own to live in, whatever the real materials, or it could no more exist than any of us could without the sense of touch, brings Mr. Goodchild to reason: the rather, because the thing soon drops its downy chin upon its scarf, and slobbers itself asleep.

Friday morning. Early fights. Gong-donkey, and correct cards. Again, a great set towards the races, though not so great a set as on Wednesday. Much packing going on too, upstairs at the gunsmith's, the wax-chandler's, and the serious stationer's; for there will be a heavy drift of Lunatics and Keepers to London by the afternoon train. The course as pretty as ever; the great pincushion as like a pincushion, but not nearly so full of pins; whole rows of pins wanting. On the great event of the day, both Lunatics and Keepers become inspired with rage; and there is a violent scuffling, and a rushing at the losing jockey, and an emergence of the said jockey from a swaying and menacing crowd, protected by friends, and looking the worse for wear; which is a rough proceeding, though animating to see from a pleasant distance. After the great event, rills begin to flow from the pincushion towards the rail-road; the rills swell into rivers; the rivers soon unite into a lake. The lake floats Mr. Goodchild into Doncaster, past the Itinerant personage in black, by the way-side telling him from the vantage ground of a legibly printed placard on a pole that for all these things the Lord will bring him to judgment. No turtle and venison ordinary this evening; that is all over. No Betting at the rooms; nothing there but the plants in pots, which have, all the week, been stood about the entry to give it an innocent appearance, and which have sorely sickened by this time.

Saturday. Mr. Idle wishes to know at breakfast, what were those dreadful groanings in his bedroom doorway in the night? Mr. Goodchild answers, Nightmare. Mr. Idle repels the calumny, and calls the waiter. The Angel is very sorry—had intended to explain; but you see, gentlemen, there was a gentleman dined downstairs with two more, and he had lost a deal of money, and he would drink a deal of wine, and in the night he "took the horrors," and got up; and as his friends could do nothing with him he laid himself down and groaned at Mr. Idle's door. "And he DID groan there," Mr. Idle says; "and you will please to imagine me inside, 'taking the horrors' too!"

So far, the picture of Doncaster on the occasion of its great sporting anniversary, offers probably a general representation of the social condition of the town, in the past as well as in the present time. The sole local phenomenon of the current year, which may be considered as entirely unprecedented in its way, and which certainly claims, on that account, some slight share of notice, consists in the actual existence of one remarkable individual, who is sojourning in Doncaster, and who, neither directly nor indirectly, has anything at all to do, in any capacity whatever, with the racing amusements of the week. Ranging throughout the entire crowd that fills the town, and including the inhabitants as well as the visitors, nobody is to be found altogether disconnected with the business of the day, excepting this one unparalleled man. He does not bet on the races, like the sporting men. He does not assist the races, like the jockeys, starters, judges, and grooms. He does not look on at the races, like Mr Goodchild and his fellow-spectators. He does not profit by the races, like the hotel-keepers and the trades-people. He does not minister to the necessities of the races, like the booth-keepers, the postillions, the waiters, and the hawkers of Lists. He does not assist the attractions of the races, like the actors at the theatre, the riders at the circus, or the posturers at the Poses Plastiques. Absolutely and literally, he is the only individual in Doncaster who stands by the brink of the full-flowing race-stream, and is not swept away by it in common with all the rest of his species. Who is this modern hermit, this recluse of the St. Leger-week, this inscrutably ungregarious being, who lives apart from the amusements and activities of his fellow-creatures? Surely, there is little difficulty in guessing that clearest and easiest of all riddles. Who could he be, but Mr. Thomas Idle?

Thomas had suffered himself to be taken to Doncaster, just as he would have suffered himself to be taken to any other place in the habitable globe which would guarantee him the temporary possession of a comfortable sofa to rest his ankle on. Once established at the hotel, with his leg on one cushion and his back against another, he formally declined taking the slightest interest in any circumstance whatever connected with the races, or with the people who were assembled to see them. Francis Goodchild, anxious that the hours should pass by his crippled travelling-companion as lightly as possible, suggested that his sofa should be moved to the window, and that he should amuse himself by looking out at the moving panorama of humanity, which the view from it of the principal street presented. Thomas, however, steadily declined profiting by the suggestion.

"The farther I am from the window," he said, "the better, Brother Francis, I shall be pleased. I have nothing in common with the one prevalent idea of all those people who are passing in the street. Why should I care to look at them?"

"I hope I have nothing in common with the prevalent idea of a great many of them, either," answered Goodchild, thinking of the sporting gentlemen whom he had met in the course of his wanderings about Doncaster. "But, surely, among all the people who are walking by the house, at this very moment, you may find——"

"Not one living creature," interposed Thomas, "who is not, in one way or another, interested in horses, and who is not, in a greater or less degree, an admirer of them. Now, I hold opinions in reference to these particular members of the quadruped creation, which may lay claim (as I believe) to the disastrous distinction of being unpartaken by any other human being, civilised or savage, over the whole surface of the earth. Taking the horse as an animal in the abstract, Francis, I cordially despise him from every point of view."

"Thomas," said Goodchild, "confinement to the house has begun to affect your biliary secretions. I shall go to the chemist's and get you some physic."

"I object," continued Thomas, quietly possessing himself of his friend's hat, which stood on a table near him,—"I object, first, to the personal appearance of the horse. I protest against the conventional idea of beauty, as attached to that animal. I think his nose too long, his forehead too low, and his legs (except in the case of the cart-horse) ridiculously thin by comparison with the size of his body. Again, considering how big an animal he is, I object to the contemptible delicacy of his constitution. Is he not the sickliest creature in creation? Does any child catch cold as easily as a horse? Does he not sprain his fetlock, for all his appearance of superior strength, as easily as I sprained my ankle? Furthermore, to take him from another point of view, what a helpless wretch he is! No fine lady requires more constant waiting on than a horse. Other animals can make their own toilette: he must have a groom. You will tell me that this is because we want to make his coat artificially glossy. Glossy! Come home with me, and see my cat,—my clever cat, who can groom herself! Look at your own dog! see how the intelligent creature curry-combs himself with his own honest teeth! Then, again, what a fool the horse is, what a poor, nervous fool! He will start at a piece of white paper in the road as if it was a lion. His one idea, when he hears a noise that he is not accustomed to, is to run away from it. What do you say to those two common instances of the sense and courage of this absurdly overpraised animal? I might multiply them to two hundred, if I chose to exert my mind and waste my breath, which I never do. I prefer coming at once to my last charge against the horse, which is the most serious of all, because it affects his moral character. I accuse him boldly, in his capacity of servant to man, of slyness and treachery. I brand him publicly, no matter how mild he may look about the eyes, or how sleek he may be about the coat, as a systematic betrayer, whenever he can get the chance, of the confidence reposed in him. What do you mean by laughing and shaking your head at me?"

"Oh, Thomas, Thomas!" said Goodchild. "You had better give me my hat; you had better let me get you that physic."

"I will let you get anything you like, including a composing draught for yourself," said Thomas, irritably alluding to his fellow-apprentice's inexhaustible activity, "if you will only sit quiet for five minutes longer, and hear me out. I say again the horse is a betrayer of the confidence reposed in him; and that opinion, let me add, is drawn from my own personal experience, and is not based on any fanciful theory whatever. You shall have two instances, two overwhelming instances. Let me start the first of these by asking, what is the distinguishing quality which the Shetland pony has arrogated to himself, and is still perpetually trumpeting through the world by means of popular report and books on Natural History? I see the answer in your face: it is the quality of being Sure-Footed. He professes to have other virtues, such as hardiness and strength, which you may discover on trial ; but the one thing which he insists on your believing, when you get on his back, is that he may be safely depended on not to tumble down with you. Very good. Some years ago, I was in Shetland with a party of friends. They insisted on taking me with them to the top of a precipice that overhung the sea. It was a great distance off, but they all determined to walk to it except me. I was wiser then than I was with you at Carrock, and I determined to be carried to the precipice. There was no carriage-road in the island, and nobody offered (in consequence, as I suppose, of the imperfectly-civilised state of the country) to bring me a sedan-chair, which is naturally what I should have liked best. A Shetland pony was produced instead. I remembered my Natural History, I recalled popular report, and I got on the little beast's back, as any other man would have done in my position, placing implicit confidence in the sureness of his feet. And how did he repay that confidence? Brother Francis, carry your mind on from morning to noon. Picture to yourself a howling wilderness of grass and bog, bounded by low stony hills. Pick out one particular spot in that imaginary scene, and sketch me in it, with outstretched arms, curved back, and heels in the air, plunging headforemost into a black patch of water and mud. Place just behind me the legs, the body, and the head of a sure-footed Shetland pony, all stretched flat on the ground, and you will have produced an accurate representation of a very lamentable fact. And the moral device, Francis, of this picture will be to testify that when gentlemen put confidence in the legs of Shetland ponies, they will find to their cost that they are leaning on nothing but broken reeds. There is my first instance—and what have you got to say to that?"

"Nothing, but that I want my hat," answered Goodchild, starting up and walking restlessly about the room.

"You shall have it in a minute," rejoined Thomas. "My—second instance"—(Goodchild groaned, and sat down again)—"My second instance is more appropriate to the present time and place, for it refers to a race-horse. Two years ago an excellent friend of mine, who was desirous of prevailing on me to take regular exercise, and who was well enough acquainted with the weakness of my legs to expect no very active compliance with his wishes on their part, offered to make me a present of one of his horses. Hearing that the animal in question had started in life on the turf, I declined accepting the gift with many thanks; adding, by way of explanation, that I looked on a race-horse as a kind of embodied hurricane, upon which no sane man of my character and habits could be expected to seat himself. My friend replied that, however appropriate my metaphor might be as applied to race-horses in general, it was singularly unsuitable as applied to the particular horse which he proposed to give me. From a foal upwards this remarkable animal had been the idlest and most sluggish of his race. Whatever capacities for speed he might possess he had kept so strictly to himself, that no amount of training had ever brought them out. He had been found hopelessly slow as a racer and hopelessly lazy as a hunter, and was fit for nothing but a quiet, easy life of it with an old gentleman or an invalid. When I heard this account of the horse, I don't mind confessing that my heart warmed to him. Visions of Thomas Idle ambling serenely on the back of a steed as lazy as himself, presenting to a restless world the soothing and composite spectacle of a kind of sluggardly Centaur, too peaceable in his habits to alarm anybody, swam attractively before my eyes. I went to look at the horse in the stable. Nice fellow! he was fast asleep with a kitten on his back. I saw him taken out for an airing by the groom. If he had had trousers on his legs I should have not known them from my own, so deliberately were they lifted up, so gently were they put down, so slowly did they get over the ground. From that moment I gratefully accepted my friend's offer. I went home; the horse followed me—by a slow train. Oh, Francis, how devoutly I believed in that horse! how carefully I looked after all his little comforts! I had never gone the length of hiring a man-servant to wait on myself; but I went to the expense of hiring one to wait upon him. If I thought a little of myself when I bought the softest saddle that could be had for money, I thought also of my horse. When the man at the shop afterwards offered me spurs and a whip, I turned from him with horror. When I sallied out for my first ride, I went purposely unarmed with the means of hurrying my steed. He proceeded at his own pace every step of the way; and when he stopped at last, and blew out both his sides with a heavy sigh, and turned his sleepy head and looked behind him, I took him home again, as I might take home an artless child who said to me, 'If you please, Sir, I am tired.' For a week this complete harmony between me and my horse lasted undisturbed. At the end of that time, when he had made quite sure of my friendly confidence in his laziness, when he had thoroughly acquainted himself with all the little weaknesses of my seat (and their name is Legion), the smouldering treachery and ingratitude of the equine nature blazed out in an instant. Without the slightest provocation from me, with nothing passing him at the time but a pony-chaise driven by an old lady, he started in one instant from a state of sluggish depression to a state of frantic high spirits. He kicked, he plunged, he shied, he pranced, he capered fearfully. I sat on him as long as I could, and when I could sit no longer, I fell off. No, Francis! this is not a circumstance to be laughed at, but to be wept over. What would be said of a Man who had requited my kindness in that way? Range over all the rest of the animal creation, and where will you find me an instance of treachery so black as this? The cow that kicks down the milking-pail may have some reason for it; she may think herself taxed too heavily to contribute to the dilution of human tea and the greasing of human bread. The tiger who springs out on me unawares has the excuse of being hungry at the time, to say nothing of the further justification of being a total stranger to me. The very flea who surprises me in my sleep may defend his act of assassination on the ground that I, in my turn, am always ready to murder him when I am awake. I defy the whole body of Natural Historians to move me, logically, off the ground that I have taken in regard to the horse. Receive back your hat, Brother Francis, and go to the chemist's, if you please; for I have now done. Ask me to take anything you like, except an interest in the Doncaster races. Ask me to look at anything you like, except an assemblage of people all animated by feelings of a friendly and admiring nature towards the horse. You are a remarkably well-informed man, and you have heard of hermits. Look upon me as a member of that ancient fraternity, and you will sensibly add to the many obligations which Thomas Idle is proud to owe to Francis Goodchild.''

Here, fatigued by the effort of excessive talking, disputatious Thomas waved one hand languidly, laid his head back on the sofa-pillow, and calmly closed his eyes.

At a later period, Mr. Goodchild assailed his travelling companion boldly from the impregnable fortress of common sense. But Thomas, though tamed in body by drastic discipline, was still as mentally unapproachable as ever on the subject of his favourite delusion.

The view from the window after Saturday's breakfast is altogether changed. The tradesmen's families have all come back again. The serious stationer's young woman of all work is shaking a duster out of the window of the combination breakfast-room; a child is playing with a doll, where Mr. Thurtell's hair was brushed; a sanitary scrubbing is in progress on the spot where Mr. Palmer's braces were put on. No signs of the Races are in the streets, but the tramps and the tumble-down carts and trucks laden with drinking-forms and tables and remnants of booths, that are making their way out of the town as fast as they can. The Angel, which has been cleared for action all the week, already begins restoring every neat and comfortable article of furniture to its own neat and comfortable place. The Angel's daughters (pleasanter angels Mr. Idle and Mr. Goodchild never saw, nor more quietly expert in their business, nor more superior to the common vice of being above it), have a little time to rest, and to air their cheerful faces among the flowers in the yard. It is market-day. The market looks unusually natural, comfortable, and wholesome; the market-people too. The town seems quite restored, when, hark! a metallic bray—The Gong-donkey!

The wretched animal has not cleared off with the rest, but is here, under the window. How much more inconceivably drunk now, how much more begrimed of paw, how much more tight of calico hide, how much more stained and daubed and dirty and dunghilly, from his horrible broom to his tender toes, who shall say! He cannot even shake the bray out of himself now, without laying his cheek so near to the mud of the street, that he pitches over after delivering it. Now, prone, in the mud, and now backing himself up against shop-windows, the owners of which come out in terror to remove him; now, in the drinking-shop, and now in the tobacconist's, where he goes to buy tobacco, and makes his way into the parlour, and where he gets a cigar, which in half-a-minute he forgets to smoke; now dancing, now dozing, now cursing, and now complimenting My Lord, the Colonel, the Noble Captain, and Your Honourable Worship, the Gong-donkey kicks up his heels, occasionally braying, until suddenly he beholds the dearest friend he has in the world coming down the street.

The dearest friend the Gong-donkey has in the world, is a sort of Jackal, in a dull mangy black hide, of such small pieces that it looks as if it were made of blacking bottles turned inside out and cobbled together. The dearest friend in the world (inconceivably drunk too) advances at the Gong-donkey, with a hand on each thigh, in a series of humorous springs and stops, wagging his head as he comes. The Gong-donkey regarding him with attention and with the warmest affection, suddenly perceives that he is the greatest enemy he has in the world, and hits him hard in the countenance. The astonished Jackal closes with the Donkey, and they roll over and over in the mud, pummelling one another. A police Inspector, supernaturally endowed with patience, who has long been looking on from the Guildhall-steps, says, to a myrmidon, "Lock 'em up! Bring 'em in!"

Appropriate finish to the Grand Race-Week. The Gong-donkey, captive and last trace of it, conveyed into limbo, where they cannot do better than keep him until next Race-Week. The Jackal is wanted too, and is much looked for, over the way and up and down. But, having had the good fortune to be undermost at the time of the capture, he has vanished into air.

On Saturday afternoon, Mr. Goodchild walks out and looks at the Course. It is quite deserted; heaps of broken crockery and bottles are raised to its memory; and correct cards and other fragments of paper are blowing about it, as the regulation little paper-books, carried by the French soldiers in their breasts, were seen, soon after the battle was fought, blowing idly about the plains of Waterloo.

Where will these present idle leaves be blown by the idle winds, and where will the last of them be one day lost and forgotten? An idle question, and an idle thought; and with it Mr. Idle fitly makes his bow, and Mr. Goodchild his, and thus ends the Lazy Tour of Two Idle Apprentices.

THE END

PICTURES FROM ITALY

Editor's Note

Dickens in 1841 crossed the Atlantic for the first time, and wrote some strong criticisms of the Americans ; which they resented, the more so because the Republic did not introduce slavery. In 1844 he crossed to Italy in order to " fade away from the public eye for a year " and also give himself time and opportunity to get new ideas and to enlarge his knowledge. One of the fruits of this tour was the uncontroversial and far happier Pictures from Italy—notably interesting features of which are : the description of the Theatre of Puppets, or Marionetti ; and the references to his brave Courier, whose name was Louis Roche. Proverbs are almost proverbially inaccurate : certainly Louis disproved the one alleging that no master is a hero to his own servant (see The Life of Dickens : Volume XIV). Also among the new ideas resulting from the " holiday" was that of The Chimes, suggested by the bells of Genoa. Pictures from Italy was serially published in " The Daily News," beginning with the first issue of that newspaper ; of which, for a short time, Charles Dickens was Editor. This edition is printed from the one carefully corrected by the author in 1867–1868.

PICTURES FROM ITALY

BY
CHARLES DICKENS

LONDON:
HAZELL, WATSON & VINEY, LTD.

PICTURES FROM ITALY

THE READER'S PASSPORT

IF the readers of this volume will be so kind as to take their credentials for the different places which are the subject of its author's reminiscences, from the Author himself, perhaps they may visit them, in fancy, the more agreeably, and with a better understanding of what they are to expect.

Many books have been written upon Italy, affording many means of studying the history of that interesting country, and the innumerable associations entwined about it. I make but little reference to that stock of information; not at all regarding it as a necessary consequence of my having had recourse to the storehouse for my own benefit, that I should reproduce its easily accessible contents before the eyes of my readers.

Neither will there be found, in these pages, any grave examination into the government or misgovernment of any portion of the country. No visitor of that beautiful land can fail to have a strong conviction on the subject; but as I chose when residing there, a Foreigner, to abstain from the discussion of any such questions with any order of Italians, so I would rather not enter on the inquiry now. During my twelve months' occupation of a house at Genoa, I never found that authorities constitutionally jealous were distrustful of me; and I should be sorry to give them occasion to regret their free courtesy, either to myself or any of my countrymen.

There is, probably, not a famous Picture or Statue in all Italy, but could be easily buried under a mountain of printed paper devoted to dissertations on it. I do not, therefore, though an earnest admirer of Painting and Sculpture, expatiate at any length on famous Pictures and Statues.

This Book is a series of faint reflections—mere shadows in the water—of places to which the imaginations of most people are attracted in a greater or less degree, on which mine had dwelt for years, and which have some interest for all. The greater part of the descriptions were written on the spot, and sent home, from time to time, in private letters. I do not mention the circumstance as an excuse for any defects they may present, for it would be none; but as a guarantee to the Reader that they were at least penned in the fulness of the subject, and with the liveliest impressions of novelty and freshness.

If they have ever a fanciful and idle air, perhaps the reader will suppose them written in the shade of a Sunny Day, in the midst of the objects of which they treat, and will like them none the worse for having such influences of the country upon them.

I hope I am not likely to be misunderstood by Professors of the Roman Catholic faith, on account of anything contained in these pages. I have done my best, in one of my former productions, to do justice to them; and I trust, in this, they will do justice to me. When I mention any exhibition that impressed me as absurd or disagreeable, I do not seek to connect it, or recognise it as necessarily connected with, any essentials of their creed. When I treat of the ceremonies of the Holy Week, I merely treat of their effect, and do not challenge the good and learned Dr. Wiseman's interpretation of their meaning. When I hint a dislike of nunneries for young girls who abjure the world before they have ever proved or known it; or doubt the *ex officio* sanctity of all Priests and Friars; I do no more than many conscientious Catholics both abroad and at home.

I have likened these Pictures to shadows in the water, and would fain hope that I have, nowhere, stirred the water so roughly, as to mar the shadows. I could never desire to be on better terms with all my friends than now, when distant mountains rise, once more, in my path. For I need not hesitate to avow, that, bent on correcting a brief mistake I made, not long ago, in disturbing the old relations between myself and my readers, and departing for a moment from my old pursuits, I am about to resume them, joyfully, in Switzerland; where during another year of absence, I can at once work out the themes I have now in my mind, without interruption: and while I keep my English audience within speaking distance, extend my knowledge of a noble country, inexpressibly attractive to me.*

This book is made as accessible as possible, because it would be a great pleasure to me if I could hope, through its means, to compare impressions with some among the multitudes who will hereafter visit the scenes described with interest and delight.

And I have only now, in passport wise, to sketch my reader's portrait, which I hope may be thus supposititiously traced for either sex:

Complexion	Fair.
Eyes	Very cheerful.
Nose	Not supercilious.
Mouth	Smiling.
Visage	Beaming.
General Expression	Extremely agreeable.

GOING THROUGH FRANCE

On a fine Sunday morning in the Midsummer time and weather of eighteen hundred and forty-four, it was, my good friend, when—

* This was written in 1846.

don't be alarmed; not when two travellers might have been observed slowly making their way over that picturesque and broken ground by which the first chapter of a Middle Aged novel is usually attained—but when an English travelling-carriage of considerable proportions, fresh from the shady halls of the Pantechnicon near Belgrave Square, London, was observed (by a very small French soldier; for I saw him look at it) to issue from the gate of the Hôtel Meurice in the Rue Rivoli at Paris.

I am no more bound to explain why the English family travelling by this carriage, inside and out, should be starting for Italy on a Sunday morning, of all good days in the week, than I am to assign a reason for all the little men in France being soldiers, and all the big men postilions; which is the invariable rule. But, they had some sort of reason for what they did, I have no doubt; and their reason for being there at all, was, as you know, that they were going to live in fair Genoa for a year; and that the head of the family purposed, in that space of time, to stroll about, wherever his restless humour carried him.

And it would have been small comfort to me to have explained to the population of Paris generally, that I was that Head and Chief; and not the radiant embodiment of good humour who sat beside me in the person of a French Courier—best of servants and most beaming of men! Truth to say, he looked a great deal more patriarchal than I, who, in the shadow of his portly presence, dwindled down to no account at all.

There was, of course, very little in the aspect of Paris—as we rattled near the dismal Morgue and over the Pont Neuf—to reproach us for our Sunday travelling. The wine-shops (every second house) were driving a roaring trade; awnings were spreading, and chairs and tables arranging, outside the cafés, preparatory to the eating of ices, and drinking of cool liquids, later in the day; shoe-blacks were busy on the bridges; shops were open; carts and waggons clattered to and fro; the narrow, up-hill, funnel-like streets across the River, were so many dense perspectives of crowd and bustle, parti-coloured night-caps, tobacco-pipes, blouses, large boots, and shaggy heads of hair; nothing at that hour denoted a day of rest, unless it were the appearance, here and there, of a family pleasure-party, crammed into a bulky old lumbering cab; or of some contemplative holiday-maker in the freest and easiest dishabille, leaning out of a low garret window, watching the drying of his newly polished shoes on the little parapet outside (if a gentleman), or the airing of her stockings in the sun (if a lady), with calm anticipation.

Once clear of the never-to-be-forgotten-or-forgiven pavement which surrounds Paris, the first three days of travelling towards Marseilles are quiet and monotonous enough. To Sens. To Avallon. To Chalons. A sketch of one day's proceedings is a sketch of all three; and here it is.

We have four horses, and one postilion, who has a very long whip, and drives his team, something like the Courier of Saint Petersburgh in the circle at Astley's or Franconi's: only he sits his own horse instead of standing on him. The immense jack-boots worn by these postilions, are sometimes a century or two old; and are so ludicrously disproportionate to the wearer's foot, that the spur, which is put where his own heel comes, is generally halfway up the leg of the boots. The man often comes out of the stable-yard, with his whip in his hand and his shoes on, and brings out, in both hands, one boot at a time, which he plants on the ground by the side of his horse, with great gravity, until everything is ready. When it is—and oh Heaven! the noise they make about it!—he gets into the boots, shoes and all, or is hoisted into them by a couple of friends; adjusts the rope harness, embossed by the labours of innumerable pigeons in the stables; makes all the horses kick and plunge; cracks his whip like a madman; shouts "En route— Hi!" and away we go. He is sure to have a contest with his horse before we have gone very far; and then he calls him a Thief, and a Brigand, and a Pig, and what not; and beats him about the head as if he were made of wood.

There is little more than one variety in the appearance of the country, for the first two days. From a dreary plain, to an interminable avenue, and from an interminable avenue to a dreary plain again. Plenty of vines there are in the open fields, but of a short low kind, and not trained in festoons, but about straight sticks. Beggars innumerable there are, everywhere; but an extraordinarily scanty population, and fewer children than I ever encountered. I don't believe we saw a hundred children between Paris and Chalons. Queer old towns, draw-bridged and walled: with odd little towers at the angles, like grotesque faces, as if the wall had put a mask on, and were staring down into the moat; other strange little towers, in gardens and fields, and down lanes, and in farm-yards: all alone, and always round, with a peaked roof, and never used for any purpose at all; ruinous buildings of all sorts; sometimes an hôtel de ville, sometimes a guard-house, sometimes a dwelling-house, sometimes a château with a rank garden, prolific in dandelion, and watched over by extinguisher-topped turrets, and blink-eyed little casements; are the standard objects, repeated over and over again. Sometimes we pass a village inn, with a crumbling wall belonging to it, and a perfect town of out-houses; and painted over the gateway, "Stabling for Sixty Horses;" as indeed there might be stabling for sixty score, were there any horses to be stabled there, or anybody resting there, or anything stirring about the place but a dangling bush, indicative of the wine inside: which flutters idly in the wind, in lazy keeping with everything else, and certainly is never in a green old age, though always so old as to be dropping to pieces. And all day long, strange little narrow waggons, in strings of six or eight, bringing cheese from Switzerland, and frequently in charge, the whole line, of one man, or even boy—and he very often asleep in the foremost cart—come jingling past: the horses drowsily ringing the bells upon their harness, and looking as if they thought (no doubt they do) their great blue woolly furniture, of immense weight and thickness, with a pair of grotesque horns growing out of the collar, very much too warm for the Midsummer weather.

Then, there is the Diligence, twice or thrice a-day; with the dusty outsides in blue frocks, like butchers; and the insides in white night-caps; and its cabriolet head on the roof, nodding and shaking, like an idiot's head; and its Young-France passengers staring out of window, with beards down to their waists, and blue spectacles awfully shading their warlike eyes, and very big sticks clenched in their National grasp. Also the Malle Poste, with only a couple of passengers, tearing along at a real good dare-devil pace, and out of sight in no time. Steady old Curés come jolting past, now and then, in such ramshackle, rusty, musty, clattering coaches as no Englishman would believe in; and bony women dawdle about in solitary places, holding cows by ropes while they feed, or digging and hoeing or doing field-work of a more laborious kind, or representing real shepherdesses with their flocks—to obtain an adequate idea of which pursuit and its followers, in any country, it is only necessary to take any pastoral poem, or picture, and imagine to yourself whatever is most exquisitely and widely unlike the descriptions therein contained.

You have been travelling along, stupidly enough, as you generally do in the last stage of the day; and the ninety-six bells upon the horses—twenty-four apiece—have been ringing sleepily in your ears for half an hour or so; and it has become a very jog-trot, monotonous, tiresome sort of business; and you have been thinking deeply about the dinner you will have at the next stage; when, down at the end of the long avenue of trees through which you are travelling, the first indication of a town appears, in the shape of some straggling cottages: and the carriage begins to rattle and roll over a horribly uneven pavement. As if the equipage were a great firework, and the mere sight of a smoking cottage chimney had lighted it, instantly it begins to crack and splutter, as if the very devil were in it. Crack, crack, crack, crack. Crack-crack-crack. Crick-crack. Crick-crack. Helo! Hola! Vite! Voleur! Brigand! Hi hi hi! En r-r-r-r-route! Whip, wheels, driver, stones, beggars, children, crack, crack, crack; helo! hola! charité pour l'amour de Dieu! crick-crack-crick-crack; crick, crick, crick; bump, jolt, crack, bump, crick-crack; round the corner, up the narrow street, down the paved hill on the other side; in the gutter; bump, bump; jolt, jog, crick, crick, crick; crack, crack, crack; into the shop-windows on the left-hand side of the street, preliminary to a sweeping turn into the wooden archway on the right; rumble, rumble, rumble; clatter, clatter, clatter; crick, crick, crick; and here we are in the yard of the Hôtel de l'Ecu d'Or; used up, gone out, smoking, spent, exhausted; but sometimes making a false start unexpectedly, with nothing coming of it—like a firework to the last!

The landlady of the Hôtel de l'Ecu d'Or is here; and the landlord of the Hôtel de l'Ecu d'Or is here; and the femme de chambre of the Hôtel de l'Ecu d'Or is here; and a gentleman in a glazed cap, with a red beard like a bosom friend, who is staying at the Hôtel de l'Ecu d'Or, is here; and Monsieur le Curé is walking up and down in a corner of the yard by himself, with a shovel hat upon his head, and a black gown on his back, and a book in one hand, and an umbrella in the other; and everybody, except Monsieur le Curé, is open-mouthed and open-eyed, for the opening of the carriage-door. The landlord of the Hôtel de l'Ecu d'Or, dotes to that extent upon the Courier, that he can hardly wait for his coming down from the box, but embraces his very legs and boot-heels as he descends. "My Courier! My brave Courier! My friend! My brother!" The landlady loves him, the femme de chambre blesses him, the garçon worships him. The Courier asks if his letter has been received? It has, it has. Are the rooms prepared? They are, they are. The best rooms for my noble Courier. The rooms of state for my gallant Courier; the whole house is at the service of my best of friends! He keeps his hand upon the carriage-door, and asks some other question to enhance the expectation. He carries a green leathern purse outside his coat, suspended by a belt. The idlers look at it; one touches it. It is full of five-franc pieces. Murmurs of admiration are heard among the boys. The landlord falls upon the Courier's neck, and folds him to his breast. He is so much fatter than he was, he says! He looks so rosy and so well!

The door is opened. Breathless expectation. The lady of the family gets out. Ah sweet lady! Beautiful lady! The sister of the lady of the family gets out. Great Heaven, Ma'amselle is charming! First little boy gets out. Ah, what a beautiful little boy! First little girl gets out. Oh, but this is an enchanting child! Second little girl gets out. The landlady, yielding to the finest impulse of our common nature, catches her up in her arms! Second little boy gets out. Oh, the sweet boy! Oh, the tender little family! The baby is handed out. Angelic baby! The baby has topped everything. All the rapture is expended on the baby! Then the two nurses tumble out; and the enthusiasm swelling into madness, the whole family are swept up-stairs as on a cloud; while the idlers press about the carriage, and look into it, and walk round it, and touch it. For it is something to touch a carriage that has held so many people. It is a legacy to leave one's children.

The rooms are on the first floor, except the nursery for the night, which is a great rambling chamber, with four or five beds in it: through a dark passage, up two steps, down four, past a pump, across a balcony, and next door to the stable. The other sleeping apartments are large and lofty; each with two small bedsteads, tastefully hung, like the windows, with red and white drapery. The sitting-room is famous. Dinner is already laid in it for three; and the napkins are folded in cocked-hat fashion. The floors are of red tile. There are no carpets, and not much furniture to speak of; but there is abundance of looking-glass, and there are large vases under glass shades, filled with artificial flowers; and there are plenty of clocks. The whole party are in motion. The brave Courier, in particular, is everywhere: looking after the beds, having wine poured down his throat by his dear brother the landlord, and picking up green cucumbers—always cucumbers; Heaven knows where he gets them—with which he walks about, one in each hand, like truncheons.

Dinner is announced. There is very thin soup; there are very large loaves—one apiece; a fish; four dishes afterwards; some poultry afterwards; a dessert afterwards; and no lack of wine. There is not much in the dishes; but they are very good, and always ready instantly. When it is nearly dark, the brave Courier, having eaten the two cucumbers, sliced up in the contents of a pretty large decanter of oil, and another of vinegar, emerges from his retreat below, and proposes a visit to the Cathedral, whose massive tower frowns down upon the court-yard of the inn. Off we go; and very solemn and grand it is, in the dim light: so dim at last, that the polite, old, lanthorn-awed Sacristan has a feeble little bit of candle in his hand, to grope among the tombs with—and looks among the grim columns, very like a lost ghost who is searching for his own.

Underneath the balcony, when we return, the inferior servants of the inn are supping in the open air, at a great table; the dish, a stew of meat and vegetables, smoking hot, and served in the iron cauldron it was boiled in. They have a pitcher of thin wine, and are very merry; merrier than the gentleman with the red beard, who is playing billiards in the light room on the left of the yard, where shadows, with cues in their hands, and cigars in their mouths, cross and recross the window, constantly. Still the thin Curé walks up and down alone, with his book and umbrella. And there he walks, and there the billiard-balls rattle, long after we are fast asleep.

We are astir at six next morning. It is a delightful day, shaming yesterday's mud upon the carriage, if anything could shame a carriage, in a land where carriages are never cleaned. Everybody is brisk; and as we finish breakfast, the horses come jingling into the yard from the Post-house. Everything taken out of the carriage is put back again. The brave Courier announces that all is ready, after walking into every room, and looking all round it, to be certain that nothing is left behind. Everybody gets in. Everybody connected with the Hôtel de l'Ecu d'Or is again enchanted. The brave Courier runs into the house for a parcel containing cold fowl, sliced ham, bread, and biscuits, for lunch; hands it into the coach; and runs back again.

What has he got in his hand now? More cucumbers? No. A long strip of paper. It's the bill.

The brave Courier has two belts on, this morning: one supporting the purse: another, a mighty good sort of leathern bottle, filled to the throat with the best light Bordeaux wine in the house. He never pays the bill till this bottle is full. Then he disputes it.

He disputes it now, violently. He is still the landlord's brother, but by another father or mother. He is not so nearly related to him as he was last night. The landlord scratches his head. The brave Courier points to certain figures in the bill, and intimates that if they remain there, the Hôtel de l'Ecu d'Or is thenceforth and for ever an hôtel de l'Ecu de cuivre. The landlord goes into a little counting-house. The brave Courier follows, forces the bill and a pen into his hand, and talks more rapidly than ever. The landlord takes the pen. The

Courier smiles. The landlord makes an alteration. The Courier cuts a joke. The landlord is affectionate, but not weakly so. He bears it like a man. He shakes hands with his brave brother, but he don't hug him. Still, he loves his brother; for he knows that he will be returning that way, one of these fine days, with another family, and he foresees that his heart will yearn towards him again. The brave Courier traverses all round the carriage once, looks at the drag, inspects the wheels, jumps up, gives the word, and away we go!

It is market morning. The market is held in the little square outside in front of the cathedral. It is crowded with men and women, in blue, in red, in green, in white; with canvassed stalls; and fluttering merchandise. The country people are grouped about, with their clean baskets before them. Here, the lace-sellers; there, the butter and egg-sellers; there, the fruit-sellers; there, the shoe-makers. The whole place looks as if it were the stage of some great theatre, and the curtain had just run up, for a picturesque ballet. And there is the cathedral to boot: scene-like: all grim, and swarthy, and mouldering, and cold: just splashing the pavement in one place with faint purple drops, as the morning sun, entering by a little window on the eastern side, struggles through some stained glass panes, on the western.

In five minutes we have passed the iron cross, with a little ragged kneeling-place of turf before it, in the outskirts of the town; and are again upon the road.

LYONS, THE RHONE, AND THE GOBLIN OF AVIGNON

CHALONS is a fair resting-place, in right of its good inn on the bank of the river, and the little steamboats, gay with green and red paint, that come and go upon it: which make up a pleasant and refreshing scene, after the dusty roads. But, unless you would like to dwell on an enormous plain, with jagged rows of irregular poplars on it, that look in the distance like so many combs with broken teeth: and unless you would like to pass your life without the possibility of going up-hill, or going up anything but stairs: you would hardly approve of Chalons as a place of residence.

You would probably like it better, however, than Lyons: which you may reach, if you will, in one of the before-mentioned steamboats, in eight hours.

What a city Lyons is! Talk about people feeling, at certain unlucky times, as if they had tumbled from the clouds! Here is a whole town that is tumbled, anyhow, out of the sky; having been first caught up, like other stones that tumble down from that region, out of fens and barren places, dismal to behold! The two great streets through which the two great rivers dash, and all the little streets whose name is Legion, were scorching, blistering, and sweltering. The houses, high and vast, dirty to excess, rotten as old cheeses, and as thickly peopled. All up the hills that hem the city in, these houses swarm; and the mites inside were lolling out of the windows, and drying their ragged clothes on poles, and crawling in and out at the doors, and coming out to pant and gasp upon the pavement, and creeping in and out among huge piles and bales of fusty, musty, stifling goods; and living, or rather not dying till their time should come, in an exhausted receiver. Every manufacturing town, melted into one, would hardly convey an impression of Lyons as it presented itself to me: for all the undrained, unscavengered qualities of a foreign town, seemed grafted, there, upon the native miseries of a manufacturing one; and it bears such fruit as I would go some miles out of my way to avoid encountering again.

In the cool of the evening: or rather in the faded heat of the day: we went to see the Cathedral, where divers old women, and a few dogs, were engaged in contemplation. There was no difference, in point of cleanliness, between its stone pavement and that of the streets; and there was a wax saint, in a little box like a berth aboard ship, with a glass front to it, whom Madame Tussaud would have nothin g to say to, on any terms, and which even Westminster Abbey might be ashamed of. If you would know all about the architecture of this church, or any other, its dates, dimensions, endowments, and history, is it not written in Mr. Murray's Guide-Book, and may you not read it there, with thanks to him, as I did!

For this reason, I should abstain from mentioning the curious clock in Lyons Cathedral, if it were not for a small mistake I made, in connection with that piece of mechanism. The keeper of the church was very anxious it should be shown; partly for the honour of the establishment and the town; and partly, perhaps, because of his deriving a percentage from the additional consideration. However that may be, it was set in motion, and thereupon a host of little doors flew open, and innumerable little figures staggered out of them, and jerked themselves back again, with that special unsteadiness of purpose, and hitching in the gait, which usually attaches to figures that are moved by clock-work. Meanwhile, the Sacristan stood explaining these wonders, and pointing them out, severally, with a wand. There was a centre puppet of the Virgin Mary; and close to her, a small pigeon-hole, out of which another and a very ill-looking puppet made one of the most sudden plunges I ever saw accomplished: instantly flopping back again at sight of her, and banging his little door violently after him. Taking this to be emblematic of the victory over Sin and Death, and not at all unwilling to show that I perfectly understood the subject, in anticipation of the showman, I rashly said, "Aha! The Evil Spirit. To be sure. He is very soon disposed of." "Pardon, Monsieur," said the Sacristan, with a polite motion of his hand towards the little door, as if introducing somebody—"The Angel Gabriel!"

Soon after daybreak next morning, we were steaming down the Arrowy Rhone, at the rate of twenty miles an hour, in a very dirty vessel full of merchandise, and with only three or four other passengers for our companions: among whom, the most remarkable was a silly, old, meek-faced, garlic-eating, immeasurably polite Chevalier, with a dirty scrap of red ribbon hanging at his button-hole, as if he

had tied it there to remind himself of something; as Tom Noddy, i
the farce, ties knots in his pocket-handkerchief.

For the last two days, we had seen great sullen hills, the first indi
cations of the Alps, towering in the distance. Now, we were rushin
on beside them: sometimes close beside them: sometimes with a
intervening slope, covered with vineyards. Villages and small town
hanging in mid-air, with great woods of olives seen through the ligh
open towers of their churches, and clouds moving slowly on, upon th
steep acclivity behind them; ruined castles perched on every emi
nence; and scattered houses in the clefts and gullies of the hills
made it very beautiful. The great height of these, too, making th
buildings look so tiny, that they had all the charm of elegant models
their excessive whiteness, as contrasted with the brown rocks, or th
sombre, deep, dull, heavy green of the olive-tree; and the puny size
and little slow walk of the Lilliputian men and women on the bank
made a charming picture. There were ferries out of number, too
bridges; the famous Pont d'Esprit, with I don't know how man
arches; towns where memorable wines are made; Vallence, wher
Napoleon studied; and the noble river, bringing at every windin
turn, new beauties into view.

There lay before us, that same afternoon, the broken bridge c
Avignon, and all the ctiy baking in the sun; yet with an under-done
pie-crust, battlemented wall, that never will be brown, though i
bake for centuries.

The grapes were hanging in clusters in the streets, and the brillian
Oleander was in full bloom everywhere. The streets are old and ver
narrow, but tolerably clean, and shaded by awnings stretched fron
house to house. Bright stuffs and handkerchiefs, curiosities, ancien
frames of carved wood, old chairs, ghostly tables, saints, virgins
angels, and staring daubs of portraits, being exposed for sale beneath
it was very quaint and lively. All this was much set off, too, by th
glimpses one caught, through a rusty gate standing ajar, of quie
sleepy court-yards, having stately old houses within, as silent a
tombs. It was all very like one of the descriptions in the Arabia
Nights. The three one-eyed Calenders might have knocked at an
one of those doors till the street rang again, and the porter who per
sisted in asking questions—the man who had the delicious purchase
put into his basket in the morning—might have opened it quit
naturally.

After breakfast next morning, we sallied forth to see the lions
Such a delicious breeze was blowing in, from the north, as made the
walk delightful: though the pavement-stones, and stones of the wall
and houses, were far too hot to have a hand laid on them comfortably

We went, first of all, up a rocky height, to the cathedral: wher
Mass was performing to an auditory very like that of Lyons, namely
several old women, a baby, and a very self-possessed dog, who hac
marked out for himself a little course or platform for exercise, be
ginning at the altar-rails and ending at the door, up and down which
constitutional walk he trotted, during the service, as methodically

and calmly, as any old gentleman out of doors. It is a bare old church, and the paintings in the roof are sadly defaced by time and damp weather; but the sun was shining in, splendidly, through the red curtains of the windows, and glittering on the altar furniture; and it looked as bright and cheerful as need be.

Going apart, in this church, to see some painting which was being executed in fresco by a French artist and his pupil, I was led to observe more closely than I might otherwise have done, a great number of votive offerings with which the walls of the different chapels were profusely hung. I will not say decorated, for they were very roughly and comically got up; most likely by poor sign-painters, who eke out their living in that way. They were all little pictures: each representing some sickness or calamity from which the person placing it there, had escaped, through the interposition of his or her patron saint, or of the Madonna; and I may refer to them as godo specimens of the class generally. They are abundant in Italy.

In a grotesque squareness of outline, and impossibility of perspective, they are not unlike the woodcuts in old books; but they were oil-paintings, and the artist, like the painter of the Primrose family, had not been sparing of his colours. In one, a lady was having a toe amputated—an operation which a saintly personage had sailed into the room, upon a couch, to superintend. In another, a lady was lying in bed, tucked up very tight and prim, and staring with much composure at a tripod, with a slop-basin on it; the usual form of washing-stand, and the only piece of furniture, besides the bedstead, in her chamber. One would never have supposed her to be labouring under any complaint, beyond the inconvenience of being miraculously wide awake, if the painter had not hit upon the idea of putting all her family on their knees in one corner, with their legs sticking out behind them on the floor, like boot-trees. Above whom, the Virgin, on a kind of blue divan, promised to restore the patient. In another case, a lady was in the very act of being run over, immediately outside the city walls, by a sort of piano-forte van. But the Madonna was there again. Whether the supernatural appearance had startled the horse (a bay griffin), or whether it was invisible to him, I don't know; but he was galloping away, ding dong, without the smallest reverence or compunction. On every picture "Ex voto " was painted in yellow capitals in the sky.

Though votive offerings were not unknown in Pagan Temples, and are evidently among the many compromises made between the false religion and the true, when the true was in its infancy, I could wish that all the other compromises were as harmless. Gratitude and Devotion are Christian qualities; and a grateful, humble, Christian spirit may dictate the observance.

Hard by the cathedral stands the ancient Palace of the Popes, of which one portion is now a common jail, and another a noisy barrack: while gloomy suites of state apartments, shut up and deserted, mock their own old state and glory, like the embalmed bodies of kings. But we neither went there, to see state rooms, nor soldiers' quarters, nor a common jail, though we dropped some money into a prisoners' box outside, whilst the prisoners, themselves, looked through the iron bars, high up, and watched us eagerly. We went to see the ruins of the dreadful rooms in which the Inquisition used to sit.

A little, old, swarthy woman, with a pair of flashing black eyes,— proof that the world hadn't conjured down the devil within her though it had had between sixty and seventy years to do it in,— came out of the Barrack Cabaret, of which she was the keeper, with some large keys in her hands, and marshalled us the way that we should go. How she told us, on the way, that she was a Government Officer (*concierge du palais apostolique*), and had been, for I don't know how many years; and how she had shown these dungeons to princes; and how she was the best of dungeon demonstrators; and how she had resided in the palace from an infant,—had been born there, if I recollect right,—I needn't relate. But such a fierce, little, rapid, sparkling, energetic she-devil I never beheld. She was alight and flaming, all the time. Her action was violent in the extreme. She never spoke, without stopping expressly for the purpose. She stamped her feet, clutched us by the arms, flung herself into attitudes, hammered against walls with her keys, for mere emphasis: now whispered as if the Inquisition were there still: now shrieked as if she were on the rack herself; and had a mysterious, hag-like way with her fore-finger, when approaching the remains of some new horror—looking back and walking stealthily, and making horrible grimaces—that might alone have qualified her to walk up and down a sick man's counterpane, to the exclusion of all other figures, through a whole fever.

Passing through the court-yard, among groups of idle soldiers, we turned off by a gate, which this She-Goblin unlocked for our admission, and locked again behind us: and entered a narrow court, rendered narrower by fallen stones and heaps of rubbish; part of it choking up the mouth of a ruined subterranean passage, that once communicated (or is said to have done so) with another castle on the opposite bank of the river. Close to this court-yard is a dungeon—we stood within it, in another minute—in the dismal tower *des oubliettes*, where Rienzi was imprisoned, fastened by an iron chain to the very wall that stands there now, but shut out from the sky which now looks down into it. A few steps brought us to the Cachots, in which the prisoners of the Inquisition were confined for forty-eight hours after their capture, without food or drink, that their constancy might be shaken, even before they were confronted with their gloomy judges. The day has not got in there yet. They are still small cells, shut in by four unyielding, close, hard walls; still profoundly dark; still massively doored and fastened, as of old.

Goblin, looking back as I have described, went softly on, into a vaulted chamber, now used as a store-room: once the chapel of the Holy Office. The place where the tribunal sat, was plain. The platform might have been removed but yesterday. Conceive the parable of the Good Samaritan having been painted on the wall of one of these

Inquisition chambers! But it was, and may be traced there yet.

High up in the jealous wall, are niches where the faltering replies of the accused were heard and noted down. Many of them had been brought out of the very cell we had just looked into, so awfully; along the same stone passage. We had trodden in their very footsteps.

I am gazing round me, with the horror that the place inspires, when Goblin clutches me by the wrist, and lays, not her skinny finger, but the handle of a key, upon her lip. She invites me, with a jerk, to follow her. I do so. She leads me out into a room adjoining—a rugged room, with a funnel-shaped, contracting roof, open at the top, to the bright day. I ask her what it is. She folds her arms, leers hideously, and stares. I ask again. She glances round, to see that all the little company are there; sits down upon a mound of stones; throws up her arms, and yells out, like a fiend, "La Salle de la Question!"

The Chamber of Torture! And the roof was made of that shape to stifle the victim's cries! Oh Goblin, Goblin, let us think of this awhile, in silence. Peace, Goblin! Sit with your short arms crossed on your short legs, upon that heap of stones, for only five minutes, and then flame out again.

Minutes! Seconds are not marked upon the Palace clock, when, with her eyes flashing fire, Goblin is up, in the middle of the chamber, describing, with her sunburnt arms, a wheel of heavy blows. Thus it ran round! cries Goblin. Mash, mash, mash! An endless routine of heavy hammers. Mash, mash, mash! upon the sufferer's limbs. See the stone trough! says Goblin. For the water torture! Gurgle, swill, bloat, burst, for the Redeemer's honour! Suck the bloody rag, deep down into your unbelieving body, Heretic, at every breath you draw! And when the executioner plucks it out, reeking with the smaller mysteries of God's own Image, know us for His chosen servants, true believers in the Sermon on the Mount, elect disciples of Him who never did a miracle but to heal: who never struck a man with palsy, blindness, deafness, dumbness, madness, any one affliction of mankind; and never stretched His blessed hand out, but to give relief and ease!

See! cries Goblin. There the furnace was. There they made the irons red-hot. Those holes supported the sharp stake, on which the tortured persons hung poised: dangling with their whole weight from the roof. "But;" and Goblin whispers this; "Monsieur has heard of this tower? Yes? Let Monsieur look down, then!"

A cold air, laden with an earthy smell, falls upon the face of Monsieur; for she has opened, while speaking, a trap-door in the wall. Monsieur looks in. Downward to the bottom, upward to the top, of a steep, dark, lofty tower: very dismal, very dark, very cold. The Executioner of the Inquisition, says Goblin, edging in her head to look down also, flung those who were past all further torturing, down here. "But look! does Monsieur see the black stains on the wall?" A glance, over his shoulder, at Goblin's keen eye, shows Monsieur—and would without the aid of the directing-key—where they are. "What are they?" "Blood!"

In October, 1791, when the Revolution was at its height here, sixty persons: men and women ("and priests," says Goblin, "priests"): were murdered, and hurled, the dying and the dead, into this dreadful pit, where a quantity of quick-lime was tumbled down upon their bodies. Those ghastly tokens of the massacre were soon no more; but while one stone of the strong building in which the deed was done, remains upon another, there they will lie in the memories of men, as plain to see as the splashing of their blood upon the wall is now.

Was it a portion of the great scheme of Retribution, that the cruel deed should be committed in this place! That a part of the atrocities and monstrous institutions, which had been, for scores of years, at work, to change men's nature, should in its last service, tempt them with the ready means of gratifying their furious and beastly rage! Should enable them to show themselves, in the height of their frenzy, no worse than a great, solemn, legal establishment, in the height of its power! No worse! Much better. They used the Tower of the Forgotten, in the name of Liberty—their liberty; an earth-born creature, nursed in the black mud of the Bastile moats and dungeons, and necessarily betraying many evidences of its unwholesome bringing-up—but the Inquisition used it in the name of Heaven.

Goblin's finger is lifted; and she steals out again, into the Chapel of the Holy Office. She stops at a certain part of the flooring. Her great effect is at hand. She waits for the rest. She darts at the brave Courier, who is explaining something; hits him a sounding rap on the hat with the largest key; and bids him be silent. She assembles us all, round a little trap-door in the floor, as round a grave.

"Voilà!" she darts down at the ring, and flings the door open with a crash, in her goblin energy, though it is no light weight. "Voilà les oubliettes! Voilà les oubliettes! Subterranean! Frightful! Black! Terrible! Deadly! Les oubliettes de l'Inquisition!"

My blood ran cold, as I looked from Goblin, down into the vaults, where these forgotten creatures, with recollections of the world outside: of wives, friends, children, brothers: starved to death, and made the stones ring with their unavailing groans. But, the thrill I felt on seeing the accursed wall below, decayed and broken through, and the sun shining in through its gaping wounds, was like a sense of victory and triumph. I felt exalted with the proud delight of living in these degenerate times, to see it. As if I were the hero of some high achievement! The light in the doleful vaults was typical of the light that has streamed in, on all persecution in God's name, but which is not yet at its noon! It cannot look more lovely to a blind man newly restored to sight, than to a traveller who sees it, calmly and majestically, treading down the darkness of that Infernal Well.

AVIGNON TO GENOA

GOBLIN, having shown *les oubliettes*, felt that her great *coup* was struck. She let the door fall with a crash, and stood upon it with her arms a-kimbo, sniffing prodigiously.

When we left the place, I accompanied her into her house, under the outer gateway of the fortress, to buy a little history of the building. Her cabaret, a dark, low room, lighted by small windows, sunk in the thick wall—in the softened light, and with its forge-like chimney; its little counter by the door, with bottles, jars, and glasses on it; its household implements and scraps of dress against the wall; and a sober-looking woman (she must have a congenial life of it, with Goblin,) knitting at the door—looked exactly like a picture by OSTADE.

I walked round the building on the outside, in a sort of dream, and yet with the delightful sense of having awakened from it, of which the light, down in the vaults, had given me the assurance. The immense thickness and giddy height of the walls, the enormous strength of the massive towers, the great extent of the building, its gigantic proportions, frowning aspect, and barbarous irregularity, awaken awe and wonder. The recollection of its opposite old uses: an impregnable fortress, a luxurious palace, a horrible prison, a place of torture, the court of the Inquisition: at one and the same time, a house of feasting, fighting, religion, and blood: gives to every stone in its huge form a fearful interest, and imparts new meaning to its incongruities. I could think of little, however, then, or long afterwards, but the sun in the dungeons. The palace coming down to be the lounging-place of noisy soldiers, and being forced to echo their rough talk, and common oaths, and to have their garments fluttering from its dirty windows, was some reduction of its state, and something to rejoice at; but the day in its cells, and the sky for the roof of its chambers of cruelty—that was its desolation and defeat! If I had seen it in a blaze from ditch to rampart, I should have felt that not that light, nor all the light in all the fire that burns, could waste it, like the sunbeams in its secret council-chamber, and its prisons.

Before I quit this Palace of the Popes, let me translate from the little history I mentioned just now, a short anecdote, quite appropriate to itself, connected with its adventures.

"An ancient tradition relates, that in 1441, a nephew of Pierre de Lude, the Pope's legate, seriously insulted some distinguished ladies of Avignon, whose relations, in revenge, seized the young man, and horribly mutilated him. For several years the legate kept *his* revenge within his own breast, but he was not the less resolved upon its gratification at last. He even made, in the fulness of time, advances towards a complete reconciliation; and when their apparent sincerity had prevailed, he invited to a splendid banquet, in this palace, certain families, whole families, whom he sought to exterminate. The utmost gaiety animated the repast; but the measures of the legate were well taken. When the dessert was on the board, a Swiss presented himself, with the announcement that a strange ambassador solicited an extraordinary audience. The legate, excusing himself, for the moment, to his guests, retired, followed by his officers.

Within a few minutes afterwards, five hundred persons were reduced to ashes: the whole of that wing of the building having been blown into the air with a terrible explosion!"

After seeing the churches (I will not trouble you with churches just now), we left Avignon that afternoon. The heat being very great, the roads outside the walls were strewn with people fast asleep in every little slip of shade, and with lazy groups, half asleep and half awake, who were waiting until the sun should be low enough to admit of their playing bowls among the burnt-up trees, and on the dusty road. The harvest here was already gathered in, and mules and horses were treading out the corn in the fields. We came, at dusk, upon a wild and hilly country, once famous for brigands; and travelled slowly up a steep ascent. So we went on, until eleven at night, when we halted at the town of Aix (within two stages of Marseilles) to sleep.

The hotel, with all the blinds and shutters closed to keep the light and heat out, was comfortable and airy next morning, and the town was very clean; but so hot, and so intensely light, that when I walked out at noon it was like coming suddenly from the darkened room into crisp blue fire. The air was so very clear, that distant hills and rocky points appeared within an hour's walk; while the town immediately at hand—with a kind of blue wind between me and it—seemed to be white hot, and to be throwing off a fiery air from the surface.

We left this town towards evening, and took the road to Marseilles. A dusty road it was; the houses shut up close; and the vines powdered white. At nearly all the cottage doors, women were peeling and slicing onions into earthen bowls for supper. So they had been doing last night all the way from Avignon. We passed one or two shady dark châteaux, surrounded by trees, and embellished with cool basins of water: which were the more refreshing to behold, from the great scarcity of such residences on the road we had travelled. As we approached Marseilles, the road began to be covered with holiday people. Outside the public-houses were parties smoking, drinking, playing draughts and cards, and (once) dancing. But dust, dust, dust, everywhere. We went on, through a long, straggling, dirty suburb, thronged with people; having on our left a dreary slope of land, on which the country-houses of the Marseilles merchants, always staring white, are jumbled and heaped without the slightest order: backs, fronts, sides, and gables towards all points of the compass; until, at last, we entered the town.

I was there, twice or thrice afterwards, in fair weather and foul; and I am afraid there is no doubt that it is a dirty and disagreeable place. But the prospect, from the fortified heights, of the beautiful Mediterranean, with its lovely rocks and islands, is most delightful. These heights are a desirable retreat, for less picturesque reasons—as an escape from a compound of vile smells perpetually arising from a great harbour full of stagnant water, and befouled by the refuse of innumerable ships with all sorts of cargoes: which, in hot weather, is dreadful in the last degree.

There were foreign sailors, of all nations, in the streets; with red shirts, blue shirts, buff shirts, tawny shirts, and shirts of orange colour; with red caps, blue caps, green caps, great beards, and no beards; in Turkish turbans, glazed English hats, and Neapolitan head-dresses. There were the townspeople sitting in clusters on the pavement, or airing themselves on the tops of their houses, or walking up and down the closest and least airy of Boulevards; and there were crowds of fierce-looking people of the lower sort, blocking up the way, constantly. In the very heart of all this stir and uproar, was the common madhouse; a low, contracted, miserable building, looking straight upon the street, without the smallest screen or court-yard; where chattering mad-men and mad-women were peeping out, through rusty bars, at the staring faces below, while the sun, darting fiercely aslant into their little cells, seemed to dry up their brains, and worry them, as if they were baited by a pack of dogs.

We were pretty well accommodated at the Hôtel du Paradis, situated in a narrow street of very high houses, with a hairdresser's shop opposite, exhibiting in one of its windows two full-length waxen ladies, twirling round and round: which so enchanted the hairdresser himself, that he and his family sat in arm-chairs, and in cool undresses, on the pavement outside, enjoying the gratification of the passers-by, with lazy dignity. The family had retired to rest when we went to bed, at midnight; but the hairdresser (a corpulent man, in drab slippers) was still sitting there, with his legs stretched out before him, and evidently couldn't bear to have the shutters put up.

Next day we went down to the harbour, where the sailors of all nations were discharging and taking in cargoes of all kinds: fruits, wines, oils, silks, stuffs, velvets, and every manner of merchandise. Taking one of a great number of lively little boats with gay-striped awnings, we rowed away, under the sterns of great ships, under tow-ropes and cables, against and among other boats, and very much too near the sides of vessels that were faint with oranges, to the *Marie Antoinette*, a handsome steamer bound for Genoa, lying near the mouth of the harbour. By-and-by, the carriage, that unwieldy "trifle from the Pantechnicon," on a flat barge, bumping against everything, and giving occasion for a prodigious quantity of oaths and grimaces, came stupidly alongside; and by five o'clock we were steaming out in the open sea. The vessel was beautifully clean; the meals were served under an awning on deck; the night was calm and clear; the quiet beauty of the sea and sky unspeakable.

We were off Nice, early next morning, and coasted along, within a few miles of the Cornice road (of which more in its place) nearly all day. We could see Genoa before three; and watching it as it gradually developed its splendid amphitheatre, terrace rising above terrace, garden above garden, palace above palace, height upon height, was ample occupation for us, till we ran into the stately harbour. Having been duly astonished, here, by the sight of a few Cappucini monks, who were watching the fair-weighing of some wood upon the wharf, we drove off to Albaro, two miles distant, where we had engaged a house.

The way lay through the main streets, but not through the Strada Nuova, or the Strada Balbi, which are the famous streets of palaces. I never in my life was so dismayed! The wonderful novelty of everything, the unusual smells, the unaccountable filth (though it is reckoned the cleanest of Italian towns), the disorderly jumbling of dirty houses, one upon the roof of another; the passages more squalid and more close than any in St. Giles's or old Paris; in and out of which, not vagabonds, but well-dressed women, with white veils and great fans, were passing and repassing; the perfect absence of resemblance in any dwelling-house, or shop, or wall, or post, or pillar, to anything one had ever seen before; and the disheartening dirt, discomfort, and decay; perfectly confounded me. I fell into a dismal reverie. I am conscious of a feverish and bewildered vision of saints and virgins' shrines at the street corners—of great numbers of friars, monks, and soldiers—of vast red curtains, waving in the door-ways of the churches—of always going up hill, and yet seeing every other street and passage going higher up—of fruit-stalls, with fresh lemons and oranges hanging in garlands made of vine-leaves—of a guard-house, and a drawbridge—and some gateways—and ven-dors of iced water, sitting with little trays upon the margin of the kennel—and this is all the consciousness I had, until I was set down in a rank, dull, weedy court-yard, attached to a kind of pink jail; and was told I lived there.

I little thought, that day, that I should ever come to have an attachment for the very stones in the streets of Genoa, and to look back upon the city with affection as connected with many hours of happiness and quiet! But these are my first impressions honestly set down; and how they changed, I will set down too. At present, let us breathe after this long-winded journey.

GENOA AND ITS NEIGHBOURHOOD

The first impressions of such a place as Albaro, the suburb of Genoa, where I am now, as my American friends would say, "located," can hardly fail, I should imagine, to be mournful and disappointing. It requires a little time and use to overcome the feeling of depression consequent, at first, on so much ruin and neglect. Novelty, pleasant to most people, is particularly delightful, I think, to me. I am not easily dispirited when I have the means of pursuing my own fancies and occupations; and I believe I have some natural aptitude for accommodating myself to circumstances. But, as yet, I stroll about here, in all the holes and corners of the neighbourhood, in a perpetual state of forlorn surprise; and returning to my villa: the Villa Bag-nerello (it sounds romantic, but Signor Bagnerello is a butcher hard by): have sufficient occupation in pondering over my new experiences, and comparing them, very much to my own amusement, with my expectations, until I wander out again.

The Villa Bagnerello: or the Pink Jail, a far more expressive name for the mansion: is in one of the most splendid situations imaginable. The noble bay of Genoa, with the deep blue Mediterranean, lies stretched out near at hand; monstrous old desolate houses and palaces are dotted all about; lofty hills, with their tops often hidden in the clouds, and with strong forts perched high up on their craggy sides, are close upon the left; and in front, stretching from the walls of the house, down to a ruined chapel which stands upon the bold and picturesque rocks on the sea-shore, are green vineyards, where you may wander all day long in partial shade, through interminable vistas of grapes, trained on a rough trellis-work across the narrow paths.

This sequestered spot is approached by lanes so very narrow, that when we arrived at the Custom-house, we found the people here had *taken the measure* of the narrowest among them, and were waiting to apply it to the carriage; which ceremony was gravely performed in the street, while we all stood by in breathless suspense. It was found to be a very tight fit, but just a possibility, and no more —as I am reminded every day, by the sight of various large holes which it punched in the walls on either side as it came along. We are more fortunate, I am told, than an old lady, who took a house in these parts not long ago, and who stuck fast in *her* carriage in a lane; and as it was impossible to open one of the doors, she was obliged to submit to the indignity of being hauled through one of the little front windows, like a harlequin.

When you have got through these narrow lanes, you come to an archway, imperfectly stopped up by a rusty old gate—my gate. The rusty old gate has a bell to correspond, which you ring as long as you like, and which nobody answers, as it has no connection whatever with the house. But there is a rusty old knocker, too— very loose, so that it slides round when you touch it—and if you learn the trick of it, and knock long enough, somebody comes. The brave Courier comes, and gives you admittance. You walk into a seedy little garden, all wild and weedy, from which the vineyard opens; cross it, enter a square hall like a cellar, walk up a cracked marble staircase, and pass into a most enormous room with a vaulted roof and whitewashed walls: not unlike a great Methodist chapel. This is the *sala*. It has five windows and five doors, and is decorated with pictures which would gladden the heart of one of those picture-cleaners in London who hang up, as a sign, a picture divided, like death and the lady, at the top of the old ballad: which always leaves you in a state of uncertainty whether the ingenious professor has cleaned one half, or dirtied the other. The furniture of this *sala* is a sort of red brocade. All the chairs are immovable, and the sofa weighs several tons.

On the same floor, and opening out of this same chamber, are dining-room, drawing-room, and divers bed-rooms: each with a multiplicity of doors and windows. Up-stairs are divers other gaunt chambers, and a kitchen; and down-stairs is another kitchen, which, with all sorts of strange contrivances for burning charcoal, looks like an alchemical laboratory. There are also some half-dozen small sitting-rooms, where the servants in this hot July, may escape from the heat of the fire, and where the brave Courier plays all sorts of musical instruments of his own manufacture, all the evening long. A mighty old, wandering, ghostly, echoing, grim, bare house it is, as ever I beheld or thought of.

There is a little vine-covered terrace, opening from the drawing-room; and under this terrace, and forming one side of the little garden is what used to be the stable. It is now a cow-house, and has three cows in it, so that we get new milk by the bucketful. There is no pasturage near, and they never go out, but are constantly lying down and surfeiting themselves with vine-leaves—perfect Italian cows enjoying the *dolce far' niente* all day long. They are presided over, and slept with, by an old man named Antonio, and his son; two burnt-sienna natives with naked legs and feet, who wear, each, a shirt, a pair of trousers, and a red sash, with a relic, or some sacred charm like the bonbon off a twelfth-cake, hanging round the neck. The old man is very anxious to convert me to the Catholic faith, and exhorts me frequently. We sit upon a stone by the door, sometimes in the evening, like Robinson Crusoe and Friday reversed; and he generally relates, towards my conversion, an abridgment of the History of Saint Peter—chiefly, I believe, from the unspeakable delight he has in his imitation of the cock.

The view, as I have said, is charming; but in the day you must keep the lattice-blinds close shut, or the sun would drive you mad; and when the sun goes down you must shut up all the windows, or the mosquitoes would tempt you to commit suicide. So at this time of the year, you don't see much of the prospect within doors. As for the flies, you don't mind them. Nor the fleas, whose size is prodigious, and whose name is Legion, and who populate the coach-house to that extent that I daily expect to see the carriage going off bodily, drawn by myriads of industrious fleas in harness, The rats are kept away, quite comfortably, by scores of lean cats, who roam about the garden for that purpose. The lizards, of course, nobody cares for; they play in the sun, and don't bite. The little scorpions are merely curious. The beetles are rather late, and have not appeared yet. The frogs are company. There is a preserve of them in the grounds of the next villa; and after nightfall, one would think that scores upon scores of women in pattens were going up and down a wet stone pavement without a moment's cessation. That is exactly the noise they make.

The ruined chapel, on the picturesque and beautiful sea-shore, was dedicated, once upon a time, to Saint John the Baptist. I believe there is a legend, that Saint John's bones were received there, with various solemnities, when they were first brought to Genoa; for Genoa possesses them to this day. When there is any uncommon tempest at sea, they are brought out and exhibited to the raging weather, which they never fail to calm. In consequence of this connection of Saint John with the city, great numbers of the common people are christened Giovanni Baptista, which latter name is pronounced in the Genoese patois "Batcheetcha," like a sneeze. To hear everybody calling everybody else Batcheetcha, on a Sunday, or festa-day, when there are crowds in the streets, is not a little singular and amusing to a stranger.

The narrow lanes have great villas opening into them, whose walls (outside walls, I mean) are profusely painted with all sorts of subjects, grim and holy. But time and the sea-air have nearly obliterated them; and they look like the entrance to Vauxhall Gardens on a sunny day. The court-yards of these houses are overgrown with grass and weeds; all sorts of hideous patches cover the bases of the statues, as if they were afflicted with a cutaneous disorder; the outer gates are rusty; and the iron bars outside the lower windows are all tumbling down. Firewood is kept in halls where costly treasures might be heaped up, mountain high; waterfalls are dry and choked; fountains, too dull to play, and too lazy to work, have just enough recollection of their identity, in their sleep, to make the neighbourhood damp; and the sirocco wind is often blowing over all these things for days together, like a gigantic oven out for a holiday.

Not long ago, there was a festa-day, in honour of the *Virgin's mother*, when the young men of the neighbourhood, having worn green wreaths of the vine in some procession or other, bathed in them, by scores. It looked very odd and pretty. Though I am bound to confess (not knowing of the festa at that time), that I thought, and was quite satisfied, they wore them as horses do—to keep the flies off.

Soon afterwards, there was another festa-day, in honour of St. Nazaro. One of the Albaro young men brought two large bouquets soon after breakfast, and coming up-stairs into the great *sala*, presented them himself. This was a polite way of begging for a contribution towards the expenses of some music in the Saint's honour, so we gave him whatever it may have been, and his messenger departed: well satisfied. At six o'clock in the evening we went to the church—close at hand—a very gaudy place, hung all over with festoons and bright draperies, and filled, from the altar to the main door, with women, all seated. They wear no bonnets here, simply a long white veil—the "mezzero;" and it was the most gauzy, ethereal-looking audience I ever saw. The young women are not generally pretty, but they walk remarkably well, and in their personal carriage and the management of their veils, display much innate grace and elegance. There were some men present: not very many: and a few of these were kneeling about the aisles, while everybody else tumbled over them. Innumerable tapers were burning in the church; the bits of silver and tin about the saints (especially in the Virgin's necklace) sparkled brilliantly; the priests were seated about the chief altar; the organ played away, lustily, and a full band did the like; while a conductor, in a little gallery opposite to the band, hammered away on the desk before him, with a scroll; and a tenor, without any voice, sang. The band played one way, the organ played another, the singer went a third, and the unfortunate conductor banged and banged, and flourished his scroll on some principle of his own: apparently well satisfied with the whole performance. I never did hear such a discordant din. The heat was intense all the time.

The men, in red caps, and with loose coats hanging on their shoulders (they never put them on), were playing bowls, and buying sweetmeats, immediately outside the church. When half-a-dozen of them finished a game, they came into the aisle, crossed themselves with the holy water, knelt on one knee for an instant, and walked off again to play another game at bowls. They are remarkably expert at this diversion, and will play in the stony lanes and streets, and on the most uneven and disastrous ground for such a purpose, with as much nicety as on a billiard-table. But the most favourite game is the national one of Mora, which they pursue with surprising ardour, and at which they will stake everything they possess. It is a destructive kind of gambling, requiring no accessories but the ten fingers, which are always—I intend no pun—at hand. Two men play together. One calls a number—say the extreme one, ten. He marks what portion of it he pleases by throwing out three, or four, or five fingers; and his adversary has, in the same instant, at hazard, and without seeing his hand, to throw out as many fingers, as will make the exact balance. Their eyes and hands become so used to this, and act with such astonishing rapidity, that an uninitiated bystander would find it very difficult, if not impossible, to follow the progress of the game. The initiated, however, of whom there is always an eager group looking on, devour it with the most intense avidity; and as they are always ready to champion one side or the other in case of a dispute, and are frequently divided in their partisanship, it is often a very noisy proceeding. It is never the quietest game in the world; for the numbers are always called in a loud sharp voice, and follow as close upon each other as they can be counted. On a holiday evening, standing at a window, or walking in a garden, or passing through the streets, or sauntering in any quiet place about the town, you will hear this game in progress in a score of wine-shops at once; and looking over any vineyard walk, or turning almost any corner, will come upon a knot of players in full cry. It is observable that most men have a propensity to throw out some particular number oftener than another; and the vigilance with which two sharp-eyed players will mutually endeavour to detect this weakness, and adapt their game to it, is very curious and entertaining. The effect is greatly heightened by the universal suddenness and vehemence of gesture; two men playing for half a farthing with an intensity as all-absorbing as if the stake were life.

Hard by here is a large Palazzo, formerly belonging to some member of the Brignole family, but just now hired by a school of Jesuits for their summer quarters. I walked into its dismantled precincts the other evening about sunset, and couldn't help pacing up and down for a little time, drowsily taking in the aspect of the place: which is repeated hereabouts in all directions.

I loitered to and fro, under a colonnade, forming two sides of a weedy, grass-grown court-yard, whereof the house formed a third side, and a low terrace-walk, overlooking the garden and the neighbouring hills, the fourth. I don't believe there was an uncracked stone in the whole pavement. In the centre was a melancholy statue, so piebald in its decay, that it looked exactly as if it had been covered with sticking-plaster, and afterwards powdered. The stables, coach-houses, offices, were all empty, all ruinous, all utterly deserted.

Doors had lost their hinges, and were holding on by their latches; windows were broken, painted plaster had peeled off, and was lying about in clods; fowls and cats had so taken possession of the out-buildings, that I couldn't help thinking of the fairy tales, and eyeing them with suspicion, as transformed retainers, waiting to be changed back again. One old Tom in particular: a scraggy brute, with a hungry green eye (a poor relation, in reality, I am inclined to think): came prowling round and round me, as if he half believed, for the moment, that I might be the hero come to marry the lady, and set all to-rights; but discovering his mistake, he suddenly gave a grim snarl, and walked away with such a tremendous tail, that he couldn't get into the little hole where he lived, but was obliged to wait outside, until his indignation and his tail had gone down together.

In a sort of summer-house, or whatever it may be, in this colonnade some Englishmen had been living, like grubs in a nut; but the Jesuits had given them notice to go, and they had gone, and *that* was shut up too. The house: a wandering, echoing, thundering barrack of a place, with the lower windows barred up, as usual, was wide open at the door: and I have no doubt I might have gone in, and gone to bed, and gone dead, and nobody a bit the wiser. Only one suite of rooms on an upper floor was tenanted; and from one of these, the voice of a young-lady vocalist, practising bravura lustily, came flaunting out upon the silent evening.

I went down into the garden, intended to be prim and quaint, with avenues, and terraces, and orange-trees, and statues, and water in stone basins; and everything was green, gaunt, weedy, straggling, under grown or over grown, mildewy, damp, redolent of all sorts of slabby, clammy, creeping, and uncomfortable life. There was nothing bright in the whole scene but a firefly—one solitary firefly—showing against the dark bushes like the last little speck of the departed Glory of the house; and even it went flitting up and down at sudden angles, and leaving a place with a jerk, and describing an irregular circle, and returning to the same place with a twitch that startled one: as if it were looking for the rest of the Glory, and wondering (Heaven knows it might!) what had become of it.

In the course of two months, the flitting shapes and shadows of my dismal entering reverie gradually resolved themselves into familiar forms and substances; and I already began to think that when the time should come, a year hence, for closing the long holiday and turning back to England, I might part from Genoa with anything but a glad heart.

It is a place that "grows upon you" every day. There seems to be always something to find out in it. There are the most extraordinary alleys and by-ways to walk about in. You can lose your way (what a comfort that is, when you are idle!) twenty times a day, if you like; and turn up again, under the most unexpected and surprising difficulties. It abounds in the strangest contrasts; things that are picturesque, ugly, mean, magnificent, delightful, and offensive, break upon the view at every turn.

They who would know how beautiful the country immediately surrounding Genoa is, should climb (in clear weather) to the top of Monte Faccio, or, at least, ride round the city walls: a feat more easily performed. No prospect can be more diversified and lovely than the changing views of the harbour, and the valleys of the two rivers, the Polcevera and the Bizagno, from the heights along which the strongly fortified walls are carried, like the great wall of China in little. In not the least picturesque part of this ride, there is a fair specimen of a real Genoese tavern, where the visitor may derive good entertainment from real Genoese dishes, such as Tagliarini; Ravioli; German sausages, strong of garlic, sliced and eaten with fresh green figs; cocks' combs and sheep-kidneys, chopped up with mutton chops and liver; small pieces of some unknown part of a calf, twisted into small shreds, fried, and served up in a great dish like whitebait; and other curiosities of that kind. They often get wine at these suburban Trattorie, from France and Spain and Portugal, which is brought over by small captains in little trading-vessels. They buy it at so much a bottle, without asking what it is, or caring to remember if anybody tells them, and usually divide it into two heaps; of which they label one Champagne, and the other Madeira. The various opposite flavours, qualities, countries, ages, and vintages that are comprised under these two general heads is quite extraordinary. The most limited range is probably from cool Gruel up to old Marsala, and down again to apple Tea.

The great majority of the streets are as narrow as any thoroughfare can well be, where people (even Italian people) are supposed to live and walk about; being mere lanes, with here and there a kind of well, or breathing-place. The houses are immensely high, painted in all sorts of colours, and are in every stage and state of damage, dirt, and lack of repair. They are commonly let off in floors, or flats, like the houses in the old town of Edinburgh, or many houses in Paris. There are few street doors; the entrance halls are, for the most part, looked upon as public property; and any moderately enterprising scavenger might make a fine fortune by now and then clearing them out. As it is impossible for coaches to penetrate into these streets, there are sedan chairs, gilded and otherwise, for hire in divers places. A great many private chairs are also kept among the nobility and gentry; and at night these are trotted to and fro in all directions, preceded by bearers of great lanthorns, made of linen stretched upon a frame. The sedans and lanthorns are the legitimate successors of the long strings of patient and much-abused mules, that go jingling their little bells through these confined streets all day long. They follow them, as regularly as the stars the sun.

When shall I forget the Streets of Palaces: the Strada Nuova and the Strada Balbi! or how the former looked one summer day, when I first saw it underneath the brightest and most intensely blue of summer skies: which its narrow perspective of immense mansions, reduced to a tapering and most precious strip of brightness, looking down upon the heavy shade below! A brightness not too common, even in July and August, to be well esteemed: for, if the Truth must out, there were not eight blue skies in as many midsummer weeks, saving, sometimes, early in the morning; when, looking out to sea, the water and the firmament were one world of deep and brilliant blue. At other times, there were clouds and haze enough to make an Englishman grumble in his own climate.

The endless details of these rich Palaces: the walls of some of them, within, alive with masterpieces by Vandyke! The great, heavy, stone balconies, one above another, and tier over tier: with here and there, one larger than the rest, towering high up—a huge marble platform; the doorless vestibules, massively barred lower windows, immense public staircases, thick marble pillars, strong dungeon-like arches, and dreary, dreaming, echoing vaulted chambers: among which the eye wanders again, and again, and again, as every palace is succeeded by another—the terrace gardens between house and house, with green arches of the vine, and groves of orange-trees, and blushing oleander in full bloom, twenty, thirty, forty feet above the street— the painted halls, mouldering, and blotting, and rotting in the damp corners, and still shining out in beautiful colours and voluptuous designs, where the walls are dry—the faded figures on the outsides of the houses, holding wreaths, and crowns, and flying upward, and downward, and standing in niches, and here and there looking fainter and more feeble than elsewhere, by contrast with some fresh little Cupids, who on a more recently decorated portion of the front, are stretching out what seems to be the semblance of a blanket, but is, indeed, a sun-dial—the steep, steep, up-hill streets of small palaces (but very large palaces for all that), with marble terraces looking down into close by-ways—the magnificent and innumerable Churches and the rapid passage from a street of stately edifices, into a maze of the vilest squalor, steaming with unwholesome stenches, and swarming with half-naked children and whole worlds of dirty people—make up, altogether, such a scene of wonder: so lively, and yet so dead: so noisy, and yet so quiet: so obtrusive, and yet so shy and lowering: so wide awake, and yet so fast asleep: that it is a sort of intoxication to a stranger to walk on, and on, and on, and look about him. A bewildering phantasmagoria, with all the inconsistency of a dream, and all the pain and all the pleasure of an extravagant reality!

The different uses to which some of these Palaces are applied, all at once, is characteristic. For instance, the English Banker (my excellent and hospitable friend) has his office in a good-sized Palazzo in the Strada Nuova. In the hall (every inch of which is elaborately painted, but which is as dirty as a police-station in London), a hook-nosed Saracen's Head with an immense quantity of black hair (there is a man attached to it) sells walking-sticks. On the other side of the doorway, a lady with a showy handkerchief for head-dress (wife to the Saracen's Head, I believe) sells articles of her own knitting; and sometimes flowers. A little further in, two or three blind men occasionally beg. Sometimes, they are visited by a man without legs, on a little go-cart, but who has such a fresh-coloured, lively face, and such a respectable, well-conditioned body, that he looks as if he had sunk into the ground up to his middle, or had come, but partially, up a flight of cellar-steps to speak to somebody. A little further in, a few men, perhaps, lie asleep in the middle of the day; or they may be chairmen waiting for their absent freight. If so, they have brought their chairs in with them, and there *they* stand also. On the left of the hall is a little room: a hatter's shop. On the first floor, is the English bank. On the first floor also, is a whole house, and a good large residence too. Heaven knows what there may be above that; but when you are there, you have only just begun to go up-stairs. And yet, coming down-stairs again, thinking of this; and passing out at a great crazy door in the back of the hall, instead of turning the other way, to get into the street again; it bangs behind you, making the dismallest and most lonesome echoes, and you stand in a yard (the yard of the same house) which seems to have been unvisited by human foot, for a hundred years. Not a sound disturbs its repose. Not a head, thrust out of any of the grim, dark, jealous windows, within sight, makes the weeds in the cracked pavement faint of heart, by suggesting the possibility of there being hands to grub them up. Opposite to you, is a giant figure carved in stone, reclining, with an urn, upon a lofty piece of artificial rockwork; and out of the urn, dangles the fag end of a leaden pipe, which, once upon a time, poured a small torrent down the rocks. But the eye-sockets of the giant are not drier than this channel is now. He seems to have given his urn, which is nearly upside down, a final tilt; and after crying, like a sepulchral child, "All gone!" to have lapsed into a stony silence.

In the streets of shops, the houses are much smaller, but of great size notwithstanding, and extremely high. They are very dirty: quite undrained, if my nose be at all reliable: and emit a peculiar fragrance, like the smell of very bad cheese, kept in very hot blankets. Notwithstanding the height of the houses, there would seem to have been a lack of room in the City, for new houses are thrust in everywhere. Wherever it has been possible to cram a tumble-down tenement into a crack or corner, in it has gone. If there be a nook or angle in the wall of a church, or a crevice in any other dead wall, of any sort, there you are sure to find some kind of habitation: looking as if it had grown there, like a fungus. Against the Government House, against the old Senate House, round about any large building, little shops stick so close, like parasite vermin to the great carcase. And for all this, look where you may: up steps, down steps, anywhere, everywhere: there are irregular houses, receding, starting forward, tumbling down, leaning against their neighbours, crippling themselves or their friends by some means or other, until one, more irregular than the rest, chokes up the way, and you can't see any further.

One of the rottenest-looking parts of the town, I think, is down by the landing-wharf: though it may be, that its being associated with a great deal of rottenness on the evening of our arrival, has stamped it deeper in my mind. Here, again, the houses are very high, and are of an infinite variety of deformed shapes, and have (as most of the houses have) something hanging out of a great many windows, and wafting its frowsy fragrance on the breeze. Sometimes, it is a curtain; sometimes, it is a carpet; sometimes, it is a bed; sometimes, a whole line-full of clothes; but there is almost always something. Before the basement of these houses, is an arcade over the pavement: very massive, dark, and low, like an old crypt. The stone, or plaster, of which it is made, has turned quite black; and against every one of these black piles, all sorts of filth and garbage seem to accumulate spontaneously. Beneath some of the arches, the sellers of maccaroni and polenta establish their stalls, which are by no means inviting. The offal of a fish-market, near at hand—that is to say, of a back lane, where people sit upon the ground and on various old bulk-heads and sheds, and sell fish when they have any to dispose of—and of a vegetable market, constructed on the same principle—are contributed to the decoration of this quarter; and as all the mercantile business is transacted here, and it is crowded all day, it has a very decided flavour about it. The Porto Franco, or Free Port (where goods brought in from foreign countries pay no duty until they are sold and taken out, as in a bonded warehouse in England), is down here also; and two portentous officials, in cocked hats, stand at the gate to search you if they choose, and to keep out Monks and Ladies. For, Sanctity as well as Beauty has been known to yield to the temptation of smuggling, and in the same way: that is to say, by concealing the smuggled property beneath the loose folds of its dress. So Sanctity and Beauty may, by no means, enter.

The streets of Genoa would be all the better for the importation of a few Priests of prepossessing appearance. Every fourth or fifth man in the streets is a Priest or a Monk; and there is pretty sure to be at least one itinerant ecclesiastic inside or outside every hackney carriage on the neighbouring roads. I have no knowledge, elsewhere, of more repulsive countenances than are to be found among these gentry. If Nature's hand-writing be at all legible, greater varieties of sloth, deceit, and intellectual torpor, could hardly be observed among any class of men in the world.

Mr. PEPYS once heard a clergyman assert in his sermon, in illustration of his respect for the Priestly office, that if he could meet a Priest and angel together, he would salute the Priest first. I am rather of the opinion of PETRARCH, who, when his pupil BOCCACCIO wrote to him in great tribulation, that he had been visited and admonished for his writings by a Carthusian Friar who claimed to be a messenger immediately commissioned by Heaven for that purpose, replied, that for his own part, he would take the liberty of testing the reality of the commission by personal observation of the Messenger's face, eyes, forehead, behaviour, and discourse. I cannot but believe myself, from similar observation, that many unaccredited celestial messengers may be seen skulking through the streets of Genoa, or droning away their lives in other Italian towns.

Perhaps the Cappuccíni, though not a learned body, are, as an order, the best friends of the people. They seem to mingle with them more immediately, as their counsellors and comforters; and to go among them more, when they are sick; and to pry less than some other orders, into the secrets of families, for the purpose of establishing a baleful ascendency over their weaker members; and to be influenced by a less fierce desire to make converts, and once made, to let them go to ruin, soul and body. They may be seen, in their coarse dress, in all parts of the town at all times, and begging in the markets early in the morning. The Jesuits too, muster strong in the streets, and go slinking noiselessly about, in pairs, like black cats.

In some of the narrow passages, distinct trades congregate. There is a street of jewellers, and there is a row of booksellers; but even down in places where nobody ever can, or ever could, penetrate in a carriage, there are mighty old palaces shut in among the gloomiest and closest walls, and almost shut out from the sun. Very few of the tradesmen have any idea of setting forth their goods, or disposing them for show. If you, a stranger, want to buy anything, you usually look round the shop till you see it; then clutch it, if it be within reach, and inquire how much. Everything is sold at the most unlikely place. If you want coffee, you go to a sweetmeat shop; and if you want meat, you will probably find it behind an old checked curtain, down half-a dozen steps, in some sequestered nook as hard to find as if the commodity were poison, and Genoa's law were death to any that uttered it.

Most of the apothecaries' shops are great lounging-places. Here, grave men with sticks, sit down in the shade for hours together, passing a meagre Genoa paper from hand to hand, and talking, drowsily and sparingly, about the News. Two or three of these are poor physicians, ready to proclaim themselves on an emergency, and tear off with any messenger who may arrive. You may know them by the way in which they stretch their necks to listen, when you enter; and by the sigh with which they fall back again into their dull corners, on finding that you only want medicine. Few people lounge in the barbers' shops; though they are very numerous, as hardly any man shaves himself. But the apothecary's has its group of loungers, who sit back among the bottles, with their hands folded over the tops of their sticks. So still and quiet, that either you don't see them in the darkened shop, or mistake them—as I did one ghostly man in bottle-green, one day, with a hat like a stopper—for Horse Medicine.

On a summer evening the Genoese are as fond of putting themselves, as their ancestors were of putting houses, in every available inch of space in and about the town. In all the lanes and alleys, and up every little ascent, and on every dwarf wall, and on every flight of steps, they cluster like bees. Meanwhile (and especially on festa-days) the bells of the churches ring incessantly; not in peals, or any known form of sound, but in a horrible, irregular, jerking, dingle, dingle, dingle: with a sudden stop at every fifteenth dingle or so, which is maddening. This performance is usually achieved by a boy up in the steeple, who takes hold of the clapper, or a little rope attached to it, and tries to dingle louder than every other boy similarly employed. The noise is supposed to be particularly obnoxious to Evil Spirits; but looking up into the steeples and seeing (and hearing) these young Christians thus engaged, one might very naturally mistake them for the Enemy.

Festa-days, early in the autumn, are very numerous. All the shops were shut up, twice within a week, for these holidays; and one night, all the houses in the neighbourhood of a particular church were illuminated, while the church itself was lighted, outside, with torches; and a grove of blazing links was erected, in an open space outside one of the city gates. This part of the ceremony is prettier and more singular a little way in the country, where you can trace the illuminated cottages all the way up a steep hill-side; and where you pass festoons of tapers, wasting away in the starlight night, before some lonely little house upon the road.

On these days, they always dress the church of the saint in whose honour the festa is holden, very gaily. Gold-embroidered festoons of different colours, hang from the arches; the altar furniture is set forth; and sometimes, even the lofty pillars are swathed from top to bottom in tight-fitting draperies. The cathedral is dedicated to St. Lorenzo. On St. Lorenzo's day, we went into it, just as the sun was setting. Although these decorations are usually in very indifferent taste, the effect, just then, was very superb indeed. For the whole building was dressed in red; and the sinking sun, streaming in, through a great red curtain in the chief doorway, made all the gorgeousness its own. When the sun went down, and it gradually grew quite dark inside, except for a few twinkling tapers on the principal altar, and some small dangling silver lamps, it was very mysterious and effective. But sitting in any of the churches towards evening, is like a mild dose of opium.

With the money collected at a festa, they usually pay for the dressing of the church, and for the hiring of the band, and for the tapers. If there be any left (which seldom happens, I believe), the souls in Purgatory get the benefit of it. They are also supposed to have the benefit of the exertions of certain small boys, who shake money-boxes before some mysterious little buildings like rural turnpikes, which (usually shut up close) fly open on Red-letter days, and disclose an image and some flowers inside.

Just without the city gate, on the Albara road, is a small house, with an altar in it, and a stationary money-box: also for the benefit of the souls in Purgatory. Still further to stimulate the charitable, there is a monstrous painting on the plaster, on either side of the grated door, representing a select party of souls, frying. One of them has a grey moustache, and an elaborate head of grey hair: as if he had been taken out of a hairdresser's window and cast into the furnace. There he is: a most grotesque and hideously comic old soul: for ever blistering in the real sun, and melting in the mimic fire, for the gratification and improvement (and the contributions) of the poor Genoese.

They are not a very joyous people, and are seldom seen to dance on their holidays: the staple places of entertainment among the women, being the churches and the public walks. They are very good-tempered, obliging, and industrious. Industry has not made them clean, for their habitations are extremely filthy, and their usual occupation on a fine Sunday morning, is to sit at their doors, hunting in each other's heads. But their dwellings are so close and confined that if those parts of the city had been beaten down by Massena in the time of the terrible Blockade, it would have at least occasioned one public benefit among many misfortunes.

The Peasant Women, with naked feet and legs, are so constantly washing clothes, in the public tanks, and in every stream and ditch, that one cannot help wondering, in the midst of all this dirt, who wears them when they are clean. The custom is to lay the wet linen which is being operated upon, on a smooth stone, and hammer away at it, with a flat wooden mallet. This they do, as furiously as if they were revenging themselves on dress in general for being connected with the Fall of Mankind.

It is not unusual to see, lying on the edge of the tank at these times, or on another flat stone, an unfortunate baby, tightly swathed up, arms and legs and all, in an enormous quantity of wrapper, so that it is unable to move a toe or finger. This custom (which we often see represented in old pictures) is universal among the common people. A child is left anywhere without the possibility of crawling away, or is accidentally knocked off a shelf, or tumbled out of bed, or is hung up to a hook now and then, and left dangling like a doll at an English rag-shop, without the least inconvenience to anybody.

I was sitting, one Sunday, soon after my arrival, in the little country church of San Martino, a couple of miles from the city, while a baptism took place. I saw the priest, and an attendant with a large taper, and a man, and a woman, and some others; but I had no more idea, until the ceremony was all over, that it was a baptism, or that the curious little stiff instrument, that was passed from one to another, in the course of the ceremony, by the handle—like a short poker—was a child, than I had that it was my own christening. I borrowed the child afterwards, for a minute or two (it was lying across the font then), and found it very red in the face but perfectly quiet, and not to be bent on any terms. The number of cripples in the streets soon ceased to surprise us.

There are plenty of Saints' and Virgin's Shrines, of course; generally at the corners of streets. The favourite memento to the Faithful, about Genoa, is a painting, representing a peasant on his knees, with a spade and some other agricultural implements beside him; and the Madonna, with the Infant Saviour in her arms, appearing to him in a cloud. This is the legend of the Madonna della Guardia: a chapel on a mountain within a few miles, which is in high repute. It seems that this peasant lived all alone by himself, tilling some land atop of the mountain, where, being a devout man, he daily said his prayers to the Virgin in the open air; for his hut was a very poor one. Upon a certain day, the Virgin appeared to him, as in the picture, and said, "Why do you pray in the open air, and without a priest?" The peasant explained because there was neither priest nor church at hand—a very uncommon complaint indeed in Italy. "I should wish, then," said the Celestial Visitor, "to have a chapel built here, in which the prayers of the Faithful may be offered up." "But, Santissima Madonna," said the peasant, "I am a poor man; and chapels cannot be built without money. They must be supported, too, Santissima; for to have a chapel and not support it liberally, is a wickedness—a deadly sin." This sentiment gave great satisfaction to the visitor. "Go!" said she. "There is such a village in the valley on the left and such another village in the valley on the right and such another village elsewhere, that will gladly contribute to the building of a chapel. Go to them! Relate what you have seen; and do not doubt that sufficient money will be forthcoming to erect my chapel, or that it will, afterwards, be handsomely maintained." All of which (miraculously) turned out to be quite true. And in proof of this prediction and revelation, there is the chapel of the Madonna della Guardia, rich and flourishing at this day.

The splendour and variety of the Genoese churches, can hardly be exaggerated. The church of the Annunciata especially: built, like many of the others, at the cost of one noble family, and now in slow progress of repair: from the outer door to the utmost height of the high cupola, is so elaborately painted and set in gold, that it looks (as SIMOND describes it, in his charming book on Italy) like a great enamelled snuff-box. Most of the richer churches contain some beautiful pictures, or other embellishments of great price, almost universally set, side by side, with sprawling effigies of maudlin monks, and the veriest trash and tinsel ever seen.

It may be a consequence of the frequent direction of the popular mind, and pocket, to the souls in Purgatory, but there is very little tenderness for the *bodies* of the dead here. For the very poor, there are, immediately outside one angle of the walls, and behind a jutting point of the fortification, near the sea, certain common pits—one for every day in the year—which all remain closed up, until the turn of each comes for its daily reception of dead bodies. Among the troops in the town, there are usually some Swiss: more or less. When any of these die, they are buried out of a fund maintained by such of their countrymen as are resident in Genoa. Their providing coffins for these men is matter of great astonishment to the authorities.

Certainly, the effect of this promiscuous and indecent splashing down of dead people in so many wells, is bad. It surrounds Death with revolting associations that insensibly become connected with those whom Death is approaching. Indifference and avoidance are the natural result; and all the softening influences of the great sorrow are harshly disturbed.

There is a ceremony when an old Cavaliêre or the like, expires, of erecting a pile of benches in the cathedral, to represent his bier; covering them over with a pall of black velvet; putting his hat and sword on the top; making a little square of seats about the whole; and sending out formal invitations to his friends and acquaintances to come and sit there, and hear Mass: which is performed at the principal Altar, decorated with an infinity of candles for that purpose.

When the better kind of people die, or are at the point of death, their nearest relations generally walk off: retiring into the country for a little change, and leaving the body to be disposed of, without any superintendence from them. The procession is usually formed, and the coffin, borne, and the funeral conducted, by a body of persons called a Confratérnita, who, as a kind of voluntary penance, undertake to perform these offices, in regular rotation for the dead; but who, mingling something of pride with their humility, are dressed in a loose garment covering their whole person, and wear a hood concealing the face: with breathing holes and apertures for the eyes. The effect of this costume is very ghastly: expecially in the case of certain Blue Confratérnita belonging to Genoa, who, to say the least of them, are very ugly customers, and who look—suddenly encountered in their pious ministration in the streets—as if they were Ghoules or Demons, bearing off the body for themselves.

Although such a custom may be liable to the abuse attendant on many Italian customs, of being recognised as a means of establishing a current account with Heaven, on which to draw, too easily, for future bad actions, or as an expiation for past misdeeds, it must be admitted to be a good one, and a practical one, and one involving unquestionably good works. A voluntary service like this, is surely better than the imposed penance (not at all an infrequent one) of giving so many licks to such and such a stone in the pavement of the cathedral; or than a vow to the Madonna to wear nothing but blue for a year or two. This is supposed to give great delight above; blue being (as is well known) the Madonna's favourite colour. Women who have devoted themselves to this act of Faith, are very commonly seen walking in the streets.

There are three theatres in the city, besides an old one now rarely opened. The most important—the Carlo Felice: the opera-house of Genoa—is a very splendid, commodious, and beautiful theatre. A company of comedians were acting there, when we arrived: and soon after their departure, a second-rate opera company came. The great season is not until the carnival time—in the spring. Nothing impressed me, so much, in my visits here (which were pretty numerous) as the uncommonly hard and cruel character of the audience, who resent the slightest defect, take nothing good-humouredly, seem to be always lying in wait for an opportunity to hiss, and spare the actresses as little as the actors. But, as there is nothing else of a public nature at which they are allowed to express the least disapprobation, perhaps they are resolved to make the most of this opportunity.

There are a great number of Piedmontese officers too, who are allowed the privilege of kicking their heels in the pit, for next to nothing: gratuitous, or cheap accommodation for these gentlemen being insisted on, by the Governor, in all public or semi-public entertainments. They are lofty critics in consequence, and infinitely more exacting than if they made the unhappy manager's fortune.

The TEATRO DIURNO, or Day Theatre, is a covered stage in the open air, where the performances take place by daylight, in the cool of the afternoon; commencing at four or five o'clock, and lasting some three hours. It is curious, sitting among the audience, to have a fine view of the neighbouring hills and houses, and to see the neighbours at their windows looking on, and to hear the bells of the churches and convents ringing at most complete cross-purposes with the scene. Beyond this, and the novelty of seeing a play in the fresh pleasant air, with the darkening evening closing in, there is nothing very exciting or characteristic in the performances. The actors are indifferent; and though they sometimes represent one of Goldoni's comedies, the staple of the Drama is French. Anything like nationality is dangerous to despotic governments, and Jesuit-beleaguered kings.

The Theatre of Puppets, or Marionetti—a famous company from Milan—is, without any exception, the drollest exhibition I ever beheld in my life. I never saw anything so exquisitely ridiculous. They *look* between four and five feet high, but are really much smaller; for when a musician in the orchestra happens to put his hat on the stage, it becomes alarmingly gigantic, and almost blots out an actor. They usually play a comedy, and a ballet. The comic man in the comedy I saw one summer night, is a waiter in an hotel. There never was such a locomotive actor, since the world began. Great pains are taken with him. He has extra joints in his legs: and a practical eye, with which he winks at the pit, in a manner that is absolutely insupportable to a stranger, but which the initiated audience, mainly composed of the common people, receive (so they do everything else) quite as a matter of course, and as if he were a man. His spirits are prodigious. He continually shakes his legs, and winks his eye. And there is a heavy father with grey hair, who sits down on the regular conventional stage-bank, and blesses his daughter in the regular conventional way, who is tremendous. No one would suppose it possible that anything short of a real man could be so tedious. It is the triumph of art.

In the ballet, an Enchanter runs away with the Bride, in the very hour of the nuptials. He brings her to his cave and tries to soothe her. They sit down on a sofa (the regular sofa! in the regular place, O.P. Second Entrance!) and a procession of musicians enters; one creature playing a drum, and knocking himself off his legs at every blow. These failing to delight her, dancers appear. Four first; then two; *the* two; the flesh-coloured two. The way in which they dance; the height to which they spring; the impossible and inhuman extent to which they pirouette; the revelation of their preposterous legs; the coming down with a pause, on the very tips of their toes, when the music requires it; the gentleman's retiring up, when it is the lady's turn; and the lady's retiring up, when it is the gentleman's turn; the final passion of a pas-de-deux; and the going off with a bound!—I shall never see a real ballet, with a composed countenance again.

I went, another night, to see these Puppets act a play called "St. Helena, or the Death of Napoleon." It began by the disclosure of Napoleon, with an immense head, seated on a sofa in his chamber at St. Helena; to whom his valet entered with this obscure announcement:

"Sir Yew ud se on Low?" (the *ow*, as in cow).

Sir Hudson (that you could have seen his regimentals!) was a perfect mammoth of a man, to Napoleon; hideously ugly; with a monstrously disproportionate face, and a great clump for the lower-jaw, to express his tyrannical and obdurate nature. He began his system of persecution, by calling his prisoner "General Buonaparte;" to which the latter replied, with the deepest tragedy, "Sir Yew ud se on Low, call me not thus. Repeat that phrase and leave me! I am, Napoleon, Emperor of France!" Sir Yew ud se on, nothing daunted, proceeded to entertain him with an ordinance of the British Government, regulating the state he should preserve, and the furniture of his rooms: and limiting his attendants to four or five persons. "Four or five for *me*!" said Napoleon. "Me! One hundred thousand men were lately at my sole command; and this English officer talks of four or five for *me*!" Throughout the piece, Napoleon (who talked very like the real Napoleon, and was, for ever, having small soliloquies by himself) was very bitter on "these English officers," and "these English soldiers;" to the great satisfaction of the audience, who were perfectly delighted to have Low bullied; and who, whenever Low said "General Buonaparte" (which he always did: always receiving the same correction), quite execrated him. It would be hard to say why; for Italians have little cause to sympathise with Napoleon, Heaven knows.

There was no plot at all, except that a French officer, disguised as an Englishman, came to propound a plan of escape; and being discovered, but not before Napoleon had magnanimously refused to steal his freedom, was immediately ordered off by Low to be hanged. In two very long speeches, which Low made memorable, by winding up with "Yas!"—to show that he was English—which brought down thunders of applause. Napoleon was so affected by this catastrophe, that he fainted away on the spot, and was carried out by two other puppets. Judging from what followed, it would appear that he never recovered the shock; for the next act showed him, in a clean shirt, in his bed (curtains crimson and white), where a lady, prematurely dressed in mourning, brought two little children, who kneeled down by the bedside, while he made a decent end; the last word on his lips being "Vatterlo."

It was unspeakably ludicrous. Buonaparte's boots were so wonderfully beyond control, and did such marvellous things of their own accord: doubling themselves up, and getting under tables, and dangling in the air, and sometimes skating away with him, out of all human knowledge, when he was in full speech—mischances which were not rendered the less absurd, by a settled melancholy depicted in his face. To put an end to one conference with Low, he had to go to a table and read a book: when it was the finest spectacle I ever beheld, to see his body bending over the volume, like a boot-jack, and his sentimental eyes glaring obstinately into the pit. He was prodigiously good, in bed, with an immense collar to his shirt, and his little hands outside the coverlet. So was Dr. Antommarchi, represented by a puppet with long lank hair, like Mawworm's, who, in consequence of some derangement of his wires, hovered about the couch like a vulture, and gave medical opinions in the air. He was almost as good as Low, though the latter was great at all times—a decided brute and villain, beyond all possibility of mistake. Low was especially fine at the last, when, hearing the doctor and the valet say, "The Emperor is dead!" he pulled out his watch, and wound up the piece (not the watch) by exclaiming, with characteristic brutality, "Ha! ha! Eleven minutes to six! The General dead! and the spy hanged!" This brought the curtain down, triumphantly.

There is not in Italy, they say (and I believe them), a lovelier residence than the Palazzo Peschiere, or Palace of the Fishponds, whither we removed as soon as our three months' tenancy of the Pink Jail at Albaro had ceased and determined.

It stands on a height within the walls of Genoa but aloof from the town: surrounded by beautiful gardens of its own, adorned with statues, vases, fountains, marble basins, terraces, walks of orange-trees and lemon-trees, groves of roses and camellias. All its apartments are beautiful in their proportions and decorations; but the great hall, some fifty feet in height, with three large windows at the end, overlooking the whole town of Genoa, the harbour, and the neighbouring sea, affords one of the most fascinating and delightful prospects in the world. Any house more cheerful and habitable than the great rooms are, within, it would be difficult to conceive; and certainly nothing more delicious than the scene without, in sunshine or in moonlight, could be imagined. It is more like an enchanted place in an Eastern story than a grave and sober lodging.

How you may wander on, from room to room, and never tire of the wild fancies on the walls and ceilings, as bright in their fresh colouring as if they had been painted yesterday; or how one floor, or even the great hall which opens on eight other rooms, is a spacious promenade; or how there are corridors and bed-chambers above, which we never use and rarely visit, and scarcely know the way through; or how there is a view of a perfectly different character on each of the four sides of the buildings; matters little. But that prospect from the hall is like a vision to me. I go back to it, in fancy, as I have done in calm reality a hundred times a day; and stand there, looking out, with the sweet scents from the garden rising up about me, in a perfect dream of happiness.

There lies all Genoa, in beautiful confusion, with its many churches, monasteries, and convents, pointing up into the sunny sky; and down below me, just where the roofs begin, a solitary convent parapet, fashioned like a gallery, with an iron across at the end, where sometimes early in the morning, I have seen a little group of dark-veiled nuns gliding sorrowfully to and fro, and stopping now and then to peep down upon the waking world in which they have no part. Old Monte Faccio, brightest of hills in good weather, but sulkiest when storms are coming on, is here, upon the left. The Fort within the walls (the good King built it to command the town, and beat the houses of the Genoese about their ears, in case they should be discontented) commands that height upon the right. The broad sea lies beyond, in front there; and that line of coast, beginning by the light-house, and tapering away a mere speck in the rosy distance, is the beautiful coast road that leads to Nice. The garden near at hand, among the roofs and houses: all red with roses and fresh with little fountains: is the Acqua Sola—a public promenade, where the military band plays gaily, and the white veils cluster thick, and the Genoese nobility ride round, and round, and round, in state-clothes and coaches at least, if not in absolute wisdom. Within a stone's-throw, as it seems, the audience of the Day Theatre sit: their faces turned this way. But as the stage is hidden, it is very odd, without a knowledge of the cause, to see their faces changed so suddenly from earnestness to laughter; and odder still, to hear the rounds upon rounds of applause, rattling in the evening air, to which the curtain falls. But, being Sunday night, they act their best and most attractive play. And now, the sun is going down, in such magnificent array of red, and green, and golden light, as neither pen nor pencil could depict; and to the ringing of the vesper bells, darkness sets in at once, without a twilight. Then, lights begin to shine in Genoa, and on the country road; and the revolving lanthorn out at sea there, flashing, for an instant, on this palace front and portico, illuminates it as if there were a bright moon bursting from behind a cloud; then, merges it in deep obscurity. And this, so far as I know, is the only reason why the Genoese avoid it after dark, and think it haunted.

My memory will haunt it, many nights, in time to come; but nothing worse, I will engage. The same Ghost will occasionally sail away, as I did one pleasant autumn evening, into the bright prospect, and sniff the morning air at Marseilles.

The corpulent hairdresser was still sitting in his slippers outside his shop-door there, but the twirling ladies in the window, with the natural inconstancy of their sex, had ceased to twirl, and were languishing, stock still, with their beautiful faces addressed to blind corners of the establishment, where it was impossible for admirers to penetrate.

The steamer had come from Genoa in a delicious run of eighteen hours, and we were going to run back again by the Cornice road from Nice: not being satisfied to have seen only the outsides of the beautiful towns that rise in picturesque white clusters from among the olive woods, and rocks, and hills, upon the margin of the Sea.

The Boat which started for Nice that night, at eight o'clock, was very small, and so crowded with goods that there was scarcely room to move; neither was there anything to eat on board, except bread; nor to drink, except coffee. But being due at Nice at about eight or so in the morning, this was of no consequence: so when we began to wink at the bright stars, in involuntary acknowledgment of their winking at us, we turned into our berths, in a crowded, but cool little cabin, and slept soundly till morning.

The Boat, being as dull and dogged a little boat as ever was built, it was within an hour of noon when we turned into Nice Harbour, where we very little expected anything but breakfast. But we were laden with wool. Wool must not remain in the Custom-house at Marseilles more than twelve months at a stretch, without paying duty. It is the custom to make fictitious removals of unsold wool to evade this law; to take it somewhere when the twelve months are nearly out; bring it straight back again; and warehouse it, as a new cargo, for nearly twelve months longer. This wool of ours, had come originally from some place in the East. It was recognised as Eastern produce, the moment we entered the harbour. Accordingly, the gay little Sunday boats, full of holiday people, which had come off to greet us, were warned away by the authorities; we were declared in quarantine; and a great flag was solemnly run up to the mast-head on the wharf, to make it known to all the town.

It was a very hot day indeed. We were unshaved, unwashed, un-dressed, unfed, and could hardly enjoy the absurdity of lying blister-ing in a lazy harbour, with the town looking on from a respectful distance, all manner of whiskered men in cocked hats discussing our fate at a remote guard-house, with gestures (we looked very hard at them through telescopes) expressive of a week's detention at least: and nothing whatever the matter all the time. But even in this crisis the brave Courier achieved a triumph. He telegraphed somebody (I saw nobody) either naturally connected with the hotel, or put en rapport with the establishment for that occasion only. The telegraph was answered, and in half an hour or less, there came a loud shout from the guard-house. The captain was wanted. Everybody helped the captain into his boat. Everybody got his luggage, and said we were going. The captain rowed away, and disappeared behind a little jutting corner of the Galley-slaves' Prison: and presently came back with something, very sulkily. The brave Courier met him at the side, and received the something as its rightful owner. It was a wicker basket, folded in a linen cloth; and in it were two great bottles of wine, a roast fowl, some salt fish chopped with garlic, a great loaf of bread, a dozen or so of peaches, and a few other trifles. When we had selected our own breakfast, the brave Courier invited a chosen party to partake of these refreshments, and assured them that they need not be deterred by motives of delicacy, as he would order a second basket to be furnished at their expense. Which he did—no one knew how—and by-and-by, the captain being again summoned, again sulkily returned with another something; over which my popular attendant presided as before: carving with a clasp-knife, his own personal property, something smaller than a Roman sword.

The whole party on board were made merry by these unexpected supplies; but none more so than a loquacious little Frenchman, who got drunk in five minutes, and a sturdy Cappuccíno Friar, who had taken everybody's fancy mightily, and was one of the best friars in the world, I verily believe.

He had a free, open countenance; and a rich brown, flowing beard; and was a remarkably handsome man, of about fifty. He had come up to us, early in the morning, and inquired whether we were sure to be at Nice by eleven; saying that he particularly wanted to know, because if we reached it by that time he would have to perform Mass, and must deal with the consecrated wafer, fasting; whereas, if there were no chance of his being in time, he would immediately breakfast. He made this communication, under the idea that the brave Courier was the captain; and indeed he looked much more like it than anybody else on board. Being assured that we should arrive in good time, he fasted, and talked, fasting, to everybody, with the most charming good humour; answering jokes at the expense of friars, with other jokes at the expense of laymen, and saying that, friar as he was, he would engage to take up the two strongest men on board, one after the other, with his teeth, and carry them along the deck. Nobody gave him the opportunity, but I dare say he could have done it; for he was a gallant, noble figure of a man, even in the Cappuccíno dress, which is the ugliest and most ungainly that can well be.

All this had given great delight to the loquacious Frenchman, who gradually patronised the Friar very much, and seemed to commiserate him as one who might have been born a Frenchman himself, but for an unfortunate destiny. Although his patronage was such as a mouse might bestow upon a lion, he had a vast opinion of its condescension; and in the warmth of that sentiment, occasionally rose on tiptoe, to slap the Friar on the back.

When the baskets arrived: it being then too late for Mass: the Friar went to work bravely: eating prodigiously of the cold meat and bread, drinking deep draughts of the wine, smoking cigars, taking snuff, sustaining an uninterrupted conversation with all hands, and occasionally running to the boat's side and hailing somebody on shore with the intelligence that we *must* be got out of this quarantine somehow or other, as he had to take part in a great religious procession in the afternoon. After this, he would come back, laughing lustily from pure good humour: while the Frenchman wrinkled his small face into ten thousand creases, and said how droll it was, and what a brave boy was that Friar! At length the heat of the sun without, and the wine within, made the Frenchman sleepy. So, in the noontide of his patronage of his gigantic protégé, he lay down among the wool, and began to snore.

It was four o'clock before we were released; and the Frenchman, dirty and woolly, and snuffy, was still sleeping when the Friar went ashore. As soon as we were free, we all hurried away, to wash and dress, that we might make a decent appearance at the procession; and I saw no more of the Frenchman until we took up our station in the main street to see it pass, when he squeezed himself into a front place, elaborately renovated; threw back his little coat, to show a broad-barred velvet waistcoat, sprinkled all over with stars; then adjusted himself and his cane so as utterly to bewilder and transfix the Friar, when he should appear.

The procession was a very long one, and included an immense number of people divided into small parties; each party chanting nasally, on its own account, without reference to any other, and producing a most dismal result. There were angels, crosses, Virgins carried on flat boards surrounded by Cupids, crowns, saints, missals, infantry, tapers, monks, nuns, relics, dignitaries of the church in green hats, walking under crimson parasols: and, here and there, a species of sacred street-lamp hoisted on a pole. We looked out anxiously for the Cappuccíni, and presently their brown robes and corded girdles were seen coming on, in a body.

I observed the little Frenchman chuckle over the idea that when the Friar saw him in the broad-barred waistcoat, he would mentally exclaim, "Is that my Patron! *That* distinguished man!" and would be covered with confusion. Ah! never was the Frenchman so deceived. As our friend the Cappuccíno advanced, with folded arms, he looked straight into the visage of the little Frenchman, with a bland, serene, composed abstraction, not to be described. There was not the faintest trace of recognition or amusement on his features; not the smallest consciousness of bread and meat, wine, snuff, or cigars. "C'est lui-même," I heard the little Frenchman say, in some doubt. Oh yes, it was himself. It was not his brother or his nephew, very like him. It was he. He walked in great state: being one of the Superiors of the Order: and looked his part to admiration. There never was anything so perfect of its kind as the contemplative way in which he allowed his placid gaze to rest on us, his late companions, as if he had never seen us in his life and didn't see us then. The Frenchman, quite humbled, took off his hat at last, but the Friar still passed on, with the same imperturbable serenity; and the broad-barred waistcoat, fading into the crowd, was seen no more.

The procession wound up with a discharge of musketry that shook all the windows in the town. Next afternoon we started for Genoa, by the famed Cornice road.

The half-French, half-Italian Vetturíno, who undertook, with his little rattling carriage and pair, to convey us thither in three days, was a careless, good-looking fellow, whose light-heartedness and singing propensities knew no bounds as long as we went on smoothly. So long, he had a word and a smile, and a flick of his whip, for all the peasant girls, and odds and ends of the Sonnambula for all the echoes.

So long, he went jingling through every little village, with bells on his horses and rings in his ears: a very meteor of gallantry and cheerfulness. But, it was highly characteristic to see him under a slight reverse of circumstances, when, in one part of the journey, we came to a narrow place where a waggon had broken down and stopped up the road. His hands were twined in his hair immediately, as if a combination of all the direst accidents in life had suddenly fallen on his devoted head. He swore in French, prayed in Italian, and went up and down, beating his feet on the ground in a very ecstasy of despair. There were various carters and mule-drivers assembled round the broken waggon, and at last some man of an original turn of mind, proposed that a general and joint effort should be made to get things to-rights again, and clear the way—an idea which I verily believe would never have presented itself to our friend, though we had remained there until now. It was done at no great cost of labour; but at every pause in the doing, his hands were wound in his hair again, as if there were no ray of hope to lighten his misery. The moment he was on his box once more, and clattering briskly down hill, he returned to the Sonnambula and the peasant girls, as if it were not in the power of misfortune to depress him.

Much of the romance of the beautiful towns and villages on this beautiful road, disappears when they are entered, for many of them are very miserable. The streets are narrow, dark, and dirty; the inhabitants lean and squalid; and the withered old women, with their wiry grey hair twisted up into a knot on the top of the head, like a pad to carry loads on, are so intensely ugly, both along the Riviera, and in Genoa, too, that, seen straggling about in dim door-ways with their spindles, or crooning together in by-corners, they are like a population of Witches—except that they certainly are not to be suspected of brooms or any other instrument of cleanliness. Neither are the pig-skins, in common use to hold wine, and hung out in the sun in all directions, by any means ornamental, as they always preserve the form of very bloated pigs, with their heads and legs cut off, dangling upside-down by their own tails.

These towns, as they are seen in the approach, however: nestling, with their clustering roofs and towers, among trees on steep hillsides, or built upon the brink of noble bays: are charming. The vegetation is, everywhere, luxuriant and beautiful, and the Palm-tree makes a novel feature in the novel scenery. In one town, San Remo—a most extraordinary place, built on gloomy open arches, so that one might ramble underneath the whole town—there are pretty terrace gardens; in other towns, there is the clang of shipwrights' hammers, and the building of small vessels on the beach. In some of the broad bays, the fleets of Europe might ride at anchor. In every case, each little group of houses presents, in the distance, some enchanting confusion of picturesque and fanciful shapes.

The road itself—now high above the glittering sea, which breaks against the foot of the precipice: now turning inland to sweep the shore of a bay: now crossing the stony bed of a mountain stream: now

low down on the beach: now winding among riven rocks of many
forms and colours: now chequered by a solitary ruined tower, one of
a chain of towers built, in old time, to protect the coast from the
invasions of the Barbary Corsairs—presents new beauties every
moment. When its own striking scenery is passed, and it trails on
through a long line of suburb, lying on the flat seashore, to Genoa,
then, the changing glimpses of that noble city and its harbour,
awaken a new source of interest; freshened by every huge, unwieldy,
half-inhabited old house in its outskirts: and coming to its climax
when the city gate is reached, and all Genoa with its beautiful
harbour, and neighbouring hills, bursts proudly on the view.

TO PARMA, MODENA, AND BOLOGNA

I STROLLED away from Genoa on the 6th of November, bound for a
good many places (England among them), but first for Piacenza; for
which town I started in the *coupé* of a machine something like a
travelling caravan, in company with the brave Courier, and a lady
with a large dog, who howled dolefully, at intervals, all night. It was
very wet, and very cold; very dark, and very dismal; we travelled at
the rate of barely four miles an hour, and stopped nowhere for refreshment. At ten o'clock next morning, we changed coaches at Ales-
sandria, where we were packed up in another coach (the body whereof
would have been small for a fly), in company with a very old priest;
a young Jesuit, his companion—who carried their breviaries and
other books, and who, in the exertion of getting into the coach, had
made a gash of pink leg between his black stocking and his black
knee-shorts, that reminded one of Hamlet in Ophelia's closet, only it
was visible on both legs—a provincial Avvocáto and a gentleman
with a red nose that had an uncommon and singular sheen upon it,
which I never observed in the human subject before. In this way we
travelled on, until four o'clock in the afternoon; the roads being still
very heavy, and the coach very slow. To mend the matter, the old
priest was troubled with cramps in his legs, so that he had to give a
terrible yell every ten minutes or so, and be hoisted out by the united
efforts of the company; the coach always stopping for him, with great
gravity. This disorder, and the roads, formed the main subject of
conversation. Finding, in the afternoon, that the *coupé* had discharged two people, and had only one passenger inside—a monstrous
ugly Tuscan, with a great purple moustache, of which no man could
see the ends when he had his hat on—I took advantage of its better
accommodation, and in company with this gentleman (who was very
conversational and good-humoured) travelled on, until nearly eleven
o'clock at night, when the driver reported that he couldn't think of
going any farther, and we accordingly made a halt at a place called
Stradella.

The inn was a series of strange galleries surrounding a yard;
where our coach, and a waggon or two, and a lot of fowls, and firewood, were all heaped up together, higgledy-piggledy; so that you

didn't know, and couldn't have taken your oath, which was a fowl and which was a cart. We followed a sleepy man with a flaring torch, into a great, cold room, where there were two immensely broad beds, on what looked like two immensely broad deal dining-tables; another deal table of similar dimensions in the middle of the bare floor; four windows; and two chairs. Somebody said it was my room; and I walked up and down it, for half an hour or so, staring at the Tuscan, the old priest, the young priest, and the Avvocáto (Red-Nose lived in the town, and had gone home), who sat upon their beds, and stared at me in return.

The rather dreary whimsicality of this stage of the proceedings, is interrupted by an announcement from the Brave (he has been cooking) that supper is ready; and to the priest's chamber (the next room and the counterpart of mine) we all adjourn. The first dish is a cabbage, boiled with a great quantity of rice in a tureen full of water, and flavoured with cheese. It is so hot, and we are so cold, that it appears almost jolly. The second dish is some little bits of pork, fried with pigs' kidneys. The third, two red fowls. The fourth, two little red turkeys. The fifth, a huge stew of garlic and truffles, and I don't know what else; and this concludes the entertainment.

Before I can sit down in my own chamber, and think it of the dampest, the door opens, and the Brave comes moving in in the middle of such a quantity of fuel that he looks like Birnam Wood taking a winter walk. He kindles this heap in a twinkling, and produces a jorum of hot brandy and water; for that bottle of his keeps company with the seasons, and now holds nothing but the purest *eau de vie*. When he has accomplished this feat, he retires for the night; and I hear him, for an hour afterwards, and indeed until I fall asleep, making jokes in some outhouse (apparently under the pillow), where he is smoking cigars with a party of confidential friends. He never was in the house in his life before; but he knows everybody everywhere, before he has been anywhere five minutes; and is certain to have attracted to himself, in the meantime, the enthusiastic devotion of the whole establishment.

This is at twelve o'clock at night. At four o'clock next morning, he is up again, fresher than a new-blown rose; making blazing fires without the least authority from the landlord; producing mugs of scalding coffee when nobody else can get anything but cold water; and going out into the dark streets, and roaring for fresh milk, on the chance of somebody with a cow getting up to supply it. While the horses are "coming," I stumble out into the town too. It seems to be all one little Piazza, with a cold damp wind blowing in and out of the arches, alternately, in a sort of pattern. But it is profoundly dark, and raining heavily; and I shouldn't know it to-morrow, if I were taken there to try. Which Heaven forbid.

The horses arrive in about an hour. In the interval, the driver swears; sometimes Christian oaths, sometimes Pagan oaths. Sometimes, when it is a long, compound oath, he begins with Christianity and merges into Paganism. Various messengers are despatched; not

so much after the horses, as after each other; for the first messenger
never comes back, and all the rest imitate him. At length the horses
appear, surrounded by all the messengers; some kicking them, and
some dragging them, and all shouting abuse to them. Then, the old
priest, the young priest, the Avvocáto, the Tuscan, and all of us,
take our places; and sleepy voices proceeding from the doors of extraordinary hutches in divers parts of the yard, cry out "Addio corrière
mio! Buon' viággio, corrière!" Salutations which the courier, with
his face one monstrous grin, returns in like manner as we go jolting
and wallowing away, through the mud.

At Piacenza, which was four or five hours' journey from the inn
at Stradella, we broke up our little company before the hotel door,
with divers manifestations of friendly feeling on all sides. The old
priest was taken with the cramp again, before he had got half-way
down the street; and the young priest laid the bundle of books on a
door-step, while he dutifully rubbed the old gentleman's legs. The
client of the Avvocáto was waiting for him at the yard-gate, and
kissed him on each cheek, with such a resounding smack, that I am
afraid he had either a very bad case, or a scantily-furnished purse.
The Tuscan, with a cigar in his mouth, went loitering off, carrying
his hat in his hand that he might the better trail up the ends of his
dishevelled moustache. And the brave Courier, as he and I strolled
away to look about us, began immediately to entertain me with the
private histories and family affairs of the whole party.

A brown, decayed, old town, Piacenza is. A deserted, solitary,
grass-grown place, with ruined ramparts; half filled-up trenches,
which afford a frowsy pasturage to the lean kine that wander about
them; and streets of stern houses, moodily frowning at the other
houses over the way. The sleepiest and shabbiest of soldiery go wandering about, with the double curse of laziness and poverty, uncouthly
wrinkling their misfitting regimentals; the dirtiest of children play
with their impromptu toys (pigs and mud) in the feeblest of gutters;
and the gauntest of dogs trot in and out of the dullest of archways,
in perpetual search of something to eat, which they never seem to
find. A mysterious and solemn Palace, guarded by two colossal
statues, twin Genii of the place, stands gravely in the midst of the
idle town; and the king with the marble legs, who flourished in the
time of the thousand and one Nights, might live contentedly inside
of it, and never have the energy, in his upper half of flesh and blood,
to want to come out.

What a strange, half-sorrowful and half-delicious doze it is, to
ramble through these places gone to sleep and basking in the sun!
Each, in its turn, appears to be, of all the mouldy, dreary, God-for-
gotten towns in the wide world, the chief. Sitting on this hillock
where a bastion used to be, and where a noisy fortress was, in the
time of the old Roman station here, I became aware that I have never
known till now, what it is to be lazy. A dormouse must surely be in
very much the same condition before he retires under the wool in his
cage; or a tortoise before he buries himself. I feel that I am getting

rusty. That any attempt to think, would be accompanied with a creaking noise. That there is nothing, anywhere, to be done, or needing to be done. That there is no more human progress, motion, effort, or advancement, of any kind beyond this. That the whole scheme stopped here centuries ago, and laid down to rest until the Day of Judgment.

Never while the brave Courier lives! Behold him jingling out of Piacenza, and staggering this way, in the tallest posting-chaise ever seen, so that he looks out of the front window as if he were peeping over a garden wall; while the postilion, concentrated essence of all the shabbiness of Italy, pauses for a moment in his animated conversation, to touch his hat to a blunt-nosed little Virgin, hardly less shabby than himself, enshrined in a plaster Punch's show outside the town.

In Genoa, and thereabouts, they train the vines on trellis-work, supported on square clumsy pillars, which, in themselves, are anything but picturesque. But, here, they twine them around trees, and let them trail among the hedges; and the vineyards are full of trees regularly planted for this purpose, each with its own vine twining and clustering about it. Their leaves are now of the brightest gold and deepest red; and never was anything so enchantingly graceful and full of beauty. Through miles of these delightful forms and colours, the road winds its way. The wild festoons, the elegant wreaths, and crowns, and garlands of all shapes; the fairy nets flung over great trees, and making them prisoners in sort; the tumbled heaps and mounds of exquisite shapes upon the ground; how rich and beautiful they are! And every now and then, a long line of trees, will be all bound and garlanded together: as if they had taken hold of one another, and were coming dancing down the field!

Parma has cheerful, stirring streets, for an Italian town; and consequently is not so characteristic as many places of less note. Always excepting the retired Piazza, where the Cathedral, Baptistery, and Campanile—ancient buildings, of a sombre brown, embellished with innumerable grotesque monsters and dreamy-looking creatures carved in marble and red stone—are clustered in a noble and magnificent repose. Their silent presence was only invaded, when I saw them, by the twittering of the many birds that were flying in and out of the crevices in the stones and little nooks in the architecture, where they had made their nests. They were busy, rising from the cold shade of Temples made with hands, into the sunny air of Heaven. Not so the worshippers within, who were listening to the same drowsy chaunt, or kneeling before the same kinds of images and tapers, or whispering, with their heads bowed down, in the selfsame dark confessionals, as I had left in Genoa and everywhere else.

The decayed and mutilated paintings with which this church is covered, have, to my thinking, a remarkably mournful and depressing influence. It is miserable to see great works of art—something of the Souls of Painters—perishing and fading away, like human forms. This cathedral is odorous with the rotting of Correggio's frescoes in the Cupola. Heaven knows how beautiful they may have been at one time. Connoisseurs fall into raptures with them now; but such a labyrinth of arms and legs; such heaps of foreshortened limbs, entangled and involved and jumbled together: no operative surgeon, gone mad, could imagine in his wildest delirium.

There is a very interesting subterranean church here: the roof supported by marble pillars, behind each of which there seemed to be at least one beggar in ambush: to say nothing of the tombs and secluded altars. From every one of these lurking-places, such crowds of phantom-looking men and women, leading other men and women with twisted limbs, or chattering jaws, or paralytic gestures, or idiotic heads, or some other sad infirmity, came hobbling out to beg, that if the ruined frescoes in the cathedral above, had been suddenly animated, and had retired to this lower church, they could hardly have made a greater confusion, or exhibited a more confounding display of arms and legs.

There is Petrarch's Monument, too; and there is the Baptistery, with its beautiful arches and immense font; and there is a gallery containing some very remarkable pictures, whereof a few were being copied by hairy-faced artists, with little velvet caps, more off their heads than on. There is the Farnese Palace, too; and in it one of the dreariest spectacles of decay that ever was seen—a grand, old, gloomy theatre, mouldering away.

It is a large wooden structure, of the horse-shoe shape; the lower seats arranged upon the Roman plan, but above them great heavy chambers, rather than boxes, where the Nobles sat, remote in their proud state. Such desolation as has fallen on this theatre, enhanced in the spectator's fancy by its gay intention and design, none but worms can be familiar with. A hundred and ten years have passed, since any play was acted here. The sky shines in through the gashes in the roof; the boxes are dropping down, wasting away, and only tenanted by rats; damp and mildew smear the faded colours, and make spectral maps upon the panels; lean rags are dangling down where there were gay festoons on the Proscenium; the stage has rotted so, that a narrow wooden gallery is thrown across it, or it would sink beneath the tread, and bury the visitor in the gloomy depth beneath. The desolation and decay impress themselves on all the senses. The air has a mouldering smell, and an earthy taste; any stray outer sounds that straggle in with some lost sunbeam, are muffled and heavy; and the worm, the maggot, and the rot have changed the surface of the wood beneath the touch, as time will seam and roughen a smooth hand. If ever Ghosts act plays, they act them on this ghostly stage.

It was most delicious weather, when we came into Modena, where the darkness of the sombre colonnades over the footways skirting the main street on either side, was made refreshing and agreeable by the bright sky, so wonderfully blue. I passed from all the glory of the day, into a dim cathedral, where High Mass was performing, feeble tapers were burning, people were kneeling in all directions before all manner of shrines, and officiating priests were crooning the usual chant, in the usual, low, dull, drawling, melancholy tone.

Thinking how strange it was, to find, in every stagnant town, this same Heart beating with the same monotonous pulsation, the centre of the same torpid, listless system, I came out by another door, and was suddenly scared to death by a blast from the shrillest trumpet that ever was blown. Immediately, came tearing round the corner, an equestrian company from Paris; marshalling themselves under the walls of the church, and flouting, with their horses' heels, the griffins, lions, tigers, and other monsters in stone and marble, decorating its exterior. First, there came a stately nobleman with a great deal of hair, and no hat, bearing an enormous banner, on which was inscribed MAZEPPA! TO-NIGHT! Then, a Mexican chief, with a great pear-shaped club on his shoulder, like Hercules. Then, six or eight Roman chariots: each with a beautiful lady in extremely short petticoats, and unnaturally pink tights, erect within: shedding beaming looks upon the crowd, in which there was a latent expression of discomposure and anxiety, for which I couldn't account, until, as the open back of each chariot presented itself, I saw the immense difficulty with which the pink legs maintained their perpendicular, over the uneven pavement of the town: which gave me quite a new idea of the ancient Romans and Britons. The procession was brought to a close, by some dozen indomitable warriors of different nations, riding two and two, and haughtily surveying the tame population of Modena : among whom, however, they occasionally condescended to scatter largesse in the form of a few handbills. After caracolling among the lions and tigers, and proclaiming that evening's entertainment with blast of trumpet, it then filed off, by the other end of the square, and left a new and greatly increased dulness behind.

When the procession had so entirely passed away, that the shrill trumpet was mild in the distance, and the tail of the last horse was hopelessly round the corner, the people who had come out of the church to stare at it, went back again. But one old lady, kneeling on the pavement within, near the door, had seen it all, and had been immensely interested, without getting up; and this old lady's eye, at that juncture, I happened to catch: to our mutual confusion. She cut our embarrassment very short, however, by crossing herself devoutly, and going down, at full length, on her face, before a figure in a fancy petticoat and a gilt crown; which was so like one of the procession-figures, that perhaps at this hour she may think the whole appearance a celestial vision. Anyhow, I must certainly have forgiven her her interest in the Circus, though I had been her Father Confessor.

There was a little fiery-eyed old man with a crooked shoulder, in the cathedral, who took it very ill that I made no effort to see the bucket (kept in an old tower) which the people of Modena took away from the people of Bologna in the fourteenth century, and about which there was war made and a mock-heroic poem by TASSONE, too. Being quite content, however, to look at the outside of the tower, and feast, in imagination, on the bucket within; and preferring to loiter in the shade of the tall Campanile, and about the cathedral; I have no personal knowledge of this bucket, even at the present time.

Indeed, we were at Bologna, before the little old man (or the Guide-Book) would have considered that we had half done justice to the wonders of Modena. But it is such a delight to me to leave new scenes behind, and still go on, encountering newer scenes—and, moreover, I have such a perverse disposition in respect of sights that are cut, and dried, and dictated—that I fear I sin against similar authorities in every place I visit.

Be this as it may, in the pleasant Cemetery at Bologna, I found myself walking next Sunday morning among the stately marble tombs and colonnades, in company with a crowd of Peasants, and escorted by a little Cicerone of that town, who was excessively anxious for the honour of the place, and most solicitous to divert my attention from the bad monuments: whereas he was never tired of extolling the good ones. Seeing this little man (a good-humoured little man he was, who seemed to have nothing in his face but shining teeth and eyes) looking wistfully at a certain plot of grass, I asked him who was buried there. "The poor people, Signore," he said, with a shrug and a smile, and stopping to look back at me—for he always went on a little before, and took off his hat to introduce every new monument. "Only the poor, Signore! It's very cheerful. It's very lively. How green it is, how cool! It's like a meadow! There are five," —holding up all the fingers of his right hand to express the number, which an Italian peasant will always do, if it be within the compass of his ten fingers,—"there are five of my little children buried there, Signore; just there; a little to the right. Well! Thanks to God! It's very cheerful. How green it is, how cool it is! It's quite a meadow!"

He looked me very hard in the face, and seeing I was sorry for him, took a pinch of snuff (every Cicerone takes snuff), and made a little bow; partly in deprecation of his having alluded to such a subject, and partly in memory of the children and of his favourite saint. It was as unaffected and as perfectly natural a little bow, as ever man made. Immediately afterwards, he took his hat off altogether, and begged to introduce me to the next monument; and his eyes and his teeth shone brighter than before.

THROUGH BOLOGNA AND FERRARA

THERE was such a very smart official in attendance at the Cemetery where the little Cicerone had buried his children, that when the little Cicerone suggested to me, in a whisper, that there would be no offence in presenting this officer, in return for some slight extra service, with a couple of pauls (about tenpence, English money), I looked incredulously at his cocked hat, wash-leather gloves, well-made uniform, and dazzling buttons, and rebuked the little Cicerone with a grave shake of the head. For, in splendour of appearance, he was at least equal to the Deputy Usher of the Black Rod; and the idea of his carrying, as Jeremy Diddler would say, "such a thing as tenpence" away with him, seemed monstrous. He took it in excellent part, however, when I made bold to give it him, and pulled off his cocked hat with a flourish that would have been a bargain at double the money.

It seemed to be his duty to describe the monuments to the people—at all events he was doing so; and when I compared him, like Gulliver in Brobdingnag, "with the Institutions of my own beloved country, I could not refrain from tears of pride and exultation." He had no pace at all; no more than a tortoise. He loitered as the people loitered, that they might gratify their curiosity; and positively allowed them, now and then, to read the inscriptions on the tombs. He was neither shabby, nor insolent, nor churlish, nor ignorant. He spoke his own language with perfect propriety, and seemed to consider himself, in his way, a kind of teacher of the people, and to entertain a just respect both for himself and them. They would no more have such a man for a Verger in Westminster Abbey, than they would let the people in (as they do at Bologna) to see the monuments for nothing.*

Again, an ancient sombre town, under the brilliant sky; with heavy arcades over the footways of the older streets, and lighter and more cheerful archways in the newer portions of the town. Again, brown piles of sacred buildings, with more birds flying in and out of chinks in the stones; and more snarling monsters for the bases of the pillars. Again, rich churches, drowsy Masses, curling incense, tinkling bells, priests in bright vestments: pictures, tapers, laced altar cloths, crosses, images, and artificial flowers.

There is a grave and learned air about the city, and a pleasant gloom upon it, that would leave it, a distinct and separate impression in the mind, among a crowd of cities, though it were not still further marked in the traveller's remembrance by the two brickleaning towers (sufficiently unsightly in themselves, it must be acknowledged) inclining cross-wise as if they were bowing stiffly to each other—a most extraordinary termination to the perspective of some of the narrow streets. The colleges, and churches too, and palaces: and above all the academy of Fine Arts, where there are a host of interesting pictures, especially by GUIDO, DOMENICHINO, and LUDOVICO CARACCI: give it a place of its own in the memory. Even though these were not, and there were nothing else to remember it by, the great Meridian on the pavement of the church of San Petronio, where the sunbeams mark the time among the kneeling people, would give it a fanciful and pleasant interest.

Bologna being very full of tourists, detained there by an inundation which rendered the road to Florence impassable, I was quartered up at the top of an hotel, in an out-of-the-way room which I never could find: containing a bed, big enough for a boarding-school, which I couldn't fall asleep in. The chief among the waiters who visited this lonely retreat, where there was no other company

* A far more liberal and just recognition of the public has arisen in Westminster Abbey since this was written.

but the swallows in the broad eaves over the window, was a man of one idea in connection with the English; and the subject of this harmless monomania, was Lord Byron. I made the discovery by accidentally remarking to him at breakfast, that the matting with which the floor was covered, was very comfortable at that season, when he immediately replied that Milor Beeron had been much attached to that kind of matting. Observing, at the same moment, that I took no milk, he exclaimed with enthusiasm, that Milor Beeron had never touched it. At first, I took it for granted, in my innocence, that he had been one of the Beeron servants; but no, he said, no, he was in the habit of speaking about my Lord, to English gentlemen; that was all. He knew all about him, he said. In proof of it, he connected him with every possible topic, from the Monte Pulciano wine at dinner (which was grown on an estate he had owned), to the big bed itself, which was the very model of his. When I left the inn, he coupled with his final bow in the yard, a parting assurance that the road by which I was going, had been Milor Beeron's favourite ride; and before the horse's feet had well begun to clatter on the pavement, he ran briskly up-stairs again, I dare say to tell some other Englishman in some other solitary room that the guest who had just departed was Lord Beeron's living image.

I had entered Bologna by night—almost midnight—and all along the road thither, after our entrance into the Papal territory: which is not, in any part, supremely well governed, Saint Peter's keys being rather rusty now: the driver had so worried about the danger of robbers in travelling after dark, and had so infected the brave Courier, and the two had been so constantly stopping and getting up and down to look after a portmanteau which was tied on behind, that I should have felt almost obliged to any one who would have had the goodness to take it away. Hence it was stipulated, that, whenever we left Bologna, we should start so as not to arrive at Ferrara later than eight at night; and a delightful afternoon and evening journey it was, albeit through a flat district which gradually became more marshy from the overflow of brooks and rivers in the recent heavy rains.

At sunset, when I was walking on alone, while the horses rested, I arrived upon a little scene, which, by one of those singular mental operations of which we are all conscious, seemed perfectly familiar to me, and which I see distinctly now. There was not much in it. In the blood red light, there was a mournful sheet of water, just stirred by the evening wind; upon its margin a few trees. In the foreground was a group of silent peasant girls leaning over the parapet of a little bridge, and looking, now up at the sky, now down into the water; in the distance, a deep bell; the shade of approaching night on everything. If I had been murdered there, in some former life, I could not have seemed to remember the place more thoroughly, or with a more emphatic chilling of the blood; and the mere remembrance of it acquired in that minute, is so strengthened by the imaginary recollection, that I hardly think I could forget it.

More solitary, more depopulated, more deserted, old Ferrara, than any city of the solemn brotherhood! The grass so grows up in the silent streets, that any one might make hay there, literally, while the sun shines. But the sun shines with diminished cheerfulness in grim Ferrara; and the people are so few who pass and re-pass through the places, that the flesh of its inhabitants might be grass indeed, and growing in the squares.

I wonder why the head coppersmith in an Italian town, always lives next door to the Hotel, or opposite: making the visitor feel as if the beating hammers were his own heart, palpitating with a deadly energy! I wonder why jealous corridors surround the bedroom on all sides, and fill it with unnecessary doors that can't be shut, and will not open, and abut on pitchy darkness! I wonder why it is not enough that these distrustful genii stand agape at one's dreams all night, but there must also be round open portholes, high in the wall, suggestive, when a mouse or rat is heard behind the wainscot, of a somebody scraping the wall with his toes, in his endeavours to reach one of these portholes and look in! I wonder why the faggots are so constructed, as to know of no effect but an agony of heat when they are lighted and replenished, and an agony of cold and suffocation at all other times! I wonder, above all, why it is the great feature of domestic architecture in Italian inns, that all the fire goes up the chimney, except the smoke!

The answer matters little. Coppersmiths, doors, portholes, smoke, and faggots, are welcome to me. Give me the smiling face of the attendant, man or woman; the courteous manner; the amiable desire to please and to be pleased; the light-hearted, pleasant, simple air— so many jewels set in dirt—and I am theirs again to-morrow!

ARIOSTO's house, TASSO's prison, a rare old Gothic cathedral, and more churches of course, are the sights of Ferrara. But the long silent streets, and the dismantled palaces, where ivy waves in lieu of banners, and where rank weeds are slowly creeping up the long-untrodden stairs, are the best sights of all.

The aspect of this dreary town, half an hour before sunrise one fine morning, when I left it, was as picturesque as it seemed unreal and spectral. It was no matter that the people were not yet out of bed; for if they had all been up and busy, they would have made but little difference in that desert of a place. It was best to see it, without a single figure in the picture; a city of the dead, without one solitary survivor. Pestilence might have ravaged streets, squares, and market-places; and sack and siege have ruined the old houses, battered down their doors and windows, and made breaches in their roofs. In one part, a great tower rose into the air; the only landmark in the melancholy view. In another, a prodigious castle, with a moat about it, stood aloof: a sullen city in itself. In the black dungeons of this castle, Parisina and her lover were beheaded in the dead of night. The red light, beginning to shine when I looked back upon it, stained its walls without, as they have, many a time, been stained within, in old days; but for any sign of life they gave, the castle and the city might have

been avoided by all human creatures, from the moment when the
axe went down upon the last of the two lovers: and might have
never vibrated to another sound

> Beyond the blow that to the block
> Pierced through with forced and sullen shock.

Coming to the Po, which was greatly swollen, and running fiercely,
we crossed it by a floating bridge of boats, and so came into the
Austrian territory, and resumed our journey: through a country of
which, for some miles, a great part was under water. The brave
Courier and the soldiery had first quarrelled, for half an hour or more,
over our eternal passport. But this was a daily relaxation with the
Brave, who was always stricken deaf when shabby functionaries in
uniform came, as they constantly did come, plunging out of wooden
boxes to look at it—or in other words to beg—and who, stone deaf
to my entreaties that the man might have a trifle given him, and
we resume our journey in peace, was wont to sit reviling the function-
ary in broken English: while the unfortunate man's face was a
portrait of mental agony framed in the coach window, from his
perfect ignorance of what was being said to his disparagement.

There was a postilion, in the course of this day's journey, as wild
and savagely good-looking a vagabond as you would desire to see.
He was a tall, stout-made, dark-complexioned fellow, with a profusion of shaggy black hair hanging all over his face, and great black
whiskers stretching down his throat. His dress was a torn suit of
rifle green, garnished here and there with red; a steeple-crowned hat,
innocent of nap, with a broken and bedraggled feather stuck in the
band; and a flaming red neckerchief hanging on his shoulders. He
was not in the saddle, but reposed, quite at his ease, on a sort of low
foot-board in front of the postchaise, down amongst the horses' tails
—convenient for having his brains kicked out, at any moment. To
this Brigand, the brave Courier, when we were at a reasonable trot,
happened to suggest the practicability of going faster. He received
the proposal with a perfect yell of derision; brandished his whip
about his head (such a whip! it was more like a home-made bow);
flung up his heels, much higher than the horses; and disappeared, in
a paroxysm, somewhere in the neighbourhood of the axletree. I fully
expected to see him lying in the road, a hundred yards behind, but up
came the steeple-crowned hat again, next minute, and he was seen
reposing, as on a sofa, entertaining himself with the idea, and crying,
"Ha ha! what next! Oh the devil! Faster too! Shoo—hoo—o—o!"
(This last ejaculation, an inexpressibly defiant hoot.) Being anxious
to reach our immediate destination that night, I ventured, by-and-
by, to repeat the experiment on my own account. It produced exactly
the same effect. Round flew the whip with the same scornful flourish,
up came the heels, down went the steeple-crowned hat, and presently
he reappeared, reposing as before and saying to himself, "Ha ha!
what next! Faster too! Oh the devil! Shoo—hoo—o—o!"

AN ITALIAN DREAM

I HAD been travelling for some days; resting very little in the night, and never in the day. The rapid and unbroken succession of novelties that had passed before me, came back like half-formed dreams; and a crowd of objects wandered in the greatest confusion through my mind, as I travelled on, by a solitary road. At intervals, some one among them would stop, as it were, in its restless flitting to and fro, and enable me to look at it, quite steadily, and behold it in full distinctness. After a few moments, it would dissolve, like a view in a magic-lantern; and while I saw some part of it quite plainly, and some faintly, and some not at all, would show me another of the many places I had lately seen, lingering behind it, and coming through it. This was no sooner visible than, in its turn, it melted into something else.

At one moment, I was standing again, before the brown old rugged churches of Modena. As I recognised the curious pillars with grim monsters for their bases, I seemed to see them, standing by themselves in the quiet square at Padua, where there were the staid old University, and the figures, demurely gowned, grouped here and there in the open space about it. Then, I was strolling in the outskirts of that pleasant city, admiring the unusual neatness of the dwelling-houses, gardens, and orchards, as I had seen them a few hours before. In their stead arose, immediately, the two towers of Bologna; and the most obstinate of all these objects, failed to hold its ground, a minute, before the monstrous moated castle of Ferrara, which, like an illustration to a wild romance, came back again in the red sunrise, lording it over the solitary, grass-grown, withered town. In short, I had that incoherent but delightful jumble in my brain, which travellers are apt to have, and are indolently willing to encourage. Every shake of the coach in which I sat, half dozing in the dark, appeared to jerk some new recollection out of its place, and to jerk some other new recollection into it; and in this state I fell asleep.

I was awakened after some time (as I thought) by the stopping of the coach. It was now quite night, and we were at the water-side. There lay here, a black boat, with a little house or cabin in it of the same mournful colour. When I had taken my seat in this, the boat was paddled by two men, towards a great light, lying in the distance on the sea.

Ever and again, there was a dismal sigh of wind. It ruffled the water, and rocked the boat, and sent the dark clouds flying before the stars. I could not but think how strange it was, to be floating away at that hour: leaving the land behind, and going on, towards this light upon the sea. It soon began to burn brighter; and from being one light became a cluster of tapers, twinkling and shining out of the water, as the boat approached towards them by a dreamy kind of track, marked out upon the sea by posts and piles.

We had floated on, five miles or so, over the dark water, when I heard it rippling in my dream, against some obstruction near at hand. Looking out attentively, I saw, through the gloom, a something black and massive—like a shore, but lying close and flat upon the water, like a raft—which we were gliding past. The chief of the two rowers said it was a burial-place.

Full of the interest and wonder which a cemetery lying out there, in the lonely sea, inspired, I turned to gaze upon it as it should recede in our path, when it was quickly shut out from my view. Before I knew by what, or how, I found that we were gliding up a street—a phantom street; the houses rising on both sides, from the water, and the black boat gliding on beneath their windows. Lights were shining from some of these casements, plumbing the depth of the black stream with their reflected rays, but all was profoundly silent.

So we advanced into this ghostly city, continuing to hold our course through narrow streets and lanes, all filled and flowing with water. Some of the corners where our way branched off, were so acute and narrow, that it seemed impossible for the slender boat to turn them; but the rowers, with a low melodious cry of warning, sent it skimming on without a pause. Sometimes, the rowers of another black boat like our own, echoed the cry, and slackening their speed (as I thought we did ours) would come flitting past us like a dark shadow. Other boats, of the same sombre hue, were lying moored, I thought, to painted pillars, near to dark mysterious doors that opened straight upon the water. Some of these were empty; in some, the rowers lay asleep; towards one, I saw some figures coming down a gloomy archway from the interior of a palace: gaily dressed, and attended by torch-bearers. It was but a glimpse I had of them; for a bridge, so low and close upon the boat that it seemed ready to fall down and crush us: one of the many bridges that perplexed the Dream: blotted them out, instantly. On we went, floating towards the heart of this strange place—with water all about us where never water was elsewhere—clusters of houses, churches, heaps of stately buildings growing out of it—and, everywhere, the same extraordinary silence. Presently, we shot across a broad and open stream; and passing, as I thought, before a spacious paved quay, where the bright lamps with which it was illuminated showed long rows of arches and pillars, of ponderous construction and great strength, but as light to the eye as garlands of hoar-frost or gossamer—and where, for the first time, I saw people walking—arrived at a flight of steps leading from the water to a large mansion, where, having passed through corridors and galleries innumerable, I lay down to rest; listening to the black boats stealing up and down below the window on the rippling water, till I fell asleep.

The glory of the day that broke upon me in this Dream; its freshness, motion, buoyancy; its sparkles of the sun in water; its clear blue sky and rustling air; no waking words can tell. But, from my window, I looked down on boats and barks; on masts, sails, cordage, flags; on groups of busy sailors, working at the cargoes of these vessels; on wide quays, strewn with bales, casks, merchandise of many kinds; on great ships, lying near at hand in stately indolence; on islands, crowned with gorgeous domes and turrets: and where golden crosses glittered in the light, atop of wondrous churches, springing from the sea! Going down upon the margin of the green sea, rolling on before the door, and filling all the streets, I came upon a place of such surpassing beauty, and such grandeur, that all the rest was poor and faded, in comparison with its absorbing loveliness.

It was a great Piazza, as I thought; anchored, like all the rest, in the deep ocean. On its broad bosom, was a Palace, more majestic and magnificent in its old age, than all the buildings of the earth, in the high prime and fulness of their youth. Cloisters and galleries: so light, they might have been the work of fairy hands: so strong that centuries had battered them in vain: wound round and round this palace, and enfolded it with a Cathedral, gorgeous in the wild luxuriant fancies of the East. At no great distance from its porch, a lofty tower, standing by itself, and rearing its proud head, alone, into the sky, looked out upon the Adriatic Sea. Near to the margin of the stream, were two ill-omened pillars of red granite; one having on its top, a figure with a sword and shield; the other, a winged lion. Not far from these again, a second tower: richest of the rich in all its decorations: even here, where all was rich: sustained aloft, a great orb, gleaming with gold and deepest blue: the Twelve Signs painted on it, and a mimic sun revolving in its course around them: while above, two bronze giants hammered out the hours upon a sounding bell. An oblong square of lofty houses of the whitest stone, surrounded by a light and beautiful arcade, formed part of this enchanted scene; and, here and there, gay masts for flags rose, tapering, from the pavement of the unsubstantial ground.

I thought I entered the Cathedral, and went in and out among its many arches: traversing its whole extent. A grand and dreamy structure, of immense proportions; golden with old mosaics; redolent of perfumes; dim with the smoke of incense; costly in treasure of precious stones and metals, glittering through iron bars; holy with the bodies of deceased saints; rainbow-hued with windows of stained glass; dark with carved woods and coloured marbles; obscure in its vast heights, and lengthened distances; shining with silver lamps and winking lights; unreal, fantastic, solemn, inconceivable throughout. I thought I entered the old palace; pacing silent galleries and council-chambers, where the old rulers of this mistress of the waters looked sternly out, in pictures, from the walls, and where her high-prowed galleys, still victorious on canvas, fought and conquered as of old. I thought I wandered through its halls of state and triumph—bare and empty now!—and musing on its pride and might, extinct: for that was past; all past: heard a voice say, "Some tokens of its ancient rule and some consoling reasons for its downfall, may be traced here, yet!"

I dreamed that I was led on, then, into some jealous rooms, communicating with a prison near the palace; separated from it by a lofty bridge crossing a narrow street; and called, I dreamed, The Bridge of Sighs.

But first I passed two jagged slits in a stone wall; the lions' mouths—now toothless—where, in the distempered horror of my sleep, I thought denunciations of innocent men to the old wicked Council, had been dropped through, many a time, when the night was dark. So, when I saw the council-room to which such prisoners were taken for examination, and the door by which they passed out, when they were condemned—a door that never closed upon a man with life and hope before him—my heart appeared to die within me.

It was smitten harder though, when, torch in hand, I descended from the cheerful day into two ranges, one below another, of dismal, awful, horrible stone cells. They were quite dark. Each had a loop-hole in its massive wall, where, in the old time, every day, a torch was placed—I dreamed—to light the prisoner within, for half an hour. The captives, by the glimmering of these brief rays, had scratched and cut inscriptions in the blackened vaults. I saw them. For their labour with a rusty nail's point, had outlived their agony and them, through many generations.

One cell, I saw, in which no man remained for more than four-and-twenty hours; being marked for dead before he entered it. Hard by, another, and a dismal one, whereto, at midnight, the confessor came—a monk brown-robed, and hooded—ghastly in the day, and free bright air, but in the midnight of that murky prison, Hope's extinguisher, and Murder's herald. I had my foot upon the spot, where, at the same dread hour, the shriven prisoner was strangled; and struck my hand upon the guilty door—low-browed and stealthy —through which the lumpish sack was carried out into a boat, and rowed away, and drowned where it was death to cast a net.

Around this dungeon stronghold, and above some part of it: licking the rough walls without, and smearing them with damp and slime within: stuffing dank weeds and refuse into chinks and crevices as if the very stones and bars had mouths to stop: furnishing a smooth road for the removal of the bodies of the secret victims of the State—a road so ready that it went along with them, and ran before them, like a cruel officer—flowed the same water that filled this Dream of mine, and made it seem one, even at the time.

Descending from the palace by a staircase, called, I thought, the Giant's—I had some imaginary recollection of an old man abdicating, coming, more slowly and more feebly, down it, when he heard the bell, proclaiming his successor—I glided off, in one of the dark boats, until we came to an old arsenal guarded by four marble lions. To make my Dream more monstrous and unlikely, one of these had words and sentences upon its body, inscribed there, at an unknown time, and in an unknown language; so that their purport was a mystery to all men.

There was little sound of hammers in this place for building ships, and little work in progress; for the greatness of the city was no more, as I have said. Indeed, it seemed a very wreck found drifting on the sea; a strange flag hoisted in its honourable stations, and strangers standing at its helm. A splendid barge in which its ancient chief had gone forth, pompously, at certain periods, to wed the ocean, lay here, I thought, no more; but, in its place, there was a tiny model, made from recollection like the city's greatness; and it told of what had been (so are the strong and weak confounded in the dust) almost as eloquently as the massive pillars, arches, roofs, reared to overshadow stately ships that had no other shadow now, upon the water or the earth.

An armoury was there yet. Plundered and despoiled; but an armoury. With a fierce standard taken from the Turks, drooping in the dull air of its cage. Rich suits of mail worn by great warriors were hoarded there; crossbows and bolts; quivers full of arrows; spears, swords, daggers, maces, shields, and heavy-headed axes. Plates of wrought steel and iron, to make the gallant horse a monster cased in metal scales; and one spring-weapon (easy to be carried in the breast) designed to do its office noiselessly, and made for shooting men with poisoned darts.

One press or case I saw, full of accursed instruments of torture: horribly contrived to cramp, and pinch, and grind and crush men's bones, and tear and twist them with the torment of a thousand deaths. Before it, were two iron helmets with breast-pieces: made to close up tight and smooth upon the heads of living sufferers; and fastened on to each, was a small knob or anvil, where the directing devil could repose his elbow at his ease, and listen, near the walled-up ear, to the lamentations and confessions of the wretch within. There was that grim resemblance in them to the human shape—they were such moulds of sweating faces, pained and cramped—that it was difficult to think them empty; and terrible distortions lingering within them, seemed to follow me, when, taking to my boat again, I rowed off to a kind of garden or public walk in the sea, where there were grass and trees. But I forgot them when I stood upon its farthest brink—I stood there, in my dream—and looked, along the ripple, to the setting sun; before me, in the sky and on the deep, a crimson flush; and behind me the whole city resolving into streaks of red and purple, on the water.

In the luxurious wonder of so rare a dream, I took but little heed of time, and had but little understanding of its flight. But there were days and nights in it; and when the sun was high, and when the rays of lamps were crooked in the running water, I was still afloat, I thought: plashing the slippery walls and houses with the cleavings of the tide, as my black boat, borne upon it, skimmed along the streets.

Sometimes, alighting at the doors of churches and vast palaces, I wandered on, from room to room, from aisle to aisle, through labyrinths of rich altars, ancient monuments; decayed apartments where the furniture, half awful, half grotesque, was mouldering away. Pictures were there, replete with such enduring beauty and expression: with such passion, truth and power: that they seemed so many young men and fresh realities among a host of spectres. I thought these, often intermingled with the old days of the city: with its beauties, tyrants, captains, patriots, merchants, courtiers, priests: nay, with its very stones, and bricks, and public places; all of which lived again, about me, on the walls. Then, coming down some marble staircase where the water lapped and oozed against the lower steps, I passed into my boat again, and went on in my dream.

Floating down narrow lanes, where carpenters, at work with plane and chisel in their shops, tossed the light shaving straight upon the water, where it lay like weed, or ebbed away before me in a tangled heap. Past open doors, decayed and rotten from long steeping in the wet, through which some scanty patch of vine shone green and bright, making unusual shadows on the pavement with its trembling leaves. Past quays and terraces, where women, gracefully veiled, were passing and repassing, and where idlers were reclining in the sunshine, on flag-stones and on flights of steps. Past bridges, where there were idlers too; loitering and looking over. Below stone balconies, erected at a giddy height, before the loftiest windows of the loftiest houses. Past plots of garden, theatres, shrines, prodigious piles of architecture—Gothic—Saracenic—fanciful with all the fancies of all times and countries. Past buildings that were high, and low, and black, and white, and straight, and crooked; mean and grand, crazy and strong. Twining among a tangled lot of boats and barges, and shooting out at last into a Grand Canal! There, in the errant fancy of my dream, I saw old Shylock passing to and fro upon a bridge, all built upon with shops and humming with the tongues of men; a form I seemed to know for Desdemona's, leaned down through a latticed blind to pluck a flower. And, in the dream, I thought that Shakespeare's spirit was abroad upon the water somewhere: stealing through the city.

At night, when two votive lamps burnt before an image of the Virgin, in a gallery outside the great cathedral, near the roof, I fancied that the great piazza of the Winged Lion was a blaze of cheerful light, and that its whole arcade was thronged with people; while crowds were diverting themselves in splendid coffee-houses opening from it—which were never shut, I thought, but open all night long. When the bronze giants struck the hour of midnight on the bell, I thought the life and animation of the city were all centred here; and as I rowed away, abreast the silent quays, I only saw them dotted, here and there, with sleeping boatmen wrapped up in their cloaks, and lying at full length upon the stones.

But close about the quays and churches, palaces and prisons: sucking at their walls, and welling up into the secret places of the town: crept the water always. Noiseless and watchful: coiled round and round it, in its many folds, like an old serpent: waiting for the time, I thought, when people should look down into its depths for any stone of the old city that had claimed to be its mistress.

Thus it floated me away, until I awoke in the old market-place at Verona. I have, many and many a time, thought since, of this strange Dream upon the water: half-wondering if it lie there yet, and if its name be VENICE.

BY VERONA, MANTUA, AND MILAN, ACROSS THE PASS OF THE SIMPLON INTO SWITZERLAND

I HAD been half afraid to go to Verona, lest it should at all put me out of conceit with Romeo and Juliet. But, I was no sooner come into the old market-place, than the misgiving vanished. It is so fanciful, quaint, and picturesque a place, formed by such an extraordinary and rich variety of fantastic buildings, that there could be nothing better at the core of even this romantic town: scene of one of the most romantic and beautiful of stories.

It was natural enough, to go straight from the Market-place, to the House of the Capulets, now degenerated into a most miserable little inn. Noisy vetturíni and muddy market-carts were disputing possession of the yard, which was ankle-deep in dirt, with a brood of splashed and bespattered geese; and there was a grim-visaged dog, viciously panting in a doorway, who would certainly have had Romeo by the leg, the moment he put it over the wall, if he had existed and been at large in those times. The orchard fell into other hands, and was parted off many years ago; but there used to be one attached to the house—or at all events there may have been,—and the hat (Cappêllo) the ancient cognizance of the family, may still be seen, carved in stone, over the gateway of the yard. The geese, the market-carts, their drivers, and the god, were somewhat in the way of the story, it must be confessed; and it would have been pleasanter to have found the house empty, and to have been able to walk through the disused rooms. But the hat was unspeakably comfortable; and the place where the garden used to be, hardly less so. Besides, the house is a distrustful, jealous-looking house as one would desire to see, though of a very moderate size. So I was quite satisfied with it, as the veritable mansion of old Capulet, and was correspondingly grateful in my acknowledgments to an extremely unsentimental middle-aged lady, the Padrona of the Hotel, who was lounging on the threshold looking at the geese; and who at least resembled the Capulets in the one particular of being very great in the "Family" way.

From Juliet's home, to Juliet's tomb, is a transition as natural to the visitor, as to fair Juliet herself, or to the proudest Juliet that ever has taught the torches to burn bright in any time. So, I went off, with a guide, to an old, old garden, once belonging to an old, old convent, I suppose; and being admitted, at a shattered gate, by a bright-eyed woman who was washing clothes, went down some walks where fresh plants and young flowers were prettily growing among fragments of old wall, and ivy-coloured mounds; and was shown a little tank, or water-trough, which the bright-eyed woman—drying her arms upon her 'kerchief, called "La tomba di Giulietta la sfortunáta." With the best disposition in the world to believe, I could do no more than believe that the bright-eyed woman believed; so I gave her that much credit, and her customary fee in ready money. It was a pleasure, rather than a disappointment, that Juliet's resting-place was forgotten. However consolatory it may have been to Yorick's Ghost, to hear the feet upon the pavement overhead, and, twenty times a day, the repetition of his name, it is better for Juliet to lie out of the track of tourists, and to have no visitors but such as come to graves in spring-rain, and sweet air, and shunshine.

Pleasant Verona! With its beautiful old palaces, and charming country in the distance, seen from terrace walks, and stately, balustraded galleries. With its Roman gates, still spanning the fair street, and casting, on the sunlight of to-day, the shade of fifteen hundred years ago. With its marble-fitted churches lofty towers, rich architecture, and quaint old quiet thoroughfares, where shouts of Montagues and Capulets once resounded,

> And made Verona's ancient citizens
> Cast by their grave, beseeming ornaments,
> To wield old partizans.

With its fast-rushing river, picturesque old bridge, great castle, waving cypresses, and prospect so delightful, and so cheerful! Pleasant Verona!

In the midst of it, in the Piazza di Brá—a spirit of old time among the familiar realities of the passing hour—is the great Roman Amphi-theatre. So well preserved, and carefully maintained, that every row of seats is there, unbroken. Over certain of the arches the old Roman numerals may yet be seen; and there are corridors, and staircases, and subterranean passages for beasts, and winding ways, above ground and below, as when the fierce thousands hurried in and out, intent upon the bloody shows of the arena. Nestling in some of the shadows and hollow places of the walls, now, are smiths with their forges, and a few small dealers of one kind or other; and there are green weeds, and leaves, and grass, upon the parapet. But little else is greatly changed.

When I had traversed all about it, with great interest, and had gone up to the topmost round of seats, and turning from the lovely panorama closed in by the distant Alps, looked down into the building, it seemed to lie before me like the inside of a prodigious hat of plaited straw, with an enormously broad brim and a shallow crown; the plaits being represented by the four-and-forty rows of seats. The comparison is a homely and fantastic one, in sober remembrance and on paper, but it was irresistibly suggested at the moment, nevertheless.

An equestrian troop had been there a short time before—the same troop, I dare say, that appeared to the old lady in the church at Modena—and had scooped out a little ring at one end of the arena; where their performances had taken place, and where the marks of their horses' feet were still fresh. I could not but picture to myself, a handful of spectators gathered together on one or two of the old stone seats, and a spangled Cavalier being gallant, or a Policinello funny, with the grim walls looking on. Above all, I thought how strangely those Roman mutes would gaze upon the favourite comic scene of the travelling English, where a British nobleman (Lord John), with a very loose stomach: dressed in a blue-tailed coat down to his heels, bright yellow breeches, and a white hat: comes abroad, riding double on a rearing horse, with an English lady (Lady Betsy) in a straw bonnet and green veil, and a red spencer; and who always carries a gigantic reticule, and a put-up parasol.

I walked through and through the town all the rest of the day, and could have walked there until now, I think. In one place, there was a very pretty modern theatre, where they had just performed the opera (always popular in Verona) of Romeo and Juliet. In another there was a collection, under a colonnade, of Greek, Roman, and Etruscan remains, presided over by an ancient man who might have been an Etruscan relic himself; for he was not strong enough to open the iron gate, when he had unlocked it, and had neither voice enough to be audible when he described the curiosities, nor sight enough to see them: he was so very old. In another place, there was a gallery of pictures: so abominably bad, that it was quite delightful to see them mouldering away. But anywhere: in the churches, among the palaces, in the streets, on the bridge, or down beside the river: it was always pleasant Verona, and in my remembrance always will be.

I read Romeo and Juliet in my own room at the inn that night— of course, no Englishman had ever read it there, before—and set out for Mantua next day at sunrise, repeating to myself (in the *coupé* of an omnibus, and next to the conductor, who was reading the Mysteries of Paris),

> There is no world without Verona's walls
> But purgatory, torture, hell itself.
> Hence-banished is banished from the world,
> And world's exile is death——

which reminded me that Romeo was only banished five-and-twenty miles after all, and rather disturbed my confidence in his energy and boldness.

Was the way to Mantua as beautiful, in his time, I wonder! Did it wind through pasture land as green, bright with the same glancing streams, and dotted with fresh clumps of graceful trees! Those purple mountains lay on the horizon, then, for certain; and the dresses of these peasant girls, who wear a great, knobbed, silver pin like an English "life preserver" through their hair behind, can hardly be much changed. The hopeful feeling of so bright a morning, and so exquisite a sunrise, can have been no stranger, even to an exiled lover's breast; and Mantua itself must have broken on him in the prospect, with its towers, and walls, and water, pretty much as on a common-place and matrimonial omnibus. He made the same sharp twists and turns, perhaps, over two rumbling drawbridges; passed through the like long, covered, wooden bridge; and leaving the marshy water behind, approached the rusty gate of stagnant Mantua.

If ever a man were suited to his place of residence, and his place of residence to him, the lean Apothecary and Mantua came together in a perfect fitness of things. It may have been more stirring then, perhaps. If so, the Apothecary was a man in advance of his time, and knew what Mantua would be, in eighteen hundred and forty-four. He fasted much, and that assisted him in his foreknowledge.

I put up at the Hotel of the Golden Lion, and was in my own room arranging plans with the brave Courier, when there came a modest little tap at the door, which opened on an outer gallery surrounding a court-yard; and an intensely shabby little man looked in, to inquire if the gentleman would have a Cicerone to show the town. His face was so very wistful and anxious, in the half-opened doorway, and there was so much poverty expressed in his faded suit and little pinched hat, and in the thread-bare worsted glove with which he held it—not expressed the less, because these were evidently his genteel clothes, hastily slipped on—that I would as soon have trodden on him as dismissed him. I engaged him on the instant, and he stepped in directly.

While I finished the discussion in which I was engaged, he stood, beaming by himself in a corner, making a feint of brushing my hat with his arm. If his fee had been as many napoleons as it was francs, there could not have shot over the twilight of his shabbiness such a gleam of sun, as lighted up the whole man, now that he was hired.

"Well!" said I, when I was ready, "shall we go out now?"

"If the gentleman pleases. It is a beautiful day. A little fresh, but charming; altogether charming. The gentleman will allow me to open the door. This is the Inn Yard. The court-yard of the Golden Lion! The gentleman will please to mind his footing on the stairs."

We were now in the street.

"This is the street of the Golden Lion. This, the outside of the Golden Lion. The interesting window up there, on the first Piano, where the pane of glass is broken, is the window of the gentleman's chamber!"

Having viewed all these remarkable objects, I inquired if there were much to see in Mantua.

"Well! Truly, no. Not much! So, so," he said, shrugging his shoulders apologetically.

"Many churches?"

"No. Nearly all suppressed by the French."

"Monasteries or convents?"

"No. The French again! Nearly all suppressed by Napoleon."

"Much business?"

"Very little business."

"Many strangers?"

"Ah Heaven!"

I thought he would have fainted.

"Then, when we have seen the two large churches yonder, what shall we do next?" said I.

He looked up the street, and down the street, and rubbed his chin timidly; and then said, glancing in my face as if a light had broken on his mind, yet with a humble appeal to my forbearance that was perfectly irresistible:

"We can take a little turn about the town, Signore !" (Si può far 'un píccolo gíro della citta).

It was impossible to be anything but delighted with the proposal, so we set off together in great good-humour. In the relief of his mind, he opened his heart, and gave up as much of Mantua as a Cicerone could.

"One must eat," he said; "but, bah ! it was a dull place, without doubt."

He made as much as possible of the Basilica of Santa Andrea—a noble church—and of an inclosed portion of the pavement, about which tapers were burning, and a few people kneeling, and under which is said to be preserved the Sangreal of the old Romances. This church disposed of, and another after it (the cathedral of San Pietro), we went to the Museum, which was shut up. "It was all the same," he said. "Bah ! There was not much inside !" Then, we went to see the Piazza del Diavolo, built by the Devil (for no particular purpose) in a single night; then, the Piazza Virgiliana; then, the statue of Virgil—*our* Poet, my little friend said, plucking up a spirit, for the moment, and putting his hat a little on one side. Then, we went to a dismal sort of farm-yard, by which a picture-gallery was approached. The moment the gate of this retreat was opened, some five hundred geese came waddling round us, stretching out their necks, and clamouring in the most hideous manner, as if they were ejaculating, "Oh ! here's somebody come to see the Pictures ! Don't go up ! Don't go up !" While we went up, they waited very quietly about the door in a crowd, cackling to one another occasionally, in a subdued tone; but the instant we appeared again, their necks came out like telescopes, and setting up a great noise, which meant, I have no doubt, "What, you would go, would you ! What do you think of it ! How do you like it !" they attended us to the outer gate, and cast us forth, derisively, into Mantua.

The geese who saved the Capitol, were, as compared to these, Pork to the learned Pig. What a gallery it was ! I would take their opinion on a question of art, in preference to the discourses of Sir Joshua Reynolds.

Now that we were standing in the street, after being thus igno- miniously escorted thither, my little friend was plainly reduced to the "píccolo gíro," or little circuit of the town, he had formerly proposed. But my suggestion that we should visit the Palazzo Tè (of which I had heard a great deal, as a strange wild place) imparted new life to him, and away we went.

The secret of the length of Midas's ears, would have been more extensively known, if that servant of his, who whispered it to the reeds, had lived in Mantua, where there are reeds and rushes enough to have published it to all the world. The Palazzo Tè stands in a swamp, among this sort of vegetation; and is, indeed, as singular a place as I ever saw.

Not for its dreariness, though it is very dreary. Nor for its dampness, though it is very damp. Nor for its desolate condition, though it is as desolate and neglected as house can be. But chiefly for the unaccountable nightmares with which its interior has been decorated (among other subjects of more delicate execution), by Giulio Romano. There is a leering Giant over a certain chimney-piece, and there are dozens of Giants (Titans warring with Jove) on the walls of another room, so inconceivably ugly and grotesque, that it is marvellous how any man can have imagined such creatures. In the chamber in which they abound, these monsters, with swollen faces and cracked cheeks, and every kind of distortion of look and limb, are depicted as staggering under the weight of falling buildings, and being overwhelmed in the ruins; upheaving masses of rock, and burying themselves beneath; vainly striving to sustain the pillars of heavy roofs that topple every kind of mad and demoniacal destruction. The figures are immensely large, and exaggerated to the utmost pitch of uncouthness; the colouring is harsh and disagreeable; and the whole effect more like (I should imagine) a violent rush of blood to the head of the spectator, than any real picture set before him by the hand of an artist. This apoplectic performance was shown by a sickly-looking woman, whose appearance was referable, I dare say, to the bad air of the marshes; but it was difficult to help feeling as if she were too much haunted by the Giants, and they were frightening her to death, all alone in that exhausted cistern of a Palace, among the reeds and rushes, with the mists hovering about outside, and stalking round and round it continually.

Our walk through Mantua showed us, in almost every street, some suppressed church: now used for a warehouse, now for nothing at all: all as crazy and dismantled as they could be, short of tumbling down bodily. The marshy town was so intensely dull and flat, that the dirt upon it seemed not to have come there in the ordinary course, but to have settled and mantled on its surface as on standing water. And yet there were some business-dealings going on, and some profits realising; for there were arcades full of Jews, where those extraordinary people were sitting outside their shops, contemplating their stores of stuffs, and woollens, and bright handkerchiefs, and trinkets: and looking, in all respects, as wary and business-like, as their brethren in Houndsditch, London.

Having selected a Vetturíno from among the neighbouring Christians, who agreed to carry us to Milan in two days and a half, and to start, next morning, as soon as the gates were opened, I returned to the Golden Lion, and dined luxuriously in my own room, in a narrow passage between two bedsteads: confronted by a smoky fire, and backed up by a chest of drawers. At six o'clock next morning we were jingling in the dark through the wet cold mist that enshrouded the town; and, before noon, the driver (a native of Mantua, and sixty years of age or thereabouts) began *to ask the way* to Milan.

It lay through Bozzolo; formerly a little republic, and now one of the most deserted and poverty-stricken of towns: where the landlord of the miserable inn (God bless him! it was his weekly custom) was distributing infinitesimal coins among a clamorous herd of women and children, whose rags were fluttering in the wind and rain outside his door, where they were gathered to receive his charity. It lay through mist, and mud and rain, and vines trained low upon the ground, all that day and the next; the first sleeping-place being Cremona, memorable for its dark brick churches, and immensely high tower, the Torrazzo—to say nothing of its violins, of which it certainly produces none in these degenerate days; and the second, Lodi. Then we went on, through more mud, mist, and rain, and marshy ground: and through such a fog, as Englishmen, strong in the faith of their own grievances, are apt to believe is nowhere to be found but in their own country, until we entered the paved streets of Milan.

The fog was so dense here, that the spire of the far-famed Cathedral might as well have been at Bombay, for anything that could be seen of it at that time. But as we halted to refresh, for a few days then, and returned to Milan again next summer, I had ample opportunities of seeing the glorious structure in all its majesty and beauty.

All Christian homage to the saint who lies within it! There are many good and true saints in the calendar, but San Carlo Borromeo has—if I may quote Mrs. Primrose on such a subject—"my warm heart." A charitable doctor to the sick, a munificent friend to the poor, and this, not in any spirit of blind bigotry, but as the bold opponent of enormous abuses in the Romish church, I honour his memory. I honour it none the less, because he was nearly slain by a priest, suborned by priests, to murder him at the altar: in acknowledgment of his endeavours to reform a false and hypocritical brotherhood of monks. Heaven shield all imitators of San Carlo Borromeo as it shielded him! A reforming Pope would need a little shielding, even now.

The subterranean chapel in which the body of San Carlo Borromeo is preserved, presents as striking and as ghastly a contrast, perhaps, as any place can show. The tapers which are lighted down there, flash and gleam on alti-rilievi in gold and silver, delicately wrought by skilful hands, and representing the principal events in the life of the saint. Jewels, and precious metals, shine and sparkle on every side. A windlass slowly removes the front of the altar; and, within it, in a gorgeous shrine of gold and silver, is seen, through alabaster, the shrivelled mummy of a man: the pontifical robes with which it is adorned, radiant with diamonds, emeralds, rubies: every costly and magnificent gem. The shrunken heap of poor earth in the midst of this great glitter, is more pitiful than if it lay upon a dunghill. There is not a ray of imprisoned light in all the flash and fire of jewels, but seems to mock the dusty holes where eyes were, once. Every thread of silk in the rich vestments seems only a provision from the worms that spin, for the behoof of worms that propagate in sepulchres.

In the old refectory of the dilapidated Convent of Santa Maria delle Grazie, is the work of art, perhaps, better known than any other in the world: the Last Supper, by Leonardo da Vinci—with a door cut through it by the intelligent Dominican friars, to facilitate their operations at dinner-time.

I am not mechanically acquainted with the art of painting, and have no other means of judging of a picture than as I see it resembling and refining upon nature, and presenting graceful combinations of forms and colours. I am, therefore, no authority whatever, in reference to the "touch" of this or that master; though I know very well (as anybody may, who chooses to think about the matter) that few very great masters can possibly have painted, in the compass of their lives, one-half of the pictures that bear their names, and that are recognised by many aspirants to a reputation for taste, as undoubted originals. But this, by the way. Of the Last Supper, I would simply observe, that in its beautiful composition and arrangement, there it is, at Milan, a wonderful picture; and that, in its original colouring, or in its original expression of any single face or feature, there it is not. Apart from the damage it has sustained from damp, decay, or neglect, it has been (as Barry shows) so retouched upon, and re-painted, and that so clumsily, that many of the heads are, now, positive deformities, with patches of paint and plaster sticking upon them like wens, and utterly distorting the expression. Where the original artist set that impress of his genius on a face, which, almost in a line or touch, separated him from meaner painters and made him what he was, succeeding bunglers, filling up, or painting across seams and cracks, have been quite unable to imitate his hand; and putting in some scowls, or frowns, or wrinkles, of their own, have blotched and spoiled the work. This is so well established as an historical fact, that I should not repeat it, at the risk of being tedious, but for having observed an English gentleman before the picture, who was at great pains to fall into what I may describe as mild convulsions, at certain minute details of expression which are not left in it. Whereas, it would be comfortable and rational for travellers and critics to arrive at a general understanding that it cannot fail to have been a work of extraordinary merit, once: when, with so few of its original beauties remaining, the grandeur of the general design is yet sufficient to sustain it, as a piece replete with interest and dignity.

We achieved the other sights of Milan, in due course, and a fine city it is, though not so unmistakably Italian as to possess the characteristic qualities of many towns far less important in themselves. The Corso, where the Milanese gentry ride up and down in carriages, and rather than not do which, they would half starve themselves at home, is a most noble public promenade, shaded by long avenues of trees. In the splendid theatre of La Scala, there was a ballet of action performed after the opera, under the title of Prometheus: in the beginning of which, some hundred or two of men and women represented our mortal race before the refinements of the arts and sciences, and loves and graces, came on earth to soften them. I never saw anything more effective. Generally speaking, the pantomimic action of the Italians is more remarkable for its sudden and impetuous character than for its delicate expression; but, in this case, the drooping monotony: the weary, miserable, listless, moping life: the sordid passions and desires of human creatures, destitute of those elevating influences to which we owe so much, and to whose promoters we render so little: were expressed in a manner really powerful and affecting. I should have thought it almost impossible to present such an idea so strongly on the stage, without the aid of speech.

Milan soon lay behind us, at five o'clock in the morning; and before the golden statue on the summit of the cathedral spire was lost in the blue sky, the Alps, stupendously confused in lofty peaks and ridges, clouds and snow, were towering in our path.

Still, we continued to advance toward them until nightfall; and, all day long, the mountain tops presented strangely shifting shapes, as the road displayed them in different points of view. The beautiful day was just declining, when we came upon the Lago Maggiore, with its lovely islands. For however fanciful and fantastic the Isola Bella may be, and is, it still is beautiful. Anything springing out of that blue water, with that scenery around it, must be.

It was ten o'clock at night when we got to Domo d'Ossola, at the foot of the Pass of the Simplon. But as the moon was shining brightly, and there was not a cloud in the starlit sky, it was no time for going to bed, or going anywhere but on. So, we got a little carriage, after some delay, and began the ascent.

It was late in November; and the snow lying four or five feet thick in the beaten road on the summit (in other parts the new drift was already deep), the air was piercing cold. But, the serenity of the night, and the grandeur of the road, with its impenetrable shadows, and deep glooms, and its sudden turns into the shining of the moon and its incessant roar of falling water, rendered the journey more and more sublime at every step.

Soon leaving the calm Italian villages below us, sleeping in the moonlight, the road began to wind among dark trees, and after a time emerged upon a barer region, very steep and toilsome, where the moon shone bright and high. By degrees, the roar of water grew louder; and the stupendous track, after crossing the torrent by a bridge, struck in between two massive perpendicular walls of rock that quite shut out the moonlight, and only left a few stars shining in the narrow strip of sky above. Then, even this was lost, in the thick darkness of a cavern in the rock, through which the way was pierced; the terrible cataract thundering and roaring close below it, and its foam and spray hanging, in a mist, about the entrance. Emerging from this cave, and coming again into the moonlight, and across a dizzy bridge, it crept and twisted upward, through the Gorge of Gondo, savage and grand beyond description, with smooth-fronted precipices, rising up on either hand, and almost meeting overhead. Thus we went, climbing on our rugged way, higher and higher all night, without a moment's weariness: lost in the contemplation of the black rocks, the tremendous heights and depths, the fields of smooth snow lying, in the clefts and hollows, and the fierce torrents thundering headlong down the deep abyss.

Towards daybreak, we came among the snow, where a keen wind was blowing fiercely. Having, with some trouble, awakened the inmates of a wooden house in this solitude: round which the wind was howling dismally, catching up the snow in wreaths and hurling it away: we got some breakfast in a room built of rough timbers, but well warmed by a stove, and well contrived (as it had need to be) for keeping out the bitter storms. A sledge being then made ready, and four horses harnessed to it, we went, ploughing, through the snow. Still upward, but now in the cold light of morning, and with the great white desert on which we travelled, plain and clear.

We were well upon the summit of the mountain: and had before us the rude cross of wood, denoting its greatest altitude above the sea: when the light of the rising sun, struck, all at once, upon the waste of snow, and turned it a deep red. The lonely grandeur of the scene was then at its height.

As we went sledging on, there came out of the Hospice founded by Napoleon, a group of Peasant travellers, with staves and knapsacks, who had rested there last night: attended by a Monk or two, their hospitable entertainers, trudging slowly forward with them, for company's sake. It was pleasant to give them good morning, and pretty, looking back a long way after them, to see them looking back at us, and hesitating presently, when one of our horses stumbled and fell, whether or no they should return and help us. But he was soon up again, with the assistance of a rough waggoner whose team had stuck fast there too; and when we had helped him out of his difficulty, in return, we left him slowly ploughing towards them, and went slowly and swiftly forward, on the brink of a steep precipice, among the mountain pines.

Taking to our wheels again, soon afterwards, we began rapidly to descend; passing under everlasting glaciers, by means of arched galleries, hung with clusters of dripping icicles; under and over foaming waterfalls; near places of refuge, and galleries of shelter against sudden danger; through caverns over whose arched roofs the avalanches slide, in spring, and bury themselves in the unknown gulf beneath. Down, over lofty bridges, and through horrible ravines: a little shifting speck in the vast desolation of ice and snow, and monstrous granite rocks; down through the deep Gorge of the Saltine, and deafened by the torrent plunging madly down, among the riven blocks of rock, into the level country, far below. Gradually down, by zig-zag roads, lying between an upward and a downward precipice, into warmer weather, calmer air, and softer scenery, until there lay before us, glittering like gold or silver in the thaw and sunshine, the metal-covered, red, green, yellow, domes and church-spires of a Swiss town.

The business of these recollections being with Italy, and my business, consequently, being to scamper back thither as fast as possible, I will not recall (though I am sorely tempted) how the Swiss villages, clustered at the feet of Giant mountains, looked like playthings; or how confusedly the houses were heaped and piled together;

or how there were very narrow streets to shut the howling winds out in the winter-time; and broken bridges, which the impetuous torrents, suddenly released in spring, had swept away. Or how there were peasant women here, with great round fur caps: looking, when they peeped out of casements and only their heads were seen, like a population of Sword-bearers to the Lord Mayor of London; or how the town of Vevey, lying on the smooth lake of Geneva, was beautiful to see; or how the statue of Saint Peter in the street at Fribourg, grasps the largest key that ever was beheld; or how Fribourg is illustrious for its two suspension bridges, and its grand cathedral organ.

Or how, between that town and Bâle, the road meandered among thriving villages of wooden cottages, with overhanging thatched roofs, and low protruding windows, glazed with small round panes of glass like crown-pieces; or how, in every little Swiss homestead, with its cart or waggon carefully stowed away beside the house, its little garden, stock of poultry, and groups of red-cheeked children, there was an air of comfort, very new and very pleasant after Italy; or how the dresses of the women changed again, and there were no more sword-bearers to be seen; and fair white stomachers, and great black, fan-shaped, gauzy-looking caps, prevailed instead.

Or how the country by the Jura mountains, sprinkled with snow, and lighted by the moon, and musical with falling water, was delightful; or how, below the windows of the great hotel of the Three Kings at Bâle, the swollen Rhine ran fast and green; or how, at Strasbourg, it was quite as fast but not as green: and was said to be foggy lower down: and, at that late time of the year, was a far less certain means of progress, than the highway road to Paris.

Or how Strasbourg itself, in its magnificent old Gothic Cathedral, and its ancient houses with their peaked roofs and gables, made a little gallery of quaint and interesting views; or how a crowd was gathered inside the cathedral at noon, to see the famous mechanical clock in motion, striking twelve. How, when it struck twelve, a whole army of puppets went through many ingenious evolutions; and, among them, a huge puppet-cock, perched on the top, crowed twelve times, loud and clear. Or how it was wonderful to see this cock at great pains to clap its wings, and strain its throat; but obviously having no connection whatever with its own voice; which was deep within the clock, a long way down.

Or how the road to Paris, was one sea of mud, and thence to the coast, a little better for a hard frost. Or how the cliffs of Dover were a pleasant sight, and England was so wonderfully neat—though dark, and lacking colour on a winter's day, it must be conceded.

Or how, a few days afterwards, it was cool, re-crossing the channel, with ice upon the decks, and snow lying pretty deep in France. Or how the Malle Poste scrambled through the snow, headlong, drawn in the hilly parts by any number of stout horses at a canter; or how there were, outside the Post-office Yard in Paris, before daybreak, extraordinary adventurers in heaps of rags, groping in the snowy streets with little rakes, in search of odds and ends.

Or how, between Paris and Marseilles, the snow being then exceeding deep, a thaw came on, and the mail waded rather than rolled for the next three hundred miles or so; breaking springs on Sunday nights, and putting out its two passengers to warm and refresh themselves pending the repairs, in miserable billiard-rooms, where hairy company, collected about stoves, were playing cards; the cards being very like themselves—extremely limp and dirty.

Or how there was detention at Marseilles from stress of weather; and steamers were advertised to go, which did not go; or how the good Steam-packet Charlemagne at length put out, and met such weather that now she threatened to run into Toulon, and now into Nice, but, the wind moderating, did neither, but ran on into Genoa harbour instead, where the familiar Bells rang sweetly in my ear. Or how there was a travelling party on board, of whom one member was very ill in the cabin next to mine, and being ill was cross, and therefore declined to give up the Dictionary, which he kept under his pillow; thereby obliging his companions to come down to him, constantly, to ask what was the Italian for a lump of sugar—a glass of brandy and water—what's o'clock? and so forth: which he always insisted on looking out, with his own sea-sick eyes, declining to entrust the book to any man alive.

Like GRUMIO, I might have told you, in detail, all this and something more—but to as little purpose—were I not deterred by the remembrance that my business is with Italy. Therefore, like GRUMIO's story, "it shall die in oblivion."

TO ROME BY PISA AND SIENA

THERE is nothing in Italy, more beautiful to me, than the coast-road between Genoa and Spezzia. On one side: sometimes far below, sometimes nearly on a level with the road, and often skirted by broken rocks of many shapes: there is the free blue sea, with here and there a picturesque felucca gliding slowly on; on the other side are lofty hills, ravines besprinkled with white cottages, patches of dark olive woods, country churches with their light open towers, and country houses gaily painted. On every bank and knoll by the wayside, the wild cactus and aloe flourish in exuberant profusion; and the gardens of the bright villages along the road, are seen, all blushing in the summer-time with clusters of the Belladonna, and are fragrant in the autumn and winter with golden oranges and lemons.

Some of the villages are inhabited, almost exclusively, by fishermen; and it is pleasant to see their great boats hauled up on the beach making little patches of shade, where they lie asleep, or where the women and children sit romping and looking out to sea, while they mend their nets upon the shore. There is one town, Camoglia, with its little harbour on the sea, hundreds of feet below the road; where families of mariners live, who, time out of mind, have owned coasting-vessels in that place, and have traded to Spain and elsewhere. Seen from the road above, it is like a tiny model on the margin of the dimpled water, shining in the sun. Descended into, by the winding mule-tracks, it is a perfect miniature of a primitive seafaring town; the saltest, roughest, most piratical little place that ever was seen. Great rusty iron rings and mooring-chains, capstans, and fragments of old masts and spars, choke up the way; hardy rough-weather boats, and seamen's clothing, flutter in the little harbour or are drawn out on the sunny stones to dry; on the parapet of the rude pier, a few amphibious-looking fellows lie asleep, with their legs dangling over the wall, as though earth or water were all one to them, and if they slipped in, they would float away, dozing comfortably among the fishes; the church is bright with trophies of the sea, and votive offerings, in commemoration of escape from storm and shipwreck. The dwellings not immediately abutting on the harbour are approached by blind low arches, and by crooked steps, as if in darkness and in difficulty of access they should be like holds of ships, or inconvenient cabins under water; and everywhere, there is a smell of fish, and sea-weed, and old rope.

The coast-road whence Camoglia is descried so far below, is famous, in the warm season, especially in some parts near Genoa, for fire-flies. Walking there on a dark night, I have seen it made one sparkling firmament by these beautiful insects: so that the distant stars were pale against the flash and glitter that spangled every olive wood and hill-side, and pervaded the whole air.

It was not in such a season, however, that we traversed this road on our way to Rome. The middle of January was only just past, and it was very gloomy and dark weather; very wet besides. In crossing the fine pass of Bracco, we encountered such a storm of mist and rain, that we travelled in a cloud the whole way. There might have been no Mediterranean in the world, for anything that we saw of it there, except when a sudden gust of wind, clearing the mist before it, for a moment, showed the agitated sea at a great depth below, lashing the distant rocks, and spouting up its foam furiously. The rain was incessant; every brook and torrent was greatly swollen; and such a deafening leaping, and roaring, and thundering of water, I never heard the like of in my life.

Hence, when we came to Spezzia, we found that the Magra, an unbridged river on the high-road to Pisa, was too high to be safely crossed in the Ferry Boat, and were fain to wait until the afternoon of next day, when it had, in some degree, subsided. Spezzia, however, is a good place to tarry at by reason, firstly, of its beautiful bay; secondly, of its ghostly Inn; thirdly, of the head-dress of the women, who wear, on one side of their head, a small doll's straw hat, stuck on to the hair; which is certainly the oddest and most roguish head-gear that ever was invented.

The Magra safely crossed in the Ferry Boat—the passage is not by any means agreeable, when the current is swollen and strong—we arrived at Carrara, within a few hours. In good time next morning, we got some ponies, and went out to see the marble quarrie .

They are four or five great glens, running up into a range of lofty hills, until they can run no longer, and are stopped by being abruptly strangled by Nature. The quarries, "or caves," as they call them there are so many openings, high up in the hills, on either side of these passes, where they blast and excavate for marble: which may turn out good or bad: may make a man's fortune very quickly, or ruin him by the great expense of working what is worth nothing. Some of these caves were opened by the ancient Romans, and remain as they left them to this hour. Many others are being worked at this moment; others are to be begun to-morrow, next week, next month; others are unbought, unthought of; and marble enough for more ages than have passed since the place was resorted to, lies hidden everywhere: patiently waiting its time of discovery.

As you toil and clamber up one of these steep gorges (having left your pony soddening his girths in water, a mile or two lower down) you hear, every now and then, echoing among the hills, in a low tone, more silent than the previous silence, a melancholy warning bugle,—a signal to the miners to withdraw. Then, there is a thundering, and echoing from hill to hill, and perhaps a splashing up of great fragments of rock into the air; and on you toil again until some other bugle sounds, in a new direction, and you stop directly, lest you should come within the range of the new explosion.

There were numbers of men, working high up in these hills—on the sides—clearing away, and sending down the broken masses of stone and earth, to make way for the blocks of marble that had been discovered. As these came rolling down from unseen hands into the narrow valley, I could not help thinking of the deep glen (just the same sort of glen) where the Roc left Sindbad the Sailor; and where the merchants from the heights above, flung down great pieces of meat for the diamonds to stick to. There were no eagles here, to darken the sun in their swoop, and pounce upon them; but it was as wild and fierce as if there had been hundreds.

But the road, the road down which the marble comes, however immense the blocks! The genius of the country, and the spirit of its institutions, pave that road: repair it, watch it, keep it going! Conceive a channel of water running over a rocky bed, beset with great heaps of stone of all shapes and sizes, winding down the middle of this valley and *that* being the road—because it was the road five hundred years ago! Imagine the clumsy carts of five hundred years ago, being used to this hour, and drawn, as they used to be, five hundred years ago, by oxen, whose ancestors were worn to death five hundred years ago, as their unhappy descendants are now, in twelve months, by the suffering and agony of this cruel work! Two pair, four pair, ten pair, twenty pair, to one block, according to its size; down it must come, this way. In their struggling from stone to stone, with their enormous loads behind them, they die frequently upon the spot; and not they alone; for their passionate drivers, sometimes tumbling down in their energy, are crushed to death beneath the wheels. But it was good five hundred years ago, and it must be good now: and a railroad down one of these steeps (the easiest thing in the world) would be flat blasphemy.

When we stood aside to see one of these cars drawn by only a pair of oxen (for it had but one small block of marble on it), coming down, I hailed, in my heart, the man who sat upon the heavy yoke, to keep it on the neck of the poor beasts—and who faced backwards: not before him—as the very Devil of true despotism. He had a great rod in his hand, with an iron point; and when they could plough and force their way through the loose bed of the torrent no longer, and came to a stop, he poked it into their bodies, beat it on their heads, screwed it round and round in their nostrils, got them on a yard or two, in the madness of intense pain; repeated all these persuasions, with increased intensity of purpose, when they stopped again; got them on, once more; forced and goaded them to an abrupter point of the descent; and when their writhing and smarting, and the weight behind them, bore them plunging down the precipice in a cloud of scattered water, whirled his rod above his head, and gave a great whoop and hallo, as if he had achieved something, and had no idea that they might shake him off, and blindly mash his brains upon the road, in the noon-tide of his triumph.

Standing in one of the many studii of Carrara, that afternoon—for it is a great workshop, full of beautifully-finished copies in marble, of almost every figure, group, and bust, we know—it seemed, at first, so strange to me that those exquisite shapes, replete with grace, and thought, and delicate repose, should grow out of all this toil, and sweat, and torture! But I soon found a parallel to it, and an explanation of it, in every virtue that springs up in miserable ground, and every good thing that has its birth in sorrow and distress. And, looking out of the Sculptor's great window, upon the marble mountains, all red and glowing in the decline of day, but stern and solemn to the last, I thought, my God! how many quarries of human hearts and souls, capable of far more beautiful results, are left shut up and mouldering away: while pleasure-travellers through life, avert their faces, as they pass, and shudder at the gloom and ruggedness that conceal them!

The then reigning Duke of Modena, to whom this territory in part belonged, claimed the proud distinction of being the only sovereign in Europe who had not recognised Louis-Philippe as King of the French! He was not a wag, but quite in earnest. He was also much opposed to railroads; and if certain lines in contemplation by other potentates, on either side of him, had been executed, would have probably enjoyed the satisfaction of having an omnibus plying to and fro across his not very vast dominions, to forward travellers from one terminus to another.

Carrara, shut in by great hills, is very picturesque and bold. Few tourists stay there; and the people are nearly all connected, in one way or other, with the working of marble. There are also villages among the caves, where the workmen live. It contains a beautiful little Theatre, newly built; and it is an interesting custom there, to form the chorus of labourers in the marble quarries, who are self-taught and sing by ear. I heard them in a comic opera, and in an act of "Norma;" and they acquitted themselves very well; unlike the common people of Italy generally, who (with some exceptions among the Neapolitans) sing vilely out of tune, and have very disagreeable singing voices.

From the summit of a lofty hill beyond Carrara, the first view of the fertile plain in which the town of Pisa lies—with Leghorn, a purple spot in the flat distance—is enchanting. Nor is it only distance that lends enchantment to the view; for the fruitful country, and rich woods of olive-trees through which the road subsequently passes, render it delightful.

The moon was shining when we approached Pisa, and for a long time we could see, behind the wall, the leaning Tower, all awry in the uncertain light; the shadowy original of the old pictures in school-books, setting forth "The Wonders of the World." Like most things connected in their first associations with school-books and school-times, it was too small. I felt it keenly. It was nothing like so high above the wall as I had hoped. It was another of the many deceptions practised by Mr. Harris, Bookseller, at the corner of St. Paul's Churchyard, London. *His* Tower was a fiction, but this was a reality—and, by comparison, a short reality. Still, it looked very well, and very strange, and was quite as much out of the perpendicular as Harris had represented it to be. The quiet air of Pisa too; the big guard-house at the gate, with only two little soldiers in it; the streets with scarcely any show of people in them; and the Arno, flowing quaintly through the centre of the town; were excellent. So, I bore no malice in my heart against Mr. Harris (remembering his good intentions), but forgave him before dinner, and went out, full of confidence, to see the Tower next morning.

I might have known better; but, somehow, I had expected to see it, casting its long shadow on a public street where people came and went all day. It was a surprise to me to find it in a grave retired place, apart from the general resort, and carpeted with smooth green turf. But, the group of buildings, clustered on and about this verdant carpet: comprising the Tower, the Baptistery, the Cathedral, and the Church of the Campo Santo: is perhaps the most remarkable and beautiful in the whole world; and from being clustered there, together away from the ordinary transactions and details of the town, they have a singularly venerable and impressive character. It is the architectural essence of a rich old city, with all its common life and common habitations pressed out, and filtered away.

Simond compares the Tower to the usual pictorial representations in children's books of the Tower of Babel. It is a happy simile, and conveys a better idea of the building than chapters of laboured description. Nothing can exceed the grace and lightness of the structure; nothing can be more remarkable than its general appearance. In the course of the ascent to the top (which is by an easy staircase), the inclination is not very apparent; but, at the summit, it becomes so, and gives one the sensation of being in a ship that has heeled over, through the action of an ebb-tide. The effect *upon the low side*, so to speak—looking over from the gallery, and seeing the shaft recede to its base—is very startling; and I saw a nervous traveller hold on to the Tower involuntarily, after glancing down, as if he had some idea of propping it up. The view within, from the ground—looking up, as through a slanted tube—is also very curious. It certainly inclines as much as the most sanguine tourist could desire. The natural impulse of ninety-nine people out of a hundred, who were about to recline upon the grass below it, to rest, and contemplate the adjacent buildings, would probably be, not to take up their position under the leaning side; it is so very much aslant.

The manifold beauties of the Cathedral and Baptistery need no recapitulation from me; though in this case, as in a hundred others, I find it difficult to separate my own delight in recalling them, from your weariness in having them recalled. There is a picture of St. Agnes, by Andrea del Sarto, in the former, and there are a variety of rich columns in the latter, that tempt me strongly.

It is, I hope, no breach of my resolution not to be tempted into elaborate descriptions, to remember the Campo Santo; where grass-grown graves are dug in earth brought more than six hundred years ago, from the Holy Land; and where there are, surrounding them, such cloisters, with such playing lights and shadows falling through their delicate tracery on the stone pavement, as surely the dullest memory could never forget. On the walls of this solemn and lovely place, are ancient frescoes, very much obliterated and decayed, but very curious. As usually happens in almost any collection of paintings of any sort, in Italy, where there are many heads, there is, in one of them, a striking accidental likeness of Napoleon. At one time, I used to please my fancy with the speculation whether these old painters, at their work, had a foreboding knowledge of the man who would one day arise to wreak such destruction upon art: whose soldiers would make targets of great pictures, and stable their horses among triumphs of architecture. But the same Corsican face is so plentiful in some parts of Italy at this day, that a more commonplace solution of the coincidence is unavoidable.

If Pisa be the seventh wonder of the world in right of its Tower, it may claim to be, at least, the second or third in right of its beggars. They waylay the unhappy visitor at every turn, escort him to every door he enters at, and lie in wait for him, with strong reinforcements, at every door by which they know he must come out. The grating of the portal on its hinges is the signal for a general shout, and the moment he appears, he is hemmed in, and fallen on, by heaps of rags and personal distortions. The beggars seem to embody all the trade and enterprise of Pisa. Nothing else is stirring, but warm air. Going through the streets, the fronts of the sleepy houses look like backs. They are all so still and quiet, and unlike houses with people in them, that the greater part of the city has the appearance of a city at day-break, or during a general siesta of the population. Or it is yet more like those backgrounds of houses in common prints, or old engravings, where windows and doors are squarely indicated, and one figure (a beggar of course) is seen walking off by itself into illimitable perspective.

Not so Leghorn (made illustrious by SMOLLETT'S grave), which is a thriving, business-like, matter-of-fact place, where idleness is shouldered out of the way by commerce. The regulations observed there, in reference to trade and merchants, are very liberal and free; and the town, of course, benefits by them. Leghorn had a bad name in connection with stabbers, and with some justice it must be allowed; for, not many years ago, there was an assassination club there, the members of which bore no ill-will to anybody in particular, but stabbed people (quite strangers to them) in the streets at night, for the pleasure and excitement of the recreation. I think the president of this amiable society was a shoemaker. He was taken, however, and the club was broken up. It would, probably, have disappeared in the natural course of events, before the railroad between Leghorn and Pisa, which is a good one, and has already begun to astonish Italy with a precedent of punctuality, order, plain dealing, and improvement—the most dangerous and heretical astonisher of all. There must have been a slight sensation, as of earthquake, surely, in the Vatican, when the first Italian railroad was thrown open.

Returning to Pisa, and hiring a good-tempered Vetturíno, and his four horses, to take us on to Rome, we travelled through pleasant Tuscan villages and cheerful scenery all day. The roadside crosses in this part of Italy are numerous and curious. There is seldom a figure on the cross, though there is sometimes a face; but they are remarkable for being garnished with little models in wood, of every possible object that can be connected with the Saviour's death. The cock that crowed when Peter had denied his Master thrice, is usually perched on the tip-top; and an ornithological phenomenon he generally is. Under him, is the inscription. Then, hung on to the cross-beam, are the spear, the reed with the sponge of vinegar and water at the end, the coat without seam for which the soldiers cast lots, the dice-box with which they threw for it, the hammer that drove in the nails, the pincers that pulled them out, the ladder which was set against the cross, the crown of thorns, the instrument of flagellation, the lanthorn with which Mary went to the tomb (I suppose), and the sword with which Peter smote the servant of the high priest,—a perfect toy-shop of little objects, repeated at every four or five miles, all along the highway.

On the evening of the second day from Pisa, we reached the beautiful old city of Siena. There was what they called a Carnival, in progress; but, as its secret lay in a score or two of melancholy people walking up and down the principal street in common toy-shop masks, and being more melancholy, if possible, than the same sort of people in England, I say no more of it. We went off, betimes next morning, to see the Cathedral, which is wonderfully picturesque inside and out, especially the latter—also the market-place, or great Piazza, which is a large square, with a great broken-nosed fountain in it: some quaint Gothic houses: and a high square brick tower; *outside* the top of which—a curious feature in such views in Italy—hangs an enormous bell. It is like a bit of Venice, without the water. There are some curious old Palazzi in the town, which is very ancient; and without having (for me) the interest of Verona, or Genoa, it is very dreamy and fantastic, and most interesting.

We went on again, as soon as we had seen these things, and going over a rather bleak country (there had been nothing but vines until now: mere walking-sticks at that season of the year), stopped, as usual, between one and two hours in the middle of the day, to rest the horses; that being a part of every Vetturíno contract. We then went on again, through a region gradually becoming bleaker and wilder, until it became as bare and desolate as any Scottish moors. Soon after dark, we halted for the night, at the osteria of La Scala: a perfectly lone house, where the family were sitting round a great fire in the kitchen, raised on a stone platform three or four feet high, and big enough for the roasting of an ox. On the upper, and only other floor of this hotel, there was a great, wild, rambling sála, with one very little window in a by-corner, and four black doors opening into four black bedrooms in various directions. To say nothing of another large black door, opening into another large black sála, with the staircase coming abruptly through a kind of trap-door in the floor, and the rafters of the roof looming above: a suspicious little press skulking in one obscure corner: and all the knives in the house lying about in various directions. The fireplace was of the purest Italian architecture, so that it was perfectly impossible to see it for the smoke. The waitress was like a dramatic brigand's wife, and wore the same style of dress upon her head. The dogs barked like mad; the echoes returned the compliments bestowed upon them; there was not another house within twelve miles; and things had a dreary, and rather a cut-throat, appearance.

They were not improved by rumours of robbers having come out, strong and boldly, within a few nights; and of their having stopped the mail very near that place. They were known to have waylaid some travellers not long before, on Mount Vesuvius itself, and were the talk at all the roadside inns. As they were no business of ours, however (for we had very little with us to lose), we made ourselves merry on the subject, and were very soon as comfortable as need be. We had the usual dinner in this solitary house; and a very good dinner it is, when you are used to it. There is something with a vegetable or some rice in it, which is a sort of shorthand or arbitrary character for soup, and which tastes very well, when you have flavoured it with plenty of grated cheese, lots of salt, and abundance of pepper. There is a half fowl of which this soup has been made. There is a stewed pigeon, with the gizzards and livers of himself and other birds stuck all around him. There is a bit of roast beef, the size of a small French roll. There are a scrap of Parmesan cheese, and five little withered apples, all huddled together on a small plate, and crowding one upon the other, as if each were trying to save itself from the chance of being eaten. Then there is coffee; and then there is bed. You don't mind brick floors; you don't mind yawning doors, nor banging windows; you don't mind your own horses being stabled under the bed: and so close, that every time a horse coughs or sneezes, he wakes you. If you are good-humoured to the people about you, and speak pleasantly, and look cheerful, take my word for it you may be well entertained in the very worst Italian Inn, and always in the most obliging manner, and you may go from one end of the country to the other (despite all stories to the contrary) without any great trial of your patience anywhere. Especially, when you get such wine in flasks, as the Orvieto, and the Monte Pulciano.

It was a bad morning when we left this place; and we went, for twelve miles, over a country as barren, as stony, and as wild, as Cornwall in England, until we came to Radicofani, where there is a ghostly, goblin inn: once a hunting-seat, belonging to the Dukes of Tuscany. It is full of such rambling corridors, and gaunt rooms, that all the murdering and phantom tales that ever were written might have originated in that one house. There are some horrible old Palazzi in Genoa: one in particular, not unlike it, outside: but there is a winding, creaking, wormy, rustling, door-opening, foot-on-stair-case-falling character about this Radicofani Hotel, such as I never saw anywhere, else. The town, such as it is, hangs on a hill-side above the house, and in front of it. The inhabitants are all beggars; and as soon as they see a carriage coming, they swoop down upon it, like so many birds of prey.

When we got on the mountain pass, which lies beyond this place, the wind (as they had forewarned us at the inn) was so terrific, that we were obliged to take my other half of the carriage, lest she should be blown over, carriage and all, and to hang to it, on the windy side (as well as we could for laughing), to prevent its going, Heaven knows where. For mere force of wind, this land-storm might have competed with an Atlantic gale, and had a reasonable chance of coming off victorious. The blast came sweeping down great gullies in a range of mountains on the right: so that we looked with positive awe at a great morass on the left, and saw that there was not a bush or twig to hold by. It seemed as if, once blown from our feet, we must be swept out to sea, or away into space. There was snow, and hail, and rain, and lightning, and thunder; and there were rolling mists, travelling with incredible velocity. It was dark, awful, and solitary to the last degree; there were mountains above mountains, veiled in angry clouds; and there was such a wrathful, rapid, violent, tumultuous hurry, everywhere, as rendered the scene unspeakably exciting and grand.

It was a relief to get out of it, notwithstanding; and to cross even the dismal, dirty Papal Frontier. After passing through two little towns; in one of which, Acquapendente, there was also a "Carnival" in progress: consisting of one man dressed and masked as a woman, and one woman dressed and masked as a man, walking ankle-deep, through the muddy streets, in a very melancholy manner: we came, at dusk, within sight of the Lake of Bolsena, on whose bank there is a little town of the same name, much celebrated for malaria. With the exception of this poor place, there is not a cottage on the banks of the lake, or near it (for nobody dare sleep there); not a boat upon its waters; not a stick or stake to break the dismal monotony of seven-and-twenty watery miles. We were late in getting in, the roads being very bad from heavy rains; and, after dark, the dulness of the scene was quite intolerable.

We entered on a very different, and a finer scene of desolation, next night, at sunset. We had passed through Montefiaschone (famous for its wine) and Viterbo (for its fountains): and after climbing up a long hill of eight or ten miles' extent, came suddenly upon the margin of a solitary lake: in one part very beautiful, with a luxuriant wood; in another, very barren, and shut in by bleak volcanic hills. Where this lake flows, there stood, of old, a city. It was swallowed up one day; and in its stead, this water rose. There are ancient traditions (common to many parts of the world) of the ruined city having been seen below, when the water was clear; but however that may be, from this spot of earth it vanished. The ground came bubbling up above it; and the water too; and here they stand, like ghosts on whom the other world closed suddenly, and who have no means of getting back again. They seem to be waiting the course of ages, for the next earthquake in that place; when they will plunge below the ground, at its first yawning, and be seen no more. The unhappy city below, is not more lost and dreary, than these fire-charred hills and the stagnant water, above. The red sun looked strangely on them, as with the knowledge that they were made for caverns and darkness; and the melancholy water oozed and sucked the mud, and crept quietly among the marshy grass and reeds, as if the overthrow of all the ancient towers and house-tops, and the death of all the ancient people born and bred there, were yet heavy on its conscience.

A short ride from this lake, brought us to Ronciglione; a little town like a large pig-sty, where we passed the night. Next morning at seven o'clock, we started for Rome.

As soon as we were out of the pig-sty, we entered on the Campagna Romana; an undulating flat (as you know), where few people can live; and where, for miles and miles, there is nothing to relieve the terrible monotony and gloom. Of all kinds of country that could, by possibility, lie outside the gates of Rome, this is the aptest and fittest burial-ground for the Dead City. So sad, so quiet, so sullen; so secret in its covering up of great masses of ruin, and hiding them; so like the waste places into which the men possessed with the devil used to go and howl, and rend themselves, in the old days of Jerusalem. We had to traverse thirty miles of this Campagna; and for two-and-twenty we went on and on, seeing nothing but now and then a lonely house, or a villainous-looking shepherd: with matted hair all over his face, and himself wrapped to the chin in a frowsy brown mantle, tending his sheep. At the end of that distance, we stopped to refresh the horses, and to get some lunch, in a common malaria-shaken, despondent little public-house, whose every inch of wall and beam, inside, was (according to custom) painted and decorated in a way so miserable that every room looked like the wrong side of another room, and, with its wretched imitation of drapery, and lop-sided little daubs of lyres, seemed to have been plundered from behind the scenes of some travelling circus.

When we were fairly going off again, we began, in a perfect fever, to strain our eyes for Rome; and when, after another mile or two, the Eternal City appeared, at length, in the distance; it looked like—I am half afraid to write the word—like LONDON!!! There it lay, under a thick cloud, with innumerable towers, and steeples, and roofs of houses, rising up into the sky, and high above them all, one Dome. I swear, that keenly as I felt the seeming absurdity of the comparison, it was so like London, at that distance, that if you could have shown it to me, in a glass, I should have taken it for nothing else.

ROME

WE entered the Eternal City, at about four o'clock in the afternoon, on the thirtieth of January, by the Porta del Popolo, and came immediately—it was a dark, muddy day, and there had been heavy rain—on the skirts of the Carnival. We did not, then, know that we were only looking at the fag end of the masks, who were driving slowly round and round the Piazza until they could find a promising opportunity for falling into the stream of carriages, and getting, in good time, into the thick of the festivity; and coming among them so abruptly, all travel-stained and weary, was not coming very well prepared to enjoy the scene.

We had crossed the Tiber by the Ponte Molle two or three miles before. It had looked as yellow as it ought to look, and hurrying on between its worn-away and miry banks, had a promising aspect of desolation and ruin. The masquerade dresses on the fringe of the Carnival, did great violence to this promise. There were no great ruins, no solemn tokens of antiquity, to be seen;—they all lie on the other side of the city. There seemed to be long streets of common-place shops and houses, such as are to be found in any European town; there were busy people, equipages, ordinary walkers to and fro; a multitude of chattering strangers. It was no more *my* Rome: the Rome of anybody's fancy, man or boy; degraded and fallen and lying asleep in the sun among a heap of ruins: than the Place de la Concorde in Paris is. A cloudy sky, a dull cold rain, and muddy streets, I was prepared for, but not for this: and I confess to having gone to bed, that night, in a very indifferent humour, and with a very considerably quenched enthusiasm.

Immediately on going out next day, we hurried off to St. Peter's. It looked immense in the distance, but distinctly and decidedly small, by comparison, on a near approach. The beauty of the Piazza, on which it stands, with its clusters of exquisite columns, and its gushing fountains—so fresh, so broad, and free, and beautiful— nothing can exaggerate. The first burst of the interior, in all its expansive majesty and glory: and, most of all, the looking up into the Dome: is a sensation never to be forgotten. But, there were preparations for a Festa; the pillars of stately marble were swathed in some impertinent frippery of red and yellow; the altar, and entrance to the subterranean chapel: which is before it: in the centre of the church: were like a goldsmith's shop, or one of the opening scenes in a very lavish pantomime. And though I had as high a sense of the beauty of the building (I hope) as it is possible to entertain, I felt no very strong emotion. I have been infinitely more affected in many English cathedrals when the organ has been playing, and in many English country churches when the congregation have been singing. I had a much greater sense of mystery and wonder, in the Cathedral of San Mark at Venice.

When we came out of the church again (we stood nearly an hour staring up into the dome: and would not have "gone over" the Cathedral then, for any money), we said to the coachman, "Go to the Coliseum." In a quarter of an hour or so, he stopped at the gate, and we went in.

It is no fiction, but plain, sober, honest Truth, to say: so suggestive and distinct is it at this hour: that, for a moment—actually in passing in—they who will, may have the whole great pile before them, as it used to be, with thousands of eager faces staring down into the arena, and such a whirl of strife, and blood, and dust going on there, as no language can describe. Its solitude, its awful beauty, and its utter desolation, strike upon the stranger the next moment, like a softened sorrow; and never in his life, perhaps, will he be so moved and overcome by any sight, not immediately connected with his own affections and afflictions.

To see it crumbling there, an inch a year; its walls and arches overgrown with green; its corridors open to the day; the long grass growing in its porches; young trees of yesterday, springing up on its ragged parapets, and bearing fruit: chance produce of the seeds dropped there by the birds who build their nests within its chinks and crannies; to see its Pit of Fight filled up with earth, and the peaceful Cross planted in the centre; to climb into its upper halls, and look down on ruin, ruin, ruin, all about it; the triumphal arches of Constantine, Septimus Severus, and Titus; the Roman Forum; the Palace of the Cæsars; the temples of the old religion, fallen down and gone; is to see the ghost of old Rome, wicked, wonderful old city, haunting the very ground on which its people trod. It is the most impressive, the most stately, the most solemn, grand, majestic, mournful sight, conceivable. Never, in its bloodiest prime, can the sight of the gigantic Coliseum, full and running over with the lustiest life, have moved one's heart, as it must move all who look upon it now, a ruin. GOD be thanked: a ruin!

As it tops the other ruins: standing there, a mountain among graves: so do its ancient influences outlive all other remnants of the old mythology and old butchery of Rome, in the nature of the fierce and cruel Roman people. The Italian face changes as the visitor approaches the city; its beauty becomes devilish; and there is scarcely one countenance in a hundred, among the common people in the streets, that would not be at home and happy in a renovated Coliseum to-morrow.

Here was Rome indeed at last; and such a Rome as no one can imagine in its full and awful grandeur! We wandered out upon the Appian Way, and then went on, through miles of ruined tombs and broken walls, with here and there a desolate and uninhabited house: past the Circus of Romulus, where the course of the chariots, the stations of the judges, competitors, and spectators are yet as plainly to be seen as in old time: past the tomb of Cecilia Metella: past all inclosure, hedge, or stake, wall or fence: away upon the open Campagna, where on that side of Rome, nothing is to be beheld but Ruin. Except where the distant Apennines bound the view upon the left, the whole wide prospect is one field of ruin. Broken aqueducts, left in the most picturesque and beautiful clusters of arches; broken temples; broken tombs. A desert of decay, sombre and desolate beyond all expression; and with a history in every stone that strews the ground.

On Sunday, the Pope assisted in the performance of High Mass at St. Peter's. The effect of the Cathedral on my mind, on that second visit, was exactly what it was at first, and what it remains after many visits. It is not religiously impressive or affecting. It is an immense edifice, with no one point for the mind to rest upon; and it tires itself with wandering round and round. The very purpose of the place, is not expressed in anything you see there, unless you examine its details—and all examination of details is incompatible with the place itself. It might be a Pantheon, or a Senate House, or a great architectural trophy, having no other object than an architectural triumph. There is a black statue of St. Peter, to be sure, under a red canopy; which is larger than life, and which is constantly having its great toe kissed by good Catholics. You cannot help seeing that: it is so very prominent and popular. But it does not heighten the effect of the temple, as a work of art; and it is not expressive—to me at least—of its high purpose.

A large space behind the altar, was fitted up with boxes, shaped like those at the Italian Opera in England, but in their decoration much more gaudy. In the centre of the kind of theatre thus railed off, was a canopied dais with the Pope's chair upon it. The pavement was covered with a carpet of the brightest green; and what with this green, and the intolerable reds and crimsons, and gold borders of the hangings, the whole concern looked like a stupendous Bonbon. On either side of the altar, was a large box for lady strangers. These were filled with ladies in black dresses and black veils. The gentlemen of the Pope's guard, in red coats, leather breeches, and jack-boots, guarded all this reserved space, with drawn swords that were very flashy in every sense; and from the altar all down the nave, a broad lane was kept clear by the Pope's Swiss guard, who wear a quaint striped surcoat, and striped tight legs, and carry halberds like those which are usually shouldered by those theatrical supernumeraries, who never *can* get off the stage fast enough, and who may be generally observed to linger in the enemy's camp after the open country, held by the opposite forces, has been split up the middle by a convulsion of Nature.

I got upon the border of the green carpet, in company with a great many other gentlemen, attired in black (no other passport is necessary), and stood there at my ease, during the performance of Mass. The singers were in a crib of wirework (like a large meat-safe or bird-cage) in one corner; and sang most atrociously. All about the green carpet, there was a slowly moving crowd of people: talking to each other: staring at the Pope through eye-glasses; defrauding one another, in moments of partial curiosity, out of precarious seats on the bases of pillars: and grinning hideously at the ladies. Dotted here and there, were little knots of friars (Francescáni, or Cappuccíni, in their coarse brown dresses and peaked hoods) making a strange contrast to the gaudy ecclesiastics of higher degree, and having their humility gratified to the utmost, by being shouldered about, and elbowed right and left, on all sides. Some of these had muddy sandals and umbrellas, and stained garments: having trudged in from the country. The faces of the greater part were as coarse and heavy as their dress; their dogged, stupid, monotonous stare at all the glory and splendour, having something in it, half miserable, and half ridiculous.

Upon the green carpet itself, and gathered round the altar, was a perfect army of cardinals and priests, in red, gold, purple, violet, white, and fine linen. Stragglers from these, went to and fro among the crowd, conversing two and two, or giving and receiving introductions, and exchanging salutations; other functionaries in black gowns, and other functionaries in court-dresses, were similarly engaged. In the midst of all these, and stealthy Jesuits creeping in and out, and the extreme restlessness of the Youth of England, who were perpetually wandering about, some few steady persons in black cassocks, who had knelt down with their faces to the wall, and were poring over their missals, became, unintentionally, a sort of humane man-traps, and with their own devout legs, tripped up other people's by the dozen.

There was a great pile of candles lying down on the floor near me, which a very old man in a rusty black gown with an open-work tippet, like a summer ornament for a fireplace in tissue-paper, made himself very busy in dispensing to all the ecclesiastics: one a-piece. They loitered about with these for some time, under their arms like walking-sticks, or in their hands like truncheons. At a certain period of the ceremony, however, each carried his candle up to the Pope, laid it across his two knees to be blessed, took it back again, and filed off.

This was done in a very attenuated procession, as you may suppose, and occupied a long time. Not because it takes long to bless a candle through and through, but because there were so many candles to be blessed. At last they were all blessed; and then they were all lighted; and then the Pope was taken up, chair and all, and carried round the church.

I must say, that I never saw anything, out of November, so like the popular English commemoration of the fifth of that month. A bundle of matches and a lantern, would have made it perfect. Nor did the Pope, himself, at all mar the resemblance, though he has a pleasant and venerable face; for, as this part of the ceremony makes him giddy and sick, he shuts his eyes when it is performed: and having his eyes shut and a great mitre on his head, and his head itself wagging to and fro as they shook him in carrying, he looked as if his mask were going to tumble off. The two immense fans which are always borne, one on either side of him, accompanied him, of course, on this occasion. As they carried him along, he blessed the people with the mystic sign; and as he passed them, they kneeled down. When he had made the round of the church, he was brought back again, and if I am not mistaken, this performance was repeated, in the whole, three times. There was, certainly, nothing solemn or effective in it; and certainly very much that was droll and tawdry. But this remark applies to the whole ceremony, except the raising of the Host, when every man in the guard dropped on one knee instantly, and dashed his naked sword on the ground; which had a fine effect.

The next time I saw the cathedral, was some two or three weeks afterwards, when I climbed up into the ball; and then, the hangings being taken down, and the carpet taken up, but all the framework left, the remnants of these decorations looked like an exploded cracker.

The Friday and Saturday having been solemn Festa days, and Sunday being always a *dies non* in carnival proceedings, we had looked forward, with some impatience and curiosity, to the beginning of the new week: Monday and Tuesday being the two last and best days of the Carnival.

On the Monday afternoon at one or two o'clock, there began to be a great rattling of carriages into the court-yard of the hotel; a hurrying to and fro of all the servants in it; and, now and then, a swift shooting across some doorway or balcony, of a straggling stranger in a fancy dress: not yet sufficiently well used to the same, to wear it with confidence, and defy public opinion. All the carriages were open, and had the linings carefully covered with white cotton or calico, to prevent their proper decorations from being spoiled by the incessant pelting of sugar-plums; and people were packing and cramming into every vehicle as it waited for its occupants, enormous sacks and baskets full of these confétti, together with such heaps of flowers, tied up in little nosegays, that some carriages were not only brimful of flowers, but literally running over: scattering, at every shake and jerk of the springs, some of their abundance on the ground. Not to be behindhand in these essential particulars, we caused two very respectable sacks of sugar-plums (each about three feet high) and a large clothes-basket full of flowers to be conveyed into our hired barouche, with all speed. And from our place of observation, in one of the upper balconies of the hotel, we contemplated these arrangements with the liveliest satisfaction. The carriages now beginning to take up their company, and move away, we got into ours, and drove off too, armed with little wire masks for our faces; the sugar-plums, like Falstaff's adulterated sack, having lime in their composition.

The Corso is a street a mile long; a street of shops, and palaces, and private houses, sometimes opening into a broad piazza. There are verandahs and balconies, of all shapes and sizes, to almost every house —not on one story alone, but often to one room or another on every story—put there in general with so little order or regularity, that if, year after year, and season after season, it had rained balconies, hailed balconies, snowed balconies, blown balconies, they could scarcely have come into existence in a more disorderly manner.

This is the great fountain-head and focus of the Carnival. But all the streets in which the Carnival is held, being vigilantly kept by dragoons, it is necessary for carriages, in the first instance, to pass, in line, down another thoroughfare, and so come into the Corso at the end remote from the Piázza del Popolo; which is one of its terminations. Accordingly, we fell into the string of coaches, and, for some time, jogged on quietly enough; now crawling on at a very slow walk; now trotting half-a-dozen yards; now backing fifty; and now stopping altogether: as the pressure in front obliged us. If any impetuous carriage dashed out of the rank and clattered forward, with the wild idea of getting on faster, it was suddenly met, or overtaken, by a trooper on horseback, who, deaf as his own drawn sword to all remonstrances, immediately escorted it back to the very end of the row, and made it a dim speck in the remotest perspective. Occasionally, we interchanged a volley of confétti with the carriage next in front, or the carriage next behind; but as yet, this capturing of stray and errant coaches by the military, was the chief amusement.

Presently, we came into a narrow street, where, besides one line of carriages going, there was another line of carriages returning. Here the sugar-plums and the nosegays began to fly about, pretty smartly; and I was fortunate enough to observe one gentleman attired as a Greek warrior, catch a light-whiskered brigand on the nose (he was in the very act of tossing up a bouquet to a young lady in a first-floor window) with a precision that was much applauded by the bystanders. As this victorious Greek was exchanging a facetious remark with a stout gentleman in a doorway—one-half black and one-half white, as if he had been peeled up the middle—who had offered him his congratulations on his achievement, he received an orange from a house-top, full on his left ear, and was much surprised, not to say discomfited. Especially, as he was standing up at the time; and in consequence of the carriage moving on suddenly, at the same moment staggered ignominiously, and buried himself among his flowers.

Some quarter of an hour of this sort of progress, brought us to the Corso; and anything so gay, so bright, and lively as the whole scene there it would be difficult to imagine. From all the innumerable balconies: from the remotest and highest, no less than from the lowest and nearest: hangings of bright red, bright green, bright blue, white and gold, were fluttering in the brilliant sunlight. From windows, and from parapets, and tops of houses, streamers of the richest colours, and draperies of the gaudiest and most sparkling hues, were floating out upon the street. The buildings seemed to have been literally turned inside out, and to have all their gaiety towards the highway. Shop-fronts were taken down, and the windows filled with company, like boxes at a shining theatre; doors were carried off their hinges, and long tapestries groves, hung with garlands of flowers and ever-greens, displayed within; builders' scaffoldings were gorgeous tem-ples, radiant in silver, gold, and crimson; and in every nook and corner, from the pavement to the chimney-tops, where women's eyes could glisten, there they danced, and laughed, and sparkled, like the light in water. Every sort of bewitching madness of dress was there. Little preposterous scarlet jackets; quaint old stomachers, more wicked than the smartest bodices; Polish pelisses, strained and tight as ripe gooseberries; tiny Greek caps, all awry, and clinging to the dark hair, Heaven knows how; every wild, quaint, bold, shy, pettish, madcap fancy had its illustration in a dress; and every fancy was as dead forgotten by its owner, in the tumult of merriment, as if the three old aqueducts that still remain entire had brought Lethe into Rome, upon their sturdy arches, that morning.

The carriages were now three abreast: in broader places four; often stationary for a long time together; always one close mass of varie-gated brightness; showing the whole street-full, through the storm of flowers, like flowers of a larger growth themselves. In some, the horses were richly caparisoned in magnificent trappings: in others they were decked from head to tail, with flowing ribbons. Some were driven by coachmen with enormous double faces: one face leering at the horses: the other cocking its extraordinary eyes into the carriage: and both rattling again, under the hail of sugar plums. Other drivers were attired as women, wearing long ringlets and no bonnets, and looking more ridiculous in any real difficulty with the horses (of which, in such a concourse, there were a great many) than tongue can tell, or pen describe. Instead of sitting *in* the carriages, upon the seats, the handsome Roman women, to see and to be seen the better, sit in the heads of the barouches, at this time of general licence, with their dainty feet upon the cushions—and oh, the flowing skirts and dainty waists, the blessed shapes and laughing faces, the free, good-humoured, gallant figures that they make! There were great vans, too, full of handsome girls—thirty, or more together, perhaps—and the broadsides that were poured into, and poured out of, these fairy fire-shops, splashed the air with flowers and bon-bons for ten minutes at a time. Carriages, delayed long in one place, would begin a deliber-ate engagement with other carriages, or with people at the lower windows; and the spectators at some upper balcony or window, joining in the fray, and attacking both parties, would empty down great bags of confétti, that descended like a cloud, and in an instant made them white as millers. Still, carriages on carriages, dresses on dresses, colours on colours, crowds upon crowds, without end. Men and boys clinging to the wheels of coaches, and holding on behind, and following in their wake, and diving in among the horses' feet to pick up scattered flowers to sell again; maskers on foot (the drollest generally) in fantastic exaggerations of court-dresses, surveying the throng through enormous eye-glasses, and always transported with an ecstasy of love, on the discovery of any particularly old lady at a window; long strings of Policinelli, laying about them with blown bladders at the ends of sticks; a waggon-full of madmen, screaming and tearing to the life; a coach-full of grave mamelukes, with their horse-tail standard set up in midst; a party of gipsy-women engaged in terrific conflict with a shipful of sailors; a man-monkey on a pole, surrounded by strange animals with pigs' faces, and lions' tails, carried under their arms, or worn gracefully over their shoulders; carriages on carriages, dresses on dresses, colours on colours, crowds upon crowds, without end. Not many actual characters sustained, or represented, perhaps, considering the number dressed, but the main pleasure of the scene consisting in its perfect good temper; in its bright, and infinite, and flashing variety; and in its entire abandonment to the mad humour of the time—an abandonment so perfect, so contagious, so irresistible, that the steadiest foreigner fights up to his middle in flowers and sugar-plums, like the wildest Roman of them all, and thinks of nothing else till half-past four o'clock, when he is suddenly reminded (to his great regret) that this is not the whole business of his existence, by hearing the trumpets sound, and seeing the dragoons begin to clear the street.

How it ever *is* cleared for the race that takes place at five, or how the horses ever go through the race, without going over the people, is more than I can say. But the carriages get out into the by-streets, or up into the Piázza del Popolo, and some people sit in temporary galleries in the latter place, and tens of thousands line the Corso on both sides, when the horses are brought out into the Piázza—to the foot of that same column which, for centuries, looked down upon the games and chariot-races in the Circus Maximus.

At a given signal they are started off. Down the live lane, the whole length of the Corso, they fly like the wind: riderless, as all the world knows: with shining ornaments upon their backs, and twisted in their plaited manes: and with heavy little balls stuck full of spikes, dangling at their sides, to goad them on. The jingling of these trappings and the rattling of their hoofs upon the hard stones; the dash and fury of their speed along the echoing street; nay, the very cannon that are fired—these noises are nothing to the roaring of the multitude: their shouts: the clapping of their hands. But it is soon over—almost instantaneously. More cannon shake the town. The horses have plunged into the carpets put across the street to stop them; the goal is reached; the prizes are won (they are given, in part, by the poor Jews, as a compromise for not running foot-races themselves); and there is an end to that day's sport.

But if the scene be bright, and gay, and crowded, on the last day but one, it attains, on the concluding day, to such a height of glittering colour, swarming life, and frolicsome uproar, that the bare recollection of it makes me giddy at this moment. The same diversions, greatly heightened and intensified in the ardour with which they are pursued, go on until the same hour. The race is repeated; the cannons are fired; the shouting and clapping of hands are renewed; the cannons are fired again; the race is over; and the prizes are won. But the carriages: ankle-deep with sugar-plums within, and so be-flowered and dusty without, as to be hardly recognisable for the same vehicles that they were, three hours ago: instead of scampering off in all directions, throng into the Corso, where they are soon wedged together in a scarcely moving mass. For the diversion of the Moccoletti, the last gay madness of the Carnival, is now at hand; and sellers of little tapers like what are called Christmas candles in England, are shouting lustily on every side, "Moccoli, Moccoli! Ecco Moccoli!"—a new item in the tumult; quite abolishing that other item of "Ecco Fióri! Ecco Fior—r—r!" which has been making itself audible over all the rest, at intervals, the whole day through.

As the bright hangings and dresses are all fading into one dull, heavy, uniform colour in the decline of the day, lights begin flashing, here and there: in the windows, on the house-tops, in the balconies, in the carriages, in the hands of the foot-passengers: little by little: gradually, gradually: more and more: until the whole long street is one great glare and blaze of fire. Then, everybody present has but one engrossing object; that is, to extinguish other people's candles, and to keep his own alight; and everybody: man, woman, or child, gentleman or lady, prince or peasant, native or foreigner: yells and screams, and roars incessantly, as a taunt to the subdued, "Senza Moccolo, Senza Moccolo!" (Without a light! Without a light!) until nothing is heard but a gigantic chorus of those two words, mingled with peals of laughter.

The spectacle, at this time, is one of the most extraordinary that can be imagined. Carriages coming slowly by, with everybody standing on the seats or on the box, holding up their lights at arm's length, for greater safety; some in paper shades; some with a bunch of undefended little tapers, kindled altogether; some with blazing torches; some with feeble little candles; men on foot, creeping along, among the wheels, watching their opportunity, to make a spring at some particular light, and dash it out: other people climbing up into carriages, to get hold of them by main force; others, chasing some unlucky wanderer, round and round his own coach, to blow out the light he had begged or stolen somewhere, before he can ascend to his own company, and enable them to light their extinguished tapers; others, with their hats off, to a carriage-door, humbly beseeching some kind-hearted lady to oblige them with a light for a cigar, and when she is in the fulness of doubt whether to comply or no, blowing out the candle she is guarding so tenderly with her little hand; other people at the windows, fishing for candles with lines and hooks, are letting down long willow-wands with handkerchiefs at the end, and flapping them out, dexterously, when the bearer is at the height of his triumph; others, biding their time in corners, with immense extinguishers like halberds, and suddenly coming down upon glorious torches; others, gathered round one coach, and sticking to it; others, raining oranges and nosegays at an obdurate little lantern, or regularly storming a pyramid of men, holding up one man among them, who carries one feeble little wick above his head, with which he defies them all! Senza Moccolo! Senza Moccolo! Beautiful women, standing up in coaches, pointing in derision at extinguished lights, and clapping their hands, as they pass on, crying, "Senza Moccolo! Senza Moccolo"; low balconies full of lovely faces and gay dresses, struggling, with assailants in the streets; some repressing them as they climb up, some bending down; some leaning over, some shrinking back— delicate arms and bosoms—graceful figures—glowing lights, fluttering dresses, Senza Moccolo, Senza Moccolo, Senza Mocco-lo-o-o-o! —when in the wildest enthusiasm of the cry, and fullest ecstasy of the sport, the Ave Maria rings from the church steeples, and the Carnival is over in an instant—put out like a taper, with a breath!

There was a masquerade at the theatre at night, as dull and senseless as a London one, and only remarkable for the summary way in which the house was cleared at eleven o'clock: which was done by a line of soldiers forming along the wall, at the back of the stage, and sweeping the whole company out before them, like a broad broom. The game of the Moccoletti (the word, in the singular, Moccoletto, is the diminutive of Moccolo, and means a little lamp or candle-snuff) is supposed by some to be a ceremony of burlesque mourning for the death of the Carnival: candles being indispensable to Catholic grief. But whether it be so, or be a remnant of the ancient Saturnalia, or an incorporation of both, or have its origin in anything else, I shall always remember it, and the frolic, as a brilliant and most captivating sight: no less remarkable for the unbroken good-humour of all concerned, down to the very lowest (and among those who scaled the carriages, were many of the commonest men and boys), than for its innocent vivacity. For, odd as it may seem to say so, of a sport so full of thoughtlessness and personal display, it is as free from any taint of immodesty as any general mingling of the two sexes can possibly be; and there seems to prevail, during its progress, a feeling of general, almost childish, simplicity and confidence which one thinks of with a pang, when the Ave Maria has rung it away, for a whole year.

Availing ourselves of a part of the quiet interval between the termination of the Carnival and the beginning of the Holy Week: when everybody had run away from the one, and few people had yet begun to run back again for the other. we went conscientiously to work, to see Rome. And, by dint of going out early every morning, and coming back late every evening, and labouring hard all day, I believe we made acquaintance with every post and pillar in the city, and the country round; and, in particular, explored so many churches, that I abandoned that part of the enterprise at last, before it was half finished, lest I should never, of my own accord, go to church again, as long as I lived. But, I managed, almost every day, at one time or other, to get back to the Coliseum, and out upon the open Campagna, beyond the Tomb of Cecilia Metella.

We often encountered, in these expeditions, a company of English Tourists, with whom I had an ardent, but ungratified longing, to establish a speaking acquaintance. They were one Mr. Davis, and a small circle of friends. It was impossible not to know Mrs. Davis's name, from her being always in great request among her party, and her party being everywhere. During the Holy Week, they were in every part of every scene of every ceremony. For a fortnight or three weeks before it, they were in every tomb, and every church, and every ruin, and every Picture Gallery; and I hardly ever observed Mrs. Davis to be silent for a moment. Deep underground, high up in St. Peter's, out on the Campagna, and stifling in the Jews' quarter, Mrs. Davis turned up, all the same. I don't think she ever saw anything, or ever looked at anything; and she had always lost something out of a straw hand-basket, and was trying to find it, with all her might and main, among an immense quantity of English halfpence, which lay, like the sands upon the sea-shore, at the bottom of it. There was a professional Cicerone always attached to the party (which had been brought over from London, fifteen or twenty strong, by contract), and if so much as looked at Mrs. Davis, she invariably cut him short by saying, "There, God bless the man, don't worrit me! I don't understand a word you say, and shouldn't if you was to talk till you was black in the face!" Mr. Davis always had a snuff-coloured great-coat on, and carried a great green umbrella in his hand, and had a slow curiosity constantly devouring him, which prompted him to do extra-ordinary things, such as taking the covers off urns in tombs, and looking in at the ashes as if they were pickles—and tracing out inscriptions with the ferrule of his umbrella, and saying, with intense thoughtfulness, "Here's a B you see, and there's a R, and this is the way we goes on in; is it!" His antiquarian habits occasioned his being frequently in the rear of the rest; and one of the agonies of Mrs. Davis, and the party in general, was an ever-present fear that Davis would be lost. This caused them to scream for him, in the strangest places, and at the most improper seasons. And when he came, slowly emerging out of some sepulchre or other, like a peaceful Ghoule, saying "Here I am!" Mrs. Davis invariably replied, "You'll be buried alive in a foreign country, Davis, and it's no use trying to prevent you!"

Mr. and Mrs. Davis, and their party, had, probably been brought from London in about nine or ten days. Eighteen hundred years ago, the Roman legions under Claudius, protested against being led into

Mr. and Mrs. Davis's country, urging that it lay beyond the limits of the world.

Among what may be called the Cubs or minor Lions of Rome, there was one that amused me mightily. It is always to be found there; and its den is on the great flight of steps that lead from the Piazza di Spágna, to the church of Trínita del Monte. In plainer words, these steps are the great place of resort for the artists' "Models," and there they are constantly waiting to be hired. The first time I went up there, I could not conceive why the faces seemed familiar to me; why they appeared to have beset me, for years, in every possible variety of action and costume; and how it came to pass that they started up before me, in Rome, in the broad day, like so many saddled and bridled nightmares. I soon found that we had made acquaintance, and improved it, for several years, on the walls of various Exhibition Galleries. There is one old gentleman, with long white hair and an immense beard, who, to my knowledge, has gone half through the catalogue of the Royal Academy. This is the venerable, or patriarchal model. He carries a long staff; and every knot and twist in that staff I have seen, faithfully delineated, innumerable times. There is another man in a blue cloak, who always pretends to be asleep in the sun (when there is any), and who, I need not say, is always very wide awake, and very attentive to the disposition of his legs. This is the *dolce far niente* model. There is another man in a brown cloak, who leans against a wall, with his arms folded in his mantle, and looks out of the corners of his eyes; which are just visible beneath his broad slouched hat. This is the assassin model. There is another man, who constantly looks over his shoulder, and is always going away, but never does. This is the haughty, or scornful model. As to Domestic Happiness, and Holy families, they should come very cheap, for there are lumps of them, all up the steps; and the cream of the thing is, that they are all the falsest vagabonds in the world, especially made up for the purpose, and having no counterparts in Rome or any other part of the habitable globe.

My recent mention of the Carnival, reminds me of its being said to be a mock mourning (in the ceremony with which it closes), for the gaieties and merry-makings before Lent; and this again reminds me of the real funerals and mourning processions of Rome, which, like those in most other parts of Italy, are rendered chiefly remarkable to a Foreigner, by the indifference with which the mere clay is universally regarded, after life has left it. And this is not from the survivors having had time to dissociate the memory of the dead from their well-remembered appearance and form on earth; for the interment follows too speedily after death, for that: almost always taking place within four-and-twenty hours, and, sometimes, within twelve.

At Rome, there is the same arrangement of Pits in a great, bleak, open, dreary space, that I have already described as existing in Genoa. When I visited it, at noonday, I saw a solitary coffin of plain deal: uncovered by any shroud or pall, and so slightly made, that the hoof of any wandering mule would have crushed it in: carelessly tumbled down, all on one side, on the door of one of the pits—and there left, by itself, in the wind and sunshine. "How does it come to be left here?" I asked the man who showed me the place. "It was brought here half an hour ago, Signore," he said. I remembered to have met the procession, on its return: straggling away at a good round pace. "When will it be put in the pit?" I asked him. "When the cart comes, and it is opened to-night," he said. "How much does it cost to be brought here in this way, instead of coming in the cart?" I asked him. "Ten scudi," he said (about two pounds, two-and-six-pence, English). "The other bodies, for whom nothing is paid, are taken to the church of the Santa Maria della Consolázione," he continued, "and brought here altogether, in the cart at night." I stood, a moment, looking at the coffin, which had two initial letters scrawled upon the top; and turned away, with an expression in my face, I suppose, of not much liking its exposure in that manner: for he said, shrugging his shoulders with great vivacity, and giving a pleasant smile, "But he's dead, Signore, he's dead. Why not?"

Among the innumerable churches, there is one I must select for separate mention. It is the church of the Ara Cœli, supposed to be built on the site of the old Temple of Jupiter Feretrius; and approached on one side, by a long steep flight of steps, which seem incomplete without some group of bearded soothsayers on the top. It is remarkable for the possession of a miraculous Bambíno, or wooden doll, representing the Infant Saviour; and I first saw this miraculous Bambíno, in legal phrase, in manner following, that is to say:

We had strolled into the church one afternoon, and were looking down its long vista of gloomy pillars (for all these ancient churches built upon the ruins of old temples, are dark and sad), when the Brave came running in, with a grin upon his face that stretched it from ear to ear, and implored us to follow him, without a moment's delay, as they were going to show the Bambíno to a select party. We accordingly hurried off to a sort of chapel, or sacristy, hard by the chief altar, but not in the church itself, where the select party, consisting of two or three Catholic gentlemen and ladies (not Italians), were already assembled: and where one hollow-cheeked young monk was lighting up divers candles, while another was putting on some clerical robes over his coarse brown habit. The candles were on a kind of altar, and above it were two delectable figures, such as you would see at any English fair, representing the Holy Virgin, and Saint Joseph, as I suppose, bending in devotion over a wooden box, or coffer; which was shut.

The hollow-cheeked monk, number One, having finished lighting the candles, went down on his knees, in a corner, before this set-piece; and the monk number Two, having put on a pair of highly ornamented and gold-bespattered gloves, lifted down the coffer, with great reverence, and set it on the altar. Then, with many genuflexions, and muttering certain prayers, he opened it, and let down the front, and took off sundry coverings of satin and lace from the inside. The ladies had been on their knees from the commencement; and the gentlemen now dropped down devoutly, as he exposed to view a little wooden doll, in face very like General Tom Thumb, the American Dwarf: gorgeously dressed in satin and gold lace, and actually blazing with rich jewels. There was scarcely a spot upon its little breast, or neck, or stomach, but was sparkling with the costly offerings of the Faithful. Presently, he lifted it out of the box, and carrying it round among the kneelers, set its face against the forehead of every one, and tendered its clumsy foot to them to kiss—a ceremony which they all performed down to a dirty little ragamuffin of a boy who had walked in from the street. When this was done, he laid it in the box again: and the company, rising, drew near, and commended the jewels in whispers. In good time, he replaced the coverings, shut up the box, put it back in its place, locked up the whole concern (Holy Family and all) behind a pair of folding-doors; took off his priestly vestments; and received the customary "small charge," while his companion, by means of an extinguisher fastened to the end of a long stick, put out the lights, one after another. The candles being all extinguished, and the money all collected, they retired, and so did the spectators.

I met this same Bambíno, in the street a short time afterwards, going, in great state, to the house of some sick person. It is taken to all parts of Rome for this purpose, constantly; but, I understand that it is not always as successful as could be wished; for, making its appearance at the bedside of weak and nervous people in extremity, accompanied by a numerous escort, it not unfrequently frightens them to death. It is most popular in cases of child-birth, where it has done such wonders, that if a lady be longer than usual in getting through her difficulties, a messenger is despatched, with all speed, to solicit the immediate attendance of the Bambíno. It is a very valuable property, and much confided in—especially by the religious body to whom it belongs.

I am happy to know that it is not considered immaculate, by some who are good Catholics, and who are behind the scenes, from what was told me by the near relation of a Priest, himself a Catholic, and a gentleman of learning and intelligence. This Priest made my informant promise that he would, on no account, allow the Bambíno to be borne into the bedroom of a sick lady, in whom they were both interested. "For," said he, "if they (the monks) trouble her with it, and intrude themselves into her room, it will certainly kill her." My informant accordingly looked out of the window when it came; and, with many thanks, declined to open the door. He endeavoured, in another case of which he had no other knowledge than such as he gained as a passer-by at the moment, to prevent its being carried into a small unwholesome chamber, where a poor girl was dying. But, he strove against it unsuccessfully, and she expired while the crowd were pressing round her bed.

Among the people who drop into St. Peter's at their leisure, to kneel on the pavement, and say a quiet prayer, there are certain schools and seminaries, priestly and otherwise, that come in, twenty or thirty strong. These boys always kneel down in single file, one behind the other, with a tall grim master in a black gown, bringing up the rear: like a pack of cards arranged to be tumbled down at a touch, with a disproportionately large Knave of clubs at the end. When they have had a minute or so at the chief altar, they scramble up, and filing off to the chapel of the Madonna, or the sacrament, flop down again in the same order; so that if anybody *did* stumble against the master, a general and sudden overthrow of the whole line must inevitably ensue.

The scene in all the churches is the strangest possible. The same monotonous, heartless, drowsy, chaunting, always going on; the same dark building, darker from the brightness of the street without; the same lamps dimly burning; the self-same people kneeling here and there; turned towards you, from one altar or other, the same priest's back, with the same large cross embroidered on it; however different in size, in shape, in wealth, in architecture, this church is from that, it is the same thing still. There are the same dirty beggars stopping in their muttered prayers to beg; the same miserable cripples exhibiting their deformity at the doors; the same blind men, rattling little pots like kitchen pepper-castors: their depositories for alms; the same preposterous crowns of silver stuck upon the painted heads of single saints and Virgins in crowded pictures, so that a little figure on a mountain has a head-dress bigger than the temple in the fore-ground, or adjacent miles of landscape; the same favourite shrine or figure, smothered with little silver hearts and crosses, and the like: the staple trade and show of all the jewellers; the same odd mixture of respect and indecorum, faith and phlegm: kneeling on the stones, and spitting on them, loudly; getting up from prayers to beg a little, or to pursue some other worldly matter: and then kneeling down again, to resume the contrite supplication at the point where it was interrupted. In one church, a kneeling lady got up from her prayer, for a moment, to offer us her card, as a teacher of Music; and in another, a sedate gentleman with a very thick walking-staff, arose from his devotions to belabour his dog, who was growling at another dog: and whose yelps and howls resounded through the church, as his master quietly relapsed into his former train of meditation—keeping his eye upon the dog, at the same time, nevertheless.

Above all, there is always a receptacle for the contributions of the Faithful, in some form or other. Sometimes, it is a money-box, set up between the worshipper, and the wooden life-size figure of the Redeemer; sometimes, it is a little chest for the maintenance of the Virgin; sometimes, an appeal on behalf of a popular Bambíno; sometimes, a bag at the end of a long stick, thrust among the people here and there, and vigilantly jingled by an active Sacristan; but there it always is, and, very often, in many shapes in the same church, and doing pretty well in all. Nor, is it wanting in the open air—the streets and roads—for, often as you are walking along, thinking about anything rather than a tin canister, that object pounces out upon you from a little house by the wayside; and on its top is painted, "For the Souls in Purgatory;" an appeal which the bearer repeats a great many times, as he rattles it before you, much as Punch rattles the cracked bell which his sanguine disposition makes an organ of.

And this reminds me that some Roman altars of peculiar sanctity, bear the inscription, "Every Mass performed at this altar frees a soul from Purgatory." I have never been able to find out the charge for one of these services, but they should needs be expensive. There are several Crosses in Rome too, the kissing of which, confers indulgences for varying terms. That in the centre of the Coliseum, is worth a hundred days; and people may be seen kissing it from morning to night. It is curious that some of these crosses seem to acquire an arbitrary popularity: this very one among them. In another part of the Coliseum there is a cross upon a marble slab, with the inscription, "Who kisses this cross shall be entitled to Two hundred and forty days' indulgence." But I saw no one person kiss it, though, day after day, I sat in the arena, and saw scores upon scores of peasants pass it, on their way to kiss the other.

To single out details from the great dream of Roman Churches, would be the wildest occupation in the world. But St. Stefano Rotondo, a damp, mildewed vault of an old church in the outskirts of Rome, will always struggle uppermost in my mind, by reason of the hideous paintings with which its walls are covered. These represent the martyrdoms of saints and early Christians; and such a panorama of horror and butchery no man could imagine in his sleep, though he were to eat a whole pig raw, for supper. Grey-bearded men being boiled, fried, grilled, crimped, singed, eaten by wild beasts, worried by dogs, buried alive, torn asunder by horses, chopped up small with hatchets: women having their breasts torn with iron pinchers, their tongues cut out, their ears screwed off, their jaws broken, their bodies stretched upon the rack, or skinned upon the stake, or crackled up and melted in the fire: these are among the mildest subjects. So insisted on, and laboured at, besides, that every sufferer gives you the same occasion for wonder as poor old Duncan awoke, in Lady Macbeth, when she marvelled at his having so much blood in him.

There is an upper chamber in the Mamertine prisons, over what is said to have been—and very possibly may have been —the dungeon of St. Peter. The chamber is now fitted up as an oratory, dedicated to that saint; and it lives, as a distinct and separate place, in my recollection, too. It is very small and low-roofed; and the dread and gloom of the ponderous obdurate old prison are on it, as if they had come up in a dark mist through the floor. Hanging on the walls, among the clustered votive offerings, are objects, at once strangely in keeping, and strangely at variance, with the place—rusty daggers, knives, pistols, clubs, divers instruments of violence and murder, brought here, fresh from use, and hung up to propitiate offended Heaven: as if the blood upon them would drain off in consecrated air, and have no voice to cry with. It is all so silent and so close, and tomb-like; and the dungeons below are so black and stealthy, and stagnant, and naked; that this little dark spot becomes a dream within a dream: and in the vision of great churches which come rolling past me like a sea, it is a small wave by itself, that melts into no other wave, and does not flow on with the rest.

It is an awful thing to think of the enormous caverns that are entered from some Roman churches, and undermine the city. Many churches have crypts and subterranean chapels of great size, which in the ancient time, were baths, and secret chambers of temples, and what not; but I do not speak of them. Beneath the church of St. Giovanni and St. Paolo, there are the jaws of a terrific range of caverns, hewn out of the rock, and said to have another outlet underneath the Coliseum—tremendous darkness of vast extent, half-buried in the earth and unexplorable, where the dull torches, flashed by the attendants, glimmer down long ranges of distant vaults branching to the right and left, like streets in a city of the dead; and show the cold damp stealing down the walls, drip-drop, drip-drop, to join the pools of water that lie here and there, and never saw, or never will see, one ray of the sun. Some accounts make these the prisons of the wild beasts destined for the amphitheatre; some the prisons of the condemned gladiators; some, both. But the legend most appalling to the fancy is, that in the upper range (for there are two stories of these caves) the Early Christians destined to be eaten at the Coliseum Shows, heard the wild beasts, hungry for them, roaring down below; until, upon the night and solitude of their captivity, there burst the sudden noon and life of the vast theatre crowded to the parapet, and of these, their dreaded neighbours, bounding in!

Below the church of San Sebastiano, two miles beyond the gate of San Sebastiano, on the Appian Way, is the entrance to the catacombs of Rome—quarries in the old time, but afterwards the hiding-places of the Christians. These ghastly passages have been explored for twenty miles; and form a chain of labyrinths, sixty miles in circumference.

A gaunt Franciscan friar, with a wild bright eye, was our only guide, down into this profound and dreadful place. The narrow ways and openings hither and thither, coupled with the dead and heavy air, soon blotted out, in all of us, any recollection of the track by which we had come: and I could not help thinking "Good Heaven, if, in a sudden fit of madness, he should dash the torches out, or if he should be seized with a fit, what would become of us!" On we wandered, among martyrs' graves: passing great subterranean vaulted roads, diverging in all directions, and choked up with heaps of stones, that thieves and murderers may not take refuge there, and form a population under Rome, even worse than that which lives between it and the sun. Graves, graves, graves; Graves of men, of women, of their little children, who ran crying to the persecutors, "We are Christians! We are Christians!" that they might be murdered with their parents; Graves with the pain of martyrdom roughly cut into their stone boundaries, and little niches, made to hold a vessel of the martyrs' blood; Graves of some who lived down here, for years together, ministering to the rest, and preaching truth, and hope, and comfort, from the rude altars, that bear witness to their fortitude at this hour; more roomy graves, but far more terrible, where hundreds, being surprised, were hemmed in and walled up: buried before Death, and killed by slow starvation.

"The Triumphs of the Faith are not above ground in our splendid churches," said the friar, looking round upon us, as we stopped to rest in one of the low passages, with bones and dust surrounding us on every side. "They are here! Among the Martyrs' Graves!" He was a gentle, earnest man, and said it from his heart; but when I thought how Christian men have dealt with one another; how, perverting our most merciful religion, they have hunted down and tortured, burnt and beheaded, strangled, slaughtered, and oppresed each other; I pictured to myself an agony surpassing any that this Dust had suffered with the breath of life yet lingering in it, and how these great and constant hearts would have been shaken—how they would have quailed and drooped—if a foreknowledge of the deeds that professing Christians would commit in the Great Name for which they died, could have rent them with its own unutterable anguish, on the cruel wheel, and bitter cross, and in the fearful fire.

Such are the spots and patches in my dream of churches, that remain apart, and keep their separate identity. I have a fainter recollection, sometimes of the relics ; of the fragments of the pillar of the Temple that was rent in twain; of the portion of the table that was spread for the Last Supper; of the well at which the woman of Samaria gave water to Our Saviour; of two columns from the house of Pontius Pilate; of the stone to which the Sacred hands were bound, when the scourging was performed; of the gridiron of Saint Lawrence, and the stone below it, marked with the frying of his fat and blood; these set a shadowy mark on some cathedrals, as an old story, or a fable might, and stop them for an instant, as they flit before me. The rest is a vast wilderness of consecrated buildings of all shapes and fancies, blending one with another; of battered pillars of old Pagan temples, dug up from the ground, and forced, like giant captives, to support the roofs of Christian churches; of pictures, bad, and wonderful, and impious, and ridiculous; of kneeling people, curling incense, tinkling bells, and sometimes (but not often) of a swelling organ: of Madonne, with their breasts stuck full of swords, arranged in a half-circle like a modern fan; of actual skeletons of dead saints, hideously attired in gaudy satins, silks, and velvets trimmed with gold: their withered crust of skull adorned with precious jewels, or with chaplets of crushed flowers; sometimes, of people gathered round the pulpit, and a monk within it stretching out the crucifix, and preaching fiercely: the sun just streaming down through some high window on the sailcloth stretched above him and across the church, to keep his high-pitched voice from being lost among the echoes of the roof. Then my tired memory comes out upon a flight of steps, where knots of people are asleep, or basking in the light; and strolls away, among the rags, and smells, and palaces, and hovels, of an old Italian street.

On one Saturday morning (the eighth of March), a man was beheaded here. Nine or ten months before, he had waylaid a Bavarian countess, travelling as a pilgrim to Rome—alone and on foot, of course—and performing, it is said, that act of piety for the fourth time. He saw her change a piece of gold at Viterbo, where he lived; followed her; bore her company on her journey for some forty miles or more, on the treacherous pretext of protecting her; attacked her, in the fulfilment of his unrelenting purpose, on the Campagna, within a very short distance of Rome, near to what is called (but what is not) the Tomb of Nero; robbed her; and beat her to death with her own pilgrim's staff. He was newly married, and gave some of her apparel to his wife: saying that he had bought it at a fair. She, however, who had seen the pilgrim-countess passing through their town, recognised some trifle as having belonged to her. Her husband then told her what he had done. She, in confession, told a priest; and the man was taken, within four days after the commission of the murder.

There are no fixed times for the administration of justice, or its execution, in this unaccountable country; and he had been in prison ever since. On the Friday, as he was dining with the other prisoners, they came and told him he was to be beheaded next morning, and took him away. It is very unusual to execute in Lent; but his crime being a very bad one, it was deemed advisable to make an example of him at that time, when great numbers of pilgrims were coming towards Rome, from all parts, for the Holy Week. I heard of this on the Friday evening, and saw the bills up at the churches, calling on the people to pray for the criminal's soul. So, I determined to go, and see him executed.

The beheading was appointed for fourteen and a-half o'clock, Roman time: or a quarter before nine in the forenoon. I had two friends with me; and as we did not know but that the crowd might be very great, we were on the spot by half-past seven. The place of execution was near the church of San Giovanni decolláto (a doubtful compliment to Saint John the Baptist) in one of the impassable back streets without any footway, of which a great part of Rome is composed—a street of rotten houses, which do not seem to belong to anybody, and do not seem to have ever been inhabited, and certainly were never built on any plan, or for any particular purpose, and have no window-sashes, and are a little like deserted breweries, and might be warehouses but for having nothing in them. Opposite to one of these, a white house, the scaffold was built. An untidy, unpainted, uncouth, crazy-looking thing of course: some seven feet high, perhaps: with a tall, gallows-shaped frame rising above it, in which was the knife, charged with a ponderous mass of iron, all ready to descend, and glittering brightly in the morning sun, whenever it looked out, now and then, from behind a cloud.

There were not many people lingering about; and these were kept at a considerable distance from the scaffold, by parties of the Pope's dragoons. Two or three hundred foot-soldiers were under arms, standing at ease in clusters here and there; and the officers were walking up and down in twos and threes, chatting together, and smoking cigars.

At the end of the street, was an open space, where there would be a dust-heap, and piles of broken crockery, and mounds of vegetable refuse, but for such things being thrown anywhere and everywhere in Rome, and favouring no particular sort of locality. We got into a kind of wash-house, belonging to a dwelling-house on this spot; and standing there in an old cart, and on a heap of cart-wheels piled against the wall, looking, through a large grated window, at the scaffold, and straight down the street beyond it, until, in consequence of its turning off abruptly to the left, our perspective was brought to a sudden termination, and had a corpulent officer, in a cocked hat, for its crowning feature.

Nine o'clock struck, and ten o'clock struck, and nothing happened. All the bells of all the churches rang as usual. A little parliament of dogs assembled in the open space, and chased each other, in and out among the soldiers. Fierce-looking Romans of the lowest class, in blue cloaks, russet cloaks, and rags uncloaked, came and went, and talked together. Women and children fluttered, on the skirts of the scanty crowd. One large muddy spot was left quite bare, like a bald place on a man's head. A cigar-merchant, with an earthen pot of charcoal ashes in one hand, went up and down, crying his wares. A pastry-merchant divided his attention between the scaffold and his customers. Boys tried to climb up walls, and tumbled down again. Priests and monks elbowed a passage for themselves among the people, and stood on tiptoe for a sight of the knife: then went away. Artists, in inconceivable hats of the middle-ages, and beards (thank Heaven!) of no age at all, flashed picturesque scowls about them from their stations in the throng. One gentleman (connected with the fine arts, I presume) went up and down in a pair of Hessian-boots, with a red beard hanging down on his breast, and his long and bright red hair, plaited into two tails, one on either side of his head, which fell over his shoulders in front of him, very nearly to his waist, and were carefully entwined and braided!

Eleven o'clock struck; and still nothing happened. A rumour got about, among the crowd that the criminal would not confess; in which case, the priests would keep him until the Ave Maria (sunset); for it is their merciful custom never finally to turn the crucifix away from a man at that pass, as one refusing to be shriven, and consequently a sinner abandoned of the Saviour, until then. People began to drop off. The officers shrugged their shoulders and looked doubtful. The dragoons, who came riding up below our window, every now and then, to order an unlucky hackney-coach or cart away, as soon as it had comfortably established itself, and was covered with exulting people (but never before), became imperious, and quick-tempered. The bald place hadn't a straggling hair upon it; and the corpulent officer, crowning the perspective, took a world of snuff.

Suddenly, there was a noise of trumpets. "Attention!" was among the foot-soldiers instantly. They were marched up to the scaffold and formed round it. The dragoons galloped to their near stations too.

The guillotine became the centre of a wood of bristling bayonets and shining sabres. The people closed round nearer, on the flank of the soldiery. A long straggling stream of men and boys, who had accompanied the procession from the prison, came pouring into the open space. The bald spot was scarcely distinguishable from the rest. The cigar and pastry-merchants resigned all thoughts of business, for the moment, and abandoning themselves wholly to pleasure, got good situations in the crowd. The perspective ended, now, in a troop of dragoons. And the corpulent officer, sword in hand, looked hard at a church close to him, which he could see, but we, the crowd, could not.

After a short delay, some monks were seen approaching to the scaffold from this church; and above their heads, coming on slowly and gloomily, the effigy of Christ upon the cross, canopied with black. This was carried round the foot of the scaffold, to the front, and turned towards the criminal, that he might see it to the last. It was hardly in its place, when he appeared on the platform, bare-footed; his hands bound; and with the collar and neck of his shirt cut away, almost to the shoulder. A young man—six-and-twenty—vigorously made, and well-shaped. Face pale; small dark moustache; and dark brown hair.

He had refused to confess, it seemed, without first having his wife brought to see him; and they had sent an escort for her, which had occasioned the delay.

He immediately kneeled down, below the knife. His neck fitting into a hole, made for the purpose, in a cross plank, was shut down, by another plank above; exactly like the pillory. Immediately below him was a leathern bag. And into it his head rolled instantly.

The executioner was holding it by the hair, and walking with it round the scaffold, showing it to the people, before one quite knew that the knife had fallen heavily, and with a rattling sound.

When it had travelled round the four sides of the scaffold, it was set upon a pole in front—a little patch of black and white, for the long street to stare at, and the flies to settle on. The eyes were turned upward, as if he had avoided the sight of the leathern bag, and looked to the crucifix. Every tinge and hue of life had left it in that instant. It was dull, cold, livid, wax. The body also.

There was a great deal of blood. When we left the window, and went close up to the scaffold, it was very dirty; one of the two men who were throwing water over it, turning to help the other lift the body into a shell, picked his way as through mire. A strange appearance was the apparent annihilation of the neck. The head was taken off so close, that it seemed as if the knife had narrowly escaped crushing the jaw, or shaving off the ear; and the body looked as if there were nothing left above the shoulder.

Nobody cared, or was at all affected. There was no manifestation of disgust, or pity, or indignation, or sorrow. My empty pockets were tried, several times, in the crowd immediately below the scaffold, as the corpse was being put into its coffin. It was an ugly, filthy, careless, sickening spectacle; meaning nothing but butchery beyond the momentary interest, to the one wretched actor. Yes! Such a sight has one meaning and one warning. Let me not forget it. The speculators in the lottery, station themselves at favourable points for counting the gouts of blood that spirt out, here or there; and buy that number. It is pretty sure to have a run upon it.

The body was carted away in due time, the knife cleansed, the scaffold taken down, and all the hideous apparatus removed. The executioner: an outlaw *ex officio* (what a satire on the Punishment!) who dare not, for his life, cross the Bridge of St. Angelo but to do his work: retreated to his lair, and the show was over.

At the head of the collections in the palaces of Rome, the Vatican of course, with its treasures of art, its enormous galleries, and stair-cases, and suites of immense chambers, ranks highest and stands fore-most. Many most noble statues, and wonderful pictures, are there; nor is it heresy to say that there is a considerable amount of rubbish there, too. When any old piece of sculpture dug out of the ground, finds a place in a gallery because it is old, and without any reference to its intrinsic merits: and finds admirers by the hundred, because it is there, and for no other reason on earth: there will be no lack of objects, very indifferent in the plain eyesight of any one who employs so vulgar a property, when he may wear the spectacles of Cant for less than nothing, and establish himself as a man of taste for the mere trouble of putting them on.

I unreservedly confess, for myself, that I cannot leave my natural perception of what is natural and true, at a palace-door, in Italy or elsewhere, as I should leave my shoes if I were travelling in the East. I cannot forget that there are certain expressions of face, natural to certain passions, and as unchangeable in their nature as the gait of a lion, or the flight of an eagle. I cannot dismiss from my certain know-ledge, such commonplace facts as the ordinary proportion of men's arms, and legs, and heads; and when I meet with performances that do violence to these experiences and recollections, no matter where they may be, I cannot honestly admire them, and think it best to say so; in spite of high critical advice that we should sometimes feign an admiration, though we have it not.

Therefore, I freely acknowledge that when I see a Jolly young Waterman representing a cherubim, or a Barclay and Perkins's Drayman depicted as an Evangelist, I see nothing to commend or admire in the performance, however great its reputed Painter. Neither am I partial to libellous Angels, who play on fiddles and bassoons, for the edification of sprawling monks apparently in liquor. Nor to those Monsieur Tonsons of galleries, Saint Francis and Saint Sebastian; both of whom I submit should have very uncom-mon and rare merits, as works of art, to justify their compound multi-plication by Italian Painters.

It seems to me, too, that the indiscriminate and determined raptures in which some critics indulge, is incompatible with the true appreciation of the really great and transcendent works. I cannot imagine, for example, how the resolute champion of undeserving pictures can soar to the amazing beauty of Titian's great picture of the Assumption of the Virgin at Venice; or how the man who is truly affected by the sublimity of that exquisite production, or who is truly sensible of the beauty of Tintoretto's great picture of the Assembly of the Blessed in the same place, can discern in Michael Angelo's Last Judgment, in the Sistine chapel, any general idea, or one pervading thought, in harmony with the stupendous subject. He who will contemplate Raphael's masterpiece, the Transfiguration, and will go away into another chamber of that same Vatican, and contemplate another design of Raphael, representing (in incredible caricature) the miraculous stopping of a great fire by Leo the Fourth—and who will say that he admires them both, as works of extraordinary genius—must, as I think, be wanting in his power of perception in one of the two instances, and, probably, in the high and lofty one.

It is easy to suggest a doubt, but I have a great doubt whether, sometimes, the rules of art are not too strictly observed, and whether it is quite well or agreeable that we should know beforehand, when this figure will be turning round, and where that figure will be lying down, and where there will be drapery in folds, and so forth. When I observe heads inferior to the subject, in pictures of merit, in Italian galleries, I do not attach that reproach to the Painter, for I have a suspicion that these great men, who were, of necessity, very much in the hands of monks and priests, painted monks and priests a great deal too often. I frequently see, in pictures of real power, heads quite below the story and the painter: and I invariably observe that those heads are of the Convent stamp, and have their counterparts among the Convent inmates of this hour; so, I have settled with myself that, in such cases, the lameness was not with the painter, but with the vanity and ignorance of certain of his employers, who would be apostles—on canvas, at all events.

The exquisite grace and beauty of Canova's statues; the wonderful gravity and repose of many of the ancient works in sculpture, both in the Capitol and the Vatican; and the strength and fire of many others; are, in their different ways, beyond all reach of words. They are specially impressive and delightful, after the works of Bernini and his disciples, in which the churches of Rome, from St. Peter's downward, abound; and which are, I verily believe, the most detestable class of productions in the wide world. I would infinitely rather (as mere works of art) look upon the three deities of the Past, the Present, and the Future, in the Chinese Collection, than upon the best of these breezy maniacs; whose every fold of drapery is blown inside-out; whose smallest vein, or artery, is as big as an ordinary forefinger; whose hair is like a nest of lively snakes; and whose attitudes put all other extravagance to shame. Insomuch that I do honestly believe, there can be no place in the world, where such intolerable abortions, begotten of the sculptor's chisel, are to be found in such profusion, as in Rome.

There is a fine collection of Egyptian antiques, in the Vatican; and the ceilings of the rooms in which they are arranged, are painted to represent a starlight sky in the Desert. It may seem an odd idea, but it is very effective. The grim, half-human monsters from the temples, look more grim and monstrous underneath the deep dark blue; it sheds a strange uncertain gloomy air on everything—a mystery adapted to the objects; and you leave them, as you find them, shrouded in a solemn night.

In the private palaces, pictures are seen to the best advantage. There are seldom so many in one place that the attention need become distracted, or the eye confused. You see them very leisurely; and are rarely interrupted by a crowd of people. There are portraits innumerable, by Titian, and Rembrandt, and Vandyke; heads by Guido, and Domenichino, and Carlo Dolci; various subjects by Correggio and Murillo, and Raphael, and Salvator Rosa, and Spagnoletto—many of which it would be difficult, indeed, to praise too highly, or to praise enough; such is their tenderness and grace; their noble elevation, purity, and beauty.

The portrait of Beatrice di Cenci, in the Palazzo Berberini, is a picture almost impossible to be forgotten. Through the transcendent sweetness and beauty of the face, there is a something shining out, that haunts me. I see it now, as I see this paper, or my pen. The head is loosely draped in white; the light hair falling down below the linen folds. She has turned suddenly towards you; and there is an expression in the eyes—although they are very tender and gentle—as if the wildness of a momentary terror, or distraction, had been struggled with and overcome, that instant; and nothing but a celestial hope, and a beautiful sorrow, and a desolate earthly helplessness remained. Some stories say that Guido painted it, the night before her execution; some other stories, that he painted it from memory, after having seen her, on her way to the scaffold. I am willing to believe that, as you see her on his canvas, so she turned towards him, in the crowd, from the first sight of the axe, and stamped upon his mind a look which he has stamped on mine as though I had stood beside him in the concourse. The guilty palace of the Cenci: blighting a whole quarter of the town, as it stands withering away by grains: had that face, to my fancy, in its dismal porch, and at its black, blind windows, and flitting up and down its dreary stairs, and growing out of the darkness of the ghostly galleries. The History is written in the Painting; written, in the dying girl's face, by Nature's own hand. And on! how in that one touch she puts to flight (instead of making kin) the puny world that claim to be related to her, in right of poor conventional forgeries!

I saw in the Palazzo Spada, the statue of Pompey; the statue at whose base Cæsar fell. A stern, tremendous figure! I imagined one of greater finish: of the last refinement: full of delicate touches: losing its distinctness, in the giddy eyes of one whose blood was ebbing before it, and settling into some such rigid majesty as this, as Death came creeping over the upturned face.

The excursions in the neighbourhood of Rome are charming, and would be full of interest were it only for the changing views they afford, of the wild Campagna. But, every inch of ground, in every direction, is rich in associations, and in natural beauties. There is Albano, with its lovely lake and wooded shore, and with its wine, that certainly has not improved since the days of Horace, and in these times hardly justifies his panegyric. There is squalid Tivoli, with the river Anio, diverted from its course, and plunging down, headlong, some eighty feet in search of it. With its picturesque Temple of the Sibyl, perched high on a crag; its minor waterfalls glancing and sparkling in the sun; and one good cavern yawning darkly, where the river takes a fearful plunge and shoots on, low down under beetling rocks. There, too, is the Villa d'Este, deserted and decaying among groves of melancholy pine and cypress trees, where it seems to be in state. Then, there is Frascati, and, on the steep above it, the ruins of Tusculum, where Cicero lived, and wrote, and adorned his favourite house (some fragments of it may yet be seen there), and where Cato was born. We saw its ruined amphitheatre on a grey, dull day, when a shrill March wind was blowing, and when the scattered stones of the old city lay strewn about the lonely eminence, as desolate and dead as the ashes of a long extinguished fire.

One day we walked out, a little party of three, to Albano, fourteen miles distant; possessed by a great desire to go there by the ancient Appian Way, long since ruined and overgrown. We started at half-past seven in the morning, and within an hour or so were out upon the open Campagna. For twelve miles we went climbing on, over an unbroken succession of mounds, and heaps, and hills, of ruin. Tombs and temples, overthrown and prostrate; small fragments of columns, friezes, pediments; great blocks of granite and marble; mouldering arches, grass-grown and decayed; ruin enough to build a spacious city from; lay strewn about us. Sometimes, loose walls, built up from these fragments by the shepherds, came across our path; sometimes, a ditch between two mounds of broken stones, obstructed our progress; sometimes, the fragments themselves, rolling from beneath our feet, made it a toilsome matter to advance; but it was always ruin. Now, we tracked a piece of the old road, above the ground; now traced it, underneath a grassy covering, as if that were its grave; but all the way was ruin. In the distance, ruined aqueducts went stalking on their giant course along the plain; and every breath of wind that swept towards us, stirred early flowers and grasses, springing up, spontaneously, on miles of ruin. The unseen larks above us, who alone disturbed the awful silence, had their nests in ruin; and the fierce herdsmen, clad in sheepskins, who now and then scowled out upon us from their sleeping nooks, were housed in ruin. The aspect of the desolate Campagna in one direction, where it was most level, reminded me of an American prairie; but what is the solitude of a region where men have never dwelt, to that of a Desert, where a mighty race have left their footprints in the earth from which they have vanished; where the resting-places of their Dead, have fallen like their Dead; and the broken hour-glass of Time is but a heap of idle dust! Returning, by the road, at sunset! and looking, from the distance, on the course we had taken in the morning, I almost feel (as I had felt when I first saw it, at that hour) as if the sun would never rise again, but looked its last, that night, upon a ruined world.

To come again on Rome, by moonlight, after such an expedition, is a fitting close to such a day. The narrow streets, devoid of footways, and choked, in every obscure corner, by heaps of dunghill-rubbish, contrast so strongly, in their cramped dimensions, and their filth, and darkness, with the broad square before some haughty church: in the centre of which, a hieroglyphic-covered obelisk, brought from Egypt in the days of the Emperors, looks strangely on the foreign scene about it; or perhaps an ancient pillar, with its honoured statue overthrown, supports a Christian saint: Marcus Aurelius giving place to Paul, and Trajan to St. Peter. Then, there are the ponderous buildings reared from the spoliation of the Coliseum shutting out the moon, like mountains: while here and there, are broken arches and rent walls, through which it gushes freely, as the life comes pouring from a wound. The little town of miserable houses, walled, and shut in by barred gates, is the quarter where the Jews are locked up nightly, when the clock strikes eight—a miserable place, densely populated, and reeking with bad odours, but where the people are industrious and money-getting. In the day-time, as you make your way along the narrow streets, you see them all at work: upon the pavement, oftener than in their dark and frouzy shops: furbishing old clothes, and driving bargains.

Crossing from these patches of thick darkness, out into the moon once more, the fountain of Trevi, welling from a hundred jets, and rolling over mimic rocks, is silvery to the eye and ear. In the narrow little throat of street, beyond, a booth, dressed out with flaring lamps, and boughs of trees, attracts a group of sulky Romans round its smoky coppers of hot broth, and cauliflower stew; its trays of fried fish, and its flasks of wine. As you rattle round the sharply-twisting corner, a lumbering sound is heard. The coachman stops abruptly, and uncovers, as a van comes slowly by, preceded by a man who bears a large cross; by a torch-bearer; and a priest: the latter chaunting as he goes. It is the Dead Cart, with the bodies of the poor, on their way to burial in the Sacred Field outside the walls, where they will be thrown into the pit that will be covered with a stone to-night, and sealed up for a year.

But whether, in this ride, you pass by obelisks, or columns: ancient temples, theatres, houses, porticoes, or forums: it is strange to see, how every fragment, whenever it is possible, has been blended into some modern structure, and made to serve some modern purpose—a wall, a dwelling-place, a granary, a stable—some use for which it never was designed, and associated with which it cannot otherwise than lamely assort. It is stranger still, to see how many ruins of the old mythology: how many fragments of obsolete legend and observance: have been incorporated into the worship of Christian altars here; and how, in numberless respects, the false faith and the true are fused into a monstrous union.

From one part of the city, looking out beyond the walls, a squat and stunted pyramid (the burial-place of Caius Cestius) makes an opaque triangle in the moonlight. But, to an English traveller, it serves to mark the grave of Shelley too, whose ashes lie beneath a little garden near it. Nearer still, almost within its shadow, lie the bones of Keats, "whose name is writ in water," that shines brightly in the landscape of a calm Italian night.

The Holy Week in Rome is supposed to offer great attractions to all visitors; but, saving for the sights of Easter Sunday, I would counsel those who go to Rome for its own interest, to avoid it at that time. The ceremonies, in general, are of the most tedious and wearisome kind; the heat and crowd at every one of them, painfully oppressive; the noise, hubbub, and confusion, quite distracting. We abandoned the pursuit of these shows, very early in the proceedings, and betook ourselves to the Ruins again. But, we plunged into the crowd for a share of the best of the sights; and what we saw, I will describe to you.

At the Sistine chapel, on the Wednesday, we saw very little, for by the time we reached it (though we were early) the besieging crowd had filled it to the door, and overflowed into the adjoining hall, where they were struggling, and squeezing, and mutually expostulating, and making great rushes every time a lady was brought out faint as if at least fifty people could be accommodated in her vacant standing-room. Hanging in the doorway of the chapel, was a heavy curtain, and this curtain, some twenty people nearest to it, in their anxiety to hear the chaunting of the Miserere, were continually plucking at, in opposition to each other, that it might not fall down and stifle the sound of the voices. The consequence was, that it occasioned the most extraordinary confusion, and seemed to wind itself about the unwary, like a Serpent. Now, a lady was wrapped up in it, and couldn't be unwound. Now, the voice of a stifling gentleman was heard inside it, beseeching to be let out. Now, two muffled arms, no man could say of which sex, struggled in it as in a sack. Now, it was carried by a rush, bodily overhead into the chapel, like an awning. Now, it came out the other way, and blinded one of the Pope's Swiss Guard, who had arrived, that moment, to set things to rights.

Being seated at a little distance, among two or three of the Pope's gentlemen, who were very weary and counting the minutes—as perhaps his Holiness was too—we had better opportunities of observing this eccentric entertainment, than of hearing the Miserere. Sometimes, there was a swell of mournful voices that sounded very pathetic and sad, and died away, into a low strain again; but that was all we heard.

At another time, there was the Exhibition of Relics in St. Peter's, which took place at between six and seven o'clock in the evening, and was striking from the cathedral being dark and gloomy, and having a great many people in it. The place into which the relics were brought, one by one, by a party of three priests, was a high balcony near the chief altar. This was the only lighted part of the church. There are always a hundred and twelve lamps burning near the altar, and there were two tall tapers, besides, near the black statue of St. Peter; but these were nothing in such an immense edifice. The gloom, and the general upturning of faces to the balcony, and the prostration of true believers on the pavement, as shining objects, like pictures or looking-glasses, were brought out and shown, had something effective in it, despite the very preposterous manner in which they were held up for the general edification, and the great elevation at which they were displayed; which one would think rather calculated to diminish the comfort derivable from a full conviction of their being genuine.

On the Thursday, we went to see the Pope convey the Sacrament from the Sistine chapel, to deposit it in the Capella Paolina, another chapel in the Vatican;—a ceremony emblematical of the entombment of the Saviour before His Resurrection. We waited in a great gallery with a great crowd of people (three-fourths of them English) for an hour or so, while they were chaunting the Miserere, in the Sistine chapel again. Both chapels opened out of the gallery; and the general attention was concentrated on the occasional opening and shutting of the door of the one for which the Pope was ultimately bound. None of these openings disclosed anything more tremendous than a man on a ladder, lighting a great quantity of candles; but at each and every opening, there was a terrific rush made at this ladder and this man, something like (I should think) a charge of the heavy British cavalry at Waterloo. The man was never brought down, however, nor the ladder; for it performed the strangest antics in the world among the crowd—where it was carried by the man, when the candles were all lighted; and finally it was stuck up against the gallery wall, in a very disorderly manner, just before the opening of the other chapel, and the commencement of a new chaunt, announced the approach of his Holiness. At this crisis, the soldiers of the guard, who had been poking the crowd into all sorts of shapes, formed down the gallery: and the procession came up, between the two lines they made.

There were a few choristers, and then a great many priests, walking two and two, and carrying—the good-looking priests at least—their lighted tapers, so as to throw the light with a good effect upon their faces: for the room was darkened. Those who were not handsome, or who had not long beards, carried *their* tapers anyhow, and abandoned themselves to spiritual contemplation. Meanwhile, the chaunting was very monotonous and dreary. The procession passed on, slowly, into the chapel, and the drone of voices went on, and came on, with it, until the Pope himself appeared, walking under a white satin canopy, and bearing the covered Sacrament in both hands; cardinals and canons clustered round him, making a brilliant show. The soldiers of the guard knelt down as he passed; all the bystanders bowed; and so he passed on into the chapel: the white satin canopy being removed from over him at the door, and a white satin parasol hoisted over his poor old head, in place of it. A few more couples brought up the rear, and passed into the chapel also. Then, the chapel door was shut; and it was all over; and everybody hurried off headlong, as for life or death, to see something else, and say it wasn't worth the trouble.

I think the most popular and most crowded sight (excepting those of Easter Sunday and Monday, which are open to all classes of people) was the Pope washing the feet of Thirteen men, representing the twelve apostles, and Judas Iscariot. The place in which this pious office is performed, is one of the chapels of St. Peter's, which is gaily decorated for the occasion; the thirteen sitting, "all of a row," on a very high bench, and looking particularly uncomfortable, with the eyes of Heaven knows how many English, French, Americans, Swiss, Germans, Russians, Swedes, Norwegians, and other foreigners, nailed to their faces all the time. They are robed in white; and on their heads they wear a stiff white cap, like a large English porter-pot, without a handle. Each carries in his hand, a nosegay, of the size of a fine cauliflower; and two of them, on this occasion, wore spectacles; which, remembering the characters they sustained, I thought a droll appendage to the costume. There was a great eye to character. St. John was represented by a good-looking young man. St. Peter, by a grave-looking old gentleman, with a flowing brown beard; and Judas Iscariot by such an enormous hypocrite (I could not make out, though, whether the expression of his face was real or assumed) that if he had acted the part to the death and had gone away and hanged himself, he would have left nothing to be desired.

As the two large boxes, appropriated to ladies at this sight, were full to the throat, and getting near was hopeless, we posted off, along with a great crowd, to be in time at the Table, where the Pope, in person, waits on these Thirteen; and after a prodigious struggle at the Vatican staircase, and several personal conflicts with the Swiss guard, the whole crowd swept into the room. It was a long gallery hung with drapery of white and red, with another great box for ladies (who are obliged to dress in black at these ceremonies, and to wear black veils), a royal box for the King of Naples and his party; and the table itself, which, set out like a ball supper, and ornamented with golden figures of the real apostles, was arranged on an elevated platform on one side of the gallery. The counterfeit apostles' knives and forks were laid out on that side of the table which was nearest to the wall, so that they might be stared at again, without let or hindrance.

The body of the room was full of male strangers; the crowd immense; the heat very great; and the pressure sometimes frightful. It was at its height, when the stream came pouring in, from the feet-washing; and then there were such shrieks and outcries, that a party of Piedmontese dragoons went to the rescue of the Swiss guard, and helped them to calm the tumult.

The ladies were particularly ferocious, in their struggles for places.

One lady of my acquaintance was seized round the waist, in the ladies' box, by a strong matron, and hoisted out of her place; and there was another lady (in a back row in the same box) who improved her position by sticking a large pin into the ladies before her.

The gentlemen about me were remarkably anxious to see what was on the table; and one Englishman seemed to have embarked the whole energy of his nature in the determination to discover whether there was any mustard. "By Jupiter there's vinegar!" I heard him say to his friend, after he had stood on tiptoe an immense time, and had been crushed and beaten on all sides. "And there's oil! I saw them distinctly, in cruets! Can any gentleman, in front there, see mustard on the table? Sir, will you oblige me! *Do* you see a Mustard-Pot?"

The apostles and Judas appearing on the platform, after much expectation, were marshalled, in line, in front of the table, with Peter at the top; and a good long stare was taken at them by the company, while twelve of them took a long smell at their nosegays, and Judas—moving his lips very obstrusively—engaged in inward prayer. Then, the Pope, clad in a scarlet robe, and wearing on his head a skull-cap of white satin, appeared in the midst of a crowd of cardinals and other dignitaries, and took in his hand a little golden ewer, from which he poured a little water over one of Peter's hands, while one attendant held a golden basin; a second, a fine cloth; a third, Peter's nosegay, which was taken from him during the operation. This his Holiness performed, with considerable expedition, on every man in the line (Judas, I observed, to be particularly overcome by his condescension); and then the whole Thirteen sat down to dinner. Grace said by the Pope. Peter in the chair.

There was white wine, and red wine: and the dinner looked very good. The courses appeared in portions, one for each apostle: and these being presented to the Pope, by Cardinals upon their knees, were by him handed to the Thirteen. The manner in which Judas grew more white-livered over his victuals, and languished, with his head on one side, as if he had no appetite, defies all description. Peter was a good, sound, old man, and went on, as the saying is, "to win;" eating everything that was given him (he got the best: being first in the row) and saying nothing to anybody. The dishes appeared to be chiefly composed of fish and vegetables. The Pope helped the Thirteen to wine also; and, during the whole dinner, somebody read something aloud, out of a large book—the Bible, I presume—which nobody could hear, and to which nobody paid the least attention. The Cardinals, and other attendants, smiled to each other, from time to time, as if the thing were a great farce; and if they thought so, there is little doubt they were perfectly right. His Holiness did what he had to do, as a sensible man gets through a troublesome ceremony, and seemed very glad when it was all over.

The Pilgrims' Supper: where lords and ladies waited on the Pilgrims, in token of humility, and dried their feet when they had been well washed by deputy: were very attractive. But, of all the many spectacles of dangerous reliance on outward observances, in themselves mere empty forms, none struck me half so much as the Scala Santa, or Holy Staircase, which I saw several times, but to the greatest advantage, or disadvantage, on Good Friday.

This holy staircase is composed of eight-and-twenty steps, said to have belonged to Pontius Pilate's house, and to be the identical stairs on which Our Saviour trod, in coming down from the judgment-seat. Pilgrims ascend it, only on their knees. It is steep; and, at the summit, is a chapel, reported to be full of relics; into which they peep through some iron bars, and then come down again, by one of two side staircases, which are not sacred, and may be walked on.

On Good Friday, there were, on a moderate computation, a hundred people, slowly shuffling up these stairs, on their knees, at one time; while others, who were going up, or had come down—and a few who had done both, and were going up again for the second time —stood loitering in the porch below, where an old gentleman in a sort of watch-box, rattled a tin canister, with a slit in the top, incessantly, to remind them that he took the money. The majority were country-people, male and female. There were four or five Jesuit priests, however, and some half-dozen well-dressed women. A whole school of boys, twenty at least, were about half-way up— evidently enjoying it very much. They were all wedged together, pretty closely; but the rest of the company gave the boys as wide a berth as possible, in consequence of their betraying some recklessness in the management of their boots.

I never in my life, saw anything at once so ridiculous, and so unpleasant, as this sight—ridiculous in the absurd incidents insepar-able from it; and unpleasant in its senseless and unmeaning degra-dation. There are two steps to begin with, and then a rather broad landing. The more rigid climbers went along this landing on their knees, as well as up the stairs; and the figures they cut, in their shuffling progress over the level surface, no description can paint. Then, to see them watch their opportunity from the porch, and cut in where there was a place next the wall! And to see one man with an umbrella (brought on purpose, for it was a fine day) hoisting himself unlawfully, from stair to stair! And to observe a demure lady of fifty-five or so, looking back, every now and then, to assure herself that her legs were properly disposed!

There were such odd differences in the speed of different people, too. Some got on as if they were doing a match against time; others stopped to say a prayer on every step. This man touched every stair with his forehead, and kissed it; that man scratched his head all the way. The boys got on brilliantly, and were up and down again before the old lady had accomplished her half-dozen stairs. But most of the penitents came down, very sprightly and fresh, as having done a real good substantial deed which it would take a good deal of sin to counterbalance; and the old gentleman in the watch-box was down upon them with his canister while they were in this humour, I promise you.

As if such a progress were not in its nature inevitably droll enough,

265*

there lay, on the top of the stairs, a wooden figure on a crucifix, resting on a sort of great iron saucer: so rickety and unsteady, that whenever an enthusiastic person kissed the figure, with more than usual devotion, or threw a coin into the saucer, with more than common readiness (for it served in this respect as a second or supplementary canister), it gave a great leap and rattle, and nearly shook the attendant lamp out: horribly frightening the people further down, and throwing the guilty party into unspeakable embarrassment.

On Easter Sunday, as well as on the preceding Thursday, the Pope bestows his benedicton on the people, from the balcony in front of St. Peter's. This Easter Sunday was a day so bright and blue: so cloudless, balmy, wonderfully bright: that all the previous bad weather vanished from the recollection in a moment. I had seen the Thursday's Benediction dropping damply on some hundreds of umbrellas, but there was not a sparkle then, in all the hundred fountains of Rome—such fountains as they are!—and on this Sunday morning they were running diamonds. The miles of miserable streets through which we drove (compelled to a certain course by the Pope's dragoons: the Roman police on such occasions) were so full of colour, that nothing in them was capable of wearing a faded aspect. The common people came out in their gayest dresses; the richer people in their smartest vehicles; Cardinals rattled to the church of the Poor Fishermen in their state carriages; shabby magnificence flaunted its thread-bare liveries and tarnished cocked hats, in the sun; and every coach in Rome was put in requisition for the Great Piazza of St. Peter's.

One hundred and fifty thousand people were there at least! Yet there was ample room. How many carriages were there, I don't know; yet there was room for them too, and to spare. The great steps of the church were densely crowded. There were many of the Contadini, from Albano (who delight in red), in that part of the square, and the mingling of bright colours in the crowd was beautiful. Below the steps the troops were ranged. In the magnificent proportions of the place they looked like a bed of flowers. Sulky Romans, lively peasants from the neighbouring country, groups of pilgrims from distant parts of Italy, sight-seeing foreigners of all nations, made a murmur in the clear air, like so many insects; and high above them all, plashing and bubbling, and making rainbow colours in the light, the two delicious fountains welled and tumbled bountifully.

A kind of bright carpet was hung over the front of the balcony; and the sides of the great window were bedecked with crimson drapery. An awning was stretched, too, over the top, to screen the old man from the hot rays of the sun. As noon approached, all eyes were turned up to this window. In due time, the chair was seen approaching to the front, with the gigantic fans of peacock's feathers, close behind. The doll within it (for the balcony is very high) then rose up, and stretched out its tiny arms, while all the male spectators in the square uncovered, and some, but not by any means the greater part, kneeled down. The guns upon the ramparts of the Castle of St. Angelo proclaimed, next moment, that the benediction was given; drums beat; trumpets sounded; arms clashed; and the great mass below, suddenly breaking into smaller heaps, and scattering here and there in rills, was stirred like parti-coloured sand.

What a bright noon it was, as we rode away! The Tiber was no longer yellow, but blue. There was a blush on the old bridges, that made them fresh and hale again. The Pantheon, with its majestic front, all seamed and furrowed like an old face, had summer light upon its battered walls. Every squalid and desolate hut in the Eternal City (bear witness every grim old palace, to the filth and misery of the plebeian neighbour that elbows it, as certain as Time has laid its grip on its patrician head!) was fresh and new with some ray of the sun. The very prison in the crowded street, a whirl of carriages and people, had some stray sense of the day, dropping through its chinks and crevices: and dismal prisoners who could not wind their faces round the barricading of the clocked-up windows, stretched out their hands, and clinging to the rusty bars, turned *them* towards the overflowing street: as if it were a cheerful fire, and could be shared in, that way.

But, when the night came on, without a cloud to dim the full moon, what a sight it was to see the Great Square full once more, and the whole church, from the cross to the ground, lighted with innumerable lanterns, tracing out the architecture, and winking and shining all round the colonnade of the piazza! And what a sense of exultation, joy, delight, it was, when the great bell struck half-past seven—on the instant—to behold one bright red mass of fire soar gallantly from the top of the cupola to the extremest summit of the cross, and the moment it leaped into its place, become the signal of a bursting out of countless lights, as great, and red, and blazing as itself, from every part of the gigantic church; so that every cornice, capital, and smallest ornament of stone, expressed itself in fire: and the black, solid groundwork of the enormous dome seemed to grow transparent as an eggshell!

A train of gunpowder, an electric chain—nothing could be fired, more suddenly and swiftly, than this second illumination; and when we had got away, and gone upon a distant height, and looked towards it two hours afterwards, there it still stood, shining and glittering in the calm night like a jewel! Not a line of its proportions wanting; not an angle blunted; not an atom of its radiance lost.

The next night—Easter Monday—there was a great display of fireworks from the Castle of St. Angelo. We hired a room in an opposite house, and made our way, to our places, in good time, through a dense mob of people choking up the square in front, and all the avenues leading to it; and so loading the bridge by which the castle is approached, that it seemed ready to sink into the rapid Tiber below. There are statues on this bridge (execrable works), and, among them, great vessels full of burning tow were placed: glaring strangely on the faces of the crowd, and not less strangely on the stone counterfeits above them.

The show began with a tremendous discharge of cannon; and then, for twenty minutes or half an hour, the whole castle was one incessant sheet of fire, and labyrinth of blazing wheels of every colour, size, and speed: while rockets streamed into the sky, not by ones or twos, or scores, but hundreds at a time. The concluding burst—the Girandola—was like the blowing up into the air of the whole massive castle, without smoke or dust.

In half an hour afterwards, the immense concourse had dispersed; the moon was looking calmly down upon her wrinkled image in the river; and half-a-dozen men and boys with bits of lighted candle in their hands: moving here and there, in search of anything worth having, that might have been dropped in the press: had the whole scene to themselves.

By way of contrast we rode out into old ruined Rome, after all this firing and booming, to take our leave of the Coliseum. I had seen it by moonlight before (I could never get through a day without going back to it), but its tremendous solitude that night is past all telling. The ghostly pillars in the Forum; the Triumphal Arches of Old Emperors; those enormous masses of ruins which were once their palaces; the grass-grown mounds that mark the graves of ruined temples; the stones of the Via Sacra, smooth with the tread of feet in ancient Rome; even these were dimmed, in their transcendent melancholy, by the dark ghost of its bloody holidays, erect and grim; haunting the old scene; despoiled by pillaging Popes and fighting Princes, but not laid; wringing wild hands of weed and grass, and bramble; and lamenting to the night in every gap and broken arch— the shadow of its awful self, immovable!

As we lay down on the grass of the Campagna, next day, on our way to Florence, hearing the larks sing, we saw that a little wooden cross had been erected on the spot where the poor Pilgrim Countess was murdered. So, we piled some loose stones about it, as the beginning of a mound to her memory, and wondered if we should ever rest there again, and look back at Rome.

A RAPID DIORAMA

WE are bound for Naples! And we cross the threshold of the Eternal City at yonder gate, the Gate of San Giovanni Laterano, where the two last objects that attract the notice of a departing visitor, and the two first objects that attract the notice of an arriving one, are a proud church and a decaying ruin—good emblems of Rome.

Our way lies over the Campagna, which looks more solemn on a bright blue day like this, than beneath a darker sky; the great extent of ruin being plainer to the eye: and the sunshine through the arches of the broken aqueducts, showing other broken arches shining through them in the melancholy distance. When we have traversed it, and look back from Albano, its dark, undulating surface lies below us like a stagnant lake, or like a broad, dull Lethe flowing round the walls of Rome, and separating it from all the world! How often have the Legions, in triumphant march, gone glittering across that purple waste, so silent and unpeopled now! How often has the train of captives looked with sinking hearts, upon the distant city, and beheld its population pouring out, to hail the return of their conqueror! What riot, sensuality and murder, have run mad in the vast palaces now heaps of brick and shattered marble! What glare of fires, and roar of popular tumult, and wail of pestilence and famine, have come sweeping over the wild plain where nothing is now heard but the wind, and where the solitary lizards gambol unmolested in the sun!

The train of wine-carts going into Rome, each driven by a shaggy peasant reclining beneath a little gipsy-fashioned canopy of sheepskin, is ended now, and we go toiling up into a higher country where there are trees. The next day brings us on the Pontine Marshes, wearily flat and lonesome, and overgrown with brushwood, and swamped with water, but with a fine road made across them, shaded by a long, long avenue. Here and there, we pass a solitary guardhouse; here and there a hovel, deserted, and walled up. Some herdsmen loiter on the banks of the stream beside the road, and sometimes a flat-bottomed boat towed by a man, comes rippling idly along it. A horseman passes occasionally, carrying a long gun cross-wise on the saddle before him, and attended by fierce dogs; but there is nothing else astir save the wind and the shadows, until we come in sight of Terracina.

How blue and bright the sea, rolling below the windows of the inn so famous in robber stories! How picturesque the great crags and points of rock overhanging to-morrow's narrow road, where galley-slaves are working in the quarries above, and the sentinels who guard them lounge on the sea-shore! All night there is the murmur of the sea beneath the stars; and, in the morning, just at daybreak, the prospect suddenly becoming expanded, as if by a miracle, reveals —in the far distance, across the sea there!—Naples with its islands, and Vesuvius spouting fire! Within a quarter of an hour, the whole is gone as if it were a vision in the clouds and there is nothing but the sea and sky.

The Neapolitan frontier crossed, after two hours' travelling; and the hungriest of soldiers and customs-house officers with difficulty appeased; we enter, by a gateless portal, into the first Neapolitan town—Fondi. Take note of Fondi, in the name of all that is wretched and beggarly.

A filthy channel of mud and refuse meanders down the centre of the miserable streets, fed by obscene rivulets that trickle from the abject houses. There is not a door, a window, or a shutter; not a roof, a wall, a post, or a pillar, in all Fondi, but is decayed, and crazy, and rotting away. The wretched history of the town, with all its sieges and pillages by Barbarossa and the rest, might have been acted last year. How the gaunt dogs that sneak about the miserable streets, come to be alive, and undevoured by the people, is one of the enigmas of the world.

A hollow-cheeked and scowling people they are! All beggars; but that's nothing. Look at them as they gather round. Some, are too indolent to come down-stairs, or are too wisely mistrustful of the stairs, perhaps, to venture: so stretch out their lean hands from upper windows, and howl; others, come flocking about us, fighting and jostling one another, and demanding incessantly, charity for the love of God, charity for the love of the Blessed Virgin, charity for the love of all the Saints. A group of miserable children, almost naked, screaming forth the same petition, discover that they can see themselves reflected in the varnish of the carriage, and begin to dance and make grimaces, that they may have the pleasure of seeing their antics repeated in this mirror. A crippled idiot, in the act of striking one of them who drowns his clamorous demand for charity, observes his angry counterpart in the panel, stops short, and thrusting out his tongue, begins to wag his head and chatter. The shrill cry raised at this, awakens half-a-dozen wild creatures wrapped in frowsy brown cloaks, who are lying on the church-steps with pots and pans for sale. These, scrambling up, approach, and beg defiantly. "I am hungry. Give me something. Listen to me, Signor. I am hungry!" Then, a ghastly old woman, fearful of being too late, comes hobbling down the street, stretching out one hand, and scratching herself all the way with the other, and screaming, long before she can be heard, "Charity, charity! I'll go and pray for you directly, beautiful lady, if you'll give me charity!" Lastly, the members of a brotherhood for burying the dead: hideously masked, and attired in shabby black robes, white at the skirts, with the splashes of many muddy winters: escorted by a dirty priest, and a congenial cross-bearer: come hurrying past. Surrounded by this motley concourse, we move out of Fondi: bad bright eyes glaring at us, out of the darkness of every crazy tenement, like glistening fragments of its filth and putrefaction.

A noble mountain-pass, with the ruins of a fort on a strong eminence, traditionally called the Fort of Fra Diavolo; the old town of Itrí, like a device in pastry, built up, almost perpendicularly, on a hill, and approached by long steep flights of steps; beautiful Mola di Gaëta, whose wines, like those of Albano, have degenerated since the days of Horace, or his taste for wine was bad: which is not likely of one who enjoyed it so much, and extolled it so well; another night upon the road at St. Agatha; a rest next day at Capua, which is picturesque, but hardly so seductive to a traveller now, as the soldiers of Prætorian Rome were wont to find the ancient city of that name; a flat road among vines festooned and looped from tree to tree; and Mount Vesuvius close at hand at last!—its cone and summit whitened with snow; and its smoke hanging over it, in the heavy atmosphere of the day, like a dense cloud. So we go, rattling down hill, into Naples.

A funeral is coming up the street, towards us. The body, on an open bier, borne on a kind of palanquin, covered with a gay cloth of crimson and gold. The mourners, in white gowns and masks. If there be death abroad, life is well represented too, for all Naples would seem to be out of doors, and tearing to and fro in carriages. Some of these, the common Vetturíno vehicles, are drawn by three horses abreast, decked with smart trappings and great abundance of brazen ornament, and always going very fast. Not that their loads are light; for the smallest of them has at least six people inside, four in front, four or five more hanging on behind, and two or three more, in a net or bag below the axle-tree, where they lie half-suffocated with mud and dust. Exhibitors of Punch, buffo singers with guitars, reciters of poetry, reciters of stories, a row of cheap exhibitions with clowns and showmen, drums, and trumpets, painted cloths representing the wonders within, and admiring crowds assembled without, assist the whirl and bustle. Ragged lazzaroni lie asleep in doorways, archways, and kennels; the gentry, gaily dressed, are dashing up and down in carriages on the Chiaja, or walking in the Public Gardens; and quiet letter-writers, perched behind their little desks and inkstands under the Portico of the Great Theatre of San Carlo, in the public street, are waiting for clients.

Here is a galley-slave in chains, who wants a letter written to a friend. He approaches a clerkly-looking man, sitting under the corner arch, and makes his bargain. He has obtained permission of the sentinel who guards him: who stands near, leaning against the wall and cracking nuts. The galley-slave dictates in the ear of the letter-writer, what he desires to say; and as he can't read writing, looks intently in his face, to read there whether he sets down faithfully what he is told. After a time, the galley-slave becomes discursive—incoherent. The secretary pauses and rubs his chin. The galley-slave is voluble and energetic. The secretary, at length, catches the idea, and with the air of a man who knows how to word it, sets it down; stopping, now and then, to glance back at his text admiringly. The galley-slave is silent. The soldier stoically cracks his nuts. Is there anything more to say? inquires the letter-writer. No more. Then listen, friend of mine. He reads it through. The galley-slave is quite enchanted. It is folded, and addressed, and given to him, and he pays the fee. The secretary falls back indolently in his chair, and takes a book. The galley-slave gathers up an empty sack. The sentinel throws away a handful of nut-shells, shoulders his musket, and away they go together.

Why do the beggars rap their chins constantly, with their right hands, when you look at them? Everything is done in pantomine in Naples, and that is the conventional sign for hunger. A man who is quarrelling with another, yonder, lays the palm of his right hand on the back of his left, and shakes the two thumbs—expressive of a donkey's ears—whereat his adversary is goaded to desperation. Two people bargaining for fish, the buyer empties an imaginary waistcoat pocket when he is told the price, and walks away without a word: having thoroughly conveyed to the seller that he considers it too dear. Two people in carriages, meeting, one touches his lips, twice or thrice, holding up the five fingers of his right hand, and gives a horizontal cut in the air with the palm. The other nods briskly, and goes his way. He has been invited to a friendly dinner at half-past five o'clock, and will certainly come.

All over Italy, a peculiar shake of the right hand from the wrist, with the forefinger stretched out, expresses a negative—the only negative beggars will ever understand. But, in Naples, those five fingers are a copious language.

All this, and every other kind of out-door life and stir, and mac-caroni-eating at sunset, and flower-selling all day long, and begging and stealing everywhere and at all hours, you see upon the bright sea-shore, where the waves of the bay sparkle merrily. But, lovers and hunters of the picturesque, let us not keep too studiously out of view the miserable depravity, degradation, and wretchedness, with which this gay Neapolitan life is inseparably associated! It is not well to find Saint Giles's so repulsive, and the Porta Capuana so attractive. A pair of naked legs and a ragged red scarf, do not make *all* the difference between what is interesting and what is coarse and odious? Painting and poetising for ever, if you will, the beauties of this most beautiful and lovely spot of earth, let us, as our duty, try to associate a new picturesque with some faint recognition of man's destiny and capabilities; more hopeful, I believe, among the ice and snow of the North Pole, than in the sun and bloom of Naples.

Capri—once made odious by the deified beast Tiberius—Ischia, Procida, and the thousand distant beauties of the Bay, lie in the blue sea yonder, changing in the mist and sunshine twenty times a-day: now close at hand, now far off, now unseen. The fairest country in the world, is spread about us. Whether we turn towards the Miseno shore of the splendid watery amphitheatre, and go by the Grotto of Posilipo to the Grotto del Cane and away to Baiæ: or take the other way, towards Vesuvius and Sorrento, it is one succession of delights. In the last-named direction, where, over doors and archways, there are countless little images of San Gennaro, with his Canute's hand stretched out, to check the fury of the Burning Mountain, we are carried pleasantly, by a railroad on the beautiful Sea Beach, past the town of Torre del Greco, built upon the ashes of the former town destroyed by an eruption of Vesuvius, within a hundred years; and past the flat-roofed houses, granaries, and maccaroni manufactories; to Castel-a-Mare, with its ruined castle, now inhabited by fishermen, standing in the sea upon a heap of rocks. Here, the railroad termin-ates; but, hence we may ride on, by an unbroken succession of enchanting bays, and beautiful scenery, sloping from the highest summit of Saint Angelo, the highest neighbouring mountain, down to the water's edge—among vineyards, olive-trees, gardens of oranges and lemons, orchards, heaped-up rocks, green gorges in the hills—and by the bases of snow-covered heights, and through small towns with handsome, dark-haired women at the doors—and pass delicious summer villas—to Sorrento, where the Poet Tasso drew his inspiration from the beauty surrounding him. Returning, we may climb the heights above Castel-a-Mare, and looking down among the boughs and leaves, see the crisp water glistening in the sun; and

clusters of white houses in distant Naples, dwindling, in the great
extent of prospect, down to dice. The coming back to the city, by the
beach again, at sunset: with the glowing sea on one side, and the
darkening mountain, with its smoke and flame, upon the other: is a
sublime conclusion to the glory of the day.

That church by the Porta Capuana—near the old fisher-market in
the dirtiest quarter of dirty Naples, where the revolt of Masaniello
began—is memorable for having been the scene of one of his earliest
proclamations to the people, and is particularly remarkable for
nothing else, unless it be its waxen and bejewelled Saint in a glass
case, with two odd hands; or the enormous number of beggars who
are constantly rapping their chins there, like a battery of castanets.
The cathedral with the beautiful door, and the columns of African
and Egyptian granite that once ornamented the temple of Apollo,
contains the famous sacred blood of San Gennaro or Januarius: which
is preserved in two phials in a silver tabernacle, and miraculously
liquefies three times a-year, to the great admiration of the people.
At the same moment, the stone (distant some miles) where the Saint
suffered martyrdom, becomes faintly red. It is said that the officiating
priests turn faintly red also, sometimes, when these miracles occur.

The old, old men who live in hovels at the entrance of these
ancient catacombs, and who, in their age and infirmity, seem waiting
here, to be buried themselves, are members of a curious body, called
the Royal Hospital, who are the official attendants at funerals. Two
of these old spectres totter away, with lighted tapers, to show the
caverns of death—as unconcerned as if they were immortal. They
were used as burying-places for three hundred years; and, in one
part, is a large pit full of skulls and bones, said to be the sad remains
of a great mortality occasioned by a plague. In the rest there is
nothing but dust. They consist, chiefly, of great wide corridors and
labyrinths, hewn out of the rock. At the end of some of these long
passages, are unexpected glimpses of the daylight, shining down
from above. It looks as ghastly and as strange: among the torches,
and the dust, and the dark vaults: as if it, too, were dead and buried.

The present burial-place lies out yonder, on a hill between the city
and Vesuvius. The old Campo Santo with its three hundred and
sixty-five pits, is only used for those who die in hospitals, and prisons,
and are unclaimed by their friends. The graceful new cemetery, at no
great distance from it, though yet unfinished, has already many
graves among its shrubs and flowers, and airy colonnades. It might
be reasonably objected elsewhere, that some of the tombs are mere-
tricious and too fanciful; but the general brightness seems to justify
it here; and Mount Vesuvius, separated from them by a lovely slope
of ground, exalts and saddens the scene.

If it be solemn to behold from this new City of the Dead, with its
dark smoke hanging in the clear sky, how much more awful and
impressive is it, viewed from the ghostly ruins of Herculaneum and
Pompeii!

Stand at the bottom of the great market-place of Pompeii, and

look up the silent streets, through the ruined temples of Jupiter and
Isis, over the broken houses with their inmost sanctuaries open to the
day, away to Mount Vesuvius, bright and snowy in the peaceful
distance; and lose all count of time, and heed of other things, in the
strange and melancholy sensation of seeing the Destroyed and the
Destroyer making this quiet picture in the sun. Then, ramble on, and
see, at every turn, the little familiar tokens of human habitation and
every-day pursuits; the chafing of the bucket-rope in the stone rim
of the exhausted well; the track of carriage-wheels in the pavement
of the street; the marks of drinking-vessels on the stone counter of
the wine-shop; the amphoræ in private cellars, stored away so many
hundred years ago, and undisturbed to this hour—all rendering the
solitude and deadly lonesomeness of the place, ten thousand times
more solemn, than if the volcano, in its fury, had swept the city from
the earth, and sunk it in the bottom of the sea.

After it was shaken by the earthquake which preceded the eruption, workmen were employed in shaping out, in stone, new ornaments for temples and other buildings that had suffered. Here lies
their work, outside the city gate, as if they would return to-morrow.

In the cellar of Diomede's house, where certain skeletons were
found huddled together, close to the door, the impression of their
bodies on the ashes, hardened with the ashes, and became stamped
and fixed there, after they had shrunk, inside, to scanty bones. So,
in the theatre of Herculaneum, a comic mask, floating on the stream
when it was hot and liquid, stamped its mimic features in it as it
hardened into stone; and now, it turns upon the stranger the fantastic
look it turned upon the audiences in that same theatre two thousand
years ago.

Next to the wonder of going up and down the streets, and in and
out of the houses, and traversing the secret chambers of the temples
of a religion that has vanished from the earth, and finding so many
fresh traces of remote antiquity: as if the course of Time had been
stopped after this desolation, and there had been no nights and days,
months, years, and centuries, since: nothing is more impressive and
terrible than the many evidences of the searching nature of the ashes,
as bespeaking their irresistible power, and the impossibility of es-
caping them. In the wine-cellars, they forced their way into the
earthen vessels: displacing the wine and choking them, to the brim,
with dust. In the tombs, they forced the ashes of the dead from the
funeral urns, and rained new ruin even into them. The mouths, and
eyes, and skulls of all the skeletons, were stuffed with this terrible
hail. In Herculaneum, where the flood was of a different and a heavier
kind, it rolled in, like a sea. Imagine a deluge of water turned to
marble, at its height—and that is what is called "the lava" here.

Some workmen were digging the gloomy well on the brink of which
we now stand, looking down, when they came on some of the stone
benches of the theatre—those steps (for such they seem) at the
bottom of the excavation—and found the buried city of Herculaneum. Presently going down, with lighted torches, we are perplexed

by great walls of monstrous thickness, rising up between the benches, shutting out the stage, obtruding their shapeless forms in absurd places, confusing the whole plan, and making it a disordered dream. We cannot, at first, believe, or picture to ourselves, that THIS came rolling in, and drowned the city; and that all that is not here, has been cut away, by the axe, like solid stone. But this perceived and understood, the horror and oppression of its presence are indescribable.

Many of the paintings on the walls in the roofless chambers of both cities, or carefully removed to the museum at Naples, are as fresh and plain, as if they had been executed yesterday. Here are subjects of still life, as provisions, dead game, bottles, glasses, and the like; familiar classical stories, or mythological fables, always forcibly and plainly told; conceits of cupids, quarrelling, sporting, working at trades; theatrical rehearsals; poets reading their productions to their friends; inscriptions chalked upon the walls; political squibs, advertisements, rough drawings by schoolboys; everything to people and restore the ancient cities, in the fancy of their wondering visitor. Furniture, too, you see, of every kind—lamps, tables, couches; vessels for eating, drinking, and cooking; workmen's tools, surgical instruments, tickets for the theatre, pieces of money, personal ornaments, bunches of keys found clenched in the grasp of skeletons, helmets of guards and warriors; little household bells, yet musical with their old domestic tones.

The least among these objects, lends its aid to swell the interest of Vesuvius, and invest it with a perfect fascination. The looking, from either ruined city, into the neighbouring grounds overgrown with beautiful vines and luxuriant trees; and remembering that house upon house, temple on temple, building after building, and street after street, are still lying underneath the roots of all the quiet cultivation, waiting to be turned up to the light of day; is something so wonderful, so full of mystery, so captivating to the imagination, that one would think it would be paramount, and yield to nothing else. To nothing but Vesuvius; but the mountain is the genius of the scene. From every indication of the ruin it has worked, we look, again, with an absorbing interest to where its smoke is rising up into the sky. It is beyond us, as we thread the ruined streets: above us, as we stand upon the ruined walls; we follow it through every vista of broken columns, as we wander through the empty court-yards of the houses; and through the garlandings and interlacings of every wanton vine. Turning away to Pæstum yonder, to see the awful structures built, the least aged of them, hundreds of years before the birth of Christ, and standing yet, erect in lonely majesty, upon the wild, malaria-blighted plain—we watch Vesuvius as it disappears from the prospect, and watch for it again, on our return, with the same thrill of interest: as the doom and destiny of all this beautiful country, biding its terrible time.

It is very warm in the sun, on this early spring-day, when we return from Pæstum, but very cold in the shade: insomuch, that although we may lunch, pleasantly, at noon, in the open air, by the gate of Pompeii, the neighbouring rivulet supplies thick ice for our wine. But, the sun is shining brightly; there is not a cloud or speck of vapour in the whole blue sky, looking down upon the bay of Naples; and the moon will be at the full to-night. No matter that the snow and ice lie thick upon the summit of Vesuvius, or that we have been on foot all day at Pompeii, or that croakers maintain that strangers should not be on the mountain by night, in such an unusual season. Let us take advantage of the fine weather; make the best of our way to Resina, the little village at the foot of the mountain; prepare ourselves, as well as we can, on so short a notice, at the guide's house; ascend at once, and have sunset half-way up, moon-light at the top, and midnight to come down in!

At four o'clock in the afternoon, there is a terrible uproar in the little stable-yard of Signior Salvatore, the recognised head-guide, with the gold band round his cap; and thirty under-guides who are all scuffling and screaming at once, are preparing half-a-dozen saddled ponies, three litters, and some stout staves, for the journey. Every one of the thirty, quarrels with the other twenty-nine, and frightens the six ponies; and as much of the village as can possibly squeeze itself into the little stable-yard, participates in the tumult, and gets trodden on by the cattle.

After much violent skirmishing, and more noise than would suffice for the storming of Naples, the procession starts. The head-guide, who is liberally paid for all the attendants, rides a little in advance of the party; the other thirty guides proceed on foot. Eight go forward with the litters that are to be used by-and-by; and the remaining two-and-twenty beg.

We ascend, gradually, by stony lanes like rough broad flights of stairs, for some time. At length, we leave these, and the vineyards on either side of them, and emerge upon a bleak bare region where the lava lies confusedly, in enormous rusty masses: as if the earth had been ploughed up by burning thunderbolts. And now, we halt to see the sun set. The change that falls upon the dreary region, and on the whole mountain, as its red light fades, and the night comes on—and the unutterable solemnity and dreariness that reign around, who that has witnessed it, can ever forget!

It is dark, when after winding, for some time, over the broken ground, we arrive at the foot of the cone: which is extremely steep, and seems to rise, almost perpendicularly, from the spot where we dismount. The only light is reflected from the snow, deep, hard, and white, with which the cone is covered. It is now intensely cold, and the air is piercing. The thirty-one have brought no torches, knowing that the moon will rise before we reach the top. Two of the litters are devoted to the two ladies; the third, to a rather heavy gentleman from Naples, whose hospitality and good-nature have attached him to the expedition, and determined him to assist in doing the honours of the mountain. The rather heavy gentleman is carried by fifteen men; each of the ladies by half-a-dozen. We who walk, make the best use of our staves; and so the whole party begin to labour upward over the snow,—as if they were toiling to the summit of an antediluvian Twelfth-cake.

We are a long time toiling up; and the head-guide looks oddly about him when one of the company—not an Italian, though an habitué of the mountain for many years: whom we will call, for our present purpose, Mr. Pickle of Portici—suggests that, as it is freezing hard, and the usual footing of ashes is covered by the snow and ice, it will surely be difficult to descend. But the sight of the litters above, tilting up and down, and jerking from this side to that, as the bearers continually slip and tumble, diverts our attention; more especially as the whole length of the rather heavy gentleman is, at that moment, presented to us alarmingly foreshortened, with his head downwards.

The rising of the moon soon afterwards, revives the flagging spirits of the bearers. Stimulating each other with their usual watchword, "Courage, friend! It is to eat maccaroni!" they press on, gallantly, for the summit.

From tingeing the top of the snow above us, with a band of light, and pouring it in a stream through the valley below, while we have been ascending in the dark, the moon soon lights the whole white mountain-side, and the broad sea down below, and tiny Naples in the distance, and every village in the country round. The whole prospect is in this lovely state, when we come upon the platform on the mountain-top—the region of Fire—an exhausted crater formed of great masses of gigantic cinders, like blocks of stone from some tremendous waterfall, burnt up; from every chink and crevice of which, hot, sulphurous smoke is pouring out: while, from another conical-shaped hill, the present crater, rising abruptly from this platform at the end, great sheets of fire are streaming forth: reddening the night with flame, blackening it with smoke, and spotting it with red-hot stones and cinders, that fly up into the air like feathers, and fall down like lead. What words can paint the gloom and grandeur of this scene!

The broken ground; the smoke; the sense of suffocation from the sulphur; the fear of falling down through the crevices in the yawning ground; the stopping, every now and then, for somebody who is missing in the dark (for the dense smoke now obscures the moon); the intolerable noise of the thirty; and the hoarse roaring of the mountain; make it a scene of such confusion, at the same time, that we reel again. But, dragging the ladies through it, and across another exhausted crater to the foot of the present Volcano, we approach close to it on the windy side, and then sit down among the hot ashes at its foot, and look up in silence; faintly estimating the action that is going on within, from its being full a hundred feet higher, at this minute, than it was six weeks ago.

There is something in the fire and roar, that generates an irresistible desire to get nearer to it. We cannot rest long, without starting off, two of us, on our hands and knees, accompanied by the head-guide, to climb to the brim of the flaming crater, and try to look in. Meanwhile, the thirty yell, as with one voice, that it is a dangerous proceeding, and call to us to come back; frightening the rest of the party out of their wits.

What with their noise, and what with the trembling of the thin crust of ground, that seems about to open underneath our feet and plunge us in the burning gulf below (which is the real danger, if there be any); and what with the flashing of the fire in our faces, and the shower of red-hot ashes that is raining down, and the choking smoke and sulphur; we may well feel giddy and irrational, like drunken men. But, we contrive to climb up to the brim, and look down, for a moment, into the Hell of boiling fire below. Then, we all three come rolling down; blackened, and singed, and scorched, and hot, and giddy: and each with his dress alight in half-a-dozen places.

You have read, a thousand times, that the usual way of descending, is, by sliding down the ashes: which, forming a gradually-increasing ledge below the feet, prevent too rapid a descent. But, when we have crossed the two exhausted craters on our way back, and are come to this precipitous place, there is (as Mr. Pickle has foretold) no vestige of ashes to be seen; the whole being a smooth sheet of ice.

In this dilemma, ten or a dozen of the guides cautiously join hands, and make a chain of men; of whom the foremost beat, as well as they can, a rough track with their sticks, down which we prepare to follow. The way being fearfully steep, and none of the party: even of the thirty: being able to keep their feet for six paces together, the ladies are taken out of their litters, and placed, each between two careful persons; while others of the thirty hold by their skirts, to prevent their falling forward—a necessary precaution, tending to the immediate and hopeless dilapidation of their apparel. The rather heavy gentleman is abjured to leave his litter too, and be escorted in a similar manner; but he resolves to be brought down as he was brought up, on the principle that his fifteen bearers are not likely to tumble all at once, and that he is safer so, than trusting to his own legs.

In this order, we begin the descent: sometimes on foot, sometimes shuffling on the ice: always proceeding much more quietly and slowly, than on our upward way: and constantly alarmed by the falling among us of somebody from behind, who endangers the footing of the whole party, and clings pertinaciously to anybody's ankles. It is impossible for the litter to be in advance, too, as the track has to be made; and its appearance behind us, overhead—with some one or other of the bearers always down, and the rather heavy gentleman with his legs always in the air—is very threatening and frightful. We have gone on thus, a very little way, painfully and anxiously, but quite merrily, and regarding it as a great success—and have all fallen several times, and have all been stopped, somehow or other, as we were sliding away—when Mr. Pickle of Portici, in the act of remarking on these uncommon circumstances as quite beyond his experience, stumbles, falls, disengages himself, with quick presence of mind, from those about him, plunges away head foremost, and rolls, over and over, down the whole surface of the cone!

Sickening as it is to look, and be so powerless to help him, I see him there, in the moonlight—I have had such a dream often—skimming over the white ice, like a cannon-ball. Almost at the same moment, there is a cry from behind; and a man who has carried a light basket of spare cloaks on his head, comes rolling past, at the same frightful speed, closely followed by a boy. At this climax of the chapter of accidents, the remaining eight-and-twenty vociferate to that degree, that a pack of wolves would be music to them!

Giddy, and bloody, and a mere bundle of rags, is Pickle of Portici when we reach the place where we dismounted, and where the horses are waiting; but, thank God, sound in limb! And never are we likely to be more glad to see a man alive and on his feet, than to see him now—making light of it too, though sorely bruised and in great pain. The boy is brought into the Hermitage on the Mountain, while we are at supper, with his head tied up; and the man is heard of, some hours afterwards. He too is bruised and stunned, but has broken no bones; the snow having, fortunately, covered all the larger blocks of rock and stone, and rendered them harmless.

After a cheerful meal, and a good rest before a blazing fire, we again take horse, and continue our descent to Salvatore's house—very slowly, by reason of our bruised friend being hardly able to keep the saddle, or endure the pain of motion. Though it is so late at night, or early in the morning, all the people of the village are waiting about the little stable-yard when we arrive, and looking up the road by which we are expected. Our appearance is hailed with a great clamour of tongues, and a general sensation for which in our modesty we are somewhat at a loss to account, until, turning into the yard, we find that one of a party of French gentlemen who were on the mountain at the same time is lying on some straw in the stable, with a broken limb: looking like Death, and suffering great torture; and that we were confidently supposed to have encountered some worse accident.

So "well returned, and Heaven be praised!" as the cheerful Vetturíno, who has borne us company all the way from Pisa, says, with all his heart! And away with his ready horses, into sleeping Naples!

It wakes again to Policinelli and pickpockets, buffo singers and beggars, rags, puppets, flowers, brightness, dirt, and universal degradation; airing its Harlequin suit in the sunshine, next day and every day; singing, starving, dancing, gaming, on the sea-shore; and leaving all labour to the burning mountain, which is ever at its work.

Our English dilettanti would be very pathetic on the subject of the national taste, if they could hear an Italian opera half as badly sung in England as we may hear the Foscari performed, to-night, in the splendid theatre of San Carlo. But, for astonishing truth and spirit in seizing and embodying the real life about it, the shabby little San Carlino Theatre—the rickety house one story high, with a staring picture outside: down among the drums and trumpets, and the tumblers, and the lady conjurer—is without a rival anywhere.

There is one extraordinary feature in the real life of Naples, at which we may take a glance before we go—the Lotteries.

They prevail in most parts of Italy, but are particularly obvious, in their effects and influences, here. They are drawn every Saturday. They bring an immense revenue to the Government; and diffuse a taste for gambling among the poorest of the poor, which is very comfortable to the coffers of the State, and very ruinous to themselves. The lowest stake is one grain; less than a farthing. One hundred numbers—from one to a hundred, inclusive—are put into a box. Five are drawn. Those are the prizes. I buy three numbers. If one of them come up, I win a small prize. If two, some hundreds of times my stake. If three, three thousand five hundred times my stake. I stake (or play as they call it) what I can upon my numbers, and buy what numbers I please. The amount I play, I pay at the lottery office, where I purchase the ticket; and it is stated on the ticket itself.

Every lottery office keeps a printed book, an Universal Lottery Diviner, where every possible accident and circumstance is provided for, and has a number against it. For instance, let us take two carlini —about sevenpence. On our way to the lottery office, we run against a black man. When we get there, we say gravely, "The Diviner." It is handed over the counter, as a serious matter of business. We look at black man. Such a number. " Give us that." We look at running against a person in the street. "Give us that." We look at the name of the street itself. "Give us that." Now, we have our three numbers.

If the roof of the theatre of San Carlo were to fall in, so many people would play upon the numbers attached to such an accident in the Diviner, that the Government would soon close those numbers, and decline to run the risk of losing any more upon them. This often happens. Not long ago, when there was a fire in the King's Palace, there was such a desperate run on fire, and king, and palace, that further stakes on the numbers attached to those words in the Golden Book were forbidden. Every accident or event, is supposed, by the ignorant populace, to be a revelation to the beholder, or party concerned, in connection with the lottery. Certain people who have a talent for dreaming fortunately, are much sought after; and there are some priests who are constantly favoured with visions of the lucky numbers.

I heard of a horse running away with a man, and dashing him down, dead, at the corner of a street. Pursuing the horse with incredible speed, was another man, who ran so fast, that he came up, immediately after the accident. He threw himself upon his knees beside the unfortunate rider, and clasped his hand with an expression of the wildest grief. "If you have life," he said, "speak one word to me! If you have one gasp of breath left, mention your age for Heaven's sake, that I may play that number in the lottery."

It is four o'clock in the afternoon, and we may go to see our lottery drawn. The ceremony takes place every Saturday, in the Tribunale, or Court of Justice—this singular, earthy-smelling room, or gallery, as mouldy as an old cellar, and as damp as a dungeon. At the upper end is a platform, with a large horse-shoe table upon it; and a President and Council sitting round—all Judges of the Law. The man on the little stool behind the President, is the Capo Lazzarone, a kind of tribune of the people, appointed on their behalf to see that all is fairly conducted: attended by a few personal friends. A ragged, swarthy fellow he is: with long matted hair hanging down all over his face: and covered, from head to foot, with most unquestionably genuine dirt. All the body of the room is filled with the commonest of the Neapolitan people: and between them and the platform, guarding the steps leading to the latter, is a small body of soldiers.

There is some delay in the arrival of the necessary number of judges; during which, the box, in which the numbers are being placed, is a source of the deepest interest.   When the box is full, the boy who is to draw the numbers out of it becomes the prominent feature of the proceedings.   He is already dressed for his part, in a tight brown Holland coat, with only one (the left) sleeve to it, which leaves his right arm bared to the shoulder, ready for plunging down into the mysterious chest.

During the hush and whisper that pervade the room, all eyes are turned on this young minister of fortune. People begin to inquire his age, with a view to the next lottery; and the number of his brothers and sisters; and the age of his father and mother; and whether he has any moles or pimples upon him; and where, and how many; when the arrival of the last judge but one (a little old man, universally dreaded as possessing the Evil Eye) makes a slight diversion, and would occasion a greater one, but that he is immediately deposed, as a source of interest, by the officiating priest, who advances gravely to his place, followed by a very dirty little boy, carrying his sacred vestments, and a pot of Holy Water.

Here is the last judge come at last, and now he takes his place at the horse-shoe table.

There is a murmur of irrepressible agitation. In the midst of it, the priest puts his head into the sacred vestments, and pulls the same over his shoulders. Then he says a silent prayer; and dipping a brush into the pot of Holy Water, sprinkles it over the box and over the boy, and gives them a double-barrelled blessing, which the box and the boy are both hoisted on the table to receive. The boy remaining on the table, the box is now carried round the front of the platform, by an attendant, who holds it up and shakes it lustily all the time; seeming to say, like the conjurer, "There is no deception, ladies and gentlemen; keep your eyes upon me, if you please!"

At last, the box is set before the boy; and the boy, first holding up his naked arm and open hand, dives down into the hole (it is made like a ballot-box) and pulls out a number, which is rolled up, round something hard, like a bonbon. This he hands to the judge next him, who unrolls a little bit, and hands it to the President, next to whom he sits. The President unrolls it, very slowly. The Capo Lazzarone leans over his shoulder. The President holds it up, unrolled, to the Capo Lazzarone. The Capo Lazzarone, looking at it eagerly, cries out, in a shrill, loud voice, "Sessantadue!" (sixty-two), expressing the two upon his fingers, as he calls it out. Alas! the Capo Lazzarone himself has not staked on sixty-two. His face is very long, and his eyes roll wildly.

As it happens to be a favourite number, however, it is pretty well received, which is not always the case. They are all drawn with the same ceremony, omitting the blessing. One blessing is enough for the whole multiplication-table. The only new incident in the proceedings, is the gradually deepening intensity of the change in the Capo Lazzarone, who has, evidently, speculated to the very utmost extent of his means; and who, when he sees the last number, and finds that it is not one of his, clasps his hands, and raises his eyes to the ceiling before proclaiming it, as though remonstrating, in a secret agony, with his patron saint, for having committed so gross a breach of confidence. I hope the Capo Lazzarone may not desert him for some other member of the Calendar, but he seems to threaten it.

Where the winners may be, nobody knows. They certainly are not present; the general disappointment filling one with pity for the poor people. They look: when we stand aside, observing them, in their passage through the court-yard down below: as miserable as the prisoners in the gaol (it forms a part of the building), who are peeping down upon them, from between their bars; or, as the fragments of human heads which are still dangling in chains outside, in memory of the good old times, when their owners were strung up there, for the popular edification.

Away from Naples in a glorious sunrise, by the road to Capua, and then on a three days' journey along by-roads, that we may see, on the way, the monastery of Monte Cassino, which is perched on the steep and lofty hill above the little town of San Germano, and is lost on a misty morning in the clouds.

So much the better, for the deep sounding of its bell, which, as we go winding up, on mules, towards the convent, is heard mysteriously in the still air, while nothing is seen but the grey mist, moving solemnly and slowly, like a funeral procession. Behold, at length the shadowy pile of building close before us: its grey walls and towers dimly seen, though so near and so vast: and the raw vapour rolling through its cloisters heavily.

There are two black shadows walking to and fro in the quadrangle, near the statues of the Patron Saint and his sister; and hopping on behind them, in and out of the old arches, is a raven, croaking in answer to the bell, and uttering, at intervals, the purest Tuscan. How like a Jesuit he looks! There never was a sly and stealthy fellow so at home as is this raven, standing now at the refectory door, with his head on one side, and pretending to glance another way, while he is scrutinizing the visitors keenly, and listening with fixed attention. What a dull-headed monk the porter becomes in comparison!

" He speaks like us!" says the porter: "quite as plainly." Quite as plainly, Porter. Nothing could be more expressive than his reception of the peasants who are entering the gate with baskets and burdens. There is a roll in his eye, and a chuckle in his throat, which should qualify him to be chosen Superior of an Order of Ravens. He knows all about it. "It's all right," he says. "We know what we know. Come along, good people. Glad to see you!"

How was this extraordinary structure ever built in such a situation, where the labour of conveying the stone, and iron, and marble, so great a height, must have been prodigious? "Caw!" says the raven, welcoming the peasants. How, being despoiled by plunder, fire and earthquake, has it risen from its ruins, and been again made what we now see it, with its church so sumptuous and magnificent? "Caw!" says the raven, welcoming the peasants. These people have a miserable appearance, and (as usual) are densely ignorant, and all beg, while the monks are chaunting in the chapel. "Caw!" says the raven. "Cuckoo!"

So we leave him, chuckling and rolling his eye at the convent gate, and wind slowly down again through the cloud. At last emerging from it, we come in sight of the village far below, and the flat green country intersected by rivulets; which is pleasant and fresh to see after the obscurity and haze of the convent—no disrespect to the raven, or the holy friars.

Away we go again, by muddy roads, and through the most shattered and tattered of villages, where there is not a whole window among all the houses, or a whole garment among all the peasants, or the least appearance of anything to eat, in any of the wretched hucksters' shops. The women wear a bright red bodice laced before and behind, a white skirt, and the Neapolitan head-dress of square folds of linen, primitively meant to carry loads on. The men and children wear anything they can get. The soldiers are as dirty and rapacious as the dogs. The inns are such hobgoblin places, that they are infinitely more attractive and amusing than the best hotels in Paris. Here is one near Valmontone (that is Valmontone, the round, walled town on the mount opposite), which is approached by a quagmire almost knee-deep. There is a wild colonnade below, and a dark yard full of empty stables and lofts, and a great long kitchen with a great long bench and a great long form, where a party of travellers, with two priests among them, are crowding round the fire while their supper is cooking. Above stairs, is a rough brick gallery to sit in, with very little windows with very small patches of knotty glass in them, and all the doors that open from it (a dozen or two) off their hinges, and a bare board on tressels for a table, at which thirty people might dine easily, and a fireplace large enough in itself for a breakfast-parlour, where, as the faggots blaze and crackle, they illuminate the ugliest and grimmest of faces, drawn in charcoal on the whitewashed chimney-sides by previous travellers. There is a flaring country lamp on the table; and, hovering about it, scratching her thick black hair continually, a yellow dwarf of a woman, who stands on tiptoe to arrange the hatchet knives, and takes a flying leap to look into the water-jug. The beds in the adjoining rooms are of the liveliest kind. There is not a solitary scrap of looking-glass in the house, and the washing apparatus is identical with the cooking utensils. But the yellow dwarf sets on the table a good flask of excellent wine, holding a quart at least; and produces, among half-a-dozen other dishes, two thirds of a roasted kid, smoking hot. She is as good-humoured, too, as dirty, which is saying a great deal. So here's long life to her, in the flask of wine, and prosperity to the establishment.

Rome gained and left behind, and with it the Pilgrims who are now repairing to their own homes again—each with his scallop shell and staff, and soliciting alms for the love of God—we come, by a fair country, to the Falls of Terni, where the whole Velino river dashes, headlong, from a rocky height, amidst shining spray and rainbows. Perugia, strongly fortified by art and nature, on a lofty eminence, rising abruptly from the plain where purple mountains mingle with the distant sky, is glowing, on its market-day, with radiant colours. They set off its sombre but rich Gothic buildings admirably.   The pavement of its market-place is strewn with country goods. All along the steep hill leading from the town, under the town wall, there is a noisy fair of calves, lambs, pigs, horses, mules, and oxen. Fowls, geese, and turkeys, flutter vigorously among their very hoofs; and buyers, sellers, and spectators, clustering everywhere, block up the road as we come shouting down upon them.

Suddenly, there is a ringing sound among our horses. The driver stops them. Sinking in his saddle, and casting up his eyes to Heaven, he delivers this apostrophe, "Oh Jove Omnipotent! here is a horse has lost his shoe!"

Notwithstanding the tremendous nature of this accident, and the utterly forlorn look and gesture (impossible in any one but an Italian Vetturíno) with which it is announced, it is not long in being repaired by a mortal Farrier, by whose assistance we reach Castiglione the same night, and Arezzo next day. Mass is, of course, performing in its fine cathedral, where the sun shines in among the clustered pillars, through rich stained-glass windows: half revealing, half concealing the kneeling figures on the pavement, and striking out paths of spotted light in the long aisles.

But, how much beauty of another kind is here, when, on a fair clear morning, we look, from the summit of a hill, on Florence! See where it lies before us in a sun-lighted valley, bright with the winding Arno, and shut in by swelling hills; its domes, and towers, and palaces, rising from the rich country in a glittering heap, and shining in the sun like gold!

Magnificently stern and sombre are the streets of beautiful Florence; and the strong old piles of building make such heaps of shadow, on the ground and in the river, that there is another and a different city of rich forms and fancies, always lying at our feet. Prodigious palaces, constructed for defence, with small distrustful windows heavily barred, and walls of great thickness formed of huge masses of rough stone, frown, in their old sulky state, on every street. In the midst of the city—in the Piazza of the Grand Duke, adorned with beautiful statues and the Fountain of Neptune—rises the Palazzo Vecchio, with its enormous overhanging battlements, and the Great Tower that watches over the whole town. In its court-yard

—worthy of the Castle of Otranto in its ponderous gloom—is a massive staircase that the heaviest waggon and the stoutest team of horses might be driven up. Within it, is a Great Saloon, faded and tarnished in its stately decorations, and mouldering by grains, but recording yet, in pictures on its walls, the triumphs of the Medici and the wars of the old Florentine people. The prison is hard by, in an adjacent court-yard of the building—a foul and dismal place, where some men are shut up close, in small cells like ovens; and where others look through bars and beg; where some are playing draughts, and some are talking to their friends, who smoke, the while, to purify the air; and some are buying wine and fruit of women-vendors; and all are squalid, dirty, and vile to look at. "They are merry enough, Signore," says the Jailer. "They are all blood-stained here," he adds, indicating, with his hand, three-fourths of the whole building. Before the hour is out, an old man, eighty years of age, quarrelling over a bargain with a young girl of seventeen, stabs her dead, in the market-place full of bright flowers; and is brought in prisoner, to swell the number.

Among the four old bridges that span the river, the Ponte Vecchio —that bridge which is covered with the shops of Jewellers and Goldsmiths—is a most enchanting feature in the scene. The space of one house, in the centre, being left open, the view beyond is shown as in a frame; and that precious glimpse of sky, and water, and rich buildings, shining so quietly among the huddled roofs and gables on the bridge, is exquisite. Above it, the Gallery of the Grand Duke crosses the river. It was built to connect the two Great Palaces by a secret passage; and it takes its jealous course among the streets and houses, with true despotism: going where it lists, and spurning every obstacle away, before it.

The Grand Duke has a worthier secret passage through the streets, in his black robe and hood, as a member of the Compagnia della Misericordia, which brotherhood includes all ranks of men. If an accident take place, their office is, to raise the sufferer, and bear him tenderly to the Hospital. If a fire break out, it is one of their functions to repair to the spot, and render their assistance and protection. It is, also, among their commonest offices, to attend and console the sick; and they neither receive money, nor eat, nor drink, in any house they visit for this purpose. Those who are on duty for the time, are all called together, on a moment's notice, by the tolling of the great bell of the Tower; and it is said that the Grand Duke has been seen, at this sound, to rise from his seat at table, and quietly withdraw to attend the summons.

In this other large Piazza, where an irregular kind of market is held, and stores of old iron and other small merchandise are set out on stalls, or scattered on the pavement, are grouped together, the Cathedral with its great Dome, the beautiful Italian Gothic Tower the Campanile, and the Baptistery with its wrought bronze doors. And here, a small untrodden square in the pavement, is "the Stone of DANTE," where (so runs the story) he was used to bring his stool, and sit in contemplation. I wonder was he ever, in his bitter exile, withheld from cursing the very stones in the streets of Florence the ungrateful, by any kind remembrance of this old musing-place, and its association with gentle thoughts of little Beatrice!

The chapel of Medici, the Good and Bad Angels, of Florence; the church of Santa Croce where Michael Angelo lies buried, and where every stone in the cloisters is eloquent on great men's deaths; innumerable churches, often masses of unfinished heavy brickwork externally, but solemn and serene within; arrest our lingering steps, in strolling through the city.

In keeping with the tombs among the cloisters, is the Museum of Natural History, famous through the world for its preparations in wax; beginning with models of leaves, seeds, plants, inferior animals; and gradually ascending, through separate organs of the human frame, up to the whole structure of that wonderful creation, exquisitely presented, as in recent death. Few admonitions of our frail mortality can be more solemn and more sad, or strike so home upon the heart, as the counterfeits of Youth and Beauty that are lying there, upon their beds, in their last sleep.

Beyond the walls, the whole sweet Valley of the Arno, the convent at Fiesole, the Tower of Galileo, BOCCACCIO'S house, old villas and retreats; innumerable spots of interest, all glowing in a landscape of surpassing beauty steeped in the richest light; are spread before us. Returning from so much brightness, how solemn and how grand the streets again, with their great, dark, mournful palaces, and many legends: not of siege, and war, and might, and Iron Hand alone, but of the triumphant growth of peaceful Arts and Sciences.

What light is shed upon the world, at this day, from amidst these rugged Palaces of Florence! Here, open to all comers, in their beautiful and calm retreats, the ancient Sculptors are immortal, side by side with Michael Angelo, Canova, Titian, Rembrandt, Raphael, Poets, Historians, Philosophers—those illustrious men of history, beside whom its crowned heads and harnessed warriors show so poor and small, and are so soon forgotten. Here, the imperishable part of noble minds survives, placid and equal, when strongholds of assault and defence are overthrown; when the tyranny of the many, or the few, or both, is but a tale; when Pride and Power are so much cloistered dust. The fire within the stern streets, and among the massive Palaces and Towers, kindled by rays from Heaven, is still burning brightly, when the flickering of war is extinguished and the household fires of generations have decayed; as thousands upon thousands of faces, rigid with the strife and passion of the hour, have faded out of the old Squares and public haunts, while the nameless Florentine Lady, preserved from oblivion by a Painter's hand, yet lives on, in enduring grace and youth.

Let us look back on Florence while we may, and when its shining Dome is seen no more, go travelling through cheerful Tuscany, with a bright remembrance of it; for Italy will be the fairer for the recollection. The summer-time being come: and Genoa, and Milan, and the Lake of Como lying far behind us: and we resting at Faido, a Swiss village, near the awful rocks and mountains, the everlasting snows and roaring cataracts, of the Great Saint Gothard; hearing the Italian tongue for the last time on this journey: let us part from Italy, with all its miseries and wrongs, affectionately, in our admiration of the beauties, natural and artificial, of which it is full to overflowing, and in our tenderness towards a people, naturally well-disposed, and patient, and sweet-tempered. Years of neglect, oppression, and misrule, have been at work, to change their nature and reduce their spirit; miserable jealousies, fomented by petty Princes to whom union was destruction, and division strength, have been a canker at their root of nationality, and have barbarized their language; but the good that was in them ever, is in them yet, and a noble people may be, one day, raised up from these ashes. Let us entertain that hope! And let us not remember Italy the less regardfully, because, in every fragment of her fallen Temples, and every stone of her deserted palaces and prisons, she helps to inculcate the lesson that the wheel of Time is rolling for an end, and that the world is, in all great essentials, better, gentler, more forbearing, and more hopeful, as it rolls!

MADE AND PRINTED IN GREAT BRITAIN
BY HAZELL, WATSON AND VINEY LTD.
LONDON AND AYLESBURY